Forbes Road

Love, War, and Revenge
on the Pennsylvania Frontier

ROBERT J. SHADE

Sunshine Hill Press

First Edition 2012

Sunshine Hill Press, LLC

2937 Novum Road
Reva, VA 22735

Copyright © 2012 Robert J. Shade

Artwork with specific permission:
Front Cover: *Long Way from Home* by David Wright
(www.davidwrightart.com)
Rear Cover: *Up Against The Fence* by Pamela Patrick White
(www.whitehistoricart.com)

Map: Western Pennsylvania 1759-63 by Stephen Templeton

Forbes Road is a work of fiction. With the exception of historical people, places, and events in the narrative, all names, characters, places, and incidents are used fictitiously. Any resemblance to current events, places, or to living persons is entirely coincidental.

ISBN: 0615590179
ISBN-13: 978-0615590172

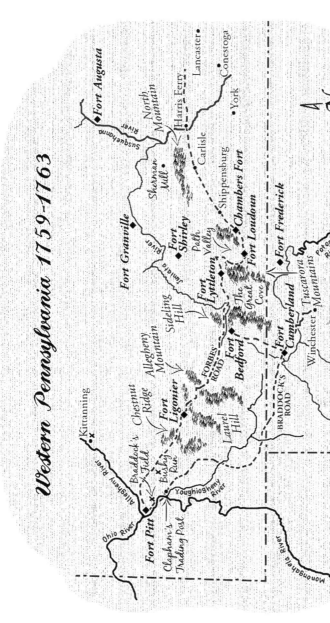

Western Pennsylvania 1759-1763

MAJOR CHARACTERS

Historical

Henry Bouquet	Colonel, 1st Battalion, 60th Foot, Commander of British military forces in Pennsylvania
James Robertson	Captain, 77th Foot
John Elder	Presbyterian Minister of Paxton
Lazarus Stewart	Captain, Paxton Militia (Paxton Rangers)
Asher Clayton	Captain, Paxton Militia (Paxton Rangers)
John Dunning	High Sheriff of Cumberland County
Guyasuta	Influential Mingo sachem
Pontiac	War captain of Ottawa in Detroit area
Neolin	Delaware spiritual leader, "The Prophet"
Simeon Ecuyer	Captain, 60th Foot, Commander of Fort Pitt
Donald Campbell	Lieutenant, 77th Foot
Allan Campbell	Major, 42nd Foot (Black Watch)
Robert Kirkwood	Private, 77th Foot, later corporal, 42nd Foot (Black Watch)
Lewis Ourry	Captain 60th Foot, Commander of Fort Bedford
Archibald Blane	Lieutenant, 60th Foot, Commander of Fort Ligonier
Thomas Stirling	Captain, 42nd Foot (Black Watch)
Wolf	Delaware war captain

Fictional

Wend Eckert	Apprentice gunsmith
Johann Eckert	Wend's father, master gunsmith appointed armorer of Fort Pitt
Mary Eckert	Wend's mother
Magistrate Gibson	Lawyer from Philadelphia, appointed legal representative at Fort Pitt
Abigail Gibson	Daughter of Magistrate Gibson
George Washburn	Tavern keeper in Carlisle
Arnold Spengler	Corporal, 60th Foot, clerk to Colonel Bouquet
Alice Downy	Boarding house proprietress in Carlisle
Joshua Baird	Civilian scout for Colonel Bouquet
Richard Grenough	Owner of border trading company
Mathew Bratton	Freight waggoner of Sherman Valley
Franklin	Black slave to Magistrate Gibson
Ross Kinnear	Border country Indian trader
Lizzie Iverson	Camp follower, nurse in 77th Foot
Mary Fraser	Lizzie Iverson's daughter
Paul Carnahan	Minister and schoolmaster of Sherman Valley
Patricia Carnahan	Wife of Rev Carnahan
Wolf Claw	War captain of Mingo band
Charlie Sawak	Conestoga Indian, peddler of tribal wares

Donovan McCartie	Tavern proprietor in Sherman Mill village
Peggy McCartie	Older daughter of Donavan McCartie
Ellen McCartie	Younger daughter of Donavan McCartie
Frank McClay	Neighbor and lay helper to Rev Carnahan
Sarah McClay	Frank's wife
Elizabeth McClay	Daughter of Sarah
Will Donaldson	Owner of largest farm in Sherman Valley
Johnny Donaldson	Son of Will Donaldson
Thomas Marsh	Gristmill proprietor of Sherman Mill
Hank Marsh	Eldest son of miller Thomas Marsh
Rose Jenson	Indentured tavern maid in Harris' Ferry
Sergeant McCulloch	Senior sergeant in 77th Foot
Simon Donegal	Corporal, 77th Foot
Esther McCulloch	Wife of the sergeant
Donald McKirdy	Senior drummer in 77th Foot
Charles McDonald	Captain of 77th Foot

CONTENTS

PART ONE

The Journey

1759

CHAPTER 1
Challenge at the Ferry

Most residents of William Penn's colony were still at their breakfasts when the two horse-drawn wagons cleared the top of a low ridge, bringing the Susquehanna River and Harris' Ferry into view. Wend Eckert, driving the second wagon, felt the first touch of the sun on his shoulders and looked back to see that the burning globe had now fully risen above the eastern horizon. He knew the withering July heat would soon have them in its grasp. Wend returned his attention to the team and noticed that the covered wagon ahead of his, which bore his parents and baby sister, was picking up speed and starting to pull away. He resettled the black, broad brimmed hat on his brown hair and slapped the horses' backs with the reins to close the distance. The pace quickened as they rolled down the mild grade of the road toward the river.

As the wagon jolted along the uneven track, Wend glanced at his ten-year-old brother seated to his left on the bench. "See, Bernd, I told you Father would rouse the horses on the way into town. He says you should always come in with a bit of dash! Hold on tight!"

"Well, you better be careful that you don't run off the road or can't pull up fast enough when we get to the landing!" Bernd grabbed the bench as the wagon bounced over a series of steep bumps. The harness trace chains rattled from the jostling and the wagon creaked under the weight of its load. "Watch out! You're not used to handling the team on a rough road. You'll be in for it if you spill the wagon or break an axel before we even get across the river!"

Wend shot back, "We broke camp before dawn to make an early morning ferry. If I drove us safely through the darkness and morning dusk, we'll be fine now that I can see the road." He concentrated on avoiding a rut, then continued, "Besides, I've handled things for the two days since we left Lancaster, so stop complaining!" He sighed to himself. The little brat was at an impish stage where he never missed an opportunity to criticize Wend, or better yet, embarrass him in front of adults.

But Wend had no intention of letting Bernd spoil the excitement of the moment. His family was moving from their home near Lancaster to Fort Pitt, the British wilderness outpost on the Ohio River which had been captured from the French in the prior year, 1758. Johann, his father, had just been appointed contract armorer to the garrison. And to Wend's great pride, at age fifteen, he was being trusted with driving the heavy wagon carrying all Johann's tools and trade supplies for the entire distance of 200 miles, two thirds of the way across the colony.

Wend looked at the village which spread out ahead of them. Scattered buildings were planted on the low-lying land along the eastern bank of the river, lacking any real focus save the ferry landing which constituted the settlement's main reason for being. The visually dominant building, sited in an open field south of the landing, was the large, two story log house which Johann had told them belonged to John Harris himself, the owner of the ferry and the trading post. A few taverns, shops, and warehouses which catered to travelers and waggoners were clustered near the landing. Randomly placed houses and small farms further back from the water completed the extent of civic development.

Wend glanced down at the water ahead and saw an opportunity to distract his brother. "Look Bernd, there's the ferry out on the river!"

Bernd shaded his eyes with his hand, and crinkled up his face. "It seems pretty small to me." Then, after further consideration, he said, "It looks like it has legs; sort of like a spider on the water."

"It's big enough, all right." Wend concentrated on the horses and the road, "And those things which look like spider legs are the poles which move the boat." He paused as he worked with the reins. "Just think: In a couple of hours we'll be in the real border country for the first time."

Despite Bernd's protestations, nothing untoward occurred as they rolled past the shops and taverns. Finally they pulled up at the building on the river bank which served as a combination ferry terminal and tavern. Their timing was near perfect, for they arrived just as the boat made its approach from the far shore. Wend saw that it was a large raft-like barge, about 40 feet in length and 10 feet wide. As the Susquehanna at this point was no more than a couple of feet deep, the ferry's motive power was ten men, five to a side, who pushed the raft along with long poles. Another man steered with a sweep oar.

Johann Eckert climbed down from his wagon to make arrangements with the ferry proprietor, who stood at the landing. Since there were only two men on horseback getting off the boat, the ferry was soon ready for them to go aboard.

Then Wend heard a loud shout from the direction of the tavern. "Hey! What is going on here?" A man strode rapidly toward the ferry proprietor, waving a brass-handled walking stick at the ferry man and Johann. He was of slight build, narrow-faced, and dressed in a fine, well-tailored brown suite. On his head he wore a powdered wig and one of those fashionable tri-cornered hats that were rarely seen out in the country. "Listen: I understood that my party was next on the boat! What are you doing loading these two wagons?"

The proprietor was still counting Johann's money. He calmly looked up at the approaching man. "So where are your rigs? If you want to go aboard you need to be ready when the boat arrives."

The agitated man clenched his teeth and pointed back at the tavern. "My good man, we were finishing our breakfast in your very own establishment. My servant is hitching up our conveyances right now. Move these wagons out of the way and we shall be right here. I have important government affairs in Carlisle and must be there for meetings early tomorrow!"

The proprietor shook his head. "Sorry, these people were ready to load and have paid in good coin. I'm running a business here, not a special service for the Governor's officials!" He turned to Johann, who had climbed back up to his wagon seat, and with a conspiratorial wink, waved him aboard the ferry. Then he turned to the city man and said, "You want to make the next ferry, you better get your wagons out here in line before some freight wagoner gets hitched up and beats you to it!"

The man in the brown suit opened his mouth as if intending to say more, but then closed it and stood scowling at the Eckert's wagons, rapidly tapping the walking stick against his right boot in frustration.

Johann Eckert deftly maneuvered his wagon up the earthen ramp onto the boat's deck. Once aboard, he carefully eased the rig to the extreme forward end. Wend relaxed on the seat of the tool wagon as Father and the ferrymen worked to secure the wagon. Meanwhile, his mother Mary and four-year old Elise climbed down from their seats to the ferry's deck. As he waited for his turn to board, Wend basked in a sense of pride and satisfaction at his competence in driving the team and heavy wagon over the long distance from Lancaster.

Then, with a single sentence, Bernd ruined his feeling of well being. "Look, Wend, there's not much room for us on the boat."

Wend looked at the ferry more closely and saw that his brother was right. There was barely enough space for his team and wagon. Then he noticed something which worried him even more. The earthen ramp up to the boat's deck was steep; much steeper than he had realized at first. He felt a surge of doubt and indecision in his stomach. *What was the proper way to load the wagon? Should he get off and lead the horses up onto the deck, or should he try to drive them up, as Johann had done?* Either way he could see the possibility of a big problem. If he led the horses at a walk, there might not be enough momentum to get the heavy wagon up the steep ramp. If he stayed aboard the wagon and drove the horses up at a rapid pace, could he get the team stopped in time to keep from running into the rear of the other wagon? Or might the horses actually balk at his command?

The unanticipated challenge deflated his confidence. Visions of an embarrassing accident crowded his mind and a knot of apprehension formed in his stomach. In his sudden doubt, he looked up, thinking that maybe Father would come to take over and save him from the necessity of making a decision. But Johann was talking with one of the men and paying him no attention.

Then suddenly things got far more complicated.

Wend glanced over in the direction of the tavern on the right and looked directly into the most incredibly blue eyes he had ever seen. The eyes were framed by golden hair under a smart hat, complemented by a small upturned nose, and nicely shaped mouth. All these features belonged to an elegantly dressed girl who had just come out of the tavern and was standing by the side of the man who had argued with the ferry proprietor. She was staring directly at Wend, her eyes seeming to bore into him, as the man indignantly described what had occurred. Wend suddenly felt a prickling on the back of his neck and quickly looked away. Sweat welled up on his face and on his hands where he held the reins. He had always had a tendency toward self-consciousness and it was now uncontrollably blossoming in the presence of this beautiful girl with the penetrating eyes.

And now the ferryman was motioning him to come onto the boat.

Wend hesitated, and after a long moment, Bernd impatiently elbowed him in the side. Then he said, in a loud voice everyone in the vicinity could hear, "Come on, Wend! They want us on the ferry."

"Be quiet. We'll go when I'm ready." Despite the embarrassment caused by Bernd's words, Wend resisted the urge to immediately start the horses forward. He sat still, forcing himself to concentrate and to plan every action he would take, working out the proper timing and thinking about what could go wrong. In his mind he felt the eyes of the girl on him, waiting to see how he would perform, and it took all his will power not to look at her again. Meanwhile, Bernd fidgeted on the seat beside him. Even the lead horse seemed to know something was up; he swung his head as far around as the harness would permit to see what Wend was doing.

Now Johann had stopped talking to the ferryman and was looking at him with concern in his eyes. Wend saw his father glance between the ramp and the remaining space on the boat and knew that he had recognized the difficulty facing his son. But he said nothing. And Wend was thankful for that because now he had worked out what he was going to do.

"Hold on, Bernd!" Wend gave the horses a first, gentle touch with the reins. That started them at a normal pace and, more importantly, got the heavy wagon rolling. Then, in the next instant, he stood up and slapped the reins down on the horses as hard as he could and at the same time shouted, "*Ha!Ha!Ha!*" at the top of his voice. It had the desired effect: The team, startled by the suddenness and urgency of his signal, literally jumped up the incline and onto the boat's deck, their racing, iron-shod hooves making a loud clattering on the planking. Wend conquered the urge to pull them up as the distance to Johann's wagon closed rapidly. He knew he had to keep up the momentum until the rear wheels were on the boat deck or the wagon's weight might force them backward down the ramp. Then, at the instant he felt the rear wheels cross to the deck, he leaned back with all his might on the reins and shouted "Whoa!" at the top of his voice. He braced himself against the front of the wagon bed and jammed his right foot down on the brake lever. For a moment he thought he had waited too long to kick the brake, but it worked out just right with the horses' noses ending up mere inches behind the front wagon. The lead horse snorted, then looked around again and Wend swore he could see surprise and grudging approval in his eyes.

Wend felt a surge of relief and dropped down onto the seat. Drops of sweat from his hatband rolled down his forehead, but the tension drained out of his body. He felt the same relief he had experienced when he successfully passed an examination by Master Dreher, the stern, demanding teacher of his former school in Lancaster.

His thoughts were interrupted by Johann's voice. "Are you going to sit there for the whole boat trip, Wend? Come down here and help us secure the wagon."

Bernd had already jumped down to the deck. Wend stood up and looked back at the landing. He was surprised to see that the girl still had her eyes on him. But as their eyes met, she frowned, then abruptly turned and walked away from the landing, following in the steps of the man in the brown suite.

The boatmen and Johann were lashing down the wagon and putting blocks at the front and back of the wheels. Wend got down and helped finish the job. As he worked, his father stood beside him and leaned down with his hand on his shoulder. He spoke quietly so only Wend could hear. "It seems you may have the makings of a good waggoner." That was all, but Wend felt a warm glow of pride spread through him to replace the feelings of insecurity which he had experienced only a few minutes before. His father was a stern taskmaster who used praise sparingly. So Wend had learned to cherish those words when he earned them.

Soon the boatmen took up their poles and moved the ferry off toward the far bank of the river. Johann struck up a conversation with the man at the steering oar, "How long will the passage take?"

"Well, the river is near a mile wide here," he replied, "So between working against this current and unloading your wagons, it will be just short of an hour until you get back on the road." He moved the oar and adjusted the boat's course into the current. "Where are you bound?"

"To Carlisle," Eckert said, meaning that was their next stop. "How far do you make it?"

The boatman hesitated and looked at the sky while he considered. "If the weather holds up and you don't waste any time along the way, you can make it by dark tonight. It's less than twenty miles and the road is not too bad this time of year."

Wend lost interest in the conversation. He watched the ferry landing slowly recede into the distance. His thoughts were on the blue eyed, blond girl he could still make out on the shore. He wondered if he would ever see her or a girl like her again. As he thought about it, he was surprised at how much he could now remember from glances of only a few seconds. He was intrigued with that idea and concentrated his thoughts to build an image like a painting of her in his mind. He realized she was tall for a girl, because she had stood nearly as high as the man who he assumed was her father. He thought about her clothing. Her dress had been blue, of a shade which blended well with her eyes. And it was of excellent quality; undoubtedly custom made by a tailor. Wend was proud that his family was reasonably well off, at least for that of a craftsman. But he had few purchased items of clothing, really only shoes, hats and a belt or two; things that Mother couldn't sew. So the girl came from a wealthy family, probably from Philadelphia. That would fit with the clothing she and her father wore. Suddenly, Wend's mind and his Germanic practicality jerked him back to reality. He thought: *Why am I standing here dreaming about a girl I saw for less than a minute? How would we ever meet? And if our paths would cross, what would an English girl from Philadelphia and a German country boy serving as his father's apprentice ever find in common?*

The answer was very clear to him: *Nothing.* Undoubtedly she would consider him on the same level as a servant and not even worthy of talking to except in the way of business.

So he resolved to put her out of his mind.

That resolution lasted all day. He concentrated his mind on the road and the team as they traveled through the rolling woodland interspersed with farms and hamlets that marked the way to Carlisle. They stopped only to rest the horses and munch on some cold food Mary had cooked the night before, arriving in a small clearing on the eastern side of the town shortly after dark. Wend and Bernd unharnessed the horses and tied them to a picket rope run between stakes. The family set up camp in the glow from the settlement's lights until Johann had a fire lighted.

Wend had never been to Carlisle, and was looking forward to seeing what he knew was the fastest growing settlement west of the Susquehanna. So he settled down to sleep in the warm blankets under the wagon with a sense of anticipation. But, with the onset of sleep, he lost control of his thoughts and his earlier resolution went by the board. His mind, unfettered by will power, took him right back to visions of the unforgettable girl at the ferry landing. It was a restless sleep, and toward dawn he woke up, surprised to find himself fully and painfully aroused.

CHAPTER 2
Carlisle Meetings

Wend and Johann strode through the bustle of Market Street, the main road through Carlisle, in mid-morning on the day after their journey from Harris' Ferry. They were on their way to meet Colonel Henry Bouquet, commandant of the First Battalion of the 60th Foot, or Royal American Regiment. Bouquet would be Johann's ultimate boss at Fort Pitt, and it had been through the colonel's recommendation that Eckert had obtained his position. Under his arm, Wend carried a small, highly polished wooden box which contained a present for the colonel.

Wend was used to the long-settled town of Lancaster. He soon observed that Carlisle was a far more intriguing place. Many of the buildings were newly finished or still under construction. Structures of roughly hewn logs stood alongside buildings of milled lumber and even stone or brick. Here and there a building was augmented by an attached tent or canvas roofed addition. There were still numerous vacant lots along the street.

One detail surprised him, and he said to Johann, "There seems to be a tavern on almost every block."

Johann smiled broadly and nodded. "What else would you expect, Wend? These Ulstermen take two things seriously: Drinking and religion!" Then he laughed out loud. "And argument is their third interest, which no doubt arises from the other two." They had come to the central square, and Johann pointed to two structures, one on the north side, the other to the south. "See those buildings? They're Presbyterian meeting houses. The Ulster people can't even agree among themselves on the same religion, so they must have separate churches, depending on their particular beliefs!"

His father's words reminded Wend that unlike Lancaster, a center of Germanic settlement, Carlisle was mainly inhabited by the English and the Scots-Irish, or Ulstermen, which was what many called the lowland Scots who had migrated to Pennsylvania via Ireland. On that island, most of the Scots had lived in the vicinity of Ulster, hence the sobriquet "Ulstermen." His father's tone of disapproval toward the Scots-Irish was typical of the attitude found in many Germans, who considered them slovenly ne'er-do-wells.

"Father, when you came back from the war, you said the Ulster made good soldiers."

"Yes, they're always ready for a scrap. But they'd be better off if they paid as much attention to their farming and trades. You can always tell an Ulsterman's farm a mile away by how unkempt it looks."

Presently they came to Washburn's Tavern, a prosperous establishment which took up the space of two lots along Market Street. On one lot was the tavern itself, a two story building of wood frame construction. The adjacent lot included a stable and open courtyard where several wagons were parked.

"This is where Bouquet keeps his headquarters in Carlisle," Johann said as he walked to the entrance. He pushed open the door and they entered a spacious common room, mostly empty of patrons given the forenoon hour. A well laid fire flickered in the massive hearth, the smell of its smoke mingling with the aroma of cooking food being prepared for the dinner meal; large windows in the front and side walls allowed sunlight to flood the room.

Johann greeted the proprietor, George Washburn, a beefy, genial man with a tavern keeper's ready smile, whom he knew from prior visits, and introduced Wend. Then he led the way through a rear door into a small room where they found two soldiers sitting behind desks, both busily writing among stacks of paper and copy books. Wend saw that one was a young lieutenant, dressed in an elegant, lace trimmed red uniform with blue facings. He knew that the blue facings, the coat's lapels and cuffs, showed that the wearer was in a regiment designated as "Royal." Regiments without that designation wore facings of colors such as green, buff, yellow, or white. The other soldier, an enlisted man, was in a similar blue faced uniform, but made of coarser, somewhat faded red material. He wore a braid knot over his right shoulder which designated him as a corporal.

Wend's eyes went to the face of the clerk, and he suddenly felt a surge of excitement. The corporal was none other than Arnold Spengler, late resident of Lancaster and fellow student at Master Richard Dreher's School. Arnold was three years his senior, a natural leader in mischief, and one of the schoolmaster's least prized students. Arnold, bored with school and his father's trade, had enlisted almost two years ago, and the last Wend had heard, he had been stationed at one of the frontier forts. The young soldier looked up from his work and upon seeing Wend, broke into a spontaneous, roguish grin. Wend was about to shout a greeting, but quickly remembered his manners, and waited for his father to speak to the lieutenant.

"Good morning, Sir," Father said, and Wend noticed that he made a slight bow to the lieutenant. "Johann Eckert, here to see Colonel Bouquet at his request."

"Ah, Eckert!" The lieutenant stood up and returned Johann's bow with a nod of his head. "I'm Lieutenant Locke, the adjutant. Glad to see that you've arrived. The colonel's been anxious for you to get to town; he has a request to make of you regarding your travel arrangements." The officer moved out from behind his writing table. "But I should let him explain the details. Let me announce you to him." After knocking, he went through another door at the side of the room and closed it behind him.

Arnold had come out from behind his table. He gave Wend a strong pat of the shoulder, and then faced Johann. "Good morning, Sir. Perhaps you don't remember me. I'm Arnold Spengler, son of Wilhelm Spengler, the cooper."

"Remember you?" Eckert mused with a look of contemplation on his face as if searching the recesses of his memory. "Would you perhaps be the Arnold Spengler who Master Dreher told me was his most recalcitrant pupil; the Arnold Spengler who was a source of despair to his father for not having the slightest interest in his trade; the Arnold Spengler whose mother Anna was frequently complaining to my Mary about the impossibility of finding him when any serious chore was necessary?" Johann paused for a second, at first grim faced, and then breaking into a crooked smile. "Yes, Arnold I know well who you are, though I am at a total loss to understand what you are doing in Colonel Bouquet's headquarters, with a corporal's knot on your shoulder no less. I would have thought it more likely to have encountered you on a punishment detail under the supervision of a corporal rather than being one."

They all laughed, Arnold somewhat sheepishly. "Actually, hard as it is to believe, I owe my job and my rank to Master Dreher," Arnold said when the laughter subsided. "After I enlisted, they found out I could read, write with a reasonable hand, and do some calculations. Lieutenant Locke started using me sometimes as a copy clerk for the colonel's correspondence. Soon they pulled me out of my company to do this full time."

"Aren't you disappointed to be a clerk instead of soldiering full time?" Wend asked.

Arnold laughed and shook his head "Are you kidding? I don't miss standing around on sentinel duty in the rain with a musket at the carry position, nor hauling sacks of provisions on work detail, nor drilling on some muddy parade ground four hours a day. By doing this I get to travel, I usually stay dry and clean, and I know the real story about what's going on in the regiment, not just the rumors which run through the barracks." He smiled, "Not to mention that they made me a corporal, mostly so I would have enough money to keep my uniform in good condition and look presentable at headquarters."

At that moment, the adjutant re-entered the room, leaving the door to Bouquet's office open, and motioned Eckert and his son to enter. Arnold moved back behind his desk, after whispering, "I'll talk to you later, Wend. Perhaps we can get together after work is done today."

Lieutenant Locke ushered them into the next room, where a middle aged, thickset man of above-average height rose from his desk to meet them. Wend noted a square-shaped head with a high forehead, framed by thick, dark hair. His eyes, topped by heavy brows, gave the impression of thoughtful intelligence; the mouth was small but well formed. However, the entire face was dominated by a nose which could most tactfully be described as "ample."

Wend felt a sense of disappointment in Colonel Bouquet's appearance. He had heard stories about the Swiss mercenary's industrious—many said brilliant—work as General Forbes' deputy in the campaign to capture Fort Duquesne. Johann had always talked about the officer with admiration. But the man in front of them now didn't seem to fit the picture Wend had in his mind of a gallant, professional military officer. Aside from the fact that he was dressed in a uniform, he would more have fit Wend's vision of a shopkeeper or tradesman.

"Eckert, good to see you," Bouquet greeted them in a quiet but warm voice tinged with the accent of his native Switzerland. He spoke in the manner of a man who uses words sparingly but to good effect. "I am very pleased you have come so promptly after my letter. I have a request to make of you and will be greatly indebted if you agree." Then the colonel looked over at Wend as if he was just noticing him, "Please excuse me for forgetting my manners, Eckert." He smiled at them both. "Unless I am mistaken, this is your son?"

"Yes sir." Johann put his hand on Wend's shoulder. "This is Wend; my eldest son and my apprentice."

Wend acknowledged Bouquet's greeting with a simple nod and "Good morning, sir."

Johann hurried to resume the conversation. "Before we talk about favors, I have something for you, as a memento of appreciation for your kind intervention in the matter of my position at Fort Pitt."

That was Wend's cue. He passed the wooden case to his father.

Johann grasped the box and, handling it almost reverently, placed it on the table. But he was in no hurry to open it. He rubbed his hands over the box in a caress, as if to wipe away dust. And in so doing, he drew attention to the brass plate at the center of the lid. It said "Presented to Colonel Henry Bouquet, 60th Foot" and below that line, "Johann Eckert, Master Gunsmith."

Then, having drawn the attention he desired, Eckert released the box's swivel catch and raised the lid. Inside, lying on luxurious looking blue felt fabric was an elegant pistol. Not an all-metal pistol, as was most common in the army, but a pistol crafted of silky-smooth, light colored wood, with an intricate grain which was shown off as a result of painstaking oiling that had produced a warm sheen. Framed by the wooden body was an iron barrel and on the right side a fine lock which had come from Germany itself.

Wend was supremely proud of the pistol, for Father had let him play a major role in the work. Johann had crafted much of the weapon itself, selecting and carving the wood to a pattern which would fit the hand well and feel balanced, sizing the barrel and ensuring its fit to the body. But Wend had done the smoothing of the wood and had performed the repeated oiling of the finish.

Wend looked at Bouquet, and could see the pleasure in his face as he contemplated the weapon. Having paused to allow his benefactor to gain an appreciation of the gift, Johann began a careful explanation of the gun's features.

Wend watched in admiration as Johann used his well-rehearsed technique for selling guns to customers. His voice was now quiet and earnest. He moved his hands lovingly over the pistol as he explained its features to Bouquet.

"You will notice, Colonel, the size of this pistol." Johann framed the pistol with his hands as it lay in the box. "That is my own innovation. It is of an intermediate size, between the bulk of a horse pistol and the lightness of a dueling pistol." He picked it up from the box. "It is just large enough to be used like a cavalry pistol, mounted in a holster on your saddle, yet it is also small enough to be carried comfortably in your belt, where a full-sized horse pistol would be too bulky." He pointed to the bore. "The same can be said for the caliber. It is sufficient to have real penetrating power, but small enough that a useful amount of shot can be carried in your saddlebags or your belt pouch. It is truly a soldier's weapon."

Bouquet took the pistol from Johann's hands with obvious relish. "Eckert, this is magnificent!" He fondled it, checking every aspect. He took up a shooting stance, aiming the pistol at an imaginary target. "I don't know how you did it, but it fits my hand well, and the balance seems perfect." He pulled back the cock and snapped the pistol. "This is as fine a gift as I ever received, Eckert. I will prize it and keep it in my kit forever."

At that moment the adjutant knocked and entered the room. "Colonel, Mr. Gibson is here to meet with you."

A look of sudden irritation swept over Bouquet's face. He reluctantly returned the pistol to its case. "Well Eckert, that brings us to the business I asked you here to discuss." He turned to Locke, and said in a sharp voice, "Please entertain Gibson for a minute while I explain my request to Eckert."

Locke nodded and shut the door as he left.

The colonel turned, put his hands on his hips, and stared after his adjutant. "As I mentioned earlier, I have a favor to ask, Johann," said Bouquet, now using Eckert's familiar name for the first time. He shook his head impatiently and burst out, "Those damned Quakers in Philadelphia! Between their parsimony and pacifism, they are driving me to distraction! First, they're forcing us to disband the Pennsylvania Provincial Regiment now that the French have moved north. And they won't even allow us to organize an official militia throughout the colony so that we have some kind of emergency defense force for the settlements. And now they've saddled me with a personal problem! This man Gibson is a lawyer; he's to be the first magistrate of the settlement around Fort Pitt. There needs to be some law there and the colony's council has engaged him for the purpose of establishing a court. Beyond that, he's to provide legal advice in negotiations with the tribal kings." Bouquet sat on the edge of his writing table and shook his head in frustration. "But you would think they would pick someone from here in Carlisle, or Shippensburg, or even York. There are plenty of magistrates from this side of the Susquehanna who understand the back country. But no! Instead they send me a city man from Philadelphia! His main qualification seems to be that he's from some important law firm with lots of contacts with the government."

Johann nodded. "It does seem a bit odd."

Bouquet looked at Eckert. "Damn right! But Johann, he needs to have help from someone with bush experience if he and his family are going to safely get to Pitt." Bouquet paused, choosing his words carefully. "You have

15

that knowledge, Johann. You helped cut that road and supervised a work crew during the expedition last year." He paused again. "You also have the patience and tact to deal with a man of Gibson's station who has no idea what he doesn't know about traveling through the backcountry."

Wend saw recognition in Johann's eyes that there really was no option but to accede to the colonel's request. "Sir, it will be our pleasure to accompany Mr. Gibson and his party. It will be an excellent opportunity for me to associate with someone who will be a major influence at Pitt."

"Good, Eckert! I knew I could count on you." Bouquet smiled broadly. "Now, let's meet Gibson." Bouquet went out the door, and they heard Locke making introductions in the anteroom. Johann exchanged glances with Wend and raised his eyebrows as if to say, "What else could I do?"

Bouquet re-entered with Gibson in tow and Wend gulped in surprise. He was looking at the brown-suited man who had argued with the proprietor at the ferry landing yesterday morning! Then, as Gibson got closer to them, Wend caught a whiff of strong liquor from his breath. But Wend brushed that aside, for racing through his mind was the idea that the fascinating girl in blue must be somewhere nearby.

After pleasantries had been completed, Bouquet turned to Gibson. "Sir, this is the man whom I mentioned to you in my letter. Johann is completely familiar with Forbes Road, experienced in border living, and an accomplished waggoner. I selected him myself to take up the post of armorer at the fort. I can recommend no better person for you to travel with on your way to Pitt."

Gibson contemplated Johann for a moment and Wend saw the lawyer's face wrinkle up into a look of distaste. He glanced back and forth between Johann and Bouquet. Then he cleared his throat and said forcefully, "Actually, Colonel, in Philadelphia I was assured that we would be traveling in company with an escort of soldiers. Might we not need armed protection in case of interference from hostile tribesmen?"

Bouquet exchanged glances with Eckert. "I don't think you have to be concerned with that, Mr. Gibson. The tribes are negotiating peace with us right now and have been on their best behavior."

"But still, Colonel, over the last year I've read accounts of attacks by war parties on farmsteads and travelers along Forbes Road. Wouldn't prudence dictate an escort?"

"Magistrate, there have been no attacks along the road for several months now," Bouquet responded. "I'll be following along behind you with a supply convoy, and I'm traveling only with my staff and contract waggoners." The colonel continued, "In fact, we are actually reducing our garrisons at Fort Pitt and other places. You will probably meet Captain Robertson's company of the 77th Foot along the road. They're coming back from Pitt to join the rest of their regiment and take part in Amherst's campaign against Fort Carillon in New York."

Now there was frustration in Gibson's eyes. "Well, Colonel, in that case, couldn't we accompany you? Perhaps we could share the hospitality of your mess? I am traveling with my young daughter, and obviously she's used to certain social amenities."

"That was my first thought, Magistrate," Bouquet countered, and Wend could see he was losing his patience. "But we are having the devil's own time getting the train ready. Supplies and wagons are coming in slowly, and the contractor is having a hard time engaging teamsters. It could be a fortnight or even longer until the convoy is ready to move." Bouquet smacked his hand down on the table in emphasis. "I doubt you want to wait around that long with the daily expense of lodging and meals. So the answer, it seems to me, is for you to travel with Eckert."

Gibson's shoulders sagged in surrender. "Of course, Colonel, if you insist: Given the circumstances, I seem to have no choice but to follow your counsel."

Johann stepped into the conversation. "Mr. Gibson, it might be a good idea for me to look over your wagons, to check their readiness. And then we need to make plans for our departure. Where are you staying, and when can we meet?"

While Gibson and Eckert made the necessary arrangements, Bouquet closed the pistol case and stowed it on a shelf behind his table. When the two men had finished, he ushered all three of his guests to the door. "Gentlemen, I am very happy to see you traveling together. May you have a safe journey and I look forward to seeing you very soon at Fort Pitt."

Wend followed the two men out of Bouquet's office. He wanted to set a time to meet with Arnold and was focusing on calculating how long it would take him to do his chores around the campsite. He noticed that Lieutenant Locke was standing in the center of the room, talking to someone seated in his chair. Arnold was pretending to work hard at his writing, but Wend could see that he was casting frequent glances at the object of Locke's attentions.

Wend's view of Locke's guest was obscured by his Johann and Mr. Gibson, who were continuing their discussions. He moved out from behind them to get to Arnold's table and was suddenly able to see the lieutenant's conversation partner and the target of Arnold's furtive glances.

It was the girl from the landing at Harris' Ferry!

Wend saw that his visualization of her in his dreams had been accurate. She was as devastatingly beautiful as he had remembered. Wend felt his heart pounding and the room growing hot. As he struggled to control his emotions he realized he was staring at her and quickly averted his eyes. But not before he noticed that she was now looking up at him in that cool, appraising manner he had noticed at the ferry.

Gibson was making introductions. "Eckert, this is my daughter, Abigail, who is also the mistress of my household, since her dear mother, bless her soul, departed us two years ago." He smiled round at all in the room. "She does a marvelous job of taking care of me, and the Lord knows I need someone to do that." He beamed down at her. "Abigail, this is Mr. Johann Eckert. We are, eh," he hesitated momentarily, "*Fortunate* that his family will be traveling with us to Fort Pitt."

Abigail rose from her chair, and greeted Wend's father with a slight curtsey. Then her father said, "And this is Master Eckert."

She turned to Wend and said very formally, "I am pleased to meet you, Sir," smiling at him and looking directly into his eyes.

Wend throttled his rising excitement and was able to control his voice as he responded to her greeting. He made a slight bow. "Nice to meet you, Miss Gibson." He would have liked to have said more to her, to have offered some pleasantry, but his imagination failed him, and in any case he worried that he would stumble in an attempt at conversation. *Better to display taciturnity than awkwardness.*

After briefly appraising him with her eyes, the girl turned away from Wend and, seating herself, resumed her conversation with Lieutenant Locke. Wend noticed they were getting along very well indeed. The officer was making the kind of light, witty talk Wend knew he could not match. And Abigail was responding to his comments with smiles and laughter which echoed through the room.

Wend was brought back to the business at hand by Arnold, who had gotten up from his desk and motioned Wend to follow him into the common room. "I'll be finished here just before supper and Locke says I can have the evening off duty. I'm staying at the fort with the quartermaster's men. Meet me there as soon as you can and I'll show you something of Carlisle tonight."

* * *

In the late afternoon Wend walked down to Carlisle Army Encampment where he found Arnold reclining on a cot in the only barracks hut which was occupied. The stockade had no permanent garrison, and aside from the young corporal, the only soldiers present turned out to be quartermasters with the job of readying the supply convoy for its trip to the west.

The corporal climbed out of his cot with a cry of greeting and together they walked to another building, a log store house. Arnold stripped off his outer coat and waistcoat, carefully folding them over some boxes. Then, in his shirtsleeves, he felt around behind the boxes. In a second he lifted an earthen jug by its handle. He pulled the cork and smelled the contents, sighing with pleasure.

"This is the real thing, Wend. These Ulstermen know how to make whiskey with a bite." He took a small swig. "Not like that weak beer and cider we used to scrounge in Lancaster." He quickly arranged some flour sacks to make comfortable seats for them. He handed the jug to Wend. "Try this, but take a small sip, not a gulp."

Wend followed his directions, but even the small amount he swallowed burned his throat like nothing he had taken before. He inadvertently shook his head as a tingling feeling flowed over his face, neck and shoulders. "Good Lord!"

Arnold laughed at the expression on Wend's face. He took the jug back for another sip.

The two spent the next hour in cheerful banter. Worried about the potency of Arnold's fiery whiskey, Wend was careful to keep his consumption to the minimum. They talked about school, about girls back in their hometown, and about Charlie Sawak, the Conestoga Indian who lived near them and who had often been their compatriot in boyhood mischief.

Arnold told Wend about his days soldiering. He had enlisted in the Royal Americans in 1757, less than a year after they had been organized. Taking the King's Shilling had been an act of defiance for him; a way to avoid joining his father in the coopering trade. It had enraged the elder Spengler and Wend knew that Arnold had not been home since enlisting. Then, in 1758, he had marched in General Forbes' 6,000 man expedition to capture French Fort Duquesne at the site where Fort Pitt now stood. During the entire campaign the young soldier had never fired his musket in anger. He had spent most of his time with an axe in his hands clearing the road which was later named after Forbes himself. As Wend knew, the campaign ended when the French, realizing the overwhelming size of the British force, blew up their stronghold

19

and retreated along the Allegheny River toward Canada. After that climax, he had been initially stationed in the garrison at Fort Ligonier, about forty miles east of Pitt. Then his company had moved to Fort Pitt itself, where Bouquet kept his main headquarters. It was there that Lieutenant Locke had discovered Arnold's abilities as a clerk and his life style had started to improve.

Wend had a question. "My father greatly admires Bouquet. I know he is Swiss, but I've never understood what led to a foreign officer having so much power in the Army."

"That's easy enough, Wend." Arnold took a pull on the jug. "It started with the organization of the Royal Americans. The Crown wanted to form a regiment made up of colonists, and decided to enlist men of German descent, because the generals calculated that they would take discipline well, certainly better than the Ulstermen or the Irish. And since it was a new regiment, they wanted experienced officers to lead it. So the government offered commissions to a core of mercenary officers, many Swiss like Bouquet. It was a good move, because these men had served in many armies and had seen a variety of tactics." The corporal paused and thought for a moment. "Bouquet commanded troops in the Dutch army during the War of the Austrian Succession, fought for the King of Sardinia, and then lead a unit of the Prince of Orange's Swiss Guards before he came here."

Wend thought a moment. "So most of the men in the 60th are Germans like us?"

Arnold laughed. "Yeah, a lot are. But this is the army; nothing ever works out quite as planned! They couldn't get enough German boys to fill out the ranks. So they had to recruit all over the colonies and even in Britain. So now you got the biggest regiment in the army, four battalions, and besides the Germans, you got Welch, Irish, Scots, and English."

There was a pause in their conversation as Wend considered his friend's words, and Arnold took the opportunity to suggest that they visit a tavern he knew about that would have music and catered to what he called a "lively clientele". By this time reasonably well fortified, the two sauntered down Market Street as the day turned to dusk. The gathering darkness was taking some of the rough edges off of the town. Lights glowed from windows of houses and taverns. Shops were closed and dark. Men were hurrying home from work. The boys felt a contentment fueled by the whiskey and their renewed fellowship. They approached a well lighted tavern and Wend saw a sign above the door which showed a man holding a lantern high to a traveler leading a horse. He pointed it out to Arnold.

"That's the Walking Horse Tavern," the soldier noted. "Best food in town and the most expensive."

Large windows opened into the common room, where they could see that each table, even those unoccupied by diners, were laid with place settings and lighted by candles. The combination of the multiple candles and the fire in the hearth created an inviting atmosphere. The tavern was doing a substantial business and servers, both male and female, moved around the tables carrying trays. Wend noted that the patrons seemed well heeled.

"Hey, look Wend!" Arnold grabbed his elbow. "There's that dandy Locke showing the Gibsons a good time."

Wend saw them at a table near the hearth. Locke, splendid in his uniform, was engaged in animated conversation with Gibson and his daughter. Magistrate Gibson sipped at a wine glass while the adjutant talked. Abigail, her hands folded in her lap, listened attentively, leaning toward him with an engaging smile and nodding as the officer talked. As they watched, Abigail broke into laughter at something Locke had said. She quickly reached out across the table and touched his hand momentarily, said something to him, then smiled coquettishly as the lieutenant resumed speaking. Wend suddenly felt a knot in his stomach at the sight of the girl playing up to the officer. Then, almost immediately, he realized that he was experiencing, for the first time in his life, the pang of jealousy.

His concentration was broken by Arnold. "God, that girl is put together in a nice way: Big blue eyes, fair hair, pretty face, and I'll wager you, long legs under those petticoats. She is going to cause a sensation when she arrives at Fort Pitt! The young subalterns will be fighting each other to spend time with her. Locke sure isn't wasting any time trying to make an impression while he has the field to himself."

He turned and started to walk and Wend caught up.

"I have to say that you certainly took her in stride." He guided Wend around a corner and down a side street. "When she and her father first came to the office today, Locke looked up from his writing table and his eyes nearly jumped out of their sockets. He practically knocked over the table in his haste to greet them and he kept looking at the girl even while shaking old man Gibson's hand. Then he went into his best 'gentleman officer' routine to impress her." He paused and shook his head. "Me, I didn't get any work done while she was in the office. Just tried to make sure she wouldn't catch me staring." Arnold turned to Wend. "But you were like an old stone face! You came out of Bouquet's office and hardly looked at her. Then, she gave you that wide smile when Gibson introduced you and you dismissed her with a curt nod and the briefest of greetings."

Wend was shocked to learn that Arnold thought he had behaved so coolly in front of Abigail. But it was also gratifying that he hadn't been taken for a tongue-tied adolescent.

As they walked down the new street, Arnold was off on another subject now. "That's the Widow Downey's house." He pointed to a two story house made of squared-off logs and with a high peaked roof. "Her husband was a shopkeeper. After he died, the shop failed. So she started doing laundry and sewing to make ends meet, and takes in borders in upstairs rooms."

Wend looked over the house, which seemed non-descript. "So, what makes the widow interesting?"

"Her boarders are always men, many of whom only stay a night or two, and tongues wagging around town have it that she provides special services, for a little extra consideration."

In his naivety, it took Wend a couple of seconds to understand that Arnold meant the widow was prostituting herself. "Is she a pretty woman?"

"Not particularly fine looking in the face, but she has a nice smile, a good figure, and great tits from what I've seen of her, mostly from a distance. But I did talk to her once. Joshua Baird stays here when he's in town, and Lieutenant Locke sent me here once to fetch him to see the colonel."

"Joshua Baird? Is he in the army?"

"He's a lot of things, but he's not a soldier. He spent years trading with the Indians; he's a crack shot with a rifle and when he's in this area he hunts game and fowl for sale to the taverns. Over the last few years, he's been on Bouquet's payroll as a scout and courier. He knows all the Indian trails through the bush and was one of the guides who helped Bouquet pick out the route for Forbes Road last year. Now that the fighting with the French is over, the colonel uses him to keep up with what is going on in the Ohio tribes."

As they walked beyond the widow's house Wend saw a brightly lit tavern a little further down the street. The music of a fiddle wafted from an open window. "What's that place?"

"That's where we're headed," Arnold smiled. "Larkin's Tavern: A place of indifferent food and drink, but one where we can afford the price of ale. More importantly, it caters, at least at night, to younger patrons and I'll guarantee you'll see a pretty face or two."

Wend felt his pocket. His access to cash was limited, but before meeting Arnold he had dug out from his stash in the tool wagon the few coins he had accumulated from doing odd jobs. He would have to be careful to make it last.

They were only a few feet from the tavern when suddenly the door swung open, spilling light into the street. A well-dressed, middle-aged man carrying a walking stick stepped out onto the small porch and descended the stairs to the sidewalk just in front of the boys. The man adjusted his broad brimmed beaver hat as he turned toward the two. He looked at Arnold, and sudden recognition flared in his eyes. "You there, soldier: Aren't you Lieutenant Locke's clerk?"

Arnold stood tall and nodded. "Yes, Mr. Grenough. Corporal Spengler, Sir."

"Thought I had the face right! Well listen sharp now: When you get to work tomorrow, tell Locke that I've just arrived from York tonight. I'll be in to see Henry about mid-morning to pay my respects and I'll buy him the noon meal." He paused a moment to reflect, then said, "You'll remember that?"

Arnold nodded again. "Absolutely, Sir, I know the colonel has been expecting that you would call on him."

"Yes, I've gotten into Carlisle days later than I expected. Getting pack trains ready at my York and Shippensburg warehouses delayed me. The man touched the walking stick to his hat brim. "Good lad, then, I'll see you tomorrow." He passed the boys and strode off toward Market Street.

Wend asked, "Who was that?"

"Richard Grenough; he owns one of the biggest Indian trading companies in Pennsylvania and he's a good friend of Bouquet's. He knows many of the tribal chiefs personally and has attended council fires out at Fort Pitt right alongside the colonel and colonial officials."

They entered the tavern, and Wend immediately knew he had never been anywhere comparable in Lancaster. Smoke from the hearth in the rear wall of the common room combined with the aromatic pipe smoke of patrons to create a foggy atmosphere and made his eyes water. A counter ran the entire distance along the wall to the right as they entered, and at the far end sat a young man playing a fiddle, with tankard and a pipe lying on a table beside him. The entire space was crowded, hot, and noisy, with shouts and laughter. Wend could see that his friend had been right about the age of the clientele. Most were older than either he or Arnold, but few seemed to be beyond their twenties. Wend was surprised to see that a fair amount of young women were present, as customers as well as servers. His eyes were drawn to the dress of the women, featuring petticoats and blouses which were much more colorful and revealing than the norm in his town.

Arnold saw Wend staring at the exposed cleavage of one of the serving girls, and with a sly smile, said, "Yes, Wend, you're not in Lancaster anymore."

They made their way through the crowd to the counter and Arnold greeted several of the patrons sitting at tables or standing about. Clearly he was a frequent visitor to Larkin's establishment. Arnold ordered beers for both, which Wend paid for in honor of his friend having supplied the jug used in their earlier drinking. Then they leaned back against the bar to take in the sights and sounds of the house. Wend felt out of his element, but was taken with the bright music played by the fiddler and almost immediately felt his spirits soaring and the urge to tap his foot with the rhythm. Several couples danced in a cleared area on the far side of the tavern.

Wend noticed that his friend was suddenly quiet, seemingly lost in thought. "Hey, what's on your mind, Arnold?"

Arnold looked at Wend, a puzzled expression on his face. "You know, I was surprised to see Grenough here at Larkin's. Doesn't seem to be his kind of place; I would have more expected to have seen him up at The Walking Horse with other people who have a lot of coin to jiggle in their pockets."

Wend thought for a second, then suggested, "Maybe he had a meeting with someone here?"

Arnold nodded. "Maybe so." Then he shrugged and turned to engage in conversation with a young man next to him, who he introduced simply as "John." Their attention was focused on the ample endowments of a red-headed girl seated at a table on the other side of the room with a male companion. Wend gathered that both Arnold and his friend knew the young lady. Presently it became clear that the girl in question was aware of their presence at the bar, for she began casting glances toward the pair, to the visible discomfort of the man at her table.

After a while Arnold turned to Wend with a crooked smile on his face. "Hey, stay here and watch my beer. John and I are going to say hello to someone." The two left without waiting for any reply, and sauntered over to the table where the couple sat.

Wend nursed his drink and watched as the pair stood talking with the couple. He noticed that the man at the table was burley and broad shouldered, with well shaped facial features framed by a shock of brown hair, pulled back around the sides of his head and tied off in a cue at the rear. He had a broad, easy smile and a twinkle in his eyes as he spoke to the girl. Wend reflected

24

that the combination probably made him very attractive to women. After a few minutes, John sat down with at the table and Arnold walked back to his drink at the counter.

Wend asked, "I guess you know that couple well?"

"I know Molly Reed well. She's the daughter of a harness maker on the edge of town and John has been seeing her on a regular basis. He considers her his girl. But the man was a stranger to me until we went over to the table. I've never seen him in here before." Arnold took a swig of his beer. "His name is Matt Bratton. He says he is a waggoner who runs freight from here to Sherman Valley in the upper part of the county."

Wend noticed that the red haired girl was sharing uneasy smiles equally between the two men at the table. "Maybe Molly doesn't think of herself as John's girl."

"Well, that's why John made a point of inviting himself to their table, to protect his interest." He paused and took another drink. "If she's trying to make him jealous, I'd wager she's doing it very successfully."

Several other people stopped by to talk to Arnold. But Wend increasingly felt out of place and alone in the crowd. Presently, he began to worry about getting back to his family's campsite before he got into too much trouble with his parents. He was about to suggest to Arnold that he leave when the real trouble began.

Wend heard shouting, furniture banging on the floor, and glass breaking. Then for a brief moment the whole crowd went quiet. He turned around to see that Arnold's friend John and the waggoner Bratton had taken their competition over Molly Reed from conversation to blows. John had risen from his seat and grabbed Bratton by the shirt; the two were grappling next to the table as Molly and other patrons formed a circle and watched in amusement. The two men's blows had just seriously started when Larkin, himself a large, muscular man, rushed to the table and drove his body between them. "If you are intent on knocking each other's heads, take it out to the back lot." He stood defiantly between the two men, a hand on each heaving chest.

A chant spread among customers in the room, "Fight out back, fight out back!" The proprietor pushed the combatants through a door to the left of the fireplace. The rest of the crowd flowed out behind. Arnold grabbed Wend's arm. "Come on, let's go out and see what happens."

At first, as the two faced off in the lot behind the tavern, Wend thought they were well matched. They were of a similar height. But it soon became clear that Bratton was much heavier and more practiced in brawling than

Arnold's friend. Moreover, he had muscular arms and large fists which could deliver hammer-like blows to an opponent's body and he rapidly demonstrated that he knew how to make every punch hit home. John's counterpunches were nearly all ineffective, even when he was able to get through Bratton's guard to land a blow. Soon Bratton began to regularly knock John off his feet and blood was running from his nose and mouth. But the youth gamely got to his feet to take more punishment. Finally, the waggoner hit John a blow to the face which landed with an audible, sickening crunch and visibly rearranged his nose. This time the youth didn't get up.

Bratton jumped on top of his prostrate victim, obviously in a blood lust. He grabbed John's shirt collar with one hand and raised his other in a big fist with the obvious intention of finishing the fight with a bone crushing slam to his face. Before Wend realized what was happening, Arnold sprang behind the big man and grabbed his arm with both hands. "Damn it! You'll kill him!" Arnold shouted, "You've won the fight, back off!"

There were loud shouts from the crowd, some urging Bratton to pummel John, others siding with Arnold. Bratton looked up, then rose and pivoted toward Spengler with a demonic grin on his face. He almost effortlessly shook the soldier off, knocking him to the ground at Wend's feet. Now in an even deeper fury, the big waggoner drew a foot back and administered a vicious kick to Arnold's stomach. "You redcoat bastard: Don't even think about interfering with my business!"

Wend instinctively went to his knees to help Arnold, who gasped and writhed in agony. But suddenly he felt himself being hoisted to his feet. Bratton grasped Wend's jacket with both hands and lifted him off his feet. The waggoner's face was mere inches from his own. Wend could smell the pungent odor of ale on his breath and the scent of his greasy hair.

The burley waggoner was looking around at the crowd and making fun of Wend. "Look at this little Dutch boy trying to help out his redcoat friend!" He faced Wend again and laughed. "You don't even belong in a place like this. I should give you a taste of my fist, but, damn, you're not worth it!"

Laughter echoed through the onlookers. And with that Bratton dropped Wend, who hit the ground on one foot, lost his balance and crumpled on top of Arnold. Embarrassment and fury ran through Wend. He balled his fists, ready to rise and lash out at his tormentor. But then he looked up at the towering man standing above him and realized any attempt to strike back would be futile.

Bratton turned and stood above John in a combative pose, but the young man lay in a stupor and it was evident to all that the fight was over. The crowd began to file back into the tavern. Clearly, John had lost not only the fight but also the allegiance of Molly. She followed Bratton into Larkin's, laughing at something he said, without a glance back at John.

Arnold, still gasping for breath, crawled over and knelt beside his friend. Larkin also lingered at the scene of the fight and produced a towel which he tossed to the corporal. "Here, clean him up, Spengler. But don't let him back in my place tonight." The tavern keeper looked down at John, who now was moving his head and had his swollen eyes open. "If it makes you feel any better, Bratton is a practiced brawler with a reputation throughout the county. You didn't have a chance with him." He looked through the door into the common room, where Bratton and Molly had resumed seats at their table. "He also is quite a favorite with girls in the towns on his freight route. I've heard plenty of stories about his amorous adventures from traveling merchants and waggoners." He turned to Arnold. "So take your friend home and let him get used to the idea that fair Molly has a new beau."

After Larkin had gone, Wend, still on the ground, looked over at Spengler as he tended to John's bloody face. He said dryly, "Arnold, are your nights with a 'lively clientele' always like this one?"

The corporal grimaced. "Things did get a little out of hand, didn't they?" He shook his head and a look of pure anger came over his face. "If that waggoner—Bratton—ever finds himself at one of the forts with me and some of my friends, he'll find out how soldiers deal with his kind. Somewhere along the way I'm going to settle the score with him."

* * *

Early the next morning, Wend was at work with his carpentry tools in the courtyard of the tavern where the Gibsons were staying. Physically, he was busy measuring the bed of their canvas covered wagon to install a brace. But in his mind he was still smarting over the rough handling and humiliation he had received the night before at the hands of Matt Bratton. Then his thoughts were interrupted by the sound of approaching footsteps. He looked up to see a black man, who Wend estimated was in his early twenties, watching him.

"Good morning, sir. Would you be called Wend?"

Wend had seen blacks before but had never spoken with one. He remembered that last night father had talked about the Gibsons having a slave and curiously took in the man's facial features, his heavy lips and broad nose before replying. "I'm Wend Eckert. Are you Mr. Gibson's man?"

"Yes sir. That's who I work for." He continued, "Mr. Gibson and your father been talking, over in the tavern, and I'm supposed to tell you to help me unload that cart and hitch up the horse."

Wend realized that Johann had convinced the magistrate to replace the Gibsons' other rig, a rickety one-horse cart. When Johann had inspected their vehicles on the previous day, it had become obvious that the lawyer had made some poor acquisitions; both vehicles were too flimsy for the ruggedness of Forbes Road. So he had convinced the lawyer to buy some milled planking and Wend had been assigned to shape and attach braces to the wagon's bed. He climbed down from his perch. "All right, let's get started. What do they call you?"

"My name is Franklin."

Wend had no idea of how to treat a slave, but after thinking it over, decided it best to consider him simply a worker like himself. He extended a hand to the black man, who hesitated momentarily, then took it with a smile. "Glad to meet you, Franklin."

They quickly unloaded the chests and boxes in the cart, stacking them against a wall of the stable. Then they worked together to get the horse harnessed. Wend saw that Franklin didn't waste any motion in his work. "Have you been long in the service of the Gibsons?"

"Mr. Gibson purchased me just before they left Philadelphia. When they found out he was going to make this trip he figured he'd need some extra help. Before that I was with a merchant; I used to drive his cart to deliver goods to his customers."

Soon after they finished, Johann and Gibson came walking from the tavern. Eckert led the magistrate to the wagon and pointed out the reinforcements Wend was making. He turned to Wend. "Mr. Gibson and I are going to visit a couple of stables I know of on the west side of town, to see if we can find a reasonably priced wagon and team which will serve his needs better than the cart. Go ahead with the work to this wagon; we should be back by the early afternoon at the latest."

Gibson crossed his arms in front of his chest, pursed his lips, and stared unhappily at the cart. "Now see here, Eckert: Are you sure about this? Do I really need to go to the expense of replacing this cart with a farm wagon and a two-horse team? The blacksmith I bought this from in Philadelphia said it was just the thing for use here in the settlements; he said farmers use these all the time."

Johann cocked his head to the left and looked over at Wend with frustration in his eyes. "Magistrate, that wasn't a total lie he told you. This thing would be good for milk delivery or carrying light loads here in the flat valley lands. But I'll tell you right now it isn't going to make it over the first mountains we come to, between the Path Valley and the Great Cove, let alone Sideling Hill or Allegheny Mountain. If you don't replace it with a proper wagon and strong team, you are going to loose some of your goods, and that's a fact!"

Gibson considered for a few seconds more, then stamped his foot in resignation and nodded his head. "Well, I guess there's no choice. You're sure we can get a credit for the horse and cart?"

Johann nodded. "There are plenty of horse and wagon traders who'll make a deal, Magistrate. And it will cost you a lot less than having to leave half of your possessions along the road somewhere up in the ridges."

With that, the two men boarded the cart and drove off down the street. Seeing them crowded together on the small bench seat, Wend got the impression of grownups playing with a child's toy.

He turned back to Franklin with a smile. "Well, it looks like they get the fun and we get the work!"

Wend felt a sense of companionship with the black man as they labored. Franklin was a great help as they fitted corner braces to the forward and rear ends of the wagon bed. Wend was leaning over, sawing a plank, when he noticed from the corner of his eye that Abigail had quietly approached and was watching him work.

Franklin acknowledged her presence with a bow of his head and by touching his right hand to his forehead. "Morning, Mistress Abigail."

She nodded curtly to Franklin, but said nothing to Wend and avoided his eyes. He ignored her as he continued his work. Abigail paced slowly around the wagon, inspecting the changes and then looking over the stacked boxes and trunks by the stable. He watched her surreptitiously. She was wearing a more casual outfit than when he had seen her previously; a light grey petticoat with a white blouse. A matching gray kerchief was over her shoulders and knotted in front and a small white cap, held in place with pins, covered the golden hair. She looked as pretty in a workday outfit as in formal traveling attire.

It was then that he looked up and saw that Abigail had approached him and was standing so close over him, her arms crossed in front of her, that he had no choice but to acknowledge her presence. They stared at each other silently for several long seconds. Finally, to end the standoff, Wend said, "Good morning, Mistress Gibson."

The girl put her hands on her hips. "I've seen you before, haven't I?" It was more a statement than a question, delivered in an imperious, almost haughty tone. "I mean before yesterday at Colonel Bouquet's office. It was at the landing at Harris' Ferry, two days ago. You were driving that wagon"—she pointed to the tool wagon— "And you were loading it onto the boat."

Wend felt a cold knot in his stomach. Was this girl going to make fun of him for what he considered his moment of indecision and hesitancy at the ferry?

But instead she said, "You and your family caused us a lot of trouble. You took the place we were promised on the ferry."

Wend stood up. "Wait a minute, Mistress Gibson. We got to the ferry just as it arrived. And no one else was in line. I heard the ferry man tell your father that he loaded fares as they arrived."

She looked at him sternly. "In the tavern, before you arrived, he said we could be next. And Franklin went out right away to hitch up the horses. Then you suddenly appeared and got ahead. The ferry proprietor should have kept his word! We could have been ready in a few more minutes."

Irritated at her manner, Wend retorted: "Well, perhaps you should have gotten up two hours before dawn, like we did, and then you'd have been in place for the ferry when it was at the landing." He thought a moment. "No doubt the proprietor meant you could go next if you were ready. People out here get started earlier than in the city."

She ignored his words. "You delayed us for over two hours, until the boat got back. And then, even driving hard, we couldn't get to Carlisle until long after dark and had to search in the night for a tavern that could put us up."

Wend allowed himself a tight smile. "If you had camped out in the clearings on the outskirts of town, like we did, you'd have been to sleep much earlier." He couldn't resist adding, "That would have been good practice anyway; you won't see any taverns along Forbes Road!"

She stared at him fiercely, then changed the subject and moderated her voice. "At any rate, I learned a lot about you from watching at the ferry landing."

"And just what do you mean by that, Mistress Gibson?"

"I'm very good at observing people and understanding what's going on in their mind."

Wend couldn't keep from laughing. "So now you have me all figured out?"

"Yes, I do." She thought for a moment. "You like to think things out before you act. You looked at the boat and saw that there wasn't much room and that the steepness of the ramp would make things difficult. I could almost hear your brain turning over like a mill, calculating just how to get your horses and wagon in place. And you didn't let yourself be hurried until you were ready to move."

Wend was unnerved by her accurate appraisal of his actions at the ferry and angered at her superior tone. Moreover, still upset over events of the previous night, he wasn't in any mood to be analyzed by a city girl. He shot back, "Come on, Mistress Gibson, are you so experienced with handling horses and wagons that you could be sure what I was thinking?"

She smirked and deflected his question. "Why do you find it hard to call me Abigail? 'Mistress Gibson' seems so formal. We are going to be traveling together for a long time. Do you plan to call me 'Mistress Gibson' all the way to Fort Pitt?"

"All right, then, *Abigail*," Wend emphasized each syllable of her name, "But you still didn't answer my question."

"No, I'm not very familiar with horses. Actually, I've spent more time with horses in the last week than I had in my entire life. But I noticed you hesitated before you started up the ramp and I watched the concentration on your face. To tell the truth, I don't think you are that experienced with horses either."

Despite her feisty words, Wend knew that he had put her on the defensive.

Then her statement about having no experience with horses before leaving Philadelphia triggered a thought in his mind. He remembered Bouquet's anger about being saddled with a city lawyer as magistrate for Pittsburgh. *There was indeed something strange about the Gibsons being sent to Pitt. And why would Gibson, with his beautiful and lively marriage-aged daughter, agree to leave a law practice and the congenial city society for service in the remote Ohio Country?*

Wend knew he couldn't ask the girl that question outright, so he searched for an oblique approach that would shed some light on the mystery. At last, he felt he had a query which would broach the subject. "Is your father looking forward to his new job at Pittsburgh? I guess it will be quite a change from Philadelphia."

Wend saw Abigail's body abruptly stiffen. In her more upright stance, he was able to see her breasts in profile as they pushed against the white blouse. They had a delicate, up thrusting curve and in his mind he could visualize the pointed nipples.

In a slow, deliberate motion she turned her head to look at him, her steely eyes boring into his own. A darkening flowed over her face. Then she answered in a tightly controlled voice, "Father welcomes the opportunity to perform a valuable service to the colony. And we are both looking forward to experiencing the adventures of living in the Ohio Country."

Abigail gave Wend a stiff, cold smile and then abruptly turned and started to walk back toward the tavern. "I must get back to my room; I have to get ready for an appointment." She turned to look directly at Wend. "I'm having lunch with a *gentleman.*" The girl put unmistakable emphasis on the word gentleman. "So I'll leave you to your work."

As they labored, Wend reflected on Abigail's reaction to his question about her father. Her words were obviously rehearsed, as if it were a query she had fielded before and one to which she wanted to present a standard, unimpeachable answer. It clearly shielded any true thoughts she had about their future home and living conditions. Wend was now certain that the Gibsons wished to keep the real motivation for their moving to Fort Pitt hidden from outsiders.

Wend turned to Franklin. "Is your Mistress always so direct in her conversation?"

Franklin looked at Wend with a conspiratorial glint in his eye. "Mistress Abigail, she always knows exactly what she wants' to say. And she's used to being in charge around the house. Back in Philadelphia they had a maid and a cook, both older than her, but there was no doubt who was giving the orders. Me, I was glad that I spent most of my time in the stables." He laughed. "But Master Wend, you know what I just said is between you and me only."

Wend nodded. He decided to ask a question which was of vital importance to him. "She seems very young to have so much authority in the family. How old is she?"

"She just turned 16 before we left the city. Master Gibson had a party: Sort of a combination going away party for them and a birthday party for her."

Wend was pleased with the way the conversation was going. He saw the opportunity to get more information about Abigail. "If she's sixteen, she must have had gentlemen calling on her for a while."

"Well, since I was only there a couple of weeks before we left, I didn't see much myself. But the cook and I got to be pretty good friends, and she told me that Miss Abigail had a good number of men callers. But they didn't often keep coming round. Maybe once or twice, then they seemed to move on."

Wend considered Franklin's words. "Why do you think that happened? She's a nice looking girl."

"Well, the word from the cook was that they were afraid of her. She's plenty smart, says her mind, and as you can see, she is used to being in control of things. It seems the young gentlemen felt uneasy with her. They generally moved on to some young girl who made them feel more comfortable."

Wend smiled at him, thinking about his sparring with Abigail. "I can see why a man might feel uncomfortable around Abigail."

Franklin nodded. "But I think there's something else which kept her from getting close to suitors. Since her mother died, she's been the lady of the household and she has been looking out for her father. It's hard for me to put my finger on it, I've been with them such a short time, but for some reason she thinks she has to protect him from something."

Franklin, perhaps realizing that he was revealing too much about his household to an outsider, stopped talking. They resumed work and in a few minutes Wend saw a familiar figure approaching. It was Lieutenant Locke, coming up Market Street from the direction of Washburn's Tavern. The lieutenant walked past without taking notice of them and entered the tavern.

Franklin leaned over to Wend. "There's that Redcoat officer again. It does appear that Mistress Abigail has a new suitor and she sure has been on her best behavior around him."

Wend remembered what Arnold had said the previous evening. "She may have had some trouble with men back in Philadelphia, where there were plenty of young ladies to choose from, but when she gets to Fort Pitt, men will be willing to overlook her strong willed nature."

"Maybe so, maybe so, Master Wend." Franklin replied in a thoughtful way. Then he smiled and winked at Wend. "But whoever takes her on is sure going to have both his hands full."

CHAPTER 3

The Great Wagon Road

The Gibson-Eckert caravan left Carlisle an hour after dawn the next morning. Magistrate Gibson, with Johann's assistance, had purchased a sturdy farm wagon and team. The two men arrived back at the inn by the time Wend and Franklin had finished strengthening the Gibsons' original wagon. Then Johann had supervised as the four men redistributed the Gibson family's possessions between the two vehicles.

Their goal for the first day was to reach the town of Shippensburg, a fast paced drive of twenty miles, possible only because of the good quality of the road. Along the way, they met considerable traffic, including numerous Conestoga freight wagons. Wend knew that the road down though the broad Cumberland Valley was part of the main north-south artery for commerce which extended through several colonies and was known as "The Great Wagon Road."

The sun was fading when Johann finally led the wagons into a campsite at the turnoff to Shippensburg. A creek ran through the meadow and Wend saw the remains of many old fires. Johann told him the spot was a favorite stopping place for travelers and army contingents. Wend and Franklin worked together to put the teams on the picket line and feed the horses. When that was done, he and Bernd cut and hauled wood for the evening fire.

Wend was just finishing stacking the wood by the family fire when Johann leaned over and whispered, "I'm concerned about that new team which Gibson bought yesterday. If there is anything infirm about them, we might be able to see it now or in the morning. And if there is a problem, Shippensburg is the last sizable town where we can get them looked after or changed." He paused to see if anyone was watching them. "Gibson won't know enough to do it himself. Why don't you go over and casually check our horses, and if you can do it without attracting a lot of attention, inspect the legs on the Gibsons' teams also."

Wend nodded and wandered over to the picket line. He made a show of inspecting the hind legs and hooves of their own animals. Then he moved to the front of the horses and did the same, moving on to the Gibson's new team when he was sure no one was watching. As he moved along, checking the animals' front legs, he saw Gibson and his daughter at their fire about 30 feet away, apparently oblivious to his presence with the horses. Gibson was seated on a log before the fire, slumped down, staring at his hands as if examining them. In his eyes was a look of weariness and sadness. Abigail stood behind him, her hands massaging his shoulders and upper arms. As Wend watched, she whispered something to her father and suddenly reached down and hugged him. He put his hands on hers and they remained in that position for a time, obviously sharing a moment of emotion.

Wend felt like an intruder spying into their personal world. He returned his attention to the horses, moving to the rear legs of the Gibson's new team.

Suddenly he was startled to hear Abigail's voice behind him. "Might I ask what's going on here? What are you doing to our horses?"

Wend turned and looked up to see her watching; her hands on her hips, a cross look on her face. He said, "I'm not doing anything to your horses. I'm just checking all the teams, yours and ours, to see if they're still firm after the day's travel."

"I can see that. I could understand you working on your own teams. Why are you so concerned about ours?"

Her tone was a repeat of the haughtiness which she had shown in the Carlisle tavern yard and Wend lost his patience. He blurted, "To tell the truth, because your father wouldn't have thought of doing it himself, or had the knowledge to check on the new team's condition. Think about it; they were purchased just yesterday. Today was their first hard travel. If there is a problem, we need to do something about it here, before we get to the really rough country where there're no horse dealers."

She shot back, "We have Franklin. He knows how to look out for our horses. And if you felt the need to look yourself, why didn't you have the consideration to tell us what you were doing?"

"Look, Abigail, Bouquet asked us to help you travel to Fort Pitt. Like you said yesterday, we'll have to work together for several weeks. If I have to discuss every routine chore with you or your father, we'll waste time. Why don't you just accept that we're trying to help and learn from people who've spent a lot of time traveling in the bush?"

"Don't be smart with me, Wend Eckert. You think you can lord it over me because we're stuck together in this caravan and you fancy yourself an expert on horses and wagons. But be careful; things will be different when we get to Fort Pitt."

Wend's anger flared. He snapped, "I don't know what they told you in Philadelphia, but think about this, Mistress Gibson: Pitt is still under construction. Even officers are living in primitive shacks and cabins. It won't be much different from life here on the road. You better get used to these conditions and working with the people around you."

Abigail's eyes grew large and fiery with anger. She clenched her jaw and balled her hands into fists as they rested on her hips.

Wend calmed himself, and thought: *She's not used to anyone talking back to her like that.* In an attempt to soothe her he started explaining what he was doing. He rubbed his hand along one horse's flank and then down the rear leg. "I'm feeling for swelling, a knot in the muscles or the animal showing any sensitivity to my touch. Then I'll check the hooves."

But Abigail was having none of it. She glared at him, her jaw jutting out. "Fine! Do what you have to!" Then she turned and stocked back to her fire.

Wend quickly finished checking the horses and hurried to give his report to Johann.

As he ate his meal by the firelight, Wend thought of the scene he had witnessed at the Gibson campfire and the weary, dejected look in their eyes. It struck him that the day's events had been an awakening for them; their first exposure to the realities of travel in the back country. Previously, the trip must have been something of an adventure, driving from tavern to tavern, seeing new towns, handling horses on well maintained roads. Now they had experienced the work of setting up camp, preparing meals, tending to the livestock, and a multitude of other chores. Franklin was a help, but he could do only a fraction of the necessary work. Moreover, their sadness reinforced his conviction that there was some cloud over the Gibson family, some hidden reason for the appointment to Fort Pitt.

Wend also reflected on his feelings about Abigail. At first sight, he had been dazzled with her beauty and sophistication, all of which had combined to arouse an animal desire in him. *And still did, he had to admit.* But events of the last two days had tempered his thoughts about her; the strong willed attitude and airs of privilege were hard to take. *Clearly his thoughts about her*

back at the ferry had been right: She considered him in the same class as a servant.
He thought: *Arnold was right—she's for those stylish officers out at Pit—not a*
working apprentice like me.

* * *

The next day, after ten hours on the road, the caravan pulled up in a tiny
hamlet planted at the convergence of two streams. On one stream was a saw-
mill and the other, smaller stream supported a gristmill. Next to the gristmill
was a substantial two story house, constructed of stone with a slate roof. A
stockade surrounded both buildings. Johann told the travelers that the proprietor of both mills and owner of the house was a man named Benjamin
Chambers. The village was known by locals variously as Falling Waters,
Chambers' Mills or simply Chambers' Fort.

While the rest of the group set up camp, Johann and Gibson went to
pay a call on Chambers. Eckert knew the man by reputation; Chambers
had been a leader in the provincial forces during the emergency of 1755-56
when, in the aftermath of the Braddock defeat, Indian raids had terrorized
the Pennsylvania settlements.

Wend and Franklin unhitched each team in sequence, watering them at
the stream and then moving them to the picket line. They joshed with each
other as they worked in the evening light. They were just starting to unhitch
the last pair when the horses, anxious to get water, surged unexpectedly as
Franklin worked to unclip the trace chains. Suddenly Wend heard a sharp cry
of surprise and pain from the black man. He seized control of the team and
saw what had happened: The movement of the horses had dragged Franklin's
arm against a sharp metal fitting on the wagon tongue, causing a deep cut on
the forearm. Franklin moaned and held the wound with his opposite hand.
Blood surged up between his fingers and flowed down his arm. With a look
of agony on his face he staggered toward where Abigail was setting up a cooking fire.

Wend called out, "Mother! Franklin's been hurt!" Mary did the doctoring
in the Eckert family and had medical supplies in her wagon. He shouted to
Bernd, "Get the medical box for Mother!"

Abigail quickly took in the situation, and turned to Wend, an angry look
on her face. "He's my servant; I'll take care of this! Come here, Franklin!" She
took the black man's unhurt arm and guiding him to a seat on a stump and

said, "Keep your hand on the wound until I get back!" Then she ran to her own wagon, returning with a basket.

Wend called to Bernd, who helped him finish unhitching the team. When the horses were all on the picket rope, they returned to find that Abigail had cleaned out Franklin's cut with water and was holding a folded piece of cloth in place to staunch the bleeding. Wend saw that the basket on the ground beside her contained medical treatment supplies such as rolled bandages, scissors, and bottles of liquid. He stood watching as she held the black man's arm and applied pressure on the wound.

She looked over at Wend and said peremptorily, "Here, don't just stand there gaping! You can at least hold this compress over the wound for me."

Miffed at her tone, Wend felt a flash of anger, but hurried to comply. Once he had taken over, Abigail searched through the basket's contents and retrieved a dark colored bottle and a shiny stiletto shaped implement. Then she irrigated Franklin's wound with liquid from the bottle. Wend smelled a whiff of alcohol as she poured the liquid.

Abigail ordered: "Hold his arm level, I want to see if there's any foreign material in the wound." Then she probed the wound with the implement. Franklin winced, his body tensing as she worked. "I know it's causing you some pain, but I need to make sure that there's no wood or metal in your flesh." She finished soon and the tenseness went out of Franklin's body. Abigail pulled some wadding and a white, rolled cloth out of the basket, and took hold of the injured arm from Wend. She placed the wadding over the wound and wrapped the cloth tightly over it and around the arm, tying it off with neat knot.

Wend was impressed. Abigail knew exactly what to do and clearly had prepared for such an emergency. He was surprised that a city girl had the foresight to put together such a complete medical kit, including tools he had never seen before.

"That's going to hurt some for the next few days, and you may have a bit of a scar, but there will be no larger problem if we can prevent mortification. So I'll need to clean the wound again tonight and then in the morning." Abigail turned back to her basket and started to put away her supplies.

Wend said, "It looks like you have some experience with medical work."

She pursed her lips and looked at him with impatience, snapping, "Now why should that surprise you?"

Wend, taken aback by her tone, sputtered, "Well, I just didn't think …"

She cut him off. "What did you think? Did you think perhaps that I've spent all my life sitting around in a parlor? Just waiting until some suitor came around to entertain me in my leisure?" She picked up the basket and stood up. "I've been running a household for years. Despite what you might think, I know how to organize things and take care of my servants."

Wend bristled and fired back tersely, "Actually, how you spent your time in Philadelphia was the least of my thoughts."

Mary had quietly watched Abigail treat the wound and the exchange between the two of them. Now she came over and put her hand on Abigail's shoulder. "Yes, indeed, Abigail; it looks to me like you got a good touch with medical work." The two women looked over Franklin's arm. Then Mary said, "You'll want to clean up after this—you have blood over your hands and on your blouse. Why don't you and your family eat with us tonight, to save you time?"

Wend beat a retreat, glad for his mother's diversion. Shortly afterward, Johann and Gibson returned from Chambers' stockade and Johann came over to Wend. "There's an area along the road tomorrow which will provide a good opportunity for hunting. I'm going to send you out on your own." He spent a few moments explaining the lay of the road ahead and discussing his plans with Wend, then said, "So get your gear ready this evening while we still have some light."

Wend gathered his hunting kit from the wagons and went to the side of the mill stream to sit on the bank. He had pulled out his hunting shirt from the baggage. Mary had made it from undyed linen, taking the effort to put a fringe on the rain flap that covered the shoulders and to sew in some sizable pockets to hold hunting supplies. He had never washed it, and now it carried the aroma of many hunts, which helped him blend with the natural scents of the forest. He also brought his rifle, pistol, and the large bag in which he kept shot and tools. He transferred several balls to one pocket of the shirt. He took out an emergency ball and put it alone in another pocket, ready for quick access. He looked over his pistol, similar in design but less elaborate than the one they had given to Bouquet, to make sure everything was in order. Then he pulled out a steel knife from its sheath, and set about sharpening its eight-inch blade using the whetstone he had brought with him.

He was busy at his work when, to his surprise, Abigail walked up and sat down on the bank beside him, settling her petticoats around her. Her feet, like his, dangled a few inches above the flowing water. She sighed. "It is very peaceful here, don't you think?"

Wend looked around at the tiny village which straddled the stream. Lights were coming on in the houses and cabins as the day's light faded. There was a gentle breeze blowing, which was starting to dispel the heat of the July day. The faint rustling of the encircling forest seemed to enhance the pervasive sense of quietness and isolation. "Yes, yes it is," he agreed. "A little while ago I saw a fish jumping over on the other side."

They sat quietly for a few moments, listening to the sounds of the evening. Wend sensed the girl was trying to make peace, but he was still smoldering at the sharpness of her earlier words. He turned to Abigail. "When you were treating Franklin, I tried to complement you. You snapped at me for my pains, as if I was insulting you. Is that your idea of politeness in Philadelphia?"

Abigail looked down at the water and Wend could see her jaw tighten. "Yes, Wend, I did lash out at you. But I got mad because you called for your mother to treat Franklin. Your first thought was that I couldn't take care of my own household."

He retorted, "Well, what did you expect? In the last two days, I've seen little evidence that you could deal with this life." Immediately Wend realized that his response sounded harsher than he intended, and he waited for her to explode again.

Instead, she set her jaw, stared straight ahead, her face turning red. Then she spoke in measured words: "Listen carefully, Wend Eckert: I admit that you're right about us. Father and I aren't inured to this traveling routine. And Father's pride would never allow him to acknowledge it, but we feel overwhelmed by the number of things which are so foreign to our experience." She looked over at Wend. "But I'm determined to learn. Last night I set up the cook fire implements and prepared a meal in the open for the first time. Today I drove the team for a good part of the journey." She stared at him fiercely. "So I'll thank you to stop giving me a hard time and allow us some credit for adapting, Sir."

Wend, surprised by her admission, simply shrugged.

"And let me explain something else: I've been interested in medicine since I was a little girl. My best friend was a girl who lived next door in Philadelphia, and her father was a doctor. We used to play in his offices when he didn't have patients. His shelves were filled with gleaming implements and medicinal bottles. I soon became intrigued and tried to figure out the purpose of all the implements. When I got older, he was kind enough to let me read books from his medical library. I learned about what kind of medicines to use and what they were derived from. Sometimes, he would let me watch as he treated patients in his office."

Abigail gazed off into the distance. "The greatest disappointment in my life was when I was old enough to understand that women were not allowed to become doctors, and that as a lawyer's daughter, society would not even consider it proper for me to work as a nurse with a doctor."

She paused to organize her thoughts. "Then, when I was fourteen, my mother died. I became the mistress of the household and managed everything. At one point we had four servants, including an indentured couple. When anyone in the house became sick, or got hurt, I treated them. And the neighbor doctor gave me advice when I was unsure about the right procedure. I even learned how to sew up a wound and how to take the stitches out at the right time. So, in the end, I had a taste of being a doctor. That's why I have my own basket of medicines and implements."

Wend nodded, but still wasn't ready to leave her off the hook. "All right, you've learned doctoring and how to manage a household. That still doesn't explain why you were harsh to me."

She sat pouting for a moment. "All right, there is more to it. The truth is, I was still upset after the way you scolded me last night at the horse line." Looking down at the water again, she said, "Then when you complimented me, I wasn't sure whether you were being honest or just condescending."

"I've tried to be open with you since we met."

"I guess I've become defensive. Back in the city, my suitors just gave me looks of amusement when I talked about medicine." She shook her head. "Even my father doesn't take me seriously. He just worries about how he's going to arrange a suitable marriage for me out here in the backwoods."

Wend said, "I've got some news for you. There aren't many doctors out here. Your friends in Philadelphia may have thought of it as a curiosity, but many women in the settlements are skilled at treating wounds and sickness; men look to them for their help." He looked her directly in the eyes. "So if you're serious about this, you're in the right place!"

Abigail said nothing for a long moment as their eyes remained locked together. Wend felt an incredible thrill run through his body. After a few seconds she slowly broke off her gaze and looked down at Wend's hands as he worked on the knife and abruptly changed the subject.

"That's a big blade. What do you use it for?"

"Father is going to send me hunting tomorrow. I'll need the knife to finish off any game I don't shoot cleanly and to clean up whatever game I can take."

She nodded, and stared curiously at the firelock which lay at his side. "I've never seen a long rifle up closely like this. The wood is beautiful, the way the rings of the grain curl around the barrel at even distances. The finish is as fine as any piece of furniture I've seen and the carvings and brass fittings are elegant. You're father can be proud of his tradecraft."

"I am very proud of my father's skill and he's taught me well. But I made this rifle myself, from start to finish." Their eyes met again, and for the first time Wend knew she was looking at him with respect.

Then Abigail's expression changed to curiosity and she pointed at the rifle. "Why does it have two triggers? It can fire only one shot."

"Some rifles have two triggers, others only one, depending on the design of the lock. The finer ones, like this one, have two triggers. The rear, curved one, is called the 'sett.' You pull that first and it activates the second trigger, the straighter one at the front. That one releases the cock, or hammer. By having the sett trigger, it is possible to safely carry the gun with the hammer cocked. Then you can take a shot at game faster and not make noise by clicking the hammer back into the cocked position just before you fire."

She nodded, then asked, "Why does the rifle have to be so long? It's almost as tall as you."

Wend gathered his thoughts and answered, "This firelock is the descendent of rifles brought from Germany over 40 years ago, called 'Jaeger' rifles." He realized she might not understand the German word. "Jaeger means hunter," he explained. "They were much shorter than the guns we use now and had a bigger bore." He used his hands to measure a distance along the rifle which was about two thirds of the length of the barrel. "But over the years, gunmakers found that a longer barrel was more efficient because the powder burned more completely over the longer length. The longer barrel also made for more accuracy at long range. Moreover, these rifles fire a smaller ball than the Jaeger rifles, for additional economy."

She reflected for a moment and then changed the subject. "You'll go into the woods alone tomorrow?"

Wend nodded. "Father knows a place where the road loops around to the north to cross a ford. I'll be able to hunt across the neck of the loop while the wagons go around the long way. I'll be alone because no one else can be spared from the wagons."

"Won't you be worried to be alone in strange country?"

He shook his head. "There are many ways to mark your place and set a course. I'll use the sun and the direction of flow in streams, the slope of the land, the location of moss on trees and rocks. Besides, all I have to do is make sure I hit the road on the other side of the loop."

They were quiet again, only the sound of his blade against the stone breaking the silence of the evening. Abigail picked up some pebbles from the ground beside her and began to toss them into the millstream one at a time, watching the ripples spread after they plopped into the water.

Just then Bernd came up behind them. "Mother says that you should come to the fire now. Supper is almost ready."

Abigail jumped up immediately. "I didn't realize we'd been here so long. I'm forgetting my manners. I need to go help your mother get ready."

Wend watched her hurry off as he gathered up his equipment. He was encouraged by the girl's effort to converse with him on a friendly basis. Still, he found it hard to shake the feeling that there was too much social distance between them for intimacy. And despite his resolution of the previous night, he had to admit to himself that intimacy, on both physical and emotional levels, was what he craved from this girl. But his suspicions were aroused. Did Abigail's change in attitude toward him stem from a genuine desire for companionship or was it spurred by her growing understanding of how much she and her father needed the help of his family? It struck him that he must guard against being manipulated by a girl who knew how to use charm and beauty to get her way.

As he walked back toward the wagons, he realized that Mary had been watching them from her place by the fire and he saw a dark, unfamiliar look on her face. He could usually read his mother's expressions, a skill he had developed long ago to stay out of trouble, but this was one he couldn't place. However, his mind didn't linger on Mary's stare; he was more intrigued with the new friendliness that Abigail was showing him and its implications for the future.

* * *

After they left Chambers' Mills, the road, which had been running generally southwest since the beginning of their journey, abruptly turned due west. The dawn sun gleamed down on their backs, dispelling the chill of the damp morning air. At first they saw farmsteads and cleared fields, with people moving about as they performed morning chores and field work. But as they progressed, these became less frequent and the forest more dense. After two hours travel, the track began to swing to the north and shortly Johann brought the caravan to a stop on the road. Wend saw his parents dismount and walk back along the line toward his wagon. He realized Johann had picked this spot for him to start his hunt and gathered his gear from where he had stowed it behind the wagon seat.

Johann had stopped to talk with Gibson, but Mary came to take Wend's place at the tool wagon's reins. Wend jumped down and pulled his hunting shirt over the lighter shirt he had worn for the morning's drive.

Now Johann had arrived. "All right, Wend, we'll continue down this road. It goes northwest for several miles until it hits the ford in a creek which runs north and south and eventually empties into the Conococheague just below Fort Loudoun. Then the road swings southward very close to the creek until it turns west again to approach Loudoun." Johann had bent over and was sketching a rough map in the dirt of the road. Wend kneeled and followed his father's tracings as the Gibsons walked up to look over their shoulders.

"You need to keep a westward track as you move through the woods. You won't be able to sit and wait for game to come to you, because you must cross the creek to the road on the other side in time to catch us. So if you aren't able to pick up any game, we'll just have to try again after we go into camp at Loudoun. But I fear the woods will be hunted out around the fort." He looked up at Wend, who nodded his understanding.

"Now, we'll rest the horses and take our meal just after we cross the ford. That will give you a little more time. When you reach the road, wait for us to come up. Mark that peak behind us," he pointed to a ridge with a distinctive outcropping. "I will stop and wait when it looks like we are directly west of it on the other side, just like we are now, if we haven't met with you by then."

Wend nodded again as he finished strapping on his equipment. He had hung his knife in its sheath just under his left shoulder, with its strap over his right shoulder. His powder horn rode on his right hip. He stuck his pistol in his belt on his left side, with the butt facing forward, so that he could grab it with his right hand. On his feet were the moccasins he had obtained in trade from his friend, the Conestoga Indian Charlie Sawak. Before leaving that morning, he had also put on his leggings, which covered his legs right up to his hips. Finally, he looped a coil of rope over his shoulder to help carry the animal's body if he was successful.

He noticed that Gibson and Abigail were looking at his hunting clothes and equipment with unconcealed curiosity. Undoubtedly this was the first time they had seen someone fully equipped for travel in the bush.

Johann gave Wend a pat on the shoulder. "Bring us some venison if you can, but don't feel ashamed if you can't take anything." With that, he and Gibson walked back to their wagons.

Abigail stood with her hands on her hips and made a show of looking up and down at his clothing. "I must say, you look very exotic." She looked down at his legs, and saw the cloth ribbons which were tied around the leggings above his knees to hold them in place. "Here, you didn't tie one of your ribbons very well," she said. "Let me fix it." Abigail kneeled and undid the ribbon of his left leg. She retied it with the same expertise she had demonstrated when tending Franklin. After she had finished, he was thrilled to feel her rub her hand gently on the back of his thigh and give him an affectionate squeeze.

Then she rose with a gleam in her eyes. "Good luck on your walk through the woods."

Mary had been watching Abigail's actions from the wagon seat above. Her narrowed eyes followed the girl as she walked away toward her wagon. Then she looked back down at Wend and cautioned, "Be careful, son. Keep your wits about you. You're traveling in a strange land."

Wend looked up into his mother's face and saw the same expression he had noted the night before. Instinctively he realized that her warning didn't just apply to the forest.

Then Johann shouted at his horses, and the whole caravan got underway. As they moved into the distance, Wend's excitement succumbed to a sudden feeling of self-doubt and isolation. But after a few seconds he shook off the chill and plunged into the forest.

Wend moved rapidly through the woods, loping like a wolf, his rifle at the carry in his right hand. His loneliness was soon replaced with exhilaration at the freedom of being out on his own after days tied to a wagon. Certain that there would be no game close to the road, he kept up his pace until he was maybe a half mile into the woods. Soon he perceived that the land was sloping ever so slightly down to the creek which lay somewhere ahead. As he moved, he developed a plan for his hunt. He slowed down to a walk, now stepping as silently as possible in the moccasins, and started to move in a zigzag pattern centered on the line he had been traveling, his eyes searching the ground. He knew that his best chance, maybe his only chance, given the shortness of the time available, was to find a game trail which animals used in search of prey or to approach water. It took him more than an hour, but he eventually met with success, cutting a lightly worn, intermittent path leading to the west, towards where the creek should run.

He stopped, and as silently as possible, cocked the hammer on his rifle's lock. Then he carefully followed the trail, looking for sign. Often he had to bend over or crawl as the path went under low lying foliage. Once he found a partial print of a deer hoof, but he couldn't tell how old it was in the dry ground. Wend moved further along the trail and was rewarded within a few minutes by the sight of the first deer droppings he had seen since leaving the road. But the path led him to a more important discovery, a spring which bubbled out from between a grouping of rocks and formed a tiny brook. The trail now followed the line of the brook, which sometimes was nothing more than an area of wet ground across which the water ran.

In a spot that was more mud than flowing water, Wend found several clear, fresh hoof marks of a good sized deer. He controlled his excitement and continued along the path. He began to move even more slowly, advancing a few steps, then stopping to listen and examine the area ahead. After an hour of this routine, he stopped to sit down on a fallen tree which lay beside the trail. He had rested for a few minutes when he looked down along the game path and was surprised to catch the faintest sign of movement in underbrush about forty yards away. It was as if a breeze had come up and moved the foliage. But there was virtually no breeze. He sat still for several long minutes, unable to convince himself he had really seen something, but not wanting to alert his prey if an animal actually was present.

Finally, Wend got up and inched toward the place where he had seen movement. He arrived near the spot and was able to see that there was a grassy opening in the undergrowth where it reached down to the brook, which had formed a small pool before flowing onward. Standing at the far side of the clearing, its head toward the water, was a buck with the beginning of the year's antler growth visible on either side of his head.

Wend could see that the animal was in a state of alertness, sensing from some sound he had made or his scent that danger was at hand, but reacting to the inborn instinct to freeze until it knew the source and direction of the threat. He had his rifle in a two handed carry position across his chest. Immediately he pulled the sett trigger. Then slowly, and as smoothly as possible, he moved the gun to the aiming position. Wend mentally drew a small triangle with one point at the base of the deer's neck and the other two points at the joints where the forelegs joined the body, and aimed for the center of the triangle. Just as he was about to fire, the buck turned almost directly toward him and appeared to stare right into his eyes. But the movement was unfortunate for the animal, because it meant the firing set-up was now perfect, and Wend squeezed the trigger. The crack of the rifle reverberated among the trees, shattering the silence of the forest.

The range of twenty yards was point blank. The rifle spit the ball to the very center of Wend's imaginary triangle, and the buck jerked back for an instant, then turned and ran for the water. It jumped though the pool and collapsed on the far bank, shuddered once, and moved no more. Wend stood perfectly still long enough to see that the animal was dead. Then, resisting the temptation to run to the deer, he reloaded his rifle.

When he had finished, Wend waded through the shallow pool to where the buck lay on the bank. He felt a surge of pride in noting that his shot was placed virtually in the dead center of the triangle he had imagined. He leaned his firelock against a tree and dragged the carcass up to solid ground.

Wend was reaching for his knife when suddenly a deep voice came from behind him. "Son, that's a good looking buck you took."

Startled, he spun on his heel and instinctively reached for his pistol. A man in hunting shirt, leggings, and a floppy hat stood leaning on his long rifle, a sly grin on his face. "Hold on lad. If I was going to shoot you, I could have put a ball into your back long since."

Wend took his hand away from the pistol but felt tenseness throughout his body. He looked at the man's face and saw that the grin did not extend to his eyes, which seemed to drill into Wend. "No harm meant, sir," Wend responded with more assurance than he felt. "It's simply that you startled me since I didn't expect anyone to be nearby." Taking stock of the situation, Wend felt confident that with his pistol at hand in his belt, he could respond faster than the stranger with his rifle grounded.

"Who would you be son, hunting alone in these woods? I haven't seen any farms around for some time."

"I'm with a train traveling west to the forts, Sir. I'll be meeting them down on the road very shortly."

"Well, that's very interesting. Interesting indeed." The man looked over at Wend's rifle. "Say, that's a good looking gun you have. Where did a lad like you get such a fine firelock?"

"I'm an apprentice to a gunsmith. I make my own weapons, sir." Wend figured that he would respond politely to the man, but give him the least information he could manage in his answers.

The man approached and looked carefully at the rifle. "That is an exceptional piece: Fine curly grained maple, double trigger lock, nice fittings. Who is your master, son?"

"His name's Eckert, sir."

The man appraised Wend with his eyes. "I've heard that name often enough; he's a Lancaster man. Most everyone who deals with guns in this colony knows the reputation of Johann Eckert." Examining the rifle more closely, he said, "Yep, that's an Eckert rifle. It has a smaller bore than most, a feature which I've seen on other guns he's made." He lifted the rifle from its resting place, holding it for a moment in both hands. "Very light, too. Easy to carry in a hunt or on horseback."

Wend stiffened as the man picked up the loaded weapon. He crossed his arms against his chest, to have his right hand closer to the butt of his pistol.

The stranger finally put Wend's rifle down, then asked, "If its not too forward, why is Eckert going out to the Ohio Country?'

Wend relaxed again as the man walked away from his rifle. "He's working for the army. As contract armourer at Fort Pitt."

"Ah, yes: The esteemed Colonel Bouquet and his redcoats. How is that gentleman?" He laughed, with a bitter tone. "Give him the regards of Ross Kinnear when you get to the fort. He'll know who I am!"

Wend said, "Actually, he's a lot closer than that. I saw him in Carlisle a few days ago. He's here to arrange the summer supply train to the forts along the road."

The man reflected for a moment, then reached down to his chest with his right hand and picked up a mouth whistle suspended on a strap and blew a long blast. "If I had to make a guess, I'd say your Eckert's son as well as his apprentice. That on target?"

Wend nodded. Then he heard the sound of many horse hooves approaching. He looked toward the sound and saw a mounted man leading a string of packhorses emerge from the brush.

"That's my partner; Flemming's his name. We're bound from York to the Ohio, with trade goods for the tribes out beyond Pitt. We were just taking a shortcut through here when we heard your shot and I came ahead to investigate." Kinnear turned and started to walk toward the pack train. Wend could smell rancid breath from the man as he walked by. "Good luck, son. We've got a fair distance to travel today and can't be taking any more time. Otherwise, I'd offer to help you get that buck down to the wagon track." He mounted his saddle horse and took the line which led to six of the packhorses.

Wend noticed that the other man, who had a full beard, led a string of six more horses, and that all twelve freight animals were very heavily loaded.

"What are you carrying Mr. Kinnear. That's quite a burden you have on those animals."

Kinnear raised an eyebrow at Wend's question and glanced back at the packs. Then he gathered the reins of his horse, settled his rifle in the crook of his arm, and made a slight frown. "Oh, we just got the usual things those Indians like to trade for: Trinkets and blankets for the women, hats and clothing for the men. We're packed with supplies for a long trip, that's all."

A thought came to Wend. "Say, you wouldn't be working for Richard Grenough's company, would you?"

Kinnear stiffened in the saddle and spun his head around to stare at Wend. "Now where would you get an idea like that?"

Wend said, "I happened to see Mr. Grenough in Carlisle a few days ago and heard him say he was organizing a couple of pack trains for the Ohio. I just thought you might be part of his company."

Kinnear raised his eyebrows and exchanged a prolonged glance with Flemming. "Na, son. To tell the truth, we're just independent partners trying to make a living. We ain't never had anything to do with Grenough, not nothing at all." Then he looked at Wend for a long moment as if he were considering an idea. He made a wry face, and said, "Take my advice, son: You and your kin be careful travelin' long Forbes Road. There's a mighty lot of things that can go wrong 'fore you get to Pitt." He clucked to his horse and rode off. Flemming stared at Wend for a moment longer, then touched his hand to his cap, and followed Kinnear without a word.

Wend watched them go and saw they were following a winding path he hadn't noticed before. Obviously it led to a crossing of the creek at the bottom of the grade and he realized that its presence would help him transport his catch. But he still couldn't shake the look of those pack horses from his mind. They were simply too heavily loaded for a trip of hundreds of miles and he wondered why his mention of Grenough had seemed to unsettle both men.

Then he remembered the knife in his hand and returned to his work of dressing the buck's carcass. When he finished, he applied himself to the problem of getting it down to the road. It was not an exceptionally large animal, and if need be he could sling it over his shoulder. But carrying it and his rifle would be awkward and he would have to stop frequently to rest and shift the load. He resolved the problem by using his knife to chop down a tall sapling and then cut it to a ten foot length. Using the rope he had brought along, he bound the carcass tightly to the sapling. Then he placed one end of the pole over his shoulder and moved a few steps with the other end dragging on the ground. It made a lot of noise, but the test satisfied him that the rig would work, so he retrieved his rifle and started dragging the his prize down the path.

He hit the creek in less than an hour and wadded across. Gaining the far bank, he saw that as his father had mentioned, the wagon road ran close to the creek.

Wend felt stiff in his legs and arms; he had been moving almost constantly for nearly five hours. Moreover, his stomach was reminding him that he hadn't eaten since before dawn. He dragged his load to a tree near the side of the road and stood the sapling upright against a branch. He sat down against the trunk and laid his rifle alongside while he pulled some salted beef from his pocket and gobbled it ravenously. As he ate, Wend reflected with pride on the success of his hunt. He admitted to himself that he had been lucky, but also felt satisfaction about his woodcraft. Forgotten now was the surge of uncertainty as he had watched the wagons roll away from him that morning. He visualized himself casually standing beside the buck as the caravan approached. Wend was glad to be able to please his father and provide meat for the two families. But he was even more excited at the prospect of having demonstrated his ability to Abigail.

As he sat under the tree with a full stomach, Wend realized how tiring the hunt and subsequent events had been. Looking down the road, he saw no sign of the caravan or any other traffic. Wend decided he would close his eyes for a few moments and his thoughts turned to Abigail. The memory of her hand on his thigh that morning and the look in her eyes led to a stirring in his groin. Wend could not resist the temptation of fantasizing about the beauty of the girl's body. Picturing her standing unclothed in front of him, he recalled the shape of her breasts under the soft white blouse she had worn in the stable-yard at Carlisle. His imagination provided the image of a slim waist above long elegant legs. With those thoughts in mind, he drifted off to sleep.

Wend! Wend! He awoke to the sound of someone shouting his name. He opened his eyes and was shocked to see his father's wagon stopped on the road directly in front of him, with Johann and Elise sitting on the bench, looking down at him. Behind were the Gibsons, likewise staring down from their rig. Franklin had climbed down from the third wagon and was fussing with the harness on his team. Mother and Bernd were straining their necks to look from the tool wagon at the rear of the caravan.

Wend hurriedly wiped the sleep from his face and got up, realizing that he had blown the opportunity to display the manly, workmanlike image he had planned to project. He stood quietly as Johann descended from the wagon seat.

Johann gave him a sharp, reproving look as he walked by. "I'm disappointed in you, Wend. Falling asleep in plain sight of the road, where anyone could have come by and taken you unawares. And many would not hesitate to relieve you of this carcass without a moment's pause." His father left it at that, and moved on to inspect the dead buck, nodding his head as he appraised the carcass. He looked at Wend, then gave him a tap on the shoulder. "Not too bad, not bad at all. That should supply us with meat for several days."

Mary came up and added her approval. "It's going to be a busy day of butchering tomorrow, but it will be nice to have some fresh meat to cook."

Wend began to relax again.

Then the Gibson's came over to see his catch. The magistrate walked around the upright sapling and carcass. He pulled out a pair of spectacles and closely inspected the hole made by the ball as if examining an exhibit in a museum. Gibson turned to Wend. "Well, I've eaten venison before, but this is the first time I've seen an animal fresh from the hunt." He looked at Johann and Wend, "I say, quite different from getting it at the butcher's shop isn't it?" He turned to Wend. "How did you find it.?"

Wend told the story of his hunt. Abigail stood by, looking with interest at the animal and listening to his explanation. She turned and looked at him with those piercing eyes and he suddenly felt a wave of self consciousness wash over him. Wend busied himself picking up his rifle and other equipment to carry back to the tool wagon.

Johann and Wend carried the carcass to the tool wagon and carefully lashed it on top of the boxes and equipment. Abigail followed them to the tool wagon and stayed on after Johann had walked back up the line of wagons. She made a face at Wend. "Phew! I hope you are going to take that hunting shirt off."

Wend started to undo the ties and hooks. "Sure, it's fragrant, but that's the mark of an experienced woodsman. I need to blend in with the woods and the scent is as important to animals as the colors."

She smiled, moved close to him, and began to help loosen the shirt. Then she spoke softly. "Remember in Carlisle how I told you that I knew how you thought things out in advance from watching you at Harris' Ferry?"

Wend laughed. "Yes, you were sure you had me all figured out."

She replied, "Well, I did. And now I know more about you. As we pulled up in the wagons, I saw you casually lying there asleep with that deer beside you and that hat of yours pulled down over your eyes, and I realized something else."

"Oh? And what would that be?"

She giggled. "You're a show off!"

Their faces were only inches apart and there was a warm twinkle in her blue eyes he had never seen before. Wend suppressed a sudden, overwhelming desire to gather her into his arms. Then he became aware that Bernd was climbing up onto the wagon seat and the rest of the caravan was ready to move. Abigail put her right hand on his side and smiled before she walked back to her wagon.

Wend climbed up to his seat. Bernd watched as Abigail walked past Franklin's wagon. Then he looked over at Wend with a little grin on his face, "Don't you think she's sort of pretty, Wend?"

Wend looked at the crafty expression on his brother's face. He knew a trap when he saw one. If he agreed, he could look forward to the little devil making an announcement of what he had said to the rest of the family when it was sure to embarrass him. "I guess she's all right. I really hadn't noticed." He was gratified to see Bernd's mischievous look change to one of disappointment at his response. Wend slapped the reins down on the horses and worked to keep up with the other wagons.

CHAPTER 4

The Fort on the Conococheague

They reached Fort Loudoun at dusk. It was a square-shaped stockade, extending about 120 feet on each side, with platforms jutting out on two opposing corners so that defenders could fire at attackers attempting to scale the walls. Inside were low huts which served as quarters, storehouses, and working space for the officers. None of the buildings were so high as to show above the top of the stockade, giving the structure a squat, low lying silhouette The most appealing attribute of the fort was its location about fifty yards from a bend on the broad, tree lined Conococheague Creek, which gave it an a picturesque, almost pastoral appearance.

Johann led the little caravan past the walls of the stockade and pulled up the wagons at a campsite near the creek. On his way to pay his call to the garrison commander with Gibson in tow, he told Wend that they would stay two nights, to rest the horses and to give Mary a full day to butcher and cook up the deer in a variety of ways which would be useful. After tending to the horses, Wend and Franklin—still favoring his injured arm—hung the deer carcass from a tripod made of saplings. The women made the decision to again set up a joint fire to save time and effort.

Shortly, Johann and Magistrate Gibson returned, accompanied by a captain in the green uniform of Pennsylvania's provincial regiment. He was the fort's commander, James Sharp. Fort Loudoun, like other posts, had been stripped down to a caretaker garrison, an under-strength company. Most of the men were nearing the end of their year-long enlistment and quite ready to go home. Sharp himself had a farm near York and was anxious for news from the settlements. Johann offered him a seat and some libation, and soon the adults were engrossed in conversation.

Wend was not ready to cool his heels by the fire. Earlier, as they had pulled into the campsite, he had noted a small building which stood midway between the fort and the creek. He wandered over in the light of the moon to investigate. He saw that it was made of logs and had several shuttered windows and a door which faced toward the stream. In curiosity, he pulled on one of the shutters and it swung open easily. In the moonlight he could make out a single room with rough furniture including tables, chairs and a cot. He wondered to what purpose the cabin was intended, located outside the protection of the fort.

He noticed that the trees on the bank of the creek just in front of the cabin had been cut down and the other brush cleared to make an access to the water. Several chairs were placed a short distance from the bank. He walked down to the edge of the creek and watched the water flow by slowly and smoothly. He had only been there only a few minutes when, to his surprise, Abigail appeared, walking around bushes which cut off sight of their campsite and the wagons.

She had a bucket in her hand. "I saw you walk over here, and thought we could be alone for a minute." Abigail put the bucket on the ground and stepped very close to him, looking up into his eyes. "Wend, there's something I need to tell you."

Wend laughed. "Well, I can't stop you! You've been telling me about myself ever since we met."

"Wend, please listen; this is serious. Ever since that day in Bouquet's office, I've been trying to find a way to relate to you. But there's been tenseness between us and my words just haven't come out quite right." She hesitated for a second. "Then, last night at Chambers' Fort and this afternoon, hearing you talk about the hunt, I realized how comfortable you are in this country. A fortnight ago, I couldn't even have imagined the life out here and all you have to do. Back in Philadelphia, my father and his friends make jokes about the settlers, calling them 'Bush People', or the 'Dutch', or the 'Ulstermen' and other names. They think it's laughable that they want to have a say in the government. But in the last few days, I've come to understand how hard you work and how many skills you need just to maintain a decent way of life."

She had on the same gray and white ensemble he had seen at the inn in Carlisle, with the addition of a white apron over her petticoat. He could smell the smoke of the cooking fire in her hair and clothes and in the moonlight he could see that her blond strands had become disheveled as she helped prepare the evening meal. He knew that if she could have seen her image in a glass she would have declared herself a mess. But to him, she looked beautiful, endearing, and totally irresistible.

He gave in to the desire which had been building in him for days and took her into his arms. She came willingly, encircling him with her own arms. Then she slid her hands up his back until she could put her fingers in the hair at the rear of his neck, fondling it with the tips of her nails, so that the ends gently tickled his skin. A thrill surged through his body. He bent over to place his lips on hers and they met eagerly.

After a few seconds, Abigail pulled back her head. For a moment, he thought that she was going to leave, but instead she took him by the hand and led him to one of the chairs by the creek and gently pushed him into the seat. She curled herself up on his lap and, again holding him with her arms, pulled herself up to his lips for a longer, more passionate kiss.

Wend felt her body lying tightly against him and her breasts pressed into his chest. He hesitantly moved to cup one in his hand and was gratified when she placed her hand on his and held it there. The reality of the sensation which he had dreamed about inevitably led to the completion of his arousal; he feared she would recoil at feeling the pressure of his member against her. He started to shift his body to prevent that, but she stopped him.

She whispered "Its all right Wend, let it stay there. Let me feel it."

After a few moments, Wend raised his head and looked at her "I have wanted to hold and kiss you for several days now. But I wasn't sure you felt the same way."

She shook her head. "Wend, I've never tried to signal my intentions so clearly to any boy before. I've smiled at you, tried to provoke you, even tried to tease you into some reaction. All to no purpose, except to get you irritated, it seemed. You would just go about your business and carry around that impassive, steely-eyed expression on your face."

"Well, Abigail, if it makes you feel better, it all worked. But you needn't have done those things. If the truth be told, I've been infatuated since I saw you at Harris' Ferry."

Abigail looked at him, smiled, and kissed him again, this time a peck rather than a lover's embrace. The she picked herself up from his lap and settled her clothes about her. Walking over to the creek, she filled the bucket. "I have to get back to the fire, or your mother is going to watch us even more closely than she is now." She giggled nervously, "But we need to steal another little visit like this again very soon."

Wend watched her walk away, her body silhouetted by the faint light from the distant fire. He sat quietly in the chair for a while, slowly relaxing from the excitement of the encounter. Wend knew he would cause suspicion if he went back to the fire so shortly after Abigail. Meanwhile, he was shocked at how rapidly his fantasy had become reality. When he had reached to kiss her, he had feared she might laugh and push him away. He had not been prepared for her readiness for physical intimacy or the urgency of her kisses.

He was particularly taken with what Abigail had said about his supposed aloofness. *Was it really possible that she had taken his shyness and awkwardness with girls for rejection and that had actually made her more interested in him?* Nothing in his life had prepared him for what he was encountering with Abigail. The only girl he had ever kissed before tonight was Martha Schaffner, back in Lancaster. Since every boy he knew had kissed Martha, that had been no more than a right of passage. He had never had a personal relationship with a girl that really meant anything to him.

Wend walked back to the fire. Captain Sharp was still gossiping with Johann and Gibson while Mary and Abigail fussed with the food. Wend sat down on a log, and Johann looked up casually and asked where he had been.

"I was exploring down by the creek." He turned to Sharp, and asked, "Sir, what's the purpose of that small cabin close to the water? It seems strange to have a building outside the stockade."

"That's a good question, son. It's actually one of the most important buildings here. It was built last year as the private residence and headquarters for General Forbes. He spent several weeks here at Loudoun, planning and making arrangements for the campaign. It's outside the fort because it gave him more ventilation and comfort, and with so many troops gathered, there was no chance of any danger from the enemy." The captain took a sip from his mug. "I'm told he used it again on his way back to Philadelphia after the expedition was over. Of course, by then he was suffering from some type of wasting disease, and a dying man, Bless his soul. He passed on a few weeks after he reached Philadelphia."

Gibson looked up from his cup. "I met Forbes at a reception just after he arrived from New York; of course, that was before he was afflicted with his disease. Think of that poor man trying to fight a campaign while in constant pain and so weak from not being able to keep food down." He stopped and gathered his thoughts. "A friend who saw him just after he came back to the city said that he looked like a living skeleton."

Johann added, "He spent most of the expedition traveling in a sling between two horses. That was why Bouquet, as the next senior officer, did so much of the real work of command. Forbes would send him dispatches from the rear and Bouquet made things happen at the front."

Sharp nodded. "There's not an officer in Pennsylvania who doesn't respect Bouquet for how he held our forces together last year, got the road built, and drove the French off the Ohio." He turned back to Wend. "But you asked about the cabin. It is now used by Bouquet every time he passes through here. As you know, we're waiting for him now with the summer supply train."

The conversation began to lag and Sharp saw that the ladies had dinner ready for the travelers. Not wanting to overstay his welcome, the captain excused himself to return to the fort and his own supper, and they settled down to eat their meal. As they finished, the quiet was broken by the sound of the sentinels of the fort calling out their hourly reports from their stations on the walls and the gate. Wend looked around the fire. The strains of the day were beginning to affect the travelers. Elise, bored by all the adult talk, was sleepily snuggling up to Mary, holding her doll in her arms in front of her. Johann and Gibson were silent, pulling on their pipes contentedly. Franklin sat on another log a little distance from the fire, lost in his own thoughts.

Wend joined him on the log. Franklin looked up from his reverie. "How you doing, Master Wend? I was just sittin' here relaxing and listening to the talk about the war. I used to hear my old master, the merchant, talking about things that happened during that campaign. It didn't affect me much."

"How long were you with the merchant, before you came to the Gibsons?"

"Over three years, Master Wend. Ever since I was sold up to Philadelphia from Charles Town, down in Carolina."

Wend had been curious about Franklin's background since Carlisle. "Carolina? What was that like?"

"My whole family was owned by the master of a plantation west of Charles Town. That's where I was born. It wasn't one of the big ones; it din't have no grand house like them down near the town. It was located on the Ashley River, far above them grand plantations. There were only a few families of black people to work the place and an old couple who worked in the house for the master."

"I don't know much about Carolina. I don't even know what they grow there. What kind of work did you do?"

"Well, after I grew up, I worked in the rice ponds; that's what we grow in the lowlands along the coast in Carolina. Before that, while I was a child, I helped wherever they told me; mostly running errands around the barns."

"So how did you come to be up here?"

"The master, he was always havin' troubles with money. He ran things himself without no overseer and spent a lot of time down at the ponds with the hands. Then one summer, four years ago now, we had a bad crop from some kind of fungus in the water. Not much could be sold. So the master sold me and a couple of other hands down to the market in Charles Town, just to get enough cash to make ends meet."

"Franklin that must have been terrible for you. Knowing you would never see your parents or the rest of your family again. How did you feel?"

"First off, I wasn't too worried. No sir, I thought I'd be sold to another plantation along the river. And sometimes the owners allow the slaves to visit to other places close by. So I figured I'd see my family now and then." Franklin paused, and looked down at the ground for a while. "But I din't count on what happened. There were a lot of the other planters havin' money troubles and weren't needin' more slaves. So a trader bought about twenty of us and shipped us on a big boat with two masts up to Philadelphia where the market was better. That's how I came to work for the first owner up here."

They were interrupted by Abigail, who arrived with her medical basket in hand to treat Franklin's arm. "What are you two discussing so earnestly?"

Wend said, "Franklin was telling me a about his life on a plantation in Carolina."

She started to unravel the black man's bandage. "Oh, I hadn't realized you came from down south. I guess I should have enquired. But you only came to us just before we started our trip, and what with the party we had and packing things up, I never thought to talk to you about it."

As he watched her work on the wound, Wend thought about what Abigail had just said. It struck him that, accustomed to servants, she simply considered Franklin another part of the environment, like her house, the furniture, or the utensils in the kitchen. Franklin's personal life wasn't of more than passing interest. He thought: *Despite her growing understanding of life in the settlements, she's still got a lot to learn.*

Soon Abigail finished with Franklin's arm, and, giving Wend a conspiratorial smile, walked off to her wagon.

Later, after a check of the horses, Wend settled into his blankets under the wagon. It was only as he was drifting off that he remembered that he hadn't told his father about the encounter with the traders in the woods. He came awake for a second, thinking that he should get up and tell the story to Johann, just because of the suspicion he had felt about the men. But then his weariness overcame him and he settled back. He resolved to tell Johann about it tomorrow. He fell asleep with lingering thoughts of Abigail, her urgent kisses and soft breasts on his mind.

* * *

The next day dawned warm and bright, promising typical July heat. Mary, intent on butchering the deer, hurried them all through breakfast, then chased off all the men save Bernd so that she and Abigail could focus on the work at hand. As they had planned the prior evening, both women had donned their shabbiest clothes for what would be a messy job. And Bernd had been deputized as assistant. Mary gathered her knives and laid out cloths and pots to receive parts of the animal. Soon the women had skinned the animal and begun to take cuts of meat off the carcass. Mary was letting Abigail do much of the job, while she instructed on the type of cuts and the techniques to get the best results. Elise sat on a log watching while she clutched her doll.

The men busied themselves making minor repairs to the wagons and harnesses. Then they shifted items around in the wagons to prepare for the trip through the mountain passes. By late afternoon, all the work on the wagons had been completed and the deer had finished its transition to dressed venison. Various parts were roasting over the fire and the women had ground up some of the meat to make sausage which could be preserved longer than plain meat. Everyone was gathered around the fire where the sausage makers worked.

Johann started to talk about the morrow's journey. "We'll be on the first part of Forbes Road itself. We go north a few miles through the Path Valley, then climb through a gap in the Tuscarora Mountains. It's a very long day to Fort Lyttleton, which is just on the other side of the pass. It will be our first real climb with these wagons and teams; we'll see how well we are loaded. So we need to have our evening meal early today, and then get packed up for a start at first light."

Later, Wend took the grease bucket from its hook underneath the tool wagon and began to lubricate the wagon wheels. He started with the Gibson's wagons, and as he had hoped, Abigail took the opportunity to join him on the far side, out of sight of the rest of the travelers. She stood over him as he worked on a wheel and put her hand on his shoulder. "Your father says we

59

all should get to bed early. But I think we're going to need another private discussion tonight."

Wend looked up and they both laughed nervously at the meaning of her comment. In guilty whispers, they hatched a conspiracy for the evening. While working on the wagons, Wend had been busily conceiving a way that they could arrange meeting in the night and he explained his idea to Abigail. When their plans were complete, she left to rejoin Mary at the cook fire.

Wend finished greasing the wagons and walked back to the tool wagon to replace the bucket on its hook. He had just crawled underneath when he realized his parents, unaware of his presence, were standing on the other side of the wagon and talking about him. They were speaking in German, which they did when they wanted to ensure they weren't overheard by the Gibsons.

He heard Mary say, "Are you blind? Can't you see what's going on between them? She's been flirting with him for days now. Or picking arguments with him, which amounts to the same thing! And Wend can't take his eyes off her; he's like a yearling buck chasing after a doe in season."

"Oh, Mary, you're exaggerating! Of course Wend is interested. She is a damned pretty girl, no doubt of that. To tell the truth, I'd be worried if he wasn't interested. But there isn't much opportunity for anything serious, considering how close together we are all living here."

"Johann, listen to me! I'm telling you, she's leading him on and she's going to break his heart. Sure, she will pay lots of attention to him while we're traveling, but as soon as we get to Fort Pitt, she's going to move on to greener pastures. Just remember how she was throwing herself at that lieutenant back at Carlisle. I'll say it again: Wend isn't experienced and she's going to break his heart."

Wend was surprised to hear his father laugh.

"Mary, every boy gets his heart broken by some girl at least once; its part of becoming a man. Good lord Mary, you broke my heart and left me mooning around like a sick calf at least twice before you finally agreed to marry me."

"Johann, what on this earth are you talking about? What did I ever do to hurt you?"

"Mary, don't tell me you can't remember how much you were carrying on with Wilhelm Spengler while I was trying to court you. And he was going around bragging about how close you two were—not that everyone in town couldn't see for themselves. And then there was that other fellow, the blond one, from the north side of town."

Wend listened, shocked to learn that his mother had been involved with Arnold's father. He simply could not envision them as a pair.

Mary stomped her foot. "Johann, we are not talking about things long past! We are talking about our son and what's happening here in this caravan. You need to do something, before this all goes too far."

"What do you want me to do? What can I do, even if you are right? Maybe we should chain Wend to the wagon and ask the Magistrate to tie up his daughter like a bitch in heat?"

"Don't make fun of me, Johann Eckert! You can at least give Wend a stern talking-to, tell him about the realities of our world, and make him understand that that city girl is never going to be part of it. She's been bred for some young lawyer or wealthy merchant or British officer, not the son of a tradesman."

Wend heard his father sigh. "All right, Mary, I will talk to him. But he has to learn how to deal with these things on his own. That is part of growing up and he is most of a man now. God knows he's been doing a man's work on this trip. He's been showing that he thinks like a man too, or haven't you noticed? He's not a child anymore and you have to get used to that."

That was the end of it and Wend watched his parents walk off together. His sat there for a few minutes, his mind a jumble of contrary emotions. He understood his mother's concerns, for he had harbored them himself. But he was becoming convinced that Abigail had it in her to be something beyond the well-bred gentleman's wife his mother described. And in his mind, he realized that he wanted to experience her love, even if it proved to be a transitory relationship as his mother expected, and he feared. What was it that Johann had said? That every boy must get his heart broken at least once? Wend concluded he must seize whatever moments he could with Abigail now, and deal with the future when the time came. If the worst happened, he would face the consequences as they emerged.

* * *

Wend lay as still as he could in his blankets under the wagon. Bernd was in a deep child's sleep beside him, breathing slowly and regularly and hadn't moved for what seemed like hours. Then Wend heard the signal he eagerly awaited— the sentry report from the fort announcing the hour of eleven o'clock.

Slowly he pulled himself from underneath the blankets and out from under the wagon. He reached back in and grabbed the rolled blanket which he had used as a pillow and slowly crept around the rear of the wagon. He looked out at the campsite and saw no movement, only the glow of the embers in the fire. More confident now, he stepped out and walked for the tree line by the creek as if he were just hurrying to relieve himself. When he reached the trees, he followed along the edge of the bushes until he was at the chairs at the bank of the creek.

He sat there, shivering despite the warmth of the evening. He was suddenly scared and worried about what would happen if he and Abigail were discovered. He was just as nervous about what would happen if they weren't discovered. Then he heard a noise from the tree line and suddenly Abigail was there, breathlessly throwing herself down in the chair next to him.

She was covered from neck to foot with a dark, flowing cape which she kept closed with her hands. "Whew!" she said in the quietest tone she could manage. "I made some noise getting out of the wagon and thought I saw Franklin stirring. But after a while, I tiptoed past and he didn't move a bit. So I think we're all right."

They looked at each other for a moment, and shared a nervous giggle. Wend took her hand and led her to the cabin. Earlier in the day, he had visited the building and confirmed that the door, like the shutters, was not locked. Now he eased the door open and drew her into the darkness. Once inside, he tossed the blanket onto a chair and took her in his arms. She had washed after the labors of the day; he could smell the fresh soap on her. He smelled something else—an unfamiliar scent. Then he guessed it was perfume, which he had heard that city girls used when they dressed up. He was consumed by desire for her and they kissed urgently. She pressed up against him until he could feel the contours of her body.

After a moment they paused and he led Abigail to the bunk. He quickly spread the blanket over the straw mattress. Abigail undid the lace at the neck of her cape and he saw she had a white shift underneath. She dropped the cloak at the bottom of the bed and loosed the top of the shift. He could plainly see the tops of her breasts; the sight of the cleavage accelerated his arousal.

Driven by his desire, he moved to embrace her again, but she gently pushed him away. She reached out and grasped the front of his shirt. "I want to look at you first," she whispered. Abigail loosened and pulled his shirt off, then paused to look at his chest. She put both of her hands on his sides, then slowly, palms against his skin, slid them up to his chest to feel the hardness of his muscles. Then she slid them down again to his waist, quickly undid his breeches and let them drop to the floor.

Abigail pulled him toward her until his nakedness was against the material of her shift. He could feel the hardness of her nipples as she kissed him passionately, first on his lips, then on his check and neck.

Now he pulled back from the embrace and asked, "When do I get to see you?"

She tossed her head and smiling, pulled the shift over her head and dropped it ceremoniously beside his shirt and breeches.

Wend saw that his fantasies had not begun to capture the full elegance of her body. She had modest, but delicately shaped breasts with nipples now hard and standing upright. Her waist was slim and her entire frame was sleek and enticing. Her legs were indeed long and sensual.

They embraced again, but soon she pulled him down to the bed. They lay on their sides in each other's arms. He could feel the delicate touch of her nipples against his chest, and the sensation sent a tingle of excitement through his body. He reached up and fondled her breasts, feeling the nipples harden even more as he moved his hand. His aroused manhood moved against her and she made a sigh of anticipation. Sliding her hand down his body, she wrapped her fingers around his member and began to stroke it rhythmically. Wend sucked in his breath with ecstasy.

She looked at him with wide eyes. "I never imagined you would be so hard!"

Wend was wild with desire. He pulled himself up to his hands and knees, and Abigail slid under him.

"Wend, come into me. Come in now!" She put her hand back onto him and helped guide him as he descended. As he entered her, she sucked in her breath and moaned with her mouth open in an almost perfect circle. He began to move up and down inside her and her moaning assumed the rhythm of his thrusts. Soon he knew that he was going to lose control. He slowed his movement in an attempt to delay the finish, but Abigail told him, "No don't slow, go ahead and come now." He resumed his frantic action, and in just a few strokes he felt himself shudder as he expelled his seed into her.

They lay trembling and smiling at each other as he slowly relaxed. After a time, Abigail reached down and pulled her cloak up over both of them. Then she shifted her body and cradled him, almost like a baby, in her arms with his head on her breasts. She kissed him all over his face like a mother to her child.

Wend savored the moment, feeling more at peace then he could ever remember. After they had been still for a time, they talked and laughed together, exchanging intimacies and expressions of passion. Inevitably, they confessed their mutual virginity and Wend felt himself happy, but somewhat surprised to find that Abigail had had no previous experience. He had been impressed with her eagerness to make love, and her competence in arousing him. He said, "You knew so well where to touch me and what would make me eager and hard. Forgive me if I say so, but it was like you had some experience in lovemaking."

"You goose! Certainly I have kissed a boy before, and there was one who, rather awkwardly, I might say, fondled my breast at a party when he caught me alone in a room. And yes, I let him do it because it felt exciting. But truly, you are my only lover. Do you remember I told you about reading the Doctor's books? Do you think they just dealt with how to sew up wounds? I made a special study of men's anatomy and it gave me a delicious feeling of guilt to do so!"

Eventually, Wend told her about the discussion between his mother and father that afternoon, tactfully leaving out Mary's most pointed comments about Abigail.

"Wend," Abigail said, "Your mother has been watching us since that night at Chambers' Mills. She's a hen protecting her first hatchling." She hugged him and then continued, "But she doesn't have to worry. You are more of a man than anyone I knew in Philadelphia. Not a one could do the things I've watched you do on this trip."

Wend thought for a moment. "You may feel that way now, but sooner or later your father's time at the fort will be over, and you'll go back to Philadelphia. Someday I'll watch you leave my world and I will have to steel my heart to get over you. I guess that's the reality of our future."

Abigail shook her head. "Wend, you don't understand. My father can never go back to Philadelphia. For us, this is exile." She turned her head, looking out into the distance, and he saw the glimmer of tears in her eyes.

He pulled her face to his and kissed her gently. "I guessed there was some problem, all the way back in the stableyard in Carlisle. Please tell me what's wrong."

She screwed up her face, as if making up her mind about whether she could trust him. Finally, she started to tell him the story. "Father was in a partnership with two other lawyers. It was one of the most respected law firms in the city. He had a reputation for brilliance in the courtroom and won almost all his cases. And he was madly in love with my mother, who was truly beautiful."

"Then mother died three years ago. It was the fever and she went quickly. I was devastated, but father was emotionally destroyed. He lost his will for everything. He couldn't make himself work and started losing cases he should have won easily. Worse, he lost confidence in himself, drinking heavily in the middle of the day, and falling to sleep many nights with an empty bottle beside him. His partners tried to help him. They made him the business manager of the firm so that he wouldn't have to take on law work."

"After a time, father saw what he had become. So he looked around for a way to prove himself again. He tried to become a merchant. Along with another man, he bought half the interest in the cargo of a merchant brig. It took almost all his reserve money. And the voyage failed; the return cargo was ruined in a storm and he had lost all his money. But the other man convinced him to try again—except father didn't have the money to invest."

Now Wend saw that she was truly crying. He wiped her eyes with his hands and kissed her. "Well, that happens all the time. That's not something which would force you to leave Philadelphia."

"Yes, father should have left it at that. But he was determined to succeed. As business manager of the law firm, he had access to their reserve funds. So he took what he needed and put it all into another cargo. He doctored the books and thought he could replace the money in the company before anyone discovered it was missing. Well, inevitably the second voyage was a failure. The ship was captured off Gibraltar by Algerian pirates. The story was in the Pennsylvania Gazette. I found father sitting at the table, with the paper before him, staring at the wall and crying. He told me that he would have to go to jail for embezzlement."

"But his partners couldn't let that happen; the firm did a great amount of work for the colony and the British. They didn't want their reputation damaged by the story getting out; they knew it would hurt their respectability with the Quakers in the colonial government. So they made a deal with father. The colony had just decided to set up the magistrate court out at Fort Pitt and they arranged for him to take it. The partners agreed not to prosecute him, but he had to promise to keep his mouth shut about what had happened and never return to Philadelphia."

"So now you know why your mother doesn't need to worry. We don't have any money, I have no dowry and no gentleman is going to think of me as a suitable match, once he knows our story. I'm going to become a woman of the settlements. Like you, my life is out here now."

She sobbed again and Wend moved to comfort her. He began caressing her, moving his hand through her tresses, fondling her breasts, kissing her. She began to respond, and stroke his back and shoulders with her hands. Soon they were both aroused, and made love again, this time with Abigail above Wend, controlling the progress of their passion. In a few minutes they reached climax and kissed madly for a moment, before collapsing in mutual exhaustion.

Finally Abigail broke the silence. "We girls used to get together and talk about making love, but I never could have imagined it would be like this. When you first entered me it hurt; it hurt more than I expected. But then I began to enjoy it. Oh, Wend, it overwhelms your body and your consciousness. Nothing else matters when the passion rises, you can think of nothing but seizing every bit of possible pleasure."

He could think of nothing to say except to agree with her. And gradually they fell asleep in each other's arms.

* * *

The damp air which precedes the arrival of dawn crept into the cabin and awakened Wend. At first he had no idea of where he was, but he felt Abigail beside him and suddenly came to full consciousness and realized their situation. It was still dark, but he could see that the stars were beginning to fade. Soon Johann would be rising to rouse the travelers for an early start. In near panic, he shook Abigail awake. "We need to get back to our wagons, right now!"

She looked confused, then he saw understanding flow into her eyes. She reached over and kissed him hurriedly, then threw the shift and cloak over her body. Her hair was wild and draped over her shoulders, but it looked beautiful to him as she scurried toward the door.

"Run along the tree and brush line until you are beyond the fire, then you can head for your wagon. I'll wait until you're sure to be inside, so that no one will see us moving at the same time."

Wend dressed as he watched her go, the full impact of their night's adventure hitting him. He knew that life would ever be the same again, and that he, Wend Eckert, had reached manhood at the tender age of fifteen. In a few minutes, he put the blanket over him like a cloak, and left the cabin. He went to the creek bank, then walked along the trees until he was opposite the camp.. Suddenly he felt the onset of panic. He saw that the fire was burning brightly, not glowing as it should be after a long night. Somebody had stoked it and put on fresh wood! Was Johann already up and around?

He walked quietly but swiftly toward the tool wagon, as if he was just coming back from relieving himself in the brush.

"Hello, Master Wend. Good mornin' to you."

Franklin was sitting beside the fire, a mug in his hands. "You want some tea, Master Wend?"

Startled, Wend blurted out, "I just had to go relieve myself." Then he sheepishly sat down at the fire opposite the black man and accepted a mug.

Franklin stoked the fire with a stick and looked at him with a knowing smile. "Yessir! The need sure comes over you right sharply the first thing in the mornin'. In fact, Mistress Abigail just come back herself."

Wend realized that Franklin had put together the entire picture. He sat on the log with panic flowing through his body.

Franklin smiled again. "Don't worry, Master Wend. I'm a man same as you. And I learned how to keep my mouth shut about certain things a long time ago."

Now the two of them shared a smile, sitting together in the light of the false dawn. Wend's thoughts were interrupted by a sound from the direction of his parent's wagon. Johann had climbed down and he could hear Elise's voice from inside the cover.

Johann nodded as he joined them at the fire and Franklin poured him a cup of tea. Wend remembered his father's stories around the campfire on the first night they had been at Loudoun. "Father, I guess the last time you left here to cross the mountains was with the army. It must have been far different."

Johann twisted around on his seat on the log, looking at the cleared area that extended all around the fort. Wend could see his eyes weren't focused; it was as if he were seeing things that weren't there. Now and then his father's eyes stopped scanning and peered in one direction as if he could make out objects in the half-dark of the dawn. Finally, his eyes returned to the fire. "Fourteen months ago it was; there were thousands of men here in camp the morning we left to start the road. Battalions of soldiers, regulars and provincials from three colonies. Hundreds of wagons. Horse picket lines wherever you looked. A city of tents, masses of fires. I was with the supply contractors, with my wagon—our tool wagon now—and I was the armorer for Armstrong's First Pennsylvania Battalion."

"In darkness like this we struck the camp. I'll never forget the sound of thousands of men moving and assembling their kit in the dark, the noise of tents coming down, metal tools being stowed in wagons, the clank of horses being hitched up, drums calling companies together; sergeants shouting to their men. It was all around me in the night, like some great storm enveloping me. It was a sound you can never forget once you've heard it; the sound of an army coming alive." Johann stopped talking, and drained the tea in his mug. Ready for business, he looked at Wend. "Let's go check the horses to make sure they're ready for today."

They walked together to the picket line and Johann made a show of looking at the horses' legs. But it soon became clear that he had other things on his mind. "Wend, I want to talk to you about something."

Wend realized that Johann was taking this opportunity to keep his promise to Mary. He put a serious expression on his face. "Yes sir?"

"What do you think about Mistress Gibson?"

"I think she's a nice girl. She sure seems to work well with mother." Wend tried to sound as casual as possible. But he had to work hard to keep a straight face. He wondered how Johann would react if he were told that his son had just spent the night in the girl's arms.

"Yes, she's a nice girl. And she is a very pretty one also, which I know that you have noticed. Your mother and I are concerned that you and she are," he paused as if searching for the right words, "Becoming too close. We're all thrown together in this caravan and many of the rules of our society have been put aside as we travel. But they have not been thrown out. That city girl is from a class above us that have money and power. In ordinary circumstances, they wouldn't associate with tradespeople like us. So while it's natural that we all may be close while we're on the road, when we get to Fort Pitt, things will be different. The girl may pay a lot of attention to you now, but she's going to be interested in men of her class when the trip is over."

Johann turned and looked directly at his son. "There's another thing; our situation here on the road doesn't allow us to observe the normal customs for chaperoning young men and women. Your mother is already upset about how often you and Abigail have been thrown together without an adult nearby. We can't change that, as long as we're on the road. But here's what I want to say that's most important: I'm counting on you to be responsible for not letting things get out of hand and to act with propriety around that young lady."

Wend noted that his father seemed relieved at having finished what he needed to say.

"So, do you understand what I'm asking of you Wend?"

Wend nodded and again said "Yes sir," He was thankful he had heard his parent's conversation the day before, and had thought about how he would handle the inevitable talk from Johann. He had decided the best strategy would be to say as little as possible. Wend had always looked up to his father and obeyed him, but things were different this time. He had no intention of stifling his relationship with Abigail, now that it had been fully consummated and now that he knew things about her background which changed her outlook on life. At any rate, the thought that his father's heart wasn't really in this admonishment bucked up Wend's spirit and mitigated the guilt he felt about his plans to be with Abigail as often as their circumstances would allow.

Johann gave Wend a light, fatherly tap on his shoulders. "Good, then let's get going and take these wagons over the mountains."

CHAPTER 5

Disaster

It took them fourteen hours to transit the Path Valley and then navigate through the mountain pass. Twice, at particularly steep grades, they had to double-up the horse teams and bring the wagons over in stages. The road was in poor shape; several times, everyone, including the women, had to push to get the wagons across rough or washed out segments. But finally, in the gathering dusk, they caught sight of Fort Lyttleton, a near twin to Fort Loudoun, lying astride a low plateau at the very northern entrance to the Great Cove. The stockade looked deserted at first, but as they moved around a curve, Wend saw the glimmer of light through the open gates and the silhouette of a sentry. Soon they had pulled up into the open area beside the walls; he thankfully slid down to the ground. Every muscle was aching as he worked with Franklin to unhitch the teams.

While the rest of the group made camp, Johann hurried to make his call on the garrison commander. Mary sent Bernd to gather wood so she could get a fire going and start to warm up food. Everyone had the same idea; get chores done, eat a meal, and get to bed as early as possible.

Johann was gone only a few minutes, but when he returned the darkness had become total. He came over to where Wend was currying the horses and told him that the fort was manned only by a caretaker garrison, a half company of twenty provincial soldiers under a young ensign. "Things are pretty slack in there. They have just about enough men to post sentries and aren't doing much to keep up the fort. The officer said that it's probably going to be abandoned in a few months anyway, since the fighting's over around here and the colony is trying to muster out as many troops as possible to save money."

As Wend was finishing up with the horses, Abigail came over to him. He was glad to see her until he noticed that she had a strained look on her face. "What's wrong?" he asked.

"Oh, God, I don't know what to do! Father is drinking again. He started to get very quiet this afternoon. I think the depth of the forest and the terrible condition of the road reminded him how isolated we'll be at Fort Pitt. He turned down your father's invitation to go along to see the fort commander and he pulled out a whiskey flask. He didn't even try to hide it from me. Now he's standing over behind our wagon, drinking by himself."

Wend was only little surprised. Abigail had told him about her father's drinking problem after his wife's death and he remembered how the Magistrate had smelled when he had come into Bouquet's office that first day. "How long since this has happened before?" he asked.

"He had a bad day on the road from Philadelphia to Harris', when it hit him that we were really leaving Philadelphia forever. He had a couple of drinks before we went to meet Colonel Bouquet and he got a little tipsy the night we had dinner with Lieutenant Locke. But he hasn't had much since we left Carlisle."

"What can you do about it?"

"I just told him he must be sober for dinner tonight. He put his arm around me and said he would stop, but I'm still worried. Once he gets started, he finds it hard to quit. And he hides it so he can take a quick swallow now and then."

Wend thought for a moment. This was a problem he hadn't encountered before. His parents never drank hard liquor, only ale, small beer, and some wine, and that mostly with meals. "Well, I think we're all going to get to bed as soon as we can, so maybe he won't be able to drink too much, particularly with us all around the same fire again tonight."

Abigail looked at him for a moment, then gave him a quick, furtive peck on his cheek. "I hope you're right. Maybe he'll pull out of this after a good sleep." Then she left to help Mary.

The women put together a simple meal and everyone ate in silence. Gibson had arrived at the fire with a tankard in his hand and Wend could guess the nature of its contents. Wend kept an eye on the magistrate as he worked on his plate; sure enough, he detected clumsiness in his movements which he had never seen before.

Johann broke the silence. "We'll want to get another early start tomorrow. We have near forty miles ahead of us to get to Bedford, and that includes one very high ridge, called Sideling Hill, and then several smaller ones. And then we have to make it across the Juniata. The road will get rougher as we go along. So we'll be doing well to put ten miles a day behind us."

Gibson asked, "Where will we camp tomorrow? Are there many settlers along the way?"

"Virtually none; so we'll be camping in the bush. There are a few clearings along the road, set up to allow troops and supply trains to stop. If one of those fits our progress, we can stop there for the night."

Gibson took a gulp of his drink. "I was surprised to see so little settlement along the road after we got through the pass."

Wend noticed that the magistrate's voice was louder than usual and he saw that Abigail was watching him with concern.

Johann finished off the food on his plate. "Magistrate, there's reasons this area is sparsely populated. The first is that the colony wouldn't allow settlement here for a long time, because it was Delaware tribal land. In 1750, when a group of Ulster-Scots tried to move in and start a settlement just north of here, the colony sent a sheriff's party to turn them out. Then they burned the homes and farmsteads to the ground. That area's called the 'Burnt Cabins' now."

Gibson's face lit up. In a very loud voice which startled everyone, he exclaimed, "Why, I should have thought of that. Our firm handled some legal matters about evicting squatters from various places in the backcountry. I didn't realize this was one of those areas."

He took a pull on his mug, and then began to loudly lecture them in the manner of a schoolmaster. Raising his right hand, gesticulating with a finger for emphasis, he said: "We can be very proud of the way our colony has dealt with the tribes. We buy the land from them before we open it to settlement. We don't just seize it from them, as other colonies have done. In fact, we make special efforts to prevent squatters from moving to the tribal lands. Actions like the one you describe show our good faith with the tribes, and kept us from having nearly as many troubles as other colonies. I think that an enlightened policy of that sort, if adopted universally, would have saved the British government much grief over the years."

Johann stared at Gibson. "Well, I guess you have a point. We didn't have much problem with the Delawares or the other tribes for a long time. But Magistrate, think about this: Once the war broke out, most of the tribes didn't waste any time before throwing in their lot with the French. I guess they figured that offered a chance of getting back some of their land. You have to reason that even when they sold out and moved west, they really would have rather stayed on their traditional lands."

The gunsmith lighted his pipe. After taking his first satisfying draw, he continued: "But that brings us to the second reason why it is so sparse out here. A few years after the burning of the cabins, the land was finally opened up to settlement. And a fair amount of people, mostly Ulster, set up farms in the valley to the south of here, the Great Cove if you will. They were doing well, but then the raids started after Braddock's defeat. In '55, a huge war party led by the French raided the valley. They killed over fifty people and captured a number more; that led a lot of settlers to give up and go back over the mountain."

"That raid was one of the events which forced the assembly, despite the Quakers' pacifism, to finally set up provincial military forces and build the forts. They built Loudoun, Lyttleton here, Shirley about twenty miles to the north, and Granville another twenty or so miles further up. They were the outer line of defense in the war, until the Forbes expedition last year."

Gibson scowled, mulling over what Johann had said. "Well, handling the tribes through legal channels and negotiations is the proper way to open up the lands here in the backcountry. And now that the war is over in this part of the colonies, the chiefs must see that dealing with us in that way is best for them."

Johann looked into the fire, skepticism written on his face. "There have been treaties before, where all the parties said things were settled. But they didn't last. There are a lot of people, in this colony and Virginia, who want to open up the Ohio Country to trading and settlement. What will that do to the tribes? They used to live here, now they've been forced into the land across the Ohio. What if we start to take that, too?"

Gibson smiled knowingly and drank from the tankard. He waved his hand to stop Johann from talking. "Listen, Eckert, I've been involved in plans for the new treaties and I can assure you that this time things will be different. The idea is to establish a line, somewhere around the Alleghenies, which will divide the white land from the tribal lands. And the army will be tasked to keep settlers from crossing into the Ohio territory. They'll man forts along the line and patrol the border. If settlers cross, they'll be dealt with like the situation at Burnt Cabins and be forced to return to the approved area. There's so much land on this side of the Alleghenies, I can't foresee a situation which will cause friction with the tribes. With the French not stirring up the tribes or providing them with weapons and powder, we can look forward to a continuing peace here in the colony."

Gibson sat back, smugness in his eyes. Wend glanced at his father, and saw disagreement written on his face. Wend was worried that Johann would respond sharply and the intoxicated lawyer wouldn't take it well. He was trying to think of something to say when Mary interrupted. "You know, this is very interesting, but I think I'm going to put Elise to bed. She's dropping off to sleep right here. And Bernd, it's also time for you."

Abigail took the cue, standing up and putting her arm on Gibson's shoulder. "Father, you were really tired when we arrived and tomorrow promises more of the same. Why don't we both go to our wagons?"

Gibson stared up at her as if he wasn't ready to retire, but looking at his daughter's face, changed his mind. "Yes, yes, probably a good idea." He rose and turned to Johann, and in overly formal, measured words, said "A good evening to you, sir."

He turned to go with Abigail, but caught his foot on the log that had been his seat, and stumbled, losing all semblance of dignity. His daughter was able to catch him, but he dropped his tankard and the contents spilled out; the pungent smell of whiskey wafted around the fire. Abigail's face flushed. She hurriedly picked up the mug and helped her father walk unsteadily to their wagon. Franklin got up and followed.

Johann stared after the Gibsons, stirring the fire with a stick. He got up and put some wood in the fire to make sure it would stay alive through the night.

Mary came back and started to clean up around the fire. "Johann, am I wrong in thinking that Gibson was not in full control of himself tonight? His voice sounded funny and I've never seen him so assertive."

Johann frowned and shook his head. "Not in full control? He damn well was in his cups! That's all we need out here; someone drinking during the day. Handling a wagon on these hills is hard enough without having strong liquor in you."

"Well, what can you do about it? You can't just go up to him and tell him to stop."

"I'm going to watch him over the next few days. If he keeps it up, I'm of a mind to leave him at Fort Bedford until the supply train comes up."

Mary thought for a moment. "Maybe his daughter will put a stop to it. She nurse maids him anyway, in case you haven't noticed, and she was watching him like a hawk tonight. You saw how she herded him out of here when he started to get pugnacious."

Wend listened while nursing a rising fear that Johann would carry out his intent of dumping the Gibsons at Bedford. He tried to change the subject before Johann got more heated about Gibson's problem. "What do think about the magistrate's idea about keeping settlers out of the Ohio Country?"

The elder Eckert snorted and shook his head again. "They sure think up lofty ideas back in Philadelphia. In truth, giving the tribes their own protected land is only just. But I can't see it working. There are too many people who have designs on that land out there."

Mary looked up from her work. "What about the magistrate's idea that the army would keep settlers off the western lands?"

"No string of forts is going to stop the flow of the people who want to get into the Ohio Country. It would be like trying to stop a wave in the ocean. And sooner or later the tribes are going to have to make the same decision; move again or fight for what they have."

Wend got up, saying he would check the picket line and then go to bed. He walked into the dark along the line of wagons. As he had hoped, Abigail was sitting on the seat of her wagon, waiting for him. She slid down to the ground; Wend gathered her in his arms and they kissed. She put her head on his shoulder and he quickly told Abigail about his father's threat to leave them at Bedford. Abigail looked up at him with fright in her eyes. "Oh, Wend, we can't let that happen! Tomorrow, while we're traveling, I'll try to explain to Father how embarrassing he was tonight, and tactfully let him know how much he upset your father. He's come to depend on him, although he doesn't like to admit it to himself. If we were traveling with a bunch of soldiers and rough waggoners nobody would help us like your family has over the last week."

"There's something else you can do. Find out where he's keeping his liquor. Get rid of it; dump it into the woods when he's not looking."

"You're right. He'll be mad as a hornet when he finds out, but I'll do anything to make sure we stay with you." She kissed him again, and pressed her body tightly against his.

And at that moment, disaster struck. Magistrate Gibson stuck his head out of the covered wagon and looked down on the embracing couple. He shouted, "What the hell is going on here!" Then, in whiskey-fueled rage, he half jumped, half fell out of the wagon, landing on his hands and knees beside the startled pair. He pushed himself to his feet and lashed out at Wend, smacking his chest and pushing him away from Abigail.

"Get your hands off my daughter! How dare you touch her in that way!" The magistrate looked between the two of them, appearing as if he was literally ready to explode. "And you, Abigail! How could you participate in something like this shamefulness? Didn't your mother and I teach you how to behave? To understand your position in society? Yet here you are, groping around with this apprentice boy! A German trade boy, of all things! My God, you are better than this! Better by far. Get off to you wagon this instant!"

Abigail defiantly tried to argue. "But Father, Wend and I are old enough to know what we're doing. Think Father! We're not in Philadelphia any-more—this is the wilderness! And this is where we are going to live! Wend is more of a man than any I ever met in Philadelphia." She stepped over and clutched Wend's arm.

But Gibson wasn't having any of it. He reached out and pushed her arm down. "Be quiet, Daughter! Immediately!" Gibson turned and shouted back toward the fire. "Eckert, get over here! Right this instant! Eckert, do you hear me? Come here right now!"

Johann came out of the night, walking slowly and warily, his eyes narrow and his jaw set, well aware that trouble was afoot. He stopped and took in the scene. Then, in a very calm voice, he asked, "What's going on, Mr. Gibson? What's so urgent?"

Gibson pointed at Wend. "This boy of yours has taken advantage of the situation to seduce my daughter, that's what is going on here. I looked out of my wagon to see them kissing and groping each other like some low-life Irish or Ulster couple in the corner of a mean, back street tavern."

Johann raised his eyebrows and looked at Wend and then at Abigail. Then he cocked his head and looked back at his son. Wend, suddenly remembering the talk he and his father had had at Loudoun that very morning, lowered his eyes. *He had put his father in a bad situation.* Johann remained silent and Wend knew he was thinking about how to deal with Gibson.

But then the magistrate again lashed out. "Damn, Eckert, don't just stand there! Even you can see the disgrace of this whole affair. What kind of upbringing have you given your boy if he even thinks about imposing himself on a girl of the quality and status of Abigail! When we get to Fort Pitt, we'll be living in officer's quarters and your family will be down in some rude cabin on tradesman's row." Gibson stamped a foot. "I knew that I should have been more insistent with Bouquet about our travel arrangements! We should be with people of our own class, not a family of low born mechanics!"

Wend was in no way ready for what happened next. Without a change in expression, Johann stepped forward until he was a foot away from Gibson. Then, without warning, he grabbed the little man by his jacket and effortlessly slammed him back against the side of the wagon.

Wend thought his father was going to hit Gibson. So did the magistrate, for his face broke into an expression of fearful anticipation. But instead, Johann spoke in controlled tones.

"Gibson, get this straight. My family comes from the province of Hesse-Cassel in the old country. We were Jaegers for the aristocracy: A post and service of the highest honor. And then we became gunsmiths, making weapons of great quality for princes and rulers. Forty years ago, my father brought his family here to the colony so that we could be our own masters and realize for ourselves the fruits of our labors. You may think that your English heritage and your law training give you privilege, but to me you're just an arrogant scribbler who bends laws and words to help rich clients. And mark this: My son is enough of a man to make your daughter forget about any lace-shirted Philadelphia dandy or stuffy army officer."

Wend stood up straight. He was proud of the way his father had controlled himself and calmly dressed down Gibson. But there was only one problem, which betrayed Johann's internal turmoil. *He had spoken in German!* Gibson hadn't understood a word, but Wend could see that the terrified lawyer had definitely gotten Johann's meaning.

At once, Johann realized his mistake; he shook his head, frowned, and then carefully repeated in English his prior statement. Wend was impressed that he was able say it almost word for word as before.

Johann released Gibson, who stood shaking and silent against the wagon. He turned to Wend and spoke quietly. "Son, go sit by the fire; I'll speak to you directly."

Wend obeyed, feeling shame for betraying his father's trust and knowing that he was about to get the scolding of his life.

As he arrived at the fire, Mary climbed down from the wagon, a worried look on her face. "Wend, what was all the shouting and arguing about over by the Gibson's wagons?"

Wend briefly explained.

His mother's face turned red, and anger filled her eyes. She opened her mouth to speak. Just then, Johann arrived at the fire. She turned to him. "I told you this was going to happen! I told you! You were supposed to talk to Wend, to head this very thing off! Who knows how far these two children have gone and now we are at odds with the Gibsons, with weeks to go on the road!"

Johann went over to his wife, put his arm around her, and spoke in a stern tone. "Go to bed now, Mother. I will work this out with Gibson. You will see. But tonight I need to spend some time with my son. I'll join you in a little while."

Mary stared at her husband, then at Wend, fuming silently and clearly wanting to say more. But in the end she turned and climbed back up into the covered wagon. Shortly, they heard her moving around and banging items in the wagon bed.

Wend steeled himself for his father's anger. But Johann stood silently by the fire and stared into the flames for a few moments. Then he picked up two mugs and filled both of them with ale. He sat down on the log beside Wend. "I told Gibson to go to bed, sober up, and that he and I would discuss the situation after tomorrow's journey." He smiled at Wend. "I expect by tomorrow evening, having experienced conditions on Sideling Hill, the good magistrate will have done some serious reconsidering of his position and his dependence on a family of 'low-born mechanics.' "

Johann turned to his son and handed him one of the mugs. "Tonight, we two Jaegers will have a quiet drink together and then get a good night's rest."

* * *

Johann Eckert had been right about the road west from Lyttleton. It was rougher than anything they had yet encountered. Wend found that he had to devote every bit of his attention to the reins, trying to avoid the worst of the bumps, holes, projecting roots, and even stumps in the wagon track. Bernd tried to play the fife which was his favorite toy, but the wagon seat was moving too violently for him to finger the instrument. He put it away and started to look for other ways to get into trouble.

The forest was dense around them. The branches of the trees had grown over the road, forming a canopy which kept out most of the sun and making it a gloomy ride. Wend was happier when they occasionally passed through open stretches where he enjoyed the heat of the sun beating down on his shoulders. For the most part, they were in rolling country and before the forenoon was half over Sideling Hill began to loom ahead of them.

It had been tense around the campsite that morning with the two families exchanging only necessary words. Magistrate Gibson, now very sober, had stocked around with a grim visage. Wend's only encouragement had been when Abigail had covertly waved and blown him a kiss. Mary had not cooked a full breakfast, but had brewed tea and toasted bread, and that was the extent of their repast. Then the party had made a fast getaway from Fort Lyttleton, leaving in the morning dusk.

Suddenly Wend was jolted out of his thoughts by a shout from Bernd, who was pointing at the road ahead. He saw that a tree had fallen across the track. Johann had stopped his wagon right before the debris. All the other vehicles had pulled up behind and Franklin was already on the ground. Wend tied off the reins to the brake lever and, consoling himself to the thought of a long session chopping wood, pulled his axe from the wagon and climbed down to the ground.

As he walked up the line of wagons, he saw that Johann was standing frozen in front of the tree, his axe in his right hand, staring at the stump. Suddenly he turned to Wend and pointing at the tree's stump, shouted, "Wend, get your rifle! Now! Do it fast!"

Wend stood transfixed for a second, looking at where his father pointed. Then he understood, and felt an ice-like chill shoot through his body and form a knot in his stomach. The tree hadn't fallen, it had been chopped down! *Somebody had intentionally blocked the road!* Now he, in his turn, screamed at Bernd as he ran back to the tool wagon, "Get my rifle! And the pistol! You take the smoothbore!"

But Bernd sat there in shock, his mouth wide open but not moving. Wend turned and looked up along the wagon line and saw that Johann already had his rifle in hand and was checking the pan. Magistrate Gibson had dismounted and was standing still, looking around, uncomprehending what was about to happen. It started while Wend watched. Flying silently, an arrow hit the magistrate as perfectly in the chest as Wend's ball had hit the buck two days before. Gibson looked down in shock, his mouth wide open, took a step and collapsed onto the ground. Wend heard a shrill scream from Abigail: "Father!"

The girl's voice was blotted out by the sound of a dozen howling screams from the woods and then Wend saw them: Black painted, nearly naked men emerging from their ambush positions, carrying guns, bows, clubs and other weapons. He looked up at Johann taking aim on one of the warriors with his rifle, a look on his face Wend had never seen before; a look which combined horror and fierce hatred as he pulled the trigger.

Finally, Bernd was moving and he called to Wend to take the rifle which was now in his hand. Wend grasped it and looked down to pull back the hammer. He was turning to face the assailants when he suddenly felt a searing, hot pain in his left side under his upper arm, and stunned, he went down on one knee. He looked up, trying to raise the rifle, to see a warrior right above him, one arm swinging in a swift motion. Then the club hit Wend fair on the temple. For a second he saw a blinding white light and then blackness instantly enveloped him as if someone had snuffed out the only candle in a windowless room.

* * *

Wend emerged from the blackness to find himself in the familiar setting of their house at Lancaster, seated in his favorite chair in front of the fireplace. Johann was in the chair across from him, reading the latest number of *The Pennsylvania Gazette*. Bernd lay on the floor nearby, tooting on his wooden fife. Mother was on the other side of the great room, working in her apron at the cooking fireplace with all her utensils hung on the wall in their usual positions. She was getting ready to serve a meal, with meat roasting on the spit over the fire. Elise sat nearby at the table, watching Mary and playing with her doll.

He was reassured by the normalcy of everything and everyone in the house. But discomfort nagged in the back of his mind. He could not dispel the feeling that something terrible had happened and this was all illusion.

As he was contemplating this thought, he was shocked to see Abigail emerge from shadows in the back of the room, dressed in the rough clothes she had worn during the butchering of the deer at Fort Loudoun. She began to help Mary prepare their meal, carrying food dishes to the table, turning the meat on the spit. Then she walked to the table to arrange the place settings.

Soon Mary called them for the meal. Father folded his paper and walked to the head of the table; they all stood at their customary places while he pronounced the blessing.

When he finished, Mary held out her hands to keep them from sitting, and said, in her best hostess manner, "We're so glad that Mistress Gibson could be with us today so that we can all share this meal together. Isn't it nice that she could spend this time with us?"

Everyone nodded and agreed; Abigail smiled back and said, "Thank you for your hospitality. I wouldn't want to be anywhere else right now."

They all sat down and Wend noticed that Abigail still had streaks of deer blood on her cheek and her apron. She saw him looking at her; they smiled at each other as she reached up and flicked a strand of hair out of her face.

The meal was pleasant, with everyone displaying their most formal manners. For once, Elise sat quietly, eating with Mary's help in cutting her food. Even Bernd was on his best behavior, and didn't seem to have any embarrassing tales to tell about Wend. Father told them at length about some of the stories he had just been reading in the paper.

As they finished eating, Mary and Abigail busied themselves by coming around to each person and picking up their plates to stack up on the counter next to the fireplace. When the women were finished, Mother stood at the side of the table, her hands clasped in front of her. "It has been wonderful to have this meal together, but we have to leave you now, Wend."

Each member of the family in turn began to say goodbye to him. He was surprised. *Why was everyone leaving, yet he must stay?* Now they were moving away from him toward the back of the house. Their movements were slow, almost wooden. He tried to rise, but for some unfathomable reason he couldn't move, as if giant hands were pressing him down into his seat. One by one everyone else disappeared into the darkness which began to close in on him, and he couldn't seem to turn his head to see where they went.

Then the blackness again enveloped him completely and he could feel himself floating.

After what seemed like an eternity, it started again. The blackness dissipated and he found himself again in the chair in front of the fire. Everything proceeded as before, until once more, everyone but Wend left the room.

As he floated off into the darkness for the second time, he desperately tried to fathom what was happening, to grasp the meaning of what he was now, in the back recesses of his mind, able to recognize as a dream. But understanding escaped him as he returned to oblivion.

He lost count of the times that the dream repeated itself.

Finally he found himself sitting in his chair again at the start of the sequence, but he realized something was different this time. Father was still in his chair with the paper, Bernd on the floor with his instrument. He looked over to see Mary again at her cooking. Abigail appeared on cue from the back of the room.

It was not until they had seated themselves at the table that he realized what was different: *It was a noise.* A noise in the background, only faintly audible. He could not place the sound. And no one else seemed to hear, for the meal and the conversation proceeded as always.

For a while he could almost ignore the sound as he paid attention to the talk at the table. But it was persistent, sometimes wavering in loudness, even fading out at times. But it always returned, slowly gaining in volume.

Soon he became totally distracted from the conversation, desperate to identify the source of this strange noise. He now perceived it as a wailing as if some animal were in distress, or howling for its mate. Then he remembered stories of the banshees that his mother had told him in his childhood. Banshees were grotesquely shaped, female demons which carried the Norse warriors off to their heaven. *That was it! His mother had told of the wailing sound made by banshees, and he guessed that must be what he was hearing.*

He returned his attention to the table, and saw that Mary was starting the talk of leaving him. As had happened every time before, each individual made their farewell and then started to walk away. But this time Wend found he could move and turn his head.

He turned around and watched them walk away. And now he saw their destination: A great tunnel had opened up through the back wall of the house, just beside the stairway. It was formed by black swirling mists. The tunnel was long, its walls undulating, now wide, now narrow. Wend felt a cold, damp draft sweep over him. The tunnel ended in an intense, blinding white light so strong he could not look directly down its path, but must take short glances through the corners of his eyes.

Bernd had entered the tunnel and was walking away toward the light. Now his parents, with Elise by their side, stepped into the tunnel. They turned and waved at Wend. Then Mary took Elise's hand and they all turned to follow Bernd down the tunnel, walking in that slow, awkward way he had noticed before.

Abigail stood beside the tunnel with a warm, enticing smile on her face. Suddenly he noticed she was no longer in the old, bloody clothes of Fort Loudoun, but had changed to the blue traveling dress and smart hat he had first seen her wearing at Harris' Ferry. She smiled again and motioned for him to follow.

He looked back up the tunnel and realized he was lying on his stomach on the floor, braced up on his elbows, watching his family walk away. He desperately tried to get up, desiring in every fiber of his body to join them, to follow them through the tunnel, but now the wailing from the banshees was becoming overpowering, washing over him like the flow of a fast mill race, pulling him back from the tunnel, overwhelming his every effort to rise and follow those he loved. It was if a great battle was underway between the pull of the tunnel and the magnetic power of the banshee's call.

Finally, his family reached the end of the tunnel and seemed to become absorbed into the light.

Abigail remained at the entrance, a look of disappointment and frustration now on her face. Again, with more urgency, she beckoned for him to join her.

With all his soul, he wanted to follow. But the wail of the banshees had reached a crescendo, crowding all thoughts out of his mind. He was pinned to the floor by the power of the sounds. Finally, Abigail made a slow wave, and moving like the others, turned toward the tunnel.

That was the last he saw of the tunnel, of Abigail, of all of them. Suddenly he felt himself being rotated onto his back, to encounter a bright light. Not the blinding white light of the tunnel, but a more benign, golden light which washed away the darkness which had filled his mind.

He blinked and opened his eyes to find himself looking up at the sun. He closed his eyes for an instant and then looked up again, to shrink in terror.

Good God! Standing over him, silhouetted by the sunlight, was a wild looking creature with a huge, indescribably misshapen head! Instantly he was certain it must be one of the banshees of his fears.

Then a measure of rationality returned to him. And the creature moved so that the glare of the sun no longer blotted out the details of its features. Suddenly he could see that it was a man. But a man dressed like none he had ever beheld. He wore a short red jacket, a small blue round cap above a face with fierce blue eyes and a scruffy red beard. Most puzzling, below that jacket he wore, of all things, a skirt; a short skirt with a dark green background, cross-threaded with a pattern of lighter colors. Below the skirt, the man wore stockings almost up to his knees in a red and white checkered design. Above his left shoulder Wend saw the butt of a musket, held in place by a cloth sling across his chest. It was the butt of the musket combined with the round cap which had given the man's head the irregular, frightening shape.

With every bit of strength he could muster, Wend blurted out, "Who are you?" his voice cracking and fading out on the last word.

"Why laddie, I'm Sergeant McCulloch, of His Majesty's 77th Highlanders."

The soldier turned and shouted, "By God Captain, this one's still breathing!"

CHAPTER 6
Highlanders

Wend spent the next hours in a semi-conscious state. He was aware of someone removing his clothing, of hands gently touching him on various parts of his body, of women's voices, and finally of being lifted and moved. It was fully dark when he regained an awareness of his surroundings, and he realized he was in blankets on the ground in front of a fire. He could see many other fires in the woods around him, with cooking pots slung from tripods over the flames. Scores of men and some women and children were sitting or standing around eating a meal. The men were dressed like the sergeant who had found him, wearing the curious skirt. But some wore leggings in place of the checked stockings.

He realized that he hurt all over. He had a throbbing headache and a fiery burning at the rear of his skull. His left side and arm were painful. He felt chilly and shivered despite the warmth of the night and the fire.

A willowy, copper haired, freckled faced girl of about Bernd's age was sitting quietly on the ground beside him, her arms around her knees, looking into the flames. He moved in his blankets and she looked over at him. Then she called, "Mum, he's opened his eyes!"

A woman came out of the darkness and knelt beside him. She had hair of a color which matched the girl's, and though she looked to be younger than his mother, the firelight showed that her angular face was tanned and creased from constant exposure to sun and wind. She smiled at Wend. "Are you back to stay with us now?"

Wend tried to speak, but his mouth seemed as dry as paper, and he couldn't get anything out.

The woman reached over to a pot on the fire and poured a mug of liquid. "Here, let's try some warm tea." She leaned over and used a spoon to get some of the liquid into his mouth.

After a few mouthfuls he repeated his efforts to talk. But all he could get out was, "I feel terrible."

The woman laughed. "I should hope so. You've been shot, clubbed in the head, and scalped. You were laying out in the weather for who knows how long. Only the Lord knows why you are still with us." She reached over and took his right hand in hers. "Here, let me show you." She gently moved his hand over to his left side. Wend felt a bandage and pain where he touched.

"A ball hit you right there. Actually, it grazed right along a rib, which I've 'na doubt is broken. But at least it kept going and didn't stay in you." She moved his hand to his left arm and he felt another bandage. "The same ball took out a piece of flesh in your arm. You must have had it against your side right where the ball hit."

She laid his hand back down. "Then you were hit with one of those great war clubs the savages carry; hit right here, on your left temple." She touched the side of his head against another bandage and Wend suddenly felt a surge of dizzying pain. "I don't know why that didn't kill you; I've seen men die from less. Your whole head was swollen and covered in dried blood when we found you." She moved her hand to the rear of his skull. "And then the warrior took your scalp at the back. I think he must have been in a hurry, probably to share in the plunder from the wagons, because he did only a partial job. Just a small circle of your hair and scalp. Right down to the skull in some places. But the flesh will eventually grow over it, though you won't ever have hair in back anymore. You'll have to grow it long on the sides and top and then pull it over the bare spot in a cue."

Wend looked around at the fires and the people. "Where am I? Who are all these people?"

"This is Captain Robertson's company of the 77th. We're marching back to Carlisle from Fort Pitt, trying to catch up with the rest of the regiment, which is in Albany. We came across you and the wagons this afternoon. At first, it looked like everyone was dead. But then Sergeant McCulloch turned you over and you started to squawk." She paused and laughed. "He said it near scared him to death when you came alive!"

"We're camped in the woods beside the road and your wagons." She spoke to the girl. "Mary, go get Mr. Robertson; he'll want to talk to the lad." She turned back to Wend. "I'm Lizzie Iverson, Sergeant Iverson's wife. That's my daughter, Mary Fraser. We'll take care of you while you're with us."

Hearing the name Mary suddenly reminded Wend of his family. "Mary is my mother's name. What about everybody else in our caravan? What happened to them?"

Lizzie put a hand softly on him. "Quiet now, the Captain will tell you all about your family. Here, take some more tea." She fed him a few more mouthfuls.

Wend heard steps and looked up to see several men approaching, followed by the little girl. An officer led the group and he sat down on the ground beside Wend, putting his arms around his knees. He was a thin faced, dark haired, tallish man in his twenties and he wore the red jacket of the other soldiers, but instead of a skirt, he had on trousers. The other men sat or stood around, looking at Wend curiously. He recognized one as the sergeant who had wakened him from his dream.

"Well, lad, you're looking a lot better than the last time I saw you. Mrs. Iverson's done a lot of work to get you clean and fixed up. Permit me to introduce myself. I'm Captain James Robertson of the 77th, and, by the grace of His Majesty, commander of this band of ruffians." The soldiers around him smiled at his characterization of them. He pointed to a younger man. "And this is Lieutenant McLean. The rest of these men are my sergeants and corporals, all very anxious to hear your story." Before Wend could speak, Robertson continued, "Actually, I know a little bit about you already. We found a bible in one of the wagons. On the leaf was written the family name 'Eckert', and the names of 5 people. Would you be one of them?"

"My name is Wend Eckert."

"Son, we also found a gunsmith's tools in one of the wagons. Sergeant Iverson says that there was an armorer named Eckert with one of the Pennsylvania battalions during the campaign last year. Is that your father?"

"Yes, he was with Armstrong's 1st Pennsylvania."

Robertson looked at one of the sergeants. "Does that match what you remember?"

Iverson, a tall burly man with a broken nose and a scar on his right cheek, nodded. "Aye, sir. He helped us repair our weapons after the retreat from Duquesne on Grant's scouting expedition."

Robertson turned back to Wend, a grim expression on his face. "All right, lad. Now I must tell you the bad news. All the rest of your party are dead or captured. We found two dead men by the wagons. One was near the first wagon in line; he was shot in two places. The second man was older and had been hit with an arrow."

Wend felt tears welling up and looked hard at the fire, to avoid looking into the eyes of the soldiers. "My father was the one at the first wagon. The other was Mr. Gibson, who was going to be the magistrate out at Pitt."

Robertson nodded. "We also found a woman with brown hair, on the other side of the first wagon. It looked like she was trying to run away. She was shot in the back."

"That was my mother, Mary Eckert. What about my sister? She was four years old"

"Yes, from the bible, that would be Elise. We didn't find her. Looks like she was carried off; we did find a young boy's body lying next to you."

"That was Bernd. He was ten. How did he die?"

"Look, son you don't need to know all these details now. Just think of him being at peace."

Wend, choked back the tears as he asked the next question. "There was a sixteen year old girl, named Abigail. She was Magistrate Gibson's daughter. What happened to her?"

Robertson looked surprised. "We didn't find a girl of that age. She must have been taken. Was there anyone else in the train?"

"A black slave to the Gibsons. He drove their second wagon."

"We didn't find anyone like that." Robertson did a mental calculation. "So it looks like the war party made off with three people." He put his hand on Wend's shoulder. "We've sent out a civilian scout who was traveling with us. He's following the track of the war party, to see what he can learn from sign on the trail. He may find out enough to guess what tribe they're from."

Just then, Wend heard a sound which made his blood run cold. From somewhere near at hand came the unmistakable banshee sound from his dream. First a long groaning sound, then the rhythmic wailing which he remembered so well. Now another banshee groaned and joined in the wailing. Startled, he pushed himself up on his right elbow. He looked at the men who had gathered around him, surprised to see them nonchalantly listening to the sound, some even nodding their heads slightly in time with the rhythm, which now seemed to sound something like a musical tune. Wend looked around and saw the source of the noise; two of the men in skirts were standing by a fire on the other side of the camp, blowing into strange instruments.

Captain Robertson was looking at him with concern. "Lad, you look as white as if you had seen a ghost. What's frightened you?"

Wend asked, "What are those instruments making the music? I've never heard anything like that."

"Why, those are bagpipes. Or just the 'pipes' as we call them. They're traditional highland instruments, which we use like regular foot regiments use the fife."

A flood of understanding and relief flowed over Wend. "Were you playing the bagpipes when you came up the road to the ambush site?"

"Why, yes. Yes, we were. From a long distance, we saw the wagons behind the fallen tree and thought you were busy trying to clear the road. We didn't have any idea you had been attacked. So to announce our presence, I had the pipers start playing. It wasn't until our point men reached the tree that we realized what had happened."

Then Wend told him about his memory of the attack, his dream, and how the sounds of the "banshees" had pulled him back from following the others into the oblivion of the swirling tunnel. Robertson and the group around the fire listened intently, fascination written on their faces.

After he had finished his story, there was a long silence. Finally Robertson put his hand on Wend's shoulder. "Well, lad, there's no denying that the sound of the pipes are wild and go right to a man's soul. It has often been said that the wail of the pipes can rouse the dead. It looks like for you they might have actually done it." The officer stood, and the group of men broke up, returning to their own fires. Robertson told Wend, "Tomorrow, we'll start to sort things out and make ready to move on. Tonight, you get a good sleep and I'll talk with you again in the morning."

Soon Wend and his nurses were alone with Sergeant Iverson. Around the other campfires, the soldiers and their families were settling in for the night. Mary brought a poultice over and began, ever so gently, to apply it to the back of his head. As it touched his open wound, he jerked with the sting of it. "I know it stings, but this will make it heal more quickly. Mother has treated other men who have been scalped. We'll keep it on there as much as possible."

After the girl was done, Lizzie Iverson knelt beside him and he saw that she had a bottle in her hand. She produced a spoon, and in a mischievous tone said, "Time to take your medicine." She spooned liquid into his mouth.

Wend felt the burning of whiskey in his throat. It was as fiery as the stuff he and Arnold had sampled back in Carlisle. He looked up at Lizzie in surprise and, grinning broadly, she fed him several more spoonfuls. "That will help you get to sleep. As much as you have been through, I thought you'd need a little spirits to kill the pain and keep your mind from pondering everything that's happened."

Then she put the bottle to her mouth and took a couple of generous pulls herself, before putting the cork back in the bottle. "The lord knows, it's helped me find a peaceful rest many a night after a day tending the wounded or with the regiment getting ready for a fight in the morning." The woman pulled the blankets up over his shoulders and tucked them around his feet.

Wend felt a warm glow spreading through his body from the alcohol, and drowsiness began to settle in. As he drifted off, he decided Mrs. Iverson unquestionably knew her business as a nurse.

* * *

Wend was awakened in the dawn by the sounds of the camp coming alive. Lizzie was moving around the fire, preparing the morning meal. Soon her daughter began dressing Wend's wounds. Lizzie brought him tea and a plate of warmed salt beef and bread. The aroma made him realize how hungry he was; little Mary sat beside him and fed him the food. He noticed that she was very thin, but seemed to always have a cheery smile on her freckled face. She worked at feeding him with great diligence and he was impressed with how much more mature she seemed than Bernd.

Wend had just finished eating, and Mary was cleaning up his face with a damp cloth, when he saw a woman pass by carrying a bundle of clothing. Suddenly he recognized that they were some of his mother's clothes. The woman took the garments to her fire and began looking through them, pressing them up against her body for size. He felt outrage at the thought that these people were looting his parents' property and started to push himself up to a sitting position.

The girl put a hand out to restrain him. "Here, what's the matter Wend? You can't get up!"

"That woman has my mother's clothing! She's taking it for her own. They're looting our wagons." Wend looked up and saw that Mary was looking at him as if he had said something nonsensical.

Lizzie had heard the exchange. She came over and sat down beside Wend. She spooned him some tea. The sergeant's wife put a hand gently on his brow. "Now lad, I know you're upset. But think on it. Your mother and father and the others are 'na needing those clothes any more. And you can't carry much of it with you. The Indians tore through those wagons like a gale in their haste to find what they could take with them and left the rest lying around on the ground. Now our people might as well get some use out of what's left. It's the army way when things like this happen." Lizzie sighed, and getting up from the ground, went to a bag lying near the fire. She pulled a piece of clothing out and showed it to Wend. He gasped as he realized it was Abigail's blue traveling dress. "This is the prettiest dress I've ever seen. I found it on the ground next to one of the wagons. I'll ne'er be able to afford something like this on the pay of a sergeant. I'd be much obliged to you if I could keep it?"

Wend was devastated by the thought of someone beside Abigail wearing the dress. But suddenly, reality washed over him like the cold shock of creek water. The woman was right. Whatever happened, Abigail would never use the dress again. And he owed this woman for the kindness she was showing him.

He looked at the clothing Lizzie and her daughter were wearing and saw how faded and worn their petticoats were. He could see where rips had been mended and patches sewn in to cover holes. The hems were permanently stained with mud and other filth from living in dirty camps.

"Of course you may keep the dress, Mrs. Iverson. Keep it with my blessing and thanks." He hurried to change the subject. "I notice your daughter's last name is Fraser. Are you remarried?"

The woman packed the blue dress back into her bag and rejoined him. "My name used to be Fraser. But my husband, Mary's father, was a sergeant and was killed during Major Grant's fight near Fort Duquesne last year. So John Iverson asked for my hand right away, and I agreed. He's a good man, if not the most handsome, what with that nose and scar of his. But he treats Mary well, as if she was his own. I could have done worse."

Captain Robertson had come over to the fire while Lizzie was talking. After conferring with her out of Wend's earshot, he sat down beside the blankets and began to discuss his plans for handling the wreckage that had been the travelers' caravan.

"My men will be cutting a small clearing in the woods, to park the wagons and clear the road. And they are digging graves. We've had your family and Mr. Gibson's bodies wrapped in blankets since yesterday, over on the other side of the wagons. I expect we'll be finished with the graves and be able to have a service for them this afternoon."

"I'm very grateful for your consideration, sir." Wend was starting to feel tears forming again.

"We'll march tomorrow morning. We have two wagons of our own, so we'll set up to carry you in one of those." He thought a moment. "Oh, and just now, Mrs. Iverson brought it to my attention that you are concerned about our people taking some of your possessions."

"I was upset at first, but after she talked to me, I think I understand."

"Good lad! But listen close now; I don't want to speak too loud. The army's a hard life for the men and their families. The Crown pays these soldiers a pittance each month and then we take back a large part of it in what we call 'stoppages', which pay for clothing, food, and some items of equipment. When all is said and done, they have only pennies to spend every month. So when someone dies, their goods are divided up among the company. Mrs. Iverson is a good woman, kind and full of Christian charity, and the best nurse in the company. Many a man is thankful for her care. But I assure you, I've also seen her moving among the dead in the hospital or on the battlefield, relieving them of their worldly goods. I can't find it in my heart to think less of her for doing it. And I hope you won't, either."

Wend nodded his agreement. But his mind had been working hard since he realized that his family's possessions were being salvaged by the soldiers and their women. He knew he must try to save one item. "I'll need your help in recovering something which is very important, sir."

"Of course, lad. I'll do everything I can. What is it you need? We've already taken care of saving some clothes for you."

Wend looked around to check that their conversation was private. "The most urgent thing is a keg of hardware, screws and such, in the last wagon, which we call the tool wagon. If you could find that, I would be forever in your debt. The truth, sir, is that it has a double bottom. And most of our money, from selling our house and land back in Lancaster, is there in gold coins."

The Captain nodded. "I'll get right to that." He stood up and walked off toward the wagons.

* * *

It was early afternoon, and Wend had just been fed some soup by Lizzie and Mary. The food was bringing on drowsiness and he was willing to let it sweep over him, for sleep helped to assuage the pain, both physical and emotional.

Captain Robertson had found, undisturbed, the hardware keg with the double bottom and had taken it under his care. So Wend, although an orphan, was now relatively well off financially, at least for the near term. It was small consolation for the loss of all that was dear to him.

As Wend was thinking about these matters and just about to finally drift off to sleep, he was roused by a shout from one of the sentinels. "Rider coming in!"

He looked up the road to the west, and saw a horseman visible on the rise about a quarter of a mile away, approaching with his horse at a walk. As he came closer, Robertson and others gathered in a group next to the road to meet the rider. The man was dressed in a hunting shirt similar to Wend's, with dark green leggings. He carried a rifle across his saddle in front of him, with powder horn, bullet pouch, and knife in slings over his shoulders. He wore a wide brimmed gray hat with one side pinned up to the crown, and a buck's tail protruded jauntily to the rear. Wend realized it must be the scout that Robertson had told him was following the war party's trail.

As the woodsman pulled up his horse and dismounted in front of Robertson, Wend noticed that he had a large bundle slung over the horse in front of the saddle, hanging down on both sides of the horse. A chill swept over Wend, for he feared what the contents might be.

Robertson and the scout were out of Wend's earshot and he watched as the man made his report to the captain. He saw that the scout was tall and wiry, with an angular face under a stubbly brown beard which matched the hair showing under his hat. As they talked, he untied the bundle from his horse and laid it gently on the ground. Wend was wide awake as the two now approached where he lay. Robertson knelt beside him and the scout sat down, accepting a cup of tea from Lizzie.

"Wend, this is a scout employed by Colonel Bouquet, who's traveling with us."

"Joshua. Joshua Baird." The man reached over and shook Wend's right hand. "Very sorry to hear about your trouble, son."

Robertson looked at Wend. "Joshua found the war party's trail, lad, and followed them for a way. And I'm afraid we have more bad news for you." The Captain paused and looked at Baird for a moment. "He found your sister's body; she's in that bundle that he brought back with him."

Wend felt tears in his eyes, then streaming down his face. Mary brought a cloth and he wiped away the wetness. The men looked away while he regained control.

Baird told the story. "They must have decided she was too much trouble to keep with them. Maybe she wouldn't stop crying, maybe she couldn't keep up, who knows? It's not unusual for them to stop after they get some distance away from the raid site and make a decision about which captives to keep. I found her body near their camp."

Robertson said, "Joshua says he saw signs of the other two with them."

Wend asked the question which had been bothering him since his rescue. "Who did this? I thought the tribes were making peace. The troubles were supposed to be over. Bouquet said that at Carlisle."

Robertson looked at Baird, then at Wend. "That's what everyone thought. The Delawares, the Shawnees, all the tribes have been at council's out at Fort Pitt. There haven't been any raids for months now. Joshua thinks the war party was from a tribe called the Mingoes." He motioned for Baird to take over.

The scout paused while he assembled his thoughts. "You have to understand, them Mingoes ain't a proper tribe, like you would normally think about. They're really a bunch of separate bands, loosely allied. There's no single chief at the top, so each group pretty much operates on its own. In fact, they were originally related to the Iroquois, up to the north. They say that the Iroquois leadership sent out several groups years ago, to live among the tribes to the south and keep them informed about affairs down here. Eventually those bands inter-married with the local tribes or adopted captives to keep up their numbers. So eventually each band took on their own character and customs. They don't necessarily follow along with what the other tribes in the area are doing. This particular band may have decided that they weren't ready for peace yet. And Mingoes are always very aggressive in taking captives to be adopted."

Wend was puzzled. "But what were they doing this far east? Wouldn't an attack like this be more likely beyond Ligonier or even Bedford?"

"Good thought, son," Baird replied. "That was my first idea also. And it kept puzzling me while I was following their trail. Until I got to their campsite. And then I realized it was also the camp they had been at before they attacked you. It had sign of them being there for several days. And even more important, it had sign of white men in the camp. Hoof marks of lots of horses. Like from a pack train. And there were parts of boxes and other things which came from the settlements."

Wend was stunned. "Did you say there might have been a pack train at the campsite?"

"Sure; looked like maybe a dozen horses tied up to one picket line, for a couple of days, from the amount of dung on the ground. Why do you ask?"

Wend told him about his experience on the hunt, of meeting the pack train there and talking with the two traders, and the heaviness of the horse packs.

Baird was looking at Wend with great interest now. "Did you get the names of the packers, son?"

"Yes; Kinnear and Fleming. Does that mean anything to you?"

"Yes, damn it! They work out of York. They're scum, as far as I'm concerned. For a long time, the colonel and I have been thinking that they trade large amounts of powder, lead for balls, guns, and steel implements to the tribes." He grimaced and changed his position on the ground. "That may explain the Mingo band's being this far to the east—a planned meeting with those traders in an area where there wouldn't be much chance of an army patrol. But more important, it may also explain why you got raided. The traders tipped off the Mingoes about your train and where you would be along the road. It ingratiated them to the band; sort of a bonus to the Indians who got some extra goods and hostages. And it served Kinnear and Fleming also—it eliminated you, or so they thought, probably the only outsider who knew they were here."

Wend was devastated. In his mind, he was at least partially responsible for the death of his family and Magistrate Gibson as well as the captivity of Abigail and Franklin. He remembered his negligence in not telling his father about the encounter with the traders. Johann might have sensed that danger existed if he had been told. And the worst part was that Wend, the one who could have alerted them, was the survivor.

Baird interrupted his thoughts. "I understand your name is Eckert. Was your father the gunsmith with Armstrong's Battalion last year?"

"Yes sir, he was."

"Well, your father did good work for me. I came into camp out at Ligonier with a broken lock on my rifle. Stupid move by me: Got it caught in a tree while on horseback, and before I could stop, the lock got pulled apart. Your father did a good job: Repaired it with a better lock than I had in the first place. You'd never know, from lookin' at the rifle that it had been replaced."

Wend looked at the scout's rifle, which he had placed against a nearby tree. He instantly recognized the lock. "That's a German, three-spring lock. It's the best quality. We bought a supply from a trading ship in Philadelphia in 1757."

Baird reached over and laid the rifle across his lap. "Well, your father fitted it like it was custom made to go with this rifle, even though the first lock was a different style. And it has never let me down since." He thought for a moment. "Were you your father's apprentice?"

"I've been working with my father in his shop since I was nine." Wend looked over at the rifle. "Hold that up and turn it over slowly so I can see both sides of the stock."

Baird complied, looking at Wend curiously.

"I'd wager that rifle was made in York county. It has the look of work by Nicholas Hachen, down Hanover way, or perhaps his apprentice, George Shroyer."

Baird looked at Robertson, then at Wend. "Why, I bought it from that old Switzer Hachen at Hanover in '56. Lord, son, how did you know from just lookin' at the gun?"

"Look at the shape of the rear ramrod finial—the brass holder which keeps the ramrod in place. Do you see the way it tapers differently from the other two? Then look at the curves on the trigger guard, particularly the reverse spur at the rear, and the fleur-de-lis carved into the top of the wrist, where you put your right hand when you're aiming. Finally, see the open C-scroll carved into the rear of the cheek piece? Those are all signature designs used by Mr. Hachen."

Baird looked over his rifle with new interest, and Robertson, listening to Wend's description of the details, had leaned over to examine the gun. The scout said, "You certainly know your rifles. I'll tell Nicholas he has an admirer next time I see him."

"I hope you won't be telling him for a while, sir. Mr. Hachen died last year, according to the word we got."

Baird looked hard at Wend for a long moment, then smiled. "Anyone ever tell you that you look like the spitting image of your father?"

"About every other person that I meet, sir."

"Can you make rifles as good as you can talk about them? Ever made one on your own?"

"Mr. Baird, I've been making and selling rifles, pistols and knives on my own for the last year. One of those wagons over there is full of gunsmith tools and parts for rifles, like blank barrels and locks. There's even a rifling machine, broken down for travel. Take a look for yourself."

Robertson had gotten up, and now Baird did the same. "I might just do that. And I'll come back and talk to you some more about what I found on the trail in a little while," Baird said as he turned to walk with Robertson.

After they left, Mary brought him some water in a cup. "Can you really make long rifles like Joshua and the other scouts use? They look so elegant, what with the carvings and the brass fittings. So different from the 'Brown Bess' the soldiers use."

"Sure. And I made myself one. It was bright maple, with double triggers. A real beauty; I won a shooting contest with it back in Lancaster. Some brave is carrying it now, I guess."

* * *

They held a funeral service in the late afternoon. The highlanders had dug five graves to the south of the road across from the company's campsite and what had now become a park for the derelict wagons. Wend had tried to sit up that afternoon, only to find that he experienced severe dizziness. So a canvas litter had been made and four highlanders carried him to the service.

The soldiers formed ranks on the road in front of the five crosses lashed together from saplings. The wives and children stood to one side and Robertson read passages from the Eckert's bible. When he had finished, the pipers played a slow, forlorn melody which echoed through the quiet of the forest. Then Robertson solemnly walked over to Wend's litter and handed him the bible. Wend had been able to control his grief until that moment, but when he felt the familiar covers of the book in his hand and saw where Robertson had neatly written in the word 'deceased' and the date beside each member of his family, he could bear it no longer and began to sob.

Later, as the evening began to close about them, Baird returned and again sat down by Wend. He pulled a short stemmed pipe and tobacco from a pocket in his shirt to set about fixing himself a smoke. Only after he had lighted the pipe and had it drawing well did he begin to tell Wend about trailing the war party.

The Mingo trail had been easy to read; they were leading several horses from the caravan carrying loot. Their camp was about five miles westward, on the eastern slope of Sideling Hill. It lay at the foot of a rock outcropping visible for miles, which clearly had been a landmark for their rendezvous with the traders. The camp showed signs of eight or ten warriors. Two trails left the site. One was the trappers heading back eastward, the other the warriors and their captives leading northwest, up to a well known walking path through the ridges.

He had found Elise's body under brush outside the camp. "You don't need to worry about her feeling much pain. I 'spect one of them came up behind her quiet-like and hit her head with a war club. I doubt she even knew what happened."

Wend nodded, knowing that if he talked about Elise, he would break down again. The scout continued his story: After finding Elise, and wrapping her body in his blanket, he had followed the party up the slope of the mountain to the crest and onto the ancient path. "It was pretty clear that they were moving fast, trying to get back into their own territory using horses to transport the goods they got from your train and the traders."

Wend composed himself. "I appreciate your telling me about all this, and about what happened to Elise. What do you think is going to happen to Abigail—the girl they took—and the black man?"

"If they didn't have their way with her right away here on the road, or at the camp, and then dispatch her, I reckon they mean to adopt her into their band. If they were Delaware or Shawnee, they might trade her to another tribe or band, just like you might trade a slave in Philadelphia. But since these are Mingoes, I figure they want her for some brave's wife. Could be they ain't got enough young women in their band. Was she good looking?"

Wend looked up at Baird, then down at the fire. "She was beautiful, with blue eyes and blond hair."

"Well, then, she might end up as their leader's wife or the wife of his son. Indians are men just like us; a pretty head makes them just as interested." The scout smiled to himself and then to Wend, with a knowing look on his face.

"What about the slave? His name was Franklin."

"Now, that's an interesting subject. The Indians are sort of taken with black men. 'Cause of their dark skin, they think of them as sort of cousins, if you will. That's probably why they took him alive, instead of just clubbing him right away down at the road. How old was this Franklin?"

Wend considered for a moment. "In his early or middle twenties, I think. He was shipped up from Carolina when he was a young man and had been in Philadelphia for about three years before this trip began."

"Well, if he's fairly young, they probably will adopt him into the tribe just like the girl. As I mentioned, those Mingo bands are always in need of more people, to keep up their numbers."

"Mr. Baird, what will the army do to get them back? When will they send a party in pursuit?"

The scout gave Wend a quick look of impatience. "Ain't in the cards, lad; Bouquet's got his hands full just keeping the forts supplied. He hasn't got enough troops to mount any kind of expedition to hunt for captives. And you got to realize there are hundreds of small bands of Indians out there in the Ohio Country. How do you find two people among all that lot? And word spreads like wildfire among the tribal society; a band of Indians hears that somebody's looking for their captives and they move to another location deeper in the territory or find some other way to hide them."

The prospect that Abigail was gone forever swept over Wend. And Abigail's situation was worse than most. With her father dead, she had no relatives who would even be thinking about her. And the Gibsons had left Philadelphia under a cloud anyway. Wend was probably the only one who cared what happened to her. He looked up from his thoughts to see Baird staring at him.

"Say, how old was this girl, anyway? Didn't the Captain say that she was about your age?"

Wend nodded.

"You got a special interest in her?" The scout looked directly into Wend's eyes for a time and the boy knew they had betrayed him. He looked back down into the fire, not wanting to discuss his relations with Abigail further. But Baird wouldn't leave it drop. He leaned closer to Wend, and in an almost conspiratorial manner said, "Yeah, you had a special interest: You're stuck on her. I can see it in your eyes."

Wend felt the tears well up and he instinctively reached up with his right hand to wipe them away.

Baird put his arm on Wend's shoulder. "Hey, listen, lad. I understand how you feel. Life has given you one cruel blow. But you got to deal with the fact that the girl is gone and get on with your life."

Wend turned on him. "No, you don't understand. We were intimate. Do you know what I mean? Intimate! I loved her."

Baird raised his hand. "Whoa, lad, rein it in!" He took a pull on his pipe, savoring the taste. Looking down at the pipe, he said in a conversational tone, "You got to hand it to those Virginians; whatever else you think of them, they know how to grow good tobacco." He took another pull and nodded his head as if signaling agreement with his own words. "Listen son, this is going to be hard to take at first, but here's the truth of it: You got to think about this girl as if you had been courting her, and things were going pretty well, and she was showing you her favors, if you take my meaning. And then something came between you. Like another good looking guy came around and she decided he was her cup of tea, and suddenly you was out of the picture. Happens to us all, somewhere along the way. Matter of fact, it's even happened to me, more than once." He shook his head and frowned. "I know that's hard to believe, but it's true." Then he continued, "Just pretend that's what has taken place, and make up your mind to move on. There are other young lasses around who can do as much damage to your heart as this one has."

Wend looked up at the scout. "There's never going to be another girl like this."

"Well, of course the first one's always in your memory, always next to your heart. Keep her memory there, private like and cherish it. Take it out once and a while and savor it all over again at quiet moments. But you still got to pull your life together. Right now you want to roll up and die, but you can't do it. No one's ever been closer to dead than you were, but the Lord kept you alive for some reason, so you better go figure out what that is."

Wend, looking deep into the flames, didn't answer.

Baird took a few more puffs on his pipe. Then, as it became clear that Wend wasn't ready to say anything, he started to talk again. "Which brings us to an interesting question: What are you going to do now that things have turned out this way?"

Wend realized the scout had targeted the very thing which he had been avoiding. In truth, for the last two days he had been living in the moment with no thought for the future.

"You got any close kin that will take you in?"

Wend thought for a moment. He realized how alone he was. "The only real family left back in Lancaster is my mother's half sister. And she's married, with four of her own. There's nobody in America on my father's side."

"Well, lad, then it's time for you to start thinking about all this. And I got a proposition for you to chew over."

Wend looked up from the fire at the scout sitting next to him. Baird was leaning back, the picture of contentment as he drew on his pipe, his feet stretched before him baking in the heat of the flames. "What kind of proposition?"

"There's a small settlement, an easy day's ride up north of Carlisle, called Sherman Mill. It's in Sherman Valley, which is starting to get populated pretty fast, now that the war is winding down. My sister and her husband live there. He's the minister for the congregation. They got a pretty fair sized house and ain't been able to have children. I know she would be grateful to have a lad like you around. But even more important, there isn't any gunsmith up there yet, and the people sure could use one. So it looks like it would be a good opening for a young fellow like you who wants to make a place for himself."

Wend thought for a moment. "You said your sister would like to have me there. What about her husband, the minister? How would he feel about it?"

"That's no problem. Her husband's my best friend. We traveled together when we was young."

"It sounds interesting. But I'd need my father's tools and supplies. They're in the wagon over there. But all the horses are either dead or stolen. How could we take the wagon along?"

"I've been thinking about that since earlier today, when I looked at the wagon. I think between me and Captain Robertson, we could find a way to get it back to Lyttleton or even Loudoun, where a team could be found. In fact, the captain let on to me that you saved some money from the ambush, which could be used to buy animals. I know people down at McDowell's Mill, which is close to Loudoun, who deal in horses. So getting you your tools is just about a done thing. Now all you need to do is say yes."

Wend thought for a moment. Accepting the scout's offer meant going to live amidst the Ulster people: A whole new world for him. He had tasted it that night in Carlisle with Arnold Spengler. The people had dressed, talked, and acted in ways so foreign to his Germanic upbringing. But what did he have to lose? The simple truth was, the scout was presenting him with a new start, something he would have to do on his own, without friends, if he didn't accept the offer. And Baird was ready to do all the work. Now that he had started thinking about it, he was desperately eager to save the tool wagon. Moreover, Wend realized he couldn't go back to Lancaster. There would be too many memories of his family, too many reminders of the life he had led before and which he could never regain.

"All right, Mr. Baird. I'm game. I'll be the gunsmith of Sherman Mill."

The scout exhaled a stream of smoke and smiled at Wend. "I thought you'd take me up, once you thought it over. Makes sense any way you look at it." He knocked the embers of tobacco from his pipe against a log, and placing it back into his pocket, climbed to his feet. "I'll go work things out with Robertson. You get some rest, 'cause tomorrow is going to be an early day. These highlanders are restless to get back on the road."

CHAPTER 7
Bouquet's Pledge

The column reached Loudoun in the afternoon two days later and made camp in the same place where the Eckerts and Gibsons had broken camp only days before. Wend was shocked to find that, after the cataclysmic events which had overtaken his life, Fort Loudoun looked exactly the same as when he had left in that misty dawn so recently. He could see the ashes of the fire where he and Abigail and his family had spent so much time. Forbes' cabin sat alone by the Conococheague as if waiting for another meeting between he and Abigail. That thought made the sadness that had been residing in him well up and he worked hard to keep from showing his tears as the soldiers and their families set up camp around him.

Mary dressed his wounds and Lizzie came over to look. With the bandages off his side, she put her hand against the bullet wound along his ribs, then carefully inspected the damage to his head. "That gouge in your side is healin' up nicely, bleeding's all stopped and it's scabbing up good-like. Not a sign of corruption. That arm's doing just as well." She clucked her tongue. "Now this place where they lifted your scalp is another matter, its 'na coming along like I'd want. It's still oozing all kinds of liquid around the edges. I'm going to try another kind of poultice, to see if that helps."

She gave instructions to Mary that meant nothing to Wend and he lost interest in the words of his nurse. He felt himself sinking into another of the gloomy periods which had frequently come over him since the massacre.

But Lizzie would not be ignored. "Hey, do you hear me? I asked you how that scalp felt!"

Wend thought for a moment. "It still has a lot of throbbing soreness. And it itches like the devil all the time. If you didn't have that dressing on it, I couldn't stop from scratching."

102

"Lord, that's the best news I've heard. The itching means that the scalp is trying to heal itself. But I'll put some liquid in the new dressing which will keep it within limits."

She was interrupted by the sound of hooves. Wend looked up to see Baird pull up his horse by the group. He looked down at Wend with a mischievous grin. "Hey, Sprout, I'm off to McDowell's Mill to find you some horses. Robertson broke into that keg of yours and gave me some wherewithal to pay for them. McDowell's is not two miles from here, so if I have any luck I'll be back about dark with a team."

He turned his attention to the women and swept his hat off in a gallant salute. "I hope Wend understands how much it pains me to have to leave the prettiest lady in the regiment, Mrs. Iverson! Wouldn't ever do it except for the pressing need to get that team."

Blushing, Lizzie drew a hand through her copper hair. "There you go again, Joshua, makin' advances to a married woman. And the wife of a highlander of all things; its lucky Sergeant Iverson is a patient man who understands your foolin' nature, or he'd have that head of yours off with his broadsword! Now get out of here and let me get on with my work."

"Well, at least promise you'll keep some of your dinner for me to taste. It will be a consolation after the hard riding I've got to do. Ain't no one who can make army rations taste palatable like you can, and that's the truth. I haven't had any of your cookin' since before Bedford, and I'm feelin' all the poorer for it."

"So, now, Joshua, we know the truth about why your bein' so flattering. You just want some dinner cooked by a woman, instead of that slop they put together over at the sergeant's fire. I would just tell you to fend for yourself, if I wasn't such a charitable person. But I'll keep some dinner for you if you promise to hold your flirting tongue around my husband. And don't be too late gettin' back, or you can forget about it."

The scout's face split into a broad smile which seemed to go from ear to ear; he returned the hat to his head and snugged it down. "Mrs. Iverson, I'll be cherishing your smile and the thought of sharing your fire all the way to McDowell's and back."

Then Baird was off, pressing his horse into a trot as soon as he left the bivouac area. Wend looked at Lizzie Iverson with fresh eyes. Suddenly it occurred to him that beneath the weathered skin of her face she was a strikingly attractive woman. The copper hair framed a long face, prominent cheekbones, widely set eyes and a small but strong chin. Even the tiny lines which radiated from the edge of her eyes seemed to add to her appearance, giving her a reflective, dignified countenance.

Mary arrived with a new poultice for his skull. She applied it gently and then replaced the wrapping over his head. Soon a cooling effect set in and drove away the itching. Wend felt his body relaxing and soon drifted off to sleep.

It seemed like only a few seconds had passed when he was awakened by shouting. He came back awake to realize that he had slept for hours, because it was nearly dusk. Sergeant Iverson and his wife were standing together before the fire, looking down the road from Chambers' Mills. Other soldiers were pointing in the same direction and talking excitedly. Iverson saw that Wend was awake and responded to his questioning look. "Freight wagons in sight coming up the road. Lots of them: It looks like Bouquet's supply train out of Carlisle, and they should be here in a few minutes."

Wend pulled himself up to a sitting position. His head felt like he was spinning. But after a few seconds, the feeling abated and he was able to watch the approach of the wagons. He counted sixteen of them; big Conestoga's with six horse teams. Some of the civilian drivers were riding on their lead horse, but most walked on the left side of their wagon, the reins led back from each pair of horses. He recognized Colonel Bouquet on horseback in the lead with Lieutenant Locke on a mount beside him. Several soldiers, muskets slung over their shoulders, marched alongside the wagons. The wagon wheels kicked up plumes of dust as they moved along the track.

The train pulled up in the open space on the other side of the fort, where Wend could see Captain Sharp and a cluster of his green coated garrison bunched up in front of the gate to watch the arrival. Soon the train had been parked in two rows and the waggoners were busy unhitching and leading their teams to a picket line on the far side of the wagon park. Bouquet and his adjutant rode over to where Sharp stood, dismounting amid salutes and shouted greetings. Orderlies came and took the horses' reins from the officers and presently Sharp walked Bouquet and Locke to Forbes' cabin by the creek. Wend saw Robertson hurry over to greet the colonel and make his report.

Wend was distracted by Mary's arrival with a bowl of stew from the cook pot. The aroma aroused a strong hunger in him. She carefully placed a cloth over his chest like a baby's bib and then began spooning the food into his mouth.

It was in this moment of relative helplessness that Wend looked up to see Arnold Spengler standing with his musket grounded in front of him, pack and bedroll on his back, watching the girl feed him the stew. The corporal looked down at him with a broad smile on his face. "Well, Eckert, you've got yourself into a real mess this time, haven't you?"

Wend felt a rush of emotion as he looked up at the first familiar face he had seen since the massacre. He fought back the tears and put a stoic expression on his face. He tried to think of something jocular to say, but couldn't do it. Instead he blurted out, "They got everyone in my family, Arnold. They're all dead and buried by the road out beyond Lyttleton."

Arnold's smile faded. "Yeah, I heard that highland captain tell Bouquet all about what happened. Wend, I'm real sorry about your family. And I used to spend so much time over at your house, I feel like a part of my life has disappeared too."

"Arnold, they took Abigail into captivity."

"Oh, yeah, the blond girl from Philadelphia—I heard that they got her and that black man. You should have seen Lieutenant Locke's face when he heard the news. After you left, he was talking about her all the time and couldn't wait to get to Pitt so he could see her again. That's a real shame, because she sure was pretty, and now she's dead or some brave's woman."

Wend looked at Mary, and asked her to let he and Arnold talk privately. She gave them a look of disappointment, but moved around to the other side of the fire. Arnold sat down beside Wend on the ground. "Arnold, I have to tell you something. She was my girl. We got to be real close on the road."

"Yes, well I don't blame you for gettin' stuck on her. She turned heads wherever she went. I even heard the colonel saying what a looker she was to Locke. But there will be other girls."

Wend saw that Arnold didn't understand. "Arnold, I was with her. All the way. I don't know why she liked me, but it happened fast, and it took place one night right here at Loudoun, over in that cabin where Bouquet is staying."

Arnold started to say something before the meaning of what Wend had said hit him. He stopped and looked over at Wend with a startled, disbelieving look on his face. "You're serious? She went the whole way with you? In that short a time?"

"Yes. And I'm going to get her back, somehow, sometime. You can wager on that! I've been thinking about it for the last two days, Arnold. There has to be some way."

Arnold slowly shook his head. "Wend, I can understand how you feel, but we haven't got the men to find captives, let alone rescue them from the midst of that hostile territory out beyond the rivers. People who have lost relatives come out to the fort all the time wanting us to do something. We just send them back east with sympathy."

Wend saw sadness in his friend's eyes and realized that Arnold pitied him for not being able to face reality. He decided to change the subject. So he told the corporal about Baird's proposal that Wend stay with his sister's family at Sherman Mill, and that his tools had been saved, so that he could earn a living.

Arnold's face brightened. "Now that sounds like a real good plan. And if you are that close to Carlisle, I can get mail to you along with our dispatches if anything turns up about the girl." Arnold got up and slung his musket over his shoulder. "I've got to get back to work. Bouquet never stops writing, even on the road like this. He's going to have dispatches for me to copy. But he said he would try to get over here to talk to you before the night is over."

Mary came back and finished feeding him. Just as she was cleaning him up, Baird rode out of the darkness leading a couple of draught horses. He threw down from his horse and smiled at Lizzie across the fire. "Said I wouldn't miss your dinner, Mrs. Iverson." Wend saw Lizzie's face light up as she gave him a quick, warm smile of her own. Then he nodded to the sergeant, who sat on a log looking up at the horses and grinning in amusement.

Iverson pointed to the team of horses. "You didn't actually pay money for that pair of nags, did you Joshua? I've eaten better looking animals than those and considered it a poor meal."

Baird looked over at the team and grimly shook his head. "They ain't beauties, and that's the truth. And I'll admit they are more than just a bit past their prime. But they're all that old man Craig had available in his stable on short notice." He turned and looked down at Wend, "Don't worry; they'll get your wagon up to Sherman Mill sure enough! And the price was right."

The scout led the three horses over to the picket line and was back in a few minutes to partake of the promised meal from Lizzie's pot. He sat enjoying the stew, and telling jokes about his trip to McDowell's when they heard the sound of footsteps from the direction of the fort. Wend looked up to see Bouquet, accompanied by Locke and Robertson, emerge into the light of the fire. Everyone save Wend stood up.

Baird held the bowl of stew in his left hand and casually raised the wooden spoon in his right hand by way of improvised salute. "Evening, Colonel. I was going to come over and report to you a little later, after I got some rations down."

Bouquet nodded at Baird and motioned everyone around the fire to retake their seats. He touched his hat to Mrs. Iverson. "I beg your leave to spend a few minutes at your fire. I would not impose on you, but I wanted to talk to young Mr. Eckert, and given his injuries, I thought it would be easier for everyone if I came to him."

The colonel turned to Wend, removed his hat, and spoke with great formality. "Young man, let me extend my most sincere sympathy on your great loss. I had only the deepest respect for your father. His service to the Crown, and to me, was of the greatest value during the late campaign. Also, on behalf of the Crown, please let me express my great sorrow over the loss of your family in the pursuit of His Majesty's service."

Wend could not find the words to reply, so he nodded acknowledgement of the colonel's words. Arnold had been standing behind the officers, carrying a folding stool. Now he placed it beside Wend and Bouquet sat down. He looked around at the gathering. "Can I ask you to leave Mr. Eckert and I for a short time?"

When they were alone, he thought for a moment, then said, "I wanted to be alone with you, Wend, for just a few moments, because I have something personal to say. I must apologize to you for my misjudgment about the safety of the road. I am the one who is to blame for these deaths and for the fact that two people are now captives, probably never to see civilization again. And so I have a debt to you because I failed you. I shall repay that debt some day, in some way I cannot know now. Do you understand, lad?"

"Sir, you don't owe me anything. Everyone, even my father, thought it was safe along Forbes Road."

"The man in command must accept responsibility for whatever happens; the good and the bad, the foreseen and the unforeseen. So I must make amends to you for my failing." Bouquet reached down to his belt and pulled out the pistol that Johann had presented him. "I shall carry this with me always; it will remind me of the man who made it, and of my debt to him and his son."

Bouquet returned the pistol to his belt. "Now there is another matter I must discuss. Your friend, Corporal Spengler, is an impudent, irascible young upstart who frequently abuses the privilege of his position on my staff." He grinned conspiratorially. "I'd send him back to his company in a minute if he didn't have the clearest writing hand in the battalion! At any rate, he approached me a short time ago and confided that you and Magistrate Gibson's daughter had, shall we say, become much more than mere traveling companions before the attack occurred. Is that truly the case?"

Wend mentally cursed Arnold for telling Bouquet about Abigail. He felt himself turning red in the face. He started to reply, but Bouquet quieted him by putting a hand on his shoulder.

"I can see from your face that it is true." He smiled at Wend. "And there is no need to feel embarrassed. Although I have never had the honor of marriage, I can assure you that I have a thorough understanding of the relationships between men and women. In fact, there is a very beautiful and graceful lady in Switzerland who I worshipped in my youth. I let my duties pull me away from her. I know I will never see her again, but she inhabits my most cherished dreams when I am alone and the night is at its darkest. So I can understand how you feel at the loss of Miss Gibson. Perhaps, since we share a common form of loss, it may be a bond between us."

He reached down and offered Wend his hand, and they held the grasp for a long moment.

"And don't be angry with your friend for telling me about your intimacy with Mistress Gibson. He only wanted to ensure that I understand your interest in her situation." Then Bouquet looked down at Wend with a crooked smile on his lips and merriment in his eyes. "Oh yes: One other thing. I should tell you that I will not inform anyone else about you and the girl. In particular, I see no reason why my adjutant, Mr. Locke, has any reason to know. I fear his confidence in himself would be irretrievably crushed if he found out that Miss Gibson had given her favors to someone else after the Herculean efforts he made toward her in Carlisle."

Wend looked up at Bouquet and broke into the first laughter he had had since the massacre. "Sir, I will trust to your discretion."

Bouquet winked, then stood up and made ready to leave. "I pledge to you that I shall pay particular attention to the case of Miss Gibson. If I get any information about her well-being, or her location, I will send it to you by way of Corporal Spengler. Be that as it may, now you must concentrate on building yourself a new life. Godspeed, son."

PART TWO

Among the Ulster

1762-1763

CHAPTER 8

Sherman Mill

Peggy McCartie, her raven hair and blue petticoat highlighted by a white cap, blouse, and apron, screwed up her face as she looked up at the firelock on the wall. "Wend Eckert, stop teasing me! How can you have such a thing as a smoothbore rifle? That's a contradiction!"

Wend stood in the center of the common room of McCartie's Tavern, critically looking at his handiwork. He had just placed a long-barreled firearm upon two pegs in the wall behind the tavern's bar. It was crafted from dark, well oiled wood, with simple but attractive carvings around the butt and wrist and trimmed with brass fittings. A leather hunting pouch, with a polished powder horn attached, hung decoratively from the firelock by means of a carrying strap looped over the barrel. Centered below the pegs was a wooden plaque with brass lettering which proclaimed, "Wend Eckert, Gunsmith." He nodded, satisfied that it made an attractive advertisement for his business. Shortly after arriving in Sherman Mill in 1759, he had hit upon this way of showing off his tradecraft. Now, in September 1762, he maintained Eckert rifles on display in several taverns throughout the border country.

"Now Peggy, why would you think I'm trying to make fun of you?"

The black haired girl, of about Wend's age, pursed her lips and glared at him. "Because, just like I said, it doesn't make any sense! And anyway, I can never tell when you're kidding; you always put on that wooden face."

Wend knew that the men of Sherman Valley universally agreed that Peggy was the prettiest woman north of Carlisle and the tavern's most valuable asset. Watching the girl work the common room, coquettishly flaunting her looks and smile was well worth a walk or ride to town after a day's labor on the farm. But all would also admit that she was a hard-worker who did more than her share in keeping up the tavern.

Wend permitted himself a tiny smile. "Peggy, I'm not trying to put you on. 'Smoothbore rifle' is an accurate name for that type of gun. It's built in the exact same style as one of my rifles, except the barrel is smooth inside."

Peggy asked impatiently, "So why would you make a firelock like that? What's the sense of it?"

"Peggy, actually it's just the thing for people, like farmers, who do most of their shooting at short ranges. At those distances its accuracy is comparable to a rifle. And they can use it with either ball or shot, depending on the kind of game they are after."

Peggy's younger sister, Ellen, looked up as she scrubbed one of the tables. "Well, it sure didn't take you long to make up another display gun after Paul Milliken bought the last one." The girl, dressed similarly to her sister, but in a gray petticoat, had dark brown hair and an angular face which would never be called pretty. But she made up for her plainness with a pleasant smile which almost never left her countenance.

Wend nodded to her: "That's the point, Ellen: It's cheaper and faster to make than a rifle, since I don't have to cut grooving into the barrel and that's what takes a lot of time."

As they were talking, Donovan McCartie entered the common room bearing a small keg of ale which he put down on the counter. Ellen pointed out the display gun to her father. "Pa, look at the new gun Wend's brought. It's a smoothbore."

"Hello, lad, I wondered when you were going to bring a new piece down. That's nice looking. The wood is quite a bit darker than the last one."

"Yes, I've used walnut instead of maple," Wend replied. "Joseph Junkin has been talking about needing a new gun but can't spare the price for a rifle, in cash or barter. So I made this smoothbore up with him in mind. I also used some less costly parts, like the single trigger lock, instead of the double trigger type I normally use. If he comes in, you might point out its features, particularly that it's cheaper than one of my rifles."

McCartie nodded. "Well, if I know Junkin, he'll go after a bargain like that."

Wend went to the counter and handed some coins to McCartie as his fee for allowing the display. The tavern keeper placed them in his money drawer behind the counter. "This reminds me: We should be making plans for the next shooting match. It's just over a month from now."

Wend considered for a moment. "Why don't you call a meeting of the merchants and we'll settle the details."

"I'll do that", McCartie answered. "Business has been slow the last few weeks and I can use the trade from a good crowd spending the day here in the village."

Every few months the merchants of the village of Sherman Mill sponsored a shooting match on cleared land behind McCartie's Tavern. The tavern keeper himself had started the custom years ago as means of attracting customers. For McCartie, not a man known for his creativity, it had been a masterstroke of marketing. Now the matches drew shooters and spectators from all over Cumberland County, making for good sport and wagering. McCartie put up prizes for different contests, with various sized targets at different ranges. From the start Wend had been one of the best shots and his skill had grown until he had become recognized as the premier marksman of Sherman Valley. Most of the time he won the largest prize, which was a keg of whiskey from the tavern. This warmed Donovan McCartie's heart, because after the event was over and the crowd dispersed, Wend secretly gave the prize back to the tavern owner.

After a few more minutes passing the time with McCartie, Wend picked up his canvas bag and went out the tavern door to the wagon road which passed through the village of Sherman Mill. Across the road from McCartie's Tavern, along Sherman Creek, was the grist mill which gave the village its name. The miller's house and outbuildings nestled alongside the mill structure. Next to the tavern was a blacksmith's establishment, with a log house, stable, forge and work shack out front. Aside from a few small cabins, the only other significant structure in the village was a two story log building which served as both a store and a house for its proprietor.

Wend slung the bag over his shoulder and walked up the hill along the wagon track to the Carnahan's place. It consisted of several buildings laid out on a small plateau above the village. The road, which went on to a few more farms up the valley, ran between the major buildings of the farmstead. On the side away from the creek was the Carnahan's two story house. Beside the house was the building, constructed by the men of the valley some years ago, which served as both the church and school house. Paul Carnahan served a similar dual role, leading the townspeople in prayer on the Lord's Day and teaching the children on weekdays. As he reached the crest of the hill Wend could see Carnahan himself through a window in the school, animatedly talking to his students as they sat in the pews, slate boards in hand.

On the other side of the road was the Carnahan's barn and outbuildings.

Wend walked past the church and into the house. Patricia Carnahan was sitting before the fire, hunched over some mending. She looked up and broke into a broad smile. Looking at her, there could be no doubt that she was Joshua Baird's sister. She was a tall woman, with brown hair and the same rawboned, lanky figure as the scout. In fact she was actually slightly taller than her brother and had a couple of inches over her own husband. When he first arrived, Wend had thought they made an unlikely pairing, but their obvious affection for each other quickly drove that perception forever from his mind. He had, in fact, never seen a couple more attuned to each others' thoughts and manners.

Three years earlier, Joshua had driven the tool wagon up the hill from Sherman Mill with the wounded Wend lying on blankets in the wagon bed and reined in the horses at the Carnahan's door. The scout strode into the house, announcing his presence with a shout. After a few minutes he emerged accompanied by Paul and Patricia. Seeing Wend's condition, the Reverend's face had assumed a grim expression, as he and Joshua prepared to lift Wend out of the wagon. Patricia's hands had flown to her face in distress at his appearance. She had taken charge, having them carry Wend upstairs to a bedroom.

Instantly, Wend became the son that Patricia Carnahan, childless at thirty-two, had thought that she never would have. Over the next weeks she nursed him with gentle and loving hands. Whereas the care given by Lizzie Iverson had been efficient and practiced, Patricia administered her treatment like a mother hen doting over her only chick.

Wend had welcomed the attention and the total absence of need to act for himself. The early weeks at the Carnahan's had been a regression for him. Since the day he had turned seven, his life had been focused on increasing acceptance of responsibility and the onset of adulthood. On that birthday he had started rising with his father at dawn and performing chores in the barn before starting off for school. Then, at nine, he had begun his apprenticeship, each day learning new skills and responsibilities. On the journey West along Forbes Road, he had eagerly felt himself becoming an adult as he handled grown-up challenges, culminating when he and Abigail had consummated their love at Fort Loudoun. But since the shock of the massacre, he had lost all sense of purpose, all desire to meet the challenges of life. It was like he had pulled the protective shell of childhood back over himself, allowing others to make decisions for him.

Patricia cared for him, washing him and experimenting with his hair until she found the best arrangement to make the missing portion of his scalp less obvious. She skillfully made him a new, more colorful Ulster-style wardrobe and cleaned and stowed away the few pieces of his clothing which had been saved from the massacre site. It was as if to convey that he had a new life now, but the old life was still there, to be brought out and remembered from time to time whenever he felt the need.

Patricia spent hours talking with Wend as he sat bundled up before the kitchen fire while she went about her chores. He learned about the wildness of her brother Joshua, who at sixteen had rebelled against the drudgery of farming and run away from home to take up the life of a hunter and trader. She told him how, several years later, Joshua had finally come back and brought his friend Paul Carnahan to her parent's farm near York. There she and the quiet young man had fallen in love, married, and then moved to the green hills of Sherman Valley. Her stories had given Wend a sense of belonging, as if the Carnahan family history were part of his own.

But it was Paul Carnahan who had pulled Wend out of his mental slump. On a day six weeks after his arrival, Carnahan had walked into the kitchen after the morning meal and, in a brusque manner, told Wend to come with him. Wend had been able to walk for a couple of weeks, but had felt little desire to leave the comfort of Patricia's domain. So he followed Carnahan with some trepidation. Paul led him to a small farm building across from the house. The reverend had parked the tool wagon alongside.

Carnahan turned to Wend. "With a little work, this will be a good place for your shop. Let's get the tools out of your wagon."

Carnahan's simple words shamed Wend for his lack of motivation. He realized that Carnahan was fulfilling the role his own father would have taken, by essentially giving him a strong kick in the rear. Together they had unloaded his tools, and Wend started spending most of his time in the shop. Outside, he and Carnahan erected a lean-to shelter for his rifling machine. Open on three sides, it had a nice view of the hill, the settlement, and the valley beyond. Wend had set up some benches under the roof, and in good weather he liked to sit there and enjoy the view, often joined by Carnahan and sometimes by Joshua Baird, who visited whenever his wanderings brought him back from the border.

Now, as Wend entered the kitchen, Patricia asked, "Did you get the display set up to your satisfaction down at McCartie's?"

"Yes. I've no doubt that Junkin will be interested. He'll mull it over for a few days, but he'll be up here to start dickering within a week."

Patricia shook her head. "You know Joseph Junkin. I'll wager he tries to pay for it with hogs, chickens, and as little cash as he can!" Then she had a thought: "Make sure you get a cow from him as part of the trade!"

Wend laughed. "Well, at least a deal like that will help out with our table this winter."

Patricia nodded. "Yes, what with all the time Paul spends with the church and the school, our farming suffers. I hate depending on the congregation for so much of our food. But of course, you bring in a lot of meat from hunting." She thought a moment. "You know, we could use someone here to run the farm; so much of our land is lying fallow."

"Maybe you could get a man to till the land and give you a share of the crops as payment." Wend picked up an apple from the fruit basket on the kitchen table. He turned to leave the house and heard Patricia laughing behind him.

She called out, "I've been trying to get Paul to do just that for years!"

Wend grinned back at Patricia, left the house, and walked across the road into his shop. There were several guns in a rack; some in for repairs and others at various stages of fabrication. A maple stocked rifle lay on his work table, ready to have its lock installed. But after reflecting for a few moments, he moved it to the storage rack and instead concentrated on several repair jobs which he needed to finish up and return to his customers.

"Good morning, Cat!" Wend looked up at the gray animal reclining on a shelf above the workbench, leisurely grooming his coat. "Did you have a good night's hunting?" A multitude of semi-wild cats inhabited the farmyard; this one, when barely out of kittenhood, had adopted Wend shortly after he had set up the workshop. For weeks he had observed Wend from a distance, as if trying to fathom who or what he was, and why he did strange things all day in the little building. Wend had simply ignored him, which apparently intrigued The Cat. Then the animal had taken their relationship to the next level, first starting to rub himself on Wends legs as he sat working. Eventually had come the day when he leapt to Wend's work table and started butting and rubbing him with his head. Wend, familiar with dogs and their mannerisms, thought this strange until he realized that it reflected some sort of possessive behavior. He found himself touched by The Cat's affection and a little embarrassed to find himself attached emotionally to the animal. But now he welcomed the companionship and was disappointed when the feline disappeared for a day or two, as was his wont several times a month. Wend's deepest secret was that he had started talking to The Cat as he sat working during the long hours of the day. Even worse, he had become convinced that The Cat understood his words.

By the time the shadows had begun to deepen, Wend had finished his repair jobs and stood up to stretch his muscles. He turned to his companion. "Well, Cat, I should get some work done on the new rifle before the light fades." The Cat, now sitting on the floor, yawned in response. Wend realized what he really wanted to do was visit the creek. He left the workshop and took the path which ran through the woods down the steep hill to Sherman Creek. The Cat scooted around him and led the way. Early on Wend had discovered a quiet nook among large rocks on the creek bank, where the water ran swiftly over some shallows and midstream rocks. He found the gentle noise of the flow soothing. This was the place where he could allow himself to again become the young German boy who had ended one life on Forbes Road. Here he could cherish the memory of his family and Abigail without feeling that he was being disloyal to the Carnahans.

Wend sat down against a small boulder and The Cat jumped up into his lap. The feline mewed, rubbing his head against Wend's hand, and then curled up. He responded by gently massaging the animal's ears, who closed his eyes and purred in pleasure. Wend relaxed as he stroked the fur, very much at peace.

But suddenly The Cat stiffened, ears cocked forward, and stared down the creek bank in the direction of the village. Then Wend heard voices. He put The Cat down and, using bushes for cover, surveyed the bank. He soon saw a couple approaching. It was Peggy McCartie and Matt Bratton, the beefy waggoner he had encountered in the tavern at Carlisle so long ago. Shortly after his arrival in the village, Wend had discovered that Bratton was the son of the blacksmith and headquartered his freight business at his father's stable. Although twenty-three, Bratton was still unmarried and living at home. And while no engagement had been announced, the valley settlers considered the eventual marriage of Peggy and Matt a matter of due course. Wend believed he was the only one who had reason to doubt Bratton's intentions, and not just because of that night in Carlisle. During his own business travels, he had heard more stories about Bratton, and he was well aware that the waggoner had continued his amorous ways on the road with a string of young ladies.

The couple disappeared into bushes about thirty feet from Wend's nest. He guessed what was about to happen and his first instinct was to escape up the path back to his shop. But he didn't want to embarrass the couple and himself by being seen or heard leaving, so he settled down behind cover. Sure enough, after a few minutes, he heard giggles and amorous sounds begin to emanate from the creek bank. There was a series of loud groans of pleasure from Bratton, followed, after an interval, by a gentle, feminine moaning sound. Then, clearly in Peggy's voice, came a series of high pitched shouts of excitement. Now Wend wished he had taken the chance of discovery to steal away. He rose slightly, thinking he might still creep to the shelter of the trees and the path. But that only brought him high enough to see Peggy's head bobbing in and out of view, black hair now cascading over her face and naked shoulders as she rhythmically rose and fell over Bratton. He settled back down, resigned to remaining in place until the couple had finished their tryst. In fact, it was over soon enough, the noisy frenzy being followed by a period of silence, then another series of giggles from Peggy. For a while he was afraid that they would rest awhile and then renew their passion, but he was soon relieved to see Peggy standing up, tying her hair back in place and pulling her bodice up around her shoulders. Noticing the growing dusk, he realized that she would have to hurry back to the tavern to help with the evening meal. Soon the couple moved off down the bank toward the mill and Wend was free to retreat to his shop.

As he walked up the path, Wend decided this would be a good night for him to visit McCartie's Tavern. Bratton had been out of town for a weeklong freighting trip and had obviously just returned to the village this afternoon. And Bratton should have brought with him a crate of blank gun barrels which Wend had ordered from the Kurtz Forge in Lancaster. He could arrange to pick them up from Bratton in the morning. Moreover, Wend was curious about what interest his new display gun would generate among the tavern's patrons.

* * *

Following supper and his stable chores, Wend again strolled down the wagon road into the village. Welcoming light flowed from the windows of the settlement's buildings, particularly McCartie's. He entered the tavern to find that a good crowd had preceded him; farmers, tradesmen, hired men from the surrounding area. He also recognized a peddler up from Shippensburg. Donovan McCartie presided from behind his bar, while the girls waited on the tables. Wend saw that Bratton was at his usual corner table, surrounded by his circle of friends. Peggy was standing by the peddler's table, tray in hand, laughing and exchanging jokes with him. Ellen was working the other side of the room and Wend was gratified to see Joseph Junkin at a table with a group of other farmers.

Wend made his way to the counter and motioned for Donovan to pour him some ale. Paul Milliken, already at the bar, was looking at the new fire-lock display. He turned to Wend. "Now that's a different style than you sold me last month. The wood's darker and it looks like the bore is larger than my gun."

Wend turned to Milliken. "Indeed, but this one's a smoothbore, meant to fire either a ball or shot. The bore is larger to accommodate a useful amount of shot." As Wend had hoped, Junkin rose from his table and joined them at the counter. He greeted the heavyset farmer, who carried the scent of his barn and animals in his clothing. The man was obviously interested in the gun; he asked questions about the lock, the bore, how much shot it would fire.

Junkin mulled over Wend's answers. "I'm sure it will be a good gun for birds and small animals, firing shot. But I wonder how good it will be with ball. How far out will it be accurate?"

Wend said, "I'm confident that it will be quite accurate out as far as you want to use it, Mr. Junkin: Say 80 or 100 yards."

Junkin looked at the gun doubtfully. "That far? I've got an old smooth-bore and it doesn't have anything like that kind of accuracy."

Wend was about to explain when he heard the loud voice of Matt Bratton. "The Dutchman's putting you on, Junkin! No smoothbore is going to have the accuracy of a rifle at 100 yards, and he knows it. He's just trying to sell you a gun."

The waggoner had approached the bar, with a tankard in his hand, a scowl on his face, and his cronies in tow. "Think about it for a minute, Mr. Junkin. Take army muskets: They're smoothbores. Everybody knows that at eighty yards you can fire directly at a man and he's as safe as if you were throwing rocks at him. Anyway, have you ever seen a fowling piece, with its smooth bore, that could hit anything with a ball at eighty yards?"

Junkin looked at Bratton, then back to the gunsmith. Wend could see the conflict in the farmer's eyes; he liked the look of the gun and the price, and he wanted to believe that it would perform as Wend had indicated. But Bratton had put a large measure of doubt in his mind and he didn't want to look foolish in front of the tavern crowd which had gathered around to listen.

Wend knew he had to do something to counter Bratton's assertions, or he would never make the sale. "Joseph, you know the quality of my work. I never claim anything that I can't prove. Pick a day and we'll take the gun up to my shooting range, test fire it at various distances, and you can judge for yourself. And I'll vouch that we'll get results similar to a rifle out to 100 yards, just as I said before."

Wend could see in Junkin's eyes that he was reassured and ready to take Wend up at his proposal.

But Bratton wasn't going to leave it alone. "I still say that gun can't hit a reasonable target at 100 yards, or even eighty. The Dutchman's just trying to get you alone and give you a sales pitch! You know what a smooth talker he is, Junkin."

Wend saw that the patrons were looking at him with rapt attention. Bratton had deftly put him on the spot. Wend paused to control his anger and to give himself time to think. This was far from the first time that Bratton had tried to bully Wend or interfere with his business relationships. It was as if he worried that Wend was a rival to his leadership of the younger set in the area. Wend wanted nothing of the kind and had made a practice of going out of his way to avoid conflict of any kind with the beefy waggoner. But that had seemed only to encourage Bratton.

Wend looked directly into Bratton's eyes; he could see that the man was seeking a challenge. But Wend was determined not to rise to the bait. He turned back to Junkin. "My offer stands, Mr. Junkin. Just let me know when you want a demonstration and I'll be glad to show you what the gun will do." Wend drained his ale and turned to leave the tavern.

Bratton stopped him with a rough hand on his shoulder. "Say, Eckert, I have an idea. If you're so confident about that firelock, why don't you show all of us what it can do? McCartie here is soon going to have another of his shooting matches. Why don't you compete with that gun, against me and my rifle, at 80 and 100 yards? You could prove to the whole county what you say is true in one afternoon."

Bratton took his hand off Wend's shoulder and took a long pull on his drink. Wend could see the triumph in his eyes. He knew that if Wend didn't accept the challenge, he would loose all hope of the sale to Junkin, and more importantly, credibility around the county. And Bratton, who had been Wend's chief rival in the shooting matches for years, was confident that with a rifle he could best Wend firing a smoothbore. He had maneuvered Wend into a tight corner.

"All right, Bratton. You're on. I'll shoot the smoothbore at all ranges you want, up to 100 yards, and at least match the shooting of any other man, with groups of four shots. Is that fair?"

Bratton's triumphant look spread from his eyes to his entire face. "That suits me perfectly, Dutchman. You can bet I'll be there and I'll be the one you have to match." With that, he led his comrades back to the corner table, and a series of laughs, audible throughout the common room, emanated from the group. The rest of the crowd at the counter broke up and the patrons returned to their tables.

McCartie moved close to Wend and leaned across the bar. "Good Lord, son; Bratton's nearly as good a shot as you are, with you both using rifles. I think he's got you on this one."

Wend could see that McCartie was worried that if Wend lost the contest he might actually have to ante up a keg of his best whiskey to Bratton. The thought of McCartie's anguish at having to part with his cherished whiskey actually made Wend laugh out loud. Men around the room looked up at the noise of Wend's laugh. He leaned over, and in a voice only Donovan could hear, said, "Don't worry about your prize. Even if I lose, there are going to be so many people here to watch the contest between a rifle and the smoothbore, you'll sell more than enough food and drink to make up for the loss of the keg!"

McCartie considered Wend's words for a minute, his face wrinkled and his eyes narrowed to slits. Then he broke out into a broad smile. "Why lad, damned if I don't think you're right. The word's going to spread all over the county and this may be the biggest match we've ever had!"

Ellen came up to the counter with an order from one of the tables. She looked at Wend with pity in her eyes, then at Donovan. "Everyone's talking about the match, Father. They think Matt is finally going to beat Wend. They all want to be here for it."

Wend smiled at Ellen. "Do you think I'm going to lose, Ellen? You think I can't beat Matt at 100 yards?"

Ellen shook her head. "Wend, I know you are the best shot in the valley. But you can't win with a smoothbore. It's as simple as that. Everyone is going to bet against you."

Wend thought for a moment. Then, as Donovan moved down to the end of the bar to fill Ellen's order, he put his arm on hers, and gently pulled her close so only she could hear him. "I'm going to give you a tip, Ellen. If you want to make some money, bet on me at the match. I'm going to beat Bratton."

He smiled at her as she stared at him in disbelief. Then he turned and walked over to Bratton's table. Bratton and his cronies looked up at Wend, surprised that he had come over. Wend carefully modulated his voice to make sure that he sounded calm as he spoke to Bratton. "I'll be down to collect my cargo tomorrow morning, first thing. You will be ready for me to pick it up, won't you?" It gratified him that Bratton seemed a little non-plussed at his casualness.

"Sure enough; any time you are ready."

Wend nodded to the waggoner, carefully placed his hat on his head at a jaunty angle, and walking deliberately, left the tavern. Once outside in the night's gloom he paused a moment where he could see Bratton's table through a window. Soon Ellen came over and started talking to the group. They all broke out into laughs. Clearly she was telling them about his advice to bet on him.

He walked up the wagon track to the Carnahan's place, satisfied that he had completed a good night's work.

CHAPTER 9

Carlisle Encounter

It was coming on dusk when Wend drove his wagon through the bustling streets of Carlisle on what had been a golden October day. He had left Sherman Mill in the pre-dawn twilight to perform several chores in the larger town. As he drove his team on the road over Kittatinny or North Mountain and through the colorful fall foliage of the eleven miles to Carlisle, he had remarked to himself how the land to the south of Sherman Valley was becoming increasingly populated. With the peace following the French War, more and more settlers were moving across the Susquehanna and into the area north of Carlisle. On every trip, he saw farmsteads being carved out of the woods, and here and there a new store or mill being established to serve the needs of the settlers.

Most of these newcomers were Ulster, realizing the dream of their own property through land acquired cheaply from the colony. Wend often reflected on how he had become, in just three years, so thoroughly integrated into the Ulster culture. He was aware that his speech patterns had changed and he had lost virtually all the accent which would have bespoke his German background. He did make it a practice to periodically speak to himself in the German dialect which his family had often used at home; he wanted to make sure he would not lose the words.

Wend soon turned onto Market Street. Carefully guiding the team through the heavy wagon and foot traffic, he soon pulled up at the stableyard at Washburn's Tavern. He unhitched his team and, after leading the pair into the stable, arranged for the stable boy to berth and feed the horses.

Wend walked into the tavern, to be greeted by Washburn himself. The beefy inn-keeper was behind the bar talking to a couple of loungers. "Hello, Eckert! It's been a while since you've been in town."

"Good afternoon, George." They shook hands over the counter. Wend had forced himself, even when he had been only seventeen and at the very beginning of his life as an independent tradesman, to start addressing other business men by their first names, even when they were years senior to him. He had realized that he couldn't negotiate successfully if the older man were allowed to dominate the relationship because of his age.

Washburn leaned on the counter. "I've got some news for you. There have been some serious inquiries about your rifle up there." He gestured to the display rifle, which just like at McCartie's Tavern, rested across two pegs on the wall behind the counter. "Lots of patrons have looked it over and there are two men who have been expressing serious interest."

The rifle was one of Wend's better efforts. The stock was beautifully grained maple, highlighted with brass fittings, scroll carvings, and an elegant pattern inscribed on the patch box cover in the butt. It had one of the locks with double triggers, marking it as a top of the line product.

Washburn lowered his voice to a whisper. "Because of the interest I've taken the liberty of adding a couple of shillings to your asking price. I think we've got a very good chance of selling it at that amount, without any real haggling."

Wend knew that Washburn was an accomplished salesman, and if he was convinced that the gun could be sold at the higher level, it was probably a done deal. Of course, Washburn would want an increased commission for selling the rifle at a dear price, but that was fine with the gunsmith.

Wend nodded, then asked, "Any mail here for me?"

Washburn held up his hand. "I nearly forgot: There's a letter here for you from Fort Pitt. It came in just a couple of days ago by military courier." He pulled out a brown envelope.

Wend saw immediately that it was from Arnold. He asked Washburn for a glass of ale and moved over to a table to read the letter. It was in Arnold's clear, round hand, practiced for years now copying Bouquet's official correspondence.

Fort Pitt
September 2nd 1762

Dear Wend,

Bouquet and his adjutant just left the headquarters office to go to supper, and I have some correspondence to copy, but I thought I'd take a few minutes off to let you know what is going on out here and to tell you what I just heard about that blond girl of yours.

Yesterday, Bouquet and his staff, including your correspondent, rode over to Mr. Clapham's trading post on the Yioghiogheny River. He and Bouquet are great friends and my colonel makes it a practice to visit him whenever he can get away. His post and store are at a pretty place right along the river where the canoes can easily land. We arrived in the early evening and the colonel and his staff officers had a long dinner in their host's house while the rest of us made camp and ate rations wherever we could.

I shared some time around a fire with a couple of traders who were back from the Ohio Country to pick up some more trade goods. They had some good whiskey and, as you would expect, they were full of stories about the various tribes. The biggest news right now is that all the Indians are getting upset about the number of settlers crossing the Alleghenies and moving into the Ohio territory itself. We turn back these pilgrims whenever we can, but there is no way we can stop even the better part of them. The tribes don't mind the traders; they want to see them and trade for the goods they have. But they get disturbed when someone comes in and starts clearing land. We just don't have enough men to stop settlers. Two years ago, after the French surrendered in Quebec and Montreal, a lot of the troops in our regiment were drafted to join in the expeditions against the French and Spanish West Indies. So we are terribly short-handed here, with only about 125 men in the fort, and it needs at least 300 to adequately man all the fighting positions.

But the traders said that there are lots of council fires among the tribes, discussing their unhappiness about the way they feel the British don't treat them as well as the French did.

There's a lot of talk about a Delaware medicine man called 'The Prophet' who is moving through the tribes saying that the Indians in the Ohio Country should band together like the Iroquois Confederation up north, so that they will have the strength to oppose the British.

After a while, the traders mentioned that they had run into a village of Mingoes under a captain named Wolf Claw. They live well into the Ohio Country, along a tributary of the Beaver River. Their village had a lot of scalps on the trophy poles, including some obviously from whites, not just other Indians. Wolf Claw was very proud that he carried a long rifle, not a trade musket like most of the warriors. The traders said they had never seen an Indian with so fine a rifle; its stock was maple with beautiful grain markings and it had a bore smaller than normal. That made my ears really perk up because I know you had made yourself a rifle like that. Then they laughed that the rifle wasn't the only pretty thing that Wolf Claw had. He had a blond wife captured from the English. Wend, they actually spoke with her, and she said she had been from Philadelphia, and was taken on Forbes Road. So there's no doubt it's your Abigail. Then they mentioned how they had been startled when they saw a warrior who looked like he was ready to go on the warpath, painted all black. Soon they realized he wasn't painted, he was a black man in his natural skin, but that he was dressed like any other man of the tribe. Obviously that was the Gibsons' man that was also taken from your caravan.

So now you can be sure that Abigail and Franklin are still alive and are living as part of the Mingo band which took them. I told the adjutant about what I had heard after we got back to Fort Pitt and he told the colonel. Bouquet questioned me about what I had heard just a little while ago.

There's other good news. Bouquet is going to spend this winter in the east, at Carlisle and Philadelphia. He is courting a lady in Philadelphia, and doesn't want to be bottled up in the fort by the snows. The adjutant and I are going along, and we will start in October. So I may get a chance to see you, if you can get down to Carlisle.

Until then,

I am your Devoted Friend,

Arnold Spengler

Wend sat in his chair, frozen by the news in Arnold's letter, the first hard information he had had about Abigail in three years. Thoughts of Abigail and his family ran rampant through his mind. But in a few moments, he forced himself back to the present. He took a stiff drink and the shock of the alcohol brought him back to the reality that he couldn't do anything about Abigail in his present circumstances and he concentrated on his chores in Carlisle. The first thing he had to do was go down to the Widow Downey's house; that was where he lodged while in town. He finished off his ale, waved to Washburn, threw his traveling bag over his shoulder, and strode out of the tavern.

Minutes later he turned the corner to the street where both the widow's house and Larkin's Tavern were located. With the events of 1759 still on his mind, he stopped for a moment outside the widow's house. This was where, at Joshua Baird's request, Captain Robertson had arranged for the army wag-goner to stop and unload Wend, while the company of highlanders halted out on Market Street. He had been gently lifted down by several soldiers while

Baird had gone in to see Alice Downey and ask her to take the both of them in for a few nights. She hurried out, accompanied by Baird, who introduced her to Lizzie Iverson. Lizzie quickly briefed Alice about Wend's wounds and how she had been treating them. The soldiers, at the widow's guidance, had carried Wend to a bed in an upstairs room. Lizzie came up with her daughter to say goodbye and then they had hurried off to the company's campsite at the fort.

Wend and Baird remained at the widow's house for two days. Wend found she was a caring woman with gentle hands as she treated his wounds and a quick smile as she talked. Dark haired and in her early thirties, she had a husky, pleasant voice. Arnold Spengler's words about her having a plain face had been true enough, but when she smiled, her face dimpled up and made you forget that she wasn't a beauty. Arnold had said she had a fair figure, and that was an understatement, for her bosom invariably drew men's covert glances.

On their first night in the house, exuberant noises from the next room made it clear to Wend that Joshua was enjoying the widow's bed and favors.

Now Wend stepped up to the widow's door and knocked. She came and pulled open the door almost immediately, her face breaking into a grin. "Wend Eckert: You're here at last! I thought I was going to have to send a letter to get you down here." She turned and led him through the central hall and into the kitchen. "I've finished the clothes you asked for; and if I do say so myself, everything turned out very well."

Wend sat down in a chair in front of the fire and nodded in response to her comments. Then a thought occurred to him. "Have you heard anything from Joshua? He's supposed to be coming back here for Patricia's birthday, but we haven't gotten any confirmation."

Alice didn't say anything for a moment as she bent over to stoke the fire. Standing up, she put her hand on her back as if help were needed to straighten out her spine. "It's always the same with that man; don't count on him till you see him." She watched the fire for a couple of seconds to make sure that her stoking had had the desired effect. "Come with me into the other room. I've got the clothing hanging in there." She led the way through the hall and into the room which served as her parlor and sewing room.

Wend followed eager to see what she had produced. Two months earlier, after much thought and several discussions with Paul Carnahan, he had decided to buy some dresses for Patricia on the occasion of her thirty-fifth birthday. As far as he knew, she had made every garment in her wardrobe from fabric purchased at the store in Sherman Mill or on trips to Carlisle. Most were utilitarian petticoats and blouses suitable for work around the house. She seemed to have only one formal dress which she wore every Sunday to services. He thought she would be pleased with the luxury of apparel made by an accomplished seamstress; clothing with a little style and elegance.

Alice proudly showed what she had made. First she pulled out two patterned petticoats, one blue and the other a light green, sized to fit Patricia. Then she showed him a pair of blouses to go with the petticoats. Wend looked over the blouses and was soon satisfied that Patricia would be well pleased.

Meanwhile, Alice had pulled down another item from the clothes rack. "Here's the dress. Do you like the fabric?"

Wend liked it very well. It was a soft grey, and he was sure it would work well both for formal events like church and other more casual events. "You've done marvelously, Alice. I really appreciate your paying so much attention to this work."

"Well, you can believe I'm going to charge you enough to show true appreciation. But we're not done. You men always think only of the main event. Women know that you've got to have nice things to go with the actual clothing to dress it up and make it more interesting. So I made a couple of scarves to go with the blouses. Here, look at these and see if you fancy them."

She pulled out two scarves of very light material. Each fabric had a different pattern. One was colored to match the blue petticoat, the other the green. She laid out each petticoat on a chair, then matched it with a blouse, and draped a scarf over the blouse.

Wend had to admit the scarves made the outfits much more attractive. And the widow was right; he never would have thought of getting the scarves.

The widow stood up and admired her own work. "If you really want to finish this off right, go get her a bonnet tomorrow that will go with the gray dress. You could buy something simple in a neutral color and it could go with the other outfits, too."

Wend considered for a moment. "That's a good idea, I might just do it." But then Wend had a sudden thought. "I have a better idea: Get Joshua to buy the bonnet when he gets here. Odds are, he won't have a suitable present for Patricia."

Alice laughed and nodded agreement. "You're absolutely right. That man won't have given a thought to a present."

* * *

It was Wend's custom, whenever he spent the night at the widow's, to do some fix-up chores on her house. She had no regular man to help her and Alice's earnings didn't cover hiring anyone to do the work for her. As a result, the house was visibly the worse for a lack of regular care. Wend had noticed that the sills of the house's front windows were deteriorating; the paint flaking and the wood starting to rot in places. Early in the morning, he sorted through the toolbox that the widow's late husband had left until he found the implements that he needed. Then he climbed a ladder and went to work scraping the paint on the window frames so that he could see which wood needed replacement.

After working for a couple of hours he heard someone shouting his name. Wend looked out into the street to see a one-horse cart stopped below him. Suddenly he recognized the driver, his face nearly covered by the wide brim of a floppy hat. Charlie Sawak—his friend from Lancaster!

Charlie was a member of the Conestoga Tribe, whose village was near Wend's and Arnold's former houses. The trio had been fast friends since early childhood. Long ago, the Conestoga's had adopted the way of the white man, earning their way by farming and producing goods for sale. These included moccasins, brooms and other items which could be sold directly to settlers or placed in various dry goods stores. That was Charlie's job; he traveled the roads of the central part of the colony, peddling tribal products.

Charlie looked up from below the brim of his hat, and shouted, "You're looking mighty domesticated there, Wend. You take a wife or are you just hiring out 'cause no one wants to buy those guns of yours?"

Wend laughed and, laying his scraper on the sill of the window, climbed down the ladder and walked over to shake his friend's hand. "Where have you been, Charlie? I haven't seen you for a couple of months. I thought you might have given up on the traveling life."

"Not likely. I'm just such a good peddler that I sold all the goods we had and spent the last few weeks at the village while the tribe built up more inventory. Now I'm on my routes again. Just came in from Shippensburg, aiming to spend a couple of days talking to the merchants here in Carlisle." He paused and looked up at the window where Wend had been working. "What are you doing down here?"

Wend told him about the clothing the widow had made for Patricia.

Charlie cast a glance up at the widow's house. He smiled knowingly at Wend. "You know, the widow has a certain kind of reputation among the traveling men of the county and is known for a welcoming disposition if a man has some money to spend. When I saw you up there, I thought maybe you were working off payment in trade for some of her favors."

Initially taken aback by his friend's coarse comment, Wend realized that he shouldn't be surprised. As Arnold had told him back in 1759, it was widely known that she had male visitors who paid extra for services beyond lodging. In fact, Joshua's relationship with her had started that way; but now there was a bond between them and she thought of the scout as her man. But it was a strange relationship; his visits were infrequent and Joshua didn't have the money to support her.

Wend ignored the comment. "Where are you going to stay while you are here?"

"I know a livery stable owner down on the west side of town who lets me sleep in the corner of his barn for a very small fee, if I pay his regular rate for my horse. I've got to live as cheaply as I can or I'll use up all the profit from our sales." He made a wry smile. "Selling brooms won't make us rich, but it does pay for some of the essentials we need to buy."

Wend reached up and put a hand on Charlie's arm, "Tell you what: Meet me over at Larkin's Tavern tonight at six and I'll spot you some dinner and a few drinks. You can catch me up on what's been happening in Lancaster."

Charlie readily agreed and then he was off to make his rounds. In another hour, Wend had finished scraping the window woodwork and had determined how much replacement wood was required. He visited a lumberyard and found some scraps which he could piece into the windows and also got some paint which matched the color scheme. In the evening he was able to call Alice out from her work in the house to show her the repaired and painted windows.

Her eyes lighted up and she gave him a hug of appreciation. Despite her reputation, Wend had always had respect and admiration for the widow. Life had dealt her a hard blow, taking away her husband and her livelihood. At twenty-nine, she had been considered too old to be a good catch for the men of the town. But she had never shown despair at her situation; instead she had eked out a living the best way she knew how, doing what she had to do, even when the only choices had been unsavory in the eyes of many.

Wend put the tools and ladder back in their place, cleaned up, and had occupied a table at Larkin's well before Charlie arrived. Given its proximity to Alice Downey's house, Wend had over the years spent a considerable time in Thomas Larkin's establishment. As he sat at his table near the counter, Wend was reminded of how much his life had changed since Arnold had first brought him here. Then, the fifteen year old German boy, in his severely cut clothes had felt himself the odd person out among the tavern's Ulster clientele. Now, three years later, he leaned back in his chair and was comfortably at home, the ale he drank relaxing and mellowing him as he watched the usual evening crowd coming in for supper or drinks. He waved at acquaintances as they entered.

Charlie entered shortly after six. He was dressed like any other customer, in coat, waistcoat and breaches, with only his jet black hair, dark skin and angular features betraying his Indian heritage. He stood looking over the common room, his eyes sweeping from left to right, then lighting on Wend, who raised his hand in casual greeting. Charlie sauntered over to the table and Wend again raised his hand in signal to the serving girl and ordered ale for his friend.

"So, was your day among the merchants successful?" Wend asked.

"Absolutely splendid: I told you my tongue was persuasive, and I've sold my stock. The merchants really like the brooms and leather goods. Tomorrow I'll be on my way back to Conestoga Town, money for the tribe in my purse."

"How are your folks doing? I haven't seen them since we left Lancaster in '59. Is everyone all right?"

Charlie's face grew dark. "My family's in good health but the real story is the tribe. We grow smaller and weaker every year. Many young people leave when they get old enough. A few have gone back to their roots and joined the Iroquois to the north or Mingo villages to the west. But most just go out and become farmers or look for work. They feel they can do better on their own and don't want to work as part of the tribal organization. When we were young children, the tribe had over a hundred people in the village; now there are not even thirty."

Wend knew something of the tribe's history; it was indeed a sad story. A hundred years ago the Conestogas had been a powerful tribe living in central Pennsylvania and northern Maryland. But a series of disasters, in the form of disease and wars with other Indians had decimated the tribe by the early 1700's. Then, as white settlement flowed around them, the remnants of the Conestoga people had made the decision to stay in their traditional territories, and coexist with the Europeans, instead of moving west, as the various branches of the Delaware tribe had done. Now the once powerful nation was merely a ghostly reminder of the past, clinging to a single village and barely making a living between agriculture and the sale of simple manufactures.

Wend could see that his friend was depressed by the thought of the Conestoga's plight. He searched for a topic that would cheer him up. In the pause which ensued, he looked around the room and noticed two men entering the tavern. Suddenly he realized the leading man had a familiar look. The other man's face was covered by a beard. A chill swept through his body and he felt the muscles of his neck and jaw tighten. The clean-shaven man was the trader Ross Kinnear! Quickly his eyes darted back to the bearded man and he immediately knew it was Fleming, Kinnear's partner. Wend's hands gripped the edge of the table and turned white from the pressure of his grip. He was looking at the white men responsible for the death of his family and the abduction of Abigail!

The traders took a table in the far corner and ordered mugs of ale. Wend looked at the men. They were in street clothing, not the hunting shirts and leggings that they had worn in the forest. Kinnear, who sat with his back to the corner, scanned the room as if looking for someone. For a moment, Wend worried that the trader would recognize him. But the man's eyes swept over him without any pause or hesitation. Then Wend realized how totally different he looked from the boy of fifteen in the bush more than three years ago, and he relaxed.

There was another factor: Kinnear and Fleming were probably not aware that he was alive. *The Pennsylvania Gazette*, the Philadelphia newspaper, had not been very accurate in its reporting of the massacre of his family and the Gibsons. The headline had titled it "The Gibson Massacre", a natural result of the status Magistrate Gibson had had as a well known lawyer in the city. It had simply referred to everyone else in the caravan as part of "The Gibson Party", and the Eckerts had been described only as a tradesman's family. More importantly, while the article had accurately mentioned the capture of Abigail and Franklin, it had implied that the rest of the party had been killed. The survival of a white male had never been published. In fact, during his travels, Wend had often come across people who had known his family and who assumed that he had perished with them.

On the other hand, Wend was now earning a reputation as a gunsmith and a marksman. Sooner or later the traders would learn that he had survived.

But for now they were showing him no undue attention. Wend realized that he needed to entertain Charlie. He beckoned to the serving girl. Soon the two friends had settled on a venison stew with potatoes and vegetables, and Wend ordered another round of ale for them. While they waited for the food to arrive, Wend asked, "Now that you've sold your load of merchandise, what are your plans?"

Charlie took a sip of his ale, savored it for a moment, then put the glass down. "When I'm not traveling, I help tend the fields around the village. When the tribe builds up some more inventory I'll be on the road again. It could be next month or six weeks from now."

Wend considered a moment. "Will you come back here on your next trip?"

Charlie shook his head. "No, now that I think of it the next trip will be special. A couple of times a year we sell our goods to Slough & Simon, the big freight company which provides supplies to the army and settlers along Forbes Road. So I'll be delivering a full load of items to their warehouse up at Harris' Ferry."

Wend smiled. "Maybe we can meet there. I've got gun displays at taverns in both Harris' and Paxton. And I plan to make a rifle delivery in Paxton about the same time as you'll be at the ferry."

Charlie nodded. "I'd like that. It's lonely on the road." He looked at Wend with a mischievous smile. "Besides, it's good to have a friend who's got enough cash to buy me dinner. I'll send you a note as soon as I can figure out when that trip will be."

The girl brought them their steaming stew and bread, and the two set to work. After a few bites, Wend stopped to take a sip of his ale and noticed a man entering the tavern. He piqued Wend's interest immediately because he was older than the norm for Larkin's and dressed in finely tailored clothing. But Wend's interest in the man rose sharply when, after pausing to glance around the room, he walked directly over to the corner table occupied by the two traders and took a seat. Soon all three were engaged in intense conversation.

Wend put his spoon down. He had never told Charlie, or any other person other than the Carnahans, about the details of the massacre on Forbes Road. Perhaps it was the ale loosening his lips, perhaps it was the fact that he was with a childhood friend, but for some reason he told Charlie about the role that he believed the outlaw traders had played in providing the Mingoes with powder and lead and their likely part in the death of his family. He told about how Kinnear and Fleming were suspected to be major suppliers of illicit goods by Bouquet and Baird, but that there was no hard evidence, only the reports of suspicious incidents.

Charlie stopped eating and listened with rapt attention. When Wend was finished, he looked over at Charlie and said, "Did you wonder why I picked this time to bring up this story?"

The Conestoga lifted his ale and took a small sip, considering his words. "Actually, I felt honored that you would share a story about things so hurtful to you. Tell me anything else you want to about events on Forbes Road."

"Charlie, I want you to look around the room casually, as if simply seeing if you know anyone. While you are doing it, take note of the three men at the table in the far corner."

Charlie took another drink and then circumspectly carried out Wend's request, his eyes asking an unspoken question. When he had finished, he asked, "All right, so what was that about?"

"The two men with their backs to the wall are Kinnear and Fleming."

Charlie's eyes widened and he started to look back at the table, but Wend quickly reached out and stopped him. "Don't look again right away, I don't want to attract their attention."

Charlie nodded, and took a few bites of his stew, then another gulp of his drink. Then he again surveyed the room, his eyes stopping a second at the corner table. "Wend, I've never seen those two men against the wall before. But I recognize the man who is with them."

Wend felt a surge of excitement. "All right, who is he?"

"An important man: I've seen him several times during my travels, and heard much about him. His name is Grenough. Richard Grenough."

Wend's head spun around, caution forgotten. Looking carefully, he now recognized the man who he had seen only as a shadowy figure outside this very tavern four years ago. Then the details of his confrontation with the traders in the forest came back to him; particularly that they had denied any connection with Grenough. Now they sat with him in friendly conversation.

Wend cautiously said, "He looks important enough in that expensive city suite and boots. The question is, what is he doing with scum like Kinnear and Fleming?"

Charlie looked hard at Wend. "It's very logical why he would be with two traders. Grenough runs the biggest trading company in the colony. He sponsors numerous pack animal expeditions into the Ohio Country every year, providing the tribes with perfectly legal goods. There are many traders working directly for him; he sponsors others by providing capital or goods and takes a share of their profit. So it's totally normal for him to be having drinks and discussing business with a couple of men like your two characters."

"Charlie, these men supply powder, lead, guns, and liquor to the tribes. All of those are restricted by government decree. Are you saying it's normal for Grenough to associate with outlaw traders?"

Charlie didn't answer immediately but instead took a spoonful of his stew and then a bite of bread. He paused for a moment to savor the food. "Wend, think about this: Maybe not every trip they make to the Ohio is about illicit goods. Maybe they make trips where they're carrying only approved items. Perhaps they use those trips as cover to promote sales of the other stuff and make arrangements with the various bands of Indians to deliver the powder. So they could work with Grenough on the legal trips."

Charlie's idea intrigued Wend and made him stop to think. Then suddenly another thought struck him. "What if they're in this with Grenough for both kinds of trips; legal and illegal. What if Grenough is sponsoring them in supplying arms to the tribes? It's got to be a lucrative business. But those things are expensive. Maybe Grenough supplies the capital to buy the powder and lead and they do the actual trading?"

Charlie stopped eating, and Wend saw that he was considering his words. Then Charlie took another bite of food, and a sip of the ale. "You know this stew is actually quite good. I'm really grateful for this dinner, Wend." He smiled. "By the way, did you notice the size of the breasts on our serving girl? Not to mention that when she leaned over the table the last time they were less than three inches from my face?"

"Come on Charlie. Don't try to change the subject. What do you think about my idea?"

"Wend, Grenough isn't just the owner of a trading company. He's an influential man in the elite circles of the colony, right up to the assembly and the governor. His name is mentioned in the Gazette all the time. And don't let that elegant suite of his fool you. He worked his way up from being simple trader years ago and he is as experienced in the forest as anyone. Because of his knowledge of the tribal leaders and culture, he has been an advisor and intermediary on many of the treaty negotiations out at Fort Pitt. The governor has entrusted him with carrying messages to the tribes. In other words, any suggestion that he is putting his personal enrichment before the best interests of the colony is going to get a hostile reception among the leaders of the government back at Philadelphia."

"So you don't think that he could be involved in supplying the tribes with powder and lead?"

Charlie looked at Wend with a gleam in his eyes and laughed quietly. He wiped his lips with his napkin. "I didn't say that he wasn't in on supplying war goods to the Indians. I just said that the government wouldn't believe he was."

Wend put his hand to his mouth, and considered Charlie's words. Then he looked over at the trio in the corner table, still engaged in serious conversation. He decided not to further pursue the subject, at least for the moment. He turned back to his friend and grinned. "By the way, you're absolutely right about that girl's bosom. Her face isn't bad, either. And she doesn't mind showing off, does she?"

For the rest of the night, Wend and Charlie had a marvelous time. Later in the evening and several drinks later, when the common room had emptied out, the serving girl came over and sat down with them, much to Charlie's delight.

Wend left Charlie and the girl just after midnight and made the short trip back to the widow's, quietly stealing up to his room without disturbing her.

The three men in the corner had left the tavern together about half past eight.

CHAPTER 10
Rumors from the West

Patricia's birthday party was well underway. Wend and the Reverend had taken care to make sure that it was a memorable occasion. It was a relatively small affair, with only the family and a few of Patricia's friends. Will and Amy Donaldson, who had the second farm to the west along the wagon track, were attending, since Amy was Patricia's closest friend. They spent many hours together, making quilts. And Frank and Sarah McClay were also present. Frank was a lay helper at church; he and his wife were long time friends with the Carnahans. Both families had brought their children, so there were twelve people in all. Wend and Carnahan had decided that the party couldn't be much of an occasion for Patricia if she had to cook and serve the guests, so they had arranged for food prepared by the tavern and for the McCartie girls to come up to the house, serve the guests, and then clean up afterwards.

As was his wont, Joshua Baird had ridden in from the Ohio just in time to attend, but sufficiently late to avoid any need to participate in the preparations.

It was a cool but comfortable November evening and all the guests were seated at an improvised plank table under a canvas tarp rigged just outside the front door of the Carnahan's house. Candles were lighted on the table, providing the needed illumination as the sun faded. Peggy and Ellen McCartie were moving around the table expertly serving the supper and drinks. Patricia sat at the head of the table, glowing in the attention being showered on her by the diners.

The members of the family had gotten together just before the guests arrived and presented Patricia with their gifts in private. Joshua had given his sister a Delaware child's doll in a colorful dress decorated with beads and multicolored dried corn. And, while in Carlisle, he had actually gone out and purchased a bonnet for her, obviously at the widow's urging. Paul had sent away for some books from Philadelphia, a very suitable present, for Patricia was an avid reader who spent evenings by the fire re-reading the books she already had. Wend's clothing was the hit of the evening; he was gratified to see a gleam in Patricia's eyes and her face flush with excitement as she had opened the paper wrappings.

Now, with the dinner well underway, there was no lack of conversation. Joshua regaled the party with his tales of the backcountry and the tribes. The men talked about the quality of the harvest and how lucky they had been that the weather had held favorable for so long into the autumn.

Wend was seated at the lower end of the table. On his left was the Reverend, at the very end of the table opposite Patricia. On Wend's right was Elizabeth McClay, a brown haired lass who was a pretty, physically mature fifteen. Wend knew her seating was no accident. It was a standing joke in the Carnahan household that Sarah McClay saw Elizabeth as a perfect match for him, except everyone knew that both Elizabeth and her mother were deadly serious about the idea. And the girl had been playing her part to the hilt throughout the evening, smiling at him, sitting very close to him on the bench, hanging on his every word. More than once her hand had brushed up against his arm or leg. Wend was making a very conscious effort to be polite and engaging, but to not show the slightest receptiveness to her advances.

The other romantic activity in progress was between Johnny Donaldson and Ellen McCarty; or at least from Johnny toward Ellen. Wend hadn't yet figured out whether Ellen was interested or just being polite. Ellen was sixteen and had lived her life in the shadow of her vivacious sister. And Johnny, who was also sixteen, wouldn't be a bad catch for her. The Donaldson's farm was the model of the valley, with several very large productive fields, and William Donaldson was tireless in maintaining his buildings and fencing. Wend was watching closely to see if Ellen was going to respond to Johnny or simply use her tavern maid skills to deflect his advances.

Suddenly Wend realized that Joshua was calling him. He roused himself from his thoughts. "Sorry, Joshua, I didn't hear you."

"Hey, Sprout; what's this that Sarah is telling me about you shooting a smoothbore at Saturday's contest? What is that foolishness all about?"

Wend smiled. "It's perfectly true. I'm going to use the gun that's on the wall down at McCartie's. I told Matt Bratton that I would shoot at least as well as he and his rifle at 80 and 100 yards."

"Oh Lord, Sprout: No more strong liquor for you when bets are bein' made. You must have been in your cups. That's the only way you of all people would take a bet like that. Whatever made you accept that offer?"

"I made that smoothbore with a rifle barrel that hasn't been grooved out. Otherwise, it's the equal of a rifle. And I will at least match Bratton; there's no doubt in my mind."

All the guests laughed or smiled and Baird clasped his hands to his face in mock dismay. But Wend noticed that the McCartie girls weren't smiling. Undoubtedly Peggy would be reporting what he said to Bratton before the morrow was out. He was about to say more, but a change in conversation came from further up the table

Frank McClay called down to Reverend Carnahan.

"Say, Paul, did you hear that George Robinson is thinking about tearing down the old fort?"

Carnahan stopped eating and looked down at his plate thoughtfully before replying. "No, why in the world does he want to do that?"

Everyone knew what they were talking about. Robinson and his brothers had been among the earliest settlers in Sherman Valley. In 1755, after the Braddock massacre, he and the other settlers had banded together to build a small blockhouse surrounded by a stockade. It was a refuge against the marauding war parties which swept through the valley in the wake of the massacre. The fort lay a little less than a mile to the northeast of where they all sat. Since then, it had been known as "Fort Robinson" or "Robinson's Fort."

McClay answered, "Robinson says he either has to pull it down or fix it. Some of the stockade has come down on its own. And he doesn't see any need for it now, with the tribes now over to the west and minding their own business."

Wend smiled to himself. The younger set of Sherman Valley would not be charmed by the idea of the fort coming down. Currently, its major function was as a secure place for picnics and romantic interludes away from parents.

"At any rate, Robinson says it just gets in the way of working that big field of his. It would be much more efficient to plow and harvest without the fort sitting there," McClay continued.

Joshua spoke up. "Frankly, I'm not sure that this is the time to take the fort down."

Amy Donaldson looked up from her plate. "Oh, come on, Joshua! Don't you think we're through with the Indian attacks? We haven't had anything happen in this valley since '56. We're so far east, and there are treaties with all the tribes now."

Baird shook his head. "The mood of the tribes can change pretty fast. I think it might be good to just fix up the place a little and leave it there for a few more years. And Robinson's Fort is in a good place to hole up if there is any trouble; it's pretty much in the middle of the valley and has good brook water right there."

Wend instinctively thought back to Arnold's letter telling about tribal unhappiness. He was sure that was what was on Joshua's mind and he looked around the table to see how the others would react.

Sarah McClay looked sharply at the scout. "You can't be serious about this, Joshua! The French have been driven away; they were the ones stirring up the tribes. And the Gazette keeps running stories about how quiet the Indians have been." She looked around the table. "God knows, we had enough trouble back in '56. Our family barely made it to the fort ahead of that war party. I still have bad dreams about that night, running along paths in the darkness, tripping and falling until we got to the Robinsons'." A look of fear came over her face. "And there were three people who didn't make it — killed and scalped right beside the stockade while we watched." She visibly shuddered. "Please don't try to scare us!"

Will Donaldson bit his lip for a moment, but then spoke up. "You know, Joshua's not the only one who is talking about staying ready. Word I hear is that John Elder and Lazarus Stewart are planning to come over to the valley and organize a company of Paxton Rangers right here."

Everyone knew of The Paxton Rangers, or as some called them, the "Paxton Boys." They were a private militia which had existed since the raids of 1755. Many settlements had similar groups, since Pennsylvania had no official militia system.

Carnahan asked in a casual tone, "Where did you hear that Frank?"

"Down at the tavern. From McCartie himself, who said he got it from Matt Bratton. Bratton saw Stewart over in Paxton, when he was picking up some cargo. He said they've got two full companies over there now and they think another company would be a good idea here in the valley. They're going to come to the shooting match to talk about it with people here." He paused to take a bite. "I'm surprised you haven't heard about it from Reverend Elder already, as close as you two are."

Carnahan put his hand on his chin. "I'm wondering why Elder thinks we need a company right now." Paul looked discretely at Joshua, who met his eyes, and then concentrated on his plate without making a comment. "I'm sure Elder will talk to me about it at the match. He probably didn't send me a letter 'cause he knew he'd be here for the shooting. Be interesting to see what he has to say."

After the main courses, they finished off the meal with a pudding. Eventually the men gathered at Wend's lean-to and brought out their tobacco and pipes. Wend opened a jug for those interested. But after a few minutes, he wandered back to the house and kitchen. Peggy was outside, joking with the other women as she cleared the table. The younger children of the Donaldsons and McClays were playing together around the barn. Wend started to walk into the kitchen, intending to compliment Ellen on the meal, but noticed that Johnny had preceded him. Through the door, he could see that Johnny and Ellen were getting along very well. Johnny had his arm around her as she worked to clean and stack some dishes. And Ellen was definitely receptive to his advance. Both were giggling at something Johnny had said.

Wend thought to himself: *Well, that answers that particular question.* He was actually quite happy that Ellen had found a suitor she liked. She had far less guile than her sister, was an industrious worker, and when not displaying the practiced veneer of a tavern maid, she had a genuinely kind and engaging personality. Wend had developed sympathy for her situation over the years, what with her sister having all the family beauty and garnering the lion's share of attention in the tavern. He hoped she could find happiness with the young farmer.

Wend cleared his throat as he entered the kitchen and Johnny hastily withdrew his arm from Ellen's waist. Wend smiled at Ellen. "Hey, I just wanted to thank you for helping out with the party. Patricia is really having a good time. And tell your mother that the food was superb; she did a very nice job."

Wend walked over to a cabinet and pulled out a small mug, then filled it with water from the kitchen bucket. He felt like he had had enough alcohol for the evening. The coolness of the water felt good in his mouth. He was about to walk outside again when Ellen said, "Wend, I overheard Joshua saying that Robinson shouldn't tear down the old fort. Why do you think he said that? What did he mean?"

Wend thought about how to answer. He didn't want to alarm her with the details of what Arnold had written him. Yet other people must be hearing the stories about the unrest in the Ohio Country—otherwise, why would

John Elder be getting ready to raise a company of militia here in Sherman Valley?

Wend gave them a low-key answer. "An army friend says there are some tribes out past the Alleghenies which aren't real happy with the British rule. It will probably blow over or get taken care of in the periodic meetings that Colonel Bouquet has with the kings. But I guess Joshua just thinks it would be a good idea to have the fort around in case of trouble. And it looks like the Reverend Elder thinks the same about being ready; otherwise I can't fathom why he would be wanting to organize a company here."

Johnny had an excited look on his face. "If they do that, I'm going to volunteer. We've got that old smoothbore you fixed the trigger on last year, and I'm a pretty good shot." He looked at Wend a little sheepishly and said, "Well, not like you, Wend, but I can hit a buck at forty yards sure-enough."

Wend looked at Ellen, who was smiling at Johnny with an approving look. "Sure, I know you are a good shot. I've seen you shooting. Nobody could do much better with that ancient piece of yours."

Johnny bristled with pride at Wend's words and looked over at Ellen. "So do you think Reverend Elder and Lazarus would take me into the Paxton Rangers? Do you think I'm old enough?"

Wend smiled. "I'm sure they will. After all, you're sixteen aren't you? There are soldiers your age in the Royal Americans." Wend gave the boy a pat on the shoulder and walked back out the door, leaving the two of them to their flirting.

Later, with the party over, Peggy and Ellen were in the final stages of cleaning up. They were loading a small hand cart with serving dishes and containers which they had brought from the tavern. Wend had helped; now he took a final look around the kitchen.

"Looks like you've got everything," he said to Peggy. Both she and Ellen looked tired. Then he realized it had indeed been a long day for them, what with their regular duties at the tavern and another five or six hours up here at the Carnahan's. He picked up the tongue of the cart. "I'll help you get this down to the tavern." The three of them started down the hill toward the village. It was a clear night with fall crispness in the air. Below them the village buildings with their illuminated windows were bathed in the gentle light of the moon.

Peggy looked at Wend. "It was nice of you and the Reverend to put on such a grand party for Patricia. No one deserves a celebration more than her.

She is a marvelous lady and everyone in the valley thinks she is the perfect wife for a man of the Lord."

Wend wholeheartedly agreed with Peggy. Patricia's popularity throughout Sherman Valley stemmed from her many acts of charity over the years. If sickness was in a family, she was there to help out. There were many large families; she had assisted the poorer ones by making clothing for the children, an act which had earned her the gratitude of many a mother at wits end just finding time to cook, keep up the house and still spend some time in the fields or the stable. When death visited a household, Patricia would be the first to arrive, driving up in the Carnahan's wagon, bringing food and a pair of strong hands to help around the house while the family grieved.

"That's a nice thing for you to say, Peggy, and very true. I don't know what I would have done without her help when I first arrived after my family died."

Ellen had been walking along quietly, lost in her own thoughts. Now she spoke up, and it was clear that Patricia Carnahan wasn't the subject of her thoughts. "Wend, did you mean what you said about Johnny being a real good shot with his father's gun?"

Wend saw the chance to put in a good word for the lad. "Of course! We've hunted together many times. He can hit his prey whether it's standing still or on the run. I think he could be a good long range marksman if the family had a rifle or even a good smoothbore like the one I have on the wall of your tavern."

Ellen looked at Wend and smiled, obviously marking up another positive factor in her perception of Johnny.

Peggy asked, "Wend, do you realize that the shooting match is only three days from now? Are you still maintaining that you'll beat Matt?"

"Sure enough: I'll take the prize."

She shook her head. "Lord Above, Wend! Give it up! You've become a joke down in the tavern. Nobody thinks you'll win."

Wend considered for a second. In this moment of camaraderie with the girls, he was tempted to tell them why he could be so confident. But they were on the opposite side in this matter, and he couldn't be straight with them, at least for now. "Like I've been saying, put your money on me and you'll have a good stake for shopping the next time you go down to Carlisle."

Peggy stopped and looked sternly at him. "Come on, Wend, I've known you for three years. You always work out everything you say and do beforehand. So how could you let Matt corner you so that you are bound to lose?"

Wend was puzzled at the sympathy reflected in Peggy's question. He was trying to shape a humorous answer when Peggy spoke again, almost like she was thinking out loud to herself. It was clear that she didn't really expect him to answer.

"Matt makes me feel so alive. When I'm with him, he makes me forget about the tavern, all the work and how boring this little village can be." She grimaced, and said, "God, how I want to get out of here to a real town." After a moment of thought, she stopped, put her hand on Wend's arm, and looked into his eyes. "I know that Matt is very competitive and he can seem like a bully. And you must know that he'll never stop crowing if he beats you. He's been looking to humiliate you since you came to the valley."

Wend locked eyes with her and said firmly, "Peggy, he's got to beat me first."

She stared at him for a moment, then shook her head and resumed walking.

Surprised at the girl's burst of candor, Wend wanted to ask Peggy why Bratton was so eager to show him up; why he felt the necessity to prove his superiority. But he knew that would be taking the conversation too far and she would never answer truthfully, even if she really knew what motivated the waggoner.

By now they had reached the tavern door, and the girls began unloading the cart. Wend took his leave there, not wanting to enter the tavern. There were still a few patrons inside, and he had no desire to join them or spend the amount of time necessary for polite conversation. Instead, he walked back up the hill, enjoying the beauty of the night and the afterglow of a memorable day.

* * *

Saturday turned out to be another fine fall day, bright and with a cool, gentle breeze. The forest around the village was a riot of red, orange, and gold with a smattering of green provided by patches of pine trees. The autumnal sun provided just enough warmth so that everyone could be comfortable without heavy coats. With the harvest over, and the farming cycle complete for the year, people were free to leave their land and socialize. By ten in the morning the crowd around McCartie's was larger than anyone had seen before.

Donovan was tending a bar set up just outside the tavern, smiling broadly as ale and whiskey flowed out of his kegs and coins flowed into his money box. His two daughters rushed to keep patrons supplied at the wooden tables which had been moved out from the common room. They were assisted by a couple of other girls from around the valley, including Elizabeth McClay and one of Jim Bernard's daughters, who Donovan had hired for the day.

Several peddlers had set up displays on blankets or the back of wagons; the ladies of the valley were perusing the wares and visiting with each other as they moved from vendor to vendor. Wend had set up a table to display his own products, including the now finished maple rifle he had been working on for display in Paxton; the smoothbore which he would use in the upcoming match; a pistol, steel knives and a range of firearm utensils and accessories such as bullet molds, powder horns, cleaning tools and supplies.

The day was also filled with excitement for the younger set. Girls in their early teens moved around in small gaggles, looking coyly at the boys, who stood or sat telling jokes and speculating about the assets and virtues of the girls. Younger children burned off energy playing games around the periphery of the crowd.

The gathering was not limited to the residents of the valley. There were many people Wend had never seen before, obviously up from towns and farms south of the mountain. John Dunning, the High Sheriff of Cumberland County, stopped by at Wend's table to say hello. Wend had met him several times on business in Carlisle. He had ridden up, ostensibly because he had gotten word that a large turnout was expected, but he conceded that he wanted to watch the match between Wend and Matt. Earlier, Reverend John Elder, Lazarus Stewart, and Clayton Asher of Paxton had ridden up the road from Carlisle, their horses splashing across the ford in the creek just below the mill. Wend noticed that they were soon in conversation with Paul Carnahan, Joshua, and George Robinson.

Matt Bratton sat at one of the tables near McCartie's bar, his cronies around him, holding court as men came by to talk and ask him about the upcoming matches. Wend frequently heard loud laughs and once made out a speaker say something about "That Dutchman ...," followed by another burst of laughter. He didn't pay much attention because he had a nearly constant stream of visitors himself.

The Paxton trio had stopped by not long after their arrival. Wend had known Reverend Elder for a long time from his frequent visits with Paul. Elder, who had been the rector at Paxton Church for decades, was the acknowledged dean of the region's Presbyterian ministers. He was also the organizer and sometimes field commander of the Paxton Rangers. He had raised the militia in 1755 during the terrible days after the Braddock massacre, when war parties ranged the country at will and the Quaker government in Philadelphia refused to take measures to protect them. Now he was a revered leader throughout the settlements of the Ulster people.

Wend was less familiar with Asher Clayton. He had been a lieutenant in the provincials during Forbes' march on the Ohio in 1758, and he was now captain of one of the Paxton companies. Wend had met him once or twice and found him to be a thoughtful and congenial man with an easy smile. Joshua had worked with him during the war and considered him a good soldier.

Lazarus Stewart was a stranger to Wend, except by reputation. He was known for his aggressiveness in leading militia patrols against the war parties in '55 and '56, and he had had considerable luck in tracking down and killing marauders. Looking at him for the first time, Wend noted he was a tall man, rangy as a wolf, with a narrow face, penetrating eyes, and a thin-lipped mouth.

Wend stood up out of respect for Reverend Elder. "Good morning, sir. It is always good to have you here with us."

Elder extended his hand: "Glad to see you, Wend. I believe you know Asher Clayton here. And this other gentleman is Lazarus Stewart, captain of our second company in Paxton."

Wend greeted the two men.

"We came by to look at your goods, Wend. That's a fine looking rifle you have there."

Wend lifted the maple-stocked rifle off the table and handed it to the reverend, who examined it with an experienced, critical eye.

"This is a fine piece of work, young man. I've seen many of your late father's guns and I must say this is every bit up to his standard."

Wend felt a flush of pride. "I plan to put that firearm on display over at Paxton, as a matter of fact."

The reverend passed the rifle over to Stewart, who inspected the lock and triggers, then sighted the weapon at a distant target. "This is very good quality. I like the lightness and the sights." He put the gun's butt on the ground and looked at the bore. "But I prefer a larger bore and a heavier ball than this one takes. If you want to be sure you're going to stop a big animal or an Indian, you need it. And by God, I want a firelock that will put a real hole in a savage!"

"Well, Mr. Stewart, my personal preference is for the smaller bore. It gives you a flatter trajectory at long distance. And a skilled marksman will place his shot where it will kill, regardless of the size." He paused to let the effect of his words register on Stewart. "But I do make guns with a large bore also, if that is what the customer desires." Wend picked up the smoothbore. "I assume this is more to your liking. It's made from a standard barrel with a half-inch bore, although this particular gun is not rifled."

Asher Clayton looked at the gun and then at Wend. "Is that the smoothbore you are going to be firing today?"

Wend nodded.

Stewart smiled craftily. "So besides the fact that you are going to be shooting with a smoothbore against a rifle, you'll be firing a larger bore than you use regularly?"

"Well, that's true, Mr. Stewart. But then I'm used to shooting with all sizes of bore."

Stewart turned to the others with a smirk on his face. "Just another reason to bet on Bratton; as if the smoothbore thing wasn't enough."

Wend decided he didn't like Stewart. Looking directly into his eyes, he said with slightly more emphasis than he meant to use, "Then you'll be betting on the wrong shooter, Captain Stewart."

Stewart met Wend's eyes for a moment, then he looked him over slowly, deliberately, obviously evaluating the youth who stood before him. "Well, we'll just have to see, won't we Dutchman?" He put strong emphasis on the word 'Dutchman", so that it sounded like a pejorative. "It's getting pretty close to the time when you'll have to make good on these assertions of yours."

Wend decided he had said enough to the militia officer. He turned to Reverend Elder. "Word around the village is that you are thinking about starting a militia company here in the valley. Is that right?"

"It's no rumor, Wend. We're here to make some preliminary arrangements and to start recruiting. We figure there are at least twenty-five or thirty men who are good candidates. And one of them would certainly be you. How about it; can we count on you?"

Wend had been thinking about that question since Patricia's party three days ago. "It makes sense to have some sort of organization if we face an emergency like '55 or '56. Yes, I'd be willing to join."

Elder looked at his compatriots and then back to Wend. "We can sure use someone who is as good a woodsman and shooter as you if there's an uprising." The reverend nodded to Wend, and the group moved on to talk with other men around the gathering.

As Wend watched the three move on, Johnny Donaldson came up, enthusiasm written on his face. "Wend, you wouldn't believe the amount of betting which is going on over at Mr. Marsh's table!"

Thomas Marsh owned the mill. He had built it back in 1756 and the village had grown up around his establishment. When the matches had begun years ago, he had taken up the duty of holding the bets made by individuals on the shooters. It gave him a way to participate in the event and put him at the center of the action. Periodically he banged a mallet on the table he used and announced to the crowd how the betting was going and who was favored.

Wend smiled at the lad. "Well, is everyone putting their money on our friend Bratton?"

"There's a few betting on you, mostly your friends. But they have no scarcity of takers to match the people who are betting for you. I think Joshua put a few coins on you. And Joseph Junkin bet a small amount! Everyone said they've never seen him bet before. Oh, I think Mr. Millikin put some money on you too. And the biggest surprise was Ellen: She put down a small bag of coins for you, betting against one of Matt's friends!"

Wend laughed. So Ellen had taken his advice. He hoped his shooting was up to snuff today, for he would hate to have her lose her money. Wend reached down into the canvas carrying bag he had on the ground beside him and pulled out a small cloth pouch.

"Johnny, do me a favor. This purse has some coins in it. Take this over to Marsh's table and see if he can get anyone to bet against me for that amount."

Johnny eagerly took the purse and headed toward the betting table. The coins in the bag represented a lot of cash for most of the residents of Sherman Valley, save for someone like Marsh himself or maybe McCartie. But Wend speculated that with the large number of visitors there might be someone from Carlisle or one of the other towns who would be able to match him.

Wend glanced around the gathering again and then down the wagon track to Carlisle. He noticed a rider gingerly maneuvering his horse through the shallow ford. The man first drew his attention because even at that distance, he appeared to sit his horse stiffly, as if he was not much used to riding. But then he noticed another thing about the rider. He was dressed, not in the manner of the Ulster-Scots, but rather in the darker, more severely cut clothing which Wend had worn in his youth. He had the look of a fellow German. Wend wondered what the man was doing in this place, at this particular time.

He watched as the rider rode up to the tavern's stable and awkwardly dismounted from his horse. After tying up the animal, he hesitated for a moment and looked around at the village and the assembled crowd. Then he fixed his eyes on Wend and his table display and walked purposely toward him.

Soon the man stood in front of Wend, his lips pursed in a serious look. He was in his mid or late forties, of below average stature, with a squint in his eyes and thinning brown hair. As Wend looked at him, he pulled out a set of Mr. Franklin's spectacles and placed them over his nose. Then he began to speak to Wend. For a moment Wend found he couldn't understand his words. Then he suddenly realized the man was talking in German. Wend was shocked to realize how long it had taken him to recognize the language. He concentrated on the man's words to ensure he could understand.

"I presume you are Mr. Eckert, the gunsmith and noted marksman?"

Wend carefully formed his response, not wanting to be embarrassed by his rustiness in using the language. "I am Wend Eckert, the gunsmith of this village. And I will be shooting in the matches this afternoon."

"My name is Henry Froehlich, of Shippensburg. I have come here to see the matches." He looked down at Wend's firearms. "May I inspect your wares?"

Wend nodded, and the man took his round hat off and placed it on the side of the table, exposing a nearly bald crown. Then he carefully picked up the Paxton rifle. He examined it with careful hands, bringing the lock and trigger assembly up very close to his eyes. He aimed the rifle into the distance, then brought it down and pulled the cock back. He worked the trigger mechanism with practiced expertise, holding the cock in his hand so that it didn't slam down when he pulled the trigger. Nodding to Wend, he handed back the rifle and picked up the smoothbore, giving it the same inspection.

Wend watched, then said, "It seems clear that you have considerable knowledge of firearms."

The man nodded at Wend. "I'll be honest with you young man. I'm speaking to you in this language because I want our conversation to be private. I'm in the same trade as you, and have been for the past thirty-five years. I knew of your father by reputation, of course. So when I heard men talking in a tavern that someone named Eckert was going to match a smoothbore against a rifle, I knew that I must come up here to this contest."

The man smiled, now in a conspiratorial way. "We both know what you are about, don't we?"

"I'm sure I don't understand what you mean, Mr. Froehlich."

He laughed. "Oh, please, Young Eckert. Don't play games with me. We're fellow journeymen in the same trade. I don't have to explain why we both know that you have an excellent chance of winning, if you are as good a shooter as men say you are."

Now it was Wend's turn to smile. "I guess not. Since this challenge was made, the only thing I worried about was that another gunsmith would get word of the match and give away my secret."

"Well, you don't have to worry about me. I must confess that I am here in the service of a very serious vice. My sinning is the scourge of my poor wife's existence, which fact she intimates to me each day, and certainly it will cause me grief when I stand in front of the Lord." The man grimaced. "My sin is that I cannot pass by a wager, particularly when it is almost certain I can win a lot of money. So that is my secret: I came here specifically to bet on your victory."

Now Wend laughed. He was beginning to like this little man. "And how much do you plan to wager on me, Mr. Froelich?"

"Well, I have brought ten pounds with me, though I don't expect to find anyone who will be able to wager that whole amount. I will have to make wagers with several people, but that is what I intend."

Froelich looked around. "Where do I make my wagers? Is there one place, or must I go find interested men on my own?"

Wend showed him Marsh's table and explained the way the wagering was done. Then he had a brilliant thought. "I suggest you find a man named Lazarus Stewart. He'll probably be glad to make a bet against me."

Froelich nodded and started to walk away. Then he remembered something and turned back to Wend. "By the way, can you show me the man who you will be shooting against? I should know your adversary. Anyway, it would be good to see if he wants to bet on himself."

Wend looked around and then saw Bratton with his friends near the betting table. "There he is, the beefy man with broad shoulders. He runs a freight service around the county."

Froelich squinted and adjusted his glasses to clearly see Bratton. "My God, I have seen that man before! It was at a tavern in Shippensburg! He was working hard to make an impression on a young tavern maid."

Wend had to suppress a laugh. "Well, that would definitely be what I would expect Bratton to be doing."

"But it turned out that he was just passing the time before other business, clearly important business indeed. After a while the noted merchant, Richard Grenough came into the tavern, and this Bratton fellow immediately broke off his attentions to the woman and sat down for a very lengthy and serious discussion with Grenough."

Wend was startled at those words. "You're sure it was Richard Grenough? He's a very important man in the colony, and I wonder what he would be doing in a tavern with a waggoner."

"I have no idea what they were talking about, but I've seen Grenough many times. He works with traders out of Shippensburg. Perhaps he was arranging with Bratton to freight in some of his goods." Froelich reached out and shook Wend's hand and then strode off purposely in the direction of Marsh's table. Soon the little man disappeared into the crowd.

Wend was stunned by the gunsmiths's information. *Bratton with Grenough: What was their connection?* And then Wend remembered something from a back corner of his mind. The first time he had seen Bratton was at Larkin's Tavern. And Grenough had been there that night; Arnold and he had encountered him leaving, with Bratton inside. He suddenly recalled Arnold's puzzlement at seeing the rich trader in a down-scale tavern like Larkin's. Wend thought furiously for a moment. *That explained it—he was there to meet with Bratton! The question was: Why?*

Wend's racing thoughts were interrupted by a call from Marsh, announcing the start of the matches. Normally there was one set of matches, with the shooting starting at sixty yards and progressing to longer ranges in increments of twenty yards, until one shooter proved dominant. But on this occasion, McCartie had set up the contest between Wend and Bratton as a special event. So Wend wasn't shooting in the regular match. He sat on the sidelines and watched as marksmen from all over the county competed. The shooting was very spirited, accurate, and not decided until the targets had been placed at 160 yards.

Then it was finally time for the match which was causing all the excitement. Marsh was acting as the referee and called the two competitors to their firing marks. There was a burst of noise from the crowd as Wend and Bratton took their places. Bratton exuded confidence, nodding and waving at friends and supporters as he took his place.

Wend went into the routine he always used when shooting in a match; he concentrated on total isolation from the world around him. He approached his mark looking straight ahead, avoiding eye contact with anyone else, his mouth set with pursed lips. He shut his ears to the clamor around him, trying to focus totally on the habitual practices and technique which he had cultivated over the years. Placing the canvas bag which contained his shooting supplies on the ground beside the mark, he opened the bag and made sure the contents were ordered as he desired. In the bag were sixteen paper containers he had made up the day before; each contained the same pre-measured load of the best quality, fine-grained black powder he could obtain. Also present was a small fabric bag containing sixteen balls, molded precisely to the smoothbore and then lightly polished to absolute smoothness. In addition, there was a brass charger containing the powder he would use for loading the pan of the lock and a small box containing an extra flint. Finally, a small wooden mallet lay next to the ammunition.

He placed the smoothbore's butt on the ground and went through his loading routine at a painstaking rate, taking one of the powder loads, tearing off the top, and carefully emptying the contents into the barrel. Then he took a greased patch from the box in the butt, and centering a ball precisely on it, placed it at the top of bore. Holding it in place with his left hand, he drove it down most of the barrel with the ramrod. Then he took the mallet and tapped the end of the ramrod several times to fully seat the ball. Finally, he used the charger to measure out the priming powder into the pan. After a final look at the weapon and the lock, he was ready for his first shot.

Only now did he look at Marsh and nod, being careful to ensure that he did not look directly at anyone else, and particularly Bratton.

Marsh announced the first phase of the match. "The first round will be at eighty yards. Each man will fire four rounds at the target. Both will fire at the same time and at their own rate."

The mark for each man was a small log. Wend carefully placed the smoothbore on the ground, and lay down. He took the gun in his hands and laid the barrel over the log, carefully drawing the cheek-piece to his face. He reached out and cocked the hammer, then precisely moved his hands to assume his practiced grasp of the weapon.

Wend looked at the target, which was a thinly sliced piece of the circular cross-section of a tree trunk. The growth rings were clearly visible, and in the exact center had been painted a red bull's eye about two inches in diameter.

Wend had shared with no one his special technique for aiming during matches. It had started as what he now considered a childish reaction to the horrible day of the massacre and the feeling of shame which had grown in him that he had not been able to get off a shot in defense of the caravan. In the anguish over the death of his family, he had incessantly gone over each second of the ambush, fixing in his mind's eye every aspect of what he had seen. In the last seconds before he had been clubbed, he had seen the assailants rising from their positions of concealment, bringing their weapons to bear. He had noted one black painted warrior almost in front of him, and had been swinging his own rifle in his direction when darkness overcame him. In the months after the attack, he had focused on remembering every detail of the warrior's face; the paint pattern, the stretched ears, the rings in the ears and nose, the shaved scalp and the precisely tied hair lock with its feather decoration. Now when he shot in matches, he used his imagination to carefully overlay the warrior's visage over the wooden target. The effort to do so helped increase his concentration, further isolating him from the crowd.

He centered the face so that the Indian's nose ring was right on the bull's eye. The center of that ring was his aiming point. Wend drew a deep breath, held it, and without consciously thinking about it, his finger squeezed off the first shot.

Mechanically, he reloaded and fired another three shots into the warrior's nose ring.

Then he forced himself to stay in his private world as he watched Marsh's oldest boy, sixteen year old Hank, run down the range and retrieve the targets for both shooters. Wend looked at his target. His shots had created one large four-cornered hole where the bull's eye had been.

Now Marsh raised both targets over his head to show the crowd. Wend allowed himself to look at Bratton's target. The pattern was a near copy of his own, but more like a triangle, flat on one side. But it was clear that they had tied. The shooting would now be extended to 100 yards.

Then Wend realized Marsh was making an announcement. "The first round is a tie! We will have a pause for a quarter of an hour. Anyone wishing to make a new wager, or change a previous one, can see me at the table!"

Wend was surprised by this. It hadn't been part of the match plan. He was disappointed, because now he could not avoid breaking his concentration and would have to rebuild it after the pause. But at the same time, he realized his mouth was bone dry and he needed some water. He turned to walk to the bucket beside McCartie's bar, but found that Ellen had brought him a cup with water. Johnny Donaldson was with her. Both were smiling broadly.

"That was terrific shooting Wend!" Johnny exclaimed. "Everyone is shocked to see how accurate your shots were placed. Didn't you hear the shouting?"

In truth, Wend had not noticed, so deep had he been in concentration. But he had an important need to know something. "Johnny, tell me how Bratton is reacting. I don't want to look at him."

"You should have seen his face when they held up the targets and yours was just as good as his! His jaw literally dropped! He looked over at you in disbelief that he couldn't hide."

Wend gulped the water. That was good news; he wanted Bratton's confidence to be shaken and it looked like the surprise of Wend's tight group had helped.

Ellen added, "Just before the match, Matt made a large bet with some little man—a Dutchman like you. So did Captain Stewart. They were joking about how they hated to take the man's money. So now they're starting to be concerned that it's their money that may be in jeopardy."

Wend laughed to himself. *So Froelich had been able to place his big bets!*

Just then Peggy came by, carrying a tray of mugs. She stopped and looked at Wend with puzzlement in her eyes. Wend couldn't resist asking, "Do you still think I'm a joke for making this bet?"

She stared at him intensely for a moment, looked over at Bratton, and then said, "You shot well, Wend." She hesitated a moment, and continued, "But it's not over yet." Then she started walking again in the direction of Bratton and his friends.

Joshua appeared out of the crowd, a large tankard in his hand. "Sprout, you got this crowd stirred up like nothin' I ever seen before. Most everyone was convinced that this match would be over after the first round and everyone would be collecting their bets on Bratton. Now, seeing that group you shot, everyone is reconsidering their position. But lot's of them figure that smoothbore must be some kind of trick gun you thought up. Is there some trick you got going here?"

Wend couldn't help breaking into a wide grin. "No trick, Joshua; just basic principles of nature and accurate shooting."

Tom Marsh stopped by their group. "Wend, I stopped the shooting because I knew your first round of firing had shocked this crowd. Now there are suddenly a lot of people who've put money on you." He slapped Wend's shoulder in emphasis. "You ready for 100 yards?"

Wend forced himself back into his shell of isolation. He loaded the smoothbore for his first shot, then indicated his readiness to Marsh, and assumed his prone position in front of the log.

For the next few minutes, Wend concentrated on making himself as machine-like as possible; a mechanical device with the sole purpose of precisely placing rounds into the bulls-eye of the wooden orb. Then, it was over. He had done his best and could do no more.

He shook off his isolation and returned to the world of the village. People were shouting and laughing, Hank Marsh was running down to the targets. Tom Marsh was standing pensively waiting for the targets; Bratton was quiet for once as he gripped his rifle in his right hand, also watching the boy, now coming back.

Marsh took the targets from Hank, his back to the crowd, which now began to quiet down. Wend could see the miller looking from target to target. Then he turned around and raised one above his head for all to see.

He shouted, "Bratton's target!"

The bull's eye was essentially obliterated by the group of holes. Bratton had shot a near perfect square.

The crowd roared, Bratton's friends began cheering and slapping him on the back.

But now Marsh held up Wend's target. "Eckert's target," He shouted.

There was a sudden silence, and then almost immediately a surge of shouting as loud as for Bratton's target, for Wend's group was a precise duplicate of the waggoner's. To demonstrate, Marsh had the boy hold both targets in front of him and used a piece of wood to measure the height and width of the shots on both targets. It was clear to everyone that there was virtually no difference.

Marsh stood up on a stump to make an announcement of the results. "The two targets show an exact tie. Under the terms of the bet for this match, which was that Eckert, with his smoothbore, could shoot as well as Bratton with a rifle at 80 and 100 yards, I declare Eckert the winner!"

A roar rose up from the crowd. Bratton turned and strode over to Wend, his face red. "There's some trick going on here. Nobody has ever seen any smoothbore shoot like that." He turned to Marsh, who was still on the stump with his hands holding the targets. "I say we check out that gun of his to find out what he's pulling on us. Eckert's a sly bastard who's always got some sleight of hand up his sleeve."

Bratton stood glaring at Wend, less than a pace away, his face distorted in anger, his fists balled up at his sides. Wend realized he had miscalculated how the waggoner would take being beaten; after all, he had bested the man many times in contests with both of them using regular rifles. But obviously this had become a blood match for Bratton.

Suddenly Sheriff Dunning was pushing his way between them. "Whoa, here! There's going to be no fighting!" He turned to the crowd and raised his arm to quiet the roar. He looked at Wend. "Lad, that was tremendous shooting. But Bratton's right about one thing. Many a man in this crowd has bet against you and after the first round of firing, word spread like wild fire that you must have some kind of trick built into that piece."

Wend worked hard to fight his growing anger. He conquered it before he spoke and answered in measured words. "Just what kind of trick do they think could be involved? I know of none possible and I'm a gunsmith."

"Well, the word is circulating that maybe you have a barrel that has been partially rifled, like the lower half, so that if you look at the bore from the outside it looks smooth. But maybe there's enough grooving in there to make it shoot straighter at longer ranges than a regular smoothbore."

Wend couldn't avoid laughing. He looked directly at Bratton and watched his face redden further as he laughed. Finally, he turned to the sheriff and handed him the gun.

"Here, it's easy enough to prove one way or another. Take the ramrod and slide it up and down in the barrel. You'll find out soon enough if there are any grooves."

Dunning took the smoothbore and performed the check. The crowd was deadly silent. Then, without saying a word, he turned to Bratton and handed him the gun and the ramrod.

"You check it."

Bratton ran the rod up and down the barrel several times, scraping it audibly against the side. A look of puzzlement came over his face.

Dunning asked, in a quiet voice, "Do you feel any rifle grooves? I certainly didn't."

Bratton literally threw the smoothbore back to the sheriff. Wend could see that he was now madder than ever. His teeth were clenched and the arteries were standing out on his neck.

Dunning turned to the crowd. "There are no rifle grooves in Eckert's piece. As far as I'm concerned, the results stand as declared!"

Now the uproar from the crowd was louder than ever.

Wend was suddenly seized by an impulse. He turned to Marsh and Bratton. "Matt, I think you still believe I'm tricking you somehow. So why don't we shoot one more time—at 120 yards. One shot only; just to settle the score."

Marsh turned to Bratton. But he didn't need to even ask the question.

"Your on, Dutchman. Set up the targets, Marsh!"

The miller leapt to the stump. "Your attention! Your attention!" He shouted, "There's a new bet. Eckert versus Bratton at 120 yards. One shot only! Fifteen minutes from now. Place your bets at the table!"

The assemblage buzzed while Marsh jumped down to run to the betting table.

Suddenly Froelich was at Wend's side. "I just won a lot of money on your last two rounds. But 120 yards? That's pushing it. Are you sure?"

Wend looked down at the gunsmith. "I'm far less a gambler than you, sir. And I have something more important than money riding on this."

The little man looked up at him and nodded. "I'm going to bet everything!" And he almost ran over to the table to find bettors.

Joshua arrived, still carrying his tankard, and obviously feeling some effect from a full day's drinking. "Sprout, after this is all over, you are going to tell me how it was done, aren't you? To tell the truth, I thought they had you when they started to run that rod up and down your barrel. But the sheriff is swearing to everyone that that smoothbore is the real thing."

Wend put his hand on the scout's shoulder. "Tonight, Joshua, when we have some quiet time up at the house."

"All right, Sprout. But good luck. Don't let that waggoner get bragging rights over you." He looked down in his tankard. "I've got to get me some more of McCartie's good whiskey!" And he was off to the bar.

Wend turned to his bag, and started to reload the smoothbore. He took the most care he had all afternoon, particularly with checking the precise placement of the patch under the ball, and he firmly seated the ball with the ramrod and mallet. Since he had now fired eight shots, he cleaned out the vent to ensure that it was not fouled so as to result in delayed ignition or a misfire of the main charge.

By the time Tom Marsh walked back to the firing line, Wend was ready and had regained his concentration. He was betting that Bratton, less practiced in controlling his emotions, was still agitated from the shock of the earlier shooting.

Marsh announced, "Bratton will shoot first, then Eckert."

Wend made sure not to look at the waggoner. It seemed that he waited a long time as Bratton aimed, but finally the shot cracked out.

Now Wend took aim. As he had all afternoon, he mentally painted the warrior's face over the target. But this time, instead of aiming for the center of the nose ring, he carefully picked out a spot just below where the ring passed through the nose, so that his firearm was aimed the tiniest bit above where he had on prior shots.

He took a breath and squeezed the trigger, then relaxed.

He stood up and dusted himself off as the boy ran down to the targets and back. Once again Marsh took a moment to examine the targets himself, but almost immediately he turned and stepped up on the stump. He held the two targets up to the crowd.

There was a roar. Bratton's shot was in the red, but at the very edge on the right side, about an inch from dead center. Wend's was off center slightly, but only by the width of a bullet hole. He had clearly won. Wend felt his body shake and the tension drain from him. It was over. Suddenly he felt sweat all over his face and chest. He hadn't realized that he had been so worried about the outcome. But now the breeze felt good.

Joshua came up and slapped him on the back, almost knocking him over.

Wend saw a scramble at the betting table and many people staring at him. He looked over at his competitor. Bratton was staring at him, again red faced; visibly shaking with anger. But Wend felt an ice-cold calm come over himself. He walked to the waggoner and made a visible show of putting out his hand. "That was a fine competition, Matt. Congratulations on your shooting; let me buy you a drink."

Bratton was having none of it. He pulled pack a fist as if to strike Wend. His friends, standing close by, grabbed his arms and hurried him off toward the bar, leaving Wend with his hand held out. Wend looked at Marsh, as if to say "I tried."

Marsh stepped over beside Wend and Joshua. "He's taking it hard, lad. And losing that last shot rubbed salt into the wound. You'd best stay out of his way for a while, Wend."

Just then Johnny Donaldson came up. He had coins in his hand. "Wend, here's your three pounds. And here's three more that you won. I bet even on the original match. And here's another pound. I only bet one pound on the last shot. But I should have bet more for you!"

* * *

Wend sat on the bench under the lean-to outside his shop after the shooting match. Grouped around on other benches were Joshua, Reverend Carnahan and Henry Froelich. Wend had invited the Shippensburg gunsmith to join them for the evening. He was planning to stay the night in the village before beginning his trip south in the morning.

Wend was drinking some whiskey from a jug he had brought up from McCartie's. He rarely drank anything stronger than ale, but tonight he had felt the need of the potent libation. The drink was having its effect. He was feeling very relaxed, more relaxed than he had felt in days.

They could see that the crowd down at McCartie's had dispersed. The only reminder of the day's events was intermittent noise from some hardy souls who where holding forth inside the tavern itself.

Wend looked at his companions and broke the silence which had reigned for a few seconds. "Well, Joseph Junkin came up to me after the match and said he definitely wants to buy the smoothbore. Said he won enough so that he can pay for it part with cash he won today, and the rest he'll pay with a gaggle of hens he's got. So we'll be eating fowl for a while!" Wend laughed.

Joshua lighted his pipe and settled his back against one of the roof supports. Suddenly he burst out, "Cut the small talk, Sprout! Tell us how you did it. I've been busting with curiosity ever since the shooting ended."

Wend looked at Froelich and the two gunsmiths smiled at each other. "It's just like I told you earlier today. There's no trick, its natural law if you understand how firelocks work."

"So why don't you explain it, Sprout. Make it simple for those of us who don't have time to study all the mysteries of firearms."

"It is quite simple. Since the smoothbore uses the same barrel as a rifle of similar bore, everything is the same except there's no grooving. And, logically, it uses the same powder charge to drive the ball. If the ball is made as tight fitting as in a rifle, and patched like a rifle bullet so the ball grabs the sides of the barrel, the ball will have similar characteristics in flight, at least out to about 100 yards. That is essentially point blank range, for either the smoothbore or a rifle. Here's the secret most people don't understand: The effect of the ball spinning from the grooves really has its greatest value after 100 yards or so, when the initial impulse of the powder explosion has lost its effect. The spinning will keep the bullet on course as it slows, whereas after a hundred yards the smooth bore's ball will start to slow and lose its stability." Wend looked at Mr. Froelich. "Do you agree, Sir?"

"Most certainly, Wend. The effect of the rifling certainly is essential for accurate shooting at 200 yards, but a well made smoothbore will do well out to a 100, or slightly further, as you so aptly demonstrated today."

Baird looked skeptically at the two gunmakers. "Wait a minute. I've seen plenty of smoothbores fired before and I never saw so much accuracy as today."

Froelich responded. "You may be correct, but I'll wager the smoothbores you saw fired were fowling pieces or muskets. Am I right?"

"Yes—I've seen plenty of both fired, and accuracy beyond seventy or eighty yards just doesn't exist."

"Yes, but that's why this is called a 'smoothbore rifle', it's built to the same standards as a rifle, not a gun made to fire shot or a musket ball. The difference is the tightness of the ball in the bore. A musket, for example, is made for rapid reloading. A well drilled soldier can load and fire three or four times in a minute. The purpose is volume of fire, not accuracy. The British don't even train soldiers to aim at anyone in particular, just level the musket and pull the trigger." Froelich bent over and traced two parallel lines in the dirt floor. "This is a musket barrel." He drew a small circle inside the two lines. "The musket ball is sized significantly smaller than the bore, to make it easier to load. Sometimes in heat of battle, soldiers don't even use their ramrod; they just drop the ball in and pound the butt against the ground until the ball goes most of the way down the barrel. But the looseness of the ball affects accuracy." He moved his finger inside the drawing of the barrel to simulate the ball.

"After the charge is fired, the ball is so loose it doesn't travel straight down the barrel. It bounces around against the walls of the barrel. So when the ball leaves the barrel, it most often leaves the muzzle at a slight angle. That's why it generally goes wide of a target directly in front of it. The same is true for most fouling pieces when you fire a ball instead of shot."

Carnahan had his hand on his chin and looked curiously at Wend. "So tell me, Wend. Did you plan, from the beginning, to draw Bratton into this contest, trusting that he wouldn't understand the accuracy of your smoothbore?"

Wend sat quietly for a second, then looked directly at the minister and held up his hand in protest. "I didn't plan anything. I was trying to tell Junkin why the smoothbore would be as accurate as he needed when Bratton interrupted. He wouldn't let me explain what Mr. Froelich and I just told you. So, since he insisted on the contest, I played along. And Bratton learned the hard way."

CHAPTER 11

Paxton Rangers

Several days after the shooting match, Wend sat at his workbench, finishing the repairs to an old rifle owned by Thomas Marsh. The lock's trigger mechanism had become worn through long use; he had replaced the internal parts and remounted the lock on the gun. But he would need to test fire it to make sure that the whole assembly worked and the spark from the pan properly flowed through the vent-hole into the barrel. He decided to also take the opportunity to check and align the sights on the new rifle he had made for display in Paxton.

Wend carried the two rifles and shooting supplies to the range behind his shop. The range paralleled the wagon track as it ran westward up the valley and Wend had cleared it for over 200 yards. Today he would be shooting at half that distance. Wend set up his shooting table, which had adjustable clamps to hold a rifle absolutely steady for purposes of performing the sight alignment. The first step would be to check the Paxton rifle's sights. He set up a wooden target at a place he had marked as precisely 100 yards. Then he aligned the rifle in the table clamps, fired five shots at the target, and was preparing to walk down and check the placement of the shots when he looked over to see that Reverend Carnahan had quietly come up and was watching as Wend worked.

Carnahan stood lighting his pipe. "The children were fidgeting, so I sent them out behind the school to play for a few minutes and let them use up some energy. They'll need to be ready to concentrate, because were going to do some ciphering for the next hour. Then I heard your shots and I thought I'd wander over and see what you were up to."

Wend grinned. "I guess you need a break as much as the young ones do." Then he had a thought. "Would you mind helping me out here? I have to test fire this rifle to check the lock. But I'd like to watch as it is fired. Could you shoot while I observe?"

Carnahan looked down range and at the rifle. "Sure, I'd be glad to help." He walked up to the table and laid his pipe on it. Wend handed him Marsh's rifle, fully loaded and ready to fire. The reverend looked a bit nervous as he handled the firearm. "It's been a long time since I did any real shooting. Don't know how well I'll do on a target so far down range."

Wend smiled at Paul's words. He couldn't remember the Reverend actually handling a rifle in the years since he had been in Sherman Valley. But he had seen him take small game and birds with a fowling piece and knew that he could handle a gun well enough. "Don't worry, Reverend. It doesn't matter whether you even hit the target. The purpose is just to make sure the lock works correctly."

Carnahan cocked the rifle, turned down range and put it to his shoulder. "Tell me when you're ready for me to fire."

Wend took a position about three feet to his side, where he could observe the operation but be clear of the smoke and fire from the pan's ignition. "Go ahead when you're ready."

Carnahan squinted, flipped the set trigger, and almost instantaneously squeezed the firing trigger. Wend watched the lock and was gratified to see that it functioned perfectly and ignition of the charge occurred precisely as he wanted.

Carnahan stared down the range toward the target, nodded to himself, and then handed the rifle back to Wend. He picked up his pipe and took a deep pull to make sure it was still lit. "I used to be able to shoot well enough, back when Joshua and I were on the road together. But it's been a long time since those days." He took another draw on the pipe. "Well, I need to get back to work, before my charges get into too much trouble. Thanks for letting me take a shot." He turned and walked back toward the schoolhouse.

Wend trudged down the firing range to retrieve the target. He would use the placement of his first group to judge the need to adjust the new rifle's sights. As he walked, he was thinking about what price he would ask for the new rifle. It was very handsome; he had selected a beautiful piece of maple for the stock and he expected that it would fetch a good amount once he offered it for sale. And his timing was right, for the fall was the time when men had the most money to spend.

He was deep in his thoughts when he reached the target and grabbed it from the stand. He didn't even look at the shot pattern until he had walked about a third of the distance back to the firing mark. But when he did, what he saw made him halt in astonishment. There was his five shot pattern, centered in a near perfect circle within the bull's eye. He knew they were his shots because of the size of the holes. The Reverend's shot was also obvious because the ball from Marsh's rifle was larger. And the hole from his shot was almost precisely in the center of the bull's eye! Wend held the target up for close examination.

The large hole was less than a half-inch from dead center.

Wend thought for a second. The Reverend had stood upright when firing, not bracing himself in any way. Moreover, he had fired almost instantly when Wend had indicated he was ready to observe the rifle's lock. In truth, it was a "snap shot." And there was only the smallest chance that it was simply luck.

But Wend didn't think it was luck. Odds were that the Reverend Paul Carnahan was a crack marksman.

* * *

On the second Saturday after the shooting match, the common room of McCartie's Tavern was cloudy with pipe smoke and overflowing with men talking, telling jokes and laughing. Wend and Joshua leaned against the bar, watching the scene. Reverend John Elder, Lazarus Stewart, Carnahan, and Tom Marsh were engaged in discussion at a table by the fireplace, while Matt Bratton and his cronies were at their usual corner table, with a number of boys standing around.

John Elder stood up. "I'm glad to see that so many men of Sherman Valley have turned out today. Reverend Carnahan called you here because we believe formation of a militia company is important to your well being and that of your families." He stopped to survey the room. "But some of you may wonder why. So I want you to hear some first-hand news from beyond the Alleghenies. Joshua Baird's just back from the Ohio Country." He turned to the scout. "Joshua, I've heard from traders that the tribes are worried about the number of settlers moving beyond the Alleghenies."

Joshua picked up his mug of ale and strolled over to the hearth. "Reverend Elder's got that right, except that the word is 'mad', not 'worried'. And they're upset about a whole lot more than just settlers: They're mad about the way that the British have treated them since the fighting stopped back in '59. Baird took a drink from his mug. "The problem is that the British suddenly have got a whole country of Indians to govern and they don't have any real experience with it. There's no real policy or system for working with the tribes. And the big wigs up in New York, particularly General Amherst, who has the primary responsibility for dealing with the Indians for the Crown, think they can just leave the tribes alone to their own business."

Bratton interrupted, "So what's wrong with that? The tribal kings are always saying they want to be left alone on their own land! Then we do that, and they're not happy. I say they just want to complain!"

Other men picked up the refrain. Joshua held up a hand to quiet the room. "The chiefs are accustomed to the way the French used to run things. Government agents visited the chiefs on a regular basis, at least every year. They sat around the council fire with them, showed them respect and made them feel important, asked them their opinion on this and that, and generally left the impression that the French colonial authorities up in Canada were thinking about them. And to seal the deal, every year they used to give every king a batch of gifts. Gunpowder, lead, tools, blankets, clothing, beads, and all sorts of other trade goods."

Marsh asked, "So the British don't do anything like that?"

"Not a bit, Tom; haven't even thought about the idea, at least in the senior army leadership, and anyway, they don't have the money for it. The British have also limited sales of gunpowder and lead to the Indians. And as far as sending out emissaries to the kings, they don't understand that either. Mostly they just summon them to council fires at Fort Pitt or up at Fort Detroit. That gives the impression that the British don't respect the tribal chiefs, which is true, 'cause they are essentially treating them like underlings, not important leaders."

Bratton spoke up again. "Look, I don't see why this concerns us. What we do know is that all the traders and others from the west have stories about war talk by the tribes. The chiefs are just complaining about the British to whip up their people for the war path!"

Lazarus stood up. "I don't see anything wrong with keeping gunpowder and lead from the savages. That damn-well sounds like the right policy to me! I'm with Bratton—let's worry less about the welfare of the Indians and more about protecting our families and property if war starts!"

Joshua turned and looked at Stewart. "Like you, I don't think we should sell or give war supplies to the tribes. But if the Crown would spend more time talking with the chiefs, and spend some money for small gifts, I'd wager we wouldn't be here talking about a militia." He shrugged his shoulders and returned to the counter.

John Elder looked around the room and quieted the men again. "Regardless of the reason, it's clear that we could face war party raids soon enough. So that gets us back to our primary question here: Should we form a militia for Sherman Valley?"

Tom Marsh stood up and all faces turned toward him. "We've had Fort Robinson since back in '55, but the fort is not enough. Think how many more families there are in the valley now and how spread out they are. We need a force which can provide protection, and strike back against a war party ranging the valley, or go to the succor of a family under attack in their cabin or stable."

Elder held both hands out in supplication. "The only answer is what we did in Paxton eight years ago: Set up your own militia. In '55 and '56, we sent our boys over here to help the people of this valley. That was when there were only a few families here. But the valley has prospered since then; look at how many new farms there are in the last few years, look at the number of you there are here today. We in Paxton will continue to help, but it's time for you to provide for your own defense here along Sherman Creek."

"Wait a minute, Reverend. I have a question." James Newhouse stood up. He was a recent settler and had a farm on the eastern side of the valley toward the Susquehanna. "Most of the Indians have moved over to the Ohio Country. Why would they attack this far eastward? Wouldn't most of the raiding be over around Pitt or Ligonier or Bedford?"

Joshua answered, "You got a point James, but keep in mind that the settlement out there is still thin. And the truth is, those farms are pretty hardscrabble. So there's a lot more plunder in this area, which is what's attractive to the typical warrior." Joshua paused a moment and laughed to himself. "And good plunder is even more attractive to Indian wives; they think of raiding parties the same way your wife thinks of a shopping trip to Carlisle!" There were guffaws around the room. "And remember, a party of eight or ten braves can move fast along the trails. A few more days walk ain't any bar to them. So I expect that this valley, the Great Cove down to the south, and the Conococheague country between Chambers' Fort and Maryland would be attractive targets."

He took another pull on his drink. "Also, remember that those tribal kings are pretty savvy. They know that, aside from the plunder they can take, the purpose of their attacks will be to put fear into the settlers so they abandon their farms and pressure the government to negotiate a peace. Yeah, if they can strike deep into the more settled areas, things will be better for them when they eventually start to talk peace."

Newhouse, an Englishman, was one of the few non-Ulster settlers in the valley. "I'm still not convinced we need to set up an armed force. If the tribes start attacking, won't the colony raise provincials, like they did in '56? And what about the regulars: Why do we have garrisons of the Royal Americans if they're not going to protect us?"

Lazarus sneered, "If you had been here as long as the rest of us, Newhouse, you'd know not to count on those Quakers in Philadelphia for anything but tax collection." There was a roar of laughter throughout the common room. "And as for the Royal Americans, they're all out on the border. We'll get precious little help from them."

Carnahan stood up, signaling for attention. "Mr. Newhouse, let me share some thoughts with you." The reverend spoke in low tones, and the room quieted as men strained to listen. "Everybody here, except you and Wend Eckert, are Ulster. We're in the valley because the colony let us have land cheap." He looked around and grinned, then continued, "And some of us didn't pay anything." There were laughs all around; at least a few of the men were squatters, having simply built their farmsteads on unclaimed land. "Be that as it may, the colony let us, and many other Ulster-Scotts all along the border, have the land in what I would call a 'Devil's Bargain'. It served their purpose to have us settle out here because they knew we'd have no choice but to organize and defend ourselves if the Indians came. And in doing that, we provide a line of defense which shields the eastern part of the colony. Those Quakers don't want to soil their hands in bloody violence, but they know there must be some armed protection for the colony. So they're letting the Ulster do the dirty work for them and they can sleep at night with a clear conscience that they haven't violated their religion."

A loud voice came from the table in the corner. "Reverend, I can't understand what we are quibbling about here. Everyone knows what happened in '55 and '56." Matt Bratton stood up. "If the choice is between doing something and taking no action, it's pretty clear that we should set up a company now. All it means is getting together to drill or train a couple of times a month. That's little enough, and at least we'll have some sort of organization if raids break out. I say let's take the damn vote and be done with it."

There was a murmur of agreement throughout the room. Reverend Carnahan nodded. "Matt has a good point. And now is the time to organize, before winter descends." He paused to look around the room, and saw no one else looking like they wanted to talk. "So let's take a vote."

The vote was essentially unanimous, in fact so lopsided in favor of forming a company that Carnahan didn't even ask for a show of negative hands, thus sparing any dissenters the embarrassment of showing their cards.

Then Reverend Elder again took the floor and discussed the organization of the company. As he spoke, it became obvious that he had done considerable planning. He pointed out that settlement now spread through the length of the valley, a distance of fifteen miles, and suggested that the company be split into two "half-companies", one centered in the village itself and covering the western part of the valley, and the second to cover the farmland to the east. Each half would be led by a lieutenant. An appropriate number of sergeants and corporals would be appointed within each half-company.

There was a nodding of heads around the room and they moved on to electing officers. Thomas Marsh, who many considered the unofficial mayor of the village and the valley settlement, was elected the captain of their company. Marsh stood up and conducted the election of the two lieutenants. After brief discussion, Ezra Gamble, a prosperous farmer who had been a sergeant in the Pennsylvania provincial regiment, was picked as the leader of the eastern group, and Paul Milliken, who also had served in the war, was elected as lieutenant of the western half company. Each of the lieutenants then appointed a sergeant and corporal for his part of the company.

Marsh then surprised Wend by appointing him a corporal, to keep records and to act as a scout. "Eckert isn't tied to a farm, can write, and he has hunted throughout the valley. He's the best choice to range the western part of the valley, looking for any sign of tribal parties."

Then he had Wend take down the names of all the men who had agreed to join the company. While he was doing that, the leaders made plans to drill and to spend time over the winter fixing up George Robinson's fort and the blockhouse within.

By early afternoon, all the arrangements and plans had been laid; the Sherman Valley company of the Paxton Rangers had become a reality.

* * *

Joshua Baird pulled up his horse and gazed at the base of a ridge which signaled the westward end of Sherman Valley. "There it is: The place where the trail starts up the ridge." He pointed the spot out to his two companions, Wend and Johnny Donaldson, who also stopped their horses and squinted in the direction of the scout's finger. They could see where the hard packed pathway through the woods turned to angle up the side of the hill.

It was two days after the militia meeting at McCartie's. The ride had been Joshua's idea; the scout was due to return to Fort Pitt almost immediately. Before leaving, he wanted to acquaint Wend with the Indian trail system in the western part of the valley where a war party would likely start its approach in a raid through the settlement.

In the dim light of dawn, Joshua and Wend had ridden out from Reverend Carnahan's house westward along the wagon track and then had stopped briefly at the Donaldson place, the most westward of the farms, to pick up Johnny.

Shortly after they left the Donaldson's, the sun had broken through the clouds and started to provide some warmth, even though the breeze persisted. An hour later, and four miles to the north, they cut the Indian walking trail. Turning westward, an hour along the well packed ground had brought the three men to the bottom of the ridge where the old trail descended into the valley. Joshua led them to the very base of the hill. "We'll dismount here and go up the hill on foot. It'll rest the horses and we can talk better on foot."

They tied their horses to trees on long leads, which enabled them to graze, and with their firearms cradled in the crook of their arms, started up the hill. Joshua briefed them as they walked. "As you can see, this is a well worn trail, but all the tribes, in their different languages, call it the 'New Path.' So it must not be as ancient as most of the others. If you follow it from here to the west, it goes over to old Fort Shirley, in the area the tribes call Aughwick. If you go eastward, it follows the valley for a while, then turns southward over Croghan's Gap and leads down to Carlisle."

As they approached the crest, Joshua suddenly stopped and Wend almost bumped into him. The scout was pointing. "Look there, on that tree."

After a moment, Wend saw what had attracted Baird's attention. It was on a tree located about four or five feet to the left of the trail, far enough so that if you weren't looking for it, it would not have been obvious. A ring of bark, nearly a foot wide, had been cut off around the trunk of the tree, about four feet above the ground. They could see that a message, in symbols, had been painted on the exposed wood. It was obviously years old, faded and barely discernible.

"It means that there's a campsite off the trail on this side." Baird walked a few steps further along the trail. "Look here!"

He pointed, and Wend could see a faint path leading off into the bush. They followed it and within forty yards came upon a small cove, carpeted with grass.

Johnny pointed, and exclaimed, "There's a hut!"

Wend's eyes followed his arm, and there, at the far edge of the clearing, was a crude structure. It was three sided, anchored by two pairs of stakes driven into the ground. The two in the rear were about five feet high, and the forward pair about four feet high. Flimsy walls of bark were stretched around the stakes and a roof of branches covered by bark sloped from the rear to the front stakes. The front side was open to the weather. It was evident that the shelter was old, and hadn't been maintained recently, for sections of the bark had fallen away, leaving gaps in the walls and some holes in the roof. They walked around the campsite and found a well-used fire circle. Joshua unearthed some small, weathered bones which apparently came from animals which had provided meals for the travelers.

After a few minutes exploring the area, Joshua located a continuation of the path which had led them down from the main trail. They followed him to a stone outcropping that provided a wide view of Sherman Valley to the east, as if someone had laid out a vast map on the ground in front of them.

Most of the land was a carpet of tree tops, virtually all now denuded of leaves by the advance of the fall season. But here and there were little islands of green, which marked groves of evergreens. Wend could make out the fields and even many of the farm buildings which dotted the western part of the valley.

Johnny stretched out his arm. "See, there's our land and farmstead!"

He was quite right. The Donaldson's place was closest and in plain view. Wend looked more to the left and shortly made out the McClay's place, the next in line along the valley. Just beyond the McClay farm was a ridge where he and Baird frequently hunted; it hid the Carnahan farm and the village itself. But east of the McClay house he could make out the Millikens' farm, and visible beyond that, the Robinson farmstead and the shape of the fort's stockade.

Baird came up close beside Wend. "I guess I don't have to tell you this is the perfect place for a war party to view the valley and make their plans."

He looked up to see if Johnny was listening, but the boy was still mesmerized by the view and not paying attention to the others. Very quietly he said, "It don't take much thought to calculate which places they're going to hit first." He looked sharply at Wend, who immediately understood what he meant.

In a louder voice he continued, "If you get wind that things are beginning to happen in the west you might want to start coming up here now and again to check if there's been any use of this site. Might give you some indication if warriors are scouting the valley and allow you to warn the farmers."

The sun was now overhead, bathing the outcropping in warmth. Joshua looked around and then leaned his rifle against a tree. He settled himself on the ground, his back against a rock. "This is as good a place as any to have our meal, before we start back down to the horses."

Wend sat down and pulled food from his haversack. Suddenly he realized how much the morning's ride and walk had tired him out. He thought to himself that he had to get away from the shop more often, to hunt and exercise his legs. He admired how Joshua, fifteen years his elder, strode through the forest with such seemingly little effort.

"Come on Johnny, stop gazing at the sights. Sit down and eat your dinner", Baird called out to the youth. "We can't laze around here all afternoon if we expect to get back to the farm before sunset."

The boy joined them on the ground and began attacking his food eagerly. Presently, Joshua looked at Wend with a twinkle in his eye, then asked Johnny, "Hey, lad, didn't I see you paying close attention to that younger McCartie girl at the shooting matches?"

Johnny focused on the meat in his hand and considered his answer. "Well, we've been friends a since we were children. Ellen's a nice girl."

"Oh, that's good to know, 'cause I thought there might be somethin' special goin' on there; particularly since I also saw you walking down along the creek, out by the island where the stream turns south, with some girl that sure looked like Ellen. Must have been a about a week ago." He turned and smiled at Wend. "It was a long way off, mind you, but I could have sworn you two was holding hands and sometimes sort of bumping into each other. Things sure looked pretty serious. But of course, I could be wrong. My eyes just ain't what they used to be." He took another bite, and looked off in the distance, but Wend could see the mischievous gleam in his eye.

Johnny squirmed and looked back and forth between the two others. "Well, now you mention it, a man could do worse than end up with a girl like

Ellen. She's a hard worker, and she ain't no flirt like her sister. You won't find her selling her favors out in the tavern stable!"

Joshua stopped eating, a little startled at the vehemence of Johnny's words. He slowly turned to the boy. "What did you mean by that? I thought the older girl was pretty much ready to settle down with Bratton. Most people say it's just a matter of time."

"Ellen says Peggy is getting tired of waiting for Bratton. She's nineteen now, and got nothing to show for hanging around with him. And besides, she ain't been that true to him."

Wend asked, "What gives you that idea?"

"I didn't get that from Ellen, you can be sure. But there's talk around the valley that Peggy's been friendly with some of the traveling men who come through here, hanging out after hours in the tavern room. I mean real friendly late into the night, and she's been seen coming out of McCartie's stable just before dawn with her clothes and hair lookin' wild."

Joshua thought for a moment. "Well, if Bratton finds out about it, there's going to be hell to pay for whoever he thinks is with her. Not to mention him takin' it out on her some way." The scout stood up. "It's time to start back while we got enough hours of light." He walked out to the edge of the outcropping for a last look at the landscape.

Wend and Johnny joined him. Johnny pointed to his family's place. "You see our cleared fields there?"

The others nodded.

"Well, we own another 150 acres that hasn't been cleared. There, just to the left of the fields. Father says that I can have that for my own place when I'm ready. I figure to start clearing some of that next year and plant crops of my own. I can have the start of a good farm by the time I'm your age, Wend."

Wend smiled and nodded. "I guess a man could also marry a nice girl and start a family in that time, couldn't he?"

A smile slowly spread over Johnny's face. "He sure could, and that's a fact."

Wend looked out at the vista, and reflected again about the layout of the farms along the valley, and a thought came to him. "Johnny, what had you figured to use as a firearm for when you are with the militia company? Your father's smoothbore that you are carrying now?"

"Yes, Wend, that's the only gun we have."

"Well, you can't go off on patrol with the rangers and leave your family without any kind of a firelock." Wend looked over at Joshua, then back to

Johnny. "Tell you what: I've got an old French musket that a customer gave me as part trade for a new gun. I'll put it back in shape and you can have it on a long term loan for use with the militia."

Johnny broke out into a huge grin at the thought of having his own weapon. "Wend, that's real fine of you. I'll be there tomorrow!"

Wend smiled at the lad's impatience. "Better make it the day after tomorrow. Like I said, it needs some work. Give me some time to make sure it's in order."

CHAPTER 12

Suspicion

The snow started about an hour after Wend rode out of Sherman Mill on the wagon road which wound eastward through the valley to the Susquehanna. He had risen early, saddled his black mare and started in the gloom of false dawn, for he had a long day's journey ahead of him. He carried the newly finished Paxton rifle in front of him across the saddle's pommel. It was encased in canvas and he had a brace of pistols in holsters slung in the front of his saddle for protection. Behind the saddle was strapped a pair of saddlebags and a blanket-roll.

Wend was on his way to put the new rifle on display in Paxton. He also planned to spend a day with Charlie Sawak, who would be delivering a load of the Conestogas' merchandise to the Slough & Simon warehouse. Because of the threat of snow, he had chosen to approach Harris' Ferry and Paxton along the road through Sherman Valley and thence southward by the river instead of crossing the mountain and going via Carlisle.

He was well past the Milliken and Junkin places, riding in the light of the gray dawn, when the first flakes began to fall. He felt the cold tingle on his neck as a flake fell and melted under his collar. The mare shook her head as the first flakes hit her. Within a half- hour the snow was coming down in a determined way and Wend knew he was facing more than a series of flurries. Luckily, the storm was approaching from behind him, so that the wind was at his back, and did not bite him severely. In fact, the gentle fall of snow, the first of the season, brought on an enchanting feeling of being alone in a white world. Soon he began to enjoy himself as he rode onward.

It was two days since Joshua had left on his way back to the Ohio Country. On the same day, a peddler had dropped off a letter for Wend from Charlie, telling him of his plans to travel to Harris'. Charlie had sent the letter several weeks before, but it had followed a circuitous path to Sherman Mill, with the result that the proposed date of meeting was only three days away when Wend received the note. So he had bustled around the house and the shop, getting ready for the trip to the Susquehanna.

The same day Johnny Donaldson had come by to pick up the French musket which Wend had promised to loan him. He brought Ellen McCartie with him, and Wend remarked to himself that their relationship was certainly maturing rapidly. Wend pulled the musket out of the rack and handed it to the young man. He could see the gleam in Johnnie's eyes as he took it in his hands and looked it over.

"I've checked out the lock and oiled the wood of the stock. You'll need to oil the stock regularly; the wood is old and will dry out fast if you don't." The youth looked at Wend and nodded. Wend continued, "Also notice it's got a wooden ramrod, instead of metal. So be careful while loading; it is easy to break off in the barrel if you aren't careful."

Johnnie had a broad grin on his face. "Thanks, Wend. I sure appreciate it. I'll take good care of the firelock."

Wend handed Johnnie a small package. "Here are some balls already molded, and a mold which will make balls to fit your barrel. It's sized so that the balls will fit tightly in the barrel, so you may get a little better accuracy than normal for a musket. And look at this: I fitted a front and rear sight on the barrel. Neither French nor British muskets have sights; they just expect the soldier to level their weapons at the enemy line."

Johnnie nodded, his eyes bright with pleasure.

Ellen was leaning on the door frame, her arms crossed in front of her chest. Wend noted an approving look on her face as she watched Johnnie. He brought Ellen into the conversation. "I haven't seen Matt around for a while. Is he out on a freighting trip? He usually notifies all the merchants in case they want to ship something or have him pick up freight somewhere."

Ellen walked further into the shop. "He's gone out with his wagon to take a new job. He's got a contract for long distance cargo hauling out to Fort Bedford."

Wend looked up from watching Johnnie inspect the musket. "That's going to take a lot of time. He'll be away for weeks at a stretch. What about our freight service between here and Carlisle?"

"He's hired Frank McKenzie to carry freight locally. Matt bought a large farm wagon down in Carlisle which Frank will use that to do the freight work for the valley." She paused for a second. "Matt told Peggy that he wasn't making enough money from just carrying cargo around here. He needs to do something which makes a greater profit, if he's going to put money aside so they can get married."

Wend thought for a moment. "How does Peggy feel about all this? Isn't she upset that he'll be away so much?"

Ellen shrugged. "Actually, she seems quite happy about the whole matter. She's getting impatient about their marriage, and if Matt can earn some real money which will make that possible, she can put up with his absence for a time. After all, she's been pressing him about getting married; now she feels maybe he's finally listening to her."

"Do you know who Matt's working for?"

Ellen thought for a moment. "No, Peggy didn't mention that when she told me about the new contract. Just that he'd be freighting to Bedford, and that it would mean a lot of money."

After a few more minutes the two left and Wend watched them walk down the hill to the tavern. He sensed that their relationship would stand the test of time. After a few moments of reflection his mind quickly returned to his preparations for the trip.

✳ ✳ ✳

Despite its pleasant beginning, the journey to Paxton turned into a near-disaster. The snow piled up rapidly, slowing progress through the valley and exhausting the horse. Wend and his mare arrived at the river well after darkness, hours later than he had planned. He still had to go seven miles southward along the banks of the river to reach the small tavern which stood at the western ferry landing. He suddenly realized how isolated they were; he could see no lights around except for a faint glimmer from a house across the river. Feeling a growing sense of anxiety, he tried to push on through the darkness and blinding snow, hoping to make the tavern. But then the weary mare slipped on a stretch of sloping road and lost her footing. Wend was able to jump off before she fell to her knees and, with great difficulty, she regained her footing. But Wend feared the condition of her legs, and knew that she was far too tired for him to ride further that night. After a search in the darkness, he found a fallen tree and built a rude lean-to of evergreen branches against it for shelter and then started a fire for some semblance of warmth. But it was of little avail; he spent a long, freezing night shivering incessantly and fearing to let sleep overcome him. After hours which seemed interminable, dawn finally arrived. But still uncertain of the horse's condition, he was forced to lead her all the miles down to the ferry landing, his feet becoming numb as he slogged through the snow and ice.

After crossing on the ferry, with the bitter cold wind cutting to his bones, he led the mare a hundred yards up the wagon track to the tavern which Charlie had designated as their meeting place. As befitted Charlie's financial situation, it was the cheapest, most run-down of the several taverns along the road leading to the landing, Wend hadn't planned to stay there, but in his exhaustion there was no question of going up to the tavern in Paxton he normally used. He looked around the stableyard, but saw no sign of Charlie's horse cart. Leading the mare into the stable, Wend was relieved to see a young stable boy attending to the animals. He quickly made arrangements for the horse, and gathering up his gear, walked across the yard to the inn itself.

The tavern keeper, a balding, heavy-set man wearing a greasy apron, was at work cleaning the common room. Wend quickly secured the use of a room and gave his name to the proprietor so Charlie would know he was there. The man led him up a narrow staircase with squeaky steps to a room which could most charitably be called shoddy. But Wend cared not a wit. He threw his gear down, took off his overcoat and stripped down to his shirt. He pulled back the bed's torn and patched quilt, to expose sheets which undeniably hadn't been washed for some passage of time. But clean sheets were the last thing he cared about at that moment. He thankfully crawled into the bed, pulling the quilt over him. For a few minutes his whole frame shook as his frozen body dealt with the shock of sudden warmth. And then the shaking abated, the warmth spread through his limbs, and gratefully, Wend dropped off to deep sleep.

Wend woke up to the gloom of dusk. For a moment he thought he had slept through the day and the night and was looking at the beginning of dawn. Then he looked out through a window and realized from the direction of the sun that it was evening. He walked to another window, where he could view the courtyard, and saw Charlie's cart parked near the side of the stable, its traces up on blocks to keep it level.

Dressing quickly and washing in the basin, he descended to the common room. It was empty save for two people. Charlie stood leaning against the bar with a mug at his hand, talking with a brown haired, buxom tavern maid. They were getting along exceedingly well, their heads close together and the girl giggling loudly at Charlie's comments.

Wend walked over to the counter. Charlie looked at him and laughed. "There he is, Rose: My friend the day sleeper!" He and the girl giggled together at the profundity of his comment. In a more serious tone, he said, "I checked your room right after I got here, which was around noon. When I knocked you didn't answer. So I went in, and despite the noise from me tripping over some of your gear on the floor, you didn't even move. Then I shook you on the shoulder and you just rolled over. So I gave you up for a lost cause and came back down here to wait until you returned to the world of the living."

Wend quickly explained the reason for his exhaustion and asked for some tea from Rose. He was by no means ready for rum or ale. And he realized that his body was screaming for food.

The girl went to warm some tea for him. "I need to eat, Charlie. What's the food like here?"

"The food is indifferent, but the price is low. In other words, it suits my purse but not my taste. However, one lives within one's means, not up to his desire."

"I need good food, Charlie." Wend thought for a moment. "We can get two things done at once. Let's hitch up your cart and drive up to Paxton. The tavern where I need to deliver my rifle is up there and has the best food in the village. They can make us a supper while I set up the gun for display. Then we'll have all day tomorrow to ourselves."

Charlie nodded. "You always make such good sense when you talk about spending your money on me, Wend. Let's get going."

Wend quickly drank his tea when it arrived and Charlie bid a temporary farewell to Rose. Working together it took them only a short time to hitch up the cart horse, the animal making it clear he was not happy about leaving the warmth of the barn, and they were on their way in less than an hour with Wend's rifle and supply bag in the rear. The two joked and traded stories as they rode. Wend noticed that it was warmer than the previous night and that the sun had melted a good deal of the snow. Paxton village was separated from Harris' by only a few farms and they soon had Reverend Elder's church, the largest building of the settlement, in sight. The town itself had several streets which crossed the main road up from Harris' and it was on the corner of one of these that the tavern which was their objective was located.

They left the horse and cart in the stableyard and headed for the inn; cheerful lights showed through its windows. Charlie pointed up at the tavern's sign, which was a bird with spread wings above a flaming fire. "What does that mean?"

"The tavern's name is 'The Phoenix', which is a bird that old legends say was born of fire." Wend decided not to mention that the predecessor of this tavern had been burnt to the ground during a Delaware war party raid of 1755. Charlie looked up at the sign again, and a dark look passed quickly over his face, but he said nothing, and they entered the common room.

Wend was gratified to see that the tavern was filled with patrons, predominantly men, but with a sprinkling of women and children, most enjoying a drink or having dinner at tables around the room. Several men stood at the bar, making spirited conversation. It wouldn't hurt to have an audience when he put the new rifle on display.

They walked up to the bar and Wend leaned the rifle, still in its cloth wrapping, against the wall. The proprietor, Jared Caldwell, entered from the door to the kitchen. He was tall and spare, with a dour expression, certainly not representing the popular image of a jolly tavern keeper. But he broke into a pleasant smile when he saw Wend. "Hello, Eckert. I've been expecting you for a couple of weeks now."

"Evening Jared; good to see you again." Wend introduced Charlie to the proprietor and returned to business. "I thought we'd have dinner here after I set up my display gun. I've been looking forward to one of your good suppers. What have you got for today?"

"I've got a good stew of beef and vegetables, but to tell the truth, the best thing in the house is some roast turkey. A hunter brought the fowl in this morning and there's enough left for a full meal for both of you, if that's your pleasure."

The two friends readily agreed and Caldwell showed them to a table. "By the way, Wend, you've been the subject of many a discussion around here since the match over at Sherman Mill last month. There're several men, Lazarus Stewart among them, who admitted they lost serious money over that bet."

Caldwell went to order their meal and a pretty young serving girl, with auburn hair and an eye-catching bosom, came over to take their order for drinks. Charlie's eyes lit up and he gave Wend a wink. "I think I'm going to like this place!"

The girl took Charlie's meaning and favored him with a broad smile. After taking their orders, she walked back to the counter in a way calculated to keep their attention. Even without raven hair, the girl's manner reminded Wend of Peggy McCartie in her most crowd pleasing mode.

FORBES ROAD

Wend left Charlie at the table and started to set up the gun display. He was conscious that he was performing in front of an audience, and he intended to make the most of it. He moved to the end of the counter, and leaving the rifle against the wall, made a small ceremony of placing his bag on the counter and removing the supplies and accessories he needed.

There were several bantering men at the counter and at least one of them knew who Wend was. "Are you going to put up one of those smooth bore guns of yours, Eckert, like you made famous last month?"

Wend smiled at the man. "I'll show you in just a moment." He took care to lay out a leather shot pouch, powder horn, his bottle of wood-oil, and a folded polishing cloth on the counter.

Wend turned and picked up the rifle. He held it up where he was sure that all eyes in the room could see it, and untied the laces. Then, when he had the attention of the crowd, he slowly slid the cover off the rifle. The candle-light showed off the grained maple to good effect and he was gratified at the nods of approval that he could see around the room. He placed the cover aside and made a show of burnishing the maple with a final coat of oil from the cloth, then placed the rifle on the pegs behind the counter. Just as he had for the smoothbore at Sherman Mill, he hung the powder horn and the shot bag over the rifle by their straps. Then he used the cloth to wipe and shine the brass of his nameplate below the rifle.

The group of men at the bar moved down to look at the display; others rose from their tables to view the rifle at close range. Wend saw that one of the new arrivals was Asher Clayton, who he hadn't noticed before.

"Hello, Eckert," the militia captain smiled and nodded to Wend. "Good to see you again. That's a nice looking rifle you got there."

Wend shook his hand, thanking him for the complement.

"By the way, that was great shooting over at Sherman Mill in McCartie's last match. I sure wish I had bet on you!"

Wend thanked Asher again, then when he was sure that his audience was as large as it would get, he went through a description of the features of his gun; the caliber, lock, double triggers, carvings and brass decorations. He could see that the men were impressed, and he felt pride welling up inside. Suddenly he felt a knot in his stomach and wished his father could be there to share the moment with him.

As he was talking, the serving girl emerged from the kitchen and squeezed past him carrying plates of food toward his table. The aroma reminded Wend of his hunger and he was seized by the overwhelming desire to get back to the

179

table. He looked over, and true to form, Charlie was talking up the girl, who was standing by the table with her hands on her hips, giggling and showing no eagerness to leave. Wend was answering questions when he felt a cold blast of air and looked up to see that the outside door had swung open and a group of men was entering the common room. He immediately recognized the first man; it was Lazarus Stewart.

Stewart and his group stopped just inside the room, taking in the scene. He looked over at Wend and the gaggle of men around him. Wend didn't want to talk to Stewart, and avoided meeting his eyes, instead concentrating on a question from one of the men inspecting the rifle. After he had finished, he broke away from the group to get back to the table and the roast fowl.

But he had no sooner turned toward the table then he realized something was going on. Stewart and his men had stopped and were looking down at Charlie. The girl had abruptly left the table and was hurrying back toward the kitchen. Charlie was looking straight ahead, his shoulders squared and his mouth clinched in a grimace.

Wend heard Stewart say, "You haven't answered my question, red man! I asked you what you were doing here!"

Wend reached the table. "Good evening, Captain Stewart," he said in his most polite and matter of fact tone, sitting down in front of his plate and taking up knife and fork. "It's good to see you again. Have you seen the new rifle I brought over tonight?"

Then Wend looked at his friend. Charlie still sat frozen on the other side of the table, his hands gripping the edge and his face showing both anger and fear.

Stewart glared down at Wend. "So this savage is traveling with you, Eckert?"

Wend took a bite of his turkey. He took his time chewing it, to let himself calm down and think about how to respond. Only when he had put his fork down did he reply. "Captain, this is my friend Charlie Sawak, from Lancaster. We grew up together. We attended the same school. I don't see any 'savage' in this room."

Stewart looked between the two diners. "Eckert, what made you think you could bring an Indian into this place? This town was attacked in '55, and this very tavern was among the buildings burned to the ground. Why do you think it's called 'The Phoenix'? The people of Paxton don't like to be reminded of the perfidy of these people."

Stewart's face was turning red. Speaking very slowly and quietly, Wend said, "I'm well aware of what happened to Paxton during the war, Captain.

And you have my sympathy." He looked over at Charlie and smiled reassuringly. "But Charlie is a Conestoga. And everyone, Captain, everyone knows that the Conestogas have been peaceful for over seventy years and have adopted our way of life. Their business is farming and commerce. I don't think of Charlie as anything but a friend. And no one in this inn, until you arrived, seemed to take exception to his presence. So, Captain, I've no idea why you are upset."

"I've been through too many attacks by the tribes, too many of their deceptions, seen too many of my friends die at the hands of the savages to believe in the idea of a so called 'friendly Indian'. And I damn well don't want his kind in this place!"

Wend fought to control his anger. He was about to reply to Stewart when Asher Clayton came up to the table. "Hello, Lazarus. What's this all about?"

Stewart looked at Clayton for a moment and motioned toward Charlie. "This is about not having to drink in the same room with a member of the race which burned our town and killed our people. And the Dutchman here has brought him amongst us on the pretext that he's a 'Peaceful Conestoga'. I'm not ready to trust any of them. We'll not be safe until there are no Indians on this side of the Alleghenies, and I'll wager I'm not alone in that sentiment."

Stewart's friends all muttered agreement.

Clayton put his hand on Stewart's shoulder. "Come on, friend. Eckert is a member of our militia. There are men of your own company who carry rifles made by him. He wouldn't bring someone here who had any designs on us. And look at all the men of his friend's race who have helped us over the years. What about John Logan, the Mingo chief, who has lived near here and always worked for peace? I think your worry is misplaced, Sir."

Stewart was about to reply when Jared Caldwell arrived at the table.

Stewart turned to the inn keeper. "Jared, I came into your place tonight, looking for fellowship among friends. Instead, I find this savage sitting at one of your tables, eating your fare, and making advances toward one of your serving girls. I thought you had standards, Sir. For God's sake, it took you months to get this place rebuilt and back in operation after the attack of '55, with your family near starving and living under canvas. Have you such a short memory that you can willingly accept the presence of a man of this sort?"

Caldwell looked down and wiped his hands on a cloth he had carried from the counter. Then he looked up at the captain. "Stewart, no one has to remind me about what happened back in '55. But look at this man: His clothes are the same cut as yours. He speaks the language as well as you or I. And he's with Eckert. Everyone knows Eckert lost his whole family out on Forbes Road. No one has more cause to bear a grudge against the tribes. So if the Dutchman considers him a friend and a suitable companion for supper, I have no objection to his presence." Caldwell looked around the room, then straight at Stewart, "And this is, indeed, my place."

There was a moment of silence as Stewart stared at Caldwell. The innkeeper spoke again. "Lazarus, if you want to eat or if you want ale, your money is good and I'm ready to serve you. You've spent many an evening here. But if you don't want to spend time here with the clientele who have already been served tonight, you can leave. There are other taverns in this village, and you know them well. So the choice is yours."

Stewart looked around the common room. By now, there was absolute silence among the diners and the men at the bar. But he could detect no groundswell of support for his position. Stymied, he turned to his companions. "Caldwell's right. There are places around here which will be more to our liking tonight."

Stewart and his group started to leave. But then he turned back to Wend. "Dutchman, there're still a lot of people here and in Sherman Valley who think you played some kind of trick on us with that smoothbore last month. Myself, I figure that you and that other Dutchman, the little man with the spectacles who won all that money, had some scheme going between you. One day we're going to get to the truth. Now you show up here in the company of this savage. It makes me think you ain't one of us. I'm going to keep an eye on you, and you can wager on that."

Stewart turned to Clayton and Caldwell and nodded. Then he and his cronies stalked out of the tavern.

Wend felt the tension start to drain out of him. He looked up at the two men beside the table. "You have my thanks for your help. We had no intention of causing any trouble by coming in here."

Asher Clayton shook his head. "Don't worry. You didn't do anything untoward. Lazarus is hard to understand. There is no better man in the field, leading a company. And he is a good man to share ale with after a hard day's work. But he's never gotten over the events of seven years ago. And he has an unyielding hatred of Indians, which sometimes clouds his judgment. Others in this town have the same feeling, but most of our people understand that the war is over, and that the hostile tribes have moved west."

Caldwell addressed Charlie. "I'm sorry for the problem you had tonight. I know the Conestogas well, and I have no argument with them. So you are welcome here. And I hope you enjoy the rest of your meal."

Charlie nodded, and thanked the tavern keeper, who returned to the counter. The militia captain walked back to his table. Charlie, like Wend, was starting to relax after the confrontation. Suddenly a smile crossed his face. "This is just like the old days as children. We're always in trouble when we get together! The only thing that would make it better is if Arnold was here!"

Wend laughed and dug into his meal. Then he thought of something. "You know, Charlie, I always try to get along with everyone. But now I have people mad at me both here and in Sherman Mill."

"So who's mad at you over where you live?"

Wend told Charlie about Matt Bratton's antipathy over the years and how it had been magnified because of the shooting match.

Charlie thought for a moment. "Well, in Bratton's case, it's clearly envy: Through your success in trade and marksmanship, you've got money and the admiration of a lot of people. Just look at how the men here took to your new rifle."

The talk about Bratton jogged Wend's mind on what Ellen McCartie had said about the waggoner's new endeavors. So he reminded Charlie of their encounter in Carlisle with Kinnear, Fleming, and Grenough and his own conviction that they were involved with illicit trading.

Charlie shook his head and smiled: "Oh, Lord, Wend! Are you still worrying about all that?"

Wend put up his hand. "Listen, now there's more to think about. Last month, an acquaintance told me he saw a meeting in Shippensburg between Grenough and Matt Bratton." He leaned over the table. "And shortly after that, Bratton announced he had a new contract to provide freight service to Fort Bedford."

"And you believe that's related to the illicit activity you think Grenough has organized?"

Wend could see that Charlie was interested. "Yes. Last night, fighting to stay awake during the snowstorm, I thought this all out. The trouble with Bratton's supposed new contract is that he will be away from Sherman Mill for long periods, and I'm certain he could make more money and avoid the hazards of Forbes Road by expanding his freight service in the area between Carlisle and Sherman Valley."

Charlie shook his head. "What makes you so sure of that?"

"Settlement has been rapid, with stores and mills being built; the area definitely needs more service. So the only thing that would be more lucrative for Bratton is working as part of Grenough's scheme. Obviously, Grenough would pay top dollar; far more than could be made by any amount of legitimate freighting. I figure that Bratton and his wagon—or wagons— will move the supplies to the west, and deliver them to the actual traders, making things more efficient where there are good roads, say out as far as the Bedford area. Moreover, the sight of a Conestoga wagon traveling the roads would invite less suspicion than long strings of pack horses being led by traders such as Kinnear and Fleming. So Bratton would pick up a large load of trade materials from one of Grenough's warehouses in Shippensburg or York. And then he would meet at some remote rendezvous with the men who would pack the goods out to the tribal areas. That would also allow Grenough to increase the number of traders he had involved in delivery of goods to the tribes and earn him more money, probably a lot more money."

Charlie shook his head and grinned. "You make out Grenough to be some kind of mastermind. What makes you think he's smart enough to set up an intricate ring like this?"

Wend said, "Years ago, Baird worked as a legitimate trader for Grenough. And Joshua says that Grenough is a genius at organizing and expanding his business. The addition of Bratton's freight service would fit in as a natural element of such an expansion."

Charlie mulled over Wend's words. "Well, it's easy enough to check at least part of Bratton's story. There's only one company which has a contract to freight supplies out to Bedford, and that's Slough & Simon. If Bratton is telling the truth and he's got a legitimate contract, he's working for them. We'll go talk to their local manager and see if they are using him. I just dropped off my goods at their warehouse today and I'm due to get paid tomorrow. Come along and we can make enquiries."

* * *

By the time they had returned to Harris', unhitched the horse and stowed the harness, Wend was beginning to feel tired again. Charlie had the same sleeping arrangement with this inn that he had had in Carlisle, and he pulled out some blankets from his cart and placed them on a pile of straw in the corner of the stable. But Charlie wasn't ready for sleep and prevailed on Wend to have one drink, so they went into the tavern. Rose Jensen, the serving girl, smiled brightly when she saw them enter, and made haste to come to their table. They ordered some hot rum with butter to buffer the cold.

Soon the other customers left and Rose joined them at their table. She and Charlie resumed their flirtatious conversation of earlier in the day. It turned out that the girl was recently arrived from England, and serving out an indenture.

Wend looked at her. She was indeed quite pretty, and he had gained a favorable impression of her intelligence. He asked, "How did it happen that you became an indenture? What did your parents think about it?"

She laughed. "My parents? They were both gone before I was five. We lived in London; Pa was a day laborer and a drunk. He just went off one day and never showed up that night. My Ma never knew whether he got killed somehow or he just decided he was tired of us. Mother lasted only a few months after that; she died of pneumonia. So I ended up in an orphanage. It was a gloomy, damp place. I lived there for more than ten years, and hated every minute."

Charlie asked, "So how did that lead to you coming here?"

"When I turned fifteen, the orphanage started putting pressure on me to find work and a place to live. I couldn't see no prospects in England. My future was being a servant in some rich household or doing an indenture in the colonies. To my mind, there was a lot more chance of something good happening over here, and I liked the thought of traveling. So here I am at this tavern for the next seven years."

As they talked, Wend was struggling to keep awake. Moreover, he could see that he clearly was not part of the conversation. He stood up and looked at Charlie. "When you are ready for bed, why don't you get your blankets and come up to my room for the night? At least it will be warmer than the stable."

Charlie made a show of considering Wend's proposal. "Actually, I'm used to sleeping on the straw and I'll be plenty warm out there. But I appreciate the offer."

Wend looked between his friend and Rose, and realized that Charlie would indeed be having a warm night in the stable.

* * *

Wend woke up hungry. He descended to the common room and tried the tavern's breakfast, finding that Charlie's appraisal of the food quality had been entirely accurate. Rose and the tavern keeper were busy serving an almost full house of travelers, mostly waggoners.

He walked out to the stable to check on the mare, and saw that several freight wagons and a smaller rig were now in the courtyard along with his friend's cart. He found Charlie still asleep in the straw, blankets pulled up to his chin, presumably recovering from a strenuous night.

The mare whinnied at seeing him, and he gave her a grooming, followed by a thorough look at her legs. In a few minutes he determined that the horse's legs were in good shape, and Wend felt he could stop worrying about her ability to carry him back to Sherman Mill after her fall on the river road. Then he foddered her and made sure the stable boy would give the stall a good cleaning.

As he was talking to the boy, several of the inn's overnight guests came in and started to harness their teams. Wend noticed Charlie was stirring in response to the noise, and he went over and sat down on a wooden chest nearby. His friend's eyes opened, and he looked around, somewhat startled until his eyes settled on Wend.

"I hope last night was everything you wanted it to be, Charlie."

Charlie broke into a huge grin. "Absolutely marvelous in every respect; I can now most highly recommend English girls to anyone who might ask."

Wend broke up in laughter. "Charlie, you certainly have become obsessed with feminine companionship. Are all traveling men like you so involved with young tavern girls?"

He expected his friend answer him with a jest. Instead, he saw his face darken and his eyes take on a staring, reflective look. After a long moment he turned to Wend. "I guess it's because I'm getting pressure from the tribal elders to get married. They have been raising the idea more and more over the last year."

Wend was puzzled. "Why is that a problem?"

Charlie looked at Wend with impatience. "Wend, there are less than thirty Conestogas left that we know about. And not all of them even live in our village. There's only one girl who is of marriageable age. So the elders want me to take her as a wife. They see me, and my seed, as the savior of the tribe, at least for this generation. If I and that girl produce enough children, a pure bloodline will continue."

"And you are unhappy with that?"

"Wend, there's no doubt the girl will make a loyal and hard working wife. But, how do I say this kindly? She is built like an ox and seems to have no spirit of fun in her. Quite simply, I can't bear the thought of having to share my life with her." He looked at Wend and grimaced. "Out here on the road, I find all these attractive, high spirited women who make my heart soar, with whom I could make a happy life of my own."

"Charlie, I can see your problem. But why not find a girl you like who will live with you in Conestoga Town. That shouldn't be a problem. It's hard to tell the difference between where you live and any other village around Lancaster. Then you could raise the children as Conestoga's. For God's sake, the other tribes do that all the time."

"If we do that, since there are so few of us, it will be the end of the tribe. The blood will be too diluted. And the elders are afraid that the children won't want to stay around the village and adopt our customs, but will try to go live among the whites. We have too many of our people doing that already. So I am trapped. I feel I must carry out my duty and be the stallion of the Conestogas."

Charlie threw the blankets off, and stood up, pulling his clothes on. "Now you know why I must take my pleasure while I can." His face suddenly showed determination; he gritted his teeth and the arteries on his neck stood out. "But mark this: When I finally do have to marry that girl, I will be true to her, and to our children, and will make them the best life I can. I'll give the Conestoga's a chance to survive."

Wend was suddenly struck by the thought that both he and his friend were mired in circumstances for which there were no easy escape. In his case, the love for a women hundreds of miles away, who didn't even know he was alive and who slept in the arms of the man who had killed his family. For Charlie, it was the fate of husbanding a woman he could never love and the hopeless task of trying to preserve the heritage of a dying culture.

Then a chilling thought ran through his mind. It occurred to him that Rose, enslaved for the next seven years in this dingy tavern, at least could see her way clear to freedom and the ability to chart her own course. He and Charlie, ostensibly free men, were in some sense locked in an invisible prison.

There was a long moment of silence as Charlie finished dressing. Suddenly, the Conestoga had a new thought; his face broke into a crooked grin and he looked over at Wend. "I don't know why we are talking about girls around here. We should be talking about Sherman Mill. There is some girl up there in the tavern who is a legend among waggoners, peddlers, and other traveling men throughout this whole area. Supposedly she has a face so beautiful it will make your heart stop, long black hair, and legs so long she could squeeze you to death with them and you would go to your Maker with a smile on your face."

Wend, lounging on the box with his back against the wall, sat up and stiffened as he realized that his friend was talking about Peggy McCartie. Suddenly he remembered Johnny Donaldson's words at the Indian campsite about Peggy's reputation.

Charlie continued, "And what's more, she is a willing wench who will share her affections for a few coins or the pick of a peddler's merchandise. Now there's a girl after my own heart, at least for an evening." He thought for a moment and then smiled again at Wend. "Maybe we should plan to get together up at your place soon!"

Wend mumbled a non-committal reply, his mind busy. Heretofore, he had perceived of Peggy as a kind of victim, being taken advantage of by Matt Bratton. Now, putting together Johnny and Charlie's comments, the evidence was overwhelming that Peggy was playing as much a double game as her boyfriend. He remembered Peggy's comment the night of Patricia's birthday party, about not wanting to be stuck in Sherman Mill all her life. Clearly, she had made up her mind not to depend solely on Matt Bratton for her passage out of the valley.

Charlie ended Wend's reverie by saying, "Let me get some breakfast, and then we'll pay a visit to Slough & Simon."

* * *

In mid-morning, the two of them stood outside the long warehouse with the sign "Slough & Simon" on the side. Charlie was recounting the money he had just received from the company's local manager. A short conversation had proven that Matt was not associated with the company, either as a contractor or as an employee. In fact, the manager knew Bratton by reputation, and had made it quite clear that the company had no place for a waggoner of his ilk. And indeed, Slough & Simon had the exclusive army contract to provide freight service to Fort Bedford.

"Well, Wend, it appears that Bratton's lying about freighting to Fort Bedford."

"So, now do you begin to believe my story?"

Charlie screwed up his face. "He may have his own reasons for lying. And there's still no real proof that he's working for Grenough in any way, or that Grenough is running an illegal trading scheme."

For a moment, Wend had his doubts. Perhaps Bratton was just giving Peggy the story about Bedford to delay serious discussion of marriage. Or maybe he had a long distance contract to freight to some place besides Bedford; but if that was the case, why would he need to lie about the destination? Another thought arose: Did he have a girl somewhere that he was spending time with, and was simply lying to keep it from Peggy?

But Wend discounted those thoughts almost as soon as they formed in his mind. There were simply too many coincidences. First, Grenough at Larkin's on the same night as Bratton. Then Grenough's meeting with Kinnear and Flemming at the same tavern. Finally, Bratton announcing his need for prolonged absences right after meeting with Grenough at Shippensburg. The pieces of the puzzle were too close to a precise fit to be ignored. Wend told Charlie, "There just seem to be too many related occurrences. I'm not going to forget about this."

Charlie shook his head. "You keep pursuing this conspiracy thing, you're going to get in trouble. Try telling this to a sheriff or magistrate and they're going to laugh you out of their office. And the word of your accusations would inevitably get back to Grenough. My advice would be to drop it!"

CHAPTER 13
The Black Mingo

Late March had arrived, and with it the hint of approaching spring. In the afternoon of a sunny Saturday, Wend was in the lean-to working at the rifling machine, cutting the grooves into a new barrel. The wind was from the west, and the day warmer than normal, so he had rolled up the canvas wind screen on the eastward side of the lean-to, which enabled him to see down the hill into the village. It was the first time he had been able to do that since putting the screens up in November, and the brightness of natural light raised his spirits.

Earlier in the afternoon The Cat had departed on a hunting expedition: just as Wend was starting to think about quitting for the day, the animal returned carrying his prey, a small mouse. The catch was still alive and wiggling futilely in the feline's mouth. The Cat proudly brandished his prize at Wend, then lay down to enjoy the pleasure of terrorizing the doomed animal.

Wend watched as The Cat played, repeatedly letting the mouse loose then catching it as it attempted to escape. Each time it would take the animal in its mouth and shake it, before repeating the process.

Wend shifted his gaze from the floor to the village. Earlier in the day, Bratton's father had been out at his forge, the banging of the hammer audible up in Wend's workshop. But now he had banked the fire, gone inside, and all was quiet. There was some activity at the mill, where two farm wagons were parked, the teams waiting patiently in their harnesses. Undoubtedly the farmers had brought in some field corn from their winter storage to be ground into feed for animals. Hank Marsh and his younger brother were out on the mill-pond dam, adjusting the slats to manage the water flow. The mill's water wheel was turning at a good pace and Wend could see dust floating up out of the mill as the stones ground the grist.

Then Wend caught sight of three riders crossing the ford below the mill-pond, their horses taking great care in the placement of their hooves to avoid stones under the water. Wend's excitement rose as, even at that distance, he recognized that the leading horseman was Joshua Baird. He stood up and walked outside to watch the arrival of the party. The Cat, frustrated that Wend was no longer paying attention to his game with the mouse, quickly dispatched the rodent and ambled out behind Wend to see what was generating so much interest.

As the trio started the climb up the hill to the Carnahan's, Wend was shocked to see that the second rider was a black man; a black man with a scalplock and dressed in Indian garb! He stood transfixed as understanding blossomed in his mind. It was Franklin! Franklin, the Gibsons' man; last seen by traders as a Mingo warrior in the far-off Ohio Country.

Wend looked back at the third rider and was astonished to see that it was a woman; a woman also dressed in Indian clothing. For a second he dared hope that it would be Abigail, but that idea was stillborn when he saw that the woman had long black hair, dark skin, and the angular features of an Indian.

Wend untied the straps of his work apron and tossed it onto the top of the rifling machine. He waved at Baird, who was grinning at him as if enjoying some unspoken joke.

Baird waved back. "Hey, Sprout," he shouted while still twenty yards off. "Look who I ran into on the road between Fort Pitt and Ligonier; a friend of yours wandering around in the bush!"

The travelers pulled up in front of the workshop and Joshua threw down from his horse, making the reins fast to one of the lean-to supports. Reverend Carnahan, who had been working in the church, preparing his sermon for the morrow, came out and joined the group. He greeted Joshua with a quiet handshake.

Franklin broke into a smile. "Well, Master Wend, I came back." His appearance, save for the skin color, was in all respects that of a warrior. His hair was shaved to his scalp, except for the lock in the rear. He wore pewter loops in his ears and nose. A kind of blanket coat covered his torso, over a shirt of coarse red material, which hung to his hips. Tan leggings ran from the hips down to the moccasins.

Wend walked up to Franklin's horse in a state of shock. He looked up at the black man, at a loss for words. Finally he exclaimed, "Lord, Franklin. You surely did. And I'm glad to see you."

Franklin dismounted. "Me, too, Mr. Wend; the last I saw you, you was lying face down on the road by the wagons, covered in blood and missing the back of your scalp. I knew you was a dead man."

"Franklin, I was as close to dead as you can get. But I was saved by the wails of Banshees who pulled me back to life, and by some men in skirts." Wend saw a puzzled look come to Franklin's eyes and put his hand on the black man's shoulder. "It's a joke, Franklin. But there's some truth to it. I'll tell you about it when we have more time."

Joshua helped the woman down from her horse. Seeing her on the ground, it was quickly evident to Wend that she was with child. Her face was pretty and round, with oval brown eyes and a pug nose. Aside from the bloat of pregnancy, she had a small wiry frame. Her eyes darted around with curiosity at the buildings of the Carnahan place.

Joshua quickly said, "This here is Mrs. Franklin. And we better get her inside. She's a right strong woman, but in her condition this has been a rough trip for her." He paused and looked at Paul. "I got to go tell Patricia I brought in some more refugees."

Franklin spoke to his wife in her own language and she looked at Wend with new interest. "I just told her you were Abigail's lover."

Wend heard steps approaching and saw Patricia and Joshua walking rapidly toward them. The Mingo woman looked at them with apprehension until Franklin spoke to her again. Then he turned to Patricia. "Ma'am, her name is Ayika, which means 'Source of Joy' in the Mingo language."

Patricia smiled at Ayika and said, "You poor dear. You must be chilled through, after riding all day. Let's go into the house and get some tea to warm you." The Mingo woman looked at Franklin, who nodded and waved her to go with Patricia.

The four men led the horses to the stable and bedded them down, then carried the saddlebags and clothing into the house. The women were sitting at the table before the fire, Ayika sipping her hot tea while looking uncomfortable in the strange surroundings. Franklin went to her side and put his hand on her shoulder. She relaxed and looked up at him.

Patricia bustled around the kitchen putting some dried meat and bread on plates. She laid one before Ayika and also motioned Franklin and Joshua to sit down and eat. Ayika nibbled at her food, but Wend could see she was hungry, and sensed her restraint was a form of politeness.

"Once she has eaten, we need to get her to bed." Patricia stood by the fireplace, her hands on her hips. "Joshua, you brought them here, so they'll sleep in your room. You and Wend can figure out sleeping arrangements for both of you in his room."

Wend feigned indignation. "Are you joking, Patricia? You know how he snores and snorts at night! Its little sleep I'll be getting as long as he's around here!"

Patricia gave her brother a puzzled look. "That reminds me, what're you doing here now? I didn't expect you back until next fall."

Baird's rascally smile spread across his face. "Wondered when you'd think of that." He looked at Wend and Carnahan. "The truth is, I got the sack from the army. Seems they ran out of money to pay for scouts. Bouquet wasn't happy about it, but said there wasn't anything he could do. The government just keeps cutting back on funding for the army here in the colonies."

"That's how I came across this pair. I was on my way back east, taking a path from Pitt to Ligonier which cuts quite a few miles off the route taken by Forbes Road, and had gone into camp for the night, twenty yards or so off the trail, when I heard a bit of talking from the path. I crawled through the bush to where I could see, and the first thing that comes into sight is this black man dressed like a Mingo. Ayika was following along behind and they were both laughing like somebody had just told a joke."

Baird had finished the food on his plate and he leaned back from the table. "So I stood up, which surprised Mr. and Mrs. Franklin to no end. He started to swing his trade musket around toward me. I knew I had to say something to stop him, so I asked him if his name was Franklin." Joshua and Franklin exchanged grins. "That sure made him pause; he grounded his musket and asked how I knew his name."

Joshua laughed and took a drink from his mug. "So I explained to him that you were alive, that I knew the story of the massacre of your caravan, and that he had been living among the Mingo. Then I invited them to my camp, so I could explain what had happened to you."

Patricia interrupted Joshua's narrative. "You men can talk about this. Right now I need to get Ayika to bed. Franklin, tell her to come with me so I can get her settled and show her where to sleep."

After the women had climbed the stairs, Joshua continued. "So we set up camp together, and over supper Franklin told me his story." He took another drink from his mug and looked over at Franklin. "So why don't you tell Wend and the Reverend what you told me that night."

Franklin looked around and nodded. He started with the aftermath of the massacre.

* * *

The attack had happened so fast that Franklin couldn't react, except to drop the ax in his hand and back up against the side of his wagon. That undoubtedly saved him; the warriors didn't see him as a threat. He stood there while Abigail cried over her father and the Mingoes emerged from their cover. Franklin counted a total of nine in the war party. Meanwhile, the warrior who had clubbed Wend went to his body, quickly pulled out a knife and, with a swift stroke sliced off a piece of his scalp. Abigail, seeing the Indian's action, put her hands over her mouth and screamed Wend's name. Other warriors took the scalps of the remaining dead travelers.

A Mingo came up to Franklin, grabbed him by the collar and pulled him over to a tree. Taking a rope of animal hair from the rucksack hung over his shoulder, he tied the black man to a tree. Then the Indian who had scalped Wend walked over and grabbed Abigail, who tried to hit him, but he caught her arm in his hand and shook her like a child. Then he smacked her in the face with his other hand and dragged her to a tree beside Franklin where he tied her. Another Mingo carried Elise, kicking and crying, over to the trees and secured her near Franklin and Abigail.

Now the Mingoes paused for celebration. Some held up the scalps they had taken, making triumphant whoops. The man who had attacked Wend returned to his motionless body and picked up the rifle from beside him, examining it. Then he showed it off to the others, who stood admiring the beauty of the maple grain and the brass fittings. Franklin would later learn that he was the captain of the Mingo band, and his name was Wolf Claw.

Shortly the Mingoes began plundering the wagons, throwing the contents out on the ground where they pawed through the items, selecting the goods which they planned to take with them. Then Wolf Claw picked out several horses, which were unharnessed and led to the side of the road. The remaining animals were killed where they stood.

Several of the warriors gathered in front of Abigail, laughing and fondling her body. One of them pulled her bonnet off, and her hair fell down about her shoulders. The Indian ran his hands through the strands, intrigued by the golden color. He said something to the others, and they laughed again.

Abigail stood trembling, her jaw muscles standing out as she gritted her teeth. But then Wolf Claw ran up and pushed back the warriors. They argued with him, but he ended the resistance by smacking one of them in the face and the others backed off and went to load the horses with their booty. Wolf Claw turned to Abigail and slowly moved his eyes from her face down to her feet. Then he smiled and gently caressed the girl's cheek with his hand as if to reassure her. After a moment he turned and walked over to where the horses were being loaded for the journey.

Meanwhile, a warrior who had been wounded by Johann's shot came out of the woods and sat against a tree beside the road. The ball had pierced his left shoulder just below the armpit and the wound was bleeding profusely. The arm hung uselessly by his side. Although he suffered quietly, Franklin could see that his whole body was tense and that he was in great pain.

Abigail looked at him and then called out to the Mingoes, repeatedly shouting that she could help the wounded man. After a while Wolf Claw came over to her. Although the rope prevented her from moving her arms, she was able to point at the wounded man with her hand. Very slowly she said, "I can help that man; I can treat his wound."

Wolf Claw cocked his head and Franklin was surprised to hear him speak in halting English. "You... can...help?" He pointed to the injured warrior.

Abigail nodded. Then she motioned for Wolf Claw to free her. "Untie me and I will fix his wound."

Wolf Claw considered for a moment, then reached out and began unraveling the rope. Once free, Abigail went to her wagon. Her medical basket had been thrown down to the ground beside one of the rear wheels, the contents strewn out on the ground. Most of the metal implements had been taken, but, aided by Wolf Claw, she was able to recover most of them from the separate piles of booty.

Abigail knelt beside the hurt Mingo, who with great effort leaned forward and looked up at Wolf Claw inquisitively. The Mingo captain reassured the man, who fell back against the tree and watched Abigail with concern in his eyes. She cleaned out the front of the wound, then checked the man's back, finding that the ball had passed entirely through his body. She cleaned the exit wound and poured some liquid from a bottle into both sides of the wound. The warrior winced when she poured the liquid into his wounds, but soon he began to show less pain and his body began to relax.

Abigail picked up some clothing which had been tossed out by the warriors and tore it into strips. Then she placed padding over the front and rear wounds and wrapped bandages around the man's chest to hold the padding in place. Finally, Abigail took the warrior's left arm, which had been hanging loosely at his side, and gently pulled it up and in front of his torso, where she lashed it in place with strips of fabric.

The entire war party gathered around, fascinated by her actions. Abigail stood up and motioned for them to get the wounded man on his feet. Two warriors helped him up and she adjusted the bandages holding his arm in place. Then she signaled for him to move around.

The Mingo took a few steps, then looked at Wolf Claw and said something which obviously meant that he could travel. Franklin was untied and a kind of noose was thrown around his neck, so that he could be controlled by one of the warriors. Wolf Claw indicated to Abigail that she was to carry her medical basket with her. Meanwhile, another warrior untied Elise and put her on his shoulders. The rest carried plunder or led horses loaded with goods from the wagons.

Wolf Claw pushed the pace as they trekked through the woods, then started to climb a high hill to the west. Soon Franklin saw a large outcropping of rocks near the top and it became clear they were heading in that direction. As they entered the Mingo camp he was shocked to see that there were two rough-looking white men sitting beside a fire, dressed in hunting clothes similar to Wend's. One man wore a heavy beard. Franklin also noticed a string of pack animals tied to a picket line near the camp area.

Wend looked at Baird and Carnahan. "Kinnear and Flemming: Those bastards! God's truth, you were dead on, Joshua. They set the Mingoes upon our caravan. And they stayed around to see the fruits of their treachery!"

Baird looked down at the flames in the hearth. "Franklin, was their evidence of trade goods around the camp?'

"Yes sir, Mr. Joshua. That's why the Mingoes had come east. I learned that later, after I was part of the tribe, but on that trip the traders brought them powder, lead, some trade muskets, steel knives and hatchets."

Franklin continued the tale. That evening, Abigail treated the injured warrior again, taking Franklin to assist her. As they walked over to where the warrior sat against a tree, she quickly whispered to Franklin, "I told Wolf Claw that you were trained to help me. That way maybe they'll keep us together rather than trading us to separate bands."

Franklin watched as she checked the man's wounds. Most of the Mingoes gathered around, watching and making comments. Abigail took out a needle and thread from her basket. "This wound has pretty much stopped bleeding. I'm going to sew up both sides now so the openings will grow together." She worked rapidly in the fading light, stitching the skin together with delicate strokes. She left a small opening at the bottom of the front and back wounds, to allow any fluid to drain. Then, working together, they rewound the man's bandages.

That night the warriors sat around their fire and shared jugs of ale and whiskey they had found in the wagons. The two white men joined their celebration. Only Wolf Claw and one other Mingo, who was sent to the crest of the hill to keep a watch, did not partake in the drinking. Franklin and Abigail had been tied to trees after ministering to the wounded man. Elise sat alongside Abigail and cuddled with her. Periodically she broke out in tears and asked about Mary. Abigail consoled her as best she could.

Within an hour, the Mingo who had been on watch came running back calling to Wolf Claw. All the others stopped and listened. Then Wolf Claw started shouting orders to the warriors.

Shortly, the clean shaven trader came over to Franklin and Abigail. He ignored Franklin. "Well, young miss, the lookout has sighted a large number of campfires down at the bottom of the hill to the westward, right along the road. Out here, that means but one thing; a party of soldiers. So we'll all be breaking camp before dawn. My mate and I will be heading back east and you'll be heading for the Ohio and learning what it means to travel fast with a war party." He laughed, and his laugh seethed with malice. "I wish you the best of luck."

Abigail, ignoring the man's tone, pleaded, "For God's sake, can't you do anything to convince them to let you take us back to the settlements with you? You're a white man: Surely you won't let us be taken away into captivity or torture?"

The man put his hands on his hips and laughed deeply. "Torture? Not likely! Don't you realize that you are as much a part of their booty as anything else they picked up down there? And Wolf Claw has already taken a real shine to you. Even if I wanted to help you, I don't think he'd part with you for anything I got. Best of all, he's grateful to me and my partner for putting him on to your caravan. That'll be something I can use in dealing with this band in the future." With that, the man left, laughing and shaking his head as he walked back to the camp fire.

It was a short night; the Mingoes woke the captives well before dawn. Leaving Elise asleep beside the tree, Abigail and Franklin checked the wounded warrior and adjusted his bandages for travel. Around them the war party was hurrying to make preparations to leave. After finishing with the warrior's treatment, Abigail went back to get Elise and found her gone. Just then Wolf Claw came up and handed both Abigail and Franklin packs made up to carry food and booty from the caravan. Abigail tried to ask about Elise, but Wolf Claw simply ignored her. Then two warriors came and put rope leashes on Franklin and Abigail, and the party started off to the westward.

The never saw Elise again.

For the next week, Wolf Claw set a fast pace as the war party made its way west using well worn paths. Franklin and Abigail were hard pressed to keep up. For the first few nights, Abigail cried in anguish, blaming herself for not keeping Elise with her, so that she might have somehow saved her. Later they learned that Elise had been dispatched because the warriors feared she would be noisy and too much of a burden if the soldiers took up pursuit.

Eventually they came to the Allegheny River and stayed for two nights with Delawares who maintained their village along a creek which emptied into the river. There the Mingoes traded the horses for canoe transportation across the river.

Now, having reached the Ohio Country, the party felt more secure and Wolf Claw set a more leisurely pace for the rest of the journey. Finally they reached the home village of the Mingo band, nestled along the bend of a wide creek. There were several bark covered long houses and some smaller buildings made of logs.

That night the whole village celebrated the success of the expedition. The evening began with Wolf Claw standing in front of a council fire and telling the story of the war party's travels and assault on the caravan. He addressed himself to the three elders while the rest of the village listened intently. Wolf Claw's narration was highly animated, illustrated with gesticulations of his hands. Frequently the listeners shouted and cheered as he spoke. Then he spread his arms wide, as if signaling the end of his story. One of the elders stood and silence spread around the fire. He spoke at some length and finished by extending his hand toward Wolf Claw. The entire gathering cheered again as Wolf Claw stood in front of the fire with his chest puffed-out and pride in his eyes.

Now Wolf Claw pointed at Franklin and Abigail and then conversed with the elders. It was clear their fate was being addressed. Wolf Claw came over and, putting his hand on Abigail's arm, had her come to her feet. He led her in front of the elders and talked at some length, apparently making a supplication. When he had finished, the old men looked back and forth between themselves and nodded together in clear acquiescence. Thus Abigail became Wolf Claw's wife. Then Franklin was brought forward and Wolf Claw again spoke. He pointed at another warrior, who stepped up in front of the fire. The man, whose name was Etchemin, put his hands on Franklin and talked to the elders. Again the old ones conferred among themselves and finally nodded to the warrior. Franklin had become Etchemin's brother, to replace one who had died of smallpox.

Then the head elder conferred the name of Sucki Wematin, or "Black Brother", on Franklin and Abigail became Chitsa Nijlon, which meant "Fair Mistress".

Franklin was initially treated as a child. He worked in the fields with the small boys, under the tutelage of the women, cultivating the corn, squash, and beans. As the months passed he learned the Mingo language and customs. After a little more than a year, as a sign of trust, he was given a bow and taught by Etchemin to make arrows. Then he was drilled on stationary targets, and when judged sufficiently skillful, was allowed to accompany the men on short hunts. On these trips, he learned tracking and the habits of the animals.

Sitting around the campfires on the hunting trips, listening to the talk of the men, Franklin gradually learned the story of the expedition to the east which had culminated in the attack on the caravan. The band had used up its stocks of powder and lead during the raids after the Braddock defeat, and then when the British had driven the French out of western Pennsylvania in 1758, they had lost their source of replenishment for these essential supplies. This situation had led the tribes, including many Mingo bands, to take up the peace path with the English. But this particular band had reasons for not being ready for peace. The most important was that the village had been ravaged by smallpox in recent years, which had reduced their numbers so much that the elders were worried about the ability to survive independently. The idea of having to consolidate with another band was unacceptable. So, over many long council fires, they made the decision to bring in new captives which could be adopted. The easiest method would have been to make war on another band of Indians somewhere in the Ohio Country. But even a small raid would have exhausted their remaining gunpowder. That had left them no choice but to deal with the outlaw traders.

Abigail's life among the Mingo had followed a pattern similar to Franklin's. She worked in the fields with the women, learned to grind meal, clean and cook game, process animal hides and make clothing. She also absorbed the Indian's knowledge of healing qualities of roots and herbs and blended it with her conventional English medical skills. Soon stories of her healing ability began to circulate among the tribal bands and villages of the Ohio Country.

Then, about a year after their adoption, a runner from a nearby Delaware village came into the Mingo town, nearly exhausted. The son of one of the Delaware elders, a lad of about twelve, had been shot by mistake while part of a hunting party. The band's spirit doctor had tried everything he knew, but the boy was dying. The elder had heard of Abigail's skill, and in his desperation was requesting the assistance of the white skinned Mingo woman.

The Mingo elders conferred and finally decided to let Abigail go to the Delaware village. But they sent two warriors with her, fearing some sort of trick from the Delawares. Abigail also requested that Franklin come with her to assist.

Led by the runner, they traveled overnight to reach the Delaware village. They found the boy laying inside a lodge, nearly unconscious and sweating in fever. Abigail immediately had the boy moved outside into the light, but that meant that the whole village gathered around to watch her work. She quickly inspected the wound, which was in the right side of the boy's chest. Franklin noticed the sheen of perspiration on her face, that her lips were pursed tightly, and that her hand was shaking slightly as she selected items from the bags they had used to bring her tools and supplies.

She whispered to Franklin in English, "I've never worked on anything this serious; the ball is lodged in muscle tissue in his chest. I'll have to dig it out without doing too much damage to the tissue around it, or the top of his lung. And the wound has already started to mortify; it will have to be cleaned out and sewn up. If I do too much damage in digging out the ball, he may bleed to death before we can stop it." She moved her eyes circumspectly around the watching Delawares, then at the boy's father, and swallowed hard. "If I don't do this right, the boy may die right here. If that happens, we may be in trouble, Franklin."

But in the end she did it with her usual competence, extracting the ball, cleaning out the damaged area, and sewing the wound with deft strokes. At first, she was sweating heavily; but as the operation progressed, she gained in confidence. While she worked, Franklin and another warrior held the boy who suffered the excruciating pain stoically.

Two days later, the boy's body temperature had returned to normal and he was sitting up and eating. The Delaware elder presented Abigail with gifts and gave the Mingo group presents for their village elders. And soon tales were told and repeated, at village and hunting party fires from the Allegheny to the Muskingham, of the golden haired Mingo doctor. And so Abigail became known as "Orenda, The Women with Magic Hands", a near mythical figure in the lore of the tribes.

Patricia had come down the stairs and rejoined the group shortly after Franklin had started his narrative. She had listened intently to his words about Abigail. Now she asked, "Franklin, has Abigail had children?"

Franklin cast his eyes at the fire, reflected for a moment, then looked nervously over at Wend as he answered Patricia. "Yes, ma'am; she had two children before I left. A man child came in the first year, a little while before she went to treat the Delaware elder's son. And then a girl was born in the second year. Both were healthy, strong children. And she carried and birthed them well, going back to work within a day after each was born."

Wend felt his jaw muscles tighten and a knot form in his stomach. He had, of course understood that Abigail was sleeping with a Mingo; he had inured himself to that reality as the price of her survival. And logically, he had realized that children would be the result of such a liaison. But now the confirmation hit him hard.

Paul Carnahan had been quietly smoking his pipe while Franklin talked. Now he had a question. "How was it that you took a Mingo wife and what made you decide to leave the village?"

"Well, Reverend, it wasn't so much that I took a wife as the elders decided I needed one."

After more than two years in the village, the elders decided it was time for Franklin to marry. Etchemin had taught Franklin the daily skills needed of a Mingo. He had become an accomplished hunter, trusted to take trips lasting several days to find and kill game using his bow. Finally he was given tentative warrior status. Etchemin and Wolf Claw had taken pleasure in presenting him with an ancient trade musket. It was a mark of trust and Franklin had been touched by their acceptance of him.

It was the elders who selected Ayika for him. She had just emerged from childhood and was a cheerful, hard-working girl, popular with the other women. The ceremony was brief, and Ayika's father gave Franklin a small dowry which helped the couple set up housekeeping.

During the period since the trip on which Abigail and Franklin had been captured, the band had been looking for another village with which to make war and secure captives. They had decided that their potential enemies must reside outside the Ohio Country; they didn't want to start a feud with a nearby village. So Wolf Claw, accompanied by other warriors, had engaged in a series of scouting trips to locate a distant village or villages, which could be the source of new blood for the band.

Eventually, they located a series of prosperous Cherokee towns many days journey to the southward. The Cherokees were a good target, since they had often warred with tribes of the Ohio Country and had sided with the British during the French War. Wolf Claw developed a plan to raid the villages during their fall hunting season. At that time most of the men would be on extended trips, catching game for drying and processing into winter food. The Mingoes' prime target would be young boys and girls.

Franklin remained behind in the village as the only able bodied man besides the elders. This was a great responsibility which made him proud, for he was to provide game and a measure of protection for the village while the war party was away.

Wolf Claw and his party were gone for more than a month. Their trip was a total success, for without the loss of any of their company, they returned with two young boys and one female captive. But they had also come back with a captured warrior, and it was the fate of this man which led to Franklin's decision to escape.

Franklin had learned that the treatment of warrior captives was just another phase of warfare for the Indians. An Indian warrior who was captured knew that he would be tortured, ultimately put to death, and that the process would be a final test of his manhood, as important as how well he had performed in battle.

On the night that the band returned, the captured warrior was tested. First he was forced to run the gauntlet. Every individual had clubs or sticks and beat the warrior unmercifully as he proceeded through the lines. He tried to move as fast as he could, but people along the way grabbed him and held him so that more blows could be administered. Franklin had to participate, but he contrived to miss the man as he came past. He noticed that Abigail was in the line with the other women, but he could see a look of distaste on her face.

After the gauntlet, the bloodied warrior was tied to a tall stake, and a fire built close to him, so that he was essentially being broiled alive. He started singing his death song to give himself courage. Then men and woman took turns torturing him. Some simply beat him with clubs; others drove burning sticks into various parts of his body. Wolf Claw took a bayonet, captured long ago on the Braddock battlefield, and heated it in the flames. When its tip glowed, he flaunted it in front of the warrior's face, then drove the point into different areas of his body. Finally, the Mingo men built the fire up around the warrior's feet so that the flames licked up his body, to his great agony. For a short time he endured with stoicism, but as the flames enveloped him, he began to scream with agony. The smell of burned meat permeated the air. Franklin gritted his teeth and forced himself to watch, for he understood that he could not be seen to be revolted by the proceedings.

His fellow Mingoes, both men and women, sat watching with satisfaction in their eyes. When the warrior finally expired, they began to critique how well he had endured the torture, talking about what he had done well, and where he could have shown more courage. But overall, they were satisfied that he had died well.

Franklin was profoundly disturbed by the torture session. He had come to like both the Mingo people and their way of life. They had treated him generously, sharing their food, companionship, and possessions. They had provided him with a wife, of whom he had become enamored. Moreover, life in the Mingo band had given him the personal freedom he could never have in the colonies.

But seeing the same people who had treated him so kindly engage in such cruelty and consider it sport had filled him with a disgust he could not banish, even after several days. He realized that sooner or later he would be included in a war party and then expected to participate fully in a torture session such as he had just witnessed. It was also clear that he could end up on the receiving end if he were captured.

Three days after the Cherokee warrior had been killed Franklin went to see Abigail. She was working alone by a kettle over a fire. The band had killed a bear and she was rending the animal's fat into oil. Strips of fat had been cut from the bear's carcass and laid on a cloth by the fire, and Abigail was slicing the strips into smaller pieces, which she then tossed into the kettle. The smell from the boiling oil was barely tolerable. Her face was red from the heat of the fire and the hot oil; her hands were covered with grease from the bear fat. She bore little semblance to the girl who had been his elegant mistress in Philadelphia.

Franklin told her about his disgust at the brutal killing of the enemy warrior and his fears of being made to fully participate in the future. Then he confided that he was considering leaving and about the plans he had started to make. He would begin by drying small portions of the meat obtained through hunting and secreting that away in a cache in a nearby tree. Franklin would also husband his gunpowder and lead. Then when he was ready, he would ostensibly leave for a long hunting trip, and it would be several days before the band would understand the reality of his absence.

Abigail agreed with his feelings about torture and told him she would help him make his preparations. Franklin asked her if she wanted him to try to think of a way for both of them to leave. She shook her head, and simply said that his only hope of success was the number of days he would gain by using the hunting trip stratagem, and that he obviously couldn't take her along on a supposed trip of that nature.

Although he had developed affection for Ayika, Franklin had no expectation of taking her with him. He was afraid to tell her about his plans, for fear she would alert the elders. Moreover, he believed she would be happier among her own people and knew that once they realized he was gone forever, the elders would arrange another match for Ayika.

But Ayika discovered his intentions. He had been hiding his supplies in a hollow log not far from the village and periodically making trips there to drop off items he planned to take with him. One day, Ayika followed him, not because she suspected him, but in the desire for lovemaking. She caught up with him just as he was depositing some items. She immediately understood his intentions. To Franklin's surprise, she didn't run off to inform the band, but instead tears came to her eyes. She asked him what she had done that he wasn't satisfied with her as his wife.

Franklin put his arms around Ayika and assured her that it was not any unhappiness with her that led him to want to leave, but that he wanted to return to his own people. That's when Ayika told him she was carrying his child. And she also told him that if he was leaving, she was going with him. Franklin flushed with happiness at Ayika's words, but then he realized his entire plan for escaping would have to be revised. Obviously, the hunting trip stratagem was out, because Ayika's going with him would lead to suspicion.

In the end, chance played into their hands. The elders, Wolf Claw, and several of the warriors left to attend a council fire called by a Delaware chief, and the rest of the band's men went on a hunting trip. Franklin contrived to stay behind as the protector of the village. That provided their opening. One morning he left camp, ostensibly for hunting in the local area, but actually to gather up his cache of supplies. Ayika slipped out of the village later in the day, meeting him at a pre-arranged spot.

Franklin knew that they would be missed by the evening. So instead of heading directly eastward along the most likely path, they hurried as far north as they could get by dusk, carefully masking their trail, and counting on the belief that any search for them would be directly to the east of the village. They spent the first night huddled together for warmth, not daring to light a fire. The next day, they cut a trail which Franklin could see would take them eastward, and they began their trek to Pennsylvania.

Three days after leaving the Mingo village, they reached the banks of the Allegheny. Now Franklin realized he had no alternative but to seek assistance at some village, in order to cross the river.

But getting across river proved far easier than Franklin had expected. They found a town of Delawares where the trail intersected the river, and it turned out that the villagers were quite accustomed to ferrying traveling parties in their canoes. Franklin arranged their passage by bartering some of his small supply of gunpowder. The Delaware canoe man told them that instead of just crossing the river, he could get them to a place where they would find a better path to go eastward.

Joshua held up his hand in signal for Franklin to pause in his story. "The place they were delivered to by canoe was Colonel Clapham's trading post on the Yioghiogheny, a long day's ride from Pitt. He's got a right nice place there, and there are some other settlers who have made their farms in the area. And as Franklin found out, it's a real popular place for Indians to come for trading or to camp when they are traveling the paths. There's also a lot of travel between Clapham's and Fort Pitt. Bouquet, Captain Ecuyer, the commandant at Pitt, and Clapham are good friends; they exchange letters and visits all the time."

Baird looked around at the listeners. "That's how we got word that a Black Mingo had been at the post. I had just been let go, and was getting ready to travel, when a post rider came in from Clapham's and mentioned in the headquarters that he had seen a black warrior at the trading post. It happened that I was in the office, talking with Captain Ecuyer's adjutant, who wanted me to carry some dispatches east."

Wend thought for a moment. "So you weren't that surprised at seeing Franklin on the trail?"

"Well Sprout, as soon as I heard about the Black Mingo, I figured it was Franklin. And I speculated that he might be making an escape. It made no sense that the Mingoes would let him come so far east on his own, to a place where he would likely be seen by white men. So I determined to keep my eye open for him on the trip back to the settlements. Truth be told, I thought I might catch up with him long 'bout Ligonier, 'cause I figured he would have started east before me."

"But I thought you said Franklin and Ayika actually caught up with you?" Carnahan asked.

"That's the truth; they were behind me because they had stayed around the post for a couple of days." Joshua waved at Franklin to fill in the listeners.

"When we landed at the trading post, I planned to move on fast. But Ayika wanted to see what was in the trading post. She had never been to a store before. So we decided to stay there for the night. There weren't any other parties of Indians at the post, so I figured I could take the chance. Besides, we had already been seen by the Delawares in the village and by whites at the post."

"So we made camp in the woods where I could see any canoe landing from the river. And then we went to see the trading post. We had several beaver pelts that I had brought along to trade for items we might need along the trail." Franklin paused, as he reflected on their visit to the trading store. "You should have seen Ayika's eyes light up! She saw many things new to her. So I traded a pelt for some jewelry she liked. And I used two others to get some dried food I knew we would need to augment what I could catch along the trail."

That night they slept comfortably for the first time since they had left the Mingo village. Without fear of pursuers, they were able to make a warm fire and cook a hot meal. But the next morning Ayika could not travel. She had a bad case of the sickness women get when they are with child. Moreover, Franklin realized she was exhausted from hard travel. So they stayed another night in their camp.

"So that's why we came up on Mr. Joshua from behind. We thought we was in the clear, and weren't worrying like we had been the whole time before we got to the Allegheny." He paused and looked around at all the listeners. "Then this white man jumps up from behind a bush with a rifle in his hands. I didn't know what to think. Then he looks at me for a moment, and says 'Hello, Franklin, I'm a friend of Wend Eckert."

"Mr. Wend, I stood there frozen like ice. Weren't anyone had called me Franklin for years. And I recognized your name right away, but knew that you were long in your grave. Then I figured that anyone who knew my English name and could connect me to you must have some story to tell me. So we agreed to join him in his camp. And there Mr. Joshua told me how you survived."

"We had a long talk that night," Joshua told the listeners. "But as Franklin talked, it became clear to me that he had no plan beyond getting back to the settlements. Most people who escape can go back to their family or at least the place they used to live. But Franklin and Ayika had no place to go and the further east they traveled the more questions people were going to ask. That's when I put it to him that he better come with me here to Sherman Mill. I thought we could shelter them, at least till they could figure out where they were going to live."

"So the next day we put Ayika up on my horse and we walked till we got to Byerly's place at Bushy Run. He's a former Sergeant in the 60th who runs a way-station between Ligonier and Fort Pitt. The army uses it as a camp where wagon convoys and troop detachments can stop over while traveling. We stayed there one night, and went on to Ligonier the next day. That's where I bought horses for Mr. and Mrs. Franklin and we traveled in style from then on."

Joshua raised an eye and looked at Wend. "Sprout, those horses took up most of my last pay from the army; I figured you'd spring for them since the main purpose of bringing Franklin back here was to give you the word on your Mingo princess."

Wend laughed. "It's all right Joshua, I'll be glad to pay for the horses. I can make it up by selling them. At least they're in better shape than the nags you bought for the tool wagon down on the Conococheague back in 1759. I practically had to pay to get rid of that team."

Meanwhile, Carnahan had a frown on his face. "Well, I hate to say it, but we've got a real problem now."

Wend was puzzled. "What do you mean by that?"

"We need to deal with Franklin's status now that he's back in the colony proper." The Reverend looked around the table. "In the eyes of the law, Wend, Franklin is still a slave."

Wend was shocked. "But he has no master! His owner was killed on Forbes Road. The only one who has any right to him is Abigail, and I know she would want him to be free."

"I'm not a lawyer, but it seems to me that Franklin is part of Magistrate Gibson's estate. So, any other relative of Gibson might have a right to his ownership. And if there are no relatives, the colony could take ownership of the possessions in the estate." Carnahan put his hand back up to his chin. "Also, if the estate had debts that are unpaid, Franklin could be sold to satisfy those obligations."

Wend was aghast; he immediately remembered Abigail's story about the reason that the Gibsons had been sent to Fort Pitt. Clearly, Magistrate Gibson's old law partners might be able to seize control of Franklin to satisfy some of the debt that Gibson had left behind! "But we can't let Franklin be sold back into slavery after all he's been through!"

Carnahan didn't say anything for a long minute. "Well, I don't know the law. But John Elder has spent a lot of time working with the government. He has contacts in Philadelphia. Let me write to him and explain our problem. Maybe he can make discreet enquiries on what Franklin's status would be and what we can do to keep him from being taken back into bondage."

Franklin jumped up and looked around at the other four people. "You been awful kind to us, and I'm glad to have been able to see Mr. Wend again and tell him about what happened."

A determined look came over his face. "But I ain't going back to bein' a slave again, no matter what! No Sir! So Ayika and I will leave tomorrow. We'll find some place where there's nobody claiming the land and make us our own home. At least the Mingoes taught me how to live in the forest."

Patricia looked at Paul, then at Franklin. "You and Ayika don't need to go anywhere. You can stay right here on the farm. Paul, there's no reason we can't raise a cabin right here close to our house. It wouldn't have to be big. And look how many acres we have that are cleared and could be farmed, but are laying fallow 'cause you spend so much time at the school and church. That would provide work for Franklin. If he were raising grain, vegetables and beans, we wouldn't have to take so much charity from the congregation. And over time, with extra hands around here, we could clear more of our land for farming. I've been after you to do it for years."

Paul Carnahan listened to the determined tone of his wife's voice, and realized it was a done deal. He looked at the other men. "Well, we do have some logs already cut which have been lying in a pile for a couple of years. That would give us material to get started, while we fell the rest of what we need. Tomorrow is the Sabbath, and we have services, but on Monday we could stake out the cabin and get started. And I'll write a letter to John Elder about Franklin after church tomorrow."

Wend smiled his thanks to Patricia. "That makes a lot of sense, Franklin. There's no need for you to go away, when there's plenty for you to do here and you can earn a living. And Patricia will be here to help Ayika with the baby when the time comes."

CHAPTER 14

Flames on the Border

The month of June 1763 came in mild and beautiful. The weather of April and May had also been favorable and the farmers of Sherman Valley had gotten an early start on their plowing and planting. By early May the fields were all showing green with young plants reaching upwards toward the sun and waving in the wind. As the spring season advanced, a positive feeling spread through the valley that the year's harvest would prove to be memorable.

Franklin had plowed and planted the Carnahan's cleared fields and had started to clear more of their land for future planting. Ayika's increasingly visible pregnancy hadn't kept her from putting in a garden for beans and squash near their cabin. Wend was surprised how much work she did in her condition.

Tom Marsh's mill was doing a great business as farmers brought in the last of the corn and grain which had been husbanded through the winter to be made into feed and flour.

Early on a bright Saturday morning, the air fresh and still in the absence of any wind, Wend stepped out of the Carnahan's house on his way across the wagon track to his workshop. He was carrying a mug of hot tea and a bowl of milk for The Cat. The birds were busily going about their business and chirping about it noisily. He was starting early because he had a lot of repair work that he wanted to finish before beginning assembly of a new rifle for Carlisle.

He looked over at Franklin's cabin and saw smoke rising straight up in the still air from the chimney. But then he saw something which made him pause. In the distance, beyond the smoke from the cabin, beyond the ridge, was another rising pillar of smoke. It became more dense as he watched, changing from a gray haze to a distinct black. The only farmstead in that direction was the Donaldson's and Wend wondered if they were burning brush from cleared land.

He turned back to the house and opened the door. Patricia was working at the fireplace; Baird and Carnahan were sitting at the table with their morning tea before them and their pipes in their hands. "Hey, come on out and take a look to the west. It appears that the Donaldsons' are burning something." The two ambled out into the sunlight. Wend looked at Joshua. "You think they're clearing land?"

Baird said nothing for a moment. He and Carnahan exchanged glances, then the scout said calmly, "It's too focused to be a burning field. Wend, saddle horses for all of us, including Franklin. Then get your rifle and hunting gear. We're going to take a ride up the wagon track. And hurry."

In that instant Wend understood. Immediately the two older men plunged back into the house to collect their arms. Wend ran over to the cabin and knocked on the door, which was immediately opened by Franklin. "Look out to the west, Franklin!" He was unable to keep the rising excitement out of his voice. As the black man looked at the smoke, Wend said, "We're riding to see what's happening. Help me saddle the horses and then we'll get rifles out of my shop."

In a few minutes, Wend had the four horses saddled and hitched to the fence in front of the stable. Franklin was running from the shop with two rifles, powder horns, and hunting pouches carrying balls. Patricia and Ayika were standing in front of the house looking at the smoke.

Reverend Carnahan came running out of the door carrying a rifle. "Patricia, harness the team, then you and Ayika take the wagon over to the fort with supplies for a couple of days."

He motioned to Wend. "Ride down to the mill and get Marsh to send one of his boys to ring the church bell and warn the valley while we ride to the Donaldsons' place. Tell Tom to gather everyone in Robinson's Fort, muster as much of the militia as he can, and we'll meet them back there when we find out what's happening."

Wend mounted the mare and urged her down the hill. The villagers had also seen the smoke. McCartie and his brood were standing beside the tavern and Marsh himself was standing out in the road, looking to the westward. Wend pulled up the mare beside the miller. "Tom, the Reverend says we'll go see what's happening up the wagon track. Have one of your boys come up and ring the bell to call out the militia. Get everyone over to Fort Robinson, ready for a couple of days, and we'll meet you there." Marsh nodded and shouted toward the mill for Hank to come out. Wend pivoted the mare and trotted back up the hill. Half way up he looked back and saw Hank Marsh, still dressed in a flour covered apron, running up the hill behind him.

Wend would always remember that ride up the wagon track; the sound of the four horses' hooves pounding at the gallop, no one saying anything, the only other noise the banging and clanking of their gear. Behind them the bell peeled its alarm, the sound diminishing as they rode further to the west. A cold knot grew in his stomach from fear of what they would find at the Donaldson farm. All the while the smoke pillar loomed in front of them, rising for a great height straight up in a solid column, but finally dispersing at the very top.

Then suddenly Baird, who had the lead, raised his hand and motioned for them all to stop. They pulled up and in the ensuing silence he cupped his hand to his right ear. "You hear that? Shots! I hear shots! Off to the right— over the ridge."

Carnahan nodded. "Yeah, I hear them. It's got to be the McClay place; it's opposite here over the hill."

The scout nodded. "We'll go over the ridge; it's shorter than trying to take the road around. Ride the horses up as far as we can, then come down on the farm dismounted. Let's go!"

He led them about seventy-five yards further along the track, then turned his horse up a game trail which Wend was familiar with from hunting. For the next ten minutes they forced the horses upward through the trees and underbrush, crouching in their saddles to avoid branches. Finally, the path died out near the top of the ridge. At any rate, the horses were becoming tired and making a lot of noise as they crashed through the bush. Baird signaled for them to dismount and they hitched their mounts to trees. Then the scout led them at a fast lope through the woods, over the top of the ridge and down the other side.

As they ran, their breath became labored and they heard more scattering shots from the direction of the McClays'.

When the men reached the bottom of the ridge, Wend saw that there was another small hill in front of them and that the McClay place was on the other side. Joshua led them almost to the top of the small hill and then gave hand signals for them to stop and lay down. He slowly crawled to the top and looked beyond. They heard another shot ring out. Baird turned and put his finger to his mouth to signal for them to be quiet. Then he waved them to come forward.

The other three men crept up the slope. Wend reached the crest and looked down on a vivid panorama like a painting in front of him. Three warriors, painted in black, red, and white, were spaced out around the farmyard, aiming their guns at the house. A fourth was behind a wood pile, his musket and a bow lying on the ground beside him, working at something on the ground. Suddenly Wend realized he was kindling a fire. The McClays were obviously forted up inside and the war party was aiming to burn them out. Periodically one of the warriors would fire a shot at the windows of the house to keep the defenders down. As the four men watched, the warrior beside the wood pile fired his flintlock to start the fire, and he was successful, for Wend shortly saw smoke emanating from the kindling, followed by visible flames.

Wend pulled the cock back on his lock and flipped the sett trigger. He brought his firearm to the ready and aimed at the warrior making the fire. Suddenly Baird reached over and pushed the barrel of Wend's rifle down. "Sprout, the Reverend will do the shooting."

Wend, astonished, whispered, "But I'm the best shot in the county . . ."

Baird quieted him. "Hush; you ain't never killed a man, Sprout."

A second after he spoke, Paul Carnahan's rifle spouted flame from the muzzle, followed almost instantly by the report. The warrior farthest from their position crumpled noiselessly.

Baird grabbed Carnahan's rifle and gave him his own. Then he took Wend's rifle and shoved the Reverend's empty gun into his hands. "Load, Sprout, fast as you can."

Just as Joshua finished speaking, Carnahan's second shot banged out and the next Indian in line fell. Carnahan and Baird again exchanged rifles, and now the scout took Franklin's rifle and gave him the empty to load.

But before he could finish handing the empty rifle to Franklin, Carnahan's third shot rang out. Now three warriors were on the ground, all lying absolutely still.

The final warrior, the one who had been making the fire, looked around, suddenly aware of what had happened. Wend could see a look of panic in his face. But it was short lived. For almost instantly another shot rang out, the Indian's face dissolved in a spray of blood, and he fell lifeless beside the fire.

Baird used the rifle in his hands to help himself to his feet and surveyed the farmyard, "Yep, that does it. That's the lot, at least right here." He sauntered down the hill, followed closely by Carnahan.

Wend had finished loading Carnahan's rifle, and he slid the ramrod back into its finials. He stood up and moved down the hill. Franklin also finished his reloading and then followed.

Joshua pounded on the McClay's front door, with Paul standing beside him. "Hey, Frank, it's all over! You can come out!"

Wend heard the scraping noise of a bolt being pulled back and then the window shutter by the front door opened a fraction. Joshua shouted again, "Frank, Sarah, its safe! Open up!"

The window opened further and Wend could see the face of Frank McClay cautiously peering out. From inside he heard the words, in a woman's voice, "Praise God, it's the Reverend and Joshua."

The door opened and Baird and Carnahan stepped inside to see if everyone was all right. Wend went to confirm that the warriors were indeed dead. First he walked to the one who had been making the fire. He was shot through the front of his head, the eyes and nose almost unidentifiable. Wend used a stick to scatter the fire embers.

The second man was lying spread-eagled on the ground beside a shed, with a pool of blood around the upper part of his body. Like the fire maker, he had been hit in the head. There was a gaping hole in the side of his temple.

The third warrior had been hit in the neck, right below the jaw. The ball had sliced open his throat and arteries as if a great hunting knife had been pulled from ear to ear across his throat, essentially decapitating him. The warrior's eyes were open and he had a look of great surprise frozen on his face.

The final Indian, who was the first who had been shot, lay in a heap behind a low bush. Carnahan's ball had taken him just forward of the right ear and passed entirely through his head. The left side, where the ball had exited, was a mass of mush.

Franklin had been walking along behind Wend, and he came up and joined Wend as he stared down at the warrior. "Shawnee," Franklin said, "Kispokos from the Deer Clan, Mr. Wend. The Kispokos consider themselves the best scouts and warriors in the tribe."

Joshua walked up. "The McClay's are all right, but pretty shook up. Sarah is beside herself, almost out of her senses, and Carnahan is sitting with her to try to calm her down." Joshua looked down at the warrior at their feet. "I make them out to be Shawnee."

Wend nodded, "That's what Franklin said." He paused for a moment, considering his words. "Four warriors, three shot through the head and one through the neck, hit by off-hand shots in the space of about twenty seconds.

Joshua, is there something you maybe want to tell me about Reverend Carnahan?"

"I expect you ought to ask him that question, Wend. It's up to him to decide what he wants to tell you."

Suddenly a voice shouted, "Wend, Wend!" Elizabeth was coming up to him at a near run. With great drama, she threw her arms around his neck and nuzzled her head against him in a great hug, the weight of her against his body. "I was so terrified Wend. But I knew you would come. I knew it!"

The girl burst into tears and Wend held her, feeling her body shake with her sobs and the wetness from her eyes run over his face. He felt embarrassed as the other two men looked on, a wry smile on Joshua's face.

"Well, Sprout, when you get finished smooching the girl, you and me and Franklin are going to finish that ride up to the Donaldsons' place. The Reverend will take the McClay's down to the fort and tell everyone what's going on."

The scout and Franklin walked away. Joshua stooped to examine each of the dead Indians in turn.

After a few more minutes Elizabeth calmed down and Wend led her back to the cabin. "You've got to help your mother get some things packed, Elizabeth. Reverend Carnahan will escort your family to the stockade. I'll see you later down at Robinson's Fort."

She looked at him and nodded her understanding, then put her arm around his neck and gave him a long kiss while at the same time making sure her bosom pressed tightly against Wend's chest. "I'm all right now. You be careful." Then she walked back into the house in a way calculated to keep Wend's attention. Wend's eyes followed, and through the door he could see Ezra, the younger boy, gathering items into a bag, while Carnahan leaned over Sarah who sat on a chair in front of the hearth, still shaking. Frank McClay sat at the end of the dining table, looking like a man in shock, his hands to his head.

Wend rejoined Joshua and Franklin and the three ran as best they could back up the high ridge, crossing the crest to where the horses were tied. They mounted and started back down to the wagon track, with Franklin leading Carnahan's horse.

Once down to the wagon road they resumed their gallop. The column of smoke was now thinner and had turned from black to gray, as if the fire was running out of fuel. Joshua pulled them up a quarter mile from the Donaldson farmstead, where they dismounted. "We'll go on foot, quietly as we can. But I don't think it will make any difference. Whatever happened at the Donaldson's is all over now."

Joshua was right. They crept up on the farmyard to find the barn and house in ashes. The barn was nothing but smoldering debris, but flames still crackled at the house and that was now the major source of smoke.

They found Will Donaldson laying by the open gate to the fenced meadow. He had obviously just let the cattle out of the barn when the war party struck. He had been hit in the back with an arrow and must have still been alive after he fell face down on the ground, for the side of his head had been crushed by the blow of a war club. A great circle of his hair had been cut from the top of his head.

The three men walked over to the house. The front and side walls had collapsed, leaving only the rear standing. The smell of wood smoke and burned meat assaulted their noses. Joshua pointed at two completely charred bodies visible in the house. Both were women. One lay on her back, with her blackened arms and legs bent into a fetal position. Most of the flesh had been burnt off the body and the hands and feet had the look of a bird's claws. The other body was barely visible under a pile of still burning debris, but identifiable as a female by the remnants of a dress. Baird said quietly, "Amy and Paula, looks like."

Then Wend saw Johnny. He was lying halfway out of what had been the doorway. Beside him lay the remains of the old musket, its stock consumed by the fire. The boy's body was burned black up to his chest, the legs contorted and shriveled into unnatural shapes by the flames, his back arched like the curve of a bow. His eyes were wide open and his face was frozen into the same look of combined terror and anger that Wend had seen for an instant on his father's countenance in the last moments on Forbes Road. The stench of burned flesh was overwhelming.

Wend felt nausea sweeping over him. He dropped his rifle and fell to his hands and knees beside the grotesque, unspeakable thing that had been his friend's body. Then he threw up his breakfast and everything else in his stomach. When that was gone, he continued to gag and heave, nothing coming up. Finally the heaves abated. He reached up to his face and wiped away the gross mess around his mouth, the taste of it making him want to throw up again. He looked up at Joshua, who stood by his side, his rifle butt grounded in front of him.

"Yeah, I did that too, the first time I saw something like this."

Baird looked around the house. "I don't see any sign of the younger kids." He walked around to what had been the back yard of the house. There was a patch of woods between the house and a small stream which fed into Sherman Creek. He cupped his hands and started to shout. "Charles! Margaret! Charles, Margaret! It's Joshua Baird! Joshua and Wend! Come on out!"

He continued shouting for a few minutes. Finally, he stopped and shook his head. "Well, maybe they are in the wreckage of the house after all—there's sure a lot of debris. We'll have to let it cool down for a few days and then sort through it to find them."

Meanwhile Franklin had been inspecting the yard between the house and the barn. Wend watched as he walked toward the woods near the barn, his eyes down at the ground. Then he disappeared into the trees. In a few moments he came out and motioned to Joshua.

Joshua followed Franklin back into the bushes and then called out to Wend, "Hey, Sprout, you may want to come here and see this!"

Wend's stomach was starting to return to normal. But he had no heart to see any more of the family dead. And at that moment he didn't care what Joshua and Franklin thought of him. "If that's the children, I'll stay here."

He heard Joshua laughing and mentally damned him for it. "Sprout, it ain't the children and you won't want to miss this."

Wend swore, embarrassed at his own squeamishness and pissed off at Joshua's seeming nonchalance and coarseness. He grabbed his rifle and used it to help himself get to his feet. Reluctantly he walked to where the other two stood looking down at something on the ground. There, sitting with his back against a tree, was a dead Shawnee warrior. He had a gunshot wound square in the middle of his chest. Blood coved the whole of his torso below the wound. His lifeless eyes stared off into the distance.

Baird pointed at the body. "Johnny sure did a job on this one before they got him."

Franklin put a hand on Wend's shoulder and pointed with the other to indicate scrape marks and traces of blood on the ground. "I 'spect he got shot out there by the barn, and either crawled back in here to die, or others dragged him out of the way."

Suddenly, Franklin cocked his head. "Mr. Joshua, I heard something. Back toward the cabin." He raised his rifle and cautiously moved back to the edge of the trees, staring toward the burning house. Then he lowered the rifle, waved Joshua to follow, and stepped out into the cleared farmyard.

Wend and Joshua followed, to see the two Donaldson children holding hands and looking at the remains of the house. Charles, the six-year old stood silent and motionless, his mouth open. But little Margaret, still dressed in her night clothes, was sobbing uncontrollably as she stared down at what had been Johnny.

They led the children away from the cabin. Wend sat down on the ground with Margaret on his lap and was eventually able to calm her down. It took a while, but they were able to draw out as much of the story as the children knew. Johnny had been out in the yard when the Indians attacked and had seen his father assaulted by the war party. He had come running into the house, shouting a warning and grabbing his musket. Then he crouched in the door, firing at the Indians and making them take cover.

His action had gained enough time for Amy to grab the family's old smoothbore and drop the two children out the back window, where they ran down to the creek and hid under bushes along the bank. From their refuge, the children had heard a few more shots and then had seen the flames rising from the building. They had lain under cover all morning until they heard Joshua's shouts. At first they had remained too scared to come out, but after a few moments Charles had cautiously led Margaret to the house.

After getting the children's story, Joshua put Wend and Franklin to work. They had no tools and no time for burying, so they laid Will's and Johnny's bodies beside the wood stack and piled firewood over them to keep the varmints at bay. With the house still burning, the remains of the women had to be left until later, when all the bodies could be properly laid to rest. At any rate, there was not enough of the charred bodies left to attract predators.

After they had finished piling wood over the two men's remains, Joshua sat down on the ground beside Charles and Margaret and lit his pipe. Wend, suddenly feeling drained, also sat down, while Franklin settled down against a tree, his rifle cradled in his arms. For a few minutes, the group sat in silence among the ruins of the Donaldson farm, the only noise the crackling of the flames finishing their consumption of the house. Wend looked over at the pasture. The Donaldson's cattle grazed contentedly at the far end, as if nothing of consequence had occurred.

Finally, Joshua spoke, his voice measured and calm. "I make it out this way. These Shawnees was supposed to be a scouting party, to check out the valley for a raid by a sizable war party later. Five men ain't enough to make a real attack. But they were impetuous. They couldn't resist easy pickin's, and they wanted to be the first back to their village with scalps and other trophies.

So they thought they could make a couple of quick hits in the western part of the valley, then scamper back along the New Path before anyone could catch them. They didn't figure we'd be on them so fast."

He took a few puffs on the pipe. "Then again, I might be wrong, and there could be more of them around. So me and Franklin are going to look around this end of the valley just to make sure this is all over." He looked at Wend. "We'll go on foot. You take the horses and the kids down to the fort, and let Carnahan and Marsh know what happened up here."

"After we finish our little walk, we'll come down to the fort. Probably be sometime tomorrow. Tell Marsh to hold that militia of his inside the stockade until then and tell him to keep tight control of them. Be just my luck to have some trigger happy farmer mistake me for a savage and put a ball into me just when I'm walking out of the bush and contemplating some warm tea."

* * *

It was mid-afternoon by the time Wend came in sight of the fort. The stockade sat on a low bluff at the edge of the Robinson's big field, with a small creek running below the bluff. The two-story blockhouse stood against the inside of the western wall. He rode the mare, leading the other three horses, with the Donaldson children riding double on the first one. With Joshua's words about trigger happy militiamen in mind, Wend approached the stockade cautiously, crossing the creek well downstream from the fort. He dismounted and walked out into view of the fort, firing his rifle as a signal. Immediately heads bobbed up over the palisade and he could see a face peering out from a window in the upper level of the blockhouse. Someone raised a gun to the air and fired in response.

Wend led the string of horses toward the stockade, with Margaret and Charles still riding. They navigated the wagon track which climbed the bluff, and he stopped in front of the gates as they were swung open. Carnahan, Marsh and Milliken immediately came out and joined him as he lifted the children down from their mount. A crowd of settlers streamed behind, anxious for any further news of the day's events.

Wend saw Ellen McCartie standing at the back of the crowd, a look of fearful anticipation in her eyes, and he stifled his initial impulse to blurt out the full story of events at the Donaldson farm. He handed the mare's reins to a boy standing nearby and, nodding to the three leaders, walked off a distance where they would be out of earshot of the others. Only then did he tell the men about the devastation at the Donaldson's, the four deaths, and Joshua's scout through the western part of the valley.

After hearing Wend's story, Carnahan herded the settlers back into the fort, quieting their clamor for more information and promising to shortly tell them what had happened. Patricia and several other women took custody of Charles and Margaret. Hank Marsh came and led the horses over to the Robinson's fenced in meadow, where the settlers' horses had been placed.

Wend pushed his way to Ellen's side, gently took her arm and led her into the stockade and over to a quiet place near the side of the blockhouse. Peggy had been standing nearby and she followed them, a grim look on her face.

Wend had been dreading this moment the entire time he had been riding down the wagon track back to Sherman Mill, through the deserted village, and along the trail to the fort. He had tried to figure out how best to tell the girl about Johnny's death but no good way had come to him. But in the end, he didn't have to say the actual words.

Ellen looked up at him with tears in her eyes. "You don't have to tell me. I know Johnny is dead. I felt it ever since that smoke appeared this morning." Total desolation came over her face and a sob wracked her body.

Wend had no idea what to do, so he took her in his arms without saying a word and felt her crumple against his body, one sob coming after another. Finally he found words. "He was a good man, Ellen: The very best. He loved you and would have made you a fine and true husband. And you won't believe me now, but someday you will come to understand that you are a lucky girl just to have had him for a little while."

She looked up at him, her body stiffening and anger supplanting the pain in her face. "How can you tell me how I feel? Or dare tell me at this, of all moments, how 'lucky' I am!" Another sob passed through her. "The only boy who ever really had any interest in me is gone. I'll never bear his children, greet him as he comes in from the fields, or sit with him in front of our own good hearth! Oh yes, I'm real lucky indeed."

She tried to pull away from him, but Wend kept his hold on her. He searched for words to make her understand and comfort her.

Peggy was leaning against the blockhouse wall, her arms crossed in front of her. She spoke with a stern tone. "Ellen, for God's sake, listen to what you are saying! And get your wits about you for a moment. Wend is trying to help you work through this. Think about what happened to him out on Forbes Road. No one in this valley knows better what you are going through than Wend. So listen to him, and take his words to heart." She looked over at Wend and said quietly, "Now, tell us about the Donaldsons."

Wend gave them a cleaned up version of what he had seen, omitting the most graphic details and the condition of Johnny's remains.

As he talked, Ellen's body lost its stiffness, she put her cheek against his face and she lay against him, allowing his arms to bear her weight. Wend searched for suitable words to describe Johnny's actions. "Johnny made a good fight of it. He got one of the Shawnees with his musket. And he bought time for the little ones to get away. Nobody could have done more. Everyone in the valley should be proud of him."

Wend, still holding Ellen, looked around the interior of the stockade. Carnahan and Marsh were talking to the crowd of villagers and farmers, explaining what had happened at the Donaldsons' and telling them about Joshua's theory that the raid was a scouting expedition which had gotten out of hand. Several men, firearms in hand, stood watch around the walls of the stockade, standing on platforms which allowed them to peer above the top of the logs, or through firing slits between the logs themselves.

Marsh concluded by telling the people that they would remain in the stockade until Joshua came in and gave his report. With that, the meeting broke up and everyone settled down for the wait. Most families had brought blankets with them, which had been spread out around the walls or under wagons which had been pulled within the stockade. Women were building fires for cooking the provisions which had been brought from their homes.

Peggy took Ellen from his arms and escorted her to the area where the McCartie family had set up camp next to their wagon. Wend, feeling exhausted, went back to the blockhouse and sat down on the ground, his back against the side of the building. He closed his eyes, but then sensed someone was standing over him. He looked up to see that Peggy was back, holding a rag in her hand.

She knelt down beside him. "Here, let me clean you up." She began to gently wipe the rag, which she had soaked in a bucket of water, over his chest.

Surprised, he asked, "What are you doing?"

"I'm cleaning the dried vomit off your waistcoat and shirt. You've got lumps of it all over you. It's already beginning to stink and soon will be worse if you leave it there."

Wend felt embarrassed and defensive. "What makes you so sure its vomit?"

She gave him a look of impatience, reached out and pulled a lump off the collar of his shirt. "After growing up in a tavern, believe me, I know what vomit looks like." She scraped at his chest again. "There, I've got what will come off. You're going to want to boil that shirt after this is all over." She cleaned the rag in the bucket beside her, and leaned over again, this time using it to softly wipe his face and neck. "I'll get the soot off you."

This time Wend didn't object, and was happy to feel the coolness of the wet cloth over his skin. He was surprised at the gentleness of Peggy's touch, almost like a mother caressing her child.

Peggy sat down beside him. "Things must be pretty grim up at the Donaldson's farm, if you lost it like that. I could see you were holding back the details from Ellen. That was very thoughtful of you, and I appreciate you protecting Johnny's memory for her."

They sat quietly for a few moments.

Peggy took a deep breath, then reached up and ran her hands through her hair. "I've never had any trouble with men, and I guess that's no secret in this valley. But Ellen is a different story. There's no denying she's plain, except for that smile of hers which gives her face a warm look. But somehow she got Johnny, a nice enough looking boy, who also happened to be the best catch hereabouts, what with the farm and the money his parents had." She turned and looked directly into Wend's eyes. "I never saw two people so much in love. It was like the Good Lord put them here in this valley for each other."

She looked off into the distance. "But now, I'm worried about her. With Johnny gone, I don't know if she's ever going to be the same. And who is going to want her? I wouldn't be surprised if she ended up a spinster, working in the tavern all her life."

Wend was touched by Peggy's concern for Ellen. He hadn't, until now, had any reason to think of her as being worried about anyone beside herself.

"I think you are underestimating her prospects, Peggy." Wend sat for a minute marshaling his thoughts. Suddenly an idea hit him. "I know a woman, down in Carlisle; a widow. She sort of reminds me of Ellen. She isn't a beauty, but she has an honest, cheerful face like your sister's. And she's very pleasant to be with, makes a man feel comfortable and respected. So men find her very attractive. Ellen has those qualities. You may be surprised to find how many other boys come to court her."

Peggy pushed herself up from the ground. She turned and looked down at Wend. "Maybe you are right about Ellen; I sure hope you are." She walked back to where her mother was tending the family cook fire.

Wend felt weariness drifting over him. He crossed his arms in front of his chest and laid his head back against the wall. In a few moments, sleep overcame him.

He woke up in darkness to find Paul Milliken leaning over him with a hand on his shoulder. "Wend, wake up; it's near midnight. I need you to relieve Frank McKenzie on watch up in the blockhouse. Get yourself some tea and go on up there."

Wend looked around the stockade. Most of the family fires had burned down to embers, and sleeping figures in blankets lay around them and under the wagons. He could see that a group of people, including Reverend Carnahan, still sat talking at a fire in the far of the fort.

Wend found Patricia, a shawl over her shoulders, tending a fire and a pot of tea in the shelter of the other side of the blockhouse. The Donaldson children were asleep on the ground beside her, bundled up in blankets. Wordlessly, she poured a mug of tea and handed it to him.

Wend looked again at the children. "Poor kids: What's going to happen to them?"

"Paul says that the Donaldsons have kin down south, around Shippensburg. They probably got a claim to the farm, and I expect they'll take in the children." She paused for a moment and gently put her hand on Margaret's hair. "In the meantime, they'll stay with us. Looks like you and Joshua will be bunking together again for a while."

"Sure enough, you are collecting quite a brood, Mother Carnahan: First me, then Franklin and Ayika, and now the Donaldson children. Not to mention Joshua since he's come back from the army. We're going to be almost like a separate village if things keep going like this."

Wend took the mug, and carrying his rifle in the other hand, walked inside the blockhouse. Frank McKenzie was up in the loft, wearily leaning against the wall and watching out through a firing loophole. Wend passed up his rifle and then climbed the ladder carefully nursing the tea mug.

Frank rubbed his eyes. "I'm glad to see you. There's nothing moving out there and it's hard to keep awake, after everything that's gone on today."

Even though he was one of Matt Bratton's gang, and worked for him in the freight business, McKenzie was friendly enough when the waggoner wasn't around. Now it was evident that he was curious about the events at the Donaldson and McClay places. "I guess you had quite a fight up there today. Do you think that there are more of those Shawnees around?"

"Baird doesn't think so, but he wanted to be sure. That's why he's out there scouting around now." Wend considered what to say about the fight at the McClay farm. "Actually, the fight with the Shawnees wasn't that much of an affair. We were lucky and took them by surprise; the Reverend did most of the shooting and he put the warriors down fast. Mostly I just loaded and watched what happened. But it's a sure thing the McClays wouldn't have lasted much longer if we hadn't arrived when we did."

McKenzie nodded. "My Pa has a lot of respect for Reverend Carnahan. He was one of the leaders in the attack on Kittanning. Pa said he was as fierce a fighter as Lazarus Stewart himself. 'Course, that was before he took up the collar and pulpit."

Wend was startled by Frank's words. Like most people in the colony, he was quite familiar with the story of the 1756 attack by a force of Ulster militia on the large Delaware village of Kittanning. It had been located on the eastern bank of the Allegheny River, well north of the forks of the Ohio. Led by Colonel Armstrong, the attack had been a reprisal for the massive Indian raids on the settlements which followed the Braddock massacre, and most of the colonists credited it with greatly reducing the number of raids. But he had lived in the Carnahan household for nearly four years and had no inkling that the Reverend had been involved, much less one of the leaders.

By dawn, clouds had covered the whole sky, and sunrise was reflected only by a dim gray light which brought no warmth. It also brought a heavy shower. Wend watched the settlers seek what shelter they could, huddling against the stockade walls or crowding under the beds of the wagons. Patricia and other women gathered up the children and ushered them into the shelter of the blockhouse. The rain lasted for an hour, just long enough to make the inside of the fort muddy, soak most of the people, and quench the fires. Then it tapered off and a weak sun appeared.

Joshua and Franklin also appeared, emerging from the woods to the west beyond the Robinson's house and barn. Wend saw them first from his perch in the loft. He watched as Baird raised his rifle over his head and fired it into the sky, then saw him look over at Franklin and the two of them break out into laughter. Suddenly he sensed that they were sharing some version of yesterday's joke about trigger happy militiamen.

Wend called out to Tom Marsh to announce the arrival of the scouts. Men ran to open the gates and everyone crowded around the entrance in a repeat of the reception Wend had received the afternoon before. The two men sauntered into the fort, soaked and dripping from the rain. As they entered, Wend noticed that each had a large bundle tied to their back.

Joshua grounded his rifle and looked at Marsh. "Well, as far as I can see, there ain't no living warrior around for miles. We saw no sign of anyone 'cept the band that attacked the Donaldsons and McClays." He unslung the bundle he had over his shoulder and motioned for Franklin to do the same. It was a trade blanket which had been bound up with cloth straps to carry other items. "These are the travelin' clothes and supplies the Shawnees cached at the old Indian shelter camp on the ridge, just off the New Path. They was planning to pick them up on their way out of the valley." Baird opened the blanket roll. There were coats, shirts, dried food, and small bags carrying other items wrapped in the blanket. Franklin opened his bundle, and it contained much the same, except for the addition of a small wooden keg.

Joshua picked up the keg and displayed it to the assemblage. "Gunpowder: Real fine quality. And made right here in the Cumberland Valley, down by York." He handed the keg to Carnahan, who read the manufacturer's name burned into the wood. Then the Reverend passed the keg around for others to see.

"Made down in York," Joshua repeated. "You can be sure it made the trip out to wherever these Shawnees got it in some outlaw trader's pack train."

Marsh, Milliken, the Reverend and Joshua talked quietly for a moment, and then the miller shouted out to the crowd that they could go back to their homes. Everyone was anxious to leave, for the farm stock had been untended for a full day. Soon teams were hitched up to the wagons and the people of Sherman Valley streamed out of the fort.

The leaders of the militia stayed behind, meeting with Joshua at Patricia's fire near the blockhouse. Joshua and Franklin sat on their haunches, tea mugs in their hands. The scout looked up at the faces around the fire. "This won't be the last attack we see. I think this is just the beginning. Franklin and I had a good talk while we were looking around. He says that for the last year he was with the Mingoes, there were all sorts of council fires among the various tribes of the Ohio Country. There was something cooking, particularly among the tribes which live around the big lakes up North. What was the name of that chief that you heard a lot about?"

"He was called Pontiac, Mr. Joshua. He was a big leader in the Ottawa tribe near Fort Detroit." Franklin looked into the flames. "He was always sending messengers with wampum belts down to the tribes in Ohio. It was all about working together to attack the forts and settlements and drive the

English back." He looked around at the eager listeners. "The Delawares was getting excited about retaking their land here in Pennsylvania. At the same time they was getting wampum from Pontiac there was a Delaware spirit man, Neolin, also called 'The Prophet', who was traveling all through the Ohio Country. He visited our village, and I heard him speak at the council fire. He said that the Master of Life had come to him in dreams and foretold that the tribes would band together and drive the British out of their lands. Then they would shuck themselves of all the things that the whites had brought, like guns, metal implements, and other trade goods, and live the way their fathers had. These predictions seemed to support what Pontiac was saying and caused much enthusiasm for war against the British."

Franklin paused for a moment to gather his thoughts. "In the part of the country where we lived, the main chief who was pushing for war was named Guyasuta. He is a Mingo, but he has considerable pull with the Delawares and Shawnees as well and there were a lot of warriors who liked what he was saying. In fact, the reason that I was able to escape with my wife was because most of the warriors in my village went to a council fire called by Guyasuta at his town."

Milliken made a face. "I think I've heard that name before, during the war."

Baird snorted. "You should have; you was in the provincials out at Ligonier during the Forbes campaign. Guyasuta was the chief who made a fool out of that Major Grant during the fight at Fort Duquesne. He ambushed Grant and killed or captured about a third of the force. Grant got himself and a bunch of the 77th taken prisoner. But Grant was lucky: The French officers protected him, and he was returned to the British after the war. But the captured highlanders were given to the Indians. After we marched into Duquesne, we found their heads on stakes outside the fort." Joshua took a deep sip of his tea. "Yeah, Guyasuta is a tough customer, and he ain't got any love for the English. So it's easy to see that he would be happy to join in with any plan for an attack on the settlements."

Marsh looked around at the group. "It's clear we must make preparation for more raids. We need to make patrols out to the west, to watch for any more sign of war parties. If we're alert, we may be able to ambush them or at the very least, gain time to get everyone into the fort."

But Milliken shook his head. "We ain't got enough men to do that kind of scouting. We got less than twenty-five men in this part of the valley. And aside from you three," he motioned toward Joshua, Franklin and Wend, "Just about everybody is a farmer. They have to finish their planting and tend their fields now, or there won't be any crops in the fall."

Marsh said, "Maybe we could get some men from the other half company—from the eastern part of the valley—to help out for a while."

Milliken shook his head. "No, Tom, that ain't going to work. The whole of that group is farmers, they won't be anymore available than the ones here in the west."

Carnahan spoke up. "It's pretty clear that we need reinforcement. I'll get word to Reverend Elder. Maybe he could send some of his Paxton men. They have a goodly number of men who aren't farmers. And they know that if there are more attacks, it will start here. So if they help us, they may head off raids across the river."

Wend said, "I'll go, Reverend, I've got a strong horse, and I can be there tonight."

Marsh thought for a moment. "No, you stay here Wend. We need you for scouting. And I'd bet that a lot of men are going to be bringing in their firearms for you to check out and put into the best working order. I'll send Hank; he rides well and I can spare him from the mill for a few days. He can go by way of Carlisle and let Sheriff Dunning know what's happened."

With those plans made, the meeting broke up. Wend looked around. Everyone else had left the fort, making haste to get back to their homes and livestock. Patricia and Ayika had loaded the wagon, and Wend worked with Franklin to get the team hitched.

Soon they were riding back to Sherman Mill, and the old fort was again deserted.

CHAPTER 15

Bouquet's Call

In a few days, Sherman Valley had returned to its normal routine. But inevitably there was a tension and watchfulness in the air which hadn't been present before. Farmers took the family firearm with them as they went to tend their fields, herd their cattle into the meadow, or carried it with them in the wagon as they traveled to the mill. Mothers held their children close to the house and kept a wary eye on the woods around the farmstead.

Tom Marsh was right about people taking more of an interest in the condition of their firearms. Within two days of the raid several men had brought in guns to Wend's shop for repair. Before the attack, the deficiencies hadn't seemed urgent; now they wanted Wend to get the work done immediately. And a farmer from the central part of the valley, whom Wend barely knew, came into Sherman Mill and plunked down the asking price for the rifle on display behind McCartie's bar; cold cash with no haggling. He told McCartie that the New Path ran right past his farm and he was taking no chances. There was a run on gun powder and lead at the village store, which was soon sold out. Men began to ask Wend how much of his own supply he could sell, but he had a limited amount, which he kept for his own work and, although not admitting it to anyone but Marsh, as a reserve for the militia in case of another, larger attack.

Four days after the raid, Lazarus Stewart, with eighteen men and Hank Marsh at his back, rode into Sherman Mill from Paxton. After discussion with Tom Marsh and Paul Milliken, the new arrivals took up residence at Robinson's Fort, from which patrols sallied forth to sweep the western end of the valley and the New Path.

Two days after the arrival of the Paxton men Matt Bratton drove his wagon in from Carlisle. He told everyone that Carlisle was rife with rumors of tribal attacks on the forts in the Ohio Country and of war parties raiding trading posts and farmsteads out beyond Ligonier. The only nearby attack so far was the one in Sherman Valley, but the whole of Cumberland County was tense with anticipation. Then the waggoner began patrolling with Lazarus and his men.

Baird also worked with the Paxton men, helping Stewart set up routes for scouting, then accompanying some of the patrols himself.

However, by late June, with no further attacks in the area, there was a growing optimism that maybe the uprising, whatever its extent on the western borders, might not reach the valley again. Stewart's men, having been on patrol for over two weeks, and having seen no signs of a war party, were beginning to grumble and talk about riding home.

Then, as June entered its last week, news reached Sherman Mill which changed everyone's outlook. It came in the form of a circular from John Dunning, High Sheriff of Cumberland County, sent to all the towns and settlements. The words told of destruction which had descended on the border settlements beyond the Alleghenies. Border forts had fallen to the tribes, trading posts had been overrun, settlers killed in their fields and homes. Both Pitt and Ligonier were under siege by hundreds of warriors. More worrisome, the plague was spreading eastward. In the last weeks, war parties had attacked around Bedford, killing whole families and driving the survivors to shelter in the fort. Farmsteads and mills stood untended, many burned to the ground. It seemed only a matter of time until the war parties descended upon the Cumberland and Sherman Valleys.

Tom Marsh called a meeting of the militia to discuss how Sherman Valley should react. The men gathered into McCartie's common room until there was standing room only.

Carnahan, Baird and Wend had gotten to the tavern early, and sat at a trestle table in front of the hearth. The meeting was a windfall for Donavan McCartie, as Peggy and Ellen rushed around the room to satisfy the thirst of all the attendees. Finally everyone seemed to have arrived, and Donavan shooed the girls out the door to the family quarters. As they left, Wend saw a look of disgust on Peggy's face at being excluded from listening to the business part of the proceedings.

Marsh, as captain of the militia, called the meeting to order. He read the contents of the sheriff's circular to the assemblage. The room became increasingly quiet and by the time he finished, there was total silence and every man had a reflective look on his face. Marsh cleared his throat and put the paper down on the table in front of him. "I guess we all understand that if it can happen in Ligonier and Bedford, this scourge can reach here. Lord knows, it already has in a small way. My feeling is that we must increase our vigilance and take what additional measures we can to be ready for the inevitable." He looked around the room. "So I am calling for your opinion on what steps we should take to meet this threat." He motioned to George Robinson. "Perhaps you can tell us about what they did here in the valley during the raids of '55 and '56."

Robinson stood up. "Of course, we were far fewer in those days. That was before the mill was here and there was no village. Only farms scattered over this part of the valley. The stockade was our first step, but the real key to the problem was working together all the time."

"The biggest fear was being attacked while you were out tending the fields; not knowing what was lurking in the bush out beyond the edge of the cleared land. Many a day I've been swinging a hoe or a scythe, but unable to shake the feeling that savages were watching me."

Wend looked around the room. He saw that Robinson's words had hit home. Most men were looking down at the tables or floor in front of them, not wanting to meet each other's eyes.

Robinson continued, "We had to do something so that we could be safe while working the fields. So we took turns guarding each other. Two or three men bearing arms would watch over a neighbor while he got essential work done. Then we would move on to another farm. It wasn't very efficient: All we could do was get the most important things finished, but it was better than being completely driven from the fields by fear."

Around the room, men were nodding in agreement. Marsh said, "That is something I believe we must organize as soon as possible." He turned to Milliken. "Paul, as lieutenant here in the west, please sit down with the farmers and put together a plan for a rotation of guards."

Bratton and Stewart were sitting at the corner table and had been whispering together. Bratton jumped up. "This talk of guarding fields is less than a half measure. It makes everyone feel good, but it will have no value if a big war party strikes a farm. Look what a war party of only five did to the Donaldsons. We've got to be aggressive in patrolling the far western end of the valley. Seek out and ambush the war parties before they descend on the farms, or perhaps even the village."

Stewart rose. "Bratton has it right. You must find a way to reach out and stop the war parties before they hit the farms."

Marsh turned to Stewart. "Lazarus, ideally we should do both; have some men range to the west, while others stand guard at the farms. But we don't have enough men under arms unless we can count on your continued help. What say you to that?"

"We've already been here more than two weeks. My lads have jobs or trades to which they must return soon. I ask you to recall Reverend Elder's words at a meeting in this very tavern last November. He pointed out that we can help Sherman Valley only after we secure our own town."

Paul Milliken spoke up. "Lazarus, Sherman Valley is like a western shield for Paxton. Protect Sherman, you help protect Paxton. That's why you are here now, that's why you should stay."

Stewart hardened his face. "I'll not deny there's some truth in what you say, Paul. But remember, many of the war parties that attacked east of the Susquehanna in '55 and '56 came not from the west, but down from the north. That could happen again, so we must be vigilant in that direction for ourselves. And I'll say it here now; we intend to pull out tomorrow."

Reverend Carnahan stood. "Lazarus, I understand that your boys are anxious to get home. But wouldn't it be possible for another group to come over? Should I send a message with you to Reverend Elder, saying how important it would be considering our shortage of manpower?"

"I'll talk to the Reverend when we get back. Perhaps Asher Clayton will be willing to lead another detachment over here. But I can promise nothing. You here in the valley must take responsibility for your protection, and I tell you simply sitting by the fence with guns in your hands won't be enough."

Marsh nodded at Stewart, then spreading his hands in supplication, asked the meeting at large for ideas. In response, groups of men throughout the room began talking at once.

In the midst of this discussion, Wend suddenly became aware of the noise of a horse's hooves approaching outside the tavern, audible through the open windows. Then the sound of the hooves stopped and in a few seconds the door of the tavern was flung wide open. Instantly, everybody stopped talking and turned their eyes toward the entrance. In the burst of light which flooded in through the doorway, the figure of a young man appeared. He was dressed in a short, shabby jacket of almost totally faded out red, with loose fitting breeches made of a course, tan fabric. Leggings of blue material covered the area from the tops of his shoes to his knees. On his head was a broad-brimmed black hat which looked like it had been crumpled and straightened out many times. A musket was slung over the man's left shoulder with its butt next to his head. A bayonet and other accouterments of a military nature were hung on straps across his chest and from his belt.

The man swung his eyes around the room as if searching for someone. Then, realizing all eyes were upon him, and seemingly enjoying the attention, he casually leaned against the frame of the door with his right shoulder. At the same time he reached up with his left hand and tilted his battered hat to a jaunty angle. His face formed a smile which complemented the hint of impudence in his eyes and lips.

"Sorry if I have interrupted a private meeting, gentlemen, but I have a dispatch of some urgency from Colonel Bouquet, of His Majesty's Royal American Regiment, for Mr. Joshua Baird."

Wend fought to keep his face impassive and finally reached up with his hand to smother the laugh which was forcing itself upon him.

In his own inimitable style, Arnold Spengler had come to Sherman Mill!

* * *

Tom Marsh was the first to recover from the unexpected arrival of the soldier. "Is Colonel Bouquet at Carlisle, then?"

Arnold looked at Marsh, and evidently decided he was a man of some substance. "When last I saw him, Sir, he was in Lancaster, stopping on his way from Philadelphia. I would expect he is in or near Carlisle by now. I was sent ahead to deliver dispatches."

Marsh started to speak again, but before he could say a word, Stewart pushed his way through the crowd until he was nearly face-to-face with Arnold, and then he turned to face the men in the room. "Here's somebody who could answer your questions about protecting the valley." He turned back to Arnold. "What is your Colonel Bouquet planning to do about this uprising? When is the 60th going to send some troops up here to protect us from the tribes?"

Arnold looked at Lazarus for a moment, as if inspecting him. Then he crossed his arms in front of his chest, still leaning casually against the door. "And whom might you be, Sir?"

"I am Captain Stewart, of the Paxton Militia. Here with a half company to assist these good people."

Arnold made no move to come to attention or otherwise show respect to Lazarus. "Well, Captain Stewart, even if I were privy to Colonel Bouquet's plans, I have no warrant from him to discuss them with you, Sir. My orders were to deliver dispatches, nothing more. You must seek the information you want from the colonel himself, Sir."

Joshua rose from his seat and made his way toward Arnold. Wend followed him.

"Let us go outside, Corporal Spengler, and you can deliver the dispatch to me." Joshua pushed past both Lazarus and Arnold, and walked out into the tavern's yard. Wend and Arnold followed.

Wend pulled the tavern door shut behind them.

Arnold shook hands with Baird and gave Wend a wide grin and friendly poke on the shoulder. "Pretty little village here, though I can't say much for your friend Captain Stewart there."

"He's no friend of mine." Wend laughed, "But I can't say your manner did anything to curry favor with him."

Joshua started to walk up the hill to the Carnahans'. "Come on, both of you. Let's go up to the house where we can have some privacy. Bring that horse with you Arnold. You can rest him in the barn."

As they walked up the wagon track, Arnold reached into a canvas bag slung on his hip and passed an envelope to Joshua. "Here's the dispatch. But since I took down the colonel's words, I can tell you what it says. You're requested to come back into service. He's going to command an expedition along Forbes Road to relieve Fort Pitt, and wants you to lead all the scouts."

Joshua nodded thoughtfully. "'Bout what I expected. Tell me, how many men of the 60th has Bouquet got ready to march from Carlisle?"

Arnold's face became very grim. "As things stand, 14 men."

Baird stopped in his tracks and looked at Spengler. "Good Lord! Surely you're not serious! That's not an expedition, that's a burial detail!"

"That's all there are here in the eastern part of the colony. A few quartermasters, some recruits and several men who were on leave when this all broke out. Plus, the adjutant and myself."

Joshua started walking up the hill again. "Then Amherst must be sending reinforcements down to him from up north. What about Gage's 80th — they're all light infantry and would be perfect for this job."

"The 80th has been disbanded. Broken up to fill up the ranks of the regiments sent down to the West Indies. Just like they did with the 3rd and 4th battalions of the 60th. That's why Bouquet has so few men to garrison the forts. The terrible truth is that Amherst has less than 800 men available for reinforcements, and that's for the whole of the border, not just here in

Pennsylvania." They reached the barn and Arnold led the horse into a stall and began stripping the saddle and other equipment from its back.

"Arnold, that's less than a battalion at wartime strength. So how many can the commanding general send down here?"

"Wait a minute, Joshua, the news gets worse. More than half of those troops are the remnants of the 42nd and 77th Highlanders. They were devastated by yellow fever in the West Indies campaign, and were shipped up to New York City to recover. Many of them are still in the hospital, and a good amount of those who have been released are so weak that they can't march. It takes weeks to rebuild your strength even after the fever is gone. The 77th is in especially bad condition, they suffered worse from the fever. Moreover, the 77th is due to be mustered out and the men sent back to Britain, but it looks like Amherst will try to hold on to them and use them to fight the insurrection."

"So in answer to your question, Bouquet will likely get only about 400 highlanders from the total troops available to Amherst. The rest will be sent to the New York border to fight the insurrection around the northwest lakes."

Joshua shook his head. "All right, when will they arrive?"

"Amherst put an advance party of three companies, two from the Black Watch and one from the 77th, on the road about ten days ago. That's around 150 men. They should be arriving in Carlisle any day now. The rest will march when they can get organized and find wagon transport for the convalescent men and the baggage for the entire group."

Wend had been taking in the discussion about troop strength, but had another question. "We just got news from the sheriff that some of the forts have been attacked. What do you know about that?"

"We've got sketchy reports from the commanders of Ligonier and Bedford. And Captain Ecuyer at Fort Pitt has been able to sneak out some messages by courier, even though he's under siege. The news is exceedingly bad; most of the smaller forts appear to have been taken and burned, their garrisons killed. Wend, the tribes struck in May and June according to some kind of cooperative plan and the uprising is massive."

Joshua had been examining Spengler's horse, running his hands over his legs and flanks. "When are you supposed to get back to Carlisle?"

"The adjutant said as soon as possible. We've got major work ahead to get this expedition organized."

"Well, lad, you had best stay the night here. This horse has been rode hard. He needs feed and rest and if you wait 'till morning to start back you won't lose much time."

They walked over to the house and Joshua introduced Arnold to Patricia. Wend explained how he and the corporal had been friends in Lancaster. In short order Patricia had them seated at the table in front of the fire, with mugs of ale.

While Arnold was talking, Reverend Carnahan arrived and joined the group at the table. He told them that the meeting at the tavern had ended without any additional decisions about how to defend the valley. Joshua quickly filled him in about the contents of Bouquet's message, the plan for a relief expedition to Fort Pitt, and the details Arnold had brought about the weakness of the army.

Carnahan thought for a moment. "Those plans are logical from the army's point of view, but the settlers are going to want the troops to stay around here to protect the settlements. After you left there was a lot of talk, led by Stewart and Bratton, about what the army should do to defend against the tribes. They don't have any idea—yet—about how weak the King's forces are."

Arnold looked around at all the faces at the table. "Bouquet has no choice but to march to Fort Pitt. There are 125 soldiers and as many as 500 settlers holed up in Pitt. And the rations available won't last very long. The fort must be relieved as soon as possible. If the tribes take the fort, there will be a massacre on the scale of the Braddock affair."

Patricia asked, "Couldn't the commander negotiate a truce with the Indians, if he agreed to evacuate the fort and march the garrison and settlers back across the Alleghenies?"

Arnold shook his head. "We don't have the details yet, but Captain Ecuyer wrote that one of the methods that the Indians used to take the small forts was to offer safety and free passage to the garrisons if they surrendered. Then they massacred them as they marched out."

Carnahan nodded. "That trick about free passage in exchange for surrendering is an old one. Remember what happened to the garrison of Fort William-Henry in New York back in 1757? The French commander, Montcalm, gave the garrison safe passage, but the Indians swarmed over them as they left the fort. Many died, including women and children. And the same thing happened at Fort Granville, up to the north of here, in 1756." He looked at Patricia and shook his head. "No, surrender is not an option."

Arnold spoke up again. "This isn't official yet, but I copied a dispatch to Amherst which contained Bouquet's proposal for a campaign against the tribes once he takes back Fort Pitt. He plans to put together a force of about 2000, made up of the highlanders and provincial forces to be raised by Virginia, Maryland, and Pennsylvania, to leave Fort Pitt and march westward through the Ohio territory to the Muskingum River. He'll attack or threaten the Indian villages, in the hope that they will sue for peace."

Carnahan turned to Joshua. "Well, I assume you are going to join Colonel Bouquet's little hike to the Forks of the Ohio. You realize it isn't going to be like '58, when he had 6000 men? There won't be a road to build, but you'll still only be 400 men, against God knows how many warriors."

"Yeah, I guess so. Hunting game for the taverns ain't making me a rich man." Joshua waved his hand at Arnold. "So you can tell Bouquet I'll be down to Carlisle in a couple of days, soon as I put my kit together."

Arnold nodded to Joshua, then looked over at Wend. "It ain't in the dispatch, but the colonel told me he thought you might want to come along as a scout too. He pointed out that if the campaign is successful, part of the peace negotiations will be to arrange the return of white captives. This may be your best chance to recover Abigail Gibson, if you're still of a mind to do so."

Wend felt his heart surge. He looked around the table; everyone was staring at him. "I don't have to think about this. I'll come to Carlisle with Joshua, ready for any service the colonel wants of me."

The corporal took a swallow from his mug. "Well, then I've accomplished my mission here in Sherman Mill. From now on, my visit is purely social."

* * *

Later, in the early evening, Wend and Arnold walked down to McCartie's to share a drink. The militia meeting was long since adjourned and the common room sparsely populated. Tom Marsh and Paul Milliken were seated before the fireplace in deep discussion; Bratton and some of his friends, including Frank McKenzie, were gathered around the corner table, telling stories and laughing.

The two went to the bar, where Wend bought Arnold a mug of rum, then Wend walked over to Marsh's table to tell him that he and Joshua would be leaving to scout for the army.

Marsh was not happy. "Wend, when that soldier said he had a message for Baird, I figured he'd be leaving. But I hadn't counted on you going."

Milliken shook his head. "You and Joshua were the main people we had available for scouting. And you're our gunsmith. Between you two leaving and the Paxton men riding out, we're going to be weaker than ever. I know Joshua has to go, but won't you reconsider?"

"Paul, I have business, long unfinished business, which can only be completed with the army's assistance. This town and the valley have become my home, and I feel guilty leaving people who have become my friends, but I must see this business through."

Marsh looked up thoughtfully. "I've heard stories, Wend, about a girl captured by the savages when your family was killed. Does this have something to do with that?"

Wend looked the miller directly in the eye. "It has everything to do with that, Sir."

Marsh grinned and put his hand on Wends arm. "Then go do what you must. You'll be missed, but we'll work things out here. And come back to us when it is all over. There's always room for a lad like you here in the valley."

Wend returned to the counter to find Arnold entertaining the McCartie girls with stories of his work on Bouquet's staff.

Peggy asked with excitement in her voice, "You've been to Philadelphia and Baltimore and New York?"

Arnold nodded. "Sure. Colonel Bouquet has bought some land in Maryland, and he had to go to Baltimore to settle legal matters. Then we traveled up to New York, to have meetings with General Amherst and General Gage. He's taking over from Amherst soon. But we spent most of the winter in Philadelphia. Bouquet had business with the governor and the council."

Wend listened as Arnold told the sisters, both now leaning against the bar in rapt interest, vignettes about the sights he had seen in the cities. Both girls had questions about what the women's fashions were like and the merchandise in the stores and shops.

Wend could see that Arnold, like most men, was taken with Peggy and was working to make an impression on her. And she was acting particularly receptive, smiling and giggling loudly, playing the coquette to the hilt. As the corporal talked, Wend carefully glanced several times at the corner table. He could see that Bratton was eying Arnold and the girls, and was not happy about what he was seeing.

In a moment when both girls briefly left to tend to chores, Wend quickly poked Arnold with his elbow. "Hey, look over in the corner, at the table."

Arnold complied, and then looked back at Wend. "Now that you mention it, that big guy looks familiar."

"He's not just familiar; that's Matt Bratton. Remember how he handled your friend John and us at Larkin's in Carlisle? That night you first took me there back in '59?"

Arnold looked at the table again, squinted, and made a face of distaste. "Oh, yes: Now I remember. I vowed to settle the score!"

"Yes, Arnold, but that's not the main point." Wend nodded toward Peggy. "She's engaged to him. I've been watching, and he is not amused by your attentions to the lady. I think he's even less amused by her interest in your tales."

Wend had thought that his warning would lead his friend to back off in his advances; but to his surprise, when Peggy returned to the counter, Arnold's voice became louder and his words more flirtatious. Moreover, Peggy clearly basked in the attention. In a few minutes, Bratton rose from the table and walked to the bar. Wend cursed to himself as Bratton advanced; he could see that the waggoner's face was showing unmistakable anger, but not any recognition of Arnold from the long ago night at Larkin's place.

"Well, Dutchman, I see you are friends with this messenger from Colonel Bouquet. Would you care to introduce me?"

Wend noticed that despite his agitation, Matt's voice was controlled. Wend made the requested introduction.

Bratton, at least a hand taller than Spengler, looked down at the soldier. "I imagine in your travels that you find many occasions to tell amusing stories to girls all over the colony."

Arnold looked up at Bratton, smiled at him and then turned to Peggy and smiled at her in turn. She reciprocated with her prettiest grin.

"Now that you mention it, it is a fact that I find many girls here in the settlements are very interested in news from back east. It provides them with a diversion from their daily chores. But I must say, not many of them are as exceptionally fair as this lass. Wouldn't you agree, sir?"

Arnold raised his mug to Peggy, who acknowledged his salute with a nod of her head.

Bratton's hand grasped the edge of the counter tightly and Wend saw that his knuckles were turning white. "Corporal, you should understand that Miss McCartie is my betrothed and I don't fancy your amorous attentions toward her."

Arnold feigned astonishment at Matt's words. He turned to Peggy. "Miss, is this true? Are you in fact betrothed to this gentleman?"

Peggy nodded. "Indeed it's true, although I regret to say that Mr. Bratton is keeping me in suspense about the date of our nuptials."

Arnold turned to Bratton with a look of mock surprise. "Why Sir, I congratulate you on your good fortune. However, I find it difficult to believe that, having gained the favors of such a beautiful and charming lady, you would delay an instant in setting the date of your vows."

Ellen, who had been standing nearby, listening intently to the exchange, suddenly laughed out loud. "Well Matt, Corporal Spengler certainly has put you in a tight spot. When are you two going to get married?"

Peggy said nothing, but smiled at Ellen and Arnold in turn, then looked at Bratton with a questioning look in her face.

Bratton realized he had become the butt of a joke and anger turned to rage on his face. His countenance reddened. Meanwhile Arnold calmly took a pull on his rum, slowly set it down, wiped his mouth, and leaned against the bar casually. His nonchalance was obviously calculated to further rouse the waggoner's ire.

Wend sighed. He was now resigned to the fact that there would be a fight.

Bratton lost all semblance of control. He poked a finger into Arnold's chest. "Damn it, Redcoat, the date of the wedding is my business. I'm telling you here and now to keep your nose out of it!"

Arnold smiled and started to respond. But it was Peggy who spoke out, in a voice more angry than Wend had ever heard her use.

"Yes, Matt, it is your business. But it's also mine! And I'm getting tired of waiting for you to set the date. All you talk about is getting more money and looking for the right time. When is that going to be?" She glared at the waggoner. 'You better tell me soon!'"

Arnold glanced at Peggy, then smiled again and said in a taunting voice, "It does seem like the lady is getting a bit impatient; don't you agree?"

Bratton looked back and forth between Peggy and Arnold. Then rage overcame him. He reared back and cocked his fist at the soldier.

But suddenly the train of events was interrupted by the noise of the tavern door slamming open against the wall. Then little Charles Donaldson burst into the room, breathless from running. He came up to Wend and tugged on his sleeve. "Mrs. Carnahan says to come quick, she needs you! Ayika is going to have her baby! And we're supposed to ask Mrs. McCartie and Mrs. Marsh come up to help, too."

Tom Marsh stood up. "I'll go fetch my wife; she'll be up directly!"

Ellen ran to the door which opened to the McCartie family quarters and called for her Mother.

Wend grabbed Arnold's sleeve. "Come on, we need to get back to the Carnahan's. There will be work for us."

The two of them, followed by Charles, went out the tavern door at the run, leaving Bratton standing alone at the bar with his fist raised and no one to hit. Peggy stood behind the counter looking at him, her angry expression now replaced by one of amusement.

As they hurried up the wagon track, Arnold gave Wend a mischievous grin. "I dare say our friend Bratton isn't going to have a very good evening with Miss McCartie!"

* * *

As is often the case with first babies, Ayika had a hard, painful time giving birth to her child. The women tended to her in Franklin's cabin and the men gathered under the lean-to at the rear. Arnold, weary after two days on the road from Lancaster, soon excused himself and, rolling up in a blanket before the Carnahan's hearth, dropped off into deep sleep.

Joshua, Paul, Wend and Franklin kept water heating in a large kettle over the outdoor fireplace next to the lean-to and spent the hours swapping stories. Sometime after midnight, following the closing of the tavern, Peggy McCartie came walking up the hill with an armful of towels and torn-up cloth in her arms and had the men put them in the water to boil before she went in to join the other women.

Wend had gone over to his workshop and gotten some canvas material and his sewing tools. He sat working to make the canvas into rifle slings like the one used by Arnold for his musket. They would allow him and Joshua to carry their weapons on their back while riding, instead of having to hold them across the saddle, thus giving them the free use of both hands.

A little while after Peggy arrived, Joshua and Franklin went out to the woodpile to replenish the supply of firewood. They worked together to split some logs into a usable size. That left Wend and Reverend Carnahan alone, sitting under the lean-to in the night.

Carnahan sat quietly smoking his pipe as Wend worked with his needle. Wend searched for a way to ask the questions which had been in his mind since the Shawnee raid. "Reverend, can we talk for a minute? About something that has been bothering me for weeks?"

Carnahan took his pipe out of his mouth and looked at Wend thoughtfully, the hint of a smile on his face. "Of course, Wend. Is this of a theological nature or something more personal?"

"It's in the nature of satisfying my curiosity." Wend put his sewing down. "I always thought I was pretty good with a rifle. But the way that you shot those warriors at the McClay place was like nothing I've ever seen. And you did it mostly with unfamiliar rifles. Then too, there was the day you fired Tom Marsh's rifle so I could check the lock. You easily hit the center of the mark. I know you spent a lot of time in the bush with Joshua, but you had to make a special effort to become that good."

Carnahan took a pull on his pipe and Wend decided to take the moment to lay out all his questions. "Besides that, in the last few months, it's become clear to me that all the men hereabouts defer to your judgment on defending the valley. Marsh and Milliken come to talk with you about the militia company. And then I heard from Frank McKenzie that you were a leader of the raid on Kittanning, eight years ago. So it's pretty clear you have a background which isn't typical of a minister."

Carnahan chuckled and knocked the ashes out of his pipe. "Well, of course you are right about that. It's not a mystery; I just don't talk about it much. Since the older people around here know the story, there's no real cause to spend a lot of time on my history."

"So where did you learn to shoot like that?"

"It's a simple story. My parents lived on a small farm down in the Conococheague area, a few miles southwest of Ben Chambers' mills. Our place was never very prosperous in terms of crops; Pa was more of a hunter by nature. But he did real well bringing in game, so we always ate well. And he made money trading pelts. Father was a good shot and he taught me well. But it turned out I had a natural eye for it and I practiced as much as my father would allow. By the time I was fourteen, I could hit targets out as far as the rifle could throw a ball. At 100 yards, I could put it dead center all the time. Just like you, my shooting won me prizes at the local contests and fairs."

"When did you and Joshua get together?"

"It was at Colonel Chambers' place, when I was seventeen. The local people had come together for a small fair and my family attended. I won in the rifle match. Joshua also shot in the match; he was a couple of years older and already a traveled and accomplished hunter and trapper. I spent the day listening to his adventures on the border. A week later, Joshua showed up at our place and invited me to go with him on a long hunting trip, collecting pelts for trade. From then on, we were partners. We spent our time roaming from the Great Cove westward to Raystown, which is now Bedford, and Loyalhanna Creek, which you know as Fort Ligonier. We even got out to the Ohio Country while it was still in French hands. We visited Indian towns such as Logstown, Kittanning, and Mingotown along the Ohio and Allegheny rivers. Of course there were no roads in those days; we used the Indian trails for our travels. But we made good money and were as prosperous as any two young men could hope."

"I saw my first raid in 1755. Joshua and I were in our late twenties by then, and experienced woodsmen. When the war started in 1754, the western areas became hostile, so we fell back east of the Alleghenies for our undertakings. We were at my parent's place when the great raid by a mixture of Frenchmen and Indians occurred in the Great Cove. We joined a ranging company going to the rescue of those settlements. But when we got there, the only thing left to do was tidy up after the warriors. They had swept through the cove, leaving a swath of destruction. Almost every family was disrupted. We buried fifty-five people—men, women, and children—on a hillside in the center of the cove, the survivors weeping as prayers were said over the graves. After that, the cove, which had been rapidly filling with farms, was barren of settlement."

Wend had many questions to ask, but let Carnahan pause for a moment to gather his thoughts.

"That was the beginning. It was a bloody time and we were almost constantly engaged in patrolling and trying to ambush war parties. We operated out of McDowell's Mill, where a private stockade had been set up. Sometimes we were successful, but more often we found burned out farmsteads with the inhabitants dead or carried off to captivity. We spent more time digging graves than fighting."

He clasped his hands tightly together in his lap. "To tell the truth, if you wanted to picture me at that time, think of Lazarus Stewart. I was bitter at the tribes for their raids and resented the government in Philadelphia for their unwillingness to protect the settlements. I was happy to become an officer of militia, leading many patrols. Joshua, as always, was Joshua; taking the good and the bad in as they came, seemingly inured to the bloodiness of it all."

"Then in the summer of '56 the raids got more frequent than before. Many of the war parties were led by the French, who kept the warriors to their work. Were it up to the Indians, they'd make one or two attacks, get some booty and captives, and then hurry back to their village to celebrate their success. But the French, of course, had a long term objective; to beat the English and drive the settlements back."

"The combination of the warriors and the French was devastating for the colony. August was the worst month of all. Several settlements and many farmsteads were hit and burned to the ground. That attacks occurred even on the eastern side of the Susquehanna seemed to accelerate the growing idea that we needed to take the war to the tribes. But the real catalyst was the taking of Fort Granville, which was located northeast of Fort Shirley, and the massacre of the people inside by a band of warriors led by the French. In late August of '56, Governor Penn ordered John Armstrong, who was a lieutenant colonel in the provincials, to assemble a force and destroy Kittanning, which was the place where many of the war parties were coming from."

Wend knew about Armstrong, and had actually seen him once in Carlisle. He had been the surveyor who had laid out the town in 1750 at the governor's request, and had stayed to become one of its first settlers and a leading citizen. With the outbreak of the war, he had been a logical choice for a commission as a senior officer in the provincial forces.

Carnahan continued, "Soon, Armstrong had got together an expedition of over 300 men, mostly militia, organized into seven companies. Joshua and I joined eagerly. The force was assembled at Fort Shirley. Since I had been to Kittanning a couple of times, and knew the layout of the village, I was made a captain and given the job of leading an advance group of about 20 men to act as pathfinders. We led the expedition over the trails to the Allegheny without being discovered by the inhabitants. Then, on the morning of the attack, my men and I were stationed at the edge of a cornfield outside the village to cut off any Indians who might try to escape that way."

"We watched the main force go in at dawn and shortly after that the village was on fire. We couldn't see much; there were blankets of smoke from the fires and black powder of the firearms. Then we suddenly saw a bunch of Indians running out of the smoke, maybe ten or twelve of them. They were shadowy, indistinct figures; it was hard to tell anything except that they weren't dressed like militia. My men began firing as soon as we saw them; in no time they were all hit and on the ground."

"Just minutes after that we heard whistles blowing in the village. That was the signal for all the detachments to assemble. We got up from our positions and started across the field toward the town. That's when I came across the woman and her child. They had been part of the group hit by our volley. I looked around and discovered that most the people we had shot were children and women. They were all dead except for this women and her child, who I guess was about a year old. The woman was lying on the ground and holding onto the baby. She had been shot in the stomach and the same ball had grazed the baby. It was clear she was going to die. But the child wasn't badly hurt. The mother looked up at me with fear in her eyes, then hugged her child more tightly. The baby was just looking around, sort of curious."

"I had just taken all this in when one of my men came up and, without saying a word, put a bullet into the woman's head. Then he reached into his belt and pulled out a hatchet. Before I could react to what he had done to the woman, he had split open the baby's head. He looked at me with a grin, and said, 'That's for Granville.' Then he continued on his way into the village."

Wend looked at Carnahan. His eyes were staring into the distance and his jaw was grinding as he recalled that morning at Kittanning. Then the Reverend shook his head. "By that time, I had seen and buried many dead women and children at the scene of raids. I thought I was pretty hard inside. But when I participated in an actual killing of helpless people, even though they were Delawares, something snapped in me. I had never been part of something like that before and the militiaman's casualness in executing the mother and child turned my stomach. Then when I actually got into the village, I saw many more children, women, and old ones who had been killed or wounded."

"The memory of that carnage remained with me. In fact, I couldn't shake it and I found it hard to sleep at night as we withdrew to the settlements. The fear in that mother's eyes and the innocence of the doomed baby haunted me every time I closed my eyes."

Wend quietly asked, "Was that when you decided to become a minister?"

Carnahan nodded. "Joshua and I went to his parent's farm near York to rest after the raid. That's when I met Patricia. We took long walks together and I was able to talk about my feelings in a way that was impossible with other men. She helped me work through my anguish. To make a long story short, I decided to become a man of the church, Patricia and I got married, I studied to be a minister, and eventually we settled in Sherman Valley."

Wend looked at Carnahan. "There's something I don't understand. If you became a minister because you were ashamed about Kittanning, it sure didn't show during the fight at the McClays' place. You shot those warriors without hesitation."

Carnahan's face showed frustration. "Wend, you haven't got it quite straight yet. Or maybe I didn't make things clear enough to you. I wasn't ashamed about Kittanning or about fighting warriors. That raid was the only way to make the tribes think twice about attacking the settlements. In a way, it was a defensive action." Carnahan gathered his thoughts for a moment. "It was more personal: I just decided that I didn't have the stomach to be part of the merciless killing of women and children. But that doesn't mean that I won't defend the people and homes of this valley."

"So how do you feel about Bouquet's plan to march into the Ohio Country? If he has to raid the villages, there are going to be a lot of women, children and old people injured and killed."

"Bouquet doesn't have any choice. Of course, it's natural that the settlers here want him to provide troops to protect them. You should have heard the angry comments about the army and the colonial government down at the tavern after you, Joshua and Arnold had left. But that is useless; it would be like trying to swat flies in the air. Even if Bouquet had half the army at his disposal, all they'd be able to do is react, to go where the Indians had been. Going after the Indian villages is the only strategy which has any chance of actually ending the raids. All warriors are worried about the survival of their own band; if they think it is threatened, they'll rush back to protect it. So if you go after the home villages the raids here will stop. It will take a while and people will die in the meantime. But that's going to happen anyway. So Bouquet, with the limited number of troops he has, must shut his eyes to that and march on the tribal homelands."

As he finished talking, Joshua came to the lean-to, carrying an armful of split wood. "You two going to sit here jabbering all night? How about making yourselves useful and carrying some wood now that Franklin and I did all the real work chopping and splitting it up."

Wend left to haul some wood and then their wait went on for more hours. Finally, in the hour before dawn, Ayika's baby came. They heard high pitched crying from inside the cabin, then silence resumed. But in just a few minutes, the door was swung open by Peggy and Patricia came out, a bundle in her arms. The men could see that there was something alive within the towels.

Patricia smiled as she carried the bundle over to Franklin. "You have a beautiful little boy, perfect in every way. Ayika did her job well, even though it was a hard birth; she's fine but exhausted."

Franklin peeked inside the toweling, a look of amazement and puzzlement on his face. "Lord, Mrs. Carnahan. I got a son. He sure looks mighty fine. I never expected anything like this could ever happen to me."

Patricia shook her head and laughed. "Well, you caused it, but Ayika made it happen. Now you better go in there and see her before she drops off to sleep and show her how much you appreciate her. Or you'll have some hard days in front of you after she gets well."

Franklin rushed into the cabin to see his wife, and the other men crowded around Patricia. Wend peeked into the bundle to see the baby. The child was fast asleep, but breathing heavily from the exertions of fighting his way out of the womb. He had seen several newborns before, but this was the first time he had seen a black or Indian baby, and he was startled that he was unable to see any difference in color or features from white children. He guessed those differences appeared later.

Wend watched as Paul Carnahan carefully pulled part of the cloth back, to look more closely at the child. The Reverend stared for a moment and then a grin spread over his face. Suddenly Wend was certain that the Reverend was seeing another baby in a far off corn-field smelling of smoke and gunpowder.

The other women emerged from the cabin, to give Franklin and Ayika privacy. They all took turns looking at the child. Then Patricia looked around at the men. "Paul, you men have been sitting around here all night with nothing to do, and you might have at least brewed some tea for these ladies, considering they've worked all these hours."

Carnahan looked nonplussed at the scolding and Joshua simply shrugged his shoulders. Wend sought to get the Reverend off the hook. "Here, I'll make some tea."

After fetching a container of tea leaves and a pot from the Carnahan house, Wend kneeled at the fire behind the lean-to. He had just set the teapot on when Peggy came and stood beside the fire, a shawl pulled up around her shoulders against the cool of the pre-dawn air. Wend could see the weariness around her eyes after the night-long vigil. He looked up at her. "It was very nice of you to come up and help out, especially after working all day."

Peggy didn't respond in the way he expected; instead she looked at him with steely, cold eyes. "I know how to help my friends and neighbors. It was the right thing to do." She stood silent for a moment, then crossed her arms in front of her. "Tom Marsh told my father last night that you are planning to leave with Joshua to scout for the army. Is that true?"

Wend nodded. "Bouquet is going to march to the Ohio, to relieve Fort Pitt. It's my chance to get out to the Indian country."

"Wend Eckert, I'm disappointed in you! I thought that after living here for almost four years, you had become one of us. But now, at the very moment that we're threatened with destruction, you choose to run off to settle personal matters. Haven't you thought about the fact that we need you here? You're the best scout and marksman in the valley and you are deserting us. It appears that you don't know how to show loyalty to your neighbors and friends. I had thought better of you."

Wend stood up, surprised at the vehemence in her words. "Peggy, it's not just about my personal matters! Bouquet thinks that marching to the Ohio Country will put fear into the tribes, and force them to stop their attacks on settlements like ours. So does the Reverend. I believe it may actually be the best way to protect the valley."

Disdain spread across her face. "Don't try to confuse the issue, Wend. You're just trying to justify chasing after that Philadelphia girl you are stuck on. Look, everybody knows why you haven't shown any interest in girls around here. The truth is, you aren't going to find that girl. All you're going to do is get yourself shot and lose the rest of your scalp! Meanwhile, there are women here who would make you a good wife and give you a fine family." She shook her head. "What a waste."

Wend stood looking at the girl, trying to think of something to say. But before he could gather his wits, Peggy abruptly turned around and walked off, her head bowed and her arms still crossed in front of her chest. He watched her as she slowly made her way down the wagon path toward the tavern.

* * *

The Cat knew Wend was leaving. He sat on his haunches atop the workbench and watched Wend pack supplies for gun repair into a canvas sack. After a few minutes, he voiced his unhappiness at Wend with a few high pitched, sharp cries. Finally, he turned around and lay down on the wooden table with his rear end toward Wend, thus performing his ultimate act of displeasure. Wend picked up his bag and slung it over his shoulder. "It's all right, Cat, I'll be back soon enough." He reached out to rub the animal behind its ears, but The Cat was having none of it. He shook his head to brush off Wend's fingers, emitted a single cry of anger, and then continued to stare off into the distance. "All right, go ahead and be mad at me. You're in good company. There seems to be a lot of others here in the valley who feel the same way."

It was dawn, just two days after Ayika had given birth to her son. Arnold had awakened shortly after the baby came, and after viewing the child and congratulating Franklin, had ridden off to Carlisle to rejoin Bouquet's staff. Now it was the turn of Wend and Joshua to leave.

Wend strode out of the shop toward the Carnahan's house through the early morning dusk. Joshua was already mounted, holding the reins to Wend's mare while talking to Paul, Patricia, Franklin and Ayika, who stood together waiting to say goodbye. Ayika had been up and working the day after giving birth.

Patricia came to Wend and threw her arms around him, tears running down her cheeks. "You come back to us, you hear?" She looked up at Baird. "You better take care of him or you'll answer to me!"

Joshua shook his head. "Here's my own sister no less, and all she can think about when I go off to war is Wend here."

"There's no sense my worrying about you, Joshua Baird. You are a total scoundrel, born to be hanged. The Good Lord won't let any Indian get you; he has his own retribution planned for you in his own good time. So I know you'll come back, same as you have every other time. Just make sure Wend stays in one piece and rides back with you."

Franklin looked up at Wend. "Remember me to Miss Abigail if you do get to see her, Mr. Wend. And bring her back if you can."

Reverend Carnahan took his pipe from his mouth as if to speak, but instead reached up silently to shake their hands. Finally he found words. "The Lord be with both of you."

It was still morning dusk as they rode down the hill into the village. The sound of their horses' hooves echoed in the stillness. No one was about, but Wend could see lights in the Marsh's house by the mill and in the tavern as the occupants prepared for the day's business. Smoke rose from the chimneys of most of the houses.

Suddenly the door of the tavern opened and Ellen McCartie came out. She ran over and they pulled up as she reached them. The girl stopped beside the mare and put a hand on Wend's leg. She looked up at him silently for a moment, as if trying to decide what to say. He could see tears had streaked her face. "Wend, I wanted to apologize for what I said to you at the fort. I was reacting out of my grief. But since then, I've realized that you were speaking the truth and were doing your best to console me about Johnny."

"Ellen, we both valued Johnny very much. Now it's up to us to keep his memory alive. I think we can do that best by honoring him in our hearts."

The girl nodded. "Wend, there are a lot of people who are angry at you; they say you are deserting us here in the valley. But I'm certain you are doing the right thing. And I know Johnny would have admired you for it. She reached down into a pocket and pulled out a small brass ring on a chain. "Here, Johnny made this for me and I wore it around my neck so it would be close to my heart. Keep it with you while you are gone, in memory of him. When you fight, his spirit will be with you. And after you're finished, bring it back to me. Then I'll be able to think that in the end, he really achieved a kind of victory."

Wend spoke gently. "Of course I will, Ellen. It's a wonderful thing for you to do. I'll wear this proudly and it will give me strength." He put the chain around his neck and dropped the ring down inside his shirt.

She nodded, turned and ran back to the tavern. Wend's eyes followed her, and then noticed that Peggy had also come out of the tavern and was standing beside the door, a broom in one hand. She was watching the proceedings with a stern look on her face. Wend looked over at Joshua, who sat staring back at him with a crooked smile and a twinkle in his eye, looking as if he was about to comment. Wend cut him off before he could speak. "Just don't say anything; I don't want to hear it, Joshua. Let's just ride. It's a long way to Carlisle."

Baird laughed out loud, but heeding Wend's words, said nothing. They roused their horses and carefully made their way across the ford. Joshua started his horse down the southbound road at a trot.

Wend pulled up his horse on the southern bank of the creek and looked back at the cluster of buildings which had been his home for four years. The mare, anxious to be off and alongside her stable mate, tossed her head, whinnied and pranced in nervous frustration. Wend pulled harder on the reins and stroked her neck to steady her. The village across the stream now lay bathed in the gentle light of the rising sun. Suddenly Wend realized how much the village, the valley and its people had come to mean to him. A thought formed in his mind: *No matter where fate led him during rest of his life, some part of him would always be an Ulsterman.*

He turned the mare southward and kicked her into a gallop to catch up with Joshua and to pursue the westward journey he had started four years earlier.

PART THREE

Call of the Pipes

1763

CHAPTER 16
Paths of the Warriors

Alice Downey stood in her doorway with her hands on her hips and a kitchen rag draped over her right shoulder. "For the last time, Joshua, there is no way you two are staying here!" Wend stood in the road, holding their horses, watching the drama unfold. Baird was up on the widow's front step, having knocked on the door until she appeared.

"Can't you see how crowded this town is, what with all the country folk come in to seek refuge from the savages?" Alice stamped her foot in frustration. "Right now I've got three families in this house, sleeping in every room. There are children running all around the house, and more people camping out in the yard. I'm spending my nights rolled up in blankets in front of the hearth. So how am I to find room for two more people now? Am I supposed to throw out paying lodgers to put you two up?"

Baird looked around in frustration. "Come on, Alice, where are we going to stay?"

"Well, the army called you to work for them. So why don't you go down to Carlisle Fort and find a place. Go see your Colonel Bouquet; you're his responsibility. Or go find a patch of field and camp out. There are plenty of people here living like that, and you've done it often enough!"

Wend reflected that the Widow was certainly right about conditions in Carlisle. The town was jammed with refugees. Farm wagons were parked in every empty lot, tents and canvas shelters had been set up in the most unlikely places alongside houses and taverns. As they rode into the settlement, they had seen pastures on the outskirts of the town filled with families living in the open.

The two scouts led their horses along Market Street to Washburn's Tavern where they could see a sentinel of the 60th Foot on duty outside the main entrance. They hitched the horses in the stableyard and entered the common room.

Inside, the tavern was in near pandemonium, crowded with men standing or sitting in groups talking animatedly. Others were drinking and eating. There were several highland officers present, some in the uniform of the 77th, others in a slightly different uniform with blue facings; Wend guessed they were from the 42nd Black Watch. Most of the civilians appeared to be contractors of various trades waiting for an audience with Bouquet.

Joshua and Wend pushed their way up to the counter. Washburn was bustling to meet the demands of his clientele, and had more serving people working than Wend had ever seen before in the tavern. The tavern keeper waved at the two from the far end of the bar and a serving man came to take their order. After a few hurried gulps, Joshua left to go to the back rooms and tell Bouquet's adjutant that he was in town. Meanwhile, Wend noticed that the rack where his display rifle usually hung was empty and concluded that Washburn had been able to sell the latest specimen, which had been in place for only a short while.

Presently Washburn came over. "Wend, I'm glad to see you. I sold that last rifle of yours a week ago, at a premium price, no questions asked! The demand for firearms is insatiable in this town. How soon can you get another ready for me to display? Or better yet, several guns. I know we can sell them rapidly!"

Wend shook his head. "No more rifles for a while, George. I'm going as a scout on Bouquet's expedition to Fort Pitt."

"You can't mean that lad! You're not serious?" The shock on Washburn's face was genuine.

'Of course I'm serious, George. Bouquet needs scouts."

"My God, lad! No one thinks Bouquet is going to be successful. Look at what happened to Braddock in '55. Then those same tribes nearly destroyed Major Grant's force at Duquesne in '58. Braddock had 1200 men at the battle, Grant had 800. And Bouquet is trying to fight his way to Pitt with only 400, put together from the fragments of three broken regiments. The wager here in town is that we'll never see a man of his battalion again after they march out." He put his hand on Wend's arm. "For God's sake, lad, this is insanity. Think about your future!"

Wend tried to think of a way to answer the tavern keeper, but words did not immediately come to mind.

Washburn shook his head. "Four years ago, at this very bar, I questioned Johann about taking his family out into that wilderness when he had a good business in Lancaster. And now it seems like you are going to follow in his footsteps." The older man squeezed Wend's arm again and spoke very quietly but forcefully. "You've built a great reputation here in the county, lad. Now there's the opportunity to make a lot of money while this emergency lasts. Why don't you go back to Sherman Valley and follow your trade. If your father had done that your family would still be alive."

Now Wend found the right words. "George, there are times when making more money isn't the right answer. In fact, I am doing this in the memory of my family. I have a score to settle. And there's the matter of a girl forced to spend her life as a prisoner of the Mingoes. So I'll take my chances, whatever the cost."

Washburn looked down at the counter, then up at Wend again. He was ready to speak when Joshua came back and grabbed Wend's elbow. "Hey, Sprout, finish your drink and come with me. Bouquet wants to see us right now." He tossed down the rest of his ale and strode off toward the military rooms. Wend nodded to Washburn and followed the scout.

They walked into the anteroom where Bouquet's current adjutant, a stout, middle aged man, very different from the elegant lieutenant Locke, waited for them standing beside his desk. Alongside him stood a young, thin highland lieutenant in the green-faced uniform of the 77th. Arnold was at a writing table, now in his dress uniform instead of the field clothing he had worn in Sherman Mill, feverishly working to copy a letter. Both men had piles of paper in front of them. Arnold looked up at Wend and gave him a wink and a nod by way of greeting, then went back to his paperwork.

The adjutant stuck his hand out to Wend. "Glad to meet you, Eckert: My name is Dow. I'm the regimental quartermaster, temporarily doubling as the adjutant. Joshua told me you'd be helping him. Of course, I've heard about your history from Corporal Spengler." He turned to the highland officer and introduced him as Donald Campbell. "The colonel will give you details, but you three are going to be working together for a while." Dow went to Bouquet's office and opened the door. He said a few words to Bouquet, and then motioned the three men to go inside.

It was the first time Wend had seen Bouquet since the night at Fort Loudoun four years earlier. Now he was standing over a map spread out on his desk, his coat off, his waistcoat unbuttoned and the collar of his white shirt open. The room was hot, even with the single window open, and the colonel showed beads of perspiration on his forehead and around his neck.

Bouquet looked up. "Joshua! I've been waiting for you!" He smiled at Wend. "And here is young Eckert. I'm especially glad to see that you have decided to join us, Sir."

The colonel leaned over the map again. Wend could see that it showed western Pennsylvania, including the mountain ridges, the towns and forts, and the path of Forbes Road. It was the first time he had ever seen the course of the road on paper.

"Gentlemen, Mr. Dow and I were discussing the tactical situation." Bouquet pointed to the western part of the map. "You should know that all of our smaller posts along the border with the Ohio Country and through the large lakes to the north—eight in all—have been taken by the Indians. Only Detroit and Niagara in the north and Pitt here in Pennsylvania remain in our hands. The tribes used trickery to take most of the forts, and where that didn't work, they burned out the garrisons, which were simply too small to put up a sustained resistance. Most of our men and their families in those forts are dead. A few men and a woman escaped from Fort LeBoef, on the Allegheny north of Pitt, and were able steal through the forest to Fort Pitt."

Bouquet looked at Joshua. "Our good friend, Colonel Will Clapham, is dead. A group of Delawares came into his trading post one day in May, demanding to buy all the powder and lead he had. That made him suspicious and he sent a messenger with a warning to Ecuyer at the fort. He also refused to sell more than a small amount to each individual. That was his last service to us. The next day the Delawares came back and murdered Clapham, his family and employees, then burned the post to the ground. Obviously they got all the powder and lead he had."

Baird shook his head in sadness. "He and his family were always good to me."

Bouquet nodded and moved his finger from the forks of the Ohio eastward. "Fort Pitt is under siege. In the last communication we got from Captain Ecuyer at Pitt, he tells us he is surrounded by at least 500 warriors. He has 150 soldiers of my regiment there and near 500 settlers have crowded into the fort. Their situation is desperate. Ecuyer reports that much of his remaining flour has gone bad and there is smallpox among the settlers. But he's most desperate for ammunition. They had serious flooding during the rains this spring and one of the powder magazines was submerged in river water. The powder that was there is ruined."

Baird pointed to the map. "What about the forts along Forbes Road, Colonel?"

Bouquet nodded. "Good question, Joshua. They were reduced to mere supply stations last year. Their garrisons are twelve men or less—just enough to manage the storage and shipment of provisions and military supplies with help from contractors. The commanders, Lieutenant Blane at Ligonier and Captain Ourry at Bedford, have organized settlers into militia companies which form the real basis of the defense. From what I can tell, the tribes are conducting a loose siege of those two forts. A few warriors watch them while war parties are raiding the surrounding countryside and destroying farms."

Baird looked at the colonel. "It'd be a Hell of a problem if either of those fell to the savages. We're going to need them as way stations."

Bouquet nodded. "Exactly, Joshua; while I organize the expedition, we must do something to protect the forts along Forbes Road. To that object, I have sent Captain Robertson and his company of the 77th down to Fort Loudoun, where the contractors Plumsted and Franks are assembling a herd of bullocks and packhorses. When that's done, Robertson and his men will escort the herd to Fort Bedford and then garrison that fort until I arrive with the main force."

"Fort Lyttleton was abandoned back in '60. But George Croghan, the trader, has raised, at his own expense, a company of twenty-five men to provide a garrison. Thus that fort can serve as a refuge for settlers in the Great Cove area and as a station on our march west."

Bouquet turned to Lieutenant Campbell. "That brings me to your role. Pick an officer, two sergeants, two corporals, and thirty men from the companies which remain here to make up a flying detachment. Mr. Baird and Mr. Eckert will lead you, by the shortest distance along the back trails, directly from Carlisle to Bedford. You will get there before Robertson and his men, burdened as they are with the herd and the necessity of following the road. Discuss the situation with Ourry: If he needs reinforcement immediately, stay there until Robertson arrives. Otherwise, resume your march and relieve Ligonier. That is your ultimate objective."

Campbell studied the map for a moment and then nodded his understanding to the colonel.

Bouquet looked up from the map. "The detachment will leave tomorrow morning at dawn. Baird and Eckert will take you as far as Bedford. Another scout, Daniel Carmichael, is at Bedford already and he will guide you onward to Ligonier." Bouquet looked directly at Joshua. "I want you back here as soon as possible, to scout when the whole expedition marches out. So don't tarry. And bring me back what intelligence you can on the activities of the war parties between Bedford and here."

Joshua pointed to features on the map. "Colonel, we'll use the old Frankstown Trail, which runs southwest to the mountains and then to Lyttleton. That'll take 'bout two days. Then we'll use the Raystown Path, and some shortcuts I know, to make our way to Bedford." Joshua pointed to the Juniata River, which flowed southward between Sideling Hill and Bedford. "What's the situation at the post at Juniata Crossing?"

"Abandoned, Joshua; the men there retired to Bedford. There were only a sergeant and four men at the crossing station, not enough to face any attack. So you'll have to find a good place to cross on your own."

The scout considered for a moment. "All right, Colonel, figure another two days to Bedford from Lyttleton. Four days total, if we don't meet any trouble. By pushing it, I 'spect that Eckert and me can be back in eight or nine days from now, the Lord willing."

Bouquet nodded and said to Campbell, "All right, that's the plan. But speed is the key, so you need to make haste in picking your men and getting rations together." The colonel reflected silently for a moment, then continued, "Maintain the greatest caution, particularly at night, of being surprised by the savages. If you are attacked, don't act defensively, for they will hide and pick you off one by one. Fix bayonets and charge! Force your way through them; they will never stand when attacked vigorously and are only dangerous to people who appear to fear them."

Bouquet made to dismiss the three of them, but as they started to leave, held up his hand for them to stop. "One more thing: As you approach Bedford, you need to know that Captain Ourry has scouting parties out dressed like Indians. But you will easily distinguish them by a white string tied around their heads and a spot of white paint on the inside of their hands, which they are to spread when they discover friends. Make sure your men know about these marks."

Campbell nodded, and the three left Bouquet's office. Wend looked back and saw that Bouquet had seated himself at his desk, his elbows on the table in front of him and his hands holding his head as he looked down at the map.

* * *

Wend walked rapidly up Market Street toward the Widow Downey's house. He was carrying spare clothing and other items from Joshua's and his own kits to be stored at the widow's while they made their trip to Bedford. He also had in a pocket the payment from Washburn for the sale of the display rifle, which he intended to leave for safekeeping with Alice. He was not paying much attention to his surroundings, his mind occupied by preparations for the impending march through the bush. Then suddenly he became aware that someone was standing in front of him.

"Hello, Mr. Wend Eckert. It's good to see you again!"

He looked up to see a young, willowy girl with copper hair, brown eyes, a small upturned nose, and a smattering of freckles over her face. He had no idea who she was or why she knew his name. He struggled to find polite words. "I'm sorry, miss, but I must admit that you have me at a disadvantage."

The girl threw back her head and laughed. "I knew it! You don't remember me." She shook her head and giggled. "And to think how many days I spent sitting beside you, feeding you, washing your wounds and changing those dressings, putting poultices on your scalp." She took a step to the side and looked at the back of his head. "You have learned to cover it up very well, Wend. No one would notice if they weren't aware of what had happened to you."

Wend's mind feverishly groped through his past. Then he realized that there was indeed something familiar about the girl. He examined her more closely, and saw that she was wearing a blue dress. Then his heart nearly stopped. Good God! It was faded, frayed, torn and mended in several places, but it was without a doubt the traveling dress he had first seen on Abigail Gibson at Harris' Ferry, and had last seen in the hands of Lizzie Iverson on Forbes Road. He looked at the girl again; at the auburn hair, the high cheekbones, the strong mouth, the thin frame. But it couldn't be Lizzie Iverson; she would be much older. Then it dawned on him.

"You're Mary; Mary Fraser, of the 77th; Lizzie Iverson's daughter!"

The girl smiled broadly, her face wrinkling so the smile seemed to spread across her entire countenance; her eyes, her cheeks, even her forehead. "Well, you finally made the right guess, but I did have to give you a lot of clues."

Wend was still non-plussed. "I'm sorry; I should have recognized you, Mary. After all the time you spent with me and all the help you and your mother were. I can't find words to apologize for not recognizing you."

"Oh, come on Wend. Don't be so serious. How could you have been expected to know me after four years? And besides, I was only eleven then, going on twelve. Now I'm nearly sixteen. I expect I've changed a wee bit since then!"

Wend looked at the pretty girl in front of him and mentally agreed. "Well, I still apologize. I am very thankful for what you did for me." Wend touched his hand to his hat in an act of belated gallantry.

Mary looked around for a second and then a twinkle came into her eyes. "Well, if you are so concerned about making amends, you could take me into this tavern for some tea. That would be very pleasant."

Wend looked around and realized that their encounter had occurred right in front of The Walking Horse Tavern. He gazed through the windows and could see numerous patrons around tables, taking their late afternoon refreshment.

Mary extended him her arm, and Wend realized he could not politely do anything else but acquiesce, so he took it and escorted her into the tavern. In any case, he was intrigued by the girl and the chance meeting. Wend opened the door and followed her into the common room. Once inside, they stood together blinking in the relative darkness of the tavern. In a moment, a male server came up to them and asked if he could help.

Wend nodded. "We need a table for some tea and pastries." As he spoke, Mary looked around at the well appointed room and again took his arm.

The serving man looked at them appraisingly, noting the girl's frayed attire, and made a brief grimace. Then he started to lead them to a table in the back of the room near the door to the kitchen. Mary said, "Oh, can't we have a table back there at the window, so we can look out at the street? And it would be so much brighter."

The server grimaced again, but showed them to the table Mary had indicated, and held her chair while she seated herself. Wend had just taken his seat when another man came up to the table.

"Excuse me, sir. But could I speak to you?" He motioned to the counter.

Wend excused himself and accompanied the man to the bar.

"Ah, Sir, my name is McCallin. I'm the proprietor of this establishment and I'm obliged to ask you, shall we say, a delicate question."

Wend stared at the man, who didn't want to meet his eyes. "Good afternoon, Sir. Eckert is my name. And what can I do for you?"

"Well, you understand, Sir, that I have to protect myself and my establishment. And right now in this town we have all sorts of people in the most embarrassing circumstances; country people fleeing from the war parties, travelers unable to proceed because of the danger, and then there are these army camp followers." The man glanced meaningfully toward Mary.

Wend looked at the girl and had to admit that she looked shabby in the old dress, tattered bonnet, and scuffed, dirt- caked shoes. Then he realized that he was not dressed in his usual town clothes; he had on the rough clothing that he had worn to ride down from Sherman Mill.

"Not to put to fine a point on it, Sir, but there have been people who have come in over the last few days, and, how shall I say this, haven't had the means to afford our custom?" Now, having said it, the tavern owner looked directly at Wend and clasped his hands in front of him, almost as if he were in prayer.

Anger welled up in Wend. His first thought was to simply gather up Mary and walk out of the tavern. He would take her to Larkin's or Washburn's where he would be welcomed by either proprietor with enthusiasm. Then, looking around the room, he saw well-dressed men and women staring at him and the girl with disdain. He glanced at Mary, who sat smiling, looking out the window, oblivious to the stares and what was occurring at the counter. Stifling his anger, he decided that there was no way he was going to cause her embarrassment or allow McCallin to spoil her enjoyment.

Wend turned to face the bar, so that his back was to the tables in the common room. He reached over, grabbed the arm of the proprietor, and pulled him close so that no one besides the two of them could see what was transpiring. Then he reached into his pocket and took out his bag of coins. He opened it and spilled the money out on the counter. He watched with considerable gratification as the tavern owner's eyes opened wide. Wend reached down and picked up several coins worth at least triple the amount that any tea and cakes could possibly cost and carefully placed them in McCallin's pocket. Then he scooped up the rest of the money and put it back into the pouch.

"I take it that there will be no more questions, Sir?" Wend put as much disdain as he could manage into the word "Sir". Then, without waiting for a response, he whispered very quietly, but with a threatening edge in his voice, to McCallin: "A few years ago, that girl and other 'camp followers' as you call them, nursed me back to health after the savages left me for dead on Forbes Road. I hold her in the highest esteem and I shall not look kindly on any slight that anyone in this tavern might visit upon her. In fact, I expect that you and your staff will afford her the most gracious service within your capacity. Do I make myself clear?"

McCallin looked at him nervously, his left eye twitching furiously, and tried to pull away from Wend's hand. Wend tightened his grip on the man's arm, looked at him as menacingly as he could manage, and repeated, "Do we understand each other?"

The proprietor visibly gulped and nodded acquiesance. Wend released McCallin's arm, turned and strode back to the table. As he walked, he made sure to scan the room and defiantly meet the eyes of every patron who was staring at the table. Each in turn looked quickly down or away as he returned their glance.

He sat down and smiled at Mary. But even as he smiled, he was still shaking with rage. Then he focused his mind and felt calmness slowly returning.

Mary looked at him and beamed. "It was very fortunate that we met. Are you in town for business, or did you come here because of the Indians, like all these other people?"

"Actually, I am here because of the Indians. Joshua Baird and I are going to scout for Colonel Bouquet's column when it leaves." He looked into her eyes, which he realized were soft and soothing, whereas Abigail's had been so piercing. "You remember Joshua, don't you?"

"How could I ever forget Joshua? He was like my uncle. And my Mum was very fond of him."

"How is your mother? She certainly did a wonderful job putting me back together!"

A cloud crossed the girl's face. "She's dead, Wend. So is Sergeant Iverson. They died of the yellow fever, during the campaign in the West Indies. We lost many, many people down there. More than we ever lost in battle. The regiment is really just a skeleton now."

"I'm terribly sorry Mary. Your mother was a marvelous woman. But how did you avoid getting the disease?"

"I didn't. I was one of the first to get it. Mum nursed me through it; I probably survived because I was young and strong." She looked down, then out the window for a moment before resuming. "Then she got the sickness, and died in just a week. The sergeant died a few days after Mum."

"Well, how are you supporting yourself now? You don't have any other relatives with the regiment."

"I work as a nurse with the surgeon. You can imagine how busy he has been with all the men down with fever. Some of our men are still recovering and are so weak that they can only travel in wagons. I also do laundry for soldiers. So between the work as a nurse and washing clothes, I make a little money and rate a woman's ration." She smiled. "Mr. Ferguson, the chaplain, watches out for me. He calls me 'a child of the regiment.' He has been schooling me and I get time off from the hospital every day to study with him." Mary lifted her chin proudly. "Would you believe I am actually learning to read and make my letters?"

"That's wonderful Mary. But I heard that the regiment is about to be disbanded. What will you do when that happens?"

Mary frowned for a moment, took a deep breath, then brightened. "Mr. Ferguson thinks I may be able to go with the 42nd. They're going to take in men from our regiment who want to remain in the service. He's been talking about that with the chaplain and surgeon of the 42nd to see if it can be arranged."

Just then the serving man arrived at their table with an elegant tea service and pastries on a platter. He carefully laid out the food and drink, and in a very courteous tone, asked if there was anything else he could get them. Wend looked up at the man, ready to be offended at the slightest smirk on his face, but could find none. "This will be fine, thank you."

Mary served Wend and herself with the tea and then pounced on the cakes. "I've never seen such pretty cakes in my life." She bit into one, savoring the taste. "These are wonderful!" She finished it with delight and then attacked another.

Wend watched the girl devour the sweets. He remembered the coarseness of the meals he had had while on the march with the highlanders and realized that the delicate pastries must be something she had rarely, if ever, experienced.

Mary paused, a cake in her hand, and said, "Now you must tell me about what has happened to you in the last four years."

So he told her about Sherman Mill, about the Carnahans, his work as a gunsmith, Franklin's return, his travels around the colony, and lastly about the raid of the war party and the fear among the settlers. After a few more cakes, she was sated with the pastry and sipped at her tea while she listened. She kept her eyes on him while he talked, and Wend noticed that she seemed to have real interest in his story, which encouraged him to keep talking.

After Wend had talked himself out, Mary put her hands to her chin. "I'm so glad to see that you have recovered from the massacre and prospered well." There was an extended pause in the conversation. Mary looked out at the waning afternoon light. "Wend, I have to get back to the camp. The surgeon's evening rounds will be soon, and I'll have to be there to go with him."

Wend started to gather up his kit. "Shall I escort you back to Carlisle Fort?"

Mary looked at Wend's gear, and said, "Oh, that would be lovely. But I think that I interrupted you from going about business. I can make my own way back, and I must hurry."

Wend realized that he did have to get to the Widow's and then back to Washburn's to be sure that the horses were settled in at the tavern's stable. He and Joshua would be walking, not riding on the mission to Bedford, and he wanted to make sure that the arrangements for the mare and Joshua's mount were complete.

"Besides, there are plenty of men from the regiment on the streets. I'll not want for help if something goes amiss!"

They left the tavern together and Wend touched his hat to her again. As he was about to turn and leave, Mary put her hand on his arm and looked up at him, her face suddenly serious. "Thank you for a lovely time. I've never been in such an elegant place before. You made me feel like a real lady taking her afternoon repast." Then she moved more closely to him, looking right into his eyes. "And it was very gallant of you to stand up to that tavern keeper on my behalf."

She squeezed his arm momentarily, then turned and walked off toward the fort, as Wend stood and watched her go. After she had gone a few yards, she turned quickly, smiled and waved back at him, then hurried on her way.

Wend stood in front of the tavern as he watched the thin, blue clad figure making her way down Market Street. He was suddenly aware of a warm glow spreading over him.

* * *

The column actually left well before dawn, the picked company marching out of Carlisle Fort by under the first glinting of false dawn. A sentry presented arms to Lieutenant Campbell as they left the sleeping encampment, and a few sleepy eyed stable boys at their early chores watched as the troops tramped down Market Street, the highlanders in a column of threes, keeping a precise cadence without the assistance of drums. The rhythmic tramp of their feet on the packed dirt echoed through the dark, empty streets. Joshua and Wend, now in their hunting shirts and leggings, walked behind the last rank, their rifles in the crooks of their arms.

After leaving the town Campbell had the men break ranks and sling their muskets over their shoulders. Joshua took the lead and set a grueling pace. Initially they followed the wagon road to the southwest through the valley. The Frankstown Trail actually started near Shippensburg, but after they had gone several miles, and the sun was fairly up, Joshua led them off the road and onto a side path which he said would angle down to intercept the trail and take miles off their journey. Moving through the country made the walking even tougher; the path was faint at best and sometimes Wend could discern no path at all. But Joshua led with confidence and just as the sun was directly overhead they cut the well-worn trader's trail and the walking became easier.

The highlanders had been picked evenly from the 77th and 42nd, the major criteria being their health and stamina. Wend had been surprised to find that the senior sergeant was McCulloch, the man who had found him lying on Forbes Road so long ago. Most of the soldiers had no trouble keeping up with the lanky scout as he strode along but Wend suffered from the pace. He realized that his long days in the workshop had not prepared him for the sustained exercise. He had trouble getting his breath; sweat covered his face and poured down his back. He welcomed the few, brief rest stops the column made, dropping to the ground in relief.

The soldiers had spent the evening before preparing for the march through the bush. Instead of kilts, all were dressed in tan breaches of rough material with leggings up to their knees. At Joshua's urging, Lieutenant Campbell had inspected each man and had him rap rags around most of their equipment—canteens, bayonets, metal buckles—to reduce noise and to prevent a glint of the sun's reflection from being seen at some distance.

By dusk they had crossed the Cumberland Valley and were at the base of the mountains which formed its western boundary. Joshua pushed on until darkness enclosed them, then led them a score of yards off the path where they made a cold camp. They dropped to the ground, ate dried rations, and except for two sentinels, dropped immediately off to the sleep of exhaustion. Wend had a fitful rest; his legs were cramping and the muscles twitching from their unaccustomed work. And just when it seemed he had finally been able to fall into a deep sleep, the rough hand of Sergeant McCulloch tugged at his shoulder to rouse him for the new day's journey.

The second days' march was even harder than the first, for on that day Joshua led them over and through the mountains. They crossed by obscure, steep and winding paths. Joshua told Campbell that at one point they were less than a mile from Forbes Road itself as it wound up from Fort Loudoun and thence through the gap. Wend labored to keep his place in the single file of soldiers, focusing his mind on simply putting one foot in front of another through the long day. The path itself became rougher, with roots, rocks and fallen logs obstructing the way constantly. But by late afternoon they had made it through the passes and the scout brought the column out of the bush onto Forbes Road itself. Wend looked around and realized that they were in the vicinity of the Burnt Cabins, just a few miles north of Lyttleton. Following a brief stop for rest and a bite of rations, they marched easily along the road, arriving at the fort shortly after dark.

The fort was populated by the militia which George Croghan had raised and a large number of families who had come in from the Great Cove to shelter within the walls. The fort itself was in a state of deterioration, though the militia company was working to make essential repairs. By the light of the settler's fires, Wend could see where new logs had been placed in the stockade and that work on the buildings inside was underway.

The garrison and the settlers rushed to gather around the troops, heartened by their first tangible evidence that the Crown was responding to the emergency and eager to get the latest news from the east. Campbell briefed them on the status of Bouquet's preparations for the march west and of the impending arrival of Captain Robertson and the herd his company was escorting to Bedford. Meanwhile, the highlanders set up camp just outside the stockade, eagerly lit fires and ate their first warm food since leaving Carlisle. Wend was too exhausted to eat more than a few bites and in less than an hour after their arrival was in deep sleep in front of a fire.

They were marching again before dawn, only the sentry at the fort's gate awake to see them go. Joshua led them to a path which ran through hilly country, several miles to the north of Forbes Road. That day they saw their first sign of warriors; Baird found an Indian camp site near the trail, similar to the one he, Wend and Johnny Donaldson had visited at the western end of Sherman Valley. The scout pointed out signs that it had been used recently— moccasin tracks, remnants of a meal, fresh ashes in the campfire circle. Then the column moved on, every man now much more aware that they were marching though a hostile land and that an encounter with a war party was a very real possibility.

By noon they were climbing Sideling Hill, which formed the western boundary of the Great Cove. Wend was acutely aware that only a few miles south was the place on Forbes Road where his family had died. But now he was glad for the hard pace that Joshua was setting, for it gave him little time to reflect on the events of that sad day. As they climbed, they were able to look down on the canopy of green, interspersed with cleared fields that marked the Cove.

That night the column camped at the crest of Sideling. Wend slept fitfully, the journey of 1759 playing and replaying in his dreams. He was reliving the massacre itself when he was jarred awake by Joshua's hand. It was totally dark, but Wend could feel the morning dampness.

"Come on Sprout, get up. King George is paying you to be a scout, so now its time for you to start earning that pay."

Wend threw his blanket off, picked up his rifle and followed Joshua through the darkness. Baird led him onward for a few hundred yards, though Wend could see only the back of the scout in the blackness and had no idea of where they were going. His feet caught on obstructions several times and once he stumbled and fell. He finally realized that they were moving along the very crest of the hill, for they did no sustained climbing. Eventually Wend became aware that the sky was lighting with false dawn. Just then Joshua stopped and Wend made out the trunk of a tree right in front of them with its first set of branches low to the ground.

"All right, Sprout; lay your rifle down and start climbing. Go up as far as the branches will hold your weight."

Wend was mortified. He had never been adept at climbing trees, and the thought of doing it in the dark terrified him. "Joshua, I'm no good at this; especially in the middle of the night. Can't I wait until there's more light?"

"Nonsense, lad. The only reason to bring you along on this trip is so you can do things my ancient bones ain't up to anymore. This paltry little tree shouldn't be any problem for a youngster like you." Joshua leaned close to Wend. "Now listen: The purpose for you going up the tree is to be there at first real light. You'll get a grand view of the Cove from the top, and I want you to survey the area for any sign of a war party, particularly smoke. A war party may feel pretty secure out here, where they don't think there is any soldiers around and settlers are hunkered down in their farms or forted up somewhere. So they may think its all right to have a comfortable camp. You saw the fresh ashes in that campsite yesterday." He gave Wend a pat. "So get on up there and wait for dawn." Joshua sat down and lay back on the ground, placing his arms behind his head.

Wend fought his panic and began to climb. Luckily the tree had many branches close together and he was able to feel his way upward. After what seemed an eternity of picking his way through the limbs, he reached a point where his every movement caused the tree top to sway and the branches he was standing on bent easily to his weight. He stopped and held on tightly to the tree, waiting for the light.

Dawn came in less than an hour; Wend's view of the rising sun from his elevated position was magnificent. But the beauty of the moment was lost on him for the growing illumination also permitted Wend to see the area directly below the tree for the first time. He was horrified to realize that his tree stood on the very edge of a steep precipice at the side of the mountain. The drop below him was hundreds of feet! Wend felt a momentary surge of dizziness and panic, closed his eyes, and held onto the tree for dear life.

A soft call came up from the ground. "Hey Sprout, are you asleep up there? You're hugging that tree as if it were your long lost Abigail."

"Joshua, are you crazy? Sending me up here in the dark was lunacy! This tree is hanging out over the side of the mountain. If I fall I'm a dead man!"

"Good Lord, Sprout, it wouldn't have done any good sending you up a tree in the middle of the woods. You wouldn't be able to see anything!" Baird rose from the ground, and looked over the side of the mountain. He screwed up his face as if he were considering a grave proposition, and said thoughtfully, "And besides, if you fall I don't expect you'll feel a thing, not as high as the hill is here."

"For God's sake, Joshua, you could have at least have told me about the drop-off before I went up the tree."

"Wouldn't have made any difference; besides, you might not have gone up there." The scout laughed, then said, "Time to stop passing the time of day and get to work. I want you to scan the woods for any sign, particularly smoke. Take your time and look real careful."

Wend did as he was told. He started looking to the north, and slowly checked all the way around to the south. He saw nothing; nothing except the green carpet of the tree tops and clearings which marked farmsteads. Then, far to the south, he made out the thin sliver of Forbes Road. But there was no smoke or other sign of a possible war party. "There's nothing visible, Joshua."

"Look again, right along the mountain, Sprout. If there's a party around, they may be up here on the ridge somewhere."

Wend inspected the slopes from north to south, then did it again. He still saw nothing, and was about to say as much to Baird. But as he looked down at the scout, he caught something with the corner of his eye. It was on the mountain slope to the south, slightly down from the very crest of the hill. It wasn't smoke, not what he saw first, it was a kind of distortion in the air. Then he realized it for what it was; shimmering, heated air above a fire. He focused on the spot; then he finally saw the smoke, a thin, rising column, almost immediately dispersed by the small breeze that had come with dawn.

"Joshua!" Wend's voice became exited. "There is a fire; down to the south, just below the crest. It's very faint; just the least amount of smoke, as if they were keeping the fire as small as possible. But it's definitely there."

"All right, Sprout. Don't get excited. Now tell me how far away it is."

"It's hard to tell; not that far. Maybe a mile at the outside; it's just down the hill from a pile of boulders."

Joshua nodded his understanding. "Just below a pile of rocks, you say? All right, you can come down now. We need to get back to the column."

Wend made his way to the ground, being careful not to look down as he descended for fear he would freeze. When he got to the bottom, Baird handed him his rifle and began to make his way away from the precipice.

Campbell had the company ready to move when they arrived back at the camp. Sergeant McCulloch was inspecting each man's kit to make sure all was ready for the day's march. Joshua briefed the officer quickly on the location of the war party and his plans to avoid them. In just a few minutes they were moving, every man taking special care to avoid making noise. Joshua took them on a detour further to the north, along the ridge, then down the hill on a cross country route. But after a couple of hours he had again brought them onto the Raystown Path and they started to make better time.

They crossed the Juniata at mid-afternoon, using a ford where the water level was between their knees and their waists, holding their firearms, powder, and food over their heads. From there Joshua said it was fourteen miles to Fort Bedford and he set a stiff pace along the well worn path.

After covering half of that distance, Joshua and Wend ran ahead to scout the path and look for any sign of the hostile war parties which were known to be ranging around Bedford. And very shortly they literally bumped into warriors at a bend in the trail. There was a tense pause as both parties spied each other and froze, at a distance of about forty yards. But instantly both scouts recovered from their shock and flung themselves into cover beside the path. Wend's heart started pounding. He had his rifle up to his shoulder in a moment and his fingers on the triggers. But Baird reached over, tapped Wend on his shoulder and pointed at the men. Then Wend saw the white headbands on all of the "warriors". There were four of them, and after a few seconds all raised their hands to show the white spot on the palm. They had encountered one of Captain Ourry's scouting parties, camouflaged as Bouquet had indicated, in Indian dress and paint. The patrol was doing the same thing as Wend and Joshua, checking out the trail for Indian sign.

One of the black painted men shouted, "That you, Joshua?" The men around him started laughing among themselves at some joke. The voice continued, "You sure are doing a damned good imitation of a scared hare hiding from the dogs. Come on out, I got some good whiskey for you here in my canteen."

Baird stood up and walked toward the patrol. "Tell you what Daniel, all that paint you got on sure makes for an improvement. Maybe you should wear it all the time."

Wend followed Baird to where the men of the patrol stood, leaning on their grounded rifles. After Joshua and the leader of the group traded another round of sociable insults, Joshua introduced Wend. The man was Daniel Carmichael, the scout who was to guide the company of highlanders on the road beyond Bedford.

Carmichael handed Joshua his canteen; he drank deeply, then stiffened in response to the effect of the alcohol. Joshua grinned and passed the container to Wend, who followed the older scout's example. The fiery liquid burned all the way down, but he welcomed the warming feeling which soon followed.

Carmichael told them that he, along with several other woodsmen from the Shippensburg area, had traveled to Bedford about a week before at Bouquet's behest. They had carried advance word to Ourry about the planned march of the highlanders. Now their orders were to sweep the path to the eastward, then scout northward and back to Bedford in a wide circle to determine the scope of war party activity. "We'll be back in the fort late tomorrow; then I can lead the highlanders west, if Ourry decides to send them onward. In the meantime, I expect they'll be ready for a day of rest after marching from Carlisle."

Baird nodded. "We'll take them down to the fort, and then leave to rejoin Bouquet tomorrow, Daniel."

The conversation continued, with Carmichael briefing Joshua on his estimate on the number of war parties around Bedford, and the scope of their depredations. "Sometimes there are a bunch of hostiles around the fort, then for a while there are none in evidence. But they always come back and announce their presence by throwing a few shots at the fort or making off with some of the settlers' livestock which have been herded up around the fort. They obviously want to keep us guessing and forted up in the stockade. But it's clear from the smoke we see every day that they are scouring the countryside, burning down the farmsteads."

One of the men pointed up the path and Wend turned to see the advance guard of the highland company approaching. Soon the entire company had joined the group of men at the bend in the path. The highlanders settled on the ground, taking drinks from their canteens while Carmichael repeated his briefing of the situation at Bedford to Lieutenant Campbell.

After a few minutes, Carmichael's party left to continue their patrol and Campbell got the company back on the march. By the time the sun was touching the western horizon, they had the fort in sight. It was sited in the center of a great cleared area, with what looked like smaller stockades and some private buildings all around the main fort. A tributary creek of the Juniata ran right by the main stockade.

As the company filed out into the open area, they could see that many settlers were camped around the fort and animals were gathered in fenced areas.

Wend found their reception at the fort exciting and gratifying. As they left the woods, Campbell stopped the company. He turned to Joshua with a wink and a smile. "Let's give the good people of Bedford something to cheer them up." He turned to a corporal who had a set of bagpipes slung over his shoulder, "McTavish, have you got enough wind left to sound the pipes?"

The corporal nodded and slipped the pipes off his back. He put the mouthpiece to his lips and started to fill the bag with air. One of the other highlanders said, "When has McTavish not had more than enough wind?" All the others laughed in unison as if at an old joke.

Campbell ordered the company to fix bayonets, then nodded to the piper. The lieutenant and McCulloch formed the men into a loose skirmish line, each man three or four feet from the next, and then waved them forward. Wend and Joshua followed behind the rank of men, the bagpipes making their wild, heart quickening music. Feeling the effect of the music, the company increased its pace from a walk to a near run across the open area.

As they swept forward, Wend could see people emerging from the campsites and the interior of the fort, gathering into groups and looking their way. Then he heard the sound of cheering and he could see settlers hugging each other as they watched the soldiers' approach, the last rays of light glinting off their bayonets.

When the detail halted before the gates of the fort, the settlers swarmed around them, men shaking the hands of the soldiers, women and young girls hugging them, small boys gawking at the troops and their accouterments. A very nice looking young girl threw her arms around Wend and said "Thank you, thank you!" Then she moved on to provide the same greeting to one of the highlanders, a young private standing next to Wend. He accepted the girl's enthusiastic greeting with relish and gave Wend a wink as she wrapped her arms around him.

Captain Ourry was, like Bouquet, a Swiss professional soldier with a heavy accent and a hearty manner. He returned Campbell's salute and shook Joshua's hand. "Well, my old friend," he said as he pumped Baird's hand, "I see that the good colonel has pressed you back into the service."

Ourry, Campbell, and Baird shortly went into the fort's headquarters to make plans. Campbell's assistant, Lieutenant McIntosh, helped by McCulloch, got the company settled in camp, and much to their pleasure, a group of women took over the chore of preparing a stew for the men of the column.

Soon Wend was sitting in front of a warm fire with the company's non-commissioned officers, enjoying the stew, good bread and ale. After the tribulations of the march, he felt contentment spreading over him. His companions ate with gusto, then leaned back and took out pipes and tobacco. In the manner of soldiers in every place and time, they started to swap jokes and tell stories about themselves and their comrades. Since the detail was made up of men from both the 77th and the Black Watch, it didn't take long until they began comparing notes about the different campaigns of the regiments, and each side vying to show that their lot had been harder than the other's. The men of the 42nd told of the great assault on Fort Ticonderoga in 1758, when half of their battalion had become casualties in General Abercrombie's ill-advised attack. The 77th men countered with the story of the massacre during Grant's reconnaissance at Fort Duquesne when the majority of the highlanders involved had been killed or captured, and how they had found the skulls of many of their comrades lined up on stakes when Duquesne finally fell.

Wend sat back quietly and took in the soldiers' words. The scene reminded him of the evenings around fires with Robertson's company after the massacre of his family and those thoughts eventually led to contemplation of the meeting with Mary Fraser at Carlisle. There was no doubt that she had grown into a pretty girl, mature for her age.

Then Sergeant McCulloch, who had been making the rounds of the company's other fires, sat down beside Wend. "Well, lad, you're looking satisfied with life."

Wend nodded to the sergeant. "Actually, I was thinking about the days after you found me out on Forbes Road. I ran into Mary Fraser before we left Carlisle. She and her mother sure took good care of me during that time."

"Ah, now, you know that girl is a lovely thing and the darling of the regiment. Her mother was the best nurse in the battalion, 'fore she died, God rest her soul." He took a gulp of ale. "And the lass is following in her mother's path. Many a man is grateful for her care when he was wounded or had the fever. And she's cradled more than a few lads' heads and held their hands as they went to meet their maker."

That reminded Wend of what Mary had said in Carlisle. "What's going to happen to her, sergeant, when the 77th is mustered out? She's all alone since Sergeant Iverson and Lizzie passed on."

McCulloch smiled and shook his head. "The truth of it is that lass could have her future settled in a moment. There's not a young buck in this regiment, and some older ones at that, but has his eye on her and is restless in the night at the thought of her sharing his blankets. Mary just has to give the word and she could be a corporal or sergeant's wife in a moment. She's nigh sixteen now; the right age to start a family."

Wend thought for a moment. "Sergeant, when I talked to her, she said that she might move to the 42nd and work with the surgeon, when your regiment goes back to Scotland. That doesn't sound like she has the idea of getting married soon."

"Aye, now that you mention it, it's true she's played the game very close. For all the men who have tried to court her, she's never given any one of them much hope. My good wife, who is very close to her, says the girl is more interested in spending time with the chaplain, learning to read, write, and do her numbers, or watching the surgeon at his trade." The sergeant took another gulp of his ale. "But I expect she'll soon have to think of settling down to make a good wife."

There was a pause, and before Wend could say anything more, Campbell and Baird came out of the darkness to stand beside McCulloch. The lieutenant said, "Sergeant, you can tell the men we'll be spending tomorrow here in camp and will leave for Ligonier at dawn the day after that. I expect they'll be glad of the respite."

Joshua stood beside the lieutenant and lighted his pipe. "Sprout, don't even think of a day off. You had better get some sleep. We're heading back to Carlisle at first light and we'll be carrying dispatches for Captain Ourry to Bouquet."

* * *

Joshua had lied. They actually started well before the sun made its appearance, before even the false dawn was lighting the sky. With only the two of them, the lanky scout set an even faster pace than he had used for the column on the way out. On the better parts of the path, he had them moving at a near run. The pair was miles away from Bedford before the sun was fair up and they waded the Juniata at mid-morning. By late afternoon they were close to the top of Sideling Hill; Joshua stopped and then led them off the path several yards to the south and sat down.

Wend gratefully joined him, and slipped his blanket roll off. "Are we going to camp here for the night?"

"Camp? Now? Not likely. I've been pushing it so we could get here with some daylight left. That campfire you spotted from the tree yesterday ought to be just down the slope from here. I want to go down and take a look: See what kind of Indians are or were there, and in what strength."

"I thought we were hurrying to follow Colonel Bouquet's orders and get back to Carlisle as soon as possible."

"Yeah, that's part of it. But the good colonel also said to get any information we could on the war parties. So we'll rest a few minutes, then go on down and scout around some."

There was still good light as they started down the eastern slope of Sideling Hill. Joshua led them in a zigzag pattern through the bush, picking out the easiest path; but the route he chose was always centered on the same direction. Wend began to think that he somehow knew the exact location of the spot they had seen the morning before. As they crept through the woods, he looked up and saw that they were heading toward a rock outcropping which formed a cliff at the very crest of the mountain. He realized it was the one he had seen from the tree. Suddenly Wend put it all together and his heart skipped a beat; he was certain that they were advancing upon the lair which Wolf Claw's Mingo band had used before attacking his family! He wanted to ask Joshua to confirm his thought but dared not since the scout had specified total silence.

After a half hour Baird motioned them to a stop and pointed ahead. Wend saw faint smoke from a fire almost directly to their front. The rock cliff was now looming over them on their right hand.

Joshua led them ahead for the next hundred yards. Finally, he motioned for them to drop to the ground and creep forward using trees and bushes for cover. Wend tried to control the noise of his breathing. He looked up and realized that the smoke was close ahead. Then Wend froze; he heard talking and laughing. Baird stopped, lay flat on the ground, and inched forward to a bush, looking out from its very base. Wend imitated him and moved to the opposite side of the bush.

There, just ahead of them, was the camp, the fire, and a band of warriors standing and sitting around in positions of relaxation. Some of them were drinking from jugs. Then Wend spotted the horses. They were tied to a picket line on the far side of the camp, partially obscured by vegetation. On the ground in front of them was a line of pack saddles, some still made up with covered loads. But stacked up nearer the fire were a number of wooden boxes which had obviously come off the horses. Then Wend saw the gunpowder; many small kegs stacked up near the boxes.

And at that moment Ross Kinnear walked out from behind the horses into the open area of the campsite. He had obviously been tending to the horses; now he approached the fire and sat down on a log. Only then did Wend notice that one of the other men sitting at the fire was Kinnear's partner, the long bearded Fleming.

He looked around the clearing and counted at least 15 warriors in the party. Wend had no idea what tribe they were from. He was trying to get more details of the camp in his mind when he felt a tug on his leg; Joshua was motioning him to withdraw. With every bit of care he could manage he crept backward from the bush.

He turned and looked up to see the astonished face of a warrior standing only ten feet from them. A thought swept through his mind: *He's just coming back from relieving himself!* At that instant the Indian started shouting at the top of his voice to warn his comrades. Wend noticed that he had no weapon on him except for a knife hung on a strap around his neck, which he now pulled out of its sheath, and then advanced toward the two scouts, still shouting at the top of his voice.

Wend instinctively pulled the pistol from his belt. In one nearly continuous motion he cocked the hammer and fired at the warrior. The ball smashed into the Indian just below his neck. Instantly he dropped the knife and looked at Wend with a stunned expression. But at almost the same moment blood spurted from the hole in his chest and the life went out of his eyes. The man pitched backward to the ground and lay still. Wend, still on his knees, was frozen by the shock of what had so rapidly occurred.

He was spurred into action by Baird's urgent shout, "Hey Sprout, you might give me a little help here if you want to keep what's left of your scalp!"

Wend jumped to his feet and saw that Joshua had turned and had his rifle aimed toward the campfire. As he watched, the scout fired and a warrior was knocked off his feet. Wend stuck the pistol back into his belt and aimed his rifle directly at Kinnear, who still sat on the log, looking in the direction of the ruckus. Wend squeezed the trigger and the rifle went off. But the trader jumped up in the instant just before he fired, and that motion saved his life. The ball went through the point where he had been sitting, completely missing him. But the shot was not wasted; it impacted into the stack of powder kegs. For a split second nothing happened. But then the stricken keg exploded with flame and others followed.

Joshua turned and started to run. "Come on Sprout, get your ass moving! And if you can manage, get that rifle reloaded while we run!"

Wend snatched a last look at the camp. The warriors were taking cover or making haste to get away from the exploding powder kegs. But Wend realized the confusion would not last long. He turned and followed Baird, now running back up toward the crest.

As he ran he grabbed his powder horn and got some powder down the barrel of his rifle. Then he reached into the pocket of his hunting shirt and got the emergency ball and dropped that into the barrel also. He pulled the ramrod out and gave the ball two quick shoves, which seemed to seat it reasonably well. Finally, he tapped some powder into the pan of the lock. That accomplished, he concentrated on keeping up with the scout.

Wend was soon gasping for breath as they went almost straight up the hill. He was convinced that the pursuing war party could follow him just by the sound of his breathing, but his gasping was uncontrollable as he struggled to maintain the pace. Just when he thought his lungs would burst, they reached the very top of the ridge, and seconds later came to the trail. Joshua literally jumped right over the path. Wend followed suite. Then, thankfully,

Baird slowed the pace and they picked their way through the woods with greater care.

"Sprout, if ever you moved without leaving a trail or sign, now's the time to do it." Soon it became clear that Joshua was searching for something, for he stopped and looked around several times. It was at one of those moments that they heard a single shout from behind them, from somewhere near where the trail lay. Baird glanced back with a grim look on his face. "They found where we crossed the path; that's one of them calling to his mates." The scout waved for Wend to follow and started off in a new direction.

A few minutes latter Joshua found what he was looking for; it was a pile of boulders at the edge of the hill's crest. In front of the giant rocks the dirt gave way to a continuous sheet of flat stone and they strode onto the hard surface. Baird climbed through a gap in the boulders and, when they got through, Wend found that they were on another flat stone area which ended in a steep drop-off down the eastern side of the hill. Baird turned and pointed to one side of the gap they had just come through. Wend saw a horizontal slit in the rocks—less than foot high, and about fifteen feet long.

"Crawl in there Sprout and I'll be right behind you."

Wend did as he was told. He flattened out and wiggled under the rock. He had not gone more than a foot when he realized there was a fissure; a drop of several feet in front of him. "There's a pit in here, Joshua!"

"Yeah, I know. Drop down in there and lay quiet. And don't make any noise if I land on top of you when I come in."

Joshua managed mostly to miss Wend when he dropped down; then he crawled along the bottom of the pit until he lay in front. The long, narrow pit was almost totally dark, barely the width of two men, and permeated by a pungent smell of slime and mold, a constant assault on Wend's nose. He put his head down and concentrated on lying absolutely still and stifling the sound of his breath.

It seemed like only a few moments until he was aware that warriors were climbing around the rocks above them. He heard at least three different voices as they inspected the boulders. Wend froze in horror, certain they would find the fissure and their hiding pit. But after a few moments, he heard noise as the Indians crossed back to the other side of the rocks and a series of laughs as if someone had made a funny remark. Another voice responded, there were more laughs, then all was quiet.

Both men continued to lie still, straining to hear any further sound from the searchers above them. To Wend, it seemed like hours they lay in the filth and stink at the bottom of the pit, but he had no way of telling the real passage of time. He gradually calmed, his breathing slowed, and his heart stopped pounding as if it were going to jump out of his chest.

It was just as he was certain that the warriors had gone away, and his body had relaxed, that Wend thought he felt something touch the fabric of his legging right at his ankle. He shrugged it off, sure that it was just his imagination and the reaction of his body after the strain of trying to remain still for so long.

That certainty lasted for only a few seconds.

For he soon felt the pressure not only at his ankle, but also on the back of his leg. And then it started to work its way upward along the rest of the limb. In an instant he knew what it was: A snake was crawling around and on top of the back of his right calf! He shivered and inadvertently gasped as he felt the reptile slither upward toward his thigh. Soon the snake's head was nearly at the point where his legging ended; another few inches and he would be at the bare skin of Wend's upper thigh. In his fright, he whispered desperately to Joshua, "There's a snake crawling up my leg!"

Baird hissed, "For God's sake, shut the fuck up!"

Wend gritted his teeth, as his body quivered uncontrollably in terror. But he retained enough rationality to perceive that the snake had stopped moving and was resting in the same position on his leg.

Above them, the evening light faded, and the pit became even blacker. Finally, he heard Joshua slightly shift his position. Then the scout said, in a quiet voice, "Now listen carefully. I think they've gone. I thought they might be playing with us, sitting up above waiting for us to come out, but I ain't heard the slightest noise for a while now. So tell me where the snake is, exactly."

Wend described the snake's position on his leg.

"All right, no matter what happens, don't move."

Joshua inched his way past where Wend lay, and he heard the scout scraping around on the floor of the pit. The snake shifted his position slightly on Wend's leg, as if alert to the movement and noise, but then was again motionless. Suddenly, Baird's hand slammed down on Wend's thigh, grabbing the snake, which started to angrily whip his body around; he could feel it snap against his leg. Then there was the sound of a rock banging against the side of the pit, and after a few more contortions, the snake stopped moving.

Joshua sighed. "Got hold of the little bastard just behind his head and smashed it with a stone!"

Wend released his breath. Joshua felt around until he got hold of his rifle, then pushed himself to his feet and with some struggle, climbed up to the rock shelf, and then slid out to the flat surface. Wend followed and in a few moments both men were sitting on the rocky ledge, their backs against the boulders.

Wend felt exhausted. But he sucked in the clean, cool night air, clearing the pit's foulness from his lungs. He looked out at the valley below them; the darkness of the night was far less intense than the blackness of the pit. He turned to Baird. "Joshua, did you know about the pit when you led us here, or were you just hoping for the best?"

"Actually, I found it a few years ago. I was traveling west, and saw this outcropping from the trail, which is not too far away. I came over to check it out as a campsite and found the hiding hole then."

Another thought struck Wend. "It's good that you didn't know there were snakes down there or we couldn't have used the place."

"Oh, I knew for sure that there were snakes. Saw one come out of the slit while I was camping here."

Wend was incredulous. "You knew there were snakes in the pit and you had us hide there? Joshua, I could have died from the poison if that creature had bit me. We both could have died."

Baird's voice was nonchalant. "Sprout, given the choice which we had facing us, I'd rather die from snakebite than from being staked out over a fire. It didn't take much thought."

Wend was silent, but Joshua's words had, for the first time, brought the seriousness of their situation as scouts home to him. He shivered for a second, contemplating how close they had actually been to the end of life, and that their only real hope had been for the easier of two painful deaths. Then another thought occurred to him. "That campsite back there; was that the same one the Mingoes were at after the attack on my family? Is that where you found my sister?"

"That's the truth of it, Sprout." Joshua slapped Wend on his leg for emphasis. "So figure it out. Our friends Kinnear and Fleming have been using that place as a rendezvous for a long time. Obviously it's a well known spot among the tribes. That was a party of Delawares." Joshua got to his feet. "Come on;

let's find a quiet place to bed down for the night, a little further from our friends down the hill. Then tomorrow we'll make fast time to Carlisle."

That night Wend slept fitfully. Given all the tenseness of the chase, he had had no time to contemplate the fact that he just killed a man until they settled into their cold camp. But in the darkness, his dreams were filled with the image of the warrior he had shot and the memory of that last startled look in his eyes as he realized death was sweeping over him.

CHAPTER 17
Battalion of the Doomed

Wend and Joshua traveled the final few miles of the trip back to Carlisle in comparative luxury, reclining in the back of a flatbed hay wagon as it bumped along the road to the town. After taking a shortcut from the Frankstown trail, nearly at the road between Shippensburg and Carlisle, they had come across a field where a band of farmers were loading hay into wagons. Some of the men were standing guard while the others worked with scythes, rakes, and pitchforks.

The farmers got them back into town in the late afternoon and the scouts went right to Washburn's to report to the colonel. Wend was surprised to find that Arnold Spengler's desk was occupied by another soldier, busily engaged in paperwork. Lieutenant Dow rose to greet the two scouts. "Baird, Eckert! Glad to see you made it back—and right on schedule, too. The colonel was asking about you earlier. He'll want to see you immediately."

The colonel was seated at his desk and talking to another man who lounged in a chair in front of him. The second man was elegantly dressed and both had glasses of libation in their hands. Bouquet and his visitor were laughing heartily over some comment the civilian had made just before the scouts' entrance. Wend was stunned to see that the visitor was Richard Grenough. He felt the hair rise on the back of his neck; he fought to show no emotion in his face and to avoid staring at the man.

Bouquet put his drink down and rose to welcome them. "Joshua, by God, and none the worse for wear!"

Baird greeted the colonel and handed over the leather dispatch case from Captain Ourry. Then he turned to Grenough. "Good afternoon, Richard," he said as he extended a hand. "Guess the last time I saw you was at Pitt a couple of years ago."

Grenough nodded and extended his hand without rising. "Glad to see you, Joshua. You are looking fit."

Joshua laughed. "Well, another thousand miles or so under my feet doesn't make that much difference at my age."

Bouquet motioned in Wend's direction. "Richard, this young man is Mr. Wend Eckert, who is working with Joshua." Bouquet thought for a moment. "You may remember the massacre of the Gibson-Eckert caravan at Sideling Hill four years ago. Mr. Eckert is the sole survivor of that incident, save for two people who were taken captive."

Grenough's head jerked around and he looked sharply at Wend. "Is that so? Well, I am surprised. Of course, I know only what I read in the Gazette, but I seem to recall that the paper's account said that no one had survived."

Wend looked at the man as steadily as he could. "Mr. Grenough, I've learned that it's unwise to count on what you read in the newspapers. It's my experience that they often get the story wrong or incomplete."

Grenough's face darkened for a second and then broke into an easy smile. "True enough young man. But in any case I am glad to see that you lived through the experience." He wrinkled up his face. "As I recall, your father was a gunsmith in Lancaster before your journey. And I've seen guns on display under that name here at Washburn's and in a tavern over at Harris'. Are you following him in the trade?"

As Wend was about to answer, Joshua spoke first. "He's got a shop up at Sherman Mill, Richard. And he's doing a good job of making a name for himself as a marksman, at the same time."

"Ah, yes. Now it all fits together. I recollect hearing about a man named Eckert who wins all the competitions up in Sherman Valley. Several men told me they had lost serious money by betting against you in some contest recently." He looked at Wend with new interest.

Bouquet brought the conversation back to matters at hand. "Richard has been giving me his ideas on dealing with the tribes after we drive them away from Fort Pitt. He thinks that if we are successful, they will be amenable to negotiations, and that this confederacy of the northern and more southern tribes won't hold together if they face a significant defeat." Bouquet took a sip of his drink and waved a hand at Grenough. "And Richard, you've always steered me in the right direction before. I'm going to be counting on both you and George Croghan when we do start to negotiate with the chiefs."

Grenough saluted the colonel with his glass. "Henry, you know I'm always at your service in these matters."

Bouquet turned back to Joshua. "So, what can you tell me about the operations of the war parties in the Cove and around Bedford?"

"Colonel, if you read those dispatches, you'll see that Captain Ourry says the siege of Bedford is very loose. His biggest problem is convincing the settlers to stay at the fort. Because they can't see immediate evidence of the Indians, they want to go back out to their farms. But once there, they come under attack by the war parties, then rush back to the shelter of the fort. Because of that cycle, Ourry is having trouble holding together his militia companies and training them."

Then Joshua told Bouquet about finding Kinnear and Fleming trading with a war party and their close escape from the Indian camp. Wend watched Grenough's face as Baird related the story and was gratified to see a twinge of concern in his eyes and around his mouth.

Bouquet pounded his fist on the desk. "I've been trying to bring those two to justice for years. The operations of these unscrupulous traders have given the tribes the ammunition for their depredations. Now Joshua's sighting of these two selling supplies to a war party gives me the solid evidence that I need. Unfortunately, there's not much we can do about it until the present emergency is over. However, I'll tell Sheriff Dunning to draw up warrants on those two, although I don't expect much to come of it since he has his hands full trying to help organize militia for the defense of the settlements."

Grenough looked around at the three others in the room and put his hand to his chin. "You know, Henry, as a matter of fact, I used to employ that pair. But over time, I found Kinnear to be an altogether unsavory and untrustworthy fellow and stopped using him and his partner years ago. I'm glad to find my judgment vindicated by events. If I hear word of their whereabouts, I'll be sure to get the information to Dunning."

Wend listened as Grenough talked, astonished at the man's casual smoothness in spinning the lie. He was tempted to ask him that if he had stopped using Kinnear and his partner years ago, then what he had been doing meeting with them at Larkin's a few months ago. Instead, he grasped for a way to disturb the man's smugness in a more oblique way. He turned to Bouquet. "Colonel, I've been thinking about this smuggling operation. It seems to me that it must be larger than just a few traders working on their own. It takes a lot of capital to get significant supplies of powder, lead, guns and then some way of concealing the goods being bought and transported west. Perhaps they're using wagons to carry the stuff back here in the settlement area and to move it to the backcountry where the traders can reload it onto packhorses in secret. I suspect that someone with wealth and connections is managing the operation."

As he spoke, Wend watched Grenough closely, and was gratified to see his eyes widen momentarily and a quick pursing of his lips.

Bouquet looked thoughtfully at Wend. "There's some logic in your idea. Those quantities of munitions would have to be gathered at a central location back here in the settlements, and indeed, transporting them by pack train back here might tempt suspicion or outright discovery. Using wagons to move them beyond the near mountains might make sense."

Joshua said, "You know, that powder keg we found at the Shawnee war party's camp up at Sherman Valley was from York. Carrying a lot of that stuff on packhorses down there would raise questions. So maybe Wend is on to something."

Bouquet nodded. "Well, as I said, we will have the sheriff investigate these matters." He paused a moment, then changed the subject. "When you two came in, Richard and I were talking about a rumor he heard. It seems that operatives of his have picked up word that we may have Indian spies to our rear as well as raiding parties to worry about in front."

Grenough nodded. "Yes, that's what I hear. There is a persistent story that the Conestoga tribe is providing information on conditions in various settlements and helping the war parties pick the easiest targets. You know that members of that tribe move around selling various craft items, and obviously have the opportunity to see what the settlers are doing and note the movements of the army. They would be valuable allies of the hostiles. As a matter of fact, I was talking with Captain Stewart of the Paxton militia a few days ago, and he was quite concerned about the presence of the Conestoga's and other so-called peaceful tribes east of the Susquehanna."

Wend felt anger welling up and was about to speak in defense of the Conestoga's. But Joshua beat him to it. "I find it hard to put any belief in that rumor, Richard. In twenty years, I've never seen the Conestoga's have much to do with other tribes. They live like white men, have intermarried with settlers, and some are Christians. What would they have to gain by turning on their neighbors?"

Bouquet nodded. "I tend to agree with Joshua, Richard. I've spent a good deal of time in Lancaster and have seen the Conestoga village. The only way that I knew they were Indians was because someone mentioned it." The colonel picked up a paper and briefly looked at it. "I have to tell you I hear all sorts of rumors about the tribes and what they are up to, every day. Most of these stories have no basis in reality or turn out to be gross exaggerations. The fact is, the settlers of this area are so terrified that they imagine a warrior behind every tree. And there's no way I can check out all of these stories."

Bouquet turned to the two scouts. "It's time to bring you up to date on events here since you left. The main point is that the rest of the highlanders we have been expecting have arrived —about 300 under Major Allan Campbell. He's actually the cousin of the Lieutenant Campbell you just took out to Bedford." He smiled briefly. "It seems that all these highland gentlemen are related to each other in some way."

"We are building up the supplies we need for Fort Pitt. Slough and Simon's wagons are gathering here and at Loudoun. I expect to march within a few days. And that brings us to your job. When we do march, you'll be the very point of our advance. Until we get beyond Bedford that will essentially mean checking out road conditions and getting word back about what work is necessary to keep the wagons moving. I just got dispatches from Captain Robertson, and he says that the wagon track is in poor repair, particularly through the mountain passes where there are lots of wash outs which will have to be fixed as we go forward. You'll pass word on those back to our advance guard, who will act as pioneers with shovels, picks and axes. After Bedford, you'll need to do some real scouting work, for that's where the war parties will be thicker, and they'll start to keep watch on our progress."

Joshua screwed up his face. "We'll need more than two men for that, Colonel."

"I've already considered that. Go to the encampment and report to Major Campbell of the 42nd. I've ordered him to assign two of his men to you, Joshua; men who have at least some experience in hunting and in the bush. And he'll also arrange for them to be mounted." Bouquet looked at Joshua and Wend. "I'm really going to be counting on you two. All our appeals for woodsmen from among the settlers have fallen on deaf ears." He laughed and shook his head. "And back during the campaign of '58, I found that these highlanders, stout as they are in battle, are almost useless as scouts and flankers in the heavy bush. Send them out a few yards off the road into the forest, and they end up getting lost. It seems that large parts of their native Scotland are treeless!"

Bouquet and Grenough laughed at the colonel's words while Joshua and Wend took their leave.

The two scouts made their way to the tavern's bar and ordered ale. Wend's mind was in turmoil. He was more than ever convinced that Grenough was behind the operations of traders like Kinnear, yet he had just witnessed how deeply the man had ingrained himself with the elite of the colony. Bouquet, and undoubtedly other important men, considered him a trusted advisor and friend. What chance did Wend have of convincing anyone of Grenough's connivance?

Joshua took a long pull on his ale. "Let's have a quick drink here, then get up to the encampment and find some supper, even if it is army food." He looked around at the crowded common room, which was filled with even more army officers than the last time they had been there. "I was glad to hear that the main detachment of the highlander's has arrived. If the rest of the 77th is here, I'd bet that Sergeant Iverson and Lizzie are with them." He looked over at Wend. "You can't have forgotten her have you, lad, after all the time she treated you on the road?"

Wend looked at his friend. He hadn't thought to tell him about his meeting with Mary Fraser or what had happened to her mother. He looked at Joshua and could see the anticipation in his face at seeing Lizzie. "Joshua, I got to tell you something."

Baird took another pull on his ale, wiped his mouth, and looked expectantly at Wend. "Yeah, what's that?"

Wend fumbled for words, and then decided to just say it flat out. "Joshua, Lizzie and her husband are dead. They died of fever down in the West Indies. I found out because I bumped into Mary Fraser just before we left for Bedford. I didn't get a chance to tell you before now."

Wend was shocked by the sudden, startled look on Joshua's face. He shut his eyes and every muscle on his jaw and neck contracted and stood out under the skin. Baird put his ale down on the counter and pushed it aside. He opened his eyes and called out to the man behind the bar. "Whiskey; the best you got!"

When the barman put the amber liquid before him, he drank it in one swallow, shuddered, and demanded more.

Then Wend saw it all clearly: The jolly bantering with Lizzie, the offhanded complements, the passing of time at her fire hadn't been because of casual friendship: *Joshua had been in love with her.*

With that realization, Wend wasn't surprised at what Joshua said next. He looked straight ahead and took a drink from the second whiskey. "Sprout, I fancied that woman more than any other. She had the kind of looks which survived the ravages of living out in the sun and the wind and the mud. I was taken with her from the first time I saw her, right here in Carlisle at the beginning of the Forbes campaign. That was when she was still Mrs. Fraser, 'fore the sergeant was killed at Duquesne. I was out on a scouting trip when her husband got killed or I would have asked her to marry me right then. But by the time I got back, she was already spoken for by Iverson. That's the way it happens in the army; any free woman gets a husband right away, so she can stay on the ration list. She didn't have no love for him; it was just necessary for her and her daughter."

Joshua was quiet for a moment, then he continued, "She was the only woman I ever met who I think could have taken my kind of life in stride. Being with the army made her tough as any man, yet at the right times she could be soft and caring. In my mind, I thought about the two of us moving down to Carolina or Tennessee, living in a cabin in the bush. I could have supported us by hunting and trapping or maybe opening a trading post, like old man Clapham did."

Wend, in embarrassment at Baird's confession, concentrated on emptying his ale. They stood in silence for a few moments. The common room was filled with pipe smoke, which floated around them in clouds and was irritating his eyes. Wend waved his hand to clear the air around his head. Then he noticed tears in Baird's eyes as he stared at the wall beyond the counter and he knew they weren't from the smoke. "Joshua, let's get down to the encampment before it gets too late and get some food like you were talking about."

"You go, Sprout. I'm going to stay here for a while. Report to Major Campbell and tell him I'll be along presently. Then go find those two men the colonel said were going to work with us."

Wend looked at the scout, not wanting to leave him alone in his present state of mind. But reluctantly he picked up his bedroll and rifle made his way down the street to the fort.

* * *

Wend found Major Campbell seated at a field desk in a large tent with its sides rolled up in concession to the July heat. He was a man of about 40 with a slim build starting to thicken with age. But on the whole he was handsome and intelligent looking. His adjutant introduced Wend, whom he greeted with a nod and a quick smile.

"Glad to see you, Eckert. The colonel told me about you and Baird. He also told me how he wants to use you as our point detachment. As he requested, we've located two men, as it turns out, both from the 77th, who have some hunting and woodland experience. And the adjutant is looking around for suitable mounts for them. We understand that you and Baird have your own horses."

Wend nodded. "They're up at Washburn's, Major."

The major nodded and continued. "Just so you understand the arrangements, Colonel Bouquet commands the whole expedition, which includes everything—soldiers, wagons, civilian waggoners. But I command the troops; it's my job to get all these men from three regiments organized into a useful battalion and take care of their support. Your group will take its direction from Bouquet, but I'll provide you with rations and anything else you need." The major looked at Wend and asked, "That clear?"

Wend nodded again.

Campbell picked up a piece of paper from a stack on his desk and put on a pair of reading glasses. He looked down at the paper. "Look for a Corporal Donegal of the 77th; he and a private named Kirkwood will work with you."

Wend made his way through the camp with some uncertainty— it was the first time he had been in a military camp, save for his days with Captain Robertson's company—and asked his way several times. But eventually he was directed to a tent with a fire in front of it at the very end of the line where the 77th was bivouacked. There he saw a man in his late twenties, reclining on the ground in front of the fire, his shoulders and head supported by a backpack and haversack, puffing peacefully on a short pipe.

Wend stood by the fire and looked down at the soldier, who returned the favor without otherwise moving. Finally, after having appraised Wend silently for some seconds, he reached up and took the pipe out of his mouth. "Now that's a bonnie shirt you got on there, laddie, what with the fringes at the top and the bottom. It does seem to have something of a ripe smell about it, though, doesn't it?"

Wend smiled. "Well, I have been living in it for the last eight days; all the way out to Bedford and back."

The soldier considered for a moment. "Ah, Bedford; I remember it well. We stayed there for several days when we marched with General Forbes." He took another pull on his pipe. "I'd guess that you are one of the scouts I'm supposed to help. The major said it would be Joshua Baird, who I remember from '58, and another man. Since you ain't Baird, you must be the other man."

Wend pulled his bedroll off his shoulder and sat down. He extended his hand to the soldier. "I'm Wend Eckert, from Sherman Valley up north of here. And you must be either Donegal or Kirkwood."

The soldier gave Wend his hand. "Simon Donegal, lad: Presently a corporal of His Majesty's 77ᵗʰ Regiment."

Now that he was seated, Wend could feel weariness beginning to flow over him. He put his bedroll behind him to use as a pillow, and lay back with his feet to the fire. "Where's the other man—Kirkwood?"

"He's out getting supper rations. 'Na doubt he'll be back soon," Donegal said as he shifted his position slightly and took another puff on his pipe.

Wend looked at his companion. Donegal had a wiry frame and a shock of thinning blond hair. Pale blue eyes surmounted a nose which had been broken somewhere along the way and not fully straightened afterward. "I hear you were picked for this job because you have some experience as a woodsman," he asked.

Donegal turned to Wend and considered for a moment, his hand on the pipe. "Well, nobody told me why they decided I was the man to work with you. But I was the gamekeeper for a lord's estate back in Scotland and that's well known in the regiment."

"Have they found horses for you and Kirkwood yet?"

Donegal pulled the pipe from his mouth and looked hard at Wend. "Horses? Horses you say? Nobody told us about horses. Are we supposed to be dragoons now?"

"Bouquet said we'd be mounted so we can range out in front of the column. Joshua and I have our own horses. You and Kirkwood were supposed to be able to ride."

"Well, I had the use of a nag sometimes for my work around the estate. But I haven't ridden since we left Scotland; seven years I make it."

"I expect you are going to get familiar with a horse again real soon." Wend was getting increasingly drowsy; he pulled his hat down to shield his eyes from the sun, which was now very low in the western sky, crossed his arms in front of his chest, and soon found himself drifting off to sleep.

He was awakened by the aroma of cooking meat. He opened his eyes to see that it was fully dark. A chicken was roasting over the fire, skewered on an improvised spit. He examined it more closely and realized that the spit was actually the metal ramrod of a musket, supported by two forked sticks driven into the ground on either side of the fire. A kilted soldier squatted beside the coals, using a bullet mold like a pair of tongs to grab the end of the spit and turn it occasionally to rotate the chicken.

Wend pulled his hat off and sat up, rubbing his eyes. He noticed that Donegal was still lying beside him in the same position as he had first found him. Wend looked over the soldier at the fire. He looked to be in his mid-twenties, and was as spare as Donegal, but had a broader chest and shoulders, and red instead of blond hair. He was sharp faced, with a crooked smile on his lips as he tended the fowl. His uniform was identical to Donegal's with the exception of his headgear. Instead of the round, blue bonnet which was the standard part of the uniform for both the 42nd and the 77th, he wore a green, brimless soft cap, pointed in front with a creased top running from front to back. A green ribbon hung from the back of the cap, down to the top of his collar. He had affixed the badge of the 77th to the right side, which gave the cap something of an official aspect.

The soldier noticed Wend's movement, and looked over at him, the smile on his face becoming even more pronounced and crooked. He laughed and said, "Ah, the youth returns from the land of sweet dreams to the bitter realities of the world."

Wend rubbed his eyes again. "You must be Kirkwood," he said.

"Aye, laddie. But seeing as their lordships, the officers, have decided that we're to spend a 'wee bit of time together, you might want to call me Bob." He walked over to Wend and extended his hand. "Robert Kirkwood, private soldier, if you please."

Wend shook the soldier's hand and looked at the roasting chicken. It was exuding a tantalizing aroma, reminding him that he hadn't eaten any warm food for two days. "It looks like army rations have improved since the last time I was with the 77th."

Donegal laughed. "You'll 'na get rations like that from the quartermaster. That's courtesy of Kirkwood himself, who happens to be the best forager in the regiment."

Kirkwood looked at the bird with satisfaction. "Thank you, Simon. Complements regarding my professional abilities are always accepted. And after carefully scouting the town, I believe I can say that the hen you are looking at may have been the last surviving member of her species in Carlisle, being held secretly in a shed by its former owner."

A half hour later, when all three men had feasted on his largess, Kirkwood looked over at Wend and said, "You talked about having been with the 77th some time before. How did that happen?"

Wend told him about his family's massacre and his rescue by Captain Robertson's company. Both men looked at him curiously and acknowledged that they had heard something about the incident via the regimental grapevine. Kirkwood looked at Wend. "Is that when you lost that part of your scalp?"

Wend nodded. "That's right. I was shot and had my head broken by a Mingo warrior's club. I would have died but for the company finding me and Lizzie Iverson's nursing."

Kirkwood thought for a moment, then nodded. "Yes, she was a great nurse and a good looking woman. Of course, I still think of her as Lizzie Fraser."

Donegal nodded. "That's right, Bob, you weren't around when Lizzie got married to Iverson."

Kirkwood laughed, "No, I had other things on my mind about that time. At any rate, they're both gone now."

Wend's mind went to Mary. "Well, at least her daughter is carrying on. She spent a lot of time nursing me also."

Donegal smiled. "Ah, now there's one pretty lass. She's nursed a lot of men in the battalion. And as Sergeant Fraser's daughter, every man in this regiment, officer, sergeant, and private soldier, has a warm spot in his heart for her. God help any man who makes unwanted advances on her."

"Why's that, Corporal?" Wend asked.

"Because she's Ian Fraser's daughter, that's why. There's 'na a man who doesn't remember what he done during Grant's raid at Fort Duquesne, and his little girl will always have the protection of the men in this regiment."

Kirkwood had lit a pipe. Now he took it out of his mouth to speak. "Simon, perhaps I should explain to the lad." He turned to Wend. "During the advance on Fort Duquesne in 1758, Bouquet sent out an advance party of 800 men from Ligonier under Major Grant to scout the situation around the French fort. When old chief Guyasuta ambushed us that morning, and things went to shit real fast, Grant became so confused that he was useless and at a loss for what to do. Fraser was the senior sergeant; he gathered up a small bunch of the highlanders and got us back to a hill. He grabbed Grant and pulled him along with us. Then he had Grant's piper play a rallying signal, which brought the men from all the companies to the hill for a stand."

Donegal exclaimed, "Those savages was swarming like bees around us."

Kirkwood nodded. "Finally, Fraser helped organize a rearguard action, holding the hill, which allowed some of the companies to withdraw. But the sergeant's own little band didn't make it. We ended up fighting them with our bayonets and broadswords. After the savages finally broke his knot of men, Fraser and the piper were the last ones standing. I watched him fall to two warriors wielding those big clubs, the ones like they got you with; they beat him to death and then took his scalp. Grant himself was captured. But in my mind, if it hadn't been for Fraser, there wouldn't have been a man of this regiment who made it back to Ligonier."

Wend looked at Kirkwood for a second. "You talk as if you were right there with Fraser. How did you get away?"

Kirkwood took a puff on his pipe, shrugged his shoulders, and said in a matter of fact tone, "I was there with Fraser to the end, and I didn't get away."

Wend was speechless and looked back and forth from one soldier to the other to see if they were putting him on.

Donegal laughed at Wend's confusion. "Kirkwood was captured by the savages. Captured and adopted into their tribe. He was with them for most of a year."

Kirkwood nodded. "I took an arrow in the leg; I tried to get away, but was overtaken. A Shawnee warrior put his hand on me and claimed me for his own. Then he fended off some of his mates who wanted to use me for their evening entertainment over a fire. Eventually I was adopted into the tribe as a replacement for his brother, who had recently been killed in a fight with the Cherokees. I lived with them for eight months before the opportunity arose for me to take my leave."

"My God, Kirkwood. How did you manage to escape?"

"My Shawnee brother took me on a long hunting trip. We met up with another band of Shawnees which also had some adopted white men among them. One of the hostages and I conspired to steal away one night. We were lucky enough to evade the pursuit, and after a couple of weeks traveling eastward, fetched up at Fort Cumberland on the Potomac in Maryland. Eventually I was able to get back to the regiment in Pennsylvania just before we marched up to New York for Amherst's campaign against Ticonderoga."

Wend had a thought. "I guess that your time with the Shawnees was why you got picked for this job. That certainly gave you some hunting and scouting skills."

Donegal spoke up. "You're probably right, lad. But then there's also his time with the rangers."

Wend looked at Kirkwood, "You were with rangers? What rangers?"

Kirkwood pulled his pipe from his mouth. "I was with Major Rogers' for a while; on that raid up to Canada to teach the Abenaki tribe a lesson." He touched the green cap on his head. "That's how I got this."

Wend was astonished. Everybody knew about Major Robert Rogers' daring raid on the Abenaki village of St. Francis in 1759. It had been in the Gazette and on everyone's lips for weeks. The Abenaki had been allied with the French and were the scourge of New England, raiding settlements for years. At General Amherst's orders, Rogers and 200 men traveled for days by boat up Lake Champlain, then on foot through deep forests and miles of swamps, to destroy the hostile village and rescue hostages. Then, while making their retreat, the ranger force had suffered greatly by starvation and the attacks of vengeful war parties.

Wend looked at Kirkwood with new respect. "How in the world did you happen to join Rogers' Rangers? I thought they were made up of woodsman from New York and New England."

"Amherst wanted to build the force up to over 200 men for the attack. So he called for volunteers from the regular and provincial regiments around Crown Point. My company commander, who was not very well disposed to me at that time, put in my name."

"Not well disposed?" Donegal laughed. "What happened was you was caught in the quartermaster's store of rum in the middle of the night. The duty officer, Lieutenant McIntosh found you sitting beside a keg with a full mug in your hand. Then you mouthed off to the lieutenant, and the captain gave you the choice of the lash or the rangers. That's what happened!"

Kirkwood shrugged and looked thoughtfully into the fire, his pipe in one hand. "Well, there's some who say that's the way it went. But it doesn't really matter; one way or the other, I went on that little trip. And the captain was happy, 'cause he got credit for sending Rogers a volunteer. So it worked out for everybody."

Donegal laughed, and emptied the ashes from his pipe into the fire. "I think the captain would have liked things even better if you hadn't come back from Rogers' raid."

Kirkwood nodded his head, considering Donegal's words. "Now that you mention it Simon, he did look sort of disappointed when I made it back to Crown Point. If that's the case, he almost got his wish. Most of the lads didn't make it back, and there was more than one moment when I thought I was going to join their ranks."

* * *

Wend woke the next morning to find that Joshua hadn't made it to the camp the night before. After the morning meal, he decided he would go to Washburn's stable to check on the horses and try to track the scout down. The encampment was bustling with activity as he walked the road toward Market Street. Companies of highlanders drilled on the parade ground, details of other soldiers were loading wagons with supplies from the storehouses in the fort, waggoners tended horses on the picket lines or worked on their rigs, women were cleaning up their cooking utensils around campfires.

After walking a short distance, Wend passed a small group of drilling soldiers. Looking at them casually, he noticed they were Royal Americans. And then he was surprised to realize that the man giving orders was Arnold Spengler. Wend stopped and watched the drill. Arnold had a stiff, pained look on his face and was shouting orders in a gruff, angry sounding voice. Several times he halted the detachment and corrected one man or another on their musket handling or marching. Presently, Arnold noticed him. He shortly halted the squad and called for another soldier to take over.

Spengler walked over to Wend, the gruff look still on his face. Then he took his musket off his shoulder and cautiously looked back to confirm that his squad had marched out of earshot. He turned back to Wend and his face broke into a boyish grin. "Will you look at this?" He reached up to his shoulder and pointed to the braided loops on his shoulder. "They're so short of men that they made me a sergeant. Me, a sergeant of all things! And I'm supposed to turn this bunch of quartermasters, recruits, and defaulters into a functioning squad of light foot."

Wend shrugged his shoulders. "Well, you've been in the army for seven years. You should be able to handle the job."

"Wend, I've been a clerk for most of that time. I even have trouble remembering all the drill commands; I study up at night just to know what to do." He looked back at his squad again. "But I cover it up by putting on a tough face and talking a hard line. And then there's Hahn, that private who Lieutenant Dow found in the jail over at Lancaster; he's the one drilling the squad right now. He has been in the regiment for five years, at Fort Bedford, and used to be a corporal. They let him come back on leave and then he tried to desert but got caught. But at least he knows how to drill the men. So when I get in trouble, I just have him run the squad while I pretend to observe from a distance." He laughed. "But the funny part is, these men actually believe that I'm a real sergeant. So, at least I must be doing a good acting job."

Wend smiled and patted his friend on the shoulder. "Well, if you keep fooling them long enough, you may come to get used to the idea yourself."

Spengler shook his head and brought his musket back up to the carry. "I have to get back to work. Lieutenant Dow wants me to march the men out to the edge of town, where we can do some open order skirmish training in the fields. They'll need it once we get out on the road and it will impress all the settlers in their refugee camps that the army is doing something."

* * *

Wend walked down to Washburn's stable to check the horses, half expecting to find Joshua there, maybe sleeping in a pile of hay. But the stable boy said he hadn't seen the scout. Inside the tavern, Washburn said Baird had been at the bar late, but had left just before closing. So Wend walked up to the Widow's, thinking he might have wangled his way in to sleep for the night.

But Alice said she hadn't seen Joshua since the first day they had come to Carlisle. Wend was in a quandary for a while but finally decided to check the jail. Sheriff Dunning was there in the front office when he entered, going over some papers with one of his deputy constables.

The High Sheriff looked up from his work. "Ah, young Eckert; I haven't seen you since that match up in Sherman Mill last November. But I had heard from Bouquet that you were in town to work as a scout." He looked down at his desk again. "Then I got this note from the colonel last evening to be on the lookout for these two traders, named Kinnear and Fleming. It says that, based on word from you and Baird, they are suspected of providing powder and lead to the tribes."

Wend shook the sheriff's hand and gave him a short rendition of their encounter with the Delawares and traders at Sideling Hill.

Dunning looked thoughtful for a moment. "Can you give me a description of these men?"

Wend briefly described the two, and told Dunning everything he knew about their operations, including his meeting with them in the woods back in 1759, their complicity in the murder of his family, and the fact that they operated from the York area. He also pointed out to the sheriff about the keg of powder found by Joshua at the camp of the war party which had attacked Sherman Valley and how it was marked with the name of a company based in York.

Dunning took down the information. "I'll keep a watch for these two, but we have so much going on, what with organizing militia and trying to get food into the town, that I can't focus on my regular duties." The sheriff put his notes on the traders in his desk drawer. "There are so many refugees in town that we are running out of food. The government in Philadelphia has appropriated some money to buy provisions, but getting the foodstuffs here is a problem, what with the army trying to get as many wagons as it can for Bouquet's convoy."

He shook his head and looked up at Wend. "But I guess you came here to collect Joshua."

"He's here? I just came on the chance he had gotten into trouble last night." Wend thought for a moment. "Is he under arrest?"

"Baird? Naw; I found him sitting out in the middle of Market Street, in his cups and musing unintelligibly. So I helped him down here, just to give him a place to stay. Ain't the first time he's spent the night here. He's still sleeping in the back."

One of Dunning's men escorted Wend to the row of cells where a snoring Joshua lay. He pulled open the unlocked door and shook Baird until his eyes opened.

Wend leaned against the bars of the cell. "You finished mooning over a woman you can't ever have?"

Joshua looked up at Wend, the look in his eyes showing he was sober enough to understand the irony of Wend's question. "Sprout, at least I know how to get over it like a man and get on with my life."

Wend laughed and swept his hand around to take in the jail. "So this is how a man takes care of his problems: Straight whiskey and a night under the care of the sheriff? I'll remember that the next time I'm feeling unhappy with life."

Joshua sat up and stretched. "You could think of worse ways to wash away troubles. Anyway, Sprout, let's get out of here. We got things to do." Joshua stood up and immediately had to grab one of the bars to steady himself. "At least, we got things to do after I take care of this head of mine. We need to go down to Washburn's and get some medicine."

* * *

Wend walked through the camp, until he found the double row of tents, pitched next to a section of the stockade, which formed the hospital. Wend could see men lying and sitting around in the tents. He noted that not many of the men seemed to be physically ill and he remembered Mary's words about how long it took to recover after being attacked by the fever. He entered the walkway which ran between the tents, and about halfway down the line, came upon a tent which was outfitted as an office. A man in his forties, with thinning blond hair sat at a table, a pair of spectacles over his nose, reviewing papers spread in front of him. He was stripped down to his shirt and an unbuttoned waistcoat in concession to the heat of the day, his uniform coat draped over another chair. A mug sat beside his right hand.

Wend paused, and the man looked up at him speculatively, eying Wends hunting shirt and leggings. "And what can I do for you, son," he asked. "Have you got an ailment?"

A little embarrassed to state his business, Wend looked around, hoping he would see Mary, but there was no evidence of her. "Are you the doctor?"

The man shrugged his shoulders and a wry look came over his face. "Well, I have a piece of paper which says I am, but then there're those who would argue the opposite. Regardless, I am the surgeon of the 42nd. Munro is my name. And who might you be?"

Wend took his hat off and introduced himself. "I was looking for Mary Fraser. Is she in the hospital today?"

Munro took off his reading glasses, nodded to himself, and smiled knowingly. "I might have guessed. A young healthy fellow like you, what else would you be doing here at hospital?" He took a drink from his mug and pointed down the row of tents. "She's in the last tent on the right, making up bandage rolls." He grinned at Wend. "But I warn you that you've got competition. You're not the only young buck here to see her." The man turned back to his papers, answering Wend's thank-you with a simple wave of his hand.

Wend found the tent and saw Mary and an older woman preparing bandages. They had a giant pot of water on a fire and were boiling strips of cloth. They stirred the water with a wooden wand. Wet cloths were hung from a line, drying in the sunlight. Others, having completed drying, were rolled up and stacked on a table. The two were in rough clothing, their sleeves rolled up to keep them from dipping into the water as they worked. Both women's faces were red and shiny from the heat of the day and the steam coming from the pot. A young highlander of the 77th was also there, lounging against a tent pole and joking with the women.

Mary looked up from her work and saw Wend. He found himself gratified to see her break into a genuine smile. She picked up a rag and wiped her face, then reached up and pushed a lock of copper hair out of her eyes. "Wend, we heard that you were back. I'm glad to see you!"

Wend touched his hat to her and then to the other nurse. "I thought to come by and say hello."

She smiled again. "The word's all over camp how you and Joshua had a brush with the savages out on Sideling Hill. I must say, you aren't looking the worse for wear."

Wend shrugged his shoulders. "It wasn't much of an affair, but we did have to run pretty fast for a while."

Mary looked over at the soldier. "Wend, this is Donald McKirdy; he's Captain McDonald's drummer. He's also stopped by to say hello. Donald, this is Wend Eckert. He's scouting for us."

McKirdy looked at Wend appraisingly and nodded. "Morning, Eckert."

Clearly, McKirdy was not at all pleased with his arrival. Realizing that his presence had interrupted an ongoing conversation, Wend decided to finish his business and take his leave as expeditiously as possible. "Uh, Mary, I wondered if you knew of someone making up breeches and leggings for the soldiers. We have two men who will need them right away to keep from getting chaffed on horseback."

"Oh, you want to see Mrs. McCulloch, the sergeant's wife. Major Campbell put her in charge of making up those items. She's over on the other side of the encampment, working with most of the women." She looked at McKirdy, then at Wend. "Here, I'll take you over there and you can tell me more about your trip out to Bedford. I'm sure Donald has to get back to his company, he's been here for a while." She rolled down her sleeves and turned to the other nurse. "I'll be back in a little while, Kathryn." She looked at McKirdy, "Please come back anytime, Donald, it's been pleasant talking to you."

McKirdy looked at Wend in a way which indicated that going back to his company had been the last thing on his mind.

Mary led him through the camp, past several companies drilling on the parade ground, then by the wagon park, which grew every day as more freight wagons arrived. There were now twenty-four or twenty-five, lined up in three rows. Two other wagons were by the quartermaster's buildings with working parties loading them.

Wend was curious about what Mary had said of McKirdy. "Isn't Donald a little old to be a drummer? I thought they were young boys. He seemed older than I am."

Mary smiled wryly. "Not in highland regiments, Wend. With all the lack of work in Scotland, there were plenty of men ready to sign on for any position. And being a drummer is a very responsible duty. They have to keep their heads in battle, stay right by their captain, and make sure they transmit the right signals." She smiled and waved at a corporal standing by one of the wagons as they passed, who gave her a large grin in return. "And they have another duty: The head drummer is sort of the High Sheriff, and the other drummers are like his deputies." She cocked her head and looked at him meaningfully. "You don't want to get on the wrong side of one of the drummers."

Wend mentally noted that he undoubtedly had just gotten on the wrong side of McKirdy.

Mary continued, "We don't lash men very often in highland regiments, but when it is ordered, the drummers carry it out."

They came upon a series of tents that had been set up side by side and now had the canvas walls rolled up. There were nearly 40 women in and around the tents, busy working coarse, tan fabric into breeches and green material into leggings. Some were cutting the fabric at tables, others seated in chairs or on the ground, sewing. Stacks of finished garments were piled up in one tent. Children of various ages played in and around the tents.

Presiding over the entire operation was a tall, heavyset, dark haired woman of indeterminate age. She was red-faced in the July heat; Wend could see patches of perspiration under her massive arms and a spreading spot between her shoulders and down her back. As Mary led him toward her, he was aware of curious looks from most of the women and embarrassed to feel a surge of his old self-consciousness spreading over him.

The heavy woman turned toward them, cocked her head, and put her hands on her hips. "Hello, Mary!" She scrutinized Wend. "Who is this bonnie young provincial you have in tow?"

"Why Mrs. McCulloch, you should recognize him. Look closer."

Mrs. McCulloch inspected Wend from head to toe. "Now that you mention it, Mary, there is something familiar about the lad. But then all these Ulstermen look the same to me!" She laughed at her own joke in a jolly way, the deepness of it shaking her all over.

Mary stamped her foot in impatience. "Oh Esther, come on. He's not Ulster, though I have to admit he dresses and talks like one: He's a Dutchman. Do you remember back to when we were in Captain Robertson's company, marching back from Pitt? Does that freshen your memory?"

Esther McCulloch squinted at Wend. "Lord above, he's 'na that German boy scalped by the savages that you and Lizzie took care of? The lad we found lying in the road that scared my husband out of his skin by coming alive suddenly?"

Mary nodded. "The very same; he's come back to us to scout with Joshua Baird on this trip."

Esther walked around to where she could see the bare spot under Wend's hair. "My, lad, you cover that bare spot up well. I wouldn't see it if I didn't know where to look!"

Several women jumped up from their work and crowded around to look at Wend's scalp, commenting on the size of the missing area. Wend's felt himself turning red as Mary took great care to explain how her mother had treated the wound and the details of the poultices she had used. But finally, after what seemed to Wend an eternity, the women tired of inspecting his wound and went back to their work.

Mary pointed out to Esther that Wend had gone out to Bedford with the flying column.

"And how's that husband of mine doing. He was certainly excited enough about getting away from us here."

"He was well enough, Mrs. McCulloch, when I left him at Bedford. He and the rest of Lieutenant Campbell's company should be in Fort Ligonier by now."

Esther nodded and asked, "And what about that scoundrel Joshua Baird? Why hasn't he come over to see us, like he used to on the Forbes campaign?" She looked over at Mary with a mischievous look in her eye. "I wager he'd be over here fast enough if you mother, God rest her soul, was still with us!"

Mary blushed, but said nothing in reply to Esther's obvious reference. Instead, she said: "Wend's here to see about some breeches and leggings for two men who are going to be working with him and Joshua. They're Simon Donegal and Bob Kirkwood; you know them, don't you?"

Esther tossed back her head and laughed deeply. "Of course I know that pair. Lord above, think of it: Joshua Baird, Donegal, and Kirkwood. Now there's a trio of unmitigated rogues for you. Some officer must have been suffering from the heat or in his cups when he came up with the idea of putting those three together." She walked over to a stack of finished breaches and tossed two pairs to Mary. Then she went over to another stack and gave her some green colored leggings. "There, take them and you're welcome to them."

Mary clutched the clothing in her arms. "Thank you Esther. Have you heard anything about when we are going to leave? I noticed that several more wagons came in yesterday, we must have almost enough to start by now."

"I don't get told much directly now, what with the sergeant gone on that little hike out to Ligonier. But with all the activity over at the quartermaster's, I'd bet that we'll leave in a few more days. And one of the drummers told me the good colonel has called a meeting of all the officers for later today. If I had to wager, I'd count on us marching soon indeed."

Wend and Mary left the sewing group. Wend assumed that Mary would want to be going back to the hospital. He turned to her and reached to take the clothing from her arms. "Thanks for your help in getting these things. I still don't know my way around the army very well."

Mary tightened her grip on the clothing and twisted away from him. "Don't you try to take this clothing away from me, Wend Eckert!" She looked at him impishly. "I'm taking these things to Joshua myself. It's been four years since I saw him, and if he won't come see me, I'll go to him!"

They walked over to the picket line where Joshua was engaged in teaching Kirkwood the mysteries of horsemanship. Donegal stood by watching.

As they approached, Joshua had his back to them. Wend called out, "Joshua, someone here to see you!" Wend watched carefully as Joshua turned around and caught sight of Mary. The scout's eyes opened wide and his face muscles instantly tightened as he recognized the girl.

Mary turned to Wend and handed him the clothing. Then she hesitated only a moment before rushing up to Baird and throwing her arms around him. She buried her head in his shoulder.

"Oh Joshua, it's been four years! I've thought about you often, but I didn't believe I'd ever see you again."

A devilish impulse came over Wend. He caught Joshua's eye as the scout stood with his arms around the girl. "Looks just like her mother, doesn't she?"

Baird flushed bright red and looked at Wend with a touch of ire in his eyes. Then he closed them and squeezed the girl for a moment. "Yes, Wend, she does indeed." He released Mary and stood back. "I thought a lot about you, too, and your mother many times since then. We had a lot of good times, Mary. And seeing you brings them all back." He paused a moment, laughed, and said, "But you're all grown up now, and I vow, you're the prettiest girl in the regiment!"

* * *

In the afternoon Joshua and Wend were summoned by one of the drummers to the meeting with Bouquet. The colonel had moved his headquarters from Washburn's to the encampment earlier in the day, and now he presided over the disparate elements of the expedition from a large tent next to Major Campbell's. They arrived to find all the officers of the three regiments, the sergeant major of the Black Watch, and the wagon master from Slough & Simon had gathered and stood waiting for the colonel to start.

Bouquet, Campbell, and the wagon master were standing around a table in the colonel's tent pointing to features on the map of western Pennsylvania. After just a few moments, Bouquet nodded at something Campbell said, and the three finished their conversation. The colonel glanced at the assemblage, picked up a single sheet of paper from the table, and stepped to the front of his tent, looking as if he were ready to speak. But then he quickly turned back to the table and picked up his spectacles, before returning to the front of the tent platform.

He placed the spectacles over his nose, glanced down at the paper and began to speak. First he spent some time telling the officers of both highland regiments how proud he was to have them with him, citing highlight's of the regiments' histories and their roles in battles of the past. Wend looked around and saw the officers nodding approval as he complemented their units. Then Bouquet nodded in the direction of the wagon master and praised the effort of Slough & Simon in gathering wagons and supplies.

Having thus finished the preliminaries, his next words got everyone's attention.

"Gentleman, we march for Fort Pitt at dawn the day after tomorrow."

Wend saw the officers stiffening and meeting each others eyes.

"The advance from here to Bedford should be routine save for the necessity to repair Forbes Road as we march. But after Bedford, we must be on our guard; we will see increasing signs of the enemy's presence and we'll likely experience probing raids on our detachments. Then, somewhere between Fort Ligonier and Pitt, we will inevitably face a massive attack by the alliance of tribes besieging the fort."

Bouquet paused to let that sink in and looked around at the assembled officers. "And gentlemen, make no mistake: These warriors know that they are fighting for their homes, their families, and their very way of life. At the very core, that is what this uprising is all about. They will fight with skill and desperation. And they will be fighting on their home territory, ground where they destroyed Braddock and Grant."

"I have no doubt that the enemy will outnumber us. But we must be prepared to destroy whatever force the tribes throw against us."

"You're all veteran officers. You know the tactics of our army. From constant practice, you can, almost effortlessly, give the orders to complete the most difficult tactical evolutions; to bring a marching unit from column into line of battle, to coordinate platoon fire against an enemy's advance. You can change front or refuse your flank under fire. When necessary you can form square to defend against cavalry or you can execute a fighting withdrawal by companies. These are the maneuvers you have used against the French and other enemies on many fields. *But for the fight against these savages, this knowledge won't help! I repeat: They won't help!* You will need to learn a new set of tactics; tactics which we have developed here in the 60th over the last eight years."

Wend looked around at the officers. Clearly Bouquet had their attention.

"Heretofore, you have considered the battalion the key formation for fighting. But in the bush, the company and even smaller units must be the prime tactical unit. Nor is it enough for an officer to comply with orders from his battalion commander: In forest warfare, each company commander, or even a leader of a half company or squad must be ready to act on his own initiative. Units will be spread so far apart that no single officer can control the entire action. Most often, massed musket fire will not have the effect we see on open battlefields. Braddock found that out fatally at the Monongahela. His last words were to the effect that we must learn to fight in the wilderness."

"That's been my task; now we must put it to practice. We'll be on the road for more than a fortnight before we get to Ligonier. I will be spending at least a day with each company, training you and your men in the tactics necessary for success against our foe. As I said, you must think on your own, but we must all operate from a common set of proven maneuvers."

Bouquet took his spectacles off and scanned the gathered officers to let his words take effect. "All right; now for some specifics." He put the spectacles back on, and started reading a list of orders, including the order of march, details of daily routine, rotation of company duties. "Finally, to conserve rations, to enable us to travel as light as possible, and because of the high level of danger we will face in the final stages of the journey, we will leave all the women and children here at Carlisle. I trust you will all understand the necessity of this action."

Wend saw many officers look up at sharply at Bouquet; a few made comments to their companions. Surgeon Munro raised his hand. "Colonel, all my nurses are women. I only have one medical orderly for the entire battalion. We have over forty men from the 77th who are still too weak to march or fully take care of themselves and will have to be carried in wagons. Can't we take some of the nurses along?"

Bouquet shook his head. "The decision is final. You will have to recruit a few nurses from among the men. Perhaps the healthiest of your patients can take on that duty." The colonel looked around. "Are there any other questions?"

There was no response. "All right gentlemen, you have your assignments and orders. Let us make preparations to depart."

* * *

That night, the four scouts sat around the cook fire, eating their boiled ration meat and chunks of bread. True to form, Kirkwood had rounded up an extra ration of rum for them and no one had questioned where he had obtained the jug. Donegal had spent the earlier part of the evening visiting friends throughout the camp.

Donegal took a pull on his mug. "There is grumbling all through the battalion. They ain't taking well to the idea of leaving the families behind. The men are unhappy, but the women are madder than a hive of bees which had their honey taken away. Esther McCulloch has gathered the women together and is holding forth on the unfairness of it all."

Joshua put his spoon down and took a swig of the rum. "Leaving the women behind ain't no big deal. In the 60th we do it every time we figure there's going to be action. Then the women get brought up when it's all over." He picked up his spoon again. "So, Esther will just have to get over it."

Kirkwood shook his head. "This is 'na the 60th, Joshua. 'Case you haven't noticed, all but about twenty of the soldiers around us are highlanders. And highland women stay close to their men. They were right there at Ticonderoga, Crown Point, and Havana. God knows enough of the women and children died of the fever down in the islands. It may be the practice to leave the women behind in English regiments, but highland wives will 'na stand for it. The English officers tried to transport our camp followers to a rear area during the New York campaign, but the women would have none of it. They hid out when the quartermaster came to move them and others stole back after they had been taken away."

Donegal nodded. "If you think the colonel's order is going to be the end of it, you got something to learn."

The corporal's prediction was right on target. The women's mutiny took place the next day just after morning muster.

The four scouts were at the picket line grooming their horses when it started. Wend and Joshua had brought their horses down from Washburn's late the day before. The mare was full of restless energy, having been in a stall for many days, and was playfully nipping the horses on either side of her and nuzzling Wend as he worked.

Suddenly Wend became aware of a hubbub on the parade ground. He looked up to see the women of the two highland regiments, over sixty strong, advancing purposefully toward the headquarters tents. Soldiers standing around were waving and shouting at the women, who shouted back. At the head of the mob was the determined and imposing figure of Esther McCulloch.

Donegal looked up at the crowd of marching women. "This is going to be interesting, Wend. I'll wager that you are about to see the limits of discipline in the British Army. Let's go over there."

By the time they arrived, the woman had reached the headquarters area and had surrounded both Bouquet's and Campbell's tents, which had the sides rolled up. The two commanders had been taken by surprise as they sat at their writing tables, and were now being verbally accosted by the shouts of the women. Moreover, it seemed as if every man in the encampment who could manage it had also gravitated to the headquarters area. The headquarters sentry, who had been standing his post in front of the tents, had been completely intimidated and had backed up into the major's tent.

Wend scanned the mob of women, looking for Mary, and then suddenly saw her. She was standing right beside Esther, shouting at Bouquet as loudly as any of the others.

Bouquet sat transfixed at his table, bewilderment on his face as he looked around at his besiegers. Campbell also remained seated, but glanced at Bouquet with a wry expression on his face. As Wend watched, Bouquet turned to Campbell and mouthed words which he could not hear above the bedlam. Campbell raised his hands and shrugged his shoulders in response.

Finally, the colonel removed the spectacles from his nose, stood up, took his coat off the chair where it had hung, and carefully and deliberately put it on, followed by his hat. Thus formally attired, he advanced to the front of the tent and confronted his tormentors.

Bouquet stood silently for a moment, directly in front of Esther and Mary, and it seemed to Wend as if the uproar grew as he stood there. Finally, he raised his hands, calling repeatedly for quiet. Slowly and reluctantly the women complied, until all sixty stood in sullen silence, awaiting the colonel's words.

Bouquet looked around at the women, then having correctly perceived that Mrs. McCulloch was the ringleader, spoke directly to her. His first words were a masterstroke of understatement. "It would appear that you ladies have some grievance to discuss?"

Wend almost broke out laughing in spite of himself. Behind him some soldier giggled loudly. Bouquet looked in the direction of the giggler, his face grimly set.

Esther stepped forward and, given her stature, actually looked down at Bouquet. "It's this order of yours, Sir, to leave us women behind. It's an outrage, that's wa' it is, and we'll not be standing for it. We've been following our men for seven years. We've always been right behind the lines, even at the hardest times. We ask that you take it back."

Bouquet looked extremely nonplussed. He glanced around at the women and the men standing behind and then shook his head. "My good lady, do you understand the conditions we will be marching under? There is a shortage of supplies and we need to get as much food and ammunition to Fort Pitt as possible. Then there is the danger from the savages: Their treatment of women who fall into their hands is unspeakable. I would be failing in my duty if I subjected you to the threat of capture and much worse." He paused and looked around. "You must understand."

"I understand that we have shared our husband's lives here in America since '56. There's plenty of times we been on short rations, just like the men. And we spent time in the swamps of South Carolina, with bugs as big as birds, marched along Forbes Road, went to Ticonderoga and many of us died at Havana and those other pestilence-ridden places in the West Indies. So what do you think is so much more dangerous on this trip? And besides, you need us: Who do you think is going to take care of the wounded, or do the washing and sewing and cooking? Who just made up 400 pairs of breeches and leggings for you? We're as much a part of the regiment as any man here." Esther waved her hand to take in the men gathered around.

There was a murmuring of agreement among the assembled woman and a shouted "You tell, 'em, Esther!" Wend wasn't sure where that last shout had come from, but he was sure the voice had been that of a male.

Bouquet tried another tack. "I pledge your separation will not be long. Once we have relieved Fort Pitt, we will send for the families."

Mary wasn't having any of it. "And who knows how long that will be? What if you get held up at Ligonier? And there's talk of marching from Fort Pitt into the Ohio Country. We could be sitting here all summer and into the fall. And how are we supposed to live without any regimental quartermaster around to provide rations?"

"No, no, you don't understand." Bouquet raised his hands again, as if to fend off the angry women. "We have hired an agent to provide you with food and ensure you have shelter."

Esther laughed out loud to Bouquet's face. "Lord above, you are going to pay some one to feed us, and you could do it much cheaper just by taking us along and giving us our standard rations!" There we loud murmurs of agreement. "Besides, I don't trust some jobber to provide us with decent rations, particularly when there's no officer around to check up on him and this whole town has a shortage of food. As it is now, the good citizens can't get enough to eat and the word is they're taking up collections in Philadelphia and Lancaster to buy food for Carlisle! We'll be sitting here on short rations when we could be well fed with the expedition."

The colonel looked around in frustration, realizing he was making no headway and that the band of women was not going to be satisfied with any of his answers. In fact, they seemed to be getting more agitated.

Major Campbell spoke up. "Colonel, if I make a suggestion: Why don't we meet with a smaller delegation of the ladies; Mrs. McCulloch and two others? I don't think we are going to make any progress with so many people around and tempers so high."

Mrs. McCulloch agreed, and the rest of the women stalked back to their tents. Two other sergeants' wives remained as part of the delegation. Campbell gave orders for the men standing around the headquarters tent to disperse.

An hour later, word began to filter around the encampment that an agreement had been reached; both sides had made concessions. The women and children would march with the convoy as far as Ligonier, where they would remain until the siege of Fort Pitt had been lifted. Everyone breathed a sigh of relief, and turned to final preparations to leave.

* * *

Wend was shaken awake by Donegal. It was still dark and the fire had burned down to embers. The glow allowed him to see Kirkwood pouring tea from a pot the corporal had brewed using the last of the fire's heat. The scouts had stricken their tent during the previous evening to facilitate a fast start.

Wend pushed his blankets aside and sat up in the darkness. As he cleared the sleep from his eyes, he became aware that he was enveloped by an indescribable clamor. Around him the expedition was preparing to march. From every direction he could hear sergeants and corporals shouting orders to their men. There was the sound of tents being struck, the clatter of metal cooking implements banging together as they were carried to the wagons, the noise of chains rattling and horses snorting as scores of teams were harnessed, the voices of women calling to their children and each other.

He saw the light of lanterns in the distance and realized they were at the headquarters and the officers' mess tents of the 42nd. He squinted, and in the flickering light could see officers standing around, some of them still in shirt-sleeves, taking tea and hand foods for breakfast.

Kirkwood handed Wend a mug of tea. The noise around him had aroused something in his memory. Then he recalled the image of his father sitting on the log before the fire in the mists of that last morning at Fort Loudoun, reminiscing about the day that Forbes' army had marched. Suddenly he understood what Johann had meant by the noise of the army being like a storm raging around him. Wend listened again to the sounds as the expedition prepared to move, and thought to himself that the noise from 400 soldiers and thirty wagons was impressive enough, but the sound from Forbes' thousands must have been incredible. Inside him grew a feeling of closeness with his father, spanning the distance of four years, so vivid that he felt he should be able to see Johann sitting on the other side of the fire. But he caught himself, for there were only the faces of Baird, Kirkwood, and Donegal faintly illuminated by the embers as they sipped their tea and nursed their own thoughts behind drowsy eyes.

An hour later they led their horses, saddled and loaded with their blanket rolls and equipment, to the line being formed along the road leading out of the encampment. In the pre-dawn light they could see companies marching to their place in line and the last of the wagons being maneuvered into position behind the ranks of soldiers. Wend looked over to where the hospital tents had been and saw the sick soldiers of the 77th laboriously climbing into wagons which had been set aside for their use. He thought he made out the form of Mary Fraser assisting the men, but in the twilight Wend could only be sure the figure was that of a woman.

In a very short time the entire expedition was in formation. The soldiers stood in ranks, the regiments in line of seniority from the right: The 42nd, nearly 300 strong, the tiny detachment of the 60th with Arnold at their front, and finally the healthy soldiers of the 77th, mustering barely a company. Behind were the rows of wagons, most hitched with six horse teams. On the left of the wagons stood the knot of women and children with packs on their backs or sacks over their shoulders, many holding walking sticks. The scouts had been directed to place themselves with the small staff, which was forming in the gap between the 42nd and the 60th. Major Campbell stood in the road in front of the ranks, conversing with the sergeant major of the 42nd. An orderly stood beside him holding his horse.

Wend looked around and realized that the earlier clamor had subsided. The soldiers were under discipline, silent in their ranks; the waggoners stood by their wagons, holding the reins of the teams; even the women and children were still and nearly quiet. Only the occasional voice of a child, the whinny of a horse, the cough of a sick soldier broke the stillness and air of anticipation which had descended on the assemblage. Indeed, the few, isolated noises seemed only to enhance the silence.

Shortly, Bouquet and Lieutenant Dow, mounted on their horses, emerged from behind one of the low buildings of the fort and rode slowly up the road toward where the staff was formed. Campbell made a last comment to the sergeant major, and then swung gracefully up into his saddle, the sergeant and the orderly falling back to join the staff.

Wend had thought that Bouquet might take the opportunity to make an address to the expedition; but he simply rode quietly along the ranks of the Black Watch, acknowledging the salutes of the company commanders as he passed. He pulled up in front of Major Campbell. Their words were easily audible from where Wend stood.

"Major, we want to disturb the good citizens of Carlisle as little as possible as we depart. So we'll march out only to the rim tap of the drums. And none of those bagpipes of yours till we get out of town."

Campbell laughed and nodded, saying, "As you desire, Sir." Then, he raised his hand in salute, and said in a more formal tone, "May I have your permission to march?"

"March your battalion, Major." Bouquet returned the salute, spurred his horse, and continued to ride toward the junction of the fort's road with Market Street.

The staff paraded behind him. The four scouts mounted and rode behind the staff. Wend heard orders shouted behind him and the companies, in sequence from the rightmost, wheeled into a column of fours, stepped off onto the road and into line.

Bouquet reached the junction with Market Street and turned westward. In a short time the entire column was marching past the buildings of the sleeping town. The only sounds were the quiet tap of the drummer in each company and the rhythmic tread of the soldiers as they marched with the smooth, disciplined step of regular troops. Behind them Wend could hear the rumble of the wagons and the rattling of safety chains as the teams moved.

If Bouquet really thought he would depart Carlisle with little notice by the inhabitants, his plan failed. Initially, there were few witnesses save men and boys with early chores, who stopped to watch solemnly. But even the muffled sound of the expedition could not go on for long without the populace taking notice. Soon lights came on, windows were thrown open, and people in nightshirts became visible. Others poured out of the tents and flimsy shacks which filled every space in the town to shelter the refugees of the countryside. Men stood along the route and lit their morning pipes, women held babies in their arms. Children holding onto their mother's skirts pointed at the soldiers as they marched past.

Major Campbell had trotted up to ride next to the expedition commander. About half way through the town, he turned to Bouquet, and Wend, only a few feet behind, could hear what he said.

"Colonel, since it seems that everyone in town is out watching us depart, may I sound the pipes? The lads would like it."

Bouquet had been looking straight ahead as he rode, seemingly lost in thought. At the major's words, he screwed up his face and looked around at the crowd as if seeing it for the first time. Then his features relaxed and with a smile of resignation he nodded permission to the major.

Campbell swung around on his horse and made a signal to the drummers of the lead company, who immediately changed from their rim-tap to a loud beat on the head of the drum. Hearing the full-throated sound, the drummers of each succeeding company followed suite. Now Campbell turned to the piper marching with the staff, who had already pulled the pipes from the sling on his back, and gave him the name of a tune. There was a groaning sound as the man filled his bag, then the musical wailing began, picked up in quick succession by the pipers of the other companies.

The citizens had been watching the battalion's march in a quiet, almost sullen manor. Wend was aware that the prevailing sentiment of the settlers and townspeople was anger that the army was not staying to provide protection, mixed with the conviction that Bouquet's mission was doomed to failure.

Then suddenly an older woman, who had been standing in front of her house, ran out into the road to the side of Bouquet's horse, and matched her pace to him. "Colonel, my daughter and her man and children got a place out on the Allegheny north of Fort Pitt. If they're still alive, they'll be holed up in the fort. So God Speed, Sir to you and your men."

Bouquet looked down at the woman, nodded to her, and slowly raised his right hand to the brim of his hat. "Thank you, my good lady. I promise you we shall not fail."

The woman reached up, touched Bouquet's boot, and then went back to the roadside.

Now a surprising thing happened, perhaps sparked by the woman's action, or perhaps ignited by the martial sound of the pipes. It started slowly. First there was just a man or woman here and there clapping to the troops as they marched. Then it spread, with groups of people cheering. And finally it seemed as if the whole crowd was swept up in the enthusiasm of the moment, shouting encouragement to each company as they swung past.

So it was that, in the end, the column disappeared into the forest to the skirling of the pipes and warmed by the cheers of the citizens of Carlisle.

CHAPTER 18
Fort Bedford

In the bright afternoon sun of July 25th, ten days after Bouquet's expedition had left Carlisle, Baird led the advance point of the convoy from the tree line into the great cleared area which surrounded Fort Bedford. The four scouts pulled up and sat their horses in the road, surveying the scene in front of them.

Wend looked around the open space, noting the differences around the fort since he and Joshua had arrived with the flying column three weeks earlier. He could make out the camp of Robertson's detachment in one of the outlying stockades. In a similar enclosure he saw the herd of cattle and horses which Robertson had brought with him. And the settler's camp of wagons and canvas shelters around the fort seemed larger than on their previous visit.

The scouts were an hour ahead of the military advance guard of the column, which labored along the road from Sideling Hill. Their task was to warn Captain Ourry of the convoy's approach so that he could make preparations to receive it and assign campsites for the various elements.

Wend reflected that the entire expedition was weary and ready for rest. After leaving Carlisle, they had initially made good progress along the wagon roads of the Cumberland Valley, reaching Fort Loudoun in three days time. There Slough & Simon had several additional wagons, loaded with supplies, waiting for them.

But after Loudoun the real struggle had begun. The road over the mountains to Lyttleton was as bad as Captain Robertson had described in his dispatch to Bouquet. The last winter had been extremely hard on the road; rains had washed out many sections as it angled up through the gap, often clinging tenuously to the side of the mountain. The soldiers had performed backbreaking work with shovels to fill in the gaps in the road, hoping their construction would hold up under the wear of more than thirty heavy Conestoga wagons.

Bouquet was in constant fear of losing wagons if the road collapsed and sent them crashing down the steep slope. But the repairs held and the convoy had made it to Lyttleton after two days of exhausting labor.

There had been hopeful rumors among the officers and sergeants that the column would rest for a full day at Lyttleton, but Bouquet hadn't heard the rumor; he allowed only a night's stop and had them on the road through the Cove at dawn the very next day. Crossing Sideling Hill was nearly as excruciating as the struggle through the mountains.

Bouquet was a man obsessed, driving the column like a waggoner whipping his team to greater effort. He moved up and down the convoy, urging companies and wagons to move faster, solving blockages, assigning troops to help push or lift stuck wagons. Each evening, he called groups of officers to his campfire, briefing them on the fighting methods of the tribes and his ideas on how to counter them.

Wend reflected that Bouquet's predictions about the first part of the journey had been entirely correct. The scouts saw no hostile sign and spent their time either riding ahead identifying problems with the road or acting as couriers along the length of the convoy. Wend had spent considerable time delivering messages and that had allowed him to see Arnold Spengler several times. The small Royal American contingent had been placed under the leadership of a Captain Basset, who had come in from a temporary assignment just before the departure from Carlisle. Arnold had grown into his responsibilities as the group's sergeant, and now wore the mantle more comfortably.

Wend had also been able to talk to Mary. She walked with the women and children during the day, just behind the last group of wagons; only the rear guard company was behind them. She wore a marching uniform of sorts, which she had assembled from cast off soldiers' clothing. The skirt was made up of tartan material, which she told Wend was actually two kilts sewn together; it ended at her ankles. She also wore a white shirt, a short soldier's red jacket, and a highlander's blue bonnet. She carried her belongings in a standard back pack and had a haversack slung from her shoulder. A pair of regulation shoes completed her outfit. She walked with a staff made from a sapling in one hand. Wend found her appearance in the outfit, unfeminine as it was, unexpectedly attractive and appealing. As the days progressed, he noticed that the skin on her face was tanning from the constant exposure to the July sun and that the freckles across her cheeks and nose were more apparent. The effect complemented her bronze hair and accentuated the high cheekbones of her face.

Wend was shaken from his thoughts as Joshua waved them forward toward the fort. "Let's go down and tell Captain Ourry he's going to have a lot of guests for supper tonight."

They spurred forward at the trot and soon were the object of attention from all over the encampment. As they approached the fort itself, Wend saw two officers striding toward the open gates. The first was Ourry, and then he quickly recognized the second as the tall, spare figure of Captain Robertson, looking little changed from four years earlier.

Joshua pulled up his horse and touched his hand to his hat. "Hello, Captain Ourry. I'm here to tell you that Bouquet and his legions are a few hours out and to deliver you some dispatches." He handed down the leather case. "There's one in there from the colonel which lays out the size of different companies and wagon brigades. But he says it's up to you to figure where the best camp sites would be."

Ourry nodded as he opened the case, removed a sheaf of papers, and paged through them. Wend could see that his mind was already working on plans for the encampment.

Baird swung down from his horse. "Captain Robertson! Good to see you again. It's been near four years since we marched together! I'm glad to see that the Lord preserved you from the fever down in the islands."

"Joshua, I'm glad to see you! By God, I feel better about this expedition already, knowing you're going to be scouting." He held out his hand to Baird. "You should go over to our camp, Joshua; you'll find a good many men you knew from Forbes' campaign and that winter we spent out at Fort Pitt."

Wend had dismounted and now Baird put a hand on his shoulder. "Captain, do you recognize this lad?"

Robertson looked at Wend, a puzzled expression on his face. Then suddenly his eyes opened wide. "My God, yes I do. You're the boy we found near dead out on the other side of Sideling Hill, four years ago!"

"He's been living up in Sherman Valley, making guns and winning bets at target shooting, Captain," Joshua told Robertson. "Now he's working with me as a scout."

Robertson nodded. "Well, I'm glad you've with us, lad. You're looking far better than the last time I saw you!" The captain looked around at the others in the group and a broad smile came over his face. "But I can't say much for the company you're keeping: Kirkwood and Donegal, the two greatest scoundrels in the regiment."

Donegal looked over at Kirkwood and feigned an expression of indignation. "Captain, how can you say that, knowing as you do that we been in on every fight and every march of the battalion since it came to the colonies?"

Kirkwood chimed in, "And got assigned to every dirty work detail that came along, Sir. And we faced up to all that cheerful like. You know that, Captain."

"Yes, and I also know no one has been on the defaulters list more than you, Kirkwood. And what about that time up in New York when you just accidentally wandered away from the regiment for a few weeks?" Robertson winked conspiratorially at Joshua and Wend before he continued. "I remember very well picking you up at that sheriff's jail after you were apprehended."

Kirkwood drew himself up to his full height. "Captain, it's my fate to be misunderstood. And things just seem to happen; that's God's truth. But I've 'na been in any trouble since we left New York for this trip, Sir."

"Kirkwood, you may not have been apprehended, but I'm sure you've been in trouble." Robertson shook his head. "Joshua, you might as well take these two blackguards and Mr. Eckert and make your camp over there with us. In any case, I expect Bouquet will have the rest of the 77th join us there."

* * *

That evening, after the various elements of the expedition had straggled into Bedford and taken up their campsites, Bouquet announced that they would remain at the fort for three days in order to rest men and animals and effect repairs to the wagons. And to the extreme pleasure of the soldiers, he authorized an extra rum ration to all and the slaughtering of cattle for fresh meat.

After finishing supper the battalion relaxed and partied in the light of the campfires. Each squad had their own fire, and in the center of the 77th's camp, a larger communal fire had been built. Wend could see the officers sharing drinks, conversation, and laughter at a fire in front of their mess tent. The battalion's musicians had come out, forming a group near the central fire, playing fiddles and bagpipes, and there was one man who made haunting music with a wooden flute.

Joshua's group sat around their fire, joined by Arnold, who had come over from the 60th's camp to visit Wend, bearing a jug of strong libation with him. They all sipped on their mugs and listened to the sound of the fiddles and pipes as they alternated between fast, bright songs and sad strains of nostalgic melodies. Twice the highlanders around them had taken up singing songs in Gaelic, the words unintelligible to Wend, but the romantic sentiment clear.

Donegal leaned over to Wend as if understanding his thoughts. "They're singing about Scotland and the highlands and the lasses they left behind, lad."

Wend nodded. He looked around at the members of the battalion and was struck by the feeling of community that pervaded the camp. Men and women walked between the fires, cracking jokes with friends or stood around in groups conversing and watching the musicians. From a nearby fire he could hear the distinctive laughter of Esther McCulloch. At another, a group of children shouted and giggled. It was as if a big family had gotten together for some traditional occasion such as a wedding party or a wake. Then he suddenly remembered something that Lizzie Iverson had told him long ago as they rode in the cargo wagon along Forbes Road: She had said the regiment was like a traveling clan, and now Wend fully understood the meaning of her words.

Shortly thereafter the dancing started. There had been some already, with couples twirling to fiddle music. But now a soldier came up to the big fire with a broadsword in each hand and laid them down on the ground, one on top of the other, in the form of an X. A piper started a rollicking tune and McKirdy, the drummer, accompanied him to keep a beat. The soldier who had placed the swords began dancing, his body directly above the apex of the blades, his feet coming down in a different sector of the crossed swords with every step. He held his arms in the air above his head as he stepped to the sound of the pipes.

A series of soldiers succeeded the original above the swords, each doing his particular version of the dance to the accompaniment of raucous cheers for those who did well, laughs and jeers for those less nimble or made awkward by the effects of their drink. Then, after some twenty or thirty minutes, Mary Fraser came up to the swords and took her turn above the blades.

The girl was still in her marching outfit, the red jacket open against the heat of the night, showing her white soldier's shirt underneath. She danced with a woman's lightness and her feet seemed to barely touch the ground as she took each step. Mary carefully placed each foot in the sectors between the swords, appearing to land only on the toes of each downward pointed foot. She took particular care with the placement of her arms and hands, mostly holding one hand above her head, the other on her hip as she pirouetted; but at certain moments she tossed both hands toward the night sky. It was evident that she had abandoned herself to the joy and thrall of the music; absorption and happiness were written all over her face as she moved to the rhythm.

In Wend's eyes, Mary made an enticing figure silhouetted against the fire's light, the leaping flames illuminating her lithe body. He could see, beneath the tartan skirt, the thinness of her waist and the gracefulness of her legs. As he watched, Wend became aware of a feeling of excitement running through him; a feeling of desire he hadn't experienced, save in his dreams, for four long years.

Wend looked around and saw that he was far from alone in his attraction to the girl. He realized that as she danced, the noise around the soldiers' fires had diminished and then virtually stopped. In fact, there was a pervasive silence, aside from the sound of the pipes and McKirdy's drum. He saw that scores of men sat frozen, their gaze fixed on Mary, hunger and desire in their eyes. Then he remembered the words of Sergeant McCulloch, spoken right here in Bedford, that many a man dreamed of the girl sharing his blankets.

Wend's thoughts were interrupted by the voice of Arnold, who sat on his left. "Now there's a choice young woman. The Lord put a lot of thought into assembling her, didn't he?" Arnold stared for a moment. "And I have a new appreciation for auburn hair!"

Wend murmured agreement to his friend and then looked up at Mary again. He saw that her hair had come loose from underneath the bonnet and had tumbled down around her neck and shoulders, light from the fire reflecting off the copper strands. The long hair framed her face, giving her an even more girlish, innocent look. A startling thought occurred to him: In her own way, she was as exciting as Abigail and he reluctantly had to admit that she was having the same effect on him that the Philadelphia girl had aroused. Then, as he looked at Mary in the firelight, he suddenly felt a chill, and with a shock recognized that he was falling in love with the highland girl.

In an instant, that realization brought a feeling of intense guilt over him. He shook himself and thought: *I can't let this happen. I am here to do a job, to find and bring Abigail back, or fail trying.* He looked straight ahead, steeling himself to bring the image of the blond girl with the piercing blue eyes into focus.

Then he heard Mary's voice nearby and looked up to see her standing in front of him, looking down with a smile as she pulled strands of hair out of her face. "Whew! I need to rest after dancing so long. She turned to Baird. "I thought I'd come and talk with you scouts, Joshua. I haven't been able to spend much time with you since we left Carlisle."

Joshua smiled broadly and motioned gallantly with his hand. "I reckon we would all be graced by your presence, fair Mary."

The girl settled herself on Wend's right, arranging the tartan skirts to cover her legs. After she had finished she looked at him coyly. "Did you like my dancing?"

For a moment Wend felt tongue tied, not knowing how to answer. But then words came. "I think everyone in the regiment liked your dancing, Mary. You were very graceful."

She smiled at him and laughed, tossed her hair, and began to put it back up under the bonnet. After finishing, she turned serious and looked at him. "I saw how you cleaned up your family's graves when we marched past. That was thoughtful of you to take the time."

Wend, surprised that she had noticed, said. "Well, I couldn't have done any less. The crosses had fallen apart; the only remains were three sticks pointing up from the ground. Small bushes and tall grass had nearly covered the graves themselves."

Joshua overheard their exchange and spoke up, a harsh tone in his voice. "Sprout, that was an act of pure sentimentality. You could have tended the graves on the way back from Pitt, when we won't be in such a hurry. It cost us over an hour and the column almost caught up with us."

Wend retorted, "Damn it, Joshua, there's no guarantee I'll be alive for the trip back. And I'll not let the forest cover up my family's graves as long as I breathe."

Donegal turned to Baird. "Come on, Joshua, drop it! Leave the lad alone. I couldn't have just ridden by my Mum and Dad if they were laying out here in the wilderness. We all pitched in and were on our way again with nothing remiss."

Kirkwood added, "Lord, Joshua, it was a good time to rest our bottoms. I still ain't used to spending hours on top of that beast. Moving around did me some good."

Wend was thankful for the highlanders' intervention. His insistence on stopping to clean the graves had been the first time he and Joshua had argued and Baird was sill sore about losing.

But it was Mary who silenced Baird. She cast him a knowing expression and said, "I've no doubt, Joshua Baird, that if it was my Mother's grave, you would have found time to stop."

Baird stared at Mary for a moment, a startled look in his eyes, before turning to gaze into the fire.

It was uncomfortably quiet for a few moments. Then, Mary turned to Arnold and asked, "Can I have taste of your jug? I'm very dry after dancing."

Arnold looked down at the whiskey jug for a second and then hesitatingly handed it to the girl.

Mary gave him a withering look. "What, Corporal, have you 'na seen a girl take a drink before?" She lifted the jug to her mouth and took a pull which would have done any man justice, then wiped her mouth and handed it back to Arnold.

Finally Mary turned back to Wend. "I told Chaplain Ferguson about your story and how Mum and I tended you. And I think you would like to meet him. You could come over to his tent sometime while I'm taking lessons and watch me read. And I'll show you how I can write. The chaplain says I have a good, fair hand with the quill."

Wend looked at the girl who sat beside him, a smile of pleasure on her face as she thought about her schooling. A thought came to his mind. "Why are you so intent on learning to read and write? Most girls don't learn that."

She thought a moment and said, "Because I want to learn about the world. In the army, I have seen a lot of places. But when the chaplain reads to me from his books, I realize how much more there is to see and know. I want to be able to read about it myself. Someday I want to have my own books." She thought for a moment. "The army has been my life, but with the reorganization happening, I'll have to leave it if arrangements can't be made for me. And if I do leave, I want to have the learning to take with me that will help me make my way in the world. Maybe I could be a nanny at some wealthy family's estate and teach the children. The chaplain and the colonel of the regiment would give me a good recommendation."

"But you don't have to leave the army. This regiment and the 42nd are full of good men. You certainly could find one you want to marry. And you are of that age." Wend looked around at the men in the encampment. As he looked, he could see more than a few faces turned their way watching them converse. "And I've been with the regiment long enough to know that there are plenty of lads here who show an interest in you."

Even in the dim firelight he could see her blush at his suggestion and her mouth tighten as she thought about his words. After a moment, she turned to him and spoke sharply. "Yes, I can be a wife in the army. And my husband will take care of me. Maybe that's what my fate will be. But I would like to think I have some choice in my own future! So maybe when the 77th is reduced, I will go over to the 42nd. Or instead maybe I'll go back to Scotland with the discharged soldiers." Mary turned, smiled at Wend, and leaned close to him so that their bodies briefly touched. She whispered, "On the other hand, I've found a lot to like in the colonies. So maybe I'll try my fortune here, if I can find a situation which will keep body and soul together."

* * *

A few minutes earlier, Captain Charles McDonald had given his men the order "To Trees!" His company of about forty men had been standing at the edge of the forest around Fort Bedford. Now the highlanders were doing their best to use cover to advance through the woods in a skirmish line. Joshua and Wend stood with the captain, watching their progress. It was two days after the expedition's arrival in Bedford, and as part of Bouquet's training program, every company was spending time learning forest warfare as practiced in the Royal Americans. The two scouts were acting as advisors to McDonald.

Joshua looked at McDonald and shook his head. "They got their hearts in it Cap'n, but they ain't quite got the hang of it yet." He looked at the officer. "Let Eckert and I coach them on the best ways to use the bush for cover."

McDonald nodded, and the two scouts walked along behind the line of soldiers. In preparation, Joshua had explained to Wend what they should show the highlanders. Now, Baird took one side of the line and Wend moved along the other side.

Wend immediately realized that the highlanders weren't getting close enough to the ground, instead often simply standing or kneeling behind a tree or bush. Wend explained to each man that the best way to remain out of sight while looking ahead was to get as low as possible, and look out from below the base of a bush or tree with low branches, because the eye of an Indian would tend to be scanning at a higher level. He moved along the line, stopping periodically to get the men on their bellies and crawling up to the best point of vantage, then picking out the next bush or tree ahead which would provide cover.

He came upon a highlander down on one knee, his musket across his chest, looking along the side of an evergreen bush. Wend came up behind the soldier. "Any self respecting warrior would see you leaning out to get a view ahead. Or glimpse your musket barrel sticking out the other side. Get down on your elbows, with your musket beside you, and look out from under that lowest branch, there on the right."

The highlander turned around and Wend discovered that it was Donald McKirdy. The drummer was scowling fiercely at him.

"Are you thinkin' you're a sergeant, or maybe an officer now, to tell me my business, Eckert? I've fought the savages before, in Carolina and here. And we didn't need you colonials telling us how to do our job!"

Wend, taken by surprise, had to think for a moment. "McKirdy, I've been hunting game in these woods all my life. And so have the savages. I'm just trying to show you how to stay in one piece: If you want to get your head blown off by some Shawnee, that's your choice."

McKirdy snarled, "I've been in three major fights since the regiment arrived in your wretched country. And I did fine without your help. So just make yourself scarce; I'll get along without your preachin'."

Wend controlled his anger. "Well, it seems like the officers want to make use of what people like Baird and I know, so you better listen up or McDonald's sergeant will have some words for you."

Wend's comments seemed to have effect, for though McKirdy scowled again, he also turned around and flattened himself on the ground, creeping up to the bottom edge of the bush.

Wend couldn't resist saying, "That's the stuff, McKirdy. Now you're looking more like a ranger!"

The drummer looked back, his face red. "I'll play this little game for now. But meanwhile, I've got some important word for you from the men of the 77th."

Wend instinctively knew what was coming next. "Are you sure you have that straight Donald? Is it from the 77th or just from you?"

"Don't mince words with me. We've been watching you. The men ain't happy with all the attention you been paying to Mary Fraser. She's a fine highland lass and belongs with her own kind. This battalion is her family and we won't see her be led astray by some fast talking, lowland Ulster scum like you."

Wend felt his face burning. He took a deep breath and held it for a few seconds before answering. "McKirdy, before you go any further, let's make a few things clear. First, while I may look like it, I'm not Ulster. I'm German, which you might have figured out if you had paid more attention to my name. In the old country, my people were jaegers and gamekeepers before they turned to gunsmithing. Hardly what you would call scum."

Wend looked down at McKirdy. "On the other hand, I've lived with the Ulster people for four years now and I'm proud to be taken for one of them.

So if they are scum, then I'm a proud bit of scum." Wend saw that it was McKirdy who was now getting red in the face. "And a second thing," he said, "I haven't made any advances to Mary Fraser. I've talked with her a few times and bought her some tea at a tavern. Mostly in the way of being kind to her for nursing me years ago when she was a child." He took a step closer to the highlander. "But it does seem that Mary likes to visit with me. If she wants to do that, it's her business. So why don't you go about your duties, drummer, and leave me to mine."

Wend turned and moved on along the line of soldiers. But McKirdy threw a parting shot, "Eckert, just don't forget what I told you. Keep away from that girl." And then finally, "Or, mind me, there'll be consequences!"

After the company had crept forward about 100 yards, Baird and McDonald called for them to stop in their hiding places and the three walked out in front to judge the degree of concealment which the highlanders were achieving. Wend was surprised in one aspect; he had anticipated that the red jackets would stand out against the green of the bush. But then he realized that the soldiers' jackets, which had been dyed with cheap coloring, had over time faded from bright red to the dull color of bricks. This shade actually made the clothing much less conspicuous than he had expected. And the tan breeches and dark leggings were precisely the right colors for blending with the forest.

After noting the progress the company was making, Joshua turned to McDonald. "Have your soldiers ever practiced loading while they are lying on the ground, particularly on their backs?"

McDonald thought for a moment. "Now that you mention it, no they haven't. Reloading while standing, or on one knee, yes; but on their backs, no."

The captain gathered his troops into a small clearing. Baird had one squad lie on the ground and discharge their muskets into the woods. Then they were instructed to roll over on their backs and attempt to reload. Both scouts had long sticks in their hands and held them parallel to the ground just a few inches over the soldiers. "Don't let your hands or any part of your body get higher than the sticks! Hold those muskets near the ground beside your body as you work." Joshua grinned and shouted, "Imagine musket and rifle balls flying over you just at the level of these sticks!"

After reloading, Baird had the men of the squad roll over and fire their muskets from the prone position, then practice reloading once more. Each squad in succession then carried out the drill. After they were finished,

McDonald again gathered the men into a semi-circle. Joshua addressed the assembled soldiers. "Now take a look at all your equipment. Make sure you arrange everything you need for reloading where you can get at it handy-like when you are in a tight position or flat on the ground. Forget the King's regulations about where it should be carried, at least until this campaign is finished." He smiled. "You been trained to load and fire as fast as possible while standing in line. It will still be important to fire fast when you fight the warriors, but you got to do it while keeping from getting shot. So think about the best way reload while you're in hiding."

Now Baird walked over to a tree at the edge of the clearing, about twenty yards from where the men of the company were standing. He pulled out his hatchet and cut a horizontal mark at the level of his head and another at the height of his knees. Then he walked back to the assembled men.

"Another thing: You've been trained to simply level your muskets at the enemy. But in bush warfare, you've got to try to hit a specific target. Now your musket ain't any great shakes at hitting a single target at distance. But it happens that fighting in the woods mostly takes place close-up; like from here to that tree I just marked. So a musket is accurate enough at that range. Sometimes it's actually better than having a rifle, since you can reload it faster. But you got to learn to fire fast at a target which you only see for a few seconds."

Baird took the musket from the hands of a corporal standing nearby. "What you want to do is just make sure you get a ball somewhere into the enemy's body. You do that, you'll be doing plenty good. You can finish him with your bayonet or hatchet." He held the musket out parallel to the ground with one hand. With the other he pointed at features on the weapon. "You well know that you don't have any sights—just look along the barrel at the target." He pointed to the marks on the tree. "Think of those marks being at the head and the knees of a warrior."

Joshua quickly swung the musket up at the tree and fired in almost the same instant. Bark flew off the tree and a hole appeared about two feet below the upper hatchet mark. "That's the way you got to do it; fast and into the man's body. You need to react as soon as you see something or you won't get a shot."

For the next two hours, McDonald had his men take turns firing at the tree. Soon it was peppered with holes. Most of the soldiers were able to get their shot within the hatchet marks, though some were shooting low, because they were lining up the top of their bayonet lug with the rear of the barrel.

Others shot fast but high. But by the second shot by each man, everyone was doing reasonably well.

After they had finished, McDonald asked, "Well, how are they doing, Joshua? Think they'll pass muster when we get out beyond Ligonier?"

Baird turned to the captain. "These highlanders do pretty well with aimed shots. I 'spect that many of them handled firelocks before they joined the army. They'll do all right when we meet the tribes." He laughed. "But you should see the lads in the English regiments. Lots of them come from London and other towns; never touched a firearm 'till they enlisted. Getting them to hit a target, even at this range, is almost a lost cause."

* * *

Later, the day's training completed, Wend dropped his gear off at the scouts' campsite and made his way in the direction of the chaplain's tent. He had it in his mind to take Mary up on her invitation to visit at her lessons.

He walked between two tents and came out on the row where Chaplain Ferguson's tent was located. He could see the tent about seventy or eighty feet away. Mary was sitting alone, in a chair under the canvas fly in front, reading a book which she held in her lap. Wend stopped to watch the girl. She was deeply engrossed in the text, oblivious to the bustle and noise around her, following the words with a finger of her right hand, and Wend could see her lips moving as she read. She came to the end of a page and turned it rapidly, not looking up or breaking the pace of the movement of her finger along the printed words.

Suddenly there was a voice from beside him. "Judging by your clothes and your age, I would say that you must be Mr. Wend Eckert, the scout."

Wend was startled to see that the chaplain had quietly come up beside him.

"Mary does like to read," Ferguson continued. "She can lose herself in almost any kind of book and her mind just seems to soak the contents up. She can quote from practically everything she's read." The chaplain turned to Wend. "But I haven't properly introduced myself. I'm Adam Ferguson, chaplain of the 77th." He held out his hand.

Wend shook his hand. "Well, Reverend, you've got it right, sir. I am Wend Eckert. I was coming to take Mary up on her invitation for me to meet you and visit her at lessons."

Ferguson nodded. "Actually, Mr. Eckert, I've been wanting to talk to you. It happens that I know quite a lot about you. Colonel Bouquet took the noon meal at the mess of the 77th yesterday; Captain Robertson and he were talking about what happened to you and your family, which filled me in on your background. Anyway, I'd been eager to learn something about you since we left Carlisle."

"Chaplin, I'm surprised that you are so interested in my story."

"Well, son, speaking plainly, I'm interested because Mary seems to have developed an infatuation with you. Mary talks about you all the time, and told me how she nursed you after the massacre." The chaplain smiled crookedly and looked at Wend to see his reaction. He laughed as he observed Wend's startled expression at hearing the words. Then he continued, "Mary is far and above the best student I've ever had, either in the army or back in Scotland where I taught many young people, most of whom came from wealthy families. It's gratifying to see how fast she learns; not only reading, but doing her numbers and her composition. I've been working with her for several years now, and inevitably I have come to think of her almost as my own relation."

Wend said, "It seems like everyone in the battalion pays special attention to her."

He put his hand on Wend's shoulder. "Yes, that's undeniable. As for myself, I've been hoping that somehow she could find a situation which would spare her the hard life of the army. Right now, in her youth, it is exciting for her. But it would be most gratifying to me if she could settle in a more comfortable home. We've talked about her becoming a governess or taking a teaching position in a well-off household. But to tell the truth, I don't fancy her in a position which could lead to spinsterhood and isolation on some large estate. She is too high spirited and outgoing."

Wend looked at the chaplain, not sure where all this was leading. "I agree with you, sir. She is such a naturally happy person that I can't see her spending her life as a strict disciplinarian, with a dour face." Wend thought about Master Dreher, at his school. "I had a very proper teacher, and he seemed to have no humor in him."

"So right, so right lad." Ferguson tightened his grip on Wend's shoulder. "I would rather see her happy in a good marriage, perhaps to a prosperous tradesman who could give her a life of her own." He looked directly into Wend's eyes. "And it has occurred to me that life in these colonies, with their less structured style of living, would offer more opportunities for a girl like Mary than the poverty of the highlands."

Wend grasped the import of the chaplain's words. He thought to himself it was like being told he was welcome to court a man's daughter. He turned to the reverend. "Yes, I think that would be good for her. And of course, she would do well living here in the colonies."

"Oh, I'm glad you agree. It's good to have someone confirm my thoughts." Ferguson paused for a moment, considering his words. Then he looked very seriously at Wend. "By the way, the colonel happened to mention that one of the reasons you are along on this march is that you had a deep interest in a young lady who was captured by the savages. Is that correct?"

Wend nodded, and in a few sentences outlined Abigail's story.

The man listened closely, nodding as Wend spoke. Then he looked at him with a wry smile. "It would seem that you have a bit of a complication facing you, doesn't it?"

Wend flushed again, for the Chaplain's words had cut right to the internal conflict which Wend had faced ever since he had watched Mary dance two days earlier. "Yes, Reverend, it seems nothing is ever as clear-cut as you would like."

"Well, lad, what is clear is that you are going to have a decision to make sometime on this campaign." He paused and looked at Mary, and then his voice became very serious and stern sounding. "That girl is very close to my heart. I would not take it kindly if you did something which could break her spirit. Let me be absolutely straight with you: Don't play with her emotions if that captive girl means more to you than her." The chaplain looked directly into his eyes, and it seemed to Wend that he was looking right into his very soul.

Wend made a point of holding the man's eyes. "I assure you, Chaplain, that I would never do anything to hurt Mary. I would rather have my own heart twisted into knots than let that happen."

Ferguson slapped Wend on the back. "Good, my son. We understand each other. Now let's go say hello to the lass."

The two walked up to where Mary sat. She looked up from her book, and beamed at both of them.

"Look who I found wandering through the camp. This lad says he was coming here to see you!"

* * *

Later that afternoon, Wend walked Mary to the hospital. He had spent about an hour visiting with the chaplain and Mary, listening to her read from her book and then had watched as she wrote sentences on a slate board as dictated by Ferguson.

The camp was alive with soldiers and waggoners making preparations to resume the march next morning. They passed by rows of wagons where contractors were checking and mending harness, going over the wagons, greasing the axels and making other minor repairs. Soldiers from all three regiments were hauling gear back to the wagons from tents and squad fires.

They were passing between two wagons when Mary stopped and put her hand on Wend's arm. He turned to face her. She was looking up at him with a serious face. "I went to your squad fire yesterday morning to see you, and Donegal told me you and Joshua had been sent out on courier duty down to Fort Cumberland on the Potomac. You didn't even tell me you were leaving!"

"Mary, I didn't have time to even think about telling you. We had to get started right away, 'cause of the distance to Cumberland. Bouquet was anxious for us to check on a company of Maryland Rangers which were due to join the column." He thought a moment. "And besides, how would I know that you wanted me to see you before leaving?"

"Wend, haven't we become good friends in the days since Carlisle?" She squeezed his arm. "I worried about you. Joshua and you were riding alone through territory where the war parties are burning farmsteads. You could have been ambushed and I might never have seen you again!"

She quickly reached up with her other arm, putting it around his neck, while still holding his arm with the other. She rose up on her toes quickly and put her lips to his, pulling him close to her. The kiss was brief, but intense, and he felt himself excited in a way he hadn't been for years.

Then she quickly pulled away. "Maybe the memory of that will make you more interested in saying goodbye to me the next time you leave!" She turned and resumed walking toward the hospital.

Wend realized he had broken out in perspiration on his forehead. He quickly caught up with her, searching for something to say after the unexpected embrace. "Well, I certainly will remember that our first kiss was an ambush by you between two freight wagons!"

Mary stopped again and turned to him, her feet spread wide and her hands on her hips. She broke into a broad smile. "You think that was our first kiss?"

Wend stopped, shocked by her reply. "Of course it was. How could I forget if we had kissed before?"

"Because, just like now, it was I that kissed you, but at the time you didn't have a clue." She laughed, enjoying his puzzlement. "It was the night after we found you lying out on Forbes Road. Mum and I worked all afternoon to clean you up and sew up that place where the ball cut your side. I saw every inch of your body as we worked and thought you were the nicest looking boy I'd ever seen. Then that night, when I was watching over you, and Mum and Sergeant Iverson were asleep, I gave you a kiss, right on the lips. You looked so helpless laying there in the firelight, all bandaged up."

She turned and started walking. "And ever since, I've wanted to see what it would be like to kiss you when you knew what was happening!"

Wend, his mind in turmoil, walked quietly beside her until they reached the hospital. The medical tents had been set up on a slight rise on the outskirts of the encampment, to take advantage of the best breeze and cleanest air. The hospital was almost empty of patients now; some of the convalescent highlanders had been left behind at Juniata Crossing, to hold that ford which was an essential element in the line of communication. Another group of them had been formed into a small company to garrison Fort Bedford under Captain Ourry, where they could at least stand sentry and man the defense positions in an emergency.

They came upon Surgeon Munro, busy with quill and ink in his office tent. Wend could see several women, including the burly figure of Esther McCulloch, working at tables as they rolled bandages and packed them in sacks for stowage in the medical wagon.

Munro looked up as the two approached his tent and nodded at both of them. "Afternoon, Eckert. Ah, Mary; done with your lessons?"

"Yes, Doctor. I'll join the others getting bandage rolls ready."

The surgeon shook his head. "There are enough hands at that work. You can help me over in the surgery tent, packing up my implements to be ready for tomorrow." He stood up to accompany Mary.

Wend was about to say goodbye to Mary and the doctor when a shout from the nurses interrupted them. He looked up and saw that the women were pointing at a group of three soldiers coming toward the hospital. One of them was obviously in distress and having trouble walking; the other two were on either side of him, supporting him as they moved, their muskets slung over their shoulders. In a second Wend realized that the approaching troops were Royal Americans and that Arnold Spengler was one of the assisting soldiers.

As the three arrived, Arnold shouted, "Doctor, this man's taken a bullet in his thigh; he's bleeding badly and we can't stop it!"

Wend looked down, and could see blood oozing from the inside of the soldier's left leg, halfway between the knee and the crotch. A crude bandage was around the leg, but it was blood red against the man's tan breaches.

Munro, his voice calm as he looked at the wound, motioned to Arnold. "Here, bring him into this tent and we'll tend him right away. Mary, help him onto the table, get his clothing away from the wound, and clean him up as best you can. I'll get cleaned up and ready to work."

Wend, Arnold, and the other soldier, Private Hahn, stood outside the surgery, watching as Munro worked on the wounded man. He was assisted by Mary and Esther McCulloch. He turned to Arnold and asked what had happened.

Arnold, still agitated, told the story. "Captain Basset had the whole Royal American detachment, twenty of us we got now, out on patrol about a mile and a half from the fort. He had us practicing moving as quiet as possible through the woods. It was all routine and then suddenly there was a war party right in front of us, up close. It wasn't an ambush; it happened almost as if they were as startled to see us as we were at sighting them."

"Both sides took cover and fired a volley at the other. For a while everyone, us and the Indians, just worked at reloading and then firing whenever we could find a target. But after a few minutes, the captain called me over and said he had a plan. He would use most of the detachment to keep the warriors busy, and told me to take a squad and work my way under cover around to the Indian's flank, hit them with a single volley, and then close with the bayonet. It all worked out pretty well. When we hit the war party's right flank, the captain had the rest of the company stand up and advance with the bayonet. All the Indians, seeing they were being attacked from two sides, turned and ran, and then I could see there were only eight or nine. We started to chase them, but the captain blew his whistle and called us all back. He said we would never catch them in the woods, and there might be an ambush."

"That's when we found out that Berger was wounded; he hadn't even realized he had been hit until he stopped chasing the war party and looked down to see blood all over his leg."

Munro came out of the surgery tent. "We've got him cleaned up, and the wound is not bad; it looks worse than it really is because of all the blood. The bullet went right through the fleshy part of his thigh, not hitting anything really serious, except for some blood vessels. At any rate, we've got control of the bleeding now and I'll sew him up shortly. But he's going to need to be in hospital for several days while we make sure the wound doesn't mortify." He paused for a moment and wiped his hands on a rag. "So there's no reason you can't go back to your company now, Sergeant."

Arnold turned to Hahn and pointed to the column of Royal Americans, which had now emerged from the woods and was walking in single file toward their camp. "Go tell Captain Basset about Berger and that I'll catch up with the company shortly."

Wend and Arnold walked side by side in the direction of the Royal American campsite. Wend reflected as they walked, "We feel secure here among all the troops, but it's obvious that there is a strong presence of war parties out in the forest all around us." He told Arnold about burned out farmsteads he and Joshua had seen on the road to Cumberland. "Now your encounter today verifies that they are lurking just outside the area we control, keeping an eye on us."

Wend looked over at Arnold, who was staring off in the distance, as if he hadn't heard his words. He seemed lost in his own world. Wend stopped talking and waited for his friend to reply.

After a while Arnold turned and looked at Wend, a peculiar expression on his face. "Wend, listen: I've been in the army seven years, and do you realize, today is the first time I've been in action? After all those years in Colonel Bouquet's office, I thought it was the last thing that would ever happen to me, until this trouble came up. You could have knocked me over with a feather when they made me a sergeant and sent me out to take charge of troops. And today, when we caught sight of those warriors, I thought I would pee in my pants, I was so scared at first. I just took cover, and started firing and loading as fast as I could, and all the time I was thinking that this couldn't be real, couldn't be happening to me."

"Yes, Arnold, but you did all right in the end, didn't you?"

Spengler reflected a moment. "Maybe you're right. It was a funny thing. When the captain put me in charge of that flanking move, I was suddenly more scared of not getting it right than of being hit." A faint look of pride came over Arnold's face. He slung his musket, which he had been carrying in his right hand, over his shoulder, and then adjusted his battered, cut down field hat. "I got to get back to the company and get them ready to move out tomorrow." He patted Wend on the shoulder and strode off at a fast pace toward his camp.

CHAPTER 19
The Mountains

The column marched in the light of dawn the next morning. The road on the first day was generally flat, as they were still in the wide valley between Sideling Hill and the onset of the Alleghenies. Bouquet planned to take advantage of the flat country to exercise the battalion as they marched. Before departure he had called all the officers together and handed out diagrams showing several screening formations he planned to use to protect the convoy. A new element was the small company of Maryland rangers under Captain Lemuel Barrett which had come back from Cumberland with Joshua and Wend; his men would patrol as flankers on either side of the formation.

Joshua had the scouts ready for the road an hour before the convoy started to depart Bedford. After saddling the mare, Wend had led her to the hospital area where Surgeon Munro and the nurses were busy packing up and loading the remaining patients, including Berger, into wagons. As he had hoped, Mary was there, now dressed again in her marching outfit. She saw him, put down the gear she was holding, and came to him.

"I didn't forget what you said about coming to say goodbye." Wend laughed nervously. "We're about to take up the lead for the convoy. I might not see you for a while."

Mary stood very close, looking up at him and smiling mischievously. The girl raised her face to him, but held back slightly, her mouth just a few inches from his. "Well, I'm glad you came. But it's your turn to kiss me. Up to now, I've done all the work."

Wend leaned over, put his arms around her, and felt her lay her body against him. He could feel the pressure of her breasts through her white shirt. Suddenly he felt a surge of desire and pressed his lips against hers with

abandon. She responded by wrapping her arms around his neck and returning the embrace with an equal passion.

Wend said nothing more, but swung up on the mare, and rode to join the
scouts. As he turned to wave back at Mary, he saw that McKirdy and other
men of Captain McDonald's company were standing by a nearby wagon and
they had obviously been watching their farewell moment.

* * *

Wend pulled up the mare and looked down at the panorama below him.
He was at the crest of a ridge on Allegheny Mountain, looking down the eastward slope as the long line of wagons struggled up the road. The captain of
the advance guard, now over the crest and a mile ahead of the main column,
had given him a dispatch to Bouquet. It was the morning of the third day
since the convoy had left Bedford. The entire second day had featured rain
showers, some quite heavy, and they had made life miserable for humans and
beasts, with wagons bogging down and everyone's clothing soaked and clinging to their bodies. And, in the periods when the rain hadn't been falling, the
July heat had ensured that the atmosphere was oppressive.

Wend looked out from the mountain, scanning the extraordinary vista.
Over the last day he had felt a sense of awe growing as they had climbed the
mountain and he had begun to appreciate its size. For years he had heard,
first from his father, then others who had crossed the Alleghenies, about their
height and ruggedness. Now he fully understood their respect for the range.
He looked out, fighting a sense of dizziness as he looked down at the great
valley in front of his eyes, so far below him that the trees of the forest blended
into a carpet, separate trees indistinguishable to his eyes.

At this particular spot the road was cut along the very side of the mountain and seemed to hang there precariously, rarely more than thirty or forty
feet from the edge. Because of the slope of the mountain, the road had been
built up with earth on the side toward the precipice to level it for wheeled
conveyances. When they had first ridden up the incline, Wend had had to
suppress queasiness as he looked down into the abyss.

From the crest, Wend could see eight or nine of the freight wagons. The
six-horse teams of each wagon were straining against the incline, while at
the same time finding their footing difficult because of the mud. Soldiers
had been stationed along the way to help any wagon which needed a push

or extraction from a hole in the road. Suddenly Wend noticed that the third wagon down the line was having difficulty, the waggoner shouting at his horses and calling to the highlanders standing beside the road for assistance. Then Wend saw the problem.

The built-up side of the road, turned to mud by the rain, had been weakened by the passage of the previous wagons and was now crumbling under the weight of the current one. As he watched, the wagon slid off the road, pulled downward by the weight of its load. The horses were scrambling, but their hooves were not getting a purchase in the deep slime. Before his eyes, the wagon swiftly pivoted around so that its rear end was aimed directly at the precipice, now not more than thirty feet away. The wagon started to roll backwards down the steep incline and the horses panicked, thrashing in their harnesses and screaming in fright as they wildly but futilely tried to get enough traction to hold the great, heavily-loaded Conestoga.

Then things got worse. The driver had been walking alongside his wagon, the end of the reins knotted together and wrapped around his torso. As the wagon dropped off the road, the slack of the reins, now lying on the ground, had been run over by the front wheel and become wrapped around the front axel so that the waggoner was snatched backward. Almost instantly, before he could cut himself free, he was dragged to the ground and pulled along by the wagon as it headed for the edge of the mountain! Wend watched as the man frantically tried to pull his knife to cut himself free, but even when he got his knife from the sheath, he was unable to reach up and slice the reins.

Instinctively, Wend spurred the mare forward toward the wagon. She whinnied in protest, finding the wet, sloping ground not to her liking and made fearful by the panicked screaming of the wagon team. But she obeyed his command; in an instant they were next to the wagon. Wend flung himself to the ground. He grabbed his hatchet from the saddle loop and released the mare; she wasted no time scurrying up the hill to the road. Then he pulled his knife from its sheath and began slashing at the reins of the wagon. In a few seconds he had the waggoner free.

Now the wagon was gaining momentum as the slope increased near the edge of the mountain. Wend swiftly returned the knife to its sheath, and climbed in behind the rearmost set of horses, just in front of the wagon itself. Although he tried to avoid the left side horse's wildly flailing hooves, he received a nasty kick to his leg. But he ignored the pain and began swinging the hatchet against the harness straps. With a few chops he had the two rearmost horses free, and after they had bolted, he got ready to work on the next pair. But he was aware that the wagon was relentlessly moving backward and saw that the precipice was now only a few feet away.

Wend swung the hatchet with increased savagery and soon the second pair was free, both running up the hill toward he road. Now the wagon was moving backward with more speed and he laid into the harness straps of the lead pair with all his strength. At that moment the wagon's rear wheels rolled over the very edge of the cliff. The wagon started to fall, the bed sliding against the edge. As the rear of the wagon started downward, the front of the bed reared skyward, pulling up on the wagon's tongue so that the harness straps tightened and increased their pull on the remaining two horses. Wend felt panic growing inside him as he realized that his fate and that of the horses were now linked, for he must free them to escape himself. He renewed his efforts and suddenly the right horse was free. Now he focused on the left horse.

The tongue was being pulled relentlessly by the falling wagon, the harness straps tightening on the horse and causing him pain. The horse screamed in fright. But Wend soon had all but one of the straps cut, and with careful aim, sliced through the last one. The horse bolted up the hill. The wagon tongue whipped upward into the air as the front of the wagon tilted skyward and finally went over the side. The tongue smacked Wend, flipping him to the ground, his feet at the very edge of the cliff.

He sat up and watched the wagon. It fell for what seemed an eternity, rolling over and over, its contents, mostly barrels of flour, emptying from inside and falling alongside the wagon, like some escort of the damned on the way to Hell. Then the wagon and its escorting barrels smashed into the forest, the wagon shattering into a thousand fragments. The flour barrels split open on impact, making white splotches on the trees and ground around the remains of the wagon.

Slowly, carefully, Wend pulled himself back from the edge, not daring to stand up until he was several feet back.

He turned, picked up his hatchet, and started walking back up the hill to the road. The horses from the team had gathered there around his mare, all of them stamping and snorting their indignation. The waggoner was still sitting on the ground where Wend had cut him free, his hands to his head.

Suddenly Wend was aware of shouting and clapping. He looked up and saw a squad of the 42nd, who had been stationed at that point along the road, shouting congratulations at him. He nodded in acknowledgement and walked toward the road to collect the mare. Then the highlanders suddenly quieted and stiffened their posture. Wend looked around, to see a group of riders approaching; it was Colonel Bouquet, Major Campbell, and Lieutenant Dow.

They pulled up and Bouquet looked down at Wend. "Mr. Eckert, we witnessed the whole affair. I must tell you that was one of the most courageous actions I have seen in almost thirty years of campaigning." Wend felt himself blushing at the colonel's words and looked over to see that Campbell was beaming at him.

"But, Mr. Eckert," Bouquet's expression had now turned very serious; "I see that you are carrying a dispatch case."

Wend pulled the strap off his shoulder and handed the case to Bouquet. The colonel took the case and extracted the message. He looked down at Wend and spoke again. "You action was indeed very brave and saved the lives of a waggoner and six horses. But in doing so, you forgot your most important duty: That was to deliver the dispatches to the officer for whom they were intended. If you had been unsuccessful, and had perished with that wagon, the dispatches would have been lost with you. And that could have meant important information might have been lost or orders not carried out, which could have affected the lives of many men and the success of an operation." Now he looked grimly down at Wend. "In the future, when you are assigned to carry messages, you will remember that your prime duty is to make the delivery and avoid hazards to your own life. Is that clear?"

Wend gulped, now flushing with embarrassment and some anger at the colonel's words. He looked around at the riders and saw Dow with a grim look on his face. Campbell's hand was up to his mouth, but Wend could see a gleam in his eyes, and he wondered if the major was laughing at him. Wend looked at the colonel "Yes, sir. I understand."

Bouquet nodded and walked his horse over to the portion of the roadway which had collapsed. "Major Campbell, we need to fix this section so it will hold up under the weight of the rest of the wagons. Maybe we can build a wall of logs to hold it up; in the worst case we may need to corduroy this portion. Get the troops already here started on shoveling dirt back into place. Then get a message to Captain Robertson; he's got a lot of engineering experience. Order him and his company up here to make a repair which will hold up."

Campbell turned to Wend. "Eckert, ride back along the line; find Robertson and his men. They're back with the second brigade of wagons. Tell him to march up here as rapidly as possible." He paused a moment to think. "You heard what the colonel said about repairs; give Robertson an appreciation of what he'll need to do here in case he needs to collect tools along the way."

Wend nodded and spurred the mare down the hill, glad to leave the scene of the accident, and of his chastisement by Bouquet, behind him.

* * *

That evening, as usual, the scouting group camped with the company composing the vanguard for the column. Wend sat in front of the cook fire in the dusk staring into the flames, still sulking over Bouquet's admonition. Donegal stood over the cook pot stirring the contents; Kirkwood and Joshua were bantering about a soldier of the 77th they had known during the Forbes campaign. Then there was a pause in the conversation and Joshua looked over at Wend. "Hey, Sprout, you've hardly said a word. What are you brooding about?"

Wend pulled himself out of his reverie. "Nothing, Joshua. I'm just tired; there was a lot of riding to do up and down the column." As courier, Wend had briefed the captain of the advance guard about the road problem and the lost wagon, so he understood the delay affecting the column. But he had not said anything about his role in the incident either to the captain or anyone else.

Baird looked like he was about to ask another question when they were distracted by sounds of many feet approaching on the road from the direction of the convoy. Soon a body of troops appeared from around a slight bend in the wagon track. Robertson was at their head, and he waved to the captain of the encamped company. The two captains met in the road while Robertson's men trooped past and then began to set up camp on the other side of the road. Wend could see that they were still carrying the shovels and axes which they had used to repair the road. It became clear that Robertson's company had been designated to take the advance for the next day.

Later, after they had eaten, Wend unrolled his blanket in preparation for sleep. The three older scouts had all pulled out their pipes and were pursuing a desultory conversation as they enjoyed their tobacco.

"Good evening." Wend looked up to see Robertson standing at the scouts' fire. He continued, "May I join you for a while?"

Robertson sat down by Wend, placing his arms around his knees just as he had the night of the massacre at Sideling Hill. He looked around the group. "The road is really suffering from the rain and the beating it took during last winter's weather. Bouquet has ordered my company to take the lead until we get to Ligonier. We're to survey the road and effect repairs in the hope of reducing delays and avoiding accidents like happened today."

Baird looked at Robertson. "What kind of accident?"

"You haven't heard? Wend here is the talk of the whole expedition after what he did over on the eastern slope. A section of the road collapsed, sending a wagon careening toward the edge of the mountain. Wend rode in and saved the driver, who had become tangled in the reins, and then cut the team loose before the wagon went over the side. He nearly went over with it."

The three other scouts stared at Wend. Kirkwood burst out, "Why, the lad's been sittin' here quiet-like all night and said 'na a word about it."

Wend looked sheepishly at the rest of them. "Well, I may be the talk of the expedition, but Bouquet dressed me down for taking a chance while I was a courier. He told me never to do it again."

Donegal took his pipe out of his mouth and laughed. "So, that's why you been so silent all this evening."

Kirkwood rolled his head back, a broad smile on his face, and guffawed even louder than Donegal. "Come on, Wend, you can't call yourself a soldier 'less you get chewed out by an officer or a sergeant at least once a day."

Robertson simply smiled and nodded. "Wend, stop worrying; while we were fixing the road, I overheard Colonel Bouquet talking to Major Campbell about what you did. He said he wished he had fifty provincial woodsmen with your spirit." The captain thought for a moment. "The colonel was just trying to make you understand the importance of courier work and that it takes priority over whatever else that goes on. I'd bet that he's already forgotten he told you that. But he'll never forget your quick action and courage."

* * *

The scouts walked along Forbes' Road as it sloped down the western side of Laurel Ridge toward Loyalhanna Creek and Fort Ligonier. It was three days since the wagon accident on Allegheny Mountain and the sixth day out of Bedford. Robertson's company was a mile or more behind, and the scouts had left their horses with the highlanders. Joshua had warned that he didn't want the horses making noise or getting in the way if they encountered warriors. So now, with the sun perhaps an hour from the noon transit, the four hugged the sides of the road. Joshua and Kirkwood were on the left, Wend and Donegal along the right, ready to take cover at the first sign of trouble.

Joshua scanned the landscape. "I'd say we ain't more than three miles from the fort. We'll move into the woods some distance from the road to pick up any sign of a war party." He looked up at the sun. "It wouldn't surprise me a bit if war bands weren't laying in the woods somewhere, planning to hit advance parties like us or small groups of soldiers repairing the road." He stopped and waved them into the bush. "Wend, you and Donegal go out seventy-five or 100 yards on the right; me and Bob will do the same on the left. Soon as you get there, head toward the fort parallel to the road. That way we'll either see sign or flush anyone watching the road."

Wend and Donegal went out the specified distance and then spread out so they maintained ten or twenty yards between them. It was hot and Wend could feel sweat across his forehead and trickling from his hair down the back of his neck. The birds, which had been chirping mightily when they had first started out in the morning, were now subdued. The same could not be said of the flies, which swarmed around them. Wend looked over at Donegal, intermittently visible as they stole through the bush. Over the last few days, as they had spent more and more time on actual scouting work, he had gained a favorable impression of Donegal's skills. The highlander knew how to move quietly and make use of cover, and his days as a gamekeeper had taught him to recognize the signs left by animals or men.

Suddenly Wend was startled by a noise off to the left. He stopped, and almost immediately a fox broke from under a log and scampered away into the forest, disappearing as fast as he had appeared. He looked at Donegal, who grinned and nodded, and they again took up their advance. But Wend had only taken a few steps when shots rang out; three shots in rapid succession, followed by two more. He had gone to ground behind a tree with the first shot, but immediately recognized that the shots were coming from across the road where Joshua and Kirkwood were scouting. He had no sooner realized this than another series of shoots rang out. He called to Donegal: "There are a lot of people over there; Joshua and Bob must have stirred up a hornet's nest." He rose to his feet. "Let's get over there and help."

Donegal nodded, and the two of them dashed toward the road. As they neared the track, it became evident that while their flanking advance had seemed to have been on level ground, they had actually been walking up a shallow ridge. But the roadway had continued to dip, so that now they came to an outcropping, with the wagon track about fifteen feet directly below them. Several large rocks were clustered at the top of the outcropping and they scooted among them to take advantage of the cover. More shots resounded, and for the first time they heard war-shouts from unseen warriors.

Wend checked the priming in his lock, pulled back the cock, and flicked the sett trigger. He heard the sound of someone crashing through the bush and looked up to see Baird and Kirkwood coming toward the road at the run, with all effort at quietness abandoned. He stood up and waved. "Over here! In the rocks!" The heads of both men jerked up, and seeing him, they changed course directly toward the outcropping. Suddenly, Wend could see their pursuers; black painted warriors, darting in and out of view between trees and bushes. *God, there must be twelve or fifteen of them!*

Wend brought his rifle up, caught sight of a painted body, and squeezed the trigger. He heard a wild cry and thought he saw the man fall, but couldn't be sure. Then he heard Donegal's musket go off beside him and saw all the Indians take to cover.

As both of them hurried to reload, Baird and Kirkwood scampered across the road and up into the rocks. Suddenly chips of rock spattered around Wend, followed by the report of a firelock from across the road. One of the warriors had taken a shot at him! He scrunched down among the boulders and completed his reloading.

Baird flopped down a few feet from Wend; he was breathing heavily, but rolled on his back and made quick work reloading his own rifle. "There's at least twelve of them; maybe more. They'll try to work some of their people around behind us in the woods—there's no shelter for us on the side away from the road. Once they get there, they can take their time and pick us off. "

Wend asked, "Should we try to make a run for it back to Robertson's company? They can't be far behind!"

Joshua rose to his knees and rested the rifle on a rock. "Not a chance. This is poor shelter, but if we try to move from here they'll run us down sure enough."

Suddenly Donegal fired at a spot in the woods across the road. "I saw some movement there," he shouted as he immediately started to reload.

"That's the stuff, Simon." Baird said. "You and Kirkwood keep up a fire. Shoot at any movement and anything that you even suspect as a warrior's position. And aim low; they'll be as close to the ground as they can get. Your shooting may keep them from moving too much. Eckert and I will save our fire for targets that are visible."

The highlanders went to work and Wend was impressed at how quickly the two veterans were able to reload and fire. He kept scanning the other side of the woods, but the enemy were keeping themselves out of sight.

Joshua said, "We got no choice 'cept to hold out here until the advance guard comes up. They got to hear the firing back there; but if they don't hurry, the war party will get behind us and then it's only a matter of time."

Wend felt a knot of fear in his stomach, similar to the way he had felt when Joshua and he had hidden in the pit up on Sideling Hill. Suddenly two warriors popped out from trees about ten yards apart and fired. Wend ducked instinctively. But Joshua ignored the bullets and fired at one of the shooters; he hit the tree next to him, spraying bark over the man. Wend cursed himself for cringing; he raised his head to look for a target and then saw another two warriors dart across the road to the west of their position.

Joshua laughed bitterly. "They didn't care about hitting anyone; they just wanted to distract us from those two crossing the road." He grimaced. "And it worked pretty well. You keep watching the road in case some more try to cross, Sprout. I'll see if I can catch one of them moving in the woods over here."

There was a period of silence, broken only when one of the highlanders fired. Wend scanned the woods and the road, detecting no immediate sign of any movement. But his skin was crawling because he knew they were now out there behind him, silently creeping to a firing position.

Then he saw the slightest movement of bushes at the base of a roadside tree. Controlling his excitement, he lined his rifle up on the spot, keeping his eyes fixed in that area. Then suddenly several Indians fired from the opposite side, but this time Wend kept steady. And almost at the same time a warrior burst from behind the bush and started across the road. Wend carefully led him with his sights and squeezed off a shot. The man lurched and tumbled to the ground, twitched once, and was still. Wend felt a thrill of exultation. By God, he had got one! But the feeling was short lived. At almost the same time, he heard a zipping noise past his head, and stone chips sprayed his face. Momentarily he heard Baird fire.

"I may have hit one," Joshua said calmly. "I think he's lying over behind that tree about 50 yards out. But I can't tell for sure."

Another shot rang out from the woods behind them. Donegal yelped, "That bastard nearly got me!" Wend looked at the highlander and saw that the ball had ripped the shoulder of his uniform jacket.

"Yeah, I saw him break cover to fire, but I hadn't finished reloading." Joshua turned to Kirkwood. "You move around and switch to watching for targets here on this side; they're the bigger threat now."

Then, as if the two shots by the warriors on the forest side had been a signal, their comrades on the far side of the road, who had heretofore been staying mainly quiet and hidden, opened up a continuous fire apparently aimed at keeping the scouts heads down.

Joshua looked over at Wend. "They know their mates over here are in position; now they're going to keep us in a cross fire. Robertson better get up here fast or these warriors are going to be admiring our hair and bragging about their exploits around the campfire tonight."

All four of the scouts crouched against the rocks as the war party's fusillade continued. Wend heard two balls whiz past him in as many seconds. The shots were unnerving enough, but now the warriors, who previously had maintained their stealth, began to shout their war cries. And Wend shuddered as he realized that the cries emanated from all around them.

Kirkwood, his voice as calm as if he were judging the completion of his dinner in a cook pot, glanced around at the other three. "Looks like they're getting ready to make a rush at us." He gave Donegal a meaningful look. Then he reached across his chest, took his bayonet from its frog and locked it onto his musket. The other highlander nodded agreement and did the same.

Donegal looked at Joshua and Wend. "Sure enough, I'd like to be hearing Robertson's piper playing the company into action right now."

Wend shivered. Even these hardened veterans were showing the stress. He reached into his belt, pulled out his hatchet, and laid it on the ground beside him. As he did so, he was surprised to see that his hand was shaking.

Suddenly the firing from the warriors across the road burst out again and the balls whizzed over and around them. Then another volley came from the woods on their side, and Kirkwood reared back suddenly. He looked down a few inches in front of him where Wend could see a ball had just grazed a rock.

Then Wend heard more shots. It took him a second to realize that these were different; they were fired from a greater distance. His heart leaped; was it Robertson finally coming up? Then the shots from the new source rang out again and a warrior broke cover in the woods just over 40 yards from their position. To Wend's astonishment, he shouted, turned his back to them and started to run away. Suddenly other Indians were up and running, not shooting any more. Then Wend heard shots ring out again from the new source and realized that they were coming from down the slope to the westward. He was puzzled; they couldn't be from Robertson's company.

Joshua looked down the road and verbalized Wend's thoughts. "That ain't Robertson's boys shootin'. It's someone else." He crawled to a nearby tree and cautiously stood up, looking down the slope in the direction of the firing. But whoever was shooting had now stopped.

Wend stood up and looked down the road to the west. In a few seconds, a man stepped out of the woods and started to walk up the road toward their position. Then more came out of the bush from both sides of the road and followed him. The four scouts all were standing now, looking at the approaching figures. Wend realized that one of the men looked familiar. He was wearing the red jacket and blue cap of a highlander. Then Wend recognized the burly figure.

Donegal laughed out loud. "Well I'll be damned. Of all people, it's Sergeant McCulloch himself! Never thought I'd be happy to see him dropping in!"

Then Wend saw that there were other highlanders following the sergeant, and recognized some of the faces as other men from the flying column which had gone out to Ligonier. He also saw that there were civilian scouts with the soldiers, carrying rifles.

Joshua motioned toward the approaching men. "Look, there's ole' Dan Carmichael." He looked at Wend. "We're damned lucky. Lieutenant Campbell must be running patrols out from Ligonier. They sure saved our skins this time."

In a moment the patrol, numbering ten men, was gathered below them on the road. Carmichael looked up at Baird, a broad smile on his face. "Joshua, I'll be damned if those Indians didn't have you up there like a treed 'coon, looking down at the barking dogs." There were laughs from the other men in the patrol. "You all can come on down now, we chased the dogs off!"

Baird didn't directly answer Carmichael, instead greeting the civilian who stood beside him. "Byerly, by God! Good to see you, Andrew! I was worried that the Indians had caught you at your place at Bushy Run, just like they hit Clapham at his trading post. Is your family all right?"

Byerly nodded. "They're fine, Joshua; safe inside Ligonier. We had a bit of excitement when this all started, but things turned out all right."

Joshua nodded. "Glad to hear it. You got a lovely wife and kids. He turned to Wend. "Sprout, meet Andrew Byerly, late sergeant of the Royal Americans. He runs the way station at Bushy Run, on the way from Ligonier to Fort Pitt. Many's the night I've shared the comfort of his place and his wife's cooking."

The four scouts descended from their roost and joined the patrol on the road. McCulloch told them that Lieutenant Campbell had been expecting Bouquet's expedition for some time and had started sending out patrols to the eastward daily in the hope of sighting the column.

Just then Donegal pointed to the road to the east. Wend glanced around and saw other men pointing. He looked up the road to see Robertson's men approaching at the run. The captain had part of the company in a wide skirmish line which extended well into the woods on both sides of the road. The rest of his men advanced in a column along the road.

Meanwhile, Joshua and Carmichael had walked over to the body of the warrior Wend had shot and were examining him. Baird looked up at Wend. "Hey, Sprout, you might want to come over and take a look."

Wend approached the warrior's body. The man had been laying face down on the road, a pool of blood oozing out from under him. Baird had rolled him over and was now squatting beside the Indian. "Look at the paint patterns and ink tattoos, Sprout. This is a Mingo warrior."

Joshua pointed to a spot on the left side of the Indian's chest, and Wend saw there was the scar of an old gunshot wound there. On the sides of the scar were the marks of crude stitching used to close the wound. Then Joshua rolled the man back over onto his chest, and pointed to the back of the same shoulder, where a similarly stitched exit wound was visible. "This remind you of anything, Sprout? A Mingo with a sewed up bullet wound through his left shoulder?"

Then it hit Wend. He remembered Franklin's story about the day of his family's massacre. This was the very same Mingo that Abigail had treated. This was the warrior his father had shot just before he himself had been killed!" Wend looked up at Joshua in astonishment.

"Yeah, Sprout; we've been fighting the same band of Mingoes that killed your family." He paused for a moment. "As far as this character is concerned, you just finished the job your father started."

CHAPTER 20

Ligonier

Robertson held everyone in place where the skirmish had occurred. Not sure whether the Indians that the scouts had fought were an isolated outpost or part of a bigger force awaiting the convoy, he placed his men in defensive positions extending into the bush on either side of the road and sent Donegal back to appraise Colonel Bouquet and Major Campbell of the situation.

Bouquet rode up within an hour. Based on Donegal's description of events, he had already ordered two more companies up to the van, and when they joined, he deployed them into a skirmish line with Robertson's company close behind in support. Thus prepared for any opposing tribal force, they cautiously covered the remaining distance to Ligonier and, to the delight of the garrison and settlers holed up inside, arrived late in the afternoon. By nightfall the entire convoy had gone into camp around the stockade.

After six hard days on the road, having crossed two mountain ranges since leaving Bedford, everyone was tired, relieved at the relative security of the fort's environs, and ready for several days of rest as had been granted at Bedford. So there was an air of expectancy throughout the encampment when Bouquet called a meeting of all officers.

After he had the scouts' fire started, Kirkwood went on a scavenging mission to investigate the availability of rum or good border whiskey at the settler's camp. Donegal and Wend worked to set up their cooking equipment. They were just about done when a messenger from headquarters arrived and requested Joshua's attendance at the officer's meeting.

After the messenger departed, Baird sat musing for a minute. Then he said to Wend, "Sprout, you better come with me. I don't think that Bouquet would be having me to this meeting if he was just going to put out routine orders for running the camp for a few days. I think he's got something else on his mind."

They walked up through the fort's entrance, across the parade ground and found the officers gathering at a small building on the other side. There was an air of joviality, exchanges of jests, and good natured bantering all around. As they joined the group, Joshua told Wend the cabin had been built for General Forbes use in 1758. Wend's mind flashed back to the similar cabin behind Fort Loudoun.

Bouquet was seated in a camp chair before the front door, flanked by Major Campbell and Lieutenant Dow. Standing by him were Lieutenant Campbell and a Lieutenant of the 60th Foot. The lieutenant in the Royal American uniform looked old for his rank, but thin and wiry, with a narrow face topped by a shock of reddish blond hair. Bouquet was in deep conversation with him and he was nodding rapidly as if agreeing with the colonel's words or acknowledging a series of orders.

When the officers had all gathered, Bouquet rose to speak. He had a sheet of paper in his hands. His first words brought a chill to the assembled men. "We march for Fort Pitt at dawn the day after tomorrow. And we have much more than a full day's work to do between now and then."

There was dead silence among the officers.

Bouquet looked around at the faces, and continued, "As you know, the scouts had a sharp fight this morning with a war party which was watching the road. Luckily, our men found a defensive position, held out, and suffered no casualties. But the enemy knows our progress and we can be assured that runners are on the way to the force surrounding Pitt. Undoubtedly their chiefs will make plans to receive us. I expect that they will think that our force is exhausted from our transit of the mountains, and won't expect us to be back on the road for several days."

"Instead, we will give them as little time as possible to make their dispositions. I plan to march rapidly over the 50 miles from here to the fort. And to do that, we cannot be encumbered by the wagons and other heavy baggage. So we will spend tomorrow transferring a good portion of the flour and other provisions from the wagons to horse packs. What can't be packed on the animals will be left here until we have relieved Pitt and can send a detachment back to bring up the wagons."

He motioned to the Royal American lieutenant. "This is Lieutenant Archie Blane, commander of Fort Ligonier and the officer in charge of the stores which are warehoused here. He has gotten ready a supply of sacks to take the flour and gunpowder. He also has a store of pack saddles to complement the ones we are carrying in our wagons. I have already talked to the wagon master, and his men will act as drovers for the horses on our march."

There was a buzz as the officers digested Bouquet's words. Then he continued, "The only way we will get the necessary work done is for every man to help in the filling of the bags. Lieutenant Dow will make assignments for each company and Blane will provide the necessary sacks to each company commander."

"That takes care of the quartermaster business. Somewhere before we get to Pitt, we will meet the tribes in battle. We can expect them to try to ambush us; that is their preferred tactic. But remember, an ambush is effective only if the target is not ready. We will be ready and deployed to receive them."

"But we'll make detailed plans for that later. The other work we must do here is to reorganize the battalion for the fight we expect. First, we know that the highland companies were assembled in haste from men who were recovered from the fever and then dispatched from New York as fast as possible. For that reason they are unequal in size. They need to be restructured to approximate uniformity. Second, we have one light infantry company from the 42nd, and another from the 77th, but the two of them together have enough men to make three small companies, which will better suit our needs for maneuvering in the bush. Major Campbell shall have the task of effecting this realignment, and I expect the cooperation of each captain."

After a few more comments, and some detailed guidance from Dow, Bouquet dismissed the meeting. Major Campbell and the company commanders gathered with Dow and Blane in serious discussion of how to carry out the morrow's work. Bouquet motioned Joshua and Wend to his side. "You two look none the worse for your encounter with the savages today."

"Well, it did get a bit hot there today, I don't mind saying," Joshua replied. "We were sure glad to see McCulloch, Carmichael and Byerly come up when they did."

Bouquet nodded. "Well, all's well that ends well. But I called you here to talk about scouting on the rest of the trip to Fort Pitt. I'm adding Byerly and another settler from this area, a man named Means, to your group. They've got intimate knowledge of this area."

"Sounds like a good idea to me, Colonel. How about Carmichael and his boys as well? That would give us enough men to sweep a much wider area."

Bouquet shook his head. "No, I can't do that. Carmichael's group has been out here longer than they had planned. They're worried about what's going on with their families; I'm sending them back east with dispatches tomorrow."

Bouquet looked at Joshua. "At any rate, I presume you have figured out that we're going to take the southern cut-off trail through Bushy Run, instead of the main wagon road which loops to the north through smoother country. That will save six or seven miles."

Joshua signaled his understanding. "Yeah, I guessed that as soon as I heard you say you were going to leave the wagons behind. But that means we'll have to travel through the ravine at Turtle Creek, Colonel. You know how narrow that is; it's a damn good place for the tribes to attack."

"I've been weighing the chances of that, Joshua. So I'm considering a quick march to Bushy Run Station and then going into camp there as if we planned to stay overnight. Then, after dark, we'll move out as quietly as possible and march through the defile overnight. It might put them off balance, and at any rate it will reduce the chances that they can make an effective attack."

There was silence as all three of them considered the plan. Finally Baird spoke. "Makes sense, Colonel. There's also the possibility that your move will split the Indian force. They won't know which way you are going, and they'll have to watch both the road up to the North and the Bushy Run trail."

Bouquet smiled and nodded. "I thought the same, Joshua. I'd rather fight a couple of hundred warriors instead of the full 500 or so that appear to be around Fort Pitt." The colonel looked up and saw that other officers were waiting to see him. "Joshua, think over what I've said. We'll talk again before the column marches and I'll give you more detailed instructions."

The two scouts turned to leave. Wend could see that Dr. Munro was among the men waiting to see Bouquet and he nodded to the surgeon as they walked past. That reminded him that he must take the time to see Mary tonight or tomorrow, before the column moved out. Since the women were staying at Ligonier, he had no idea when he would see her again.

* * *

Following the meeting, Joshua decided to walk over to the settler's campsite to visit with Byerly and his family. Wend went to the picket line to tend the horses. The mare was glad of the visit and the oats he fed her. He gave her a good brushing down, then walked back to the scouts' campfire where Kirkwood and Donegal had the evening meal ready. They were just finishing their plates when Wend looked up to see a group of highlanders approaching.

Kirkwood quipped, "Those lads look like they have a mission and they're none too happy about it."

The men stopped in front of the flames, staring down wordlessly at Wend. He noticed that McKirdy was at the center of the group, anger and determination written across his face. Wend looked at the other soldiers, noting that they were all privates from Captain McDonald's company of the 77th.

Donegal casually looked at the men and then glanced at Kirkwood and Wend. "Well, Bob, it looks like McDonald's boys are honoring us with a visit." He popped the remains of a biscuit into his mouth and slowly chewed it, as the silence deepened. Then Donegal smiled up at the men and said, "I wish we had some good whiskey to offer you lads, but Bob Kirkwood here hasn't had enough time to round up anything worth tasting."

McKirdy stepped forward. "You know damn well this ain't about having a drink. Eckert, I'm here to call you out. Back at Bedford, I made it clear you were to stay away from Mary. She's mine, Eckert. In good time, we'll be married. All the men of the regiment got that clear in their minds. But you wouldn't listen. You were seen spending time with her at the chaplain's tent and doing more with her—a lot more—at the hospital the morning we marched from Bedford."

Donegal looked at Wend, a grin on his face. "Why Wend, I didn't have no idea. You and Mary Fraser? You are quite a devil, ain't you? And me thinkin' you didn't have any thought but for that girl who's a hostage with the Indians."

Wend felt himself flushing. But he ignored Donegal and said, "McKirdy, the girl made a point of asking me to visit with her. And things developed naturally. To me it looks like she doesn't have quite the same picture of her future as you do. Maybe you ought to go see her and clear matters up."

"I'll talk to her in my own good time. But before then, I'm going to straighten this matter with you. And I'm doing that tonight."

It was now very quiet around the campfire, the only noise the crackling of the flames. Wend broke the silence. "And how do you plan to 'straighten matters' out with me, McKirdy?"

The drummer pointed down toward Loyalhanna Creek. "Down by the stream, Eckert. There's a row of settlers" cabins that were burned down to clear the field of fire from the fort. I want to see you there right after lights out. We'll settle this then."

"You mean fight it out, McKirdy? You think you can change how a girl feels about someone with fists? That's nonsense."

"Like I said Eckert; I'll work things out with the lass later. For now, I'm going to convince you that you ain't spending any more time with her. So you be there or we'll come fetch you."

"Look, McKirdy; we're going to fight the tribes in a few days. Both of us may be dead soon enough and this won't matter a wit when animals are picking at our bones. Besides, the women are staying here when the column marches and we may not see them for weeks or months. We can work this out after we finish with the Indians."

McKirdy's mouth broke into a crooked grin. "I guess you've not heard the latest news, Eckert. The surgeon went to Bouquet and told him he couldn't get along without some nurses, particularly if we were going into battle. So, three women are marching with us—Esther McCulloch, Kathryn McWray, and Mary Fraser."

Wend was silenced by the words. He decided on another tack. "McKirdy, there's going to be real trouble if Robertson or Major Campbell find out fighting's going on tonight, what with all the work that has to be done tomorrow. You'll face punishment."

One of McKirdy's companions snarled, "And how are they going to find out, Eckert? The word is out around the battalion that you are a bit of an officers' favorite; are you going to go crying to them?"

McKirdy laughed and shook his head. "I'm a drummer, and who do you think the officers get their word from on what's going on in the ranks? Believe me; the officers won't get any word about a fight. And besides, they know enough to stay out of a soldiers' personal argument." He paused a moment. "So, Eckert, we'll see you down by the water right after lights out." He turned and walked off, followed by his friends.

As they left, Joshua walked out of the darkness and sat down at the fire. He pulled out his pipe and pointed at the departing highlanders with its stem. "That looked like a very serious discussion. What did your friends want?"

"They were inviting Wend here to a party tonight, down by the burned out settlers' cabins," Donegal responded, "The kind where somebody ends up with a bloody face."

"Or worse," added Kirkwood. "Probably worse, seeing as its McKirdy," Donegal said thoughtfully. "He's got a reputation as a tough brawler."

Baird lit his pipe and took a deep pull, savoring the taste. "What's the occasion? How did the Sprout here get on his bad side?"

Donegal smiled broadly and slapped Wend on the back. "Seems Wend has been moving in on the lass McKirdy fancies as his own."

Joshua laughed heartily, his eyes twinkling. "I ain't surprised in the least. Our Sprout here is a fine one with the young girls. Every time I turn around, he's got some female hangin' around his neck. Back in Sherman Valley, young Elizabeth McClay attached herself to him every time there was some get-together and damn if he didn't have another one giving him a ring as we was riding out for this expedition." He laughed again and took another draw on the pipe. "And who is the lass that is causing this fracas?"

"Mary Fraser, no less." Kirkwood said.

Baird's head snapped around. He said nothing for a long moment as the amusement drained out of his face. "Is this true, Wend?"

Wend chose his words carefully. "It happened natural-like, Joshua. It seems she's been carrying thoughts of me since the massacre. And I have to admit my affection for her has been building since Carlisle. It seems some-body saw us with our arms around each other back in Bedford."

"Sprout, you was a fool thinkin' you could carry on a romance in the middle of an army camp without the word getting around." He considered a moment. "Especially with Mary Fraser, the darling of the regiment. But I should have figured it out before this; the lass weren't coming round to see us all the time just because of old times."

Wend looked into the fire "It doesn't matter, Joshua. I'm not going down there to fight with McKirdy. A woman has to make up her own mind about which man she wants."

Donegal shook his head. "You may be right about the woman part of it, Wend. But what you got to worry about right now is the man side. Up to now, what with the way you saved that waggoner up on Allegheny Mountain and your scouting work, you got a good reputation. But if you don't fight McKirdy, you'll lose respect in this regiment. And McKirdy and his mates will find a way to get at you anyway. They'll come up on you unawares between a couple of wagons or somewhere in the woods, and take care of business."

Joshua said, "He's right Sprout. Best get it over with now, one way or another. You don't fight tonight you might as well go back east with Carmichael and his men tomorrow."

"We'll go with you to keep things fair, lad," Donegal looked around at Joshua and Kirkwood, who both nodded. "But you'll have to fight McKirdy on your own."

* * *

They arrived at the burned-out cabins to find that about twenty men had already gathered. The moon had risen, providing a modicum of light. Several torches had been emplaced in the ground, and men held others, the light shielded from the main encampment by a fold in the land. Kirkwood looked around and said, "These lads are mostly from MacDonald's company."

Donegal nodded. "I'd not expect anything else. And look: I'd wager that every drummer in the regiment is here too."

McKirdy saw the scouts approaching and began stripping his shirt. "Let's get started, Eckert. I want to finish with you and get some sleep before Bouquet's big work party tomorrow."

There were laughs all around as the men formed a circle about the combatants. Donegal patted Wend on his back. "Best take off your shirt. You don't want to get blood all over it."

As he pulled his shirt off, Wend felt dreamlike. He had no desire to fight this man and he had no experience in brawling. As a child he had had a few schoolyard fights, but none since he had left Master Dreher's school.

McKirdy bent over into a crouch, his arms spread wide, ready to either punch or grapple Wend as opportunity presented itself. Wend assumed a similar position. He suddenly realized that he had no strategy ready; he could only react to the highlander's moves.

Now McKirdy started to circle around to his right, forcing Wend to do the same. Suddenly he lunged, and Wend reared back to avoid his grasp. McKirdy took the opportunity to lash out with this right fist and land a blow on Wend's left cheek and mouth. The punch had the combined force of his arm and the momentum of his lunge; Wend felt his head rattle. Then the salty taste of blood flooded into his mouth.

While he was still stinging from the crunch of McKirdy's blow, the high-lander landed another using his left fist. This time the target was Wend's right eye and the side of his nose. He felt the impact; his vision went blurry for a second and then he felt blood draining from his nose, running down across his lips and his chin.

Instinctively he raised his fists to protect his head and that was fortunate, for it kept McKirdy's next blow from landing on his face. But the effect of the first two blows had shaken Wend back to the reality of his situation. He knew that he must come up with a plan to defend himself. No, he suddenly thought, that's not good enough. He must do something to attack McKirdy. He realized that he could never defeat the drummer by exchanging blows with him; McKirdy was stronger and more experienced in fighting. Wend lashed out with his fists in a spasm of punches, not expecting any of them to land, just hoping to buy himself more time to let his brain flesh out some plan. McKirdy backed off and went back into a crouch, a little wary at Wend's sudden activity.

Then it came to Wend: *My only chance is to get him off his feet and into a position where he can't use his fists.* Then, from somewhere deep in his brain, came the kernel of an idea. And as they circled a full blown tactic formed in his mind.

He crouched even lower to give McKirdy less of a target, and began to accentuate his circling motion, making it harder for the highlander either to hit him or throw him to the ground. He knew he had to buy time and make his opponent think that he was avoiding him at all costs.

So he continued to circle, at times backing off even further from McKirdy. That invited jeers from the crowd and McKirdy moved forward to close him. But it served Wend's purpose. He continued to avoid McKirdy; the drummer lunged at him a couple of times but Wend successfully jumped back or to the side. There were more jeers from the watchers. Then McKirdy attacked with a flurry of punches and Wend was able to parry all but one, a smack on the side of his head which set his ear burning but did no other damage.

Finally, McKirdy started to bait Wend. "You fuckin' coward. You won't fight. All you're doing is running from me." The men around the circle shouted agreement with the drummer. But Wend deepened his crouch and kept his hands near his face.

In response, McKirdy relaxed and eased his crouch, now standing nearly upright. "Look at this bloody provincial; worried about his pretty face. He's too terrified to come at me. And him thinking he is man enough for the likes of Mary Fraser!"

Wend knew that he would never get a better chance to attack. He was already as low as he could get, and wound up like a cat. Now he flung his arms as wide as possible and sprang with all the force in his legs, propelling his body in a slightly upward direction. His head impacted McKirdy right in his belly and he snapped his arms around McKirdy's thighs with as much force as he could muster, and pulled upward. At the same time, he started pumping his legs to keep up the momentum of his lunge. He was gratified by the sound of a loud grunt from McKirdy as his head smashed into the other man's belly. Then, with great relief, Wend felt the highlander's feet leave the ground, and his body start to fall backward.

The moment McKirdy's back hit the ground, Wend jumped up onto his chest. He hit the highlander once in the face with his right fist, then with his left. He thought: Now is the time to pound his face into a bloody pulp!

He could hear Kirkwood, Donegal, and Baird, shouting at him. "That's it, Wend! Now give it to him!"

He struck the highlander with another series of blows. But then another thought seized him. Wend jumped to his feet, and stood back from the highlander's prone body.

Quickly McKirdy was on his feet, a look of surprise on his face. The soldier had bloody eyes and a trickle of blood from the left side of his mouth from Wend's pummeling.

Wend spread his arms, to quiet the shouts of the men in the circle. "McKirdy, you've bloodied me and now I've shown that I can take you down. We're about even. Let's stop this right here, and call it a draw. We've got work to do tomorrow and a hard march after that!"

McKirdy looked around, and for a moment Wend thought he was considering his words. But then the highlander laughed wickedly and looked at Wend with pity in his eyes. "You're daft, Eckert, if you think I'm going to stop it now. I'm here to fix you proper so you won't even think of going near the girl again." He returned to his fighting crouch and brought his fists up.

Wend despaired. He had used up the only trick in his arsenal and had given up his advantage in the hope that he could end the fight with talk. Suddenly he understood that there had never been any option except to pound McKirdy senseless. And it was clear to him now that the fight would end in only one way; the highlander smashing him up until he was unable to resist. It was only a matter of time.

Suddenly a loud, rough voice came out of the darkness. "Now lads, what is it we have going on here?"

The two combatants and the entire crowd of watchers turned toward the sound of the voice. Then the heavy-shouldered figure of Sergeant McCulloch emerged into the flickering light of the torches. There was total silence. McCulloch spoke again. "Nobody going to tell me what this is all about? Cat got everyone's tongue?"

Finally, McKirdy spoke out. "Come on Sergeant, you can see what's happening here. This is a private matter; nothing you or the officers have to be concerned with. Why don't you go back to your fire, have a drink and a pipe, and let us finish our business."

The sergeant's mouth broke into a broad smile, but Wend could see that it didn't extend to his eyes. They were steely and his brow furrowed. He walked to the center of the lighted area and put his hands on his hips as he surveyed the faces of all the men. "Now McKirdy, me lad, it seems like you are forgetting who it is that runs this regiment. The officers run the tactics, and the drummers beat out the orders and carry messages and act like constables. Because of that, sometimes the drummers forget themselves, and get the idea that maybe they got some special power. But we all know it ain't the officers, it ain't the drummers, it's really the sergeants what make the regiment work, don't we McKirdy? Always has been that way, always will be." McCulloch swung around until he was right in McKirdy's face. "Ain't that a fact, drummer?"

Wend watched as McKirdy stared angrily up at the sergeant for a moment, his hands balled into fists. Then the drummer lowered his eyes. After a pause, he said, "Yes Sergeant. No one doubts you run the regiment."

McCulloch smiled broadly again. "That's the stuff, McKirdy." He turned to the gathering. "Now all you lads get back to your fires, crawl into your blankets, and think sweet thoughts of your mothers and girls back in Scotland. And the only fighting we're going to do from here on out is against the savages."

* * *

The four scouts walked back to their fire. No one had said a word since McCulloch had broken up the fight. Wend sat down and stared into the fire while Kirkwood stoked the embers and threw some new firewood into the flames. Joshua fired up his pipe and puffed contently. Donegal got a rag, soaked it in water from a canteen, and handed it to Wend. "You might want to get some of the blood off your face before it dries."

Wend took the rag and started wiping around his eyes, nose, and mouth. Finally, Kirkwood asked the question which had been hanging in the air since they had left the burnt-out cabins. "Lad, why didn't you finish off McKirdy when you had the chance? You had him down with the wind knocked out of him, and another few hard punches would have had him senseless. But then you just stood up and let him recover."

All three of them were looking at him now, Kirkwood's question echoing in their eyes. Wend looked at each of the faces in turn, and then thought about the moment when he had decided to get up from his position astride the drummer. "It sound's stupid now to say it, but it just struck me that I didn't have any real quarrel with McKirdy. It was all on his side. And I thought maybe once I had shown him that I wasn't afraid to fight, and had put him down, that we could leave things at that and abide by Mary's choice on who she wanted to be with."

Joshua made a face, but didn't say anything. Kirkwood scrunched up his face and shook his head. Donegal took out his pipe, lighted it with an ember, and then turned to Wend. "You still don't have the real picture about what this was all about. If you were a highlander competing for Mary's favors, there probably wouldn't have been a fight. McKirdy and his bunch would likely abide by her decision; if he had tried to take you on his friends might have even told him to forget it. But you are an outsider, coming along like a thief to steal something they consider their own."

He took a couple of puffs on the pipe. "You understand what I'm saying, lad?"

Wend felt anger welling up inside him. "I understand that I should have pounded McKirdy until his face was pulp and left him laying there for his friends to carry back to camp. That's what I learned tonight. I'll not make the mistake of trying to reason with an ass like him again!"

Joshua looked at Wend with a twinkle in his eyes, and reaching under a blanket, pulled out a small jug of whiskey. "Here, I got this from Byerly earlier this evening. Take a few pulls. It will make you feel better in the morning."

Kirkwood eyed the jug. "Now, you been holding out on us, have you Baird?"

Joshua looked up at him. "Not holding out; just saving it for the right occasion. You two can take your turns after Wend is done."

The three of them laughed and went back to their pipes. Wend sipped the whiskey, and soon felt a warm glow, which helped assuage the pain he felt all over his body.

That's when they saw Mary making her way along the line of fires, walking quietly in the night, still dressed in her marching outfit, with a canvas bag slung from a strap over her shoulder. She came up to the fire and all four of them stared up at her wordlessly for a moment, startled at seeing her there after lights out.

Mary looked down at Wend, a grin on her face. "It occurred to me that you could use a wee bit of medical help tonight, so I brought some supplies along. And looking at your face, I can see that I was right."

Joshua looked between Mary and Wend, grimaced, and tapped out his pipe. He stood up. "I need to go tend the horses. With all the excitement tonight, I didn't get down to the picket line."

Donegal also stood up. "Yeah, I'll go with you Joshua."

Kirkwood sighed. "This is probably a good time to do a little foraging. I'll bet it's still lively over by the settlers' camp."

Then they were alone by the fire. Mary went to her knees, reached into her bag, and pulled out some clean rags. She opened a water bottle, put it on the ground beside him, and then put her hand on his chin and moved his head around gently as she surveyed the damage. "You've got blood smeared all over."

With a light touch she cleaned him and when the blood was gone, said, "There's nothing serious, no stitches needed. There are some small cuts by your eye and around your nose and mouth, but you won't have any permanent scars."

Mary looked into his eyes, her head framed by the firelight, and Wend thought he had never seen a woman look more alluring. The flickering light accentuated her cheekbones and glinted off her copper hair. Her eyes were great cat-like ovals in the dim light. She leaned forward and put her lips on his, wrapped her arms around his neck, and gave him a lingering kiss. He returned it with fervor, feeling arousal coursing through his body like the swift current of a mountain stream.

Suddenly he was aware of the squad fires all around and that there were still men awake, sitting at the fires and stealing looks at the two of them. "People are watching us, Mary."

"I know. And the word will get back to a certain drummer before morning. And then he'll know my true feelings beyond a doubt." She sat down beside him, put her arms around his right arm, and laid her head on his shoulder.

Wend reached up with his left hand and grasped one of hers. "Mary, I didn't want to fight McKirdy. I want to be with you, but fighting over a woman is not my style."

Mary hugged his arm. "I understand; but you must realize that these men have a code of their own. And you did fight, so at least you earned some respect from them."

"But I was about to be beaten when McCulloch broke up the fight. They'll probably think that he came down there just to protect me."

Mary shook her head and laughed. "You've still got a lot to learn about the regiment. There are things going on that are bigger than your argument with McKirdy. McCulloch went down there because he wanted to settle some problems of his own with McKirdy and the other drummers."

Wend was puzzled. "All right, what kind of problems?"

"Listen, the regiment has been all dispersed, spread out in barracks and the hospital, with many men billeted in private homes since we got back from Havana. The organization had almost fallen apart, particularly with everyone expecting that we were going to be disbanded and shipped back to Scotland. Then when this Indian war broke out, General Amherst simply gathered up all the fit men and marched them off as soon as possible. They were thrown together into new companies, with unfamiliar mates, and the lines of discipline weren't as strong as they used to be. So the drummers have seized more power than they ever had before and McKirdy has been their ringleader." She paused to consider her words. "McCulloch, as the senior sergeant, has been looking for ways to break the power of the drummers and to show them who really is in charge. Your fight with McKirdy just gave him the opportunity he wanted."

Wend shook his head. "You're right; there's much about the army that is a mystery to me. But I guess I'll learn. At any rate, I'm glad he showed up when he did."

She put her hand to his mouth to quiet him, and they shared the silence of the night and the crackling of the fire for a few moments. Finally Wend said, "I was surprised to hear that you are coming with the column to Fort Pitt."

"Yes, the surgeon prevailed upon Colonel Bouquet to take three of the nurses along. To hear him talk about it, Bouquet was fit to be tied, at first refusing outright any such request. But then Munro said he simply couldn't give care to wounded soldiers without us, and that if we didn't come, he might as well stay behind. So finally Bouquet gave in, but only for three instead of the six which Munro wanted to take."

Wend looked at her. "Mary, I understand why the colonel objected. There's going to be a battle. Aren't you worried about yourself? What if we lose and the tribes smash the expedition?" He thought about how to phrase his next words. "They can be very brutal with prisoners."

The girl reared back, and withdrew her arms. "You don't think I can take care of myself? I've been at battles before." She leaned over slightly, reached into a slit in the side of her tartan skirt and groped around for a moment. Then she pulled out an object and brought it up to the light. Wend was shocked to see that it was a small pistol, its barrel and lock gleaming in the firelight.

"My God, where did you get that?"

"My Mum carried it under her petticoats, same as me. She got it when we were down in Carolina, just after we crossed the ocean. She took it off of a Cherokee lying on a battlefield that didn't have any need for it anymore. Pa took it to a gunsmith in Charles Town who said it was originally Spanish."

Wend took it in his hands, and examined it. "I've never seen one this small. How do you get balls for it?"

"I've got a mold for the bullets back in my kit. I always carry extras with me when we are on the march." Now she reached into another slit on the other side of the skirt, and pulled out a dagger. "This was Mum's also. Pa filed it down from a regular sized dagger to make it easier for her to conceal. I got a sheath which laces to my leg."

Wend couldn't think of anything to say for a moment. Mary looked at him sharply, a prideful smile on her face. "You need to get used to the idea that I'm different from the girls back in Carlisle or even the farm girls in Sherman Valley. I'm army, and I'm as much a part of the regiment as any man around those fires out there."

Mary returned her weapons to their places under the skirt, then gently pushed him down to a reclining position, and covered him with his blanket. She gave him a hug, her cheek against his, and then stood up and placed the medical bag over her shoulder. "The best thing for you now is sleep, and I'd better get back to my fire before Esther or the sergeant come looking for me."

CHAPTER 21
The Way to Bushy Run Station

In the late afternoon of the next day, Mary Fraser sat on Wend's saddle on the ground in front of the picket line, keeping him company as he groomed the mare and Joshua's horse.

Early that morning, Bouquet had sent the six scouts on a foot patrol to the westward searching for signs of war parties. They had arrived back in camp only a few minutes before. Baird had gone to brief the colonel and had sent Wend to care for the horses. The girl had come running down from the hospital when she saw him making his way through the bustle of the camp toward the horses.

Wend had told her about the results of their scouting trip and that most of the Indians seemed to have fallen back toward Fort Pitt. Then she had happily recounted the day's preparations within the encampment. In addition to the repacking of the supplies, some soldiers had been detailed to set up a comfortable camp for the women and children since it was clear that they would spend a considerable time at Ligonier.

"Oh, and you'll like this, Wend," Mary said impishly. "They did a lot of reorganizing of the companies, particularly in the 77th. Captain Robertson, as the senior officer of the regiment, got to make the final decisions and he took Sergeant McCulloch's word on what changes to make."

Wend said, "I heard they were going to make three smaller light companies out of the two which already existed from the 42nd and 77th."

"Yes, but this will please you even more: McCulloch took the opportunity to rearrange the assignments of all the drummers, to break their power. So now your friend McKirdy has been moved from MacDonald's company, where all his friends are, to Robertson's light infantry company where McCulloch can keep a close eye on him."

"I expect McKirdy is none too happy. What other changes did they make?" Wend asked.

Mary replied, "Well, Robertson organized a strong Grenadier company within the 77th, and put Lieutenant Campbell— the officer who led the flying column out here to Ligonier—in charge of it. She paused a moment. "And the last of the sick men of our regiment have been moved to the barracks and are going to stay here and help garrison the fort."

Wend finished his work on the horses and looked around at the encampment which surrounded them. The work of transferring supplies had been completed; the soldiers, waggoners, and settlers were settling in around their campfires as the evening dusk deepened. Wend put the horse brush away in a bag, reached down and took Mary's hand. "Let's walk for a while Mary, and take some time for ourselves while we can. The next few days are going to be very busy." She stood up and wrapped her arms around his left arm. He led them over to the wagon park, which was now deserted, feeling the physical desire for her well up within him as they walked with her body leaning up against his side.

In the dark among the wagons, Wend leaned back against the side of one of the Conestoga's and pulled Mary to him. She willingly leaned against him, pressing her body upon his so that he could feel the pressure of her breasts on his chest. The touch of her nipples sent his skin tingling and heightened his arousal. He pushed his lips down against hers and cupped his right hand over her breast. Mary sighed at the touch of his hand. Wend began to think of leading her up into one of the empty wagons; his desire to consummate their passion was becoming irresistible.

Then he felt Mary's body stiffen, and she slid her hands up onto his chest and gently but insistently pushed herself away from him. Wend looked down at her, feeling frustration well up within.

"Wend, we can't let this go too far." Mary smiled at him, but her voice was serious and her eyes held a look of determination. She stood back from him. "I've pledged to myself that the first man I make love with will be my husband. There are girls in the army, of my age or even younger, who given way to their lust and have been with several men. I've watched what they became, and I want no part of that. Long ago, when my Mum was still alive, I promised to her and God himself that I would be different. And I'm not going to break that pledge now, even though I truly love you, Wend." Mary reached up and kissed him again passionately.

Wend started to speak; he had to tell her how he felt. But she reached up and put her hand over his mouth. "Let me finish." She pursed her lips before resuming. "There's still a complication between us; it's the very reason you are here with the army. And I know the name of the complication is Abigail, that English girl from Philadelphia. You are pledged to find her. I've known about it since I heard you tell Joshua about her, long ago right after the massacre."

Wend looked at her; she had an earnest look on her countenance, her eyes seeming to pierce into his soul. Before he could speak, she said, "I would willingly spend the rest of my life with you Wend, if I knew you really were in love with me. But you can't answer that question now; you don't really know your own heart. You won't until you've done your best to find Abigail and decide if she means as much to you as she did four years ago. Otherwise, she would always be there, casting a shadow like a ghost over our lives." Wend realized there were tears in her eyes.

She gave him a quick kiss, then pulled back from him, turned and ran away into the night toward the lines of campfires. Wend took a step, intending to catch her and tell her that he loved her; then he stopped. *It would be no use, she wouldn't believe him.* And he knew she was right; he must resolve the turmoil within himself before he could return her love with the same intensity she had just shown him.

* * *

The whole expedition lay in the darkness of the night, sleeping on their arms in the same formation which they had spent the day marching from Ligonier. The companies were drawn up in a protective perimeter around more than 340 packhorses, tethered for the night along the path where the animals had been halted, their cargo packs removed and lying on the ground beside them. There were no fires; supper had been cold salt beef and bread from the soldiers' haversacks. The heat of the August night pressed down on the sleeping men and animals. Swarms of flies and mosquitoes hovered and pounced, making sleep hard even for exhausted soldiers.

Wend and the other scouts lay along the trail with Robertson's light company at the front of the column, the other light companies, the Royal Americans, and Barrett's Rangers close at hand. The regular infantry companies were on either side of the pack train, forming a shield. The rear of the column was held by the grenadiers. Each company had thrown out a small group of pickets to warn of any night attack which the tribes might mount.

It had been a long day. The drummers had roused the expedition well before dawn and Bouquet's intent had been to march as soon after sunrise as possible. But getting the packhorses loaded and organized had proven much more difficult than he had anticipated. So finally, after a sustained flurry of packing, repacking, and last minute adjustments at the picket line, the column departed Ligonier with no fanfare in mid-morning. The garrison, the settlers and the regimental families, knowing all too well what faced the soldiers, had watched them go in silence.

The scouting group had led the way throughout the day on foot, their horses left behind at the fort. Bouquet had ordered Joshua to move no more than a few hundred yards ahead of the column's van. He maintained one of the light companies within quick striking distance behind the scouts to support them if they ran into a war party.

The rest of the expedition marched in a rectangular formation designed by Bouquet. The light companies formed the front of the box; the horse train was in the center, screened on all sides by the regular foot companies. Barrett's rangers had been split into two groups positioned as flankers out in the bush on either side of the forward part of the convoy, ready to intercept and warn of any war party coming in to the attack from an angle.

Thus prepared, but having made a late start, the column made only ten miles good on the first day out of Ligonier.

Now Wend lay in the night with his rifle at his side, sweltering and pestered incessantly by the insects. He was between Joshua and Donegal. Baird was asleep, breathing deeply and seemingly impervious to the weather and bugs. But Wend could sense, from his movement and breathing that Donegal was still awake. Wend cursed and slapped a mosquito from the back of his neck and heard the highlander laugh quietly.

"Welcome to the pleasures of Army campaigning, lad," he whispered.

Wend responded, "I'd be fine if I could get some sleep. But I'm soaked with my own sweat and it feels like these night creatures are crawling all over my skin." He thought for a moment, "If we have to go through much more of this, we aren't going to be in any shape to meet the Indians."

"Ah, lad, that's where you've got it wrong. This is all part of the normal preparation for a fight. There's an army rule that says you have to suffer for a good and sufficient time before you're allowed to get killed. If it ain't hot like this, it's so cold you can hardly bear it, or you been rained on for days and got mud all over you. And you can only get to a battlefield after you've been marching until your feet feel like they were dead already. Yeah, I'm sure it says all that in the King's regulations somewhere."

Wend chuckled at the highlander's sarcasm. "I guess you've seen it all, after seven years, Simon."

"That I have, lad. Truth to tell, I'll be glad when this is over and I have a discharge in my hand."

"You must be looking forward to seeing Scotland again when the regiment is disbanded. What will you do when you get home?"

There was a pause before the highlander spoke again. "I don't believe I'll be going home again, lad. There's no work there and I don't have no close relatives to draw me. I was never married and my Mum died the year after we sailed for the colonies." There was another pause. "So I plan to take a land grant and stay here. The government is offering us all land if we decide not to go back to the highlands. The word is, it's cheaper to give us 100 acres than to pay our passage."

"Where will you go? Have you decided?"

"Na, lad; I'll have to think it over when the time comes. But a lot of the lads are going to take land in New York, up around the lakes, or in Canada. We campaigned there, and it was right nice country. Maybe I'll go with them up north."

A thought occurred to Wend. "Why not stay here in Pennsylvania, Simon? You could come back to Sherman Valley with me and Joshua, not that he stays around that much. But there's good land there; good for farming and hunting. And the people are welcoming. They took me in, even though my family comes from German stock." Wend thought a moment and then said, "You could at least ride back with us when we finish here, and see for yourself. You can stay at the Carnahan place, where I live."

Donegal laughed quietly. "I might just take you up on that, Wend." He was silent for a few moments as if thinking things over. "That is, if we're alive after the next few days, lad. When the fighting's done we can think about going to see your valley."

* * *

Dawn finally came, and Bouquet had the men, still tired after a restless night, on the road soon after sunrise. They took a cold breakfast as best they could. There were few of the problems of the previous morning; the pack-horse men now getting the hang of their work. The column moved rapidly over the miles and in late morning reached the junction of Forbes Road and the trail which led to Bushy Run Station.

Andrew Byerly stared down the trail as the scouting group reached the turn-off. "There're only a few miles now to my place, Joshua. The whole column can be there by mid-afternoon if Bouquet keeps the horses moving at a good pace."

Joshua nodded thoughtfully, then turned to the others and waved them onward. "Spread out on either side of the road. Keep a sharp watch; I'm expecting to see sign of war parties soon. They will be looking for the convoy."

Joshua had it right. By noon they were seeing moccasin tracks and other signs of the Indians' recent presence. And then, with the sun directly over-head, Kirkwood, who had come out into a small clearing, called out. They all gathered where he was standing, looking at the sky to the westward. He reached up and pointed. "I see smoke. Smoke from campfires."

Wend looked up into the sky; immediately he saw what Kirkwood was talking about. A wispy, flat layer of smoke floated over the tree line ahead at some distance. He looked more closely and he could see that the haze was fed by a multitude of narrow, almost imperceptible columns of smoke as if from fires intentionally kept small.

All six scouts stood silent, working out in their minds what it meant. Joshua spoke first. "War party fires; lots of fires, and the bastards are so confident that they don't care whether we see them. There must be hundreds of warriors up ahead."

Wend felt a chill run up his spine. Byerly said, "We got to notify the colonel and Major Campbell about this as soon as possible. They'll want to change the way the troops are deployed."

Joshua turned to Donegal. "Byerly's right, Simon: Run back to Robertson and ask him to come up as fast as he can. Tell him we'll wait here." Baird looked around. "Take cover and be ready in case a war party finds us before Robertson gets up!" The scouts advanced to the edge of the clearing and took the best cover available. But they didn't have to wait long. Robertson's company emerged from the trail in just a few minutes, advancing at the run with muskets held across their chests, and he immediately had them take cover in a line with the scouts at the forward edge of the clearing.

Robertson stood in the clearing with Joshua, looking at the smoke cloud ahead. "I sent word out to Barrett's flankers to close in to where they can see us and then hold up. Bouquet should be here fast; he was riding behind us. He's the one who must make the decision on how to proceed."

In a few minutes Wend caught movement in the forest to the left and right and saw the rangers coming in from their flanking positions. They had just finished taking cover when he heard hooves and he looked up to see that Bouquet and his staff had arrived. The colonel and Lieutenant Dow dismounted with their eyes on the sky ahead. As Bouquet stood taking it in Robertson and Joshua joined him.

Robertson said, "Perhaps this is a strong advance force, to observe our progress? We're still well east of Bushy Run and Turtle Creek Gorge."

Bouquet spoke thoughtfully, his eyes fixed on the smoke. "No, the chiefs have come further east than I expected. Make no mistake, this is their main force." His eyes furrowed for a few seconds and he gritted his teeth. "So much for our plan for the rest of today, but no matter. We must fight them here and let nothing stop our push to the fort." He turned to Dow. "Send a messenger back to Major Campbell. Tell him to send up all the light troops—the two other light companies and the Royal Americans. Tell him to hurry. And have him make sure the pack train bunches up tightly to reduce the perimeter we must defend. But above all, keep the train moving!"

Soon the three remaining light units started coming up, and Bouquet personally deployed them. He moved Robertson's company to the left of the road, and put the 42nd company and the detachment of the 60th on the right. Wend watched as Arnold herded his men into position on the far flank, like a mother hen shepherding her brood. Bouquet motioned the third light company to form a close reserve.

In a short time the head of the pack train came up the path, the drovers hurrying their horses. Wend could see the regular companies had closed up on either side of the pack horses, ready to shield them from any flank attack. Major Campbell arrived just ahead of the train, and conferred with Bouquet. Wend wondered about Mary and the other nurses; he couldn't see them, but knew they were at the rear of the train, with several horses carrying bandages and other medical supplies.

Bouquet mounted and motioned the light troops to advance. He turned to Dow. "You take the advance. Keep all the light units in close support of each other." He motioned to Campbell and said, "Get back and take charge of the train and escort. Make sure they stay closed up behind the advance."

The six scouts led the way along the path, only a very short distance ahead of the light infantry. Behind the light companies, the whole formation was on alert, moving as one entity.

* * *

They marched for over an hour. The flat cloud of smoke ahead of them slowly dissipated, as if the fires had been extinguished. Wend looked up at the sun and could see that it had passed the zenith. He figured it was just after one o'clock. They had just come down from a small hill with steep slopes and were crossing another low knoll when Byerly looked up and said, "See that high ridge ahead?" Wend looked through the trees and saw a high, hump-backed ridge a few hundred yards ahead of them which lay athwart the path. He nodded. "Well, that marks about a mile to Bushy Run Station. We can be there in twenty minutes after we get over that hill."

Joshua had been walking slightly ahead. Now he stopped abruptly, staring at the ridge ahead, then scanning along its crest slowly. Wend and the others came up to him and stopped. "Andrew, I don't like the look of that damn hill up there." He turned to take in all the scouts and Wend could see concern written all over his face. "Spread out on either side of the trail. Move ahead cautiously and keep your eyes open, particularly on that ridge."

Baird's concern was contagious and Wend felt a knot tighten in his stomach as he walked forward, making an extra effort to take advantage of trees and bushes as he moved. He kept his eyes on the hill. He became aware of the stifling heat; he could feel sweat all over his body. And Wend suddenly realized how quiet it was in the woods.

Minutes later, with the hill less than 100 yards away, he thought he saw movement near the top of the ridge. He blinked, and looked at the spot again. But all was motionless there. Just as he thought he had given way to his imagination he caught another movement, this one well below the crest. And he swore that he had seen sunlight glint off of something metallic. He wiped sweat of his brow, thinking that maybe moisture had gotten into his eye.

He had just put his hand back down to his rifle when the ridge erupted into a mass of smoke.

Then there was the sound of balls zipping around and over the scouts, followed immediately by the report of scores of guns being fired. Wend flung himself to the ground and crawled behind the thick trunk of a tree. He looked up at the ridge, and could see that some warriors were now plainly visible, moving to new positions. He saw one stop, shake his hand and shout a war cry before disappearing back into the vegetation.

Wend looked back at the troops behind his position. At the first sound of shots from the hill, the light companies had started to react. Almost simultaneously the two advanced companies, one on each side of the path, fired a volley at the hill and quickly started to reload. The reserve company came up almost in line with the other two, and its captain gave the order to fire; the company discharged their muskets in near unison. The other two companies, now reloaded, fired again. Then acting with the same thought, all three captains ordered "Fix Bayonets!"

Robertson's company was the first ready, and without waiting for the other two, he ordered them forward at the run. Their line passed close by Wend, so he could see the faces plainly. Robertson, at the front, had a grim look, his sword in his hand, motioning the rest forward. He saw McKirdy, drum strapped to his back, musket at the charge, shouting at the top of his voice in Gaelic. Behind the line, Sergeant McCulloch followed, and Wend swore he had a broad, demonic grin spread across his face.

Then they were gone up the hill and on his right the light company of the Black Watch swept by, howling in unison and brandishing their bayonets. Wend heard a sergeant shouting over and over, "Faster you bastards! Are you going to let the 77th beat us to the hill?"

The reserve light company followed along behind, its captain holding them back and waiting to drive home the charge wherever needed. Lieutenant Dow followed along close behind, his sword and pistol drawn. Wend looked over on the right flank and he could see that the Royal Americans, with Captain Bassett in the lead and Arnold behind closing the files, had moved up onto higher ground. They stopped and fired a volley which swept diagonally across the ridge, just ahead of the advancing light companies. Then as he watched, they fixed bayonets and drove into the Indian position on the left flank, thus providing essential support to the frontal charge of the highlanders. At nearly the same instant, a band of the Rangers, who had been walking far out on the flank, appeared from the forest and followed the Royal Americans into the fray, swinging their hatchets.

Watching the assault develop, Wend was struck by the idea that he was seeing a machine at work, with the various companies all parts of the machine. Then he thought further and told himself it must be considered a thinking machine. Each captain had acted independently, making his own decisions, yet the whole entity had worked in concert to make the attack on the ridge. He looked back up the path and could see Bouquet, now dismounted and standing calmly beside his horse, watching the action develop. The pack train had halted behind him.

Wend realized that the colonel had not yet given an order, but the response to the Indian attack had taken place instantly, as if practiced repeatedly. Then he recalled Bouquet's words at the meeting back in Carlisle, when he explained that each unit must act on its own, but from the same set of principles. And now he had just seen that concept in action. This assault was the result of all those nights the colonel spent talking with his officers and the training of the companies during the march, when everyone would have much rather have been resting.

Wend turned back to the hill, and could see that the advance was now halfway to the crest. Some warriors were firing down on the troops, others were falling back. Wend suddenly felt guilt at being a passive spectator. He raised his rifle, caught one of the retreating Indians in his sights and fired. The man's arms flayed out, and he dropped to the ground. Wend started to reload and looked over at Joshua, kneeling beside a tree about ten feet away on his left, also reloading his rifle.

"Hey Sprout, nice shot! I was beginning to wonder when you were going to stop gawking and get into the fight."

In a few more minutes, the light companies had driven the warriors away from the hill. Silence returned to the woods. Joshua stood up from his position and waved the scouts to join the soldiers, who had taken cover at the crest. The group climbed the hill and headed to where Robertson stood surveying the situation.

The captain turned to Baird. "Well, Joshua, we drove them off; the devils disappeared into the bush."

The scout scanned the forest. "I'll wager they'll be back at another place, and soon, Captain."

Wend looked around. There were bodies of Indian warriors lying on the ridge; obviously the charge had moved so swiftly that the Indians had been unable to carry off their dead. But Wend also saw that the warriors had been able to make the charge costly to the highlanders; several of the men on the ridge were clutching wounds. He looked down the slope, and saw more high-landers on the ground, some moving in agony, others lying very still. Among the wounded was Dow, who lay wounded halfway up the hill, two soldiers kneeling over him.

As he was still surveying the aftermath of the assault, Wend heard a shot fired. Then several more; they were coming from a spot well down the left flank of the horse train. In a few seconds, a volley of musket fire issued from one of the companies protecting the train; then Wend saw a half company charging with fixed bayonets toward the area where the Indian gunfire had erupted.

He heard Joshua speak, "Well Captain, there's your answer —another bunch of warriors down to the south. And I'll bet that the ones you just drove away from here are running through the woods getting ready to hit us somewhere else. No telling how many more war parties will be attacking the column on the sides and the rear."

That became the pattern for the rest of the day. The battle developed into a series of independent skirmishes, as the war parties moved all around the column, striking from random directions. In each case, the unit nearest the eruption drove the attackers off, either with gunfire or the bayonet. Rarely did the fighting actually become hand-to-hand; the war parties mostly faded into the forest in the face of a determined charge, as Bouquet had always maintained that they would. In the circumstances, the battle could have no overall direction; decisions were made by captains, lieutenants, and sergeants as attacks developed.

As the fighting along the perimeter began, Robertson had pulled his company down from the hill and faced to the left flank, to meet the threat from the south. He commandeered the scouting group to operate with him as marksmen. The rifleman developed a technique for covering the highland-ers as they charged: When the Indians exposed themselves to fire or shifted position, Joshua, Wend, Byerly, and Means would take aimed shots to hit them or at least drive them back to cover. Then, unable to fire on the assault-ing soldiers, the warriors had only two choices: stand and face the bayonets or retreat to find another attack site. Inevitably they chose to fight in another place.

Wend soon lost track of the number of attacks they had driven off and the movement of the company along the perimeter to face each outbreak. At one point, he looked over his shoulder and saw that Bouquet had led the pack train up to the top of a mound-like hill on the north side of the trail. Later he looked at the spot and saw that the pack horse men were pulling the loads off the horses; before he could figure out what that was about, his attention was drawn to face another attack.

It was much later in the afternoon, with the sun low in the sky and partially obscured by the clouds of smoke, when Joshua took an arrow below his left hip. Wend had seen arrows occasionally flying past; he had not taken much notice of them as he kept busy shooting or reloading. So when he had heard a sharp grunt from Baird, he had glanced over and been surprised to see the shaft sticking from the scout's side.

Baird looked down, a startled expression on his face. He grimaced and tried to try to pull the arrow out. But he winced as he yanked on the shaft. Wend could see that he couldn't move it. "Hey Sprout, come on over and help me with this!"

Wend crawled over to where Joshua kneeled and tried to extract the arrow. The scout moaned and twisted in pain. "It won't move, Joshua. It must be caught on a bone or something."

Baird looked down at the arrow. "All right, Sprout; break the shaft off, but leave a couple of inches sticking out from the skin so the surgeon has something to work with."

Joshua winced and sucked in his breath as Wend complied. Then he pulled himself upright against the tree. He tried to put weight on his left leg. "Sprout, this ain't going to work. I can hardly move that leg."

Wend looked around and saw the position where the horses had been drawn up. "We've got to get you to the surgeon, Joshua. Come on, I'll help you." Wend slung his rifle over his shoulder and supported Baird on his left side to take the weight off the leg. Joshua used his rifle as a walking stick. Working together and moving slowly, they traveled to the hill where the pack train had gathered and where Wend assumed the surgeon must have taken up station. As they approached the hill, they saw what Bouquet had been arranging; the horse drovers and some soldiers were stacking up the flour bags in a large circle to form a crude stockade. They found the doctor and the nurses inside tending a large number of wounded soldiers.

Wend helped Joshua to the ground where other wounded lay or sat. Esther McCulloch, seeing the two, walked over and kneeled down to examine him. The nurse took out a knife and slit open Joshua's hunting shirt around the arrow shaft and looked around the area of the wound. She shook her head. "They've given you a good one this time, Joshua. I'll go tell Monro. But he's got so many to work on that it will be a while until he can come extract the arrow head."

She left, and Wend, suddenly feeling exhausted, sat down by Joshua. He watched as the soldiers and drovers continued to stack up the bags. There was a constant sound of shots, and from time to time he heard the zipping sound of balls flying nearby.

They had only been there a few moments when Mary hurried over, concern written all over her face. She went to her knees by Joshua, and pulled open the slit in Joshua's shirt so she could see the wound. She looked for a moment, then shook her head. "That's going to take a while to heal, after we get the head out. You aren't going to be doing a lot of walking anytime soon, Joshua."

Joshua had closed his eyes; he was beginning to shiver and shake. Mary untied Baird's bedroll and threw the blanket over him.

The girl turned to Wend, and began to laugh, finally putting her hand over her mouth. She said, "I wish you could see yourself. Your face is all covered with gun powder. You look like a black man, with your eyes and teeth showing through!"

Wend reached up to wipe off his face. She laughed again. "That won't do any good. It'll just smear. You need water to clean it off, and we haven't got enough to do that. There isn't any water near here, so all we have is what's in the canteens. And we're saving the little we have for the wounded."

She suddenly exclaimed, "You've been injured!" She reached down and held up Wend's left hand.

Wend was surprised to see blood all over the hand. Looking closely, he could see where a bullet had grazed him just below the wrist. Blood and black powder were mixed, and some blood was still oozing from the wound. He had never felt any pain.

Mary held up his hand for examination. "It must have happened just a little while ago." She pulled some rags from her shoulder bag. "Here, give me your canteen." The girl poured out a little water onto the rag and quickly cleaned the wound. The she put a folded pad onto the cut and wrapped it with a bandage.

Having finished, she stood up, put her hands on her hips, and looked down at him, breaking into her impish smile. "It's a good thing I've been around every time the Indians injure you. What would you do without me?"

Wend was trying to come up with an appropriately sarcastic reply when the ball hit her. It came in through one of the openings that had been left in the stockade for access and passed through her right side, just at her waist. Wend heard the zip of the shot and then felt blood and particles of flesh spray over his face. Immediately afterward, he saw the hole in her jacket and bright red liquid oozing from her side. Then he looked up and saw surprise written over Mary's face, her eyes and mouth open wide. She dropped to her knees, then crumpled over onto her left side with a groan. She moved her mouth as if trying to talk but the only result was another groan.

Wend looked down and saw that blood was now spurting from the girl's wound. He looked around in panic for Esther or Kathryn, the other nurse, or for Dr. Munro. They were far away and he realized something must be done immediately to stop Mary's bleeding. He looked down at his left hand and an idea came to him. Wend rose to his knees and jammed the hand into her side, putting the bandage right into her wound. He pressed harder and harder until most of the bleeding was staunched. At the same time he screamed continuously for help.

It seemed to take forever, but presently Esther came running up, dismay all over her face. Munro followed behind her. Esther pulled Wend's hand out of the wound and pushed him out of the way. She placed a sanitary dressing over the wound and held it tight against Mary's waist. Then the surgeon took over, examining the wound. Mary had curled up in pain, her eyes closed; a quiet whimper issued from her lips. Wend could see that she was turning pale.

The doctor worked swiftly; they got her jacket off and cut away a portion of her shirt. In a few minutes they had cleansed Mary's wound. Munro looked up at her face. "She's fainted and that's probably just as well." He turned to Esther and Wend. "The ball took out a lot of flesh as it passed through her, but didn't hit anything vital. If we can keep the bleeding under control, and make sure the wound stays clean, she'll be all right, though she's going to carry a nasty scar for the rest of her life. The important thing is to avoid mortification." Then he was gone to treat other wounded.

Wend sat beside Mary as she lay peacefully. He looked around the inside of the little stockade and realized there were nearly forty wounded men laying or sitting around. At one side of the hospital area he saw a long line of bodies laid out. Wend looked down at his hand and saw that the bandage, white just a few minutes ago, was now totally stained with Mary's blood.

* * *

Dusk came shortly after Mary was hit. Wend had been sitting beside the sleeping girl since her wounding; he was unsure how long he had been there.

He had watched more wounded men come into the hospital area, some staggering in on their own feet; others were assisted or carried by their mates. Then he heard the beat of drums just outside the stockade; he pulled himself to his feet and walked to an opening in the flour bag wall. Major Campbell was standing not far away with three drummers in line beside him beating what Wend recognized was the recall signal. Wend looked through the forest and could see the companies disengaging from the fight and falling back toward the stockade.

As they approached, Campbell waved them to positions around the exterior of the stockade. Soon the makeshift fort was ringed by a defensive perimeter of troops. The men took whatever cover was available behind fallen logs, trees and bushes. As Wend watched, he saw Robertson's company straggling toward the western end of the circle. He expected that the remainder of the scouting group would be there and he reckoned he should rejoin them.

He was about to return to the spot where Joshua and Mary lay to pick up his firelock when he heard Campbell calling him. "Eckert, I'm glad you're here! Stay with me and act as courier while I place the companies for the night."

The next hour was hectic. The major kept Wend moving, either following him or running with messages to the various company officers. Campbell moved in a complete circle around the fort, making sure that the units took effective defensive positions about 20-30 yards out from the walls and that they were mutually supporting. By the time he was satisfied it was quite dark. While following him around the fort, Wend became aware how weary the troops were; he realized that they had been moving and fighting constantly since early in the afternoon, more than seven hours ago. And before that they had marched for many miles. Men settled into positions in the bush and could hardly keep their eyes open. Some fell asleep within minutes.

Finally the major was finished and Wend was able to go back into the stockade to retrieve his rifle. Joshua and the girl were both still unconscious. Wend was feeling the strain of the last hour, and sat down beside Mary. He decided he would stay within the fort to clean the barrel of his rifle, which had become increasingly fouled with black powder residue during the afternoon and consequently harder to load. He would return to Robertson's company to spend the night when he had finished.

Wend looked around and saw that, while campfires had been forbidden for the companies outside the stockade, a few small fires had been lighted inside the fort at positions which would not give the Indians a view of the interior. One such fire was for the benefit of the surgeon, to enable him to work on serious cases. Wend saw that another had been started for use by Bouquet at a spot at the other side of the enclosure. He saw the colonel sitting by the fire and Lieutenant Dow lying on blankets across from Bouquet with massive bandages around his middle. A group of the senior officers were standing or sitting around Bouquet.

Wend had just finished cleaning his rifle barrel when he felt a hand on his shoulder. He looked up to see a highland private standing above him. "You are wanted at the colonel's fire, Eckert. Make lively, they asked for you straight away."

Wend picked up his rifle and strode quickly to the knot of officers, curiosity rising at why he had been summoned. As he approached, he saw that the circle of officers consisted of Major Campbell, Captain Robertson, Captain Basset of the 60th, and Barrett of the Rangers. Dow lay with his eyes closed, apparently asleep. Then he noticed that Arnold Spengler sat on the ground beside Bouquet, a message book in his hands, taking dictation from the colonel. Wend guessed that Arnold had been pulled back to do clerical duty as result of the adjutant being wounded.

Wend pulled himself up to his full height and stepped up to the fire. Bouquet glanced up from his dictation and looked Wend over. "Eckert, I'm glad to see that you are in good shape." He looked into the fire for a moment, then continued. "Wend, I have to tell you that while our men have performed magnificently today, the expedition is in a bad way. Over fifty men were lost and we are still surrounded by hundreds of warriors. In fact, their numbers seem to have increased during the afternoon. There is no water source available within our lines for the wounded. The war parties have killed many of the pack horses and many others have run off in panic at the noise. Burdened with over fifty seriously wounded, we can't make a fighting advance toward Fort Pitt. Nor can we retreat toward Ligonier; the Indians would hound us on all sides and pick us off as we marched. The outcome would be worse than what happened to Braddock's army."

Bouquet looked around at the officers and then at Wend. His face hardened with determination. "So our only chance tomorrow is to destroy the tribal force."

The colonel paused to let his words sink in. For his part, Wend was shocked. He had not realized the gravity of their situation. He looked around at the officers, and saw worry in their eyes. Some looked down into the fire while others were eyeing him with curiosity.

Bouquet continued. "Campbell, Barrett and I have been discussing the situation. I have an idea which might work, and the others here agree. But we need to confirm something about the terrain of this hill. Bouquet picked up a small stick and drew a circle in the dirt beside the fire. "Here is our position on the hill." He put an X on one side. "There is the largest mass of Indians, down to the south." Now he drew a long loop which ran southward from the eastern end of the hill. "That finger is a low fold in the ground which runs out from this hill, long and narrow. I noticed it in passing just before the Indians attacked. But I didn't have time to examine it closely; I don't know how high it is, nor how far south it extends. What we are planning requires that it be high enough and sufficiently long to shelter the movement of several companies from the Indian's view for a surprise flank attack on them."

Wend felt a chill come over him. He suddenly understood why he had been called to this meeting.

"Wend, that's where we need your services. You are the best scout we have who is still in good shape. Joshua has been immobilized. I have already sent Byerly on an important mission; he is even now outside the lines, leading a few men to a small creek he knows about to bring water for the wounded. All of Barrett's rangers have been wounded or are exhausted." Bouquet looked directly into Wend's eyes. "You have the woodcraft necessary to creep out along that finger of land and determine if it meets our needs. And I know you possess the intelligence and courage to keep your wits about you; that was evident to me when you saved that waggoner and his horses on Allegheny Mountain."

Wend looked around the fire and could see that all the officers and Arnold were now staring at him. Wend felt himself shudder. The last thing he wanted to do was go crawling into the night alone. What he wanted to do was go back to the hospital, curl up, and watch over Mary and Joshua.

Bouquet looked up at him, the request hanging in the air around the fire. Wend nodded at the colonel. Then he was startled to hear himself speak calmly as if it were another person talking. "When do you want me to go?"

"Let's give the Indians time to settle in for the night; they have to be nearly as weary as we are. You should leave, say, in about an hour."

* * *

The small group of men had gathered in the darkness at the very eastern end of the hill, just behind the lines of the company which guarded that position. Campbell had come to arrange for Wend's departure with the captain of the company. Arnold and Donegal were also along to see Wend off. Donegal had told Wend that Kirkwood had volunteered to go with Byerly on the hunt for water.

Wend handed his rifle and pistols to Donegal. Silence would be the key; if he ran into trouble, his only defense could be his knife. A shot fired outside the lines would give him away and make it evident to the Indians that something was being planned. Whereas if he killed a warrior with a knife, the Indians would think that he was a messenger or deserter trying to quietly make his escape to Ligonier. He also stripped off his powder horn and all other equipment which might make noise.

The major left the group to explain to the company officers about Wend's mission outside the lines and of the need for them to be watching for his return. Wend sat with his friends, no one saying much.

Then Arnold cleared his throat. "Wend, the colonel told you that we were in a hard place here, but he couldn't show you or anyone else the depth of his fears. But he dictated a letter to me for General Amherst, ready to be sent back to Ligonier by a messenger. It essentially gives him a report of what has transpired today and implies that we may well be destroyed on the morrow. It's like he's leaving a last record for posterity. Taking down that letter and realizing how worried Bouquet is scared me more than anything in my life." He looked at Wend. "I just wanted you to know the importance of what you are doing."

Then Campbell was back and it was time to go. Wend gave his hat to Donegal, and started to move toward the side of the hill. The major stopped him with a hand on his shoulder and silently held out his right hand to Wend. "I just wanted to say lad, that I admire your courage. God be with you."

Wend couldn't speak. He simply nodded, and with extreme care, slipped quietly down the steep side of the hill, which was at this point like a low bluff. Once at the bottom he lay perfectly still on the ground for several minutes. The darkness was impenetrable; he would have to operate mainly by feel and hearing.

Taking a deep breath, Wend started to inch forward using his hands like the antenna of an insect to feel his way through the heavy undergrowth and trees. As he moved, he kept the base of the hill on his right to keep himself oriented in a southward direction. After a few minutes he came to the trail and crossed it quickly. Once on the other side, he noted that the side of the hill was losing its steepness, giving way to a gentler incline. Wend realized that this was the beginning of the fold of land which Bouquet had been talking about. He must determine if its height was enough to shield a flanking party. But it struck him that he hadn't thought out a way to measure the height of the hill. Then he realized he must climb the slope to find out. He turned and crawled up the incline. In a few minutes he perceived that he had reached the crest. He was suddenly surprised to see a glow of light ahead and slightly to his right. For a moment he was puzzled at the source. Then he recognized that what he was seeing was the glimmer from the fires within the flour bag stockade. As he watched, it came to him that he had found a way to accurately measure the height of the fold.

Wend crawled back down until he was at the base of the hill. Then he quietly stood up. Looking in the direction of the stockade, he could see no light. That meant that the crest was above the level of his head, and high enough to cover the movement of troops, at least at this point. But he would have to continue southward and make several more observations to ensure that the height of the fold extended far enough for Bouquet's purposes.

He traveled what he guessed to be another 100 yards, standing up three more times to observe. On the third one, he was able to see just a hint of light from the fires, and he knew he had reached the point were the hill was exactly at the height of his eyes. There was no sense in going any further south.

Wend lay down, resting a moment to get ready for the return trip. Suddenly he froze; he heard a voice, then another. It was two warriors talking and laughing. Their words were muffled but he reckoned they could be no more than 20 yards away. His prowling had brought him to the Indian lines or maybe even within them!

Wend lay still for a few seconds dealing with the lash of fear which had welled up within him. Then he started to inch back toward the British lines, exerting every possible effort to move quietly. He stopped every few yards to listen for any sound. He had gone perhaps twenty yards when he heard the sound he feared most; the movement of bushes, the crackle of a twig. It was the noise of a warrior approaching from his front, moving through the woods taking normal care to be quiet but not the special effort necessary to be totally silent. Wend froze. If he was lucky, the warrior would walk right by, unaware that an enemy lurked on the ground. The noises got louder and Wend's heart began to beat like a drum. It was clear that the Indian was heading right toward him!

Wend slowly reached up and pulled his knife from its sheath on the left side of his chest. At the same time the sound of the warrior's movement ceased and total silence ensued in the forest. Wend lay frozen for what seemed like an eternity. Had the warrior walked past him silently?

He was contemplating this possibility when he heard a sharp intake of breath right beside him and suddenly a hand grabbed his right arm. Wend instinctively pulled away and was able to break loose. He rose to his knees. He realized he must silence the warrior immediately, or others would come to help. He lunged in the direction of the enemy, swinging his knife in a wide arc hoping to slash him. He was lucky and felt the tip graze across the Indian's body. Now he had an idea of where the man was and lunged forward to grapple his body, hoping to get into position to sink his knife into a vital spot. Then he perceived that the warrior had turned slightly after the knife had slashed him, and that he now had his arms around the upper part of the man's body. Wend twisted and was able to get right behind him. He must keep the Indian from shouting out! He reached up with his left hand and put it over the warrior's mouth. The Indian reacted immediately, first trying to push his hand away; but Wend exerted all his strength to hold it in place. Then the man opened his mouth and bit Wend's hand. Wend groaned but ignored the excruciating pain and pushed his hand further into the Indian's mouth; as long as he had his teeth into Wend, he couldn't shout. He brought his right hand up and dug the blade of his knife into the warrior's throat and pulled it across his neck. He felt the knife jerking as it cut through skin, muscle and arteries. Then a cascade of hot blood drenched his hand, face, and shirt.

The warrior shuddered and Wend could feel the man's body jerking as he gagged on his own blood. They remained in their tight embrace until the man twitched, made a final gurgling sound, and became very still. Wend felt all the tension go out of the Indian's body. His own body quivered in involuntary repulsion.

Wend gasped for breath and felt his heart racing. He wanted to lie still to recover and control his shivering, but he worried that other warriors had heard the struggle and would be coming to investigate. He carefully disengaged himself from the body and crawled silently toward the British lines, fearful that he would hear pursuit at any moment. But in a few minutes he reached the side of the trail without any indication that he was being followed and he stopped to rest and listen. All was quiet.

With increased confidence, he scurried across the trail, and was soon at the bottom of the bluff. The company of highlanders was in position about twenty-five yards away, over the top of the hill. He climbed the bluff, careful to make no sound, fearing a trigger happy sentinel would hear him. At the top, he called out his name in a whisper; they had agreed that was as good a password as any. He saw a highlander come out from behind cover and advance toward his position. "Eckert, is that you?"

Wend whispered his name again, stood up and joined the highlander, who led him back through the lines to where Donegal and Arnold still waited. Exultation and relief welled up within him. He had made it; more importantly, he had the answer to the colonel's question.

* * *

Wend, escorted by Donegal and Arnold, arrived at Bouquet's fire to find that he was watching as Esther McCulloch changed the dressings on Lieutenant Dow, who still was unconscious. She was taking great joy in chastising the colonel as she worked. "And you were the one, Sir, who wanted to leave the women behind in Carlisle. Now who would there be here to take care of the likes of Mr. Dow here? Some bumble-handed highlander, who hardly knew how to make up a dressing, that's who! And then you argued with Mr. Munro at Ligonier when he wanted to bring all the nurses along. Well, I wish that we had the other three nurses here now." She waved her hand toward the hospital area behind them in the darkness. "I'll tell you clearly, Colonel, Sir, we could sure use them with all those wounded you have managed to accumulate today and little Mary Fraser herself lying wounded."

Bouquet sat patiently waiting for Esther to finish, but Wend could see the muscles in his face working to control the aggravation at her words. Then he looked up and saw Wend and the other two scouts at the edge of the firelight. "Ah, thank you greatly Mrs. McCulloch, for you help with the lieutenant's bandages. But they're fine now and I must talk with Mr. Eckert."

Esther hustled off in a few moments, and Wend could hear her brassy voice in the darkness, talking to another patient. Bouquet had a look of relief in his face and Wend was sure it was as much due to Esther's departure as his arrival. Bouquet immediately sent Donegal and Arnold to summon the other senior officers from their companies. After they left, he waved Wend to come closer, and he fidgeted while the colonel silently looked at him for a moment. Nervous at Bouquet's stare, Wend broke the silence and briefed him quickly on the results of his excursion.

Bouquet remained silent, but nodded his understanding. Finally he spoke in a quiet voice. "Son, do you realize that your face and shirt are covered in blood? Wend looked down at the front of his hunting shirt, and saw for the first time the extent of the stains. He reflexively put his hand to his face and could feel sticky liquid all over. He looked down at his right hand and the cuff of his sleeve, and realized they were similarly stained.

"Sorry, Sir; I tried to remain undetected. But I had to deal with one warrior. I assure you it was done silently. They won't find the body until the morning and they'll probably think a courier got him, Colonel."

Bouquet smiled wryly and shook his head. "You had to deal with one warrior? Lad, you say it as casually as if you were accustomed to doing that every night." He looked away into the darkness for a moment. "You don't have to apologize to me, Wend. I'll always be grateful for your service tonight."

The colonel sighed and slid a hand over his eyes, as if wiping away weariness. Then he looked away, lost in his own thoughts. Wend sat down, his back against a tree. He felt very tired and realized how long the day had been.

Suddenly he heard Bouquet calling him. "Eckert! Eckert, can you hear me?" Wend looked up and realized that he had dropped off to sleep. He looked around the campfire. Campbell, Robertson, McDonald, Bassett, and Barrett had arrived and stood or sat around the fire. They were looking at him in anticipation.

"Mr. Eckert, please tell these gentlemen what you found tonight."

"Well, sir," Wend said, "There is definitely a low fold of ground extending from the eastern end of the hill. And it runs out about a hundred yards south of the trail at a height of six feet or more."

Campbell spoke out. "That high? You're sure Eckert? How did you determine that?"

Wend told him about using the glimmer from the fires, and saw the heads of all the officers nodding as he explained. He amplified what he had said. "The further south you get, the gentler the hill's incline becomes. But the slope is longer to the crest."

The major asked, "You're sure it will cover more than a hundred men?"

Wend nodded. "I've no doubt of it, Sir."

Bouquet said, "All right, gentlemen; Eckert's confirmation is what we needed to finish our plans." He reached down with his stick and again drew the circle representing the fort. Then he marked lines in the dirt showing the positions of the companies around the fort. The scene would never fade from Wend's memory: Bouquet sitting by the fire with the stick in his hand as he laid out the plan, the weary, stubble bearded, powder stained faces of the officers lighted by the flames as they stood and kneeled around the flickering fire, nodding as the colonel made each point.

"Here is our scheme. First, the two light companies near the western side—Robertson's and the Black Watch company— will pull out of line, run up to the trail, and head eastward as if heading back to Ligonier. Robertson, mind you, they must look like they are near panic. Then the other companies along the perimeter will fall back and close up the gap opened by the light companies. Bassett, your Royal Americans are in the center, and I want you to make sure that your company and the others on the south side, which face the largest group of warriors, look like discipline is failing."

Bassett studied the diagram. "How far back do you want us to retreat?"

Bouquet looked up. "Fall back until your men are nearly against the flour bags."

Bassett shook his head. "The line around the fort will be awfully thin. And there'll be no margin for maneuver once they hit us."

Bouquet nodded. "Yes, but these actions, taken together, should convince the Indians that we are giving up the fight and attempting a retreat. I'm gambling that that is what they are expecting to happen tomorrow. When they see us pulling back, I believe that they will rush in for the kill, just like at Braddock's fight." He looked up at the officers. "The two light companies will be led by Major Campbell. Alan, as we discussed earlier, lead them along the trail and over the edge of the hill. As soon as you are out of sight, you will turn south and, under cover of the fold which Mr. Eckert has explored, form your men for a flank attack."

Bouquet used his stick to point to the area just south of the fort. "I expect that the largest part of the Indians will concentrate just in front of the fort, rushing to break our lines." He looked at Campbell. "You will hold your men in readiness behind the fold of land until that occurs, then be ready to strike their flank with several volleys of musket fire followed by the bayonet."

"McDonald, your company and the one next to you, on the western end of the circle, are to be ready to pivot out on the Indian's other flank after Campbell's men attack. We may be able to catch the mass of warriors between the two forces. Campbell will be the hammer and you will be the anvil."

Bouquet looked over at Campbell. "Eckert will go with you and the light companies as scout and messenger. He turned to Barrett. "You and your rangers—as many as are able—will go with the flanking force also, to take station on their left flank as they advance, and pick off warriors who attempt to escape by fleeing directly south."

McDonald asked, "When do we start this action?"

The colonel scanned the faces of his officers. "I'll pick the opportune moment. We will let the Indians attack us several times after dawn with no strong countering attacks from us. That should inflate their confidence. When the time is right, I will signal with three blasts of a whistle, followed by drummers beating recall. When you hear that sequence, you will all act out your parts without further orders."

"Are there any questions or comments?" He looked around at the faces.

Lemuel Barrett squinted at the diagram in the dirt and glanced up at Bouquet. "Colonel, it goes without saying that if the flanking action fails, or is even late, the warriors will undoubtedly break through our weakened lines and get into the fort among our wounded."

Bouquet stared back at the ranger officer for a moment, and then nodded. "True enough, Lemuel. The timing of Major Campbell's attack must be precise. But if we don't try this, we'll not last the day tomorrow and they'll be into the fort anyway." Then he looked around to see if anyone else wanted to speak, but all were silent.

"All right, may God go with you and give you good fortune on the morrow."

CHAPTER 22

Wave of Steel

Wend left flour-bag the fort and walked to rejoin the scouting group, which was bedded down with Robertson's company. He was settling in with Kirkwood and Donegal when McCulloch came over and tapped him on the shoulder. "Here, Eckert, come with me." The sergeant led Wend back up the hill to the flour bag fort. Just inside one of the openings was a stack of muskets and other equipment from dead and wounded soldiers, dimly illuminated from fires within the walls of the stockade.

McCulloch picked up one of the muskets, checked it quickly, and handed it to Wend. "Robertson tells me you are coming with us tomorrow for the attack. Well, lad, it is muskets and bayonets we'll be needing, not riflemen." He picked up a belt and handed that to Wend. It was equipped with a double frog, so that it held both the bayonet and a hatchet. "Here, put this over your right shoulder. Wend complied with the sergeant's words, and then saw that he was searching for something else among the discarded equipment. At last he found what he was looking for and put a cartridge box on a strap in Wend's hand. "Put this over your other shoulder, so that it hangs down on your right hip."

The sergeant stood looking at Wend and his new kit items. "All right lad, now put the butt of Bessie on the ground alongside your right foot and then shift the barrel to your left hand." Wend did so and then McCulloch had him pull the bayonet from its frog with his right hand. He showed Wend how to slide the bayonet over the barrel and lock it in place on the lug.

"Now listen, lad, this is the key to using the bayonet: When we advance, first, make sure you keep your alignment with the men on either side of you. That's your best protection. Second, if the savages actually stand and fight, make sure no enemy gets inside the tip of your bayonet. That's the only time they can get at you with a hatchet or club." He paused for a moment. "And I don't care what you've heard about a charge with the bayonet, or what you've seen in paintings. It's 'na a mad rush forward. It's a steady advance, so everyone can stay in line and what the enemy sees looks like a solid hedge of blades or the crest of an ocean wave coming at him. The best charge is one where the other side takes one look at that line and decides they got business somewhere else. Now, you got the idea, Eckert?"

Wend indicated his understanding

"All, right. Let's get back to the lines and get some rest. I've na a doubt we're going to need it for tomorrow."

Wend lay down next to his fellow scouts, the musket on the ground next to him. Suddenly he realized how late it was and that dawn could not be more than three or four hours away. He closed his eyes, to welcome the sleep he knew he needed.

But sleep would not come. Instead, his mind refused to release the events of the day. It forced him to relive again and again the wounding of Joshua and Mary. But mostly he found himself obsessed with the terror of the fight in the darkness with the warrior. In the last few days, he had shot several men, but tonight was the first time he had killed with cold steel. The feel of the knife jerking and grating through the warrior's throat would not leave him. The man's blood on his face and hand had a metallic smell which he could not ignore. Wend realized that mere luck had put him into the right position to dispatch the Indian and how easily things could have gone the other way. Then his imagination took him a step further. Perhaps tomorrow would bring his own turn. What if Bouquet's plan failed and the battalion was destroyed? He pictured himself running through the forest in desperation, warriors howling in pursuit and then inevitably catching him. Wend imagined he could feel the blade of a knife slicing through his neck, his own blood spraying over him and flooding into his mouth. Would his last conscious sensation be the feel of the blood draining out of him and of a warrior's scalping knife taking the rest of his hair? With that thought, the scar tissue at the back of his head began to tingle and he started to shiver uncontrollably.

Unable to shake the fearful images, he lay awake, dreading the arrival of dawn and the events of the coming day. Wend reached inside his shirt and touched the brass ring which Ellen McCartie had given him on that last morning in Sherman Mill. The feel of the smooth, cool metal lead him to think about Johnny Donaldson and the way the youth had died, fighting with desperate courage in the attempt to save his family. The memory of his friend's defiance brought a sense of determination and calmness over him which stilled some of his overwhelming anxiety. And after a while he felt the damp coolness of the pre-dawn moving in and descending over him like a blanket. It tempered the oppressive heat of the night and he suddenly felt a merciful weariness possessing him.

"Eckert! Eckert! Wake up, lad!"

Wend opened his eyes to see Donegal lying beside him with a hand on his shoulder. Trees and bushes were visible in the grey light of dawn and a hint of actual daylight showed against the top of the trees to the eastward.

"Will you look at him, Kirkwood? You'd think he was asleep back in his own bed instead of lying on this dirt, feasted on by the bugs, and surrounded by an army of savages."

Kirkwood was nibbling on bread and salt beef he had pulled from his haversack. "Dreaming like a baby, he was, with not a worry in the world." He gave a wink to Donegal, then turned to Wend. "You might be wanting to get a bite and look to that musket McCulloch gave you before our friends out there in the bush come calling, which shouldn't take too long now, I'll wager."

The men of Robertson's company were attending to their morning needs, checking out their weapons and eating some of their meager rations. Down the line Robertson himself was in close conversation with McCulloch. Wend wanted to see how Joshua and Mary were doing, and realized that Kirkwood was right—undoubtedly the battle would resume very shortly.

He found both of them lying awake. Joshua was half sitting up, using a flour bag as a prop, smoking his pipe. Mary was lying on blankets; some of her color had returned and she smiled thinly at Wend's approach. Joshua pulled the pipe from his mouth. "'Mornin', Sprout. Esther McCulloch tells me you had a busy time of it last night."

"Well, Bouquet asked me to pay our friends out in the forest a social call while you were sleeping."

Joshua didn't respond directly, but reached down and pulled up the side of his hunting shirt. There was a large bandage down around his hip. "While you were out taking in the countryside, Dr. Munro sliced me up and got that arrow out." He reached into a pocket. "I thought I'd keep it as a memento of the day." He held up the brass arrowhead attached to two inches of shaft for Wend to see. "Any rate, he did a good job by the light of the fire and I'll be good as new in a few days."

Wend turned to Mary and went to his knees beside her. "You're looking a lot better than the last time I saw you."

Mary didn't say anything for a moment. She reached out and took Wend's hand. "Esther told me how you stopped the bleeding after I was hit by stuffing your hand into my wound. It seems it was really your turn to take care of me."

"Well, I just slowed things down until the surgeon got here. How do you feel now?"

"I'm much better Wend, but I'm dying for something to drink. My mouth feels as dry as paper. The only water I've had since yesterday was a little that Andrew Byerly and some other men got us last night and it was full of mud. They had to crawl outside the lines to a tiny spring and carry it back in their canteens. The best they could do was to give a single swallow to each of the wounded." She looked around at the men lying and sitting around her. "The lack of water is driving these wounded nearly mad."

Wend pulled his canteen off his shoulder, opened it, and handed it to Mary. "Here, take a sip and then keep it beside you. I just had a good drink before coming up here."

She looked at him gratefully and took a short sip. "Wend, Esther said you were also outside the lines last night. She said that Colonel Bouquet sent you on a scouting trip."

"Yes, it was just a little look around outside the perimeter: Nothing that serious."

"Wend, you're lying. Your face and shirt are covered with dried blood. And besides, the colonel told Esther this morning that you had to kill a warrior with your knife. And he said that your scouting was essential to his plans for today."

Wend pressed Mary's hand. "I'll have to leave in a moment. The fighting could start again at any time." He looked around and thought of Barrett's words about the warriors getting inside the fort. "Mary, do you have your pistol ready?"

Mary reached down and pulled up the edge of her blanket. Wend could see her little pistol and the dagger lying next to her. "Don't worry, Wend. I understand the situation. If they get in here, I'll be ready for whatever I have to do."

Joshua laughed. "It's all right, Sprout. Mary and I will take care of things. I loaded my rifle this morning and primed up my pistol. If any warrior comes through that gap in the wall, he'll get a surprise."

Wend felt a lump in his throat and a loss for words. He just leaned over and brushed his lips against Mary's. She reached up and pulled him down to her for a longer embrace.

Suddenly he realized that wounded men around them were clapping and cheering at the two of them. He looked around sheepishly, but Mary just smiled and squeezed his hand again. Finally he found words. "Whatever happens today, Mary, I'll be with you afterward."

She broke into a broad smile with twinkles in her eyes, and Wend knew then that his heart was forever hers.

* * *

Wend returned to the 77th as the sun rose clearly above the tree line. He had barely arrived when the assaults began. Although the Indians were on all sides of the perimeter, it was clear that most of them had gathered to the south of the flour bag fort. Robertson's company was near the westernmost section of the circle, and they received a smaller proportion of the warrior's attention than those directly to the south.

Major Campbell had passed the order to fire sparingly and to use the least force necessary to repel each assault. Some of the men were frustrated at the restrictions but Wend realized that it was part of Bouquet's plan to convince the tribal chiefs that the British were weakening.

In reaction to the apparently fainthearted resistance, the war parties, keeping up a steady rate of fire using both guns and arrows, gradually crept closer to the soldiers' positions and became less concerned with concealing themselves. By mid-morning, Wend could often see warriors moving from position to position, seemingly not worried about being fired upon.

It was also in the middle of the morning when the Indians began taunting the soldiers. From behind trees and bushes came shouted threats, spoken in rudimentary English, describing the impending torture and death of the defenders once the warriors had broken the expedition. One voice made repeated threats directly to Bouquet: He would be burned alive, or skinned. His head would be on a stake before the end of the day.

Andrew Byerly looked around at the four other scouts as they crouched or lay in their positions of concealment. "I've no doubt that's old King Keekyuskung himself baiting the colonel. I've seen and heard him often enough speaking during council fires at Fort Pitt. He's met with Bouquet often, and he knows that the colonel will recognize who is making the threats."

A little before noon, drummers within the fort beat the call for officers. Moving as much as possible under cover, the captains of all the companies ran back and entered the stockade. They had been gone only a few minutes when they returned. Wend wondered if some new plan had been hatched, but quickly realized that it was another part of Bouquet's trickery; the Indians would see the gathering of officers and speculate that orders were being given for some movement.

Robertson rejoined the company. "All right lads, listen up. Everyone make a show of preparing to depart. Let the enemy see that you are putting on your packs and bedrolls."

Wend saw that the other companies were doing the same thing. He knew that Bouquet was banking on the Indians seeing what they wanted to see; a defeated force preparing to retreat. Then, from near one of the openings in the stockade, Wend heard three sharp blasts on a whistle, followed by a drummer beating recall.

Robertson jumped up. "Now, lads, follow me smartly! Eckert: Stay close to me!"

The light company ran up the hill in disorder toward the trail. Some of the men pretended to limp, as if favoring wounds. Robertson momentarily halted them on the trail. Wend looked up to see that the Black Watch's light company, which had been on the northwest side of the fort come up and join them. In a few moments, Major Campbell arrived and queried Robertson: "All set?"

Robertson nodded. Campbell waved to both captains and the two companies moved off at the run along the trail toward the east and Ligonier. Wend glanced back and could see the remaining companies in the perimeter spreading out to cover the gaps left by the light companies. It was only a brief look, because the major had already reached the point where the trail dropped over the edge of the hill into the depression which Wend had scouted. He noticed that, as luck would have it, the foliage thickened at that point and the column would become invisible as soon as it started to descend the bank of the hill. Thus the Indians would believe that the troops were still heading eastward.

As soon as he reached the bottom of the hill, Campbell shouted, "Lads, drop your packs and bedrolls here! You'll want to be free to move as fast as possible."

Wend dropped his own kit in the pile and looked around. Now, for the first time, he saw the fold of land in daylight. He breathed a sigh of relief; his assessment of its height and length had been accurate.

As soon as the men had discarded their equipment, Campbell turned right and headed south. The major led the column forward until the first troops were three quarters of the way to the point where the fold merged into level land. He turned and held up his hand to stop the column. Then he passed whispered word for the companies to each form two ranks and for the highlanders to kneel. This was quickly accomplished, the 77th on the left and the 42nd on the right. The company commanders moved along the ranks; soon each had divided his company into two equal firing platoons which were then numbered from one to four running from right to left of the line. The men began checking the pans on their muskets. As they did so, Barrett and his rangers, now numbering only ten or twelve men, rushed past to take up their positions as sharpshooters on the left flank.

Wend felt a tap on his shoulder. Campbell motioned for him to follow. He led them up the gentle slope, dropping to his knees halfway up to the crest. Together they crawled to the top of the hill. There, under cover of a large bush, they could see the fort, the British lines, and the whole area to the south of the company positions.

Wend could see that the companies had retreated until the soldiers' backs were nearly to the flour bags. And the Indians had taken the bait! From their vantage, hundreds were in plain sight. Some were still firing at the lines. A mass of warriors were surging toward the fort for a final attack, waving their weapons and shouting war cries. The nearest of the warriors were only twenty or thirty yards away but none of them were looking in the direction of the flanking column.

Wend saw a gleam in Campbell's eyes. "We've got them, Eckert!" The major turned and signaled to the company officers to bring their men forward. Immediately the two ranks of men rose and swept up the hill.

Campbell stood straight up; the time for stealth was over. The officers called their men to attention. Campbell grabbed Wend's arm and pulled him into the gap between the two companies. "We will fire by platoons! Make ready!"

The company commanders echoed Campbell's orders. When both companies were ready, the men were ordered to "Present", and the troops leveled their muskets. Breaking strict discipline, Campbell shouted out, "Men, we're on a hill! Pick out your man, but aim low. Aim low, I say!"

Wend knew that the tendency of a shooter on a hill was to fire above a target, so he understood the major's concern.

"First platoon fire!" At Campbell's order, the rightmost platoon released a volley in almost perfect unison, sending a sheet of lead through the forest.

"Fourth platoon fire!" The left flank platoon of Robertson's company fired, the men of the 77th executing the volley with the same precision that the Black Watch men had done.

"Second platoon fire!" The left half of the Black Watch fired.

"Third platoon fire!" Now the right half of the 77th company fired. Wend took aim at a warrior, and fired with the last platoon.

He was unable to see the results of his shot, for a vast cloud of black powder smoke billowed in front of the ranks. Wend concentrated on reloading his musket. As he worked, the first platoon fired again over on the right flank to start the second cycle of shooting. Wend feared that he couldn't get reloaded in time to fire with his platoon, for the other two platoons fired almost instantaneously after the first had fired. But when it was the turn of the third platoon, he was relieved to get his shot off in concert with others.

"Cease firing!" Campbell took a step forward, and drew his sword with a flourish. Taken by the excitement of the moment, he shouted in a voice Wend swore could be heard all the way to Fort Pitt, "FIX BAYONETS!"

Now, as he had been instructed by Sergeant McCulloch, Wend grounded his musket and shifted the barrel to his left hand. He reached across with his right to pull the bayonet from the frog and noticed for the first time the identity of the highlander to his left. It was McKirdy!

Momentarily disconcerted by the discovery, Wend fumbled with his bayonet for a moment, but finally got it locked onto the musket barrel. He looked up and saw Campbell standing in front of the lines. The smoke swirled around his body, giving him an ethereal appearance. The major looked up and down the ranks. Wend could see that he was smiling broadly, as if he were savoring the moment and wanted to record it for his memory. Then he ordered "Charge Bayonets!"

The order meant for the highlanders to level their muskets, the bayonets aimed directly at the enemy. It was part of the drill for the soldiers to shout a loud "HA!" in unison as they snapped the muskets to the level position. Wend had seen it practiced many times on the drill field and the accompanying shout had been perfunctory. But now the shout was like a wild beast's roar of defiance echoing through the forest. It continued unabated for long moments, the highlanders shouting at the top of their voices, mostly in Gaelic.

By now the smoke of the firing had dissipated. Wend could see that the Indians all across the field had stopped in their tracks and turned to stare at the screaming highlanders brandishing their bayoneted muskets. He could also see that more than a few warriors were lying dead or wounded on the ground.

And then Campbell ordered the advance.

As they stepped off, McKirdy scowled fiercely at Wend. "Eckert, if you let a savage get inside the tip of your bayonet I'll finish you off myself after I kill the damned Indian!"

Wend didn't respond. Instead, he concentrated on maintaining his alignment with McKirdy and the Black Watch soldier on his right as the charge picked up speed. Seconds later they approached the first party of warriors. Most of this group, watching the wave of steel blades approaching, turned and ran. Some carried wounded friends as they retreated. A few, braver or more foolish than the others, stood in resistance, swinging their hatchets or clubs. Too late these Indians realized the futility of their actions, for their handheld weapons had no chance of reaching over the combined length of the bayonets and muskets to get to the highlanders. The soldiers impaled them with short, jabbing lunges of their bayonets, then literally walked over them as the advance continued.

Now, the remainder of the warriors, having witnessed the death of their comrades, turned en masse and ran west, away from the relentlessly advancing line of bayonets. But now the second phase of Bouquet's plan began to unfold. Two companies, led by Captain McDonald, pivoted out from the end of the perimeter, attempting to block the flight of the warriors. As they pivoted, McDonald ordered a volley from both companies which sent a sheet of lead across the mass of fleeing Indians. The effect was devastating. Wend watched as scores of Indians fell to the storm of balls. The rest momentarily stopped running and looked around, not sure how to make their escape. Some turned and ran to the south. After a moment's hesitation, the rest continued west.

Having fired, McDonald ordered his men to charge with the bayonet. The largest group of warriors was now between the advancing line of Campbell's men and the place where McDonald's companies were still working to complete their pivot. Those Indians who had turned south met with less resistance, for the only force to oppose them was Barrett's rangers, who downed a few with their rifle fire but could not stop the larger number from escaping.

Wend soon realized that McDonald's pivot action was not moving fast enough to cut off all of the enemy. The fleetest of the warriors, some of whom had dropped their guns and other weapons as they ran, would clearly make it past his position before he could swing far enough to block them. He also noticed that there were so many Indians that some of the southernmost would overlap the length of the blocking line and be able to move past McDonald's right flank even when he was in position.

As it was, McDonald's line ended up impacting the mass of retreating warriors on their flank instead of being able to get into blocking position. Moreover, his line's alignment weakened, allowing fleeing Indians to get inside the line of bayonets, and hand to hand fighting ensued. However, this still slowed up the retreating warriors so that they were taken from behind by Campbell's line.

As the two lines closed, Wend looked over and saw that McDonald, a step ahead of his men, was being attacked by two warriors wielding hatchets. With a powerful swing of his sword, the officer sliced into one, who fell to the ground. However, in the process, McDonald lost balance and fell to his knees. The second warrior grabbed him by the collar with his left hand and raised his hatchet with his right, ready to strike.

Without thinking, Wend took his musket in his left hand and pulled his pistol from his belt with his right. And without stopping to consciously aim, he snapped off a shot at the warrior standing over McDonald. The range was at least thirty yards; Wend had no real hope of the shot hitting his target. But he was astonished to see the Indian's head explode in a spray of blood which cascaded all over McDonald. The warrior's lifeless body flopped on top of the officer.

Now the charge turned into a pursuit of the broken and fleeing enemy force. McDonald's men formed a line on the right of Campbell's and the four companies ran after the warriors, shouting and screaming at the top of their lungs. They drove the warriors over the hill where the battle had begun the previous day and well beyond. Finally, with the entire line exhausted, Campbell called a halt. Men dropped to their knees, gasping for breath. Others stood breathing heavily, using their grounded muskets for support. After a few minutes, the major ordered the four companies to reload and take defensive positions. But it didn't matter; Wend looked around and the Indians were clearly gone.

McKirdy was still next in line to Wend, sheltering himself behind a half-fallen tree. Wend lay behind a small bush. The drummer looked over at him with a strange look on his face and called his name. Wend wondered what kind of harassment the highlander was now going to send his way. Instead of answering immediately, he pulled his bayonet from the musket's muzzle and slid it back into the frog. Finally, he answered defiantly, "Yeah, McKirdy, what is it now?"

The highlander answered in a quiet voice. "I saw what you did back there to save Captain McDonald. No man in the regiment could have made that pistol shot." He paused for a moment. "I've been the captain's drummer since we left Scotland, until Ligonier, that is. He's a good man who's always treated me right. You got my thanks for what you did." He hesitated a moment and then extended his right hand to Wend. "I figure things are clear between us now."

Wend reached out and took the highlander's hand. A smile passed between the two of them.

* * *

Wend slowly walked back over the battlefield toward the flour bag fort. He was surprised at how he felt. The charge had been a great success and he thought he should be joyous at their deliverance and victory. Instead he simply felt relief and the lifting of a great burden off his shoulders. Beyond that he felt physically drained. The musket was a heavy load in his hands and every step was a labor, his feet like great stones which must be dragged along.

More than anything, he wanted to go back and see how Joshua and Mary had faired. Just before they had charged, he had seen that the Indian attack had advanced right up to the fort, and he prayed that none of the warriors had breached the stockade.

He was surprised to hear his name being called and looked up to see Private Hahn from the Royal Americans approaching him.

"Mr. Eckert! I'm glad I found you. Come quick! Sergeant Spengler has been hit and he's in a bad way. He wants to see you right away."

Hahn led the way at a run. "We were in the center of the attack and the savages hit us hard. They were right among us for a while. Sergeant Spengler was in the thick of the fight. He hit two of them with his hatchet. Finally we drove them away. Then another war party fired at us from cover and Sergeant Spengler took a ball right in the middle of the chest."

Wend found Arnold laying just a few feet in front of one the gaps in the stockade. Several men of his company were gathered around him, standing and kneeling. Wend went to his knees beside his friend. Arnold's eyes were closed; blood was on his lips and trickling down his chin from the side of his mouth. The front of his field uniform was soaked with blood.

"Arnold, Arnold!" Wend feared he was too late, but then Spengler's eyes slowly opened, and a crooked smile formed on his face.

"We stopped them, Wend. They tried their best to roll over our line, but by God, they didn't get through us; they couldn't get through the 60th! He coughed, and more blood oozed from his lips. "But I'm done. I can't move and it's getting real dark. I can barely make you out." He coughed again. "Reach inside my waistcoat, Wend. There's a bible there."

Wend complied and found a small, pocket size Bible, written in German. "I've got it, Arnold."

"My mother gave that to me when I left to join the regiment. You'll see she wrote me a note." Arnold closed his eyes for a moment and groaned. Then he opened them again, and when he spoke, it was in German. Wend leaned down to make sure he got the words. "Take the bible and my other things back to my Mother in Lancaster, Wend. The rest of my stuff is in the regiment's wagon at Ligonier."

Wend grasped Arnold's hand and answered in the old language, "Yes, yes, I promise. I'll go see your mother when this is all over."

"Wend, tell her about me. Tell her I was a good soldier and proud of it. Tell her what we did here today. My Pa was always saying I was wild and would never amount to anything; he was unhappy I didn't want to be a cooper like him. But Mother understood I wanted to do something on my own. Tell her about today and leave her with a good memory of me, Wend."

And before Wend could say anymore, Arnold Spengler was gone forever.

Wend knelt beside his friend's body, closed his eyes and said a brief prayer. One by one, the soldiers quietly left Arnold's side, until only Wend and Hahn were left. Then the private looked over at Wend. "I been in the regiment five years, Mr. Eckert. And I served with a lot of sergeants: Some were good, some were just plain mean. But I got to tell you, he was the best I ever had. He was fair with every man; he knew how to look after us and keep us out of trouble with the officers. And he treated me just like all the others, even though they brought me back from jail after I deserted. I won't forget him anytime soon."

* * *

Wend walked up into the fort with a heavy heart. There he found a beehive of activity. Soldiers and pack-horse men were working to make up litters for the wounded. Others were starting to pull down the flour bags from the

394

walls and to stack them into piles. Over at Bouquet's fire, a gaggle of officers were gathered, listening to instructions from the colonel. Wend found his two friends just as he had left them.

Joshua looked up, watching him inquisitively as he approached. "Why so glum, Sprout? I hear that the Indians are on the run and not likely to stop until they get back to their villages!"

Wend told them about Arnold's death. After they shared a quiet moment, Mary said, "The colonel told everyone we're going to move down to Bushy Run Station as soon as possible, where we can get water. It can't come any too soon for these wounded men."

Wend nodded, then sat beside Mary, and took her hand. He told her about the charge, and how Bouquet's plan had worked out. "There are many warriors dead on the field Mary. But there could have been even more." He told her about how McDonald's force hadn't been able to get fully into position to completely block the Indian's escape.

Mary nodded and looked into the distance. Then she screwed up her face as if a thought had just occurred to her. "Did you say there are a lot of Indian bodies still lying out there?"

Wend nodded. "Enough. They couldn't carry their dead off as usual. We pressed them too hard."

Mary pursed her lips, smiled up at him sweetly and squeezed his hand. "Wend, will you do something for me, please?" She stretched out the last word so that it had a pleading sound.

He looked down at her, feeling the warmth of just being with her spread through him. "Of course, anything you want."

"Well, will you get me some jewelry from one of the dead warriors? I've seen them wearing rings in their ears and nose, and I always thought it would be wonderful to have some. Will you do it for me, please?"

Wend looked at her in shock. The idea of robbing the dead, even Indian dead, repulsed him and chased the warmth he had just felt out of his consciousness. "Mary, I just don't feel right doing that, not taking things off of the dead."

Mary gave him a look of frustration. "Wend, that's nonsense. And it's not like I'm asking you to go out and bring back a scalp! It doesn't matter to the dead what you take. Where do think my mother got this pistol? Even the clothes I'm wearing belonged to dead soldiers. I'd go out there and get the rings myself, if I could." She pressed his hand. "If you don't do it, some soldier or ranger will get them for himself anyway."

Wend looked down at her and the pleading look on her face. He thought: *In many ways, she is far harder inside than me.* But he realized he couldn't refuse her. So, with a leaden heart, he walked out onto the battlefield and strode over to the heaviest concentration of dead warriors.

Soon enough he found what he was looking for; a dead Shawnee with pewter jewelry in both his ears and nose. There was a hole from a musket ball in his side, and a puncture wound from a bayonet in his stomach. The man's open eyes stared up at Wend. Shivering with revulsion at his task, he was able to pull the rings from the nose and right ear, but the ring in the left ear would not come free. Wend pulled out his knife and cut it free, shaking even more violently as he held onto the warrior's ear. Quickly he put the trinkets into his pocket and started back toward the fort.

He had gone only about ten yards when he saw something on the ground which brought him to a dead stop, his heart pumping wildly. He slowly walked forward, not believing his own eyes. But he could not deny what lay before him. It was a long rifle, made from bright, curly maple. Not just any rifle. It was the very rifle he had made as a youth, long ago in his father's shop at Lancaster and had last had in his hands that terrible day of the massacre in 1759. He dropped to his knees and examined the weapon. No, there was no question about it. It was scratched from use, and a line of marks had been cut into the butt like someone had been keeping score of something, and there were brass tacks along the top of the cheek piece. But there was no doubt it was his rifle!

A flood of recollections overwhelmed him: The day he had brought the piece of maple for the stock into the shop from the woods; Johann standing over him as he chiseled and planed the wood into shape; machining the rifle grooves into the barrel; the care he had taken in assembling and aligning each part; the unforgettable moment of pride when his father had examined the finished weapon and declared it the work of a journeyman. Above all, he found himself thrust back to the warm days of life in Lancaster and suddenly the memory of his family rushed through him.

After a long time on his knees, he stood up with the gun in his hands. Then he came back to the present and realized that if the rifle was here, it must have been brought by Wolf Claw. He quickly looked around for a body nearby. But no dead warrior lay in close proximity. He walked around, examining the nearest bodies. He was no expert, but none of them seemed to have Mingo markings—they were all Delaware or Shawnee. So somehow Wolf Claw had lost or dropped the rifle in the course of the battle. Maybe he had

had to drop it to fight with his hatchet or club. Or maybe, like others Wend had seen, he had thrown it down to allow himself to run faster.

He was suddenly buoyed by a thought. Events were catching up with Wolf Claw and his band. They had lost at least one warrior, and maybe more, during the skirmish on Forbes Road near Ligonier. Probably others had been killed at this battle. And now Wolf Claw had lost his prize rifle. Wend pictured him leading his men back to their village, missing brother warriors and without the weapon he had bragged about and shown off to visitors. It would not be a happy homecoming.

* * *

Andrew Byerly stood silently looking at the ashes of his buildings and the wreckage of his other property. Gathered around him, also surveying the wreckage, stood Wend, Means, Donegal, and Kirkwood. Colonel Bouquet had sent the scouting group ahead to the station, with Robertson's company in support, while the rest of the expedition picked itself up and prepared to advance. Kirkwood broke the silence. "Well, they didn't miss anything, did they?"

Byerly shook his head. He swore in his native German, using words which only Wend could understand. Then he spat and said in English, "I'll bloody well just have to start over, won't I now?"

Wend looked at Byerly. "Well, Andrew, at least you can be confident that you'll have lots of business. The army is going to be using this road for a long time, what with the campaign Bouquet plans against the Ohio country."

Byerly nodded. "I guess that's true enough. I wonder if there are men at Pitt or Ligonier I can hire out to help rebuild? We'll just have to see about that."

Donegal turned to Kirkwood. "Why don't you earn some of the King's good coin they are paying you? Run back and tell Captain Robertson there ain't no savages in sight around Bushy Run and that it's clear for him and his men to come up."

As the highlander ran back up the path to meet Robertson's men, Wend looked back toward the battlefield, a mile distant, and at the pillars of smoke which rose to the sky. Several great bonfires were consuming the better part of the flour and other supplies which had been born by the packhorses. Because the Indians had killed or driven away over half of the animals, Bouquet had been forced to make the decision to destroy most of the flour and other supplies. He needed most of the surviving horses to carry the litters of the wounded. The rest of the horses were being loaded with a few days of supplies for Pitt.

In just a few minutes Robertson's company arrived. The men immediately went to the stream which flowed by Byerly's place to satisfy their burning thirst, replenish their canteens, and wash off the powder which covered their faces and hands.

As the advance party settled in to rest, Wend heard the sound of the bagpipes from the direction of the battlefield. But the music was not the bright skirling he had heard so often on the march; it was slow and mournful, and punctuated by the solemn beating of massed drums. Then he realized he had heard them played this way before; at his family's burial. Donegal saw the look on his face. "That's it, laddie, they're playing a dirge for the fallen." All the scouts lowered their eyes in respect as the pipes wailed their haunting music.

Kirkwood spoke softly, and with a trace of bitterness. "They didn't have time to bury the dead. They just carried them to a spot on that ridgeline where the tribes first attacked us from, lined them up on the ground, and covered the bodies with tree branches and other brush to provide some protection from the animals. I heard one of the officers say they would try to get back to bury them proper after Fort Pitt is relieved."

Donegal grimaced. "That's a hell of an end for brave men and friends we marched with for all these years."

Wend thought of Arnold lying out there under brush and forest debris and shuddered. He touched his friend's bible, now in a pocket of his shirt, and mentally reaffirmed the pledge to take it back to his mother.

A few moments later Wend heard the sound of the pipes and drums shift abruptly from the funeral music to the skirling and beat of a marching tune. Within half an hour, the leading elements of the convoy began to arrive and take up campsites around the ruined station. In an hour, the entire expedition had reached Bushy Run to take sustenance from the creek. The cool water finally brought a measure of relief to the long suffering wounded. That evening and night the whole force lay around the remains of the station, exhausted and licking its wounds.

* * *

Henry Bouquet sat on a tree stump, the early morning sun over his shoulder. His officers were gathered around him. Byerly and Wend had also been called to the meeting and Bouquet had arranged for Joshua to be carried over from the hospital area.

"Gentlemen, we must make plans for our final march to Pitt. Our problem: We actually know less about our situation than we did before the battle." He stopped for a moment to allow that to register. "Questions: First, what has happened to the tribal force? Are they ahead of us, regrouping to fight again? Or have they returned to their encampments around Pitt, waiting for us there? Or did we damage them so much that they are heading back for their villages?" He shook his head. "I suspect that the latter is the case, but I cannot be sure."

"There is another concern. The people in Fort Pitt will have seen the Indians, or at least the major part of them, leave to fight our force. They have no idea about the outcome. If they thought we had lost, there might be sentiment to force Captain Ecuyer to surrender if the Indians returned to the fort. It would be just like the chiefs to try and trick him into thinking we have been destroyed."

"Finally, we have the logistics of the march to deal with. With so many wounded in litters, our progress will be very slow. Even without interference from the tribes, I don't believe we can make it to the fort in less than four days. Look at how laborious our movement from the battlefield to here was yesterday."

Wend looked around and saw the officers nodding their heads. It struck him again how much they were dependent on Bouquet's planning. While everyone else had spent the night physically and mentally recovering from the exertions of the last two days, the colonel's mind had been wrestling with the future of the expedition.

Bouquet let the impact of his words sink in to the gathered men. "So here is my plan. We will leave here today in late morning. Prior to that, our scouting group and Barrett's Rangers will patrol out ahead, searching for any signs that the tribes have been able to regroup for a continued fight. He looked at Byerly and Barrett. "Rejoin us where we camp tonight and let me know what you find."

"Assuming we don't have any opposition and can march onward, tomorrow morning we will send the scouting group to Fort Pitt to let them know we are on the way." He turned to Andrew and Wend. "Andrew, you know all the back paths to Pitt. I want you to get there safely and brief Captain Ecuyer about our progress. If the Indians still have Pitt surrounded, you will have to do your best to slip through the lines." He turned to Barrett. "You and your men will stay with the force and act as our scouts for the rest of the journey."

Bouquet turned to Joshua. "Is there anything else you would recommend to cover our scouting needs between here and The Forks?"

Joshua thought for a moment. "Just one thing, Colonel: You need someone with Barrett's company who knows the ground from here to Pitt. Why don't you have Means work with them as guide instead of going with Byerly's group?"

Bouquet nodded. "Good idea, Joshua." He turned to Byerly. "You should be fine with the four of you. But the important thing is to get there and give encouragement to Ecuyer and his people."

With the scouting and courier arrangements complete, Bouquet turned the meeting over to Major Campbell, who worked out the detailed marching arrangements. After a few moments, the officers returned to their units to make preparations.

The Indians attacked just minutes after the meeting had broken up.

The scouting group had been assembling their gear when a volley of shots rang out. Everyone in the encampment froze and looked around to locate the source of the firing. Wend looked up in the direction of the shots and saw a line of warriors standing in plain view among the trees on a high ridge, a cloud of black powder floating in front of them. He immediately understood why they were not taking cover; the ridge crest was well over 150 yards away.

Byerly looked at Wend. "I'm thinking that this ain't no major attack. Those devils are just taunting us; they know they can't do much damage from that distance. I'd wager they are a band that was up to the northern side of the flour bag stockade and didn't get chased away by Campbell's charge. Now they're just showing us they weren't cowed by the highlanders. But doing it from a distance where they can't be hurt."

While they talked, Major Campbell was organizing the light companies to attack the war party. Wend picked up his rifle and turned to Byerly. "You and Means bring your rifles and come with me. I think we can teach them a lesson!" He ran over to a wrecked wagon which lay next to the debris of Byerly's burned-out barn and rested his rifle on the top of the bed. Byerly and Means joined him in a few seconds.

Andrew shook his head. "That's a hell of a long way. I'd guess at least 175 yards."

Wend looked up at the war party. The warriors had reloaded and fired another spray of shots into the encampment, where everyone had taken whatever cover was available. A few men banged away in the direction of the Indians but musket fire was a futile gesture and the warriors just brandished their guns and war clubs by way of further taunting the soldiers.

Wend pulled the sett trigger of his rifle and concentrated on blocking out everything going on around him as if he were in a contest back at Sherman Mill. He put his sights on a warrior in the center of the group, then slowly raised the end of the barrel until he was sighting about the space of a man's head above the Indian. He took a deep breath and slowly squeezed the trigger, praying that the man wouldn't move in that instant. The rifle went off even before he expected. *Had he jerked the trigger and ruined the shot?* Cursing silently to himself, he looked up. The warrior was still standing. He swore again, sure he had missed. Then suddenly the Indian's head fell backward and he collapsed. By God, he had hit him square!

Byerly sucked in his breath. "Lord Above; that was one hell of a shot, son!" He reached over and pulled Wend's rifle from his hand and gave him his own. "Here, give it another go with mine!"

Wend took the rifle and leveled it at the ridge. The Indians were still stunned by his first shot; one had leaned over to look at the body of the fallen warrior. Realizing that Byerly's rifle had a larger bore and fired a heavier ball than his own, Wend adjusted his aiming point to a place a couple of feet over the leaning warrior, and squeezed off the shot. The warrior dropped to his knees, and clamped a hand on the side of his chest, before falling on top of his comrade.

Now Means reached over and exchanged rifles with Wend. He aimed at the ridge again, but by now the whole war party had dived for cover. He couldn't find a target. Then a pair of warriors jumped out and dragged the two men he had hit from sight. They moved so fast that Wend had no valid shot to take, and in seconds the entire war band had disappeared from the ridge line.

Meanwhile, Campbell had formed his men and was charging up the hill. Shortly they reached the crest, and advanced beyond, searching for the war party.

Wend became aware of a hubbub in the encampment. He looked around and realized that he was the object of cheering and clapping by soldiers, packers, and even the rangers. He felt his face and neck burning.

Lemuel Barrett walked over from his campfire and extended his hand. "Eckert, that first shot would have been exceptionally fine on a marked range, but here, firing uphill, without a clear idea of the distance, why I would have said that was near impossible. And then you did it again! Lad, they'll be telling stories about that for years to come."

Shortly, Campbell and the light companies returned. He reported to Bouquet that the band of warriors which had fired on the encampment had run away and that there was no sign of any other Indians. Bouquet considered the situation and saw no reason to change the plans he had made that morning. The scouts and rangers left immediately after Campbell returned, and the entire expedition was on the road to Fort Pitt before noon.

In later years, when pressed by his children and grandchildren or by others who had heard he was at the famous Battle of Bushy Run, Wend Eckert would tell his eager listeners about the fierceness of the Indian attacks, the valor of the highlanders, the sagacity of Colonel Bouquet and how the desperate flanking action had saved the day. He told them about Andrew Byerly fearlessly creeping out among the Indians to fetch water for the wounded. Listeners would see wetness in his eyes when he described how Arnold Spengler, headquarters clerk turned sergeant, died leading his squad of Royal Americans in a valiant defense of the wounded in the flour-bag fort. But he was always hesitant to talk about his own part in the fight. And when someone inevitably would ask what he had done in the battle, Wend put on the expressionless, stoic German face he was known for, and simply said, "Why, not that much. But I did fire the last shot of Bushy Run."

PART FOUR

The Ohio Country

1763

CHAPTER 23
Forks of the Ohio

Two hours after sunrise the four scouts took cover at the tree line atop a large hill north of the Monongahela River and looked westward upon Fort Pitt. It was the morning of the third day since leaving Bouquet's column. Andrew Byerly had cautiously led them along barely perceptible trails and sometimes cross-country to the very edge of the cleared area around the fort.

Wend Eckert scanned the plain before them and felt a thrill. From this vantage point he got the impression of looking down at a great, infinitely detailed map. Below lay the five-sided fort, sited at the very juncture of the Monongahela and Allegheny rivers. He could see the Ohio, the child of that coupling, flowing into the distance. The vista itself was impressive, but to Wend it had a very personal meaning: He had finally completed the journey which had started four years earlier.

The fort seemed peaceful, with smoke wafting skyward from chimneys of buildings within the walls. Wend was impressed with its size and the five great bastions which were clearly visible. But he also noted that the fort seemed at the center of a vast plain of desolation. It was surrounded by the charred debris of many structures, which Wend realized were the remains of the settlement which had grown up around the fort. Wend had now spent enough time with the army to understand that the buildings had been razed to provide a clear field of fire from the fort and to eliminate cover for the besieging Indians. He could see where unpaved streets and alleyways had run between the buildings. Surrounding the burned-out settlement were gardens and fields, their wildness showing the lack of care in the months since their owners had fled to shelter in the fortification. Also plainly visible to the northward was a gap in the forest, from whence emerged the final leg of Forbes Road, which then wound its way down past the burned out village to the gates of the fort.

Almost as if he were reading Wend's mind, Byerly tapped him on the shoulder and pointed down to the wreckage of the settlement. "That's what's left of the Upper Town, as it's called. There were near 200 houses and other buildings before the war started. That's where most of the settlers lived." Then Byerly pointed across the fort and toward the Allegheny. "The Lower Town was down on the other side of the fort, between the west walls and the Allegheny River. It was a pretty lively place; you could get just about whatever you were looking for there." He hesitated a moment, and smiled. "And sometimes you would find something you weren't looking for, if you take my meaning."

Kirkwood had been silent, taking in the sight. Then he sighed audibly. "This is the hill where Major Grant's fight ended five years ago. It wasn't far from here where the Senecas caught me. I never thought I'd be back here. One thing's sure: It's a lot more peaceful now than it was on that day."

Donegal had been looking around the whole area. "Speaking of peaceful, I don't see any sign of warriors."

Byerly nodded. "Donegal is right. They do seem to be absent." He pointed across the Allegheny. "That looks like an Indian village on the other side. It wasn't there before this all got started. But it seems deserted; I don't see any movement."

At that moment a faint noise came up from the fort. Wend listened for a moment and realized it was the sound of the sentries calling out their reports. He turned to Byerly. "I guess maybe the warriors have indeed left. We didn't see any fresh sign on the trails yesterday."

Byerly stood up. "Yep, I'll wager they are headed back to their villages, just like the colonel expected." He stood up and scanned the whole area again. "Let's wander down to the fort, and give the residents the good news about the column."

* * *

Wend stood on the parapet of the northeastern bastion of Fort Pitt, surrounded by the other three scouts. It was mid-afternoon on the day after their arrival. They felt rested and relaxed, strangely detached from the hubbub around them. Below where they stood, the fort's commander, Captain Ecuyer, was forming the companies of his garrison along the road just in front of the main entrance where the gates had been thrown open. A crowd of settlers were literally running up Forbes Road toward the place where it emerged from the forest, shouting to each other in their excitement. Other civilians, only slightly less exuberant, stood gathered to the rear of the garrison's formation. Men and women were hugging each other and clapping one another on the back. Children, freed from the confines of the fortifications, were playing and chasing each other around the wreckage of the Upper Town. Behind the scouts, from within the fort, the bell of the chapel peeled incessantly in celebration.

The genesis of all this excitement was the welcome sound of bagpipes and drums which had become audible only a few minutes previously, echoing through the forest and the open space around the fort. As the scouts watched, the head of Bouquet's column emerged from the woods. Wend could see that the pipes and drums had been massed into a single band marching at the head of the battalion. Immediately behind were several companies of the Black Watch and 77th in formation, making a brave sight as they paraded in perfect order. The skirling of the pipes aroused the same thrill in Wend as always. But behind the band and marching units he could see the rest of the convoy straggling along. It consisted of soldiers carrying litters for the wounded, pairs of horses supporting stretchers between them, and a few packhorses with the supplies which had been salvaged. Here and there were groups of walking wounded, some supported by more healthy comrades. The sight was a sobering counterweight to the thrill of the pipes and brought home to Wend how desperate the battle had been and the terrible bill which they had paid to defeat the tribes.

All this did little to dampen the enthusiasm of the settlers who had been bottled up in the fort for more than ten weeks with no news from the outside. The crowd had now reached the column and was striding along beside the soldiers, cheering and clapping loudly. Some civilians had moved in to relieve soldiers carrying the litters and Wend could see men and women hugging the highlanders as they marched.

Wend looked back down at Ecuyer, now standing in front of his garrison, ready to receive his battalion commander. He reflected on their meeting with the captain, after the scouting group had arrived at the fort.

The officer of the day had rushed to the fort's entrance to meet the scouts as they arrived. A bustling crowd of soldiers and settlers had gathered just inside the main gate upon the news of approaching strangers, which had spread through the fort like wildfire. The young lieutenant quickly led the scouts from the crowd to Captain Ecuyer's office, where they found the garrison commander seated in a chair before the hearth, his right leg bandaged and propped up on a cushioned stool. Wend later learned that he had been hit with an arrow during one of the Indians' periodic attacks. Byerly, who was well known to Ecuyer both as a former sergeant of the regiment and as proprietor of Bushy Run, quickly imparted the story of the battle and the approach of the relief column.

Ecuyer's face gradually changed from an expression of concern to relief as he listened. When Byerly had finished, he shook his head and said, in words tinged with the same Swiss accent as Bouquet, "Gentlemen, I have to tell you that the last few days have been the worst of the entire siege. We didn't know whether doom or deliverance was at hand." Then he arose and hobbled over to his desk chair and sat down. "On August 2nd, a week ago, the Indian warriors, who had been ringing the fort, gathered together on the plain, then moved off down Forbes Road. Only a few warriors remained as far as we could tell. Their woman and children, encamped in a temporary village across the river, also remained behind." He looked around at the scouts and explained, "They were so sure that they were going to take the fort that many of the bands had brought their families along to help carry the captured booty back to their home villages."

Wend thought for a moment and a question came to him. "Captain, could you tell how many warriors were in the force which left?"

Ecuyer looked up from his desk. "Well, we easily counted at least 400. There may have been more we didn't see." He took a drink of water from a glass on his desk. "The next five days were unbearably tense. It was obvious that the Indians had left to attack an approaching relief column."

"Then, late on the 7th, the Indians returned to their siege lines. Upriver, we saw a large number crossing the Allegheny to the village in canoes. Shortly thereafter, a single warrior ran out into the open near the front gate. He was unarmed but carrying a canvas sack. We didn't fire on him as he proceeded nearly to the gate where he dropped the bag. Then he brandished his fist, turned, and deliberately walked back to the tribal lines."

Ecuyer grimaced, then continued, "We sent a sergeant out to retrieve the sack. When he returned, we found it contained several scalps, a highland bonnet, and insignia from our regiment, the Black Watch, and the 77th. The implication was clear: The Indians wanted us to believe they had met Bouquet's relief force and defeated it." He shook his head. "I had no way of knowing if it was the truth or a clever ruse."

Byerly spoke up. "Well, Captain, Bouquet had that figured pretty near right. He thought the sachems would try to trick you some way into believing they had beaten the expedition."

Wend watched as the captain nodded and looked down at his desk again. "I knew that we had only a few days of provisions left. Clearly, if they had indeed destroyed or turned back Bouquet's column, we were doomed and would eventually have to surrender or break out from the fort and try to fight our way eastward along Forbes Road."

'That night, I was called to the west wall of the fort by the duty officer. He pointed out that the tribes were having a huge council fire in their great village. I looked at it across the river through my long glass. I could see shadowy masses of Indians around the fire. And, silhouetted against the flames, I watched a series of speakers talking to the gathering. We imagined, given what we knew at that time, that the leaders of the tribal force were holding a council of war to decide what action to take against us."

"Later that night a delegation of settlers called upon me, demanding that we begin parlaying with the tribal chiefs. They wanted us to attempt to negotiate surrender of the fort and safe passage to the east. They knew that the Indians had given us that option back in June, and that I had refused the offer. I told them that doing so would be making a decision to die; I reminded them of the massacres after the surrenders of Fort William-Henry and Fort Granville. That sobered them; they had all heard about that. I told them that there was a good chance that the Indians were lying about destroying the relief force and that we must wait at least a few days to see what developed."

Wend spoke up. "Captain, it seems to me that the tribal leaders must have decided at that council fire that their time was running out—with each passing day it was more likely that you would get a message from Bouquet, and learn the truth." He looked around at the assembled men. "They had to quickly settle on one of only two choices: Fight again or retreat to their villages."

Byerly said, "Eckert's right: And this time they would have had to fight the combined force of Bouquet's column and the fort's garrison." Then he smiled and continued, "And after what Bouquet did to them at Bushy Run, I say those chiefs didn't have no stomach for another fight."

Ecuyer looked at Wend. "Yes, gentlemen. I think that's precisely what happened. The next morning—yesterday—we woke up and found that the Indians had departed in the dark of night. We were alone here at the forks. Their lines were abandoned and the village deserted. So then we dared to begin hoping that it was the tribes which had been defeated and we would soon see the relief column." Ecuyer paused and smiled crookedly. "I was having a meeting of my officers here in headquarters, trying to decide if we should send a patrol out along Forbes Road in an attempt to make contact with Bouquet's force, when you four came strolling down from Grant's Hill."

* * *

After the column's arrival, Bouquet had directed Major Campbell to have all the companies go into camp on the sloping glacis to the east of Fort Pitt. The wounded were carried to the hospital within the fort.

Wend, Donegal, and Kirkwood carried Mary's litter through the fort's entranceway to the hospital area. Surgeon Munro and Chaplin Ferguson were working with the garrison doctor to get the new arrivals settled. As the only woman among the injured, Mary was put into a hastily cleared storeroom off of the main hospital ward to afford privacy. A cot had been placed along one wall to give her a little comfort. The room was smelly and dusty and had only one small window, high on the wall. But at least it provided her a quantity of natural light.

Wend sat down beside Mary on a wooden box. The girl appeared to be making progress in her recovery. But, as usual, she was in an irrepressible, cheery mood and Wend felt happy just being with her. Reaching into a bag, she pulled out the jewelry that Wend had taken off the dead Shawnee. "Look what I did with this during the march from the battlefield."

Mary held up a shiny, silver chain made of tiny links. At the bottom hung the Indian's nose ring, which she had attached to the chain using a thin piece of wire. She had artfully twisted and wound the wire so that it made a strong, attractive holder for the pewter ring. "This chain was my mother's, one of the few pieces of jewelry she had. I've been carrying it in my haversack since she died."

Wend complemented her on the chain and ring, then looked around the room. "This is a gloomy place. How long does the doctor think it will take until you can be up and around?"

"Oh, I've sure been in worse places! At least I've got a roof over my head and no wind blowing on me." She reached out and grasped Wend's hand. "I think it will be a while. There's still a lot of pain, particularly deep in the wound, and bumping along in that litter for five days didn't help things."

Wend squeezed her hand. "I'll get you some water and a mug. And you'll need a candle for some light when night comes." He stood up to go get the items, but Mary kept a hold on his hand. "Aren't you forgetting something, Wend?" She looked up at him impishly.

Wend was at a loss. "I can't think of anything. What else do you need?"

Mary put on a pouting face. "We've been alone for five minutes and you haven't given me a kiss!" She pulled him down and wrapped her arms around him. "I've missed you for the last three days. And you can't even remember to hug me. What kind of a beau are you?"

* * *

Wend walked out of Mary's room into the hospital ward. He found Joshua on a cot, being confronted by Esther McCulloch. "There is no way you are getting up. That hip of yours is not near healed enough."

Baird protested, "For God's sake, Esther. Dr. Munro did a good job sewing it up. And I'll do a lot better out in the clean air around a campfire then lying in this stinking, pestilent hole! Get me my moccasins and you can give this cot to someone who needs it more than me!"

"Joshua, you move around too much now and that will just slow the time until you get full use of that leg back. And you might break open the wound again. So lay back and stop causing me trouble. You've been a pain ever since we left Bushy Run. It's going to be weeks before you are able to get around like you did before."

Joshua, frustrated at Esther's words, looked up and saw Wend. "Hey, Sprout, tell this bossy lady that I don't need to be here cooling my heels and looking up at the ceiling. I'll do a lot better out in camp with you and Donegal."

Wend laughed. "Joshua, you know you can't fight Mrs. McCulloch. You better do as she says. Besides, you need to make sure that leg heals right. What are you going to do if you end up with a bum leg? No more ranging for you. You'll have no choice but to go back to Carlisle, get a regular job, and marry Alice Downey."

Baird's face showed a quick look of pure horror. "All right, Sprout. You and Esther win." He settled back on the cot. Then he remembered something. "Hey, Wend, that old rifle you picked up on the battlefield; it's over there in the corner along with mine. I carried the damn thing in the litter with me all the way from Bushy Run."

Wend walked over and examined the firelock closely. There was no doubt it was going to need considerable attention before he could use it again. He went back to Joshua's cot with the rifle in his hands. "I've got to find the armorer and see if I can use his shop and tools to get this back into shape."

Joshua shook his head. "You won't be doing that anytime soon. You are going to be busy for the next few weeks."

Wend looked curiously at Baird. "What do you mean by that?"

"Bouquet came by my fire last night to have a talk. He's worried about getting this fort properly provisioned and ready to support any advance on the Indian villages. In case you forgot, most of the supplies got destroyed on the battlefield. So after a couple of days rest, he is going to have Major Campbell lead the highlanders back to Ligonier to pick up the supply wagons and escort them back here. You scouts will be going with them. So don't get too comfortable."

*　*　*

Joshua's words were accurate, but only told part of the story. When the highland battalion left, straggling along with it was a mass of civilians. Bouquet was indeed worried about the shortage of provisions available at both Pitt and Ligonier, since so much had been destroyed at Bushy Run. And replacement supplies would have to be brought by another convoy all the way from the Cumberland Valley. Accordingly, he ordered women and children back to Ligonier and eventually further eastward until the emergency ended. The only women left at Pitt were nurses, a few officers' wives, and Mary, still in no condition to travel.

The initial trip back to Ligonier was only the first of several made by the highlanders and the scouts to bring up provisions and war supplies such as powder and lead. Later, detachments were sent back to Bedford to escort the civilians eastward and then convoy wagonloads of goods westward.

All this activity kept Wend busy through the remainder of the summer. By late September, he felt that he was as familiar with the western part of Forbes Road as he was with the wagon track through Sherman Valley. At the same time, the constant marching and riding—he had retrieved the mare from Ligonier—had strengthened him. He could now stride along the road, trails, and through the forest itself as tirelessly as any man. The sun had burnished his face and hands; Mary told him that his face looked as dark as some warriors.

They had had little contact with Indians. There had been isolated, hit and run ambushes of convoys by roving war parties, but no concerted campaign of attacks such as had occurred in the spring and early summer. And the frequency of attacks diminished further as fall approached. At worst they were a nuisance, except to the few soldiers unfortunate enough to be wounded or killed.

* * *

On a late September morning, with a hint of fall in the air, Bouquet led a small mounted party from Fort Pitt along the trail which paralleled the Monongahela and then the Yioghiogheny. The cavalcade consisted of Bouquet, his adjutant, Captain Stirling of the 42nd, the four members of the scouting group, and several enlisted soldiers of the Royal Americans, who came along as escorts and personal aides for the officers. Joshua had recovered enough to ride with the group, although he still limped when on foot. Byerly and Means had been relieved of their military duties and were back rebuilding their homes. All told, there were twelve riders and several packhorses with baggage, and the party made good time, reaching the ruins of Colonel Clapham's trading post in the very late afternoon.

Bouquet wanted to pay final respects to his old friend, who along with his family had been among the first to perish in the onset of the tribal rebellion. Upon their arrival, Bouquet surveyed the wreckage of the once thriving post and small village. The little settlement was surrounded by alternating patches of forest and small cleared areas which had been fields and gardens. Visibly saddened, he spent time alone at the row of graves which had been marked with crude crosses made of saplings. Then he had the Royal Americans clean up the grave area and emplace permanent crosses which had been made by the carpenter at Pitt.

Meanwhile, the rest of the party set up tents and built fires along the river, for Bouquet planned to remain the night and ride back in the morning. At the scout's fire, Kirkwood soon had a stew simmering. The four scouts sat quietly by the flames, passed around a jug, and watched the river water roll by endlessly as dusk settled over the camp. Donegal told a story about his days as a gamekeeper back in Scotland. Kirkwood regaled them with hilarious tales about his time with Major Rogers' Rangers. As portrayed by the highlander, the major was as much a rogue as himself, at least when off duty.

Wend looked around, impressed by the beauty and quietness of the spot. The post had been sited at a bend in the river where a small creek flowed into the Yioghiogheny. It was easy to see why Clapham had chosen to live here.

Bouquet and the two other officers sat at their own fire in front of Bouquet's tent, smoking pipes and socializing. Wend watched the group, curious about Stirling, the captain from the Black Watch. He was a new arrival, not having marched with the expedition that had fought at Bushy Run. Instead, he had come to Fort Pitt just a few days ago with one of the supply convoys from Carlisle. Of average height, he had a slight, delicate build, with a handsome face of fine, almost childlike features. This made him look quite young, and Wend thought he was probably in his mid-twenties. Later, Wend would be surprised to find that the officer was actually in his thirties.

Wend noticed that the colonel seemed somewhat preoccupied and expectant. A couple of times he rose from his camp stool and strolled to the very bank of the river, gazing out on the water and upstream. Wend reflected that he looked like he was expecting something or someone.

It turned out that was exactly the case. More than an hour later, after the men had eaten and full darkness had arrived, Wend looked out on the river. The moon had just come up and was reflecting on the flowing water. And as he looked down-river, Wend thought he caught sight of something moving along the near bank of the stream. Startled, he jumped up and walked to the edge of the river to get a clear look. Bouquet, seeing his action, also rose and moved quickly to the riverbank.

Wend saw that he was right; a canoe was coming toward them. He squinted, and thought he could make out three figures in the boat. Now most of the men in the party were up and watching as the craft approached. Some of the men had picked up their weapons and were checking the locks on the muskets.

Bouquet motioned to them to return to their fires. "Stay calm; put your muskets down. Show no hostility." Then by way of explanation he added, "This is not unexpected." Soon Bouquet stood alone by the river, quietly waiting for the visitors.

In a few minutes the canoe grounded in the shallows of the stream and all three occupants jumped out. The two men who had been paddling pulled the canoe onto dry land. Wend saw that the third man was considerably older than the other two and very dignified in his bearing; clearly he was looking at a chief, a priest, or an elder. The Indian leader raised a hand, walked directly to Bouquet and they exchanged greetings. The two paddlers squatted beside the canoe, totally silent and taking great care to ignore the soldiers and scouts.

Bouquet led the visitor to his fire and they took their seats. The colonel's adjutant left the fire, and stood attentively by the tent, out of earshot. The three men at the fire, Bouquet, the Indian, and Stirling, conferred for over an hour. Most of the talking was done by the sachem, who accompanied his words with descriptive hand gestures. Bouquet seemed to mostly ask questions and nod frequently as the Indian made his points. Stirling said virtually nothing, but listened carefully.

Joshua poked Wend in the ribs, and whispered, "I recognize that man. He's an elder in the Turtle Clan of the Delaware. I saw him often enough at council fires at Fort Pitt before the war broke out. He was always one of the more friendly leaders of that tribe." Baird thought for a moment. "My guess is, he's telling Bouquet what's going on among the factions in the Ohio Country. The colonel has always had his ways of keeping informed about the tribes."

Not long after that, the elder stood up and Bouquet escorted him back to where the canoe and the other two Indians waited. After a few more words between the two, the canoe departed, the paddlers turning it downstream. Soon it disappeared into the darkness along the bank.

Bouquet stood watching the canoe depart and then turned and called out to Joshua and Wend, motioning for them to come to his fire.

When they had arrived, he indicated for them to sit down. Baird settled into the camp stool vacated by the Delaware and Wend sat down on the ground. Silence reigned for a moment, as Bouquet gathered his thoughts. Wend watched as the fire flickered before them. Then the colonel looked over at Baird. "I take it that you recognized my visitor, Joshua."

Baird nodded. "I 'spect he came here to tell you about what's happening out in the Ohio Country among the tribes."

"As usual, you have it correct Joshua." Bouquet looked around at the three men. "He brought some useful information. The tribes are shocked by their defeat at Bushy Run. At least three of their kings or war captains were killed; many women are singing the death song for their men. He also told me that the war chief who led the attack on this settlement and killed Will Clapham and his family was called 'Wolf'."

Joshua said, "Yeah, I've heard of Wolf. He has the reputation of being pretty ruthless on the warpath."

"Well, Wolf is finished with the warpath permanently; our visitor said he was killed in the final charge at Bushy Run." Bouquet smiled and looked at each of the faces around the fire. "I find that very satisfying."

After letting that register with his listeners, Bouquet continued. "The sachem also told me that most of the bands have suspended their ranging to the east, at least for the fall and winter. They're concentrating on harvesting their crops and hunting to lay in provisions for the cold months."

"But for our purposes, the most important thing is that there is great dissension among the tribal leaders about how to proceed in the spring. Do they continue the rebellion or do they make peace?" Bouquet extended his hands out to the fire to ward off the chill of the night.

Joshua said thoughtfully, "With them arguing, now would be the time for us to march into the Ohio Country. I've no doubt the approach of a strong force would convince them to put down their arms rather than hazard their villages."

The colonel grimaced. "That was my intention. But we have lost that opportunity for this year." He motioned to Captain Stirling. "Thomas, tell Baird and Eckert about the word you brought with you from the east."

Stirling, who had been looking down at the fire as he listened, glanced up at the two scouts. "Well, I brought dispatches from the army command in New York, which say that the provincial forces that were expected to join us won't be ready until next spring at the earliest. Virginia and Maryland between them promise at least 1500 men by then, but that doesn't do us any good now. As usual, Pennsylvania won't be much help. The Quakers are talking about a provincial battalion to man the forts and protect the settlements, but not to be used for operations in the Ohio territory."

Bouquet said, "And I don't have anything like the force we would need to advance on the villages now. I must send the remnants of the 77th back east to be disbanded; and even if I had the entire Black Watch, it wouldn't be enough for the job." He frowned. "As it is, we will be hard pressed just to get ready for the winter ourselves."

Wend was discouraged. "So all the effort we have made this summer was for naught?"

Bouquet looked at Wend and shook his head. "No, far from it; we have raised the siege on Fort Pitt and resupplied the fort, which was our initial objective. Just as important, our victory at Bushy Run has shaken the sense of invincibility which the Indians gained from their victories over Braddock and Grant. The battle has also relieved the pressure on the settlements, at least for this year." He glanced meaningfully at Wend. "And I have an idea of how we can help convince the Indians to forebear from attacks next spring, and it is undoubtedly a proposition that will please you."

Wend was puzzled, and knew that his face showed it. Bouquet smiled, and looked around at the three men, their faces illuminated by the firelight. "What I intend involves all three of you and will keep you busy for the next few weeks. I've had this plan in my head for a while, but the news our visitor brought tonight makes me certain that it is viable."

A crooked smile spread over Joshua's face. "Colonel, just a guess, but is this plan of yours going to entail a lot of walking for us?"

Bouquet eyed Baird for a moment. "You've been working with me too long, Joshua. I feel like you sense my thoughts before they are even fully formed." He paused a moment. "Yes, there will be plenty of walking. I intend to send a company of the 42nd, under Captain Stirling, on what essentially will be a diplomatic mission into the Ohio Country. He will carry a wampum belt signifying his status as an emissary. The purpose will be to give the Indians, particularly their leaders, an ultimatum. Specifically, he will make it clear that we plan to advance on them next spring with massive force and they must make a choice: Accept peace or be ready for a fight to the death."

"You and your scouts will go with the captain, to guide him to the villages of the important tribal leaders. I expect this mission will keep you busy until the end of November." Bouquet looked over at Wend and raised an eyebrow. "In the course of your travels, you will encounter many villages, including naturally those of the Mingoes. There is some chance that you could resolve certain personal matters."

A thrill passed through Wend's body. Suddenly he remembered Bouquet's promise, so long ago, by a fire like this one at Fort Loudoun, to make amends to Wend for the loss of his family. And now he was attempting to make good on that promise! Wend nodded his understanding to the colonel.

Bouquet turned to Stirling. "Thomas, you must convey a certain attitude toward the elders of the various villages and any kings you encounter. You must reinforce the humiliation they feel at their defeat and present the appearance that we are supremely confident in our strength and our ability to crush them next year." The colonel laughed to himself before proceeding. "In other words, you must conduct yourself with some of that aristocratic arrogance for which you British are so well known."

Stirling looked up at Bouquet sharply, not sure how to take the colonel's words. Then he saw the wry smile on the senior officer's face and a look of understanding spread over his own countenance. He made a quick smile, puffed out his chest, and lifted his chin so that he seemed to be looking down his nose at the colonel. Then he replied in a haughty tone, "I understand exactly what you mean, Sir. After all, I will someday be Lord Stirling of Ardoch, and I have been brought up to understand my exalted place in the hierarchy of the British nobility."

Bouquet nodded enthusiastically. "That's the stuff! I see that we understand each other precisely, Thomas."

* * *

Five days after the visit to Clapham's trading post, Wend was hard at work in the armorer's shop at Fort Pitt. He was just completing the final steps in rehabilitating his old rifle. First he had totally disassembled it. Then he had cleaned and rebuilt the lock. He had used solvent to clean the inside of the barrel and had carefully run the bit of the armorer's rifling machine through its length to make sure the spiral grooves were clean and undamaged. The stock had been completely refinished after he had removed the tacks that Wolf Claw had inserted along the top of the cheek piece. He had applied many light coats of oil to restore the natural beauty of the wood. The only visible reminder that it had been in Wolf Claw's possession was the row of notches along the butt. Now he was carefully aligning the barrel to the stock. When that was done, he would be ready to test fire the rifle to prove both the functioning of the lock and its accuracy.

Wend felt a great satisfaction at being able to put his hands to familiar, useful work. It also served to keep his mind from worrying about Mary. It was nearly two months after the battle, but her wound was still giving her problems. At first she had seemed to heal rapidly, and after three weeks in the hospital, she had been able to spend some time up and around. She had even resumed her school sessions with Ferguson and light chores in the hospital. Several times between his trips on Forbes Road, Wend had helped her go up to one of the bastions so they could sit together on camp stools. They had spent some wonderful hours there, sometimes just talking, other times sharing one of the books Mary was reading. These intimate periods cemented his feelings for her.

But then her recovery had seemed to stall. There had come flare-ups of internal pain, accompanied by fever and weakness. Several times the doctor had put her back to bed in the hospital. Usually in a day or two she had seemed better and resumed her normal routine. But yesterday she had had a serious relapse, nearly fainting while she was helping in the hospital. Munro had put her back into her room with alternating fever and chills.

Wend sat with her for a time, keeping her company. She had tried to be cheerful and keep up a conversation, but she had soon grown weary and dropped off to sleep. Wend had gently kissed her cheek and gone off to help with the preparations for Stirling's expedition into the Ohio Country.

In fact, the onset of the expedition had precipitated important decisions by Donegal and Kirkwood. Donegal had notified Captain Robertson that he would accept his discharge at Fort Pitt and Joshua had appealed to Bouquet to take the highlander on as a civilian scout, an idea to which the colonel had eagerly agreed. Shortly afterward, Kirkwood had made a surprising announcement: He would transfer to the 42nd rather than return to Scotland with the 77th!

Wend had been astonished and said as much to the private. "Bob, as many times as you have railed against the officers and sergeants, and as much trouble as you have had, I never thought you would have been one of those to stay with the army. Why, you told me yourself that you got sent to jail for desertion up in New York! Why wouldn't you leave now when you have the chance and get paid for it as well?"

"Well, like your friend Spengler, I was a cooper before I joined the army. But I never liked it much. At any rate, I ain't quite ready to go back to the old country and spend the rest of my days making barrels." Kirkwood waved his arm at the other scouts. "Besides, I don't feel like letting you three have all the fun among the Indian tribes with Captain Stirling." He paused for a moment as if considering his next words. "And it don't hurt that the Sergeant Major of the 42nd said they would make me a corporal, 'cause of my experience."

"You a corporal?" Donegal made a show of laughing heartily. "That goes to prove what I've always thought: That 42nd, them what holds their noses so high and prides themselves so much on being a 'Royal Regiment', they actually got lower standards than the 77th! Wait 'till I tell Sergeant McCulloch about this; he'll be chuckling all the way back to Edinburgh!"

Joshua looked thoughtful for a few moments. Then he said, in a philosophical tone, "Well, he'll be a corporal for at least a few weeks, until the Black Watch figures out where all the missing rations and rum is going. But at least we four will eat well on this little hike we're going to take. 'Course, it could be that Captain Stirling knows how to keep his personal stores safeguarded better than most officers."

Kirkwood gave them a sly smile. "I already got that taken care of; me and the captain's steward, a fellow named McKay, understand each other pretty well. I slipped him some goods I found laying around unattended in the quartermaster's stores as sort of an advance payment and he's promised us a little consideration on this trip."

Now, as he stood in the shop, fixing the rifle barrel in place, Wend smiled again as he remembered the expression of satisfaction on Kirkwood's face when he told them about his deal with the officer's steward. He was glad that the highlander would be along on their new mission. The man certainly knew how to lighten up any moment. Then Wend made ready to take the firelock outside the walls of the fort so he could check the alignment by live firing at a target. He had just gathered up all the materials he needed when Esther McCulloch came bustling into the shop.

"Wend, Mary needs to see you at the hospital."

Wend replied without looking at the nurse. "All right, tell her that I'll be over a little later. I've got to check out this rifle so I can take it with me on the trip to Ohio. It has to be done today, because we're leaving at dawn tomorrow. It won't be two hours and I'll be there."

"Wend, you don't understand. She's worsening. Her fever won't go away and her wound seems to be inflamed."

Wend turned to stare at Esther. Her face was grim and showed something Wend had never seen there before: Outright fear. Wend felt a hand clutch at his heart. He immediately put down his tool bag and followed Esther without another word.

* * *

Surgeon Munro and Chaplin Ferguson were standing outside Mary's room wearing stern faces. Munro put a hand on Wend's shoulder. "Lad, I'll tell you straight: There's something bad wrong inside her. I've done everything I know and she's just getting weaker. This morning, the fever went even higher than yesterday and I can feel softness under her scar and swelling around the wound area. I don't know what's going on; I've never seen anything quite like this."

Wend looked into the surgeon's eyes and saw that the man had no hope. "She's not going to make it?"

Munro was sweating heavily, and not from the temperature, for a cool breeze was coming in through a window. He pulled out a handkerchief and mopped his face and neck. "Not if she goes on like this. It is out of my hands. She's more the chaplain's business than mine now."

Ferguson looked at Wend and said softly, "Mary's been asking for you all day. She says she wants to have some time alone with you." He shook his head. "You've got to be cheerful with her; don't let her see you are distressed or that you think she's going to die."

Wend felt himself begin to shake as full understanding of what was going on swept over him. He looked around at the three of them, Munro, Ferguson, and Esther; none of them would meet his eyes. He thought, *God, they know this is the last time I'm going to see Mary.* He gritted his teeth and pushed open the door to the girl's room.

As soon as he entered, he shut the door and with great effort put a grin on his face. He pulled up the crate which served as a visitor's chair beside her cot. He didn't know what to say to her. Then Joshua's words popped into his memory. "How's the prettiest redheaded girl in the regiment doing today?"

Mary smiled at him. He could see that her face was flushed with the fever and her eyes were unnaturally bright. Wend was surprised to see that she had put on her Indian jewelry; the shiny rings hung from her ears and the chain around her neck. She had brushed and put up her hair. But he looked more closely and he could see beads of perspiration on her forehead.

He said, "You're looking better today! I'll bet you'll be up and around in a day or two!" He leaned over and kissed her, then sat down and took her hand. He could feel the heat of the fever in her flesh.

"Don't try to put on an act in front of me, Wend Eckert. Even with that stone face of yours, I can see you know how bad things are." He looked down at her and realized that there were tears in her eyes. "I've been nursing all my life and I know when the patient is going to die."

"Oh, come on Mary. I just talked with the surgeon. Things aren't that bad. Munro was very optimistic."

She shook her head and spoke softly. "Please, please Wend. You needn't act cheerful and lie to me. I'm on my deathbed and you know it too." She looked over at the door. "I don't want us to be disturbed. Please turn the lock in that door."

He did as she requested, and then resumed his seat beside her.

"Wend, you know that I have loved you since I was a little girl. I thought you were beautiful the first time I saw you and my heart went out to you while I watched the brave way you faced up to the loss of your family. After that, you were in my dreams wherever we marched; at Albany, Ticonderoga, and the West Indies. When we were ordered back to Carlisle because of this rebellion, I walked the streets hoping to come across you. Then God answered my prayers and with his blessing, we have come to mean much to each other."

Wend shook his head. "No, Mary. That's far too much of an understatement. I love you with all my heart."

"Yes, I think you do. And that's why I'm going to ask you for something." She looked up at him beseechingly.

Wend squeezed her hand and said, "Of course Mary; anything in my power."

Suddenly she pushed herself up to a sitting position and threw her arms around him. "Wend, I promised God and my mother that I wouldn't allow myself to become a harlot; that I wouldn't give myself to any man until I was married. But I'll never live to be married. This is as close as I'll ever get. Wend, please make love to me. I want to die a woman. You are my only passion and I think that they both will understand and forgive me."

Wend had no idea how to respond. "But Mary, you're so weak; I don't want to hurt you!"

She shook her head. "I'll just get weaker from now on; this is the only time." Now tears were flowing from her eyes. "Do I look so terrible that you don't want me?" She reached down and unfastened the top of her night shirt and it fell away from her shoulders.

Wend looked down and for the first time saw her breasts and nipples. She again wrapped her arms around him and pulled herself against his chest. Then she began unlacing his shirt.

Wend gently helped her back to a reclining position on the bed, then stood up and began taking off his clothing. Mary lay smiling, watching as he undressed. She reached up and brushed the tears from her eyes.

Wend made love to her with all the tenderness he could muster, taking care to keep his weight off her body. She was hot all over, and at first he worried that he would not become aroused, but to his surprise Mary was able to help him, first stroking his chest, then moving her hands down his body until she touched his member. He caressed her small, firm breasts, feeling the nipples harden. Then slowly, tentatively, he entered her; she first made a small grimace, feeling the pain of initial penetration. But then he was inside her and began to move back and forth slowly. Gradually she changed her expression and began to moan in pleasure. He felt urgency coming over him, but he held back, keeping his motion slow and smooth, for he knew that this lovemaking must be all for her benefit. Presently he could feel that she was becoming more excited and he allowed his movement to become more rapid. Her moans came more closely together. Finally, he lost control of his body and reached climax. Mary wrapped her arms and legs around him with a sudden burst of strength and cried out with pleasure, then crushed her lips against his with an incredible frenzy. "Wend! Wend! Oh I love you so much!" She whispered the words, but they held clear passion.

They lay in embrace for long minutes; Wend thought it must have been a half-hour. Then he saw sleep coming to her, and thought to quietly leave her there. As he stood by the cot, putting on his clothes, she reached out and put her hand on his leg. She said sleepily, "Are you going to leave me now?"

Wend sat down on the crate. "Just for a little while. The mission to the Ohio Country is supposed to depart tomorrow morning. I'm going to tell Colonel Bouquet that I need to stay here with you. Then we'll be together as long as providence gives us."

Mary roused herself and reached out, grabbing his hand. "No, Wend, you mustn't do that! It's a wonderful thing for you to say, but I'm finished; there's no future with me. You must go try to find Abigail. If you can bring her back, you have a chance at a life together."

Wend looked down at her, tears now welling up in his own eyes. "I'll never leave you, as long as there is hope. And if the worst comes, I'll not let you die here alone in this wretched storeroom!"

"No, no, you must go! You are that girl's only chance. Besides, I won't be alone. There are many people here I love. The regiment is my family. I'll be with Esther and Mr. Ferguson and the others."

Wend sat, looking at her, unable to muster any words.

She squeezed his hand again. "Wend you've made me the happiest woman in the world. I'll cherish this hour we've had for as long as I have remaining. But I want you to remember me the way I am now, not as some pale shell of myself gasping out my last breaths. So kiss me now and go on your way."

Wend kissed her, a long, lingering embrace, and then quietly left the room. But he was determined that he would find a way to stay with her.

He found Ferguson out in the main ward of the hospital and pulled him aside. "Chaplain, I need your help. I love Mary, and I must stay here with her as long as she's alive. So please come with me to Bouquet's headquarters to help explain to him why I must remain behind."

Ferguson looked at Wend for a long moment, then asked, "Does Mary know what you plan to do?"

Wend shook his head. "No, she told me to go on the mission with Captain Stirling to the Ohio Country. She wants me to find Abigail if I can; but Good Lord, chaplain; she deserves to have someone who loves her at her side in her last days. I can't possibly leave."

"She told you to leave her?" Ferguson stood silently, considering Wend's words for a long minute. He put his hand to his chin as he thought, and in doing that he suddenly reminded Wend of Reverend Carnahan, back at Sherman Mill. Then he slowly shook his head. "No, Wend, Mary is right. In a few days at most, she'll be gone. But she's army and she understands death because she has seen so much of it in her short time. She knows that death is just another phase of life, no matter when it comes. However, God, in his wisdom, has given you more time. You will spend the rest of your life wondering how things would have turned out if you don't take this opportunity to find that other girl. You must go on the expedition."

Wend stood silently, not quite willing to accept the Chaplain's words. Then Ferguson put his hand on his shoulder. "Son, you've done everything you can for Mary. You've shown her your devotion; I know that has made her happy beyond measure. Now go and get on with the rest of your life."

* * *

Shortly after dawn the next morning, Captain Thomas Stirling of His Majesty's 42nd Foot, his lieutenant, forty-five highlanders, and four scouts including Joshua Baird, Simon Donegal, Corporal Robert Kirkwood, and Wend Eckert were ferried across the Allegheny River in several bateaux to start their mission to carry Bouquet's message to the tribes of the Ohio woodlands. One of the boats towed a large raft carrying a string of pack horses with enough supplies for sixty days.

Wend sat in a bateau as it crossed the river, his eyes focused on the far bank, toward where he knew that a golden haired, blue eyed girl, long the obsession of his life, lived in a distant village with her husband and children. But as the oarsmen of the boat relentlessly pulled him onward, his heart and mind remained in the fort on the receding shore, held there by the memory of a brave girl living out the last days of her life in a small, dark storeroom.

CHAPTER 24
The Village on Slippery Rock Creek

T he bateaux put Stirling's company ashore at the Indian village which had grown up across from Fort Pitt during the siege. While the troops unloaded their gear and the packhorses, Joshua led the scouts on a quick sweep through the town, to confirm that it was deserted. Wend found the place spooky, with many signs of recent habitation and items left behind by the Indians seeming to reflect a hasty departure. By the time they had satisfied themselves that the town was empty and returned to the landing, the last of the boats were on their way back to Pitt and the company had completed their preparations to march. Then, after a few words with the captain, Joshua led the column through the village in single file and then to the trail which followed the Ohio to the old Indian village of Logstown.

The path was well worn and the tough highlanders moved fast. By late afternoon Wend estimated that they had covered nearly seventeen miles. The scouts, about a mile ahead of the company, had reached a hill which looked over the Ohio and the remains of a town nestled along the shore.

"There are actually two villages here." Joshua pointed down the slope. "The first is by the river, and that was begun near forty years ago, as a meeting place between the tribes and the French traders. It started out mostly Delaware, but soon a mixture of tribes was living here together. Then, 'bout the time the French war started, most of the people left the village and moved inland. Those who stayed behind built another, smaller village on the slope of this hill above where any flooding might occur." He pointed, and after a moment Wend could make out the shape of lodges not far below where they stood.

Donegal said, "I don't see any movement. Both places look empty."

Joshua nodded. "There was a small population here until the rebellion started last spring, but Captain Ecuyer says his scouts think the last of the people left just before the attacks started. They apparently were afraid that the English could come downriver and strike at them." He paused a moment. "So let's go down and see if that's the case. Stirling is planning to camp here tonight."

After a short exploration, it became clear that the villages were indeed uninhabited and Joshua sent Kirkwood back to the column as a messenger. By dusk, Stirling had the camp set up near the river. After the evening meal, he called Baird and Wend to his fire and asked for Joshua's thoughts on their mission.

There were five men around the fire; the two scouts, Lieutenant Eddington, Sergeant Leslie, and the captain. Stirling held a roughly drawn map of the country between the Allegheny and the Muskingum. He quickly gave the other four men a summary of his orders from Bouquet. Then he spoke to Joshua. "The colonel told me we were to go no further westward than the basin of the Beaver. He believes if we get out the message to the tribal bands in that area, they'll pass it to the west." He paused and looked at his map. "This map is too general to show me the detail of the area we are to travel; can you fill us in, Mr. Baird?"

Joshua nodded and rose to his feet. He found a stick, and began to draw a map in the dirt. "Here's the Ohio, Captain, and here we are at Logstown. Just a bit to the west, the Beaver River flows into the Ohio." Baird drew a line from the Ohio northward. Then he drew a series of lines, like branches of a tree, off of the Beaver. "These are creeks which flow into the Beaver. There are a passel of villages along the Beaver itself, and along all those creeks. Many of the villages are Delaware, but the tribes are all mingled in this area. You got Shawnee, Wyandotte, Mingo and other tribal villages all through the area. So if we go up the Beaver and out along these creeks we'll get the word to villages of all the tribes throughout the Ohio country. And the colonel's right: We talk to a few bands of each tribe and the word will spread pretty fast in all directions."

Stirling nodded. "All right, Mr. Baird, that seems reasonable. Now once we have climbed the Beaver, how do we return? Do we retrace our steps?"

Joshua did some more drawing on the ground. "As you can see here, after a good distance northward, the Beaver starts to swing westward sharply. At that point, we'll leave the river and follow a trail which goes northward overland. About twenty-five or thirty miles north of here, there's a cluster of several villages called 'The Kuskuskies'. That's almost directly west of Kittanning; he marked a point on the eastern side of the Allegheny River far north of Pitt.

"Any rate, after visiting those villages, we turn east and move through the territory between the Beaver and the Allegheny itself. There's a trail which leads directly toward Kittanning, with plenty of villages along the way. Then we turn southward and eventually end up down at the forks, after making a big loop."

Sergeant Leslie cleared his throat. "Begin' your pardon, Sir. Can I ask a question?" When Stirling nodded, the sergeant continued. "The lads 'ave been asking questions, Sir. Fact is, there be lots of savages out here." He motioned his arm over Joshua's map. "And there is 'na but fifty of us." He paused and looked at the faces around the fire. "What's to keep them from rising up and overwhelming us?"

Stirling nodded his understanding. "Quite right, Sergeant, that's a natural question; but several factors are on our side. First, we're carrying a wampum belt which shows our peaceful intent. The tribes respect that. There were several negotiating missions into the Ohio Country during the late French war, and the tribal kings respected and protected those emissaries. And when we enter villages we'll also carry a white flag, which the Indians have learned is the European sign of truce." Stirling paused again to consider his words. "Second, Bouquet is convinced that whatever unity existed among the tribes and bands has been fractured by the defeat at Bushy Run. Some kings want to make peace while others are for continuing the war. That means the sachems will want to hear what we say and then talk it over among themselves over the winter. Finally, Mr. Baird says that this is the time when the men of the villages are busy harvesting crops and going on what they call the 'Long Hunt', to lay in meat supplies for the winter. That's an essential chore for them, and they don't have time for war unless it's forced on them."

Joshua nodded. "That's the truth of it, Leslie. Most of the warriors are going to be south and west of here, in less settled places which are their hunting grounds. If they don't take game now they're going to starve over the winter. So aside from the women and children, we'll be seeing a few older warriors, boys, and elders at the villages. Our biggest danger, in my mind, is running into a war party on its way back from the Pennsylvania settlements who think we are hostile."

Stirling smiled. "And that reminds me. We have one other very important factor in our favor. And that's Mr. Baird himself. He has spent a lot of time here in the Ohio Country, has met many of the important tribal leaders, and knows the ground well. He also speaks the Delaware language, which will be essential to our mission." He motioned to Eddington and Leslie. "We welcome his advice and will be relying on it for our navigation and communication with the tribes."

Joshua looked uncomfortable at Stirling's words, and Wend swore he could see the scout blush.

Then Stirling spoke again. "All right, that's it for tonight. We'll march at dawn tomorrow. Eddington, you and the sergeant check the company and the sentinels on watch. He turned to Wend. "Mr. Eckert, please stay here with me for a moment. I want to talk with you."

When they were alone, Stirling motioned to his steward who had been sitting on a log out of earshot. "McKay, bring us some of that brandy in my stock." While he waited for the steward to return, Stirling pulled out a long stemmed, graceful pipe, then filled and lighted it. As he did so, he occasionally eyed Wend, as if appraising him, but said nothing.

Wend, surprised at the captain's request to see him privately, also kept his silence and returned the officer's glances, refusing to be intimidated. Soon McKay returned with two small pewter cups and a bottle. He handed a cup to each man and then filled both. Stirling nodded, and the steward withdrew to his log.

The captain took a long pull on his pipe, savored the smoke for a moment, and then blew it out in a long exhalation. He turned to Wend. "The day before we departed from Pitt, Colonel Bouquet and I spent several hours together. He gave me his official orders and personal advice for this mission. In addition, he gave me some private, unofficial instructions about you. Rather intriguing, I might say. Sorry to hear about your family; the massacre and all that." Stirling took a sip of his brandy. "He also explained about your relationship with this girl from Philadelphia who is in the hands of the Mingoes. I believe her name is Abigail. Apparently she's rather a beauty." He looked at Wend, as if expecting him to say something.

Wend refused to be drawn out. He simply nodded in reply.

Stirling continued. "The colonel said that if we came across her, and if conditions made it at all feasible, we should attempt to bring her back with us."

Wend nodded to Stirling again. "I would be very grateful if that could be arranged, Sir."

Now it was Stirling's time to sit quietly. After a moment, he spoke again. "After talking with the colonel, and seeing his interest in you, I made certain enquiries. It seems your actions at Bushy Run were rather heroic, at least as described by officers who were there."

Wend felt himself start to blush. "I just did what seemed necessary, Sir."

"Well, let's see." Sterling put his cup down, and raised a finger of his hand. "One: You crawl out among the savages in the middle of the night to prove that the terrain is suitable for covering a flank action. Two: In the darkness, you fight hand to hand with a warrior and kill him with your knife. Three: You charge with the flanking troops. Four: As told to me by McDonald, you save his life by snapping off a one-handed pistol shot in the middle of the advance. Five: You pick off two warriors with rifle fire at an unbelievable range." Sterling took another pull on his pipe. "I'd say most of that was beyond the 'necessary' for a civilian scout."

Wend took a sip of the brandy. It had a strong, but pleasant taste. And the act helped provide an excuse for not commenting on Sterling's words immediately. He realized that the officer was, for some reason, intentionally trying to draw him out. He looked at the captain over the rim of his cup and saw that Sterling was staring back at him, a wry look on his face.

Then, when it became clear that Wend wasn't going to make an immediate reply, Sterling spoke again. "It also appears that you are something of a lothario. It is common knowledge in the battalion that you have been having a romance with one of the camp girls of the 77th. How does that square with your quest to retrieve this Philadelphia girl from the Indians? How do you plan to deal with the affections of two women?"

Wend felt a flash of resentment at Sterling's description of Mary. But he remembered he was dealing with a member of the aristocracy and steeled himself to hold his temper. He took another sip from the cup and carefully swallowed before answering. Then he looked directly into Sterling's eyes and spoke as steadily and deliberately as he could manage. "Sir, it doesn't much matter now. The army girl is dead, or soon will be, from a wound she got at Bushy Run. At any rate, all that matters for our purposes is that I feel a duty to try to give Miss Abigail Gibson a chance to resume life among our society. Right now she has no idea that I'm alive. We were in love when she was abducted four years ago and maybe we still are. But then we'll see about our feelings when and if we find her, won't we?"

Stirling looked at Wend for a long moment and then his mouth twisted into a tight smile. "Well said, Eckert. You are a cool one, aren't you? You've taken my probing without showing any emotion." The officer took another draw on his pipe. "If I may ask, how old are you?"

"I'll be twenty, in a few weeks time."

"Twenty? Well, you should learn to play whist or other games of chance. You'd be a great success at bluffing. I've never seen a face harder to read than yours."

Then Stirling nodded his head and pointed at Wend with the stem of his pipe. "All right, Eckert. It's clear that you are a brave man, accomplished beyond your years, and from what I hear, a damn good woodsman. And Bouquet made it clear he has great affection for you. So let me be straight with you, one man to another. I'll do everything in my power to help you if we come across that girl in the course of our travels. But I'll not let your personal interests hinder this mission in any way, nor will I alter our path through the wilderness to attempt to find her."

Wend drained his cup and felt the liquid burn its way down his throat. "I'd not think to ask anything more, Captain."

* * *

They came upon their first village the next day. It was a small town of the Delaware near the junction of the Beaver and the Ohio, nestled on the eastern bank of the smaller stream. Initially, the scouts observed the village from a hill, establishing the layout, approximate size, and level of activity. From their vantage point, they could see people moving around, undertaking normal chores, apparently not aware of the soldiers. Around the village were several fields and they could see people working at harvest.

The visit set the pattern for most of their subsequent encounters. Stirling, who had obviously thought out his moves in advance, then divided the force. One half-company and the scouts moved to enter the village. The second half-company and the pack train, under Eddington, was placed in a location where they could rapidly provide assistance if trouble broke out in the village.

Their entrance was made with calculated ceremony. Sergeant Leslie formed the half-company into marching order, and, Stirling in the lead, they paraded into the town with the bagpipes and drums playing. A highlander in the front rank carried a white flag. McKay, marching just behind Stirling, displayed the wampum belt prominently in his hands.

They arrived to find that the inhabitants had fled. The detachment had paraded into an empty village: Empty save for one elderly man, who stood impassively waiting for the British at the ceremonial fire ring of stones at the center of the village. Stirling halted the men in company front on the opposite side of the fire ring from the Indian. He then ordered the detachment to ground arms, another signal of non-hostile intent.

Joshua walked up beside the captain. "I've seen that man at council meetings at Pitt and Ligonier. He's undoubtedly the elder of this village. The other people have taken cover in the woods around us. I'll tell him we're here to talk."

Joshua spoke to the elder in Delaware. The Indian listened attentively, then nodded and spoke at some length in reply. "Captain, he says he is disturbed that the English have come brazenly marching into his home. They have scared his women and children into hiding. If their warriors were not away on the hunt, they would drive us away trailing blood. But he says that since we're here, he will listen to what the English officer has to say."

Stirling looked at the ranks of his half-company, an amused expression on his face. "Well, given the odds, I'd say he doesn't have much choice but to listen." He stared at the elder for a moment. "Right, Mr. Baird: Tell him I'm here representing the English King's great war-leader Bouquet, who vanquished their warriors at Bushy Run. Tell him that Bouquet, with a great army like the one Forbes used to beat the French in '58, will march into these lands next spring. He will be ready to crush the tribes and their towns in reprisal for their perfidy in attacking British forts and helpless farmers."

Joshua translated Stirling's words. The Elder maintained his expressionless visage, but looked at Stirling's face as the scout translated.

When Joshua had finished, Stirling continued. "Tell him that Bouquet and his great army will march to the Muskingum. If the leaders of the tribes assemble there to meet with him, and restrain their warriors, he will tell them on what terms peace can be made."

Baird translated and then looked back at Stirling, who continued, "Make it clear to him that if the tribes offer any resistance, Bouquet will destroy everything in his path as he marches inland. He will kill warriors, women, and the young ones, just as the Delaware have done in the English settlements. And then tell him to pass what we have said on to the king of his clan and the other villages in this area."

Baird told that to the elder. Then Baird said to Stirling, "He'll undoubtedly say something in reply; probably a long speech."

The Delaware nodded that he understood the Captain's words. He stood silent for a moment, looking back and forth between Stirling and the scout.

Joshua was right. The elder launched into long dissertation, amply punctuated with hand gestures. Baird summarized for Stirling: "He's gone through all the normal complaints of the tribes, Sir. They made a treaty with the British after the French war and the British have not kept their word. The forts along the border were supposed to be abandoned by now and there were to be no settlers beyond the Alleghenies. Instead, he says, Fort Pitt is bigger than ever and there are settlers clearing farms all through the forests. There are towns of whites growing around the forts. He says if the English had kept their word, there would have been no war. But the English Father has broken all his promises. The Delaware, on the other hand, have kept all the promises they made, at least until it became clear that the English wouldn't be true to the treaties."

Sterling nodded his head. "Sir William Johnson, the Indian Commissioner, and others would probably say the old man is right. But I'm a soldier, simply acting as a messenger. I'll let Bouquet and the diplomats sort this all out."

Joshua looked at Stirling. "Truth be told, Captain, there's a lot the Elder here has got right. But like you said, Sir, that ain't our business right now. For our purposes, he says he'll send a messenger to tell his king what you said. And he wishes we would leave now, so his people can come back and get on with their chores."

Stirling laughed, doffed his hat and made a half-bow to the Indian. Then he turned to Leslie. "All right, Sergeant. March the detachment off, smart like now."

As they marched out, the pipes and drums again playing, Wend looked back at the lone elder. Except now he wasn't alone. Another old man and several young boys stood beside him, and they were carrying weapons. They had apparently come out of the forest as soon as the highlanders had started to withdraw.

* * *

For the next three weeks they worked their way up the Beaver River and its tributary creeks. Joshua had been right; there were many villages, some quite large. They visited at least one village every day, and sometimes two or three. The next several visits they made were very similar to the first one at the Delaware town; most of the people fled at the approach of the soldiers, leaving only leaders to deal with the English. But after a few days, when word had run ahead that the soldiers were not making war on the villages, the townspeople stopped fleeing at the sound of the pipes. Instead, they crowded around as the column marched in and listened to the exchange between Stirling and their leaders. Young children eyed the highlanders curiously from behind the skirts of their mothers. The highlanders eyed the Indian women, who in their turn made a great show of ignoring the soldiers' stares.

Soon the march of the company became routine, the scouts ranging out ahead to find villages, plan the approach route, and identify a place for the reserve half-company to stand in support. Once a week, Stirling gave the company a day off, spending the day in camp, resting and taking care of their equipment. On those days, the scouts hunted for game to augment the army rations. It soon became clear why the men of the villages were absent, for they bagged only small animals. Clearly, the game had been thinned out by hunters from the villages in the area.

Wend's biggest concern was Joshua. After the first week, it became apparent that Baird was having trouble with his left hip and leg. Outwardly, the arrow wound had healed well, although there was a nasty scar on his hip. But Wend noticed a change in his stride; the lanky scout had always moved with an effortless, smooth, animal-like lope which ate up the miles. Now he showed a limp, and Wend frequently saw tightness around his jaw and beads of sweat around his brow as he walked, as if he was suppressing pain. It was most evident when going uphill or over obstacles where Baird had to lift the leg high or put his whole weight on the left side. Soon his discomfort became evident to the other scouts. No one talked about it, but they frequently exchanged glances with each other when Joshua was obviously in pain or laboring to keep the pace.

In time Stirling also recognized Baird's problem. He took an opportunity to discuss the veteran scout's condition with Wend, who provided him with the background on what had happened to Joshua at Bushy Run. Stirling nodded thoughtfully and said, "Baird's knowledge is essential to our mission. But we can't let him further injure that leg; he'll slow us down. So we'll have to use his knowledge and your legs. Eckert, you'll have to take the active role in leading the advance."

Stirling started keeping Joshua by his side much of the time as the column marched, which meant that the walking was easier than if he had been scouting on the point. He told Joshua that he wanted him nearby for advice as they pressed more deeply into the Ohio Country. And to Wend's surprise, Joshua made no protest, accepting the captain's explanation. It was tacit proof that Baird was admitting his limitations to himself. Every morning, Joshua would brief Wend on the lay of the land ahead from memory and tell him where he thought villages might be. At first Wend felt uncomfortable with this new responsibility, but he soon grew accustomed to reading the terrain and making decisions about the direction of the march. As the days passed, he developed an instinct regarding where the villages likely would be sited.

* * *

Wend, Donegal, and Kirkwood reached the crest of a tree covered ridge and found a small rock outcropping which provided a vantage point on the valley below. It was early afternoon and they had already visited one village in the morning. The expedition was in its fifth week; this was the fourth day since they had left the region of the Kuskuskies villages. Now they were heading eastward, back toward the Allegheny River. The company was behind them, marching on a well-used trail along a broad stream which Joshua called Slippery Rock Creek. It wound from valley to valley and they had found numerous villages nestled along the stream.

The three scouts laid aside their firearms and sat down to rest and scan this latest valley. Wend pulled out his water bottle and took a deep swallow of the clear liquid. He had just put the cork back when Kirkwood pointed his arm and said, "There's a town. Looks like a fairly small band."

Wend shifted his position so that he could look below. It was early November and the trees were nearly bare of leaves, which made their scouting job easier. He could see that the creek formed a looping bend on one edge of what was a bowl shaped cove among the hills. First he picked out three sizable clearings which were obviously fields and a smaller open plot which he figured was a vegetable garden. Then he saw the village itself, nestled inside the loop of the creek so that the stream flowed around on two sides of it. A wide strip of evergreen trees separated the lodges from the fields. As Wend watched, he could see people moving around in the village and a group of women and children walking out to the garden, some with baskets in their arms.

Donegal said, "Pretty little place isn't it?" He considered it a moment. "I wouldn't mind finding a little valley like that for my own farm."

Wend smiled to himself. Now that Donegal was out of the army, and due his 100 acres from the Crown, he was obsessed with speculating about his future farm. Around the campfire at night he incessantly talked about where in the colonies might be the best place for him to settle.

Kirkwood looked at Donegal. "Tell you what, Simon. 'Being as you like this place so much, why don't we just drop you off in the village? We'll give you some rations to get you started and you can stay right here and go native-like." He paused and winked at Wend. "Then at least we would 'na have to listen to your mouth runnin' on every night about your bloody farm. You'd be happy here and we'd get some peace and quiet."

"Will you listen to him, Wend?" Donegal shook his head. "Tell you the truth, I think he's just full of envy. Kirkwood here was eager to enlist in the 42nd, and now that he's done it he realizes what he's in for—spending the next five years or so under the tender mercies of dear Sergeant Leslie. Instead, he could be having his own place here in the colonies, living like the landed gentry back in the old country."

Wend grabbed his rifle and stood up. "Come on you two; let's go back and tell Stirling about this place. He'll want to waste no time going in and conducting his business so that we can get on to a good campsite tonight."

The scouts climbed down from the hill and intercepted the company on the trail about a quarter of a mile from the village. Wend made his report to Stirling. "A small village Captain; four long lodges and some other buildings. There are a few canoes along the creek. Not more than twenty-five or thirty people in sight."

Wend dropped to his knees and drew a map in the dirt, as Lieutenant Eddington, Sergeant Leslie, and the other scouts gathered around. "The village is on a point of land with the creek flowing on both sides. The trail goes right along the inland side of the village, so it will be an easy approach and departure for us, Captain. The fields are here, between the village and the ridges which form the valley. Here's your place for the reserve half-company." He pointed to the patch of evergreens which separated the fields from the village.

Stirling nodded. "Good work, Eckert." He turned to the group around him. "We'll go right in: Leslie, show the white flag, have McKay get the wampum belt, and call the drummer and piper to the head of the column."

And so, in the manner which had become routine, they paraded into the village, the scouts walking along after the half-company, the villagers gathering together in front of the fire ring. They were soon joined by the group Wend had seen working in the vegetable garden.

The were met by three elders, standing in front of the ceremonial fire ring and next to a typical trophy rack decorated with scalps and other prizes of war which the band obviously displayed with great pride. Wend stood beside Joshua as the detachment went through its drill of forming company front across from the elders and then grounding arms. He looked around and noted that there were two or three warriors present in the village; one of them stood near the elders, as if he were part of the leadership. While he was considering this, Joshua nudged him in the arm. "In case you ain't aware of it, Sprout, this is a Mingo village."

Joshua walked up to where Stirling stood to serve as translator. As he started the formalities of greeting the leaders, Wend scanned the Indians. Most were huddled together behind the elders. Wend saw no sign of Abigail. Then he turned to the group which had just come in from the garden.

And almost immediately encountered the piercing blue eyes and golden hair he had dreamed of for four years. Abigail stood near the side of a lodge, a basket in one hand. Her blond hair, bleached by the sun until it was even lighter than before, was pulled tight around her head and tied behind in a single braid which hung all the way to her waist. Her face was tanned by the long days in the open, which made the blue of her eyes stand out even more than he remembered. She wore a long gray-toned shift of coarse material, belted at her waist. Over her shoulders was a kind of shawl made from part of a trade blanket. Beside her stood a little boy and an even smaller girl, who clung to her hand.

Wend's heart stopped and he sucked in his breath. Abigail was staring at the ranks of highlanders. Presently she shifted her eyes to where he stood slightly apart from them. For a moment, Abigail examined him with detached interest. Then he saw her eyes widen, her mouth open in astonishment, and he knew that she had recognized him. He put his rifle in the crook of his arm and walked towards where she stood.

Stirling caught sight of Wend's movement, an unexpected break in their routine. His eyes followed Wend with an irritated look and then he, too, saw Abigail. Wend watched the officer's eyebrows rise as he quickly took in her appearance. Then Stirling turned his gaze to Wend and cocked his head as if asking a question. Wend nodded back to the captain and continued on his way towards Abigail.

As he approached, the little girl made a fearful face and snuggled closer to her mother. Abigail bent over and said something in the Mingo language which quieted the child.

Wend stopped in front of Abigail. She slowly shook her head in disbelief and looked for a moment like she was going to say something. But, remaining quiet, she quickly put the basket down and then stood up with her free hand over her mouth.

Wend had long wondered what he would say if he ever found Abigail and had never been able to work out the proper words. But suddenly words came to him. "Well, Abigail, it looks like for once I've managed to leave you speechless."

"Oh, Wend! My God, it is you! I had no idea, no hope! I saw you dead and scalped on the road with my own eyes!" She was clearly in shock. "How can you be here now?"

He smiled tightly at her. "It turns out that I'm pretty hard to kill, Abigail." Wend took her by the arm and gently led her to a log nearby where she sat down. Her little girl crawled up into her lap and the boy sat beside her, his eyes fixated on the stranger.

Wend sat down and looked at her. Up close, he could see the signs of the life she had been leading. Her face was weathered and there were permanent lines around her eyes and mouth. Her hands were dirty and the fingers were scarred from working with knives and handling crops in the fields. He saw that her teeth were stained, probably from chewing hides to soften them. And her body and clothing smelled of wood smoke and animal grease.

But above all her fundamental beauty remained and took his breath away in the same way it had at Harris' Ferry.

Abigail reached out and took his hand, pressing it tightly.

He said to her, "I was dead for all purposes, but soldiers saved me just as the last of my life was flowing away."

He saw a spark of memory in her eyes. "Now I understand! The Mingoes saw the campfires of soldiers in the distance the night we were captured. They were afraid they would come after us when they found the massacre. That's why they killed Elise and fled as fast as possible westward. But those same soldiers must have found you."

Wend nodded and motioned toward Stirling's men. "Yes, highlanders like these discovered me."

She looked over at the company, then back at Wend. "Are you a soldier now?"

"No, after the attack, I was taken in by a minister and his wife. I live with them at a place called Sherman Mill, in a valley north of Carlisle." He looked into her eyes. "I'm scouting for the army. It was my way to find you." He paused for a moment. "But we know a lot about what has happened to you and how you live. Franklin told us; he came back with Ayika, and he lives with us now."

"Franklin made it back and found you? That seems incredible." She looked at him with all of the sharpness he remembered in her.

"I know it seems unlikely. But Franklin and Ayika stopped at a trading post near Fort Pitt. And because it was unusual to see a black Indian, word was sent over to Pitt. That scout"—he pointed to Joshua—"Is the brother of my stepmother, and was at Pitt when the news arrived. So he knew Franklin's story and was able to find them on the trail east of the river and bring them to Sherman Mill."

Wend squeezed her hand again. "But the important thing is that I'm here now and these soldiers are ready to help me take you and your children back to Pennsylvania." He paused a moment, framing his next words. "And back to a life with me, if you still share the feeling we had at Fort Loudoun and on Forbes Road."

Abigail returned the pressure of his hand. "Wend, of course I feel the same way about you! Never doubt that! There has been this huge hole in my heart because I thought you were dead. I live with a man—he's the warrior standing by the elders—who I can never love. It's like an arranged marriage such as they do among royalty in the old country: A marriage for the purpose of producing children. But he treats me kindly, more kindly than I've seen some men treat their wives back in Philadelphia. And I do respect him. He's the war captain of the village and he does what he thinks is best for his people. But I could never love him in the way we loved each other."

"Then gather up you children and you all can leave with us. You can come back to Sherman Mill and the life we both have longed to lead."

"God, Wend, how I have dreamed about going back to Pennsylvania." She paused, and her eyes stared into the distance. "Do you know what one of my most cherished dreams is? It often comes to me during the cold nights of winter, when the freezing wind is blowing right through the cracks in the lodge and my children are shivering and cuddling against me trying to keep warm. I think of being in a carriage with you back in Philadelphia, dressed in a beautiful gown and a warm coat. I hold on to your arm as we ride down a paved street to an elegant tavern and there we have a marvelous supper: A meal I didn't have to cook, served to me by somebody else."

She turned to Wend and tears were running down her cheeks. "But my love, I can't go back to the old life."

"For God's sake, Abigail; why not?"

"Wend, I've thought about it, over and over. Our society would never accept me; I've slept with a man they consider a savage. And worse, I've had his children. And think about the children. If I take them back, they'll always be treated with disdain as half-casts. When they're older they will realize that people are looking down their noses at them. I can't subject them to that. Here, at least, they are accepted as full members of their society. And there's something more, Wend," she paused and looked up at him. "I'm carrying another child; another child of Wolf Claw's."

He looked down at the girl in her lap, who clearly showed her Indian heritage, with black hair, brown eyes, and dark skin. Then he looked at the boy. And suddenly he realized there was something different about him, something he hadn't noticed because he had been so focused on Abigail. The boy's hair was brown, not black. And his eyes were blue!

Abigail saw him staring at the boy. "Yes, Wend, he's your son. Or rather, our son." You left me with a child, who will always be my reminder of our love."

Wend sat, stunned for a moment at the revelation. Then he looked at Abigail, and felt his hope fading. Desperate, he said, "Abigail, I don't give a damn about what people think of you or the children. All that matters to me is that we are together. We can go to some place where our history isn't known; Virginia or perhaps Carolina. We can be a family. You know that I will treat all of your children like my own! And it's even more important that you come with me now that I know that we've had a child."

"Wend, I have no doubt you would be wonderful with the children. But that's not enough. Think clearly! Society would always look askance at us. And even our white son would come under suspicion, having lived with the Mingoes." She paused a moment. "But if I'm honest, I must admit something else."

She squeezed his arm tightly. "Over the years, I have come to be part of these people. I have shared the good times and bad with them and have become accepted as a full member of their tribe. I serve a necessary purpose as the doctor for this village, and indeed for villages all over this part of the country. You may not understand this, but that has come to provide me with great personal gratification. There are men, women, and children who are alive today because of what I have done." She looked up at him. "Wend, they think of me as a sort of priestess with a magical touch." She paused. "In fact, that's what my name, Orenda, means."

Wend looked at her eyes, and saw the pride there. "I think I understand what you are saying," he said reluctantly.

"And there's more, Wend. In the Mingo culture women have a great role to play in decision making. I'm a member of the woman's council. We have a say in all the major decisions of the tribe. The men don't make war, or leave on a long hunt, or move the village to a new place unless we approve their plans." She paused and thought about the right words. "But I also have another role, something no one else here can provide. Wend, these people carry impassive faces, yet down deep all of them feel desperation because they know that their way of life is in great danger. They see waves of settlers coming over the mountains and fear what it means. Since I come from that world, I can advise them on how Europeans think and how to deal with them. So you must realize that I have important functions here that I could never have back in our English society. And Wend, I have gotten accustomed to that role. I'm not sure that I could go back to a life where women are excluded from being a part of anything that really matters."

Wend felt frustration and anger welling up in him. He spoke to her sharply, "Abigail, I can understand that you feel gratification at being a useful member of this village and helping to make decisions. But my God, these are the people who killed your father and my family! You've seen how cruel they can be to their captives; you know full well that's why Franklin made his escape. And Franklin told me how you cried for days after they murdered Elise. Has your heart been hardened so much by this life," he hesitated a moment, "And by your obvious affection for this band, that you can forget about that?"

Abigail hugged his arm with both of hers and put her head on his shoulder. Tears were pouring down her face. "Oh Wend, Wend, don't hate me! Sometimes I feel so torn up inside about that part of what has happened. And you must believe that I refuse to participate in what they do to the captives." She shook her head as if trying to be free of something. Then she looked up at him with pleading eyes. "I know it must be hard, but please try to accept my feelings, and who I have become." She lifted her chin, defiantly challenging him. "If you really love me, you'll be able to do it." Then suddenly her countenance turned from one of defiance to desperation. She grasped his arm even more tightly and hugged herself against him. "Wend, I need to know that someone from my old life understands me and respects what I am doing. You are the only one who can supply that comfort to me."

With great effort, Wend throttled the turbulence he felt inside. He looked at the girl and thought about all she had said. He had to admit that she was right about what the children faced back in the English world.

Particularly after all the recent raids by war parties and the hundreds of people killed. There would be great hatred against Indians and the children might become a target. Suddenly he saw the face of Lazarus Stewart and remembered the night at the Phoenix Tavern when he had harassed Charlie Sawak. Then he thought of Abigail's satisfaction about participating in the life of the Mingo village. Out of the recesses of his mind, he recalled her words long ago beside the stream at Chamber's Mills, when she revealed her disappointment at realizing she could never be a doctor. So the tragedy of the massacre had, in an unlikely twist of fate, enabled her to achieve that desire.

Wend gritted his teeth and stood up. "I guess there's nothing more to say. Except that I will love you until the day I die. And don't ever doubt my respect for you and the choices you have made."

Abigail looked up at him reflectively, bit her lip, and said, "You know, in the end, it turns out that your Mother was right: It may have been for the wrong reason, but she somehow understood we would never be together."

There was a silence and Wend shifted the rifle in his hands. As he did so Abigail stared closely at the firelock.

"My God, that's Wolf Claw's rifle; I mean the rifle which he took off you at the caravan. He lost it at the battle with the British, when he was shot in the arm."

Wend looked down at his rifle, then at her. "Yes, I found it lying on the battlefield, right after we chased all the warriors away."

Abigail nodded. "He was hit right at the end of the battle. Then the British charged and he had to leave the rifle. He barely escaped. I'm treating his wound; he still can't use his right arm much. That's why he's here instead of with the other men at the hunting grounds."

Wend cradled the firelock in his arm. "I was in that charge, Abigail. And before that I killed at least one warrior of this band." He looked at her directly. "And I tell you this now: If I ever get Wolf Claw in my sights he'll be a dead man. Now there is something you'll have to understand about me."

Wend looked over at the elders and Wolf Claw. He could see that the talks with Stirling were wrapping up. He knew their time was short. He looked at Wolf Claw again, examining his face. Suddenly a shock ran through his body: He was looking at the face he remembered from the day of the massacre; the face of the Mingo he had seen in the woods and which he had so many times conjured up for use as a target at shooting matches!

Beyond Wolf Claw was the village trophy rack. Wend could see scalps hanging there and an idea suddenly came to him. He turned to Abigail and motioned toward the rack. "Are my family's scalps hanging there?"

She nodded; a questioning look came to her face.

"Will you point them out to me? I want to take them back and give them a proper burial."

Abigail looked at the rack and then back at him. Slowly her face broke into a smile. "Yes, I'll help you. And take my father's with you. That would make me very happy. At least I won't have to see them anymore when I walk through the village."

Wend took her by the arm and they walked toward the fire ring and Wolf Claw. She carried the little girl in her other arm and the boy came along, holding onto her skirt. Stirling, the elders, and Wolf Claw turned to watch as they approached, puzzlement showing in their faces. Wend stopped in front of Wolf Claw, staring him right in the eyes. Wolf Claw looked at Wend, then at his wife, her hand still in Wend's. Confusion and anger came over his face. Wend forced himself to smile at the warrior and then ostentatiously shifted the position of his rifle in the crook of his arm. Wolf Claw looked down at the rifle and recognition flowed into his eyes; recognition followed by a look of pure hatred. Wend saw his good hand clasp into a fist and the warrior's face start turning red.

Wend thought: *If he's mad now, wait until he sees what I do next.* He turned to Abigail. "Tell him his eyes don't deceive him; that is his rifle and explain how I got it."

Abigail translated and then said, "I told him that and I also told him you are the man who made the rifle and the one he thought he killed the day he captured me. And then I said God had raised you up to avenge the people he killed that day." She looked at Wend and grinned. "I thought you would like that part."

Wend laughed out loud. "Indeed, Abigail. Now tell him that as the start of this avenging business, I'm taking the scalps of my family from him."

She spoke in Mingo and suddenly the faces of Wolf Claw, the elders, and the two other warriors exploded in rage. One of the elders raised his arm and shouted something. Joshua had also understood her words, and Wend heard him suck in his breath and say: "For Christ sake, Sprout!"

Strangely, amidst the agitation all around, Wend felt a great calmness flow over him. He turned to Abigail and asked, "Can you point out the right scalps?"

She pointed out all four of his family's scalps and then her father's. Wend pulled out his knife in a flash, and quickly cut down the first, dropping it into his haversack. Suddenly there were more shouts from the elders and the warriors and a wave of anguished cries from the crowd of women. Several villagers moved toward Wend as if to stop him. He looked at Wolf Claw and saw that the warrior had a fierce look on his face and had pulled his knife out of its sheath with his good hand. Then, brandishing the knife, he took a step toward Wend.

Wend turned to face Wolf Claw. Each of them stood frozen, knife in hand. Wend felt a flash of desire to plunge his blade into the Mingo's heart. But he controlled himself and instead looked into the warrior's face and said, "If you weren't wounded, I'd finish you now." Abigail didn't even attempt to translate but Wend was sure Wolf Claw had understood.

Meanwhile, Stirling sprang into action. He whipped his sword out of its scabbard, at the same time ordering "Prepare to Fix Bayonets!" In the instant the men had complied, he called, "Fix Bayonets!" Twenty-three blades sprang from their frogs, followed by the metal clanking as the highlanders slid them onto the barrels and tightened them on the lugs. Stirling's next order, "Charge Bayonets!" was followed by the echoing "Ha!" from twenty-three throats as the muskets were leveled.

All the Mingoes immediately froze and stared at the massed bayonets pointed in their direction. It became deathly silent throughout the village. Wend swiftly retrieved the remaining four scalps.

He had just finished when Abigail called out. "Wend, there's one more you want to take. Your scalp is also hanging there. Wend looked to where she pointed and felt a chill to realize that he was looking at his own hair and a circular part of his scalp. He reached up and cut it down. As he touched the scalp, an uncontrollable shiver passed through his body.

Then Wolf Claw spoke and Wend could feel the seething hatred in his words. Abigail translated, her voice wavering. "He says someday you and he will meet when there are no soldiers to protect you. And then he will smash your head with his war club and rip out your cowardly heart with his knife and bring the rest of your scalp back to the trophy rack."

Wend waited a moment to harden the look on his face and find the right words. "Tell him that he will never again be close enough to take my scalp." He brandished his rifle in front of Wolf Claw's eyes. "Tell him I am a German Jaeger and this is my weapon. When the time comes, I will take my vengeance at long distance and he will never hear the ball which blows his head apart. He will die like a mindless dog, not a warrior."

As they spoke, Stirling, his sword on his shoulder, had walked up close to Wend. The captain looked around at Wolf Claw, who still had a look of anguish on his face but had put his knife back into the sheath, and then at Abigail, giving her a charming smile. Then he leaned over to Wend, and in a stage whisper everyone could hear, said with an air of exaggerated nonchalance, "Mr. Eckert, I know Colonel Bouquet told us to make a display of arrogance, but I dare say you have carried the idea to the very limit." Stirling looked around at the furious faces of the warriors and elders and made a quick wink to Wend. "I believe it is superfluous to say that we have overstayed our welcome here."

Wend nodded and he heard Abigail laughing behind him. Stirling looked at her and the children around her. Then he asked Wend, "Are we taking anyone with us?"

"No, she'll stay here. I'd like just a moment with her and then we can leave."

Stirling nodded. "Very well then, make it brief."

Wend turned to Abigail. He felt a lump growing in his throat. "Will you be all right? Will Wolf Claw take revenge on you for helping me?"

"He'll be angry for a while. But nothing will happen." She grinned impishly. "This is not the first time I've defied him, and it won't be the last. Besides, they lost four warriors at the battle. My children—and the one on the way—are too important to the survival of this village. So don't worry over me."

Wend reached out his hand, and she took it. Their eyes met and Wend could clearly see her tears. Then he had a thought. "The last night on Forbes Road, we made your father furious. Now we've done it to your husband. It seems we're fated to cause trouble!"

Abigail smiled at his joke. "Perhaps you're right. But believe this, Wend: Knowing that you are alive will sustain me. Every morning beside the fire, when I see the sun rise over the horizon, I'll know you're out there somewhere to the east. And I'll always cherish our love and the time we had together."

She dropped her hand. Went felt wetness around his eyes and over his cheeks. He quickly walked back beside the ranks of the highlanders.

Stirling, still standing near Wolf Claw, slid his sword back into the scabbard. He gave the warrior a nod and a touch of his hat. Then a devilish smile came over his face. He turned to face Abigail. With a flourish, he doffed his highland bonnet and swept it across his chest, at the same time bowing deeply to Abigail. He looked up at her with a gallant smile and said, "Captain Thomas Stirling, of His Majesty's 42nd Foot. Your servant, Ma'am."

Abigail, her face already red from the tears, flushed even more. A look of surprise and pleasure came over her face. But she remembered her manners and dropped a perfect curtsey to Stirling as if they were in some ballroom at Philadelphia. "It is my pleasure at meeting you, sir."

As they marched out, Wend looked back and saw that Abigail was still watching them, the baby girl in her arms and the boy at her side. She stood there tall and straight, the afternoon sun behind her, framing her graceful body and accentuating the color of her hair. And in that instant he understood that Abigail Gibson of Philadelphia was now but a memory; the girl he had known and once possessed had from this day forward truly become Orenda, The Golden Priestess of the Mingo.

CHAPTER 25

Vengeance on the Allegheny

That night, after they had finished their rations and the men were relaxing around the fires, McKay brought word that Stirling wanted to see Wend. Wend walked over, expecting that the captain wanted to make plans for the morrow's march. He arrived at the officers' fire, which was separated from the others by a short distance, to see that Lieutenant Eddington was not there and that Stirling sat alone, a pewter cup in his hand. He motioned for Wend to sit down.

After Wend had settled himself, Stirling leaned over and handed him a cup and then poured some liquor into it. He looked at the bottle, holding it up to the light. "Damn, Eckert. Things are getting serious! This is the very last of the brandy. It's clear that this expedition is going to have to end pretty quickly now." He grinned at Wend, amused at his own joke.

Wend sipped the drink and felt the tingle of it going down his throat. The two men sat for a few moments savoring the libation and the warmth of the fire amidst the chill of the November night.

Finally, Stirling broke the silence. "I called you over because I wanted to see how you were bearing up after today's events. Clearly, things did not turn out as you would have desired."

Wend sighed. After leaving the Mingo village he had focused intensely on his scouting duties as a way to avoid thinking about what had occurred. But as they made camp and night settled around them, he could not avoid the sense of loneliness and regret which had descended upon him as a result of Abigail's decision. He had pulled himself into a shell of silence, avoiding participation in the scouts' usual evening banter. The others, aware of his misery, had left him alone.

But now Stirling had brought the issue directly into play. "No, Captain. I'd be lying if I didn't admit that my worst fears were realized. I knew that

Abigail had children, which would complicate matters. And I worried that she would no longer share the love I maintained for her. But I have always thought that if she could be given the opportunity to safely leave with her children she would grasp the opportunity, particularly if she was still in love with me. But I hadn't ever reckoned that she would actually decide to remain behind even when professing her affection for me."

Stirling eyed his cup a moment. "Eckert, I have to confess that when Colonel Bouquet told me about your quest to find this girl, my initial reaction was that you were acting irrationally; an obsessed man refusing to face reality. I thought that you should have long since gotten on with your life. But I tell you this now with all my heart: Having seen the breathtaking beauty and spirit of that girl, I believe that had I been in your position, I would have pursued her to the very ends of the earth."

Wend looked up at the captain. The officer smiled and raised his cup. "Here's a toast to the memory of an elegant lady, Eckert."

Wend nodded and raised his cup. Both men silently took a sip of the brandy.

"One additional question, Eckert: The young boy at the girl's side. I saw him only briefly, but it was evident to me that he didn't have Indian features. Is the boy yours?"

"Yes, that's what Abigail said. And considering his age, it would be likely indeed."

Stirling made a face and shook his head. "Good Lord, Eckert; it would have been hard for me to leave my son behind. That must have been a bad moment for you."

Wend nodded. "It was a shock to learn that I had a child. And you are right; when Abigail told me she wanted to stay with the Mingoes, I briefly had the idea of taking the boy with us. But in almost the same moment I realized that a child of that age should be with his mother. And the thought of the terror he would have experienced at leaving her side immediately made me drop the idea. But now I have another regret; the realization that I'll never see my son grow up." Wend grimaced and pounded his free hand on the ground. "And in the tenseness of the moment I didn't even remember to ask his name."

They were both silent for a long moment. Then Stirling topped off both of their cups and looked sadly at the empty bottle. "Damn, that's it. No more brandy! Eckert, you'll have to get me some of that backcountry whiskey I know the men are carrying!" He laughed to himself. "As a matter of fact, over the last few days, I've been talking with Baird as we marched. He is a droll fellow, isn't he?" The captain smiled at Wend. "And we spent some time reflecting on your situation. Baird relates that you seem to have a way with the young ladies. I believe the way he put it was, 'Girls like to drape themselves over Eckert'." Stirling grinned broadly and took a sip of his drink. "A rather desirable attribute, I might take the liberty of saying. One which would seem to bode well for your future interests in that direction."

Wend shook his head. "Joshua does tend to exaggerate."

"But it does seem that you've had bad luck. And not just with this girl Abigail. Baird told me the details about the army girl you were with; Mary Fraser, I believe it is. He made it clear that she wasn't any ordinary camp follower, as I had originally believed. In fact, he spoke about her with a rather touching fondness; a fondness echoed by Donegal and Kirkwood. It seems the girl was intelligent and beautiful in her own way; the darling of the 77th."

Wend smiled at Stirling. "She was indeed a lovely young girl." He started to speak again, intending to tell the captain more about Mary, but Stirling held up his hand to quiet him.

"Hold on; I want to tell you something which may surprise you and put all this in perspective. Colonel Bouquet and you have something in common, at least in matters of the heart. For a long time, he was courting a woman in Philadelphia; a certain Miss Anne Willing, a comely woman of exceeding charm and some wealth. While far younger than he, she showed clear receptiveness to his advances. In fact, he had given his heart to her and confided to friends that he would ask for her hand the next time he visited Philadelphia. But it turned out that Miss Willing was ultimately *not* willing. She threw him over for another, younger man. And what's more, she did it without bothering to inform him. Bouquet had to find it out by letter from a friend of his while he was soldering out here. It was a devastating blow to him. That happened last year and he's been dealing with it quietly, very manfully, ever since." Stirling paused for effect.

Wend was shocked. "I had no idea, Sir."

"I dare say you didn't. But it was all over the whispering set in Philadelphia. Think of the embarrassment to Bouquet when he faced society on his trips back to the city. But the point is this: Even bearing that burden he didn't let disappointment interfere with his duties. Instead, he bore down and won the most significant victory over the tribes our army has ever achieved."

Wend nodded, not sure where the captain was headed.

"My purpose in telling you the story, Eckert, is just this: I need to know if you can you handle your disappointment with the same courage that Bouquet did. You must be in top mental form to act as my leading scout for the rest of this mission. We can't have you wallowing in self-pity over Miss Gibson's decision while the rest of the company is depending on you. So you need to tell me right now if you are up to it." Stirling cocked his head and sat looking at Wend with questioning eyes and a crooked smile on his lips.

Wend felt anger churning inside. He sat up and slammed his cup to the ground, ready to lash out at Stirling. But then he got control of his emotions and said, as slowly and precisely as he could manage, "Captain, I'm going to tell you this straight out: I don't care if you are a high-born officer. I feel insulted that you would ask me that question. I've been content to think that you've been satisfied with my service so far. But if you think that I can't keep my personal problems to myself, you've got another damn thing coming." He thought for a second. "You army officers don't have a monopoly on self-control. So just watch how I perform my duties from here to Pitt."

Stirling's face broke into a grin. "Marvelous, Eckert, just bloody marvelous!" He reached over and gave Wend a pat on the shoulder. "I was hoping that's how you would react, but needed to probe your state of mind." He smiled engagingly. "Forgive me if I was a little rough on you." He hesitated, then said, "But more importantly, now that this matter of Miss Gibson is settled, you must move forward. I know you are a gunsmith from near Carlisle. A man your age, secure in his trade, should be starting a family. There must be some suitable women there for you."

"You're right, Sir. It is time for me to go back to Sherman Mill and pick up the pieces of my business." Wend thought for a moment. "And indeed, our talk here tonight has made me think about what I'm looking for in a woman. Until now, I've followed my heart, and it seems that has led me only to a dead end. So, Captain, from here on, I'll be looking for a practical situation with a good woman. There are more considerations in picking the right woman than simple emotion."

"Well, Eckert, that's a reasonable enough conclusion." Stirling winked at Wend. "At least about the settling on a woman." Then suddenly he became serious. "But listen *very* carefully: You are totally wrong about the dead end part. Your pursuit of your heart's desire has led you to something else, something you should cherish: The admiration of many men who know what you did on Bouquet's campaign. And over the last few weeks, you certainly have earned my respect."

Wend flushed at the compliment. But before he could respond, Stirling said, "Now let's have McKay round up Mr. Baird and we'll plot ourselves a course to the last of the villages we must visit and then through this wilderness back to Fort Pitt."

* * *

After returning to the scouts' fire, Wend wrapped himself in his blankets and lay looking into the flames. The discussion with Stirling had stirred his mind about the women in his life and about his future. He thought about the girls who had moved him, comparing Abigail and Mary. Until now, he had focused on the necessity of making a choice between them. But events had made that choice for him. And as he reflected on them, he suddenly realized that what was important for him to think about now was not their differences, which were many and obvious, but their similarities. What was it about both of them which had interested him so much? They were both physically attractive. As Stirling had said, Abigail was flat out beautiful; beautiful in a classic way. She would take men's breath away whether in a ball room, wearing satins and jewelry, or like today, in rough clothing in the middle of the wilderness. Mary Fraser had been pretty, but in a totally different, rough-cut way. Both were intelligent. Abigail was cool, perceptive, sophisticated. Mary lusted to absorb learning in the manner of a sponge, excited about every experience the world had to offer. Then it hit him—despite their differences, they did have something in common: They were both strong, independent women, prepared to face the challenges of life on their own terms. And in that instant, it came to him that in both cases that attribute was what had attracted him to them.

As the heat of the fire brought on drowsiness, Wend's thoughts turned to the girls of Sherman Valley, mentally comparing them to Abigail and Mary. He thought of Elizabeth McClay and her possessive, calculating advances, her readiness to say or do anything to endear herself to him. Then there was Ellen McCartie, whom he admired for her honesty, charitable personality, and warm smile. But both seemed to have a single objective; marriage, children, and a comfortable home. Neither girl seemed to have the driving personal goals of either Mary or Abigail.

Then a startling thought occurred to him: The only girl who seemed to have the same spark was—of all people—Peggy McCartie. Although

ostensibly tied to Bratton, she certainly had a mind of her own and an undeniable streak of independence. On a couple of occasions, she had made clear
to Wend her desire to leave Sherman Mill for a more exciting life. He had
long suspected that her reputed activity as a tart had the objective of obtain-
ing her own financial resources to guarantee her ability to leave the village.
And there was no denying that the tall, blue eyed, raven haired girl was as
beautiful as either Abigail or Mary.

As sleep closed in, Wend drifted off, amused at the irony that, on this
most consequential of days in his life, the day he finally resolved his quest to
find Abigail, his last thoughts were about the fiancée of his greatest enemy
and the girl who had angrily berated him on his decision to march with
Bouquet's expedition.

* * *

The three scouts stopped on the trail as they reached the crest of a high
ridge, grounded their firelocks and, looking eastward, were rewarded by a
dramatic view of the Allegheny River. It was the second morning after they
had left the Mingo village; Stirling's company was about a half-mile behind
them on the trail.

Wend had been briefed by Baird on what to expect during the day's march,
and so was not surprised by the vista. He said to his two companions, "The old
town of Kittanning should be across the river a couple of miles up to the north,
and Joshua said there's a small Delaware village just out of sight down-stream.
There's a trail along the river which will be our way southward back to Pitt."

Kirkwood asked, "What else is supposed to be here along this side of the
river?"

Wend looked at the corporal. "Nothing else, Bob. At least Baird didn't
tell me to expect anything more."

Kirkwood shrugged and pointed toward the river almost directly ahead
of them. "Well, someone's down there close to the river bank."

Donegal chimed in: "And making themselves at home. By the amount of
smoke, that's a right comfortable fire they got."

Wend looked where Kirkwood had indicated and saw a column of smoke
that he hadn't noticed. He puzzled for a moment. "Perhaps some travelers
stopped along the river or maybe there's a small village built since Baird's last
visit?"

"Maybe. But it could also be a war party just coming back from the settlement area," Kirkwood said. "You know Baird has been worried about us bumping into something like that. They'll 'na be knowin' that we're here on a peaceful mission."

Donegal nodded. "Whatever it is, it looks to be just where we have to go to find the river path."

Wend made up his mind. "Your right. We need to go down and investigate—as stealthily as possible. Stirling may want to find a way to avoid that place." He picked up his rifle and led out down the path toward the river.

It took them a half-hour to make their approach, moving quietly in single file. When Wend judged that they were only a couple of hundred yards from the smoke column, he noticed that the path led up another, much lower ridge. He stopped and motioned the other two scouts to join him.

"If we climb the hill, we should be able to look down at that fire from a fairly short distance. At least close enough to get a good idea of who is there." Wend led the way off the path and the three of them crept forward with the practiced silence gained from weeks of scouting. Still, it was slow work because all the trees and bushes except for patches of evergreens were barren of leaves, and effective cover was hard to find. Even with their best effort, Wend realized that any enemy looking for them would have found it an easy task.

But no one was looking for them. They reached the low ridge's crest to find that they had a clear view of the river and the site of the fire, which was in the center of a substantial clearing less than thirty yards from the water. The three of them took shelter on their knees in a small grove of pines. What they saw was not a village, nor a war party camped on their way back from beyond the Allegheny Mountains. What they saw was twenty or twenty-five warriors busily engaged in commerce with a group of traders. Beyond that, along the river, was a row of canoes pulled up on the bank. Piled up around the fire were many pelts brought by the Indians. And next to the traders' canoes were supplies of goods: Blankets, hats, clothing, and wooden boxes containing metal implements. But Wend's eyes were immediately drawn to the numerous kegs of gunpowder stacked up between the riverbank and the fire.

Kirkwood quietly remarked, "This place is busier than the market at Carlisle."

"Lord Above!" Donegal whispered. "Will you look at that? There's enough powder there to keep several war parties busy all next summer!"

But the highlander's words were wasted on Wend. For he had eyes only for the two white men who were running the trading activity: Ross Kinnear and Flemming! *By God, he had caught Grenough's men in action!* Wend felt rage sweeping over him. Then, to his surprise, another white man appeared from behind a group of bushes close to the canoes; a man he had never seen. He was dressed in a short green coat, which went only a little below his hips, breeches, and riding boots. He was hatless and displayed a thick shock of red hair, redder even than Mary's had been.

Donegal tugged on Wend's sleeve, interrupting his thoughts. "We need to get back to the company and tell Stirling about this—right now!"

Kirkwood started to get up from his knees. "Simon's right; its time to get moving. Someone's liable to spot us."

But Wend had already made up his mind about what he had to do: *There would be no wasting of this opportunity.* He said quietly, "I'm not leaving yet."

Steadying his rifle on a small branch in front of him, he cocked the hammer and pulled the set trigger. Then he trained his sights on Flemming, who stood talking with a warrior no more than eighty yards away from where Wend knelt. It was an easy shot; he squeezed the trigger and watched the trader's head explode in a spray of blood which spattered over the Indian.

Donegal looked at Wend in stunned surprise. "For God's Sake! For God's Sake, Eckert! Are you out of your mind?"

Wend pulled the loaded rifle from the shocked highlander's hand and gave him the empty firelock. Then he stood up and left his hiding place so that he was in plain view of the assemblage below. All the men there were still frozen, looking at Flemming's crumpled body as it lay on the ground. Then, en masse, they turned toward the hill, looking upward to see where the lethal shot had come from. Ross Kinnear stood by a tree, holding a pelt in his hands which a warrior had just handed to him. He looked up the hill directly into Wend's eyes.

Wend shouted at the top of his lungs: "Ross Kinnear! My name is Wend Eckert and you're a dead man!" He saw the trader's mouth open in astonishment. Then Wend put the rifle to his shoulder and fired. The ball went right into Kinnear's mouth, blowing his entire jaw off, then passing out the rear of his neck and kicking up dust from the ground behind him.

Kinnear fell to the ground, the pelt lying across the still twitching body. The Indians around him took whatever cover that could be found. But Wend saw that the red-haired man was still standing transfixed in disbelief near the row of canoes. He grabbed the musket from Kirkwood and aimed it at the third trader. He had no hope of hitting him, but intended to at least shake him up. The Brown Bess jerked against his shoulder and a spray of dirt erupted beside the red-head. In panic, he ran to the row of canoes, jumped into one, and paddled frantically out into the stream.

As Wend stood watching the canoe, he heard the quiet, unemotional voice of Kirkwood beside him. "Wend, my lad, do you think we could be leaving now? The people down below seem a little agitated."

Donegal, who had now calmed down, added, "Aye, that's the truth. They're leaving cover and picking up their weapons and I don't think they're intending to come up here just to tell you how much they admire your shooting."

Wend was still staring at the man in the canoe. He shook himself out of the trance which had overcome him and took a final look at the scene below. "Yes, we'd better run."

Donegal turned and ran for the path, saying, "Now there's the first sensible thing you've said in the last few minutes."

They crashed through the brush for several minutes and then were out to the hard-packed trail, heading back toward Stirling's company. Wend glanced behind and saw several warriors appear on the ridge crest where they had stood, less than 100 yards behind them. There was no attempting to reload; they would have to slow down too much, even if they did it on the move. He took quick inventory: After his frenzy of shooting, the only loaded weapons they had were a pistol in each of their belts.

Donegal, who was leading, turned his head and shouted, "Why don't we try hiding in the bush after we go over the next ridge?"

Wend shook his head. "No, the only chance is to get back to the company. Just keep running!"

Kirkwood called from behind, "Wend's got it right. The bush is too thin this time of year. We'd not find a good hiding spot and, anyway, they'd see where we turned off the path!"

All three men stopped talking and concentrated on running as fast as the conditions on the trail would allow. They were spurred on by a stream of shouts and whoops from their pursuers. Finally, after what seemed an eternity, but which Wend later calculated could have been not more than seven or eight minutes, they met the advance guard of four highlanders casually advancing along the path. Donegal screamed word of the pursuit to the corporal in charge, and all seven men ran as a group back to the main body.

Seeing the men running toward him, Stirling immediately formed his men to receive an attack; shouting "To Trees!" and placing a half-company on either side of he trail. He sent the pack train into the bush, guarded by the men who had been the advance guard.

Wend, Donegal, and Kirkwood flung themselves to the ground in exhaustion. Instantly Stirling and Baird stood above them.

"Would you care to tell me what's going on?" Stirling asked in a voice which had a tense edge to it.

Wend said simply, "We came across outlaw traders providing powder to the Indians. Then I shot the traders."

"You what?" Stirling was clearly shocked. Then he asked again, incredulity in his voice, "You attacked a group of white men and Indians trading for powder?"

"Yes, that's it." Wend gasped for breath. "And now there's a party of warriors coming after us."

"Damn! I can imagine why they would." The captain rolled his eyes upward as if looking for guidance from the gods. "Eckert, why didn't you come back and advise me of what was going on? Has it possibly escaped your attention that we are on a diplomatic mission, not a punitive expedition?" He thought some more and then turned to Lieutenant Eddington. "Have the men fix bayonets, look to their locks, and make ready to receive an attack." He pointed at his lieutenant. "But make sure no one fires unless I give the order."

Joshua quietly spoke up. "Sprout, was that Kinnear and Flemming you shot?"

Wend nodded. "Yes—they're both dead."

"Now this is very important, Sprout: Did you hit any of the warriors?"

Wend shook his head. "Just the two white men, Joshua." Wend thought for a moment. "And Joshua, there was a third man. One who I've never seen. He escaped in a canoe."

Baird turned to Stirling. "Captain, we may be lucky here. Since he didn't kill any Indians, I think maybe we can negotiate. We can tell them that what happened was a matter of personal revenge: Those two traders were involved in the death of Wend's family. The warriors will understand that. I'll tell them that there was no intent to hurt any of their people."

Stirling nodded his understanding. "Yes, it makes sense. You take a man with the white flag and McKay with the wampum belt. Go out and meet the pursuers and see what you can do." He reflected a moment. "We can fight our way out of this if we have to, but I'd rather keep things peaceful."

Joshua was gone almost half an hour. But then he came sauntering back down the trail with the other two men, all three looking very relaxed.

"Its all right, Captain. They accepted our story. And as we was talking, they all figured out that with the traders dead or chased away, they get all the goods and also keep their pelts. So they decided they was happy with the outcome."

Stirling's face was very stern. Then he asked, "They're absolutely clear that we had no intent of hostilities against them?"

"Yep, Captain. They understand it was a matter of honor." He paused, and a smile came over his face. "Oh yes, something else." He turned and looked at Wend. "The head man complemented you on your shooting."

There was a silence for a moment as Stirling considered the situation. Joshua quickly explained to him the details of the traders' role in the massacre of Wend's family. Then he also pointed out that Bouquet was eager to put them out of business. Stirling nodded as Baird made each point.

When Joshua had finished, Stirling stood silent for a moment, looking between Joshua and Wend. Then he said, "Eckert, you may have had a valid grudge against those two men, but it doesn't excuse the fact that you jeopardized the entire purpose of our mission and the safety this company. I admire you personally, Eckert, but by God, you've exhausted my patience. I'm inclined to put you on report you for this rash, undisciplined act. In fact, there's a good case for charging you with murder."

The word "murder" hit Wend hard. He had shot men on the campaign, even killed one hand to hand, but that had all been in combat; it had been kill or be killed. This day he had, for the first time in his life, taken lives in cold blood. Suddenly he felt a steely cold fist in his stomach; then it seemed to reach up and grab his heart. In a flash of intuition, he realized that the coldness inside would always be there, grabbing him again whenever he though of this day.

Then Donegal spoke up. "Beggin' your pardon, Captain. But Eckert is 'na tellin' you the whole story. He didn't have no choice but to start shootin' back there."

Stirling looked at Donegal. "No choice? What the Devil do you mean?"

Donegal continued, "That's it, Sir. The truth is, he's shielding Corporal Kirkwood. When we was taking cover to spy on them traders and Indians,

Kirkwood moved too slow and they saw him moving along the ridge. He gave away our position." He looked over at the corporal meaningfully.

Kirkwood stared at Donegal for a long moment, pursed his lips, and then shrugged his shoulders. "Yes Sir, Captain. I hate to admit it, but Donegal's right. I was clumsy—and they saw me. The whole gang of them was picking up their firelocks and getting ready to come after us. Eckert started shooting to distract them and give us a chance to get away."

Joshua looked at Stirling with a crooked smile. "That being the case, Captain, this wasn't anything but a skirmish in hostile territory. And those white men were tradin' with the enemy. There ain't no murder in a battle."

Stirling turned to Wend and asked, "And what do you say, Eckert? Was this a skirmish?"

Wend exchanged glances with Donegal and Kirkwood, who looked at him expectantly. He chose his words carefully. "If felt like it to me, Sir."

Stirling stood staring at the three scouts, his arms crossed and a wry look on his face. Finally he spoke. "All right, I'll accept that explanation. Mind you, I don't believe it, but I will accept it." He paused and glanced over at Joshua. "In fact, things do seem to have turned out well enough. But given the circumstances, we're not going to make any more visits to villages. We'll head straight back to Fort Pitt by way of the trail along the river."

He turned to Wend, who still sat alongside the trail. "Now, Mr. Eckert, have you quite finished taking care of your personal business on the King's time?"

Wend nodded sheepishly. "Yes, Captain."

"Good. Now I suggest you take your two partners in crime and go find me a path down to the river that won't cause us to aggravate the natives more than we already have."

CHAPTER 26
A Soldier's Grave

After the return of Stirling's company from the Ohio Country in early December, Wend found Fort Pitt a changed place; the military establishment had hunkered down for the winter. The 77th Highlanders had marched out, headed for New York, disbandment and transportation back to Scotland. Any extraneous civilians and military persons had also been sent east for the cold season. The militia companies which had helped man the fort during the emergency had been mustered out. The winter garrison would consist of only three companies of the 60th and three of the 42nd plus a cadre of essential civilian tradesmen.

The morning after they arrived back at the fort Stirling took Joshua and Wend with him to make his report to Bouquet. The colonel himself was making preparations to leave for Philadelphia, where he would be able to coordinate preparations among the various colonies for the advance to the Muskingum, scheduled for the spring of the next year. They spent an hour in his office discussing the outcome of their travels through the Ohio villages.

Bouquet was very satisfied that the intended message had been delivered to the tribes. He said to Stirling, "Congratulations, Sir. Your mission has come out better than I had expected. Even before your return, I had word from my Shawnee and Delaware informers that the debate about whether to continue the raids next spring has intensified. I dare to hope there will be fewer war parties attacking the settlements next spring."

Stirling said, "There will be even fewer if we can march westward as soon as the snows melt and the land dries. If the tribes see that we have gathered a force and are preparing to advance, they'll hold their warriors back from traveling east."

Bouquet nodded. "Yes, but I fear the usual delays in recruiting and assembling the necessary provincial forces. And getting sufficient supplies staged here at Pitt will be even more challenging. That's why I'm making haste to get back to Philadelphia. I must not let Maryland, Virginia, and Pennsylvania lose their resolution over the winter."

Joshua nodded. "Beggin' your pardon, Colonel: There's another matter which is gonna' influence the campaign; that bein' the tribes' need for powder and lead. There ain't the smallest question in my mind that they're short after the raiding of last summer and the fight at Bushy Run. And the long hunt has done nothin' but worsened their situation. Eckert's encounter with those two outlaw traders out by the Allegheny made that clear. They're going to be desperate to get their hands on more by next spring."

Bouquet motioned to the scout. "You're absolutely right, Joshua. We've got to find out how the tribes are getting their munitions and put an end to it." He turned to Wend. "Eckert, I've been thinking over what you said in my office in July; that someone with great resources and organization is behind this trade—not just small-time traders like the late Kinnear and Flemming. I think you are right on target, Wend. I wish we could find that person, or persons and shut them down. Doing that would go a long way to reducing the tribes' ability to fight next year."

Wend nearly burst out with Grenough's name. But then caution seized him and he bit his lip. He remembered Charlie Sawak's admonition that no one would believe him. And Wend realized that was particularly true in Bouquet's case; he and Grenough were great friends. He would need far more evidence than he possessed now to convince the colonel.

After Stirling's briefing had been completed, Bouquet asked Wend to remain behind. When they were alone, the colonel settled behind his desk and moved some papers around. He motioned Wend to take a seat. Finally, he looked up. "I'm sorry to hear that your personal quest did not end as you would have desired."

Wend sighed. "Obviously, I would have wanted another outcome."

The colonel reflected for a moment. "As far as the young lady and her decision to remain with the Mingoes, I think you should not blame yourself. Her reaction to captivity is not unusual. Our experience is that more than half the female hostages choose to remain with their captors, particularly when they have been among them for more than a year, or have had children."

Wend nodded and said, "I had a long talk with Captain Stirling about that. I'm becoming reconciled to the situation."

He thought for a moment and said quietly, as much to himself as to the colonel, "But there's something else I have to face. For four years, my life was aimed at finding Abigail. So now her decision has done more than leave emptiness in my heart; it has left me without a clear purpose in my life. I've become used to having a driving force beyond the simple pursuit of my trade and making money."

There was a long silence, then Bouquet said, "There's much to what you just said; I've always found that higher purpose you speak about in service to a nation and devotion to the efficiency and well-being of my command. But every man must find his own personal motivation."

Wend smiled and shook his head. "I shouldn't bore you with my musings, Sir. The main thing is, I must thank you for the opportunity you provided me to resolve the situation. I shall always be grateful to you for your consideration."

Bouquet raised his hand. "As I told you long ago at Fort Loudoun, it was my obligation. But your assistance during the course of the relief expedition, and the battle near Bushy Run, placed me even more in your debt."

Then Bouquet's face suddenly lit up in a smile. "There's something else you should know—something I was told by my Indian informants. It seems that word has spread among the Ohio tribes about your actions at the Mingo village on Slippery Rock Creek. They've given you a name when they talk about you around the campfires."

"There's a name for me among the tribes?"

"Yes, but you might not be too happy about it. They call you 'The Scalp Stealer'." The colonel laughed and slapped his hand down on the desk. "And I assure you they don't mean it in a complementary way! But I would have given a month's pay to have seen you confront Wolf Claw in his own village and the expression on his face as you took down those scalps."

Wend's face became very serious. "They can think what they will of me. All I did was reclaim a missing part of my family. And I'll be fully satisfied only when I bury those scalps in the right place and make my family whole again."

Bouquet slowly nodded, and then simply extended his hand. "God go with you, Wend Eckert."

Wend shook hands with the colonel and took his leave. He looked back as he left the office and saw that Bouquet had placed his spectacles on his nose and had already gone back to addressing the pile of papers on his desk. He remembered what Stirling had told him about Bouquet's loss of Anne Willing's favors; it struck Wend how lonely Bouquet must be. He faced not only the isolation that is the lot of every senior military commander but also the lack of any close family or romantic relationship. Then Wend realized that the colonel's only constant companions were a multitude of crushing problems and inescapable responsibilities.

* * *

By the next day, Wend, Joshua, and Donegal, their participation in the campaign finished, had completed preparations to leave. Kirkwood had been permanently assigned to Captain Stirling's company, which would be wintering over in the fort. Wend had made enquiries about the fate of Mary but no one remained who could tell him about her final days. He asked at the hospital, but the staff had changed. Surgeon Munro and Esther McCulloch had left with the 77th and even the doctor of the 60th was new, having arrived during November. The storeroom where Wend had last seen Mary had reverted to its original use.

So, on a crisp, blustery day the three companions led their riding horses and a packhorse with provisions out through the gate of Fort Pitt. They wore heavy gray army overcoats which Kirkwood had requisitioned—through his own special methods—for them. Kirkwood walked with them. They headed for the fort's cemetery to find Mary's grave.

The burial ground was sizable, for it contained many graves of soldiers killed during Grant's battle. They stood looking at the rows of crude wooden crosses, many of which were falling apart. Donegal said, "We buried the remains of many a good man here, back in '58. Not that we found many whole bodies, mind you. It was skulls sitting on stakes, all lined up by the Indians. And we searched through the bush up on the hill for bodies, finding mostly just bones scattered by the varmints. But we did the best we could. Aye, there's a good part of the 77th right here and it will always be part of the garrison of Fort Pitt, in a manner of speaking."

They found where a line of new graves had been dug, representing wounded from Bushy Run who had died after reaching the fort. To Wend's dismay, aside from the bare wooden crosses, few of the graves had any identification. After a search he knew he would never be able to identify Mary's resting place.

Wend stood in front of the cemetery, his fists clutched in anger. The gusty wind swirled dry brown leaves around them and over the graves. He cursed and then turned to his companions, unable to hide his bitterness. "So this is how Mary ends. She was pretty, intelligent, and lively. She helped uncounted men and brightened their lives." Wend recalled the vision of Mary happily dancing by the fire at Bedford, her auburn hair down around her shoulders, scores of soldiers longingly watching her, and tears came to his eyes. "The girl served the King as well and as bravely as any soldier. And damn it, this is her reward: A bloody unmarked grave on a desolate plain at the end of the world."

Donegal put his hand on Wend's shoulder. "It's not as bad as all that, lad. She's in good company here; men she marched with and sang with and fought with. Mind you, laddie, there are more soldiers of the 77th here than anywhere else in the world. And she's with her Dad, Wend, for he's in that row back there; I put him there myself. I found his name on the cartridge box lying with the bones. So she'll 'na be lonely, lad. And she died knowin' you'll be keeping the memory of her all your life."

Wend looked over at Joshua and saw the tough scout was blinking away tears in his eyes, the same way as the night at Washburn's when he found out that Lizzie had died.

But after a few seconds Joshua wiped his eyes and said in a gruff voice, "Sprout, I'm tired of waiting for you to put some steel into your spine. You've been moping around since that English girl told you she was staying with the Mingo. And now you're here cryin' over Mary. Fact is, I ain't sure whether you're mourning the girl or just feelin' sorry for yourself." He turned and pointed down Forbes Road toward the distant mountains. "Sprout, it's time we were gettin' on with things."

Wend set his stone face and stood silently trying to control the flare of anger which ignited at Joshua's words. Then something inside him snapped like a broken spring in a rifle lock. He was fed up with people telling him to get on with his life. He had listened patiently with Stirling and then Bouquet; now he was even getting it from Baird! He wanted to scream out to the world to stop giving him advice. But the words came out differently. "Damn it, Joshua! I may or may not be feeling sorry for myself. But there's something I've wanted to say to you for a long time and I'm telling you right now: There's no more calling me Sprout! The Sprout died somewhere along Forbes Road, probably in that night after the first day at Bushy Run. So you can call me Wend, or you can call me Eckert. You can call me Dutchman, like everyone else in Sherman Valley. You can even call me Asshole, when that's your fancy! But mark my words; the Sprout is over and done with."

The four of them stood frozen in the aftermath of Wend's outburst. Joshua reared back and glared at Wend, his jaw set, his face reddening; he opened his mouth as if preparing to speak, but in the end, he said nothing. Then Donegal's eyes twinkled and he looked like he was going to start giggling, but instead the highlander put a hand over his mouth and stared into the distance toward Grant's Hill.

Finally, Kirkwood, who also had a gleam in his eyes, broke the tense silence. "You all had better get moving. The days are short enough as it is, this late in the season. And you got to cover ground fast if you want to get over the mountains before the heavy snows come. You'll be lucky if you do anyway, this time of year."

Donegal turned to his mate. "After all these years together and all the miles we marched, Bob, I feel bad about leaving you behind with a strange regiment. Are you going to be all right?"

"Ah, Simon, don't be having worries about me. I'll do fine with these Black Watch lads. And the best part is, Captain Stirling is talking about making me the quartermaster of his company. Now won't that be a fine thing? Think about it: Me with the key to all the provisions and in charge of keeping the account books! What more could a man of my talents and desires be wanting?"

Joshua broke off from staring at Wend. He said, "Kirkwood's right: We need to get moving—'specially since we're carrying dispatches for Bouquet. He told me that one is very important; he gave it to us because he knew we'd be traveling fast. It's to Richard Grenough, no less. He's been appointed as a commissioner to advise the colonel on negotiations with the tribal chiefs next year. The colonel has some ideas for the campaign and a proposed treaty that he wants Grenough to see so they can discuss plans back in Carlisle."

The sound of Grenough's name startled Wend. "You say he's going to have a major role in the campaign next year?"

"Aye, that's the truth of it. And of course, there ain't no one; not even me—if you could believe it—who knows more about the chief's and the politics of the tribes than Grenough. It's a smart choice."

But Wend hardly heard what Joshua was saying. The mention of Grenough, coupled with the lines of graves in front of him, brought to his mind another set of graves: A row of five along Forbes Road in the foothills of Sideling Hill. Grenough's organization had put his family and Abigail's father in those graves and his gunpowder undoubtedly drove the shot which put Mary in hers. Suddenly he recalled the promise he had made in front of his father's cross on the march westward. Wend had gone down to his knee and vowed that he would take vengeance on the murderers of his family. He had started by eliminating Kinnear and Flemming. But Wend now realized that completing the vow would mean visiting revenge on Grenough and every one of his men—including Matt Bratton and the red-haired trader who had escaped. And his resolution was reinforced by Bouquet's words the day before about the need to cut off the supply of war goods to the tribes. In all of Pennsylvania, he, Wend Eckert, was the only person who fully understood the rich trader's culpability and the scope of his activities. He knew he was playing from a weak hand and that he would have to wait for the right opportunities. But he would not rest until he destroyed Grenough and his entire conspiracy. In that instant, the listlessness which had gripped him since leaving the Mingo village was gone.

Wend slung his rifle over his shoulder and strode over to the mare. She had been in the stable for a long time and was full of pent-up energy; as he approached she stamped a fore-foot and tossed her head in eagerness to be off. He gathered the reins and turned for one last look at the graveyard where Mary lay, fixing a picture of the place in his mind and mentally making his final farewell. Then he swung up into the saddle and looked down on the others. "You're right, Joshua. We've all got things to do east of the mountains. I have to take Arnold Spengler's things to Lancaster." He thought again about Grenough and his far-flung network, "And I have overdue work waiting for me in Sherman Mill, Carlisle, York and probably Shippensburg. So let's ride; if we push the pace, by tonight we can camp halfway to Byerly's place on Bushy Run."

Wend swung the mare's head around toward Forbes Road and spurred her forward. The powerful horse easily came to the gallop. Behind him he heard Donegal laughing and Baird shout after him, "For God's sake, *Sprout*...I mean, *Eckert*, I said we had to move fast, but let's not get carried away!"

As Kirkwood stood watching, Baird and Donegal mounted their horses and hurried in Eckert's wake, Donegal leading the packhorse. After the mare had galloped 100 yards and burned off some of her excess energy, Wend reined her in to wait for the others. They soon caught up and the three men walked their horses at a pace which could be sustained for the long miles ahead. In a few minutes, they navigated a turn in the road and approached the end of the cleared area around Pitt. Just before the forest enveloped them, Wend looked back to where Kirkwood still stood and thought he saw a hand raised toward them, but couldn't be sure. Then he saw the highlander adjust his bonnet, tighten his jacket, turn and trudge slowly back toward the hulking fortress—a solitary figure hunched over against the flying leaves and other debris kicked up by the frigid wind.

THE END OF FORBES ROAD

AUTHOR'S NOTES

AND ACKNOWLEDGEMENTS

Throbbed The seeds for this book were planted in 1994 when I drove my family from our home in Northern Virginia up through central Pennsylvania for a camping trip. We took Route 30 westward to Route 522, which we then followed northward to our campsite above Lewistown. I was intrigued to see a series of historical markers noting the existence of colonial era forts along the way. These were Forts Loudoun, Littleton, Shirley, and finally Granville at Lewistown, all built in 1756. I was struck by the fact that they were spaced at distances which would have reflected a hard day's travel in colonial times. Therefore they clearly denoted a line of defense and I realized that at one point in time this route marked the western frontier of Pennsylvania. Although born in the state, I grew up in Maryland and didn't have much knowledge of The Keystone State's history. And while I had always been intrigued by the French and Indian War, I had thought of the action as mostly centered in New York and northward.

With my interest aroused, I started doing research and soon came across Francis Parkman's *The Conspiracy of Pontiac*, which introduced me to Henry Bouquet and the role of the Royal Americans in the colony. I was also gratified to find out that the British Army's highland regiments, which I had always admired for their warrior ethos and unmatched unit cohesion, had played a major role in the area from 1758 to 1765. In short, I was hooked and began serious research.

As a military officer, I soon became impressed with Henry Bouquet's professionalism in both tactics and logistics. My studies also introduced me to the extraordinary achievement of the British in building Forbes Road within the space of a few months in 1758 and the daring competence of Bouquet's fight at Bushy Run and relief of Fort Pitt in 1763. I also was surprised at how little public awareness there was about the historical importance of Pontiac's

Rebellion, the first coordinated effort of the Native Americans to push back against the waves of European settlers in the middle colonies. It was indeed a forgotten war, except to academics studying the era and history enthusiasts of western Pennsylvania. Thus was born the idea of writing a fictional story which would highlight the achievements of Bouquet, the role of the highlanders, and the war-fighting prowess of the Ohio Country tribes.

Bouquet's victory at Bushy Run in 1763 laid the foundation for a successful, and essentially bloodless, expedition into the Ohio Country in late 1764. The force consisted of the Black Watch and several battalions of provincial troops and militia, the majority from Virginia. As the colonel had anticipated, the tribal leaders were impressed by the size of his force—over 1500 men—and determined that negotiation was the better part of valor. They met with Bouquet on the Muskingham River and agreed to peace terms which included handover of European hostages. Eventually they turned over more than 200, but in fact many other whites remained with their Indian families. Bouquet returned to the universal gratitude of the colonists and King George III. Pennsylvania rewarded him with a resolution of thanks and a large land grant. King George personally made the decision to promote Bouquet to Brigadier General, an unprecedented honor for a foreigner in British service. Along with his promotion, Bouquet was assigned command of British forces in the southern colonies. Then, at the height of his career, misfortune overtook him. He took ship for his new headquarters in Pensacola in 1765; enroute the vessel stopped in Havana and Bouquet contracted yellow fever. He died onboard the ship on September 2, 1765 while at anchor off Pensacola. The general's unmarked grave is somewhere below the modern streets of that city. Bouquet never married; as noted in the narrative, he lost Anne (Also called Nancy) Willing to a younger man in 1762. However, at the time he departed Philadelphia for Pensacola, he was courting another lady. But this much can be said of Henry Bouquet: In the decade before the American Revolution, his record undoubtedly made him the most respected military officer in the colonies. By contrast, the record of that ambitious young Virginia officer, George Washington, was considered mixed at best.

My top-line objective for this book was to craft a tale which combined both absorbing fiction and good history. To that end, I have worked to make sure that the fictional story logically fit the actual timelines, places, and events of the French and Indian War and the beginning of Pontiac's War as it unfolded in Pennsylvania. For example, in early 1759 the commander of

Fort Pitt actually did write to Colonel Bouquet requesting the engagement of a gunsmith to function as armorer for the garrison. So it is entirely possible that Johann Eckert and his family would have been traveling to Pittsburgh in July of that year. It is also fact that in July Captain Robertson's company of the 77th Foot was marching eastward along Forbes Road to rejoin the rest of their regiment. The small cabin outside the stockade at Fort Loudoun where Wend and Abigail consummated their love actually existed (There was also one for Forbes at Ligonier). The march of the battalion in Part Three of the book adheres to the schedule of Bouquet's westward advance as laid out in his papers.

But, in any work of fiction, there are places where the author must stray from history to make his narrative work, and *Forbes Road* is no exception. I hereby plead mea culpa, and here are some my most grievous sins:

- According to the written orders Bouquet gave to Lieutenant Campbell, who commanded the relief column to Ligonier, the man who actually guided the highlanders was a Mr. Daniel Carmichael of Shippensburg. In the text he was displaced by Joshua and Wend for the first leg of the journey, but the reader will realize I made reparations by giving him a role beyond Fort Bedford.

- The incident at Bushy Run Station where the small war party fired down on the British from a high ridge after the battle was over is a matter of record. However, for dramatic purposes the timing has been changed in the narrative from the evening of the second day of battle to the next morning.

- The march of the Black Watch company through the Beaver River country to spread the word of Bouquet's ultimatum, and incidentally enable Wend to search for Abigail is fiction. However, Bouquet did in fact make diplomatic overtures to the tribal leaders through his Native American network of contacts in the Ohio Country, just not via a military expedition.

- Robert Kirkwood did transfer to the Black Watch following the disbandment of the 77th. However, he was assigned to Captain Graham's company at Fort Pitt, not Stirling's. I've included him in Stirling's company for simplification of the narrative.

- Captain Thomas Stirling of the Black Watch, like James Robertson of the 77th, is indeed a historical personage. But he was not in America in late 1763. Instead he was in Scotland recuperating from a wound and fever contracted in the Caribbean. However, he did return to his regimental duties in America in 1765. I put him into this story for several reasons. First, I wanted a sympathetic aristocratic officer as a mentor for Wend after Robertson and the 77th were out of the picture. Second, Stirling was indeed ordered by Bouquet to lead a similar expedition in 1765. He commanded a force of 100 men from the 42nd who were tasked to travel hundreds of miles westward along the Ohio River to take over Fort de Chartres on the Mississippi from the French (Among his detachment was a soldier named Robert Kirkwood). Thus he was obviously a competent officer ready for independent command responsibilities. Third, Stirling later took command of the 1st Battalion of the Black Watch just before the outbreak of the American Revolution and led it through most of the war. A discerning reader might have calculated that Wend Eckert would be a mature thirty years of age in 1775, and thus would inevitably become involved in the halcyon events of 1775-1783, perhaps even encountering some of his old friends from the highland regiments.

- I have found no reference which authoritatively states whether or not there were dependents with Bouquet's composite battalion. It was, in fact, the policy to leave women and children behind in a safe area. However, there are stories of women in significant numbers defying this policy and accompanying combat units into the wilderness. Thus it is not beyond the realm of possibility that the highlanders' women did march to Ligonier as described in the story and that a few women were at Bushy Run. In any case, I wanted to illustrate the important role of women as auxiliaries in the British army and of course needed the availability of Mary Fraser to present Wend with a romantic conflict. This was the genesis of the confrontation between Bouquet and the women of the battalion at Carlisle. Beyond that, after nearly thirty years association with the military, I can confidently assure the reader that virtually every unit has its version of the formidable Mrs. Esther McCulloch.

Because of the ad hoc nature of Bouquet's march to relieve Fort Pitt, there are gaps in the history records which have engendered speculation and controversies among historians attempting to tell the story. The following paragraphs discuss how I have dealt with a few of the most important.

Composition of the British Force at Bushy Run. Bouquet left no comprehensive muster of the force at Bushy Run. It is known that the total number present was in the neighborhood of 450-60 including regular soldiers, rangers, and volunteers. Several older accounts assumed the presence of as many as 150 soldiers of the 60th Foot, or Royal Americans, within this total. More recent analysis show that the overwhelming number of soldiers were highlanders of the 42nd and 77th, with less than 20 rank and file of the 60th present at the battle (The usual number cited is 16). The mistake of earlier historians appears to be in not counting the three companies of highlanders which Amherst sent down to Bouquet from New York as an advance force in the total order of battle and then assuming men from the 60th made up the difference. The definitive calculation can be reviewed in Rev. Don Daudelin's essay *Numbers and Tactics at Bushy Run* (Western Pennsylvania History Magazine, April 1985). McCulloch's *Sons of the Mountains,* cited below, details the composition of the highland contingent and, in general, supports Daudelin's computations.

Native American Force. There is a significant controversy regarding how many tribal warriors were engaged at Bushy Run. Bouquet believed he had encountered 500 or more. Some historians use the quote of Delaware warrior Killbuck in a conversation with British Indian Commissioner Sir William Johnson that "We were 99 strong" (Also quoted as 110 strong) to assert that that was the entire force. But those same historians know that the Native Americans didn't line up and take muster. The warriors tended to discuss matters in terms of their own tribe. Most likely Killbuck was saying that there were 99 Delawares present, or present from his clan of the Delawares, or perhaps in the group of warriors he was traveling among. Most students of the battle believe that there were around 400 warriors, on the basis that observers at Fort Pitt saw that many departing from the siege to meet the approaching British. A thoughtful and balanced analysis of the numbers controversy is contained in David Dixon's *Never Come to Peace Again*, which I found one of the most even-handed references on Pontiac's War.

Was the British Expedition Ambushed at Bushy Run? Most general narratives of the battle state the British troops were ambushed. It is technically true that the tribal force fired first from concealed positions. However, it is also clear from his writings that Bouquet expected to be attacked in the vicinity of Bushy Run or Turtle Creek and made plans accordingly. In his memoirs, Robert Kirkwood specifically says that the British saw smoke from the fires of the war parties shortly before the battle began. Thus we have a variation of what tacticians call a *meeting battle*, the only surprise element being that the British didn't know precisely where and when the battle would begin. Moreover, Kirkwood makes it clear that Bouquet deployed his forces into a formation designed to receive the anticipated attack and then easily go over to the counterattack.

How was the surprise flanking action at Bushy Run conceived? No one knows for certain how or when the tactical plan for the second day's battle was formulated. Most accounts simply attribute it to Bouquet, which is logical in the sense that the commander gets the credit for success and must accept the responsibility for disasters. Controversy has arisen from the claim by some colonists—first raised well after the battle and after Bouquet's death—that the plan for tricking the tribes into thinking the force was retreating and then hitting them with a flanking attack was devised by Lemuel Barrett, the captain of the ranger company. Having been personally involved in many military planning sessions, I can say that it is seldom that any individual conceives the entire scope of a plan; rather it develops from the inputs of many people and the commander or a senior staff officer synthesizes the ideas into an actionable tactical concept. Thus it is likely that the plan of attack was developed during a tense meeting of Bouquet and his key lieutenants, probably in the evening of the first day or in the night hours when the British leaders had fully assessed the gravity of their situation. No one knows how the British determined the best location from which to launch the flank attack and that, of course, gave me the opportunity to put Wend Eckert into the picture. Regardless of how the flanking action was conceived, Henry Bouquet deserves the credit for having the guts to take the enormous risks that that plan entailed and for competent execution of the tactic. A lot of British officers would have hunkered down in position hoping that a contest of attrition would somehow allow them to survive or would have attempted a desperate retreat. Either course would have been disastrous. As per the motto of the British SAS, "Who Dares, Wins."

But there is another issue which should be discussed. As played out in the body of the manuscript, I believe that the plan did not work entirely as originally conceived. Specifically, I am persuaded that Bouquet was attempting what we would call today a "double envelopment." In his report, the colonel just says that Major Campbell's flanking force drove the mass of Indians across the front of the main British position and then two additional companies advanced and poured volleys of musket fire into the flank of the tightly packed group of fleeing warriors. This is an intellectually unsatisfying use of those companies. Considering Bouquet's need to ensure that the Native American force was incapable of reforming to further hinder the drive on Pitt, it is more logical to think that the plan actually called for these two companies to pivot out and block the fleeing Indian force. In that scenario, the tribal warriors would have been under devastating attack from three sides—the flanking light companies from the east, the main line of the British to the north, and the pivot companies on the west. For some reason the pivot did not come off; perhaps it was a simple error of timing or maybe because the attack of Indians against the main British front was too wide and powerful for the pivot companies to complete their movement. Then, in his report to Amherst, Bouquet wasn't about to muddy the waters by writing, "Yeah, Boss, we did well, but it could have been a lot better if . . ."

Use of Germ Warfare. For some historians and Native American advocates the main point of interest regarding Pontiac's War and Bouquet's relief expedition is the accusation that Amherst and Bouquet conducted germ warfare by distributing smallpox-infected blankets to tribal leaders in an attempt to instigate an epidemic. This assertion is solely based on a letter between the two officers which discussed the feasibility of such an action. In fact the only documented case is that Captain Ecuyer, commanding officer of Fort Pitt, acting on his own initiative and without Bouquet's knowledge, gave some infected blankets to Indian emissaries during negotiations early in the siege of Pittsburgh. As Dixon discusses in *Never Come to Peace Again*, there is no evidence that these blankets actually caused any infection or accelerated the epidemic which was already present in the tribal areas, having originated from routine, peaceful contact with Europeans. I did not include any mention of this issue in the manuscript because Wend wouldn't have had any reason to know about or be involved in such activity.

In researching this story, I initially found few books which specifically focused on the events of 1763. But then the approach of the 250th anniversary of the French and Indian War sparked a veritable landslide of works on the general period. I must acknowledge several books which provided key information and helped spark ideas for the storyline. First and foremost is the Pennsylvania Historical and Museum Commission's six volume, *The Papers of Henry Bouquet,* which is the mandatory first stop for studying both the good colonel and the military history of this period. As noted earlier, a detailed, balanced study of Pontiac's War is contained in Dixon's *Never Come to Peace Again* (University of Oklahoma Press, 2005). I particularly wanted to pay tribute to the highlanders of the 42nd and 77th regiments and make sure that their story was told sympathetically. My job was made vastly easier by the appearance in 2006 of Lieutenant Colonel Ian Macpherson McCulloch's magnificent two-volume telling of the highlanders' service in the colonies, *Sons of the Mountains* (Purple Mountain Press). McCulloch teamed up with Timothy Todish in 2004 to publish an annotated and interpretative version of Robert Kirkwood's memoirs, *Through So Many Dangers,* (Also Purple Mountain Press) which was originally published by the former soldier in 1775 to capitalize on British public interest in North America spurred by the rebelliousness of the colonists. The contents of this book were important for two reasons. First, it reinforced my growing conviction that on the first day at Bushy Run the British command was quite aware that a hostile tribal force was directly in their front and it also helped cement my understanding of the disposition which Bouquet had formed to meet the enemy. Second, reading of Kirkwood's adventures with Rogers' Rangers convinced me that he was an ideal candidate to be included in the fictitious scouting group which I had already conceived to tell the story of Wend and Joshua.

Two other books proved invaluable in providing background to both the military and civilian environment which Bouquet and my fictional characters inhabited. The first is *Forts on the Pennsylvania Frontier, 1753-1758,* by William A. Hunter (Wennawoods Publishing, 1999). The second is Charles Stotz' *Outposts of the War for Empire: the French and English in Western Pennsylvania: Their Armies, Their Forts, Their People* (University of Pittsburgh Press, 2005). Finally, although an old book, Charles Sipes' *The Indian Wars of Pennsylvania* (Wennawoods Publishing) provided a superb timeline and was a good jumping off place for studying the Native American side of the story.

On a personal level, I owe a great deal of gratitude to many people who provided assistance in the formulation of *Forbes Road.* I am especially indebted to Mr. David Miller, the former, long serving, Site Educator (Historian) of Bushy Run Battlefield, who provided invaluable information on the battle, steered me to some critical reference material, and took valuable time from his busy professional life to make a detailed critique of the original draft of *Forbes Road*. David Wright, whose award winning art chronicles our early history, graciously allowed the use of his painting, *Long Way From Home*, for the cover and advertising material. Pamela Patrick White made her painting *Up Against The Fence* available for the rear cover and extended permission for several of her other works to be used for promotional activity. Major John Chapman, USMC (Ret), was the first outside reader of the manuscript and as such supplied a very necessary fresh look. I also thank Mr. Roddy Dean for his interest, comments, and encouragement. Above all, I thank my wife Cathy, who accepted her husband's obsessive behavior with exceptional grace and patience, read every word of the novel several times, and offered a loving combination of critical advice and unfailing encouragement throughout the process.

Robert Shade
October, 2011

Made in the USA
San Bernardino, CA
13 April 2016